THE
REED
RIVERS
TRILOGY

USA Today and International Bestselling Author
Lauren Rowe

Reed Rivers Trilogy Copyright © 2019 by Lauren Rowe

Published by SoCoRo Publishing

Cover design © Shannon Passmore - Shannof Designs

Illustrated by Jessica Florence

All rights reserved. No part of this book may be reproduced or transmitted in any form without written permission from the publisher, except by reviewers who may quote brief excerpts in connection with a review.

Bad Liar

USA Today and International Bestselling Author

Lauren Rowe

PLAYLIST

Music Playlist for Bad Liar

"I Had a Dad"—Jane's Addiction
"Father of Mine"—Everclear
"Hustle"—Pink
"Bad Guy"—Billie Eilish
"Truth Hurts"—Lizzo
"Bad Liar"—Selena Gomez

ONE
REED

Fifteen years ago

As the sorority girl in the purple wig kneels before me, her mouth working enthusiastically on me, I lean back in my armchair and try to clear my mind. I don't want to think about my father's lifeless body dangling in his prison cell while this girl is sucking me off. Actually, I don't want to think about that under any circumstances, obviously. But after getting that horrible call this morning, I can't stop imagining the grisly scene. I thought getting this pretty girl onto her knees would distract me from the images ravaging my mind.

Apparently not.

I should probably pull her off me. Pay her the usual fifty bucks and explain I'm just not feeling it tonight. But my dick is rock hard in her mouth, despite the chaos swirling inside my mind... So, fuck it. I sit back, close my eyes, and will her talented mouth to coax my racing mind into a temporary state of amnesia.

This girl isn't a professional, despite appearances, even though she's presently sucking my cock for cash. She's a student here at UCLA, the same as me—a fresh-faced sorority girl I met at a costume party at my fraternity house a month ago. The theme of the party was "Hookers and Pimps," and she was dressed like *Pretty Woman*. So, naturally, there was no shortage of raunchy jokes throughout the night... all of which ultimately led to her following me to my room upstairs and giving me head like a pro.

When the girl finished her task that night, I patted her head, congratulated her on a job well done, and handed her a fifty. I was joking, of course. Being an ass. Acting like a john. But damned if this pretty woman didn't surprise me by taking my fifty with gusto, stuffing it into her push-up bra, and purring, "Call me whenever you've got another fifty to spend." And I've been paying her for sex ever since. Fifty bucks for a blowjob and a hundred to fuck her. Plus, twenty bucks to eat her out—that last item being completely backwards and stupid, I know. This girl should be paying *me* to lick her into a frenzy, especially considering how well I do it. How hard I make her come, each and every time. But it's okay. I figure I've spent far more than twenty bucks on far stupider things in my nineteen years than making a pretty girl come like a freight train.

I gotta say, this whole *Pretty Woman* experience has taught me something interesting about myself. Something I didn't know before. Namely, that I get off paying for sex. It doesn't matter which of us is having the orgasm, or what particular sex act we're doing. I've realized I like paying for it because it makes things uncomplicated. We both know what we're getting, and what we're not. Specifically, we know feelings aren't involved. I'm not her Prince Charming, and she knows it, which, in turn, immunizes me from hearing any of the usual deal-breakers women say to me around the one-month mark. The stuff that sends me running for the hills. *Let down your guard, Reed. I want you to let me in, Reed. Am I your girlfriend or not, Reed?* And, of course, the biggest deal-breaker of them all: *I think I'm falling in love with you, Reed.*

I touch my fake whore's purple hair as she continues her enthusiastic work, trying in vain to clear my tortured mind. But it's no use. Even with her working on me, I can't stop imagining my father's lifeless body dangling in his prison cell.

Why'd he do it?

I understand what *specifically* triggered him to wrap that cord around his neck this morning: the feds tracking down the last of his secret offshore accounts. I'm just having a hard time comprehending how *that* particular event finally pushed my father over the edge, after everything that's happened over the past ten years.

I mean, shit, my father didn't kill himself during my parents' bitter divorce and custody battle. Or, right after that, when Mom suffered a catastrophic mental breakdown and had to be institutionalized. Dad didn't off himself six years ago, after the jury sent him to prison for financial fraud. Or when Dad's photo was splashed across the news as the poster boy for "corporate greed." If my father was going to hang himself, why not do it during any of that? Or, at least, during those first few years of his incarceration, when he was forced to sit back and watch his thirteen-year-old getting passed around from one distant relative to another before finally landing in a home for teenage rejects at age fourteen. Honestly, if Dad was going to end it all, I would have preferred he'd have done it then, when his son got shipped off to that horrible hell of a group home. At least, that way, I would have felt like Dad actually gave a shit about me, more than his stolen fortune.

But, no. Apparently, being an incarcerated felon with an ex-wife in the loony bin and a fourteen-year-old basket-case of a son in foster care was perfectly survivable to Terrence Rivers. Just as long as he still had his secret pot of gold. But, God forbid, the man was stripped of his last illicit penny, and, suddenly, his life just wasn't worth living anymore. Asshole.

Well, news flash, Dad: you're not the only one who went flat broke today. Thanks to the purportedly "untraceable" trust fund you set aside for me, the one that was supposed to transfer to me on my twenty-first birthday, I'm now as poor as the poorest guy in my fraternity house. But am I going to kill myself over today's reversal of fortune? No. Because unlike you, Dad, I know that no matter what life throws at me—which, by the way, has been a fucking lot in my nineteen years—I'll always come out on top in the end. Despite what I've been through these past ten years, despite what I've had to steel myself against, to fight against, to overcome, I've never lost sight of my future destiny—the one I've seen in my dreams—and I won't let anyone keep me from achieving it. *Not even you.*

Thanks to you, people hear my last name and think things like "liar" and "thief" and "fraud." But one day, after I've built my empire from nothing but my blood, sweat, and tears and relentlessness, people will hear the name Rivers and think words like "mogul" and "winner" and "self-made man." And if not any of those things, then, at least, they'll think "Hey, there's that asshole who's living the life of my dreams." Because if I can't earn the world's respect, thanks to your name, then I'll settle for earning their *envy*.

At that last thought, I grip my fake whore's fake hair, shove myself even farther down her supple throat, and release with a loud groan. A moment later, as I pull out of her, I'm trembling—but not from physical exertion. No, in this moment, I'm quaking from the resolve flooding my veins.

"I don't need him," I grit out through clenched teeth. And, by God, for the first time in my life, I'm positive it's the truth. In fact, I don't need anyone. At my comment, the sorority girl looks up at me quizzically. But before she says a word, I pull a fifty from my wallet and toss it onto the brown carpet at her knees. "Well done, Pretty Woman. Now run along. I've got something important to do."

She looks surprised. "*Now?* It's midnight."

"And I'm running late."

She makes a face that lets me know she's offended—and for a split-second, I think she's going to tell me to fuck off, as she should. But, nope. The spineless sorority girl who so desperately wants to be liked rises and slides into my lap. "What's wrong with you tonight? You've been acting weird all night."

I've got no interest in baring my soul to this girl. Or to anyone, for that matter. I say nothing.

Sighing, she puts her arms around my neck and presses her nose against mine. "Let's not play Pretty Woman anymore. I'm tired of that game. It was fun at first, but not anymore."

Shit. I have a feeling a deal-breaker will be coming my way, any minute now.

"Tell me what's wrong," she coos, stroking my cheek. "You look so sad—like you could cry. Come on, Reed. Tell me what's going on. Let me in."

And there it is. Right on cue. *Let me in.* With a deep exhale, I grab her wrist to stop her from caressing my cheek. "You're reading me all wrong, Audrey. That BJ was just so damned good, it almost brought me to tears."

She holds my gaze for a moment, her blue eyes telling me she's not buying my bullshit. But does she push back? No. Of course not. Because she's a doormat. With a deep sigh, she stands, slides off her purple wig, revealing her blonde tresses underneath, and drags her tight little ass toward the door. "Call me tomorrow?" she asks, her hand on the knob.

A puff of scorn escapes my nose. I won't be calling this girl tomorrow, or ever again. Not now that I know she wants more than I'm willing to give her. But seeing as how I've got bigger fish to fry than setting a pretty girl straight about her foolish, unrequited crush on me, I reply, "Not knowing what tomorrow will bring is one of life's greatest pleasures."

She scoffs, and a part of me hopes she'll finally grow a pair and tell me to fuck off. But, no. Passive little Audrey Meisner rolls her eyes, blows me a kiss, and slips quietly out the door, never to return to my room again, unbeknownst to her.

When the girl is gone, I shove earbuds into my ears and blast my current obsession—an indie band I stumbled across on YouTube. I swear, if these guys would only market themselves properly, they'd be the biggest thing going. Music blaring, I grab a whiskey bottle and a joint and flop back into my chair, determined to get shitfaced and stupid until I pass out cold.

But after only a couple swigs of whiskey, before I've even lit up the joint, I suddenly remember something a fraternity brother said a couple months ago during a poker game at the house—a comment that suddenly makes me want to add him to the guest list for my solo pity party.

Josh Faraday.

He's the richest guy in my fraternity house. Maybe even at UCLA, thanks to a massive inheritance he got last year, split down the middle with his fraternal twin. But money isn't why I'm suddenly thinking about calling Josh. It's the shocking thing he said.

I was sitting next to Josh at the rowdy poker table when another fraternity brother, a hard-partier named Alonso, stumbled through the front door, looking like a drunken hobo in a back alley. So, of course, everyone started slinging insults at Alonso. Telling him he looked like roadkill, etcetera. It was all the usual stuff—except for what Josh said.

"Damn, Alonso," Josh threw out. "You look as fucked-up as my father did the last time I saw him... and he'd just blown his brains out."

I was shocked by Josh's comment. Before then, I'd known Josh's dad had passed away right before Josh had started UCLA, but I'd assumed, like everyone else, that Josh's dad had died of natural causes. And also that Josh, understandably heartbroken about his loss, didn't want to talk about it. Not that I would have asked Josh about his father's death, regardless. I never ask anyone questions about their parents, lest they get the bright idea to ask me about mine. But, now, sitting here in my fraternity room with nobody but my buddies Jack and Mary Juana, I'm suddenly hell-bent on asking Josh a thousand questions about the shocking thing he said while sitting next to me at the poker table that night.

My heart clanging, I rip my earbuds out and grab my mobile.

"Are you at the house?" I ask Josh, interrupting his greeting.

"No, I'm in my car, about fifteen minutes away. What's up?"

I swallow hard. "Don't mention this to anyone, but my dad's been in prison the past six years, and, today, I found out he hanged himself. I'm hoping you've got some words of wisdom about how to handle the situation."

With a heavy sigh, Josh says he's sorry to hear the bad news, and that he's turning his car around. "About that confidentiality thing, though...?" he says. "You're on speaker right now in my car, and Henn's sitting here. Sorry. I didn't think to mention it before you started talking. But don't worry. Henn's a steel trap."

Henn's voice says, "Absolutely."

"Henn's the best guy in the world to have around in any kind of shit storm, Reed. Would it be okay for me to bring him along to hang out? I think, once you get to know him, you'll be glad I did."

I pause. I've interacted now and again with Peter "Henn" Hennessy —a funny, nerdy hacker dude from our pledge class—but always in loud, boisterous groups. I'm not sure tonight is the night I want to get to know him better.

As if reading my mind, Josh says, "Other than my brother, Henn's the only person I've talked to about my dad. Honestly, I don't know what I would have done without Henny this past year. He's been the best friend a guy could ask for. My rock."

Emotion unexpectedly rises inside me, constricting my throat. I've never had a "best friend" before, let alone a "rock." But, sitting here now, I feel near-desperation to have both. I take a deep breath and push my emotion down—something I've grown accustomed to doing these past ten years. "Henn can come, as long as he's down to get shitfaced. That's the price of admission to this particular pity party."

"I'm down," Henn says. "Whatever you need, I'm in."

"That goes double for me," Josh adds. "Whatever you need, we're here for you."

"Thanks. I'll tell you exactly what I need. Three things. One, to get shitfaced and stoned out of my fucking mind tonight, until the images in my head fade to black. Two, to talk to someone before I pass out who can help me make sense of this fucked-up situation. And three, and this is the biggie: I need to figure out a Plan B."

"A Plan B? For what?"

I take a deep, steadying breath. "For conquering the world, all by myself."

TWO
GEORGINA

Present day

As I walk past swarms of students on my way through campus, I get a call from my stepsister, Alessandra. Well, my *former* stepsister, technically. As busy as we both are—Alessandra's majoring in music in Boston while I'm majoring in journalism here at UCLA, plus, we both work part-time jobs—we still manage to talk multiple times per day.

"Are you headed to that career-thing for journalism students now?" Alessandra asks.

I press my phone into my ear to hear my stepsister's soft voice above the din of campus life around me. "I'm walking there now. But the event isn't for journalism students. It's for music students. CeeCee Rafael is the only journalist on the panel."

"Who are the other panelists?"

"Bigwigs in the music industry, I guess."

Alessandra gasps, which isn't a surprise, considering she's obsessed with music. "Who are the bigwigs?"

"I don't know. I saw CeeCee's name and looked no further. Hold on." I quickly locate the event flyer and text it to Alessandra. "I'm praying I'll be the only journalism major with the brilliant idea to crash a music school event to get a job."

"Pure genius."

"Only if it works."

I have reason to be skeptical, unfortunately, based on the countless résumés I've sent out over the past two months, to no avail. Thankfully, I've got my bartending gig to fall back on after graduation next week, and my boss, Bernie, has already said I can pick up additional shifts through the summer. It was a nice offer, and I appreciate it, but if I'm being honest, bartending with my degree in hand would be soul crushing. Plus, working at the bar throughout the summer would be a tough commute if I have to move back to my dad's house in the Valley after graduation, which I'm planning to do.

"CeeCee won't care about your grades once she meets you," Alessandra assures me. "Just come right out and explain why your grades tanked last year. She's known for being really active with cancer charities. Oh my God! Georgie! I'm looking at the event flyer, and it says—"

Bam.

After turning a corner, I walk smack into the broad chest of the one person I have no desire to see: UCLA football god, Bryce McKellar. I first met Bryce months ago, while waiting in line for coffee on-campus, and sparks instantly flew. He wasn't just physically gorgeous, but charismatic and cocky, too. Best of all, he had a bit of a dark edge to him. A dick-vibe. Which, unfortunately, is my thing, I'm not proud to say. But since I stupidly thought my relationship with Shawn, the biggest dick of them all, was still intact, I took off after getting my coffee and didn't stick around to flirt with Bryce.

Of course, once I found out Shawn was a lying, cheating dirt-bag dick, I kept an eye out for Mr. Football, hoping to bump into him again. But, unfortunately, I never did… until a few days ago… which was when, out of the blue, like manna from heaven, I spotted Bryce standing outside Royce Hall, looking even hotter than he had at the coffee place months before. And, to my thrill, when Bryce's eyes landed on mine, they lit up, every bit as much as they had during our first encounter at the coffee place.

Immediately, Bryce jogged over to me that day on-campus, and we made flirty small talk. "I've actually been keeping an eye out for you," Bryce told me, flashing me his dazzling smile. But since we were both in a rush—Bryce to get to class and me to get to the campus gym to teach a spin class—he quickly got my number and promised he'd text me "really soon." Which he did. Ten minutes later, as a matter of fact. And then again that same afternoon. And, again, later that night. But each time Bryce texted, he'd caught me at a bad time, and I could never text with him for long. "Damn, you're even busier than I am," Bryce texted. To which I replied, "Hustle beats talent, when talent doesn't hustle, baby."

We agreed to touch base the next day with an actual phone call, so we could compare our busy schedules and find a time to "connect"... which I prayed was code for "find a good time to have sex." Because, Lordy, I'm ready to have some good, fun sex with a smoking hot guy. No strings attached. I haven't had sex since Shawn, and I think I'm suffering from physical withdrawals. But since the last thing I want is another relationship right now, especially with another athlete, "no strings fun" is the only thing on my menu.

Unfortunately, though, things didn't go according to my big plans. When Bryce and I finally had that phone conversation the following day —for a full hour, in fact—it quickly became apparent we weren't on the same page. Not at all. As it turned out, Mr. Football wasn't the sexy, cocky, bad boy I'd been projecting onto him. In fact, much to my dismay, he made it clear during our call he's been raised by his God-fearing momma to be a one-woman kind of guy. To always, *always* look for a girl who, get this, is "wife material."

And it only got worse from there. As I sat there silently freaking out on my end of the line, Bryce went on to proclaim he's not looking for an "easy" woman, like all the girls who throw themselves at him, day in and out, but, instead, wants a faithful, loyal girl who'll "support him religiously" through the NFL draft and beyond. Someone he can trust. Someone he can lean on. Someone who'll love him, unconditionally, and not care about all the money and fame coming his way. All of which I thought was a bit much to say during our first phone conversation. I mean, come on, is it really so wrong for a young, horny girl to want a smoking hot guy for nothing but his dazzling smile and hot body?

But Bryce had more bombs to drop during that crazy-ass phone call.

As I sat in stunned silence, thinking maybe I was being punked, he asked, "Do you believe in love at first sight, Georgie?"

"Uh, no," I replied honestly, my insides knotting at how badly I'd misjudged him. "Why? Do you?" Obviously, I shouldn't have said that last part. Indeed, the moment my question left my lips, I knew I'd messed up.

"Not before I met you," Bryce replied. And I swear I threw up, just a little bit, into my mouth. Just like that, the lady-boner I'd had for Bryce McKellar at the coffee place sagged to my knees, and I couldn't get off the call fast enough.

I knew in that moment I'd have to come clean with Bryce and confess I'm not the future wife he thinks I am. That, in fact, at this particular stage of my life, I'm probably closer to the "easy women" who throw themselves at him, thanks to the past couple of years that have left me emotionally drained and determined to fly solo for a while. But right then, I was too stunned to make that particular speech to Bryce. And so, I got off the phone without saying any of it—and also without confirming any plans to "connect" with him any time soon.

But now, Bryce is here. Holding my shoulders so I don't crumple to the ground after bouncing off his hard chest. And, this time, I can't simply hang up my phone to avoid him.

"Bryce," I gasp out, teetering in his firm grasp.

"Are you okay?" he replies, chuckling.

"Yeah. Sorry. I was running."

"I could see that." He grins. "I was just about to text you, actually."

"Oh, yeah? Wow. Hang on." I pick my phone up off the ground—noting, thankfully, that the screen didn't crack upon impact—and breathlessly tell my stepsister I've got to call her back.

"Did you say *Bryce*?" Alessandra says.

"I did."

"As in, Mr. Football?"

"Correct."

"Only pretend to hang up. I want to listen in."

"Okay, bye."

As instructed, I pretend to disconnect the call, and return to Bryce, my stomach churning and my mind racing.

Bryce says, "I was going to text and ask what you're doing tonight."

"Sorry, I'm working at the bar until about two thirty."

"Hey, that works for me," he says. "I'm a night owl."

Shit. Fuck. "I can't. I've got class on Friday mornings, so I always race home after my Thursday-night shift to catch a few hours of sleep." I look at my watch. "Shoot. I'm running late for an event in North Campus. Gotta go!" And off I go, resolved to call Bryce tomorrow to tell him the truth: *I'm not looking for a relationship. I'm not looking to support any guy's dreams "religiously" or otherwise at this particular time. In summary, I'm just not feeling it.*

The moment I'm out of earshot of Bryce, I bring my phone to my ear. "Ally?"

Alessandra laughs. "*Coward.*"

"I know. I'll call him tomorrow and set him straight."

"You realize you're the only girl at UCLA who'd ever turn that boy down, right?"

"Dude, he's looking for a freaking wife."

"Running away all the time, you're only going to make him want you more. I'm sure he's used to girls throwing themselves at him."

"Oh, he is. And they can have him. He's way too big a momma's boy for me."

"Oh, the horror. A genuinely nice guy."

"You know what I mean. I'm still in my bad-boy phase, as I should be. It's what's going to make me ready for Mr. Right whenever he finally comes along in six point five years."

"I'm shocked you don't want to give Bryce a quick test drive before you cut him loose. Even if he's a Cling-On, why not at least hit that hard body *hard* before turning him away? He's panty-melting, Georgie. I looked him up after you told me about him, and almost had a stroke at his hotness."

"I know. If only he'd played it the least bit cool with me, the way he did at the coffee place that first time, I would have been hitting that hard body *hard* as early as this week. As it is, I can't run away fast enough." I sigh audibly at the heartbreaking situation. "Now, what were we talking about before I bumped into Mr. Love at First Sight?"

"Reed Rivers. I was freaking out he's listed as one of the panelists."

"I didn't hear any of that. Who's Reed Rivers?"

"The founder of River Records—the record label."

"Never heard of it."

"Well, you've sure as hell heard of their bands and artists. Hang on. I'll consult the mighty Google." Alessandra pauses briefly. And then, "Holy shit. The River Records roster is insanity. They've got *both* Red Card Riot *and* 22 Goats. Plus, Danger Doctor Jones, Laila Fitzgerald, 2Real, Aloha Carmichael, Fugitive Summer, Watch Party... "

"Holy crap."

"Right? The list goes on and on. That's only the top tier of the roster, but the next tier down is still pretty damned impressive."

"Those are all my favorites."

"Those are all *everyone's* favorites. It's why every student at my school would sell their soul to get signed by River Records."

"Including you?"

"Dude, I'd sell my soul, kidneys, and freaking virginity to get signed."

I cringe. "Please, don't joke about selling your virginity. I took a class on sex trafficking this quarter that was horrifying."

"I was kidding. Obviously."

"I know. But that would be a disgusting way to lose your virginity—to some pervy old guy you don't even *like*. Also, careful what you put out into the universe. From what I've heard, the music industry is full of predators, every bit as much as the movie business. Creeps who'd happily promise a sweet little virgin like you the sun and moon, just to get into your pants."

Alessandra laughs. "Interesting your momma bear comes out to protect my virginity, but not my soul and kidneys."

"Only one scenario seems like a real-world possibility."

If I know Alessandra, she's rolling her eyes at me right now. But smiling, too. "Okay, Georgie," she says. "I promise I won't sell my virginity to anyone, okay? Well, except to Reed Rivers. I can't make the same promise when it comes to him. That man can have anything he wants."

"Stop."

She giggles. "Google him, and you'll see what I mean. Honestly, Reed wouldn't need to promise me the sun and moon in exchange for my V-card. Just an Uber ride home. Actually, not even that. I'd demand nothing from him. Take my virginity, Reed Rivers! Please!"

I can't help giggling with her. "How old is he?"

"Mid-thirties, I think. No older than forty."

Oh, my sweet Alessandra. The girl's got daddy issues, that's for sure, every bit as much as I've got mommy issues. When our parents got together, Alessandra had just lost her father in a hit and run, and I'd just lost my mother in a car accident. And both our parents wrongly thought they could find comfort and solace and a fresh start in marrying another grieving person.

Unfortunately, they quickly found out that was a bad idea. That marriage in the midst of deep grief, especially to a person with whom they had nothing in common, actually made both of them feel ten times worse in their times of need. But, whatever. As confusing and chaotic, and short-lived, as the marriage of my father and Alessandra's mother turned out to be, I wouldn't undo it, even if I could. Because it brought me my beloved sister, Alessandra.

By the time I reach the lecture hall for the music event, my breathing is slightly elevated from jogging across campus, so I take a nearby seat on a bench to finish my phone call. "So, which three songs of yours do you want me to load onto a flash drive to give to the record label guy? I'm going to get you signed to River Records, baby. Absolutely no selling your virginity required."

Alessandra sighs. "Oh, Georgie. You're so sweet. But getting me signed to River Records, especially at an event like this, would be like hitting a golf ball on Earth and landing a hole-in-one on the moon. Last year, the most amazing singer-songwriter at my school won a contest where the grand prize was having Reed personally listen to her music. And guess what? He listened and turned her down."

"That's because she's not *you*."

"She's better than me."

"Impossible. But for the sake of argument, let's say she's *as good as* you, then the reason she got turned down was she didn't have a hypewoman, like me, singing her praises."

"The odds are miniscule you'll get the chance to talk to him at all. And, if you do, it'll be four seconds where you won't have the chance to dazzle him with your patented Georgina Ricci magic. If the situation were different—if you were going to be meeting him one-on-one, I'd put money on you being able to charm him, like you do everyone else. It's a well-known fact he loves beautiful women, so I'm positive you'd be able to grab his attention. But, as it is, this event is going to be packed with hundreds of music students, all of them toting flash drives in their pockets."

My shoulders droop. "Maybe, but there's no harm in me at least trying, right?"

"*Wrong.* I don't want you speeding through a conversation with CeeCee because you're preoccupied with trying to talk to Reed for me. I've got two *years* before graduation. You've got a week. Just this once, kick my dreams to the curb and look out for number one, girl."

I watch a group of students enter the lecture hall and glance at my watch. "Ally, I hear what you're saying. But I can't be in the same building as a man who could *literally* make your dreams come true, and not—"

"Stop," Alessandra says firmly. "You need a good-paying journalism job, Georgie. Not just for yourself, but for your dad, too. Now, stop arguing with me about this and go in there and get CeeCee Rafael to take your writing samples and make all your dreams come true."

THREE
REED

As I park my car in a structure at UCLA, I continue grumbling on the phone to my longtime attorney, Leonard. The entire drive here, we've been talking about the latest batch of frivolous lawsuits and settlement demands leveled against my various businesses—my record label, real estate holdings, nightclubs, and more—and I'm beyond annoyed.

"It's the way of the world when you've got extra-deep pockets," Leonard says. "These plaintiffs' attorneys are hoping you'll settle their bogus claims quickly for a nominal sum, rather than paying me quadruple the amount to fight them."

"Well, they can suck my dick. I don't settle meritless claims, Leonard."

"Yes, I know. And as your attorney, may I say it's the thing I like best about you."

"Not my sparkling personality?"

"That's a distant second." I hear papers rustling on Leonard's end of the call. "Okay, let's talk about that copyright infringement suit against Red Card Riot for a second. Also bullshit?"

"Total and complete. That same chord progression can be found in everything from Mozart to Bruno Mars."

"Well, then, it should be easy to get the case dismissed on a motion.

I'll just need to attach a declaration by a musicologist, explaining what you just said. Know anyone?"

"Angela McGavin. She's the head of UCLA's music school. Coincidentally, I'll be seeing her at an event on-campus in about a half-hour. I'll chat with her about it then."

"Perfect. Lemme know. What's the event?"

"I'll be speaking on a panel, telling wide-eyed music students about the business side of the industry."

"Look at you, giving back to the college kiddies who are hoping to follow in your illustrious footsteps."

"I'm not doing it out of the goodness of my heart. I got roped into it by CeeCee."

Leonard chuckles. "Ah, the indomitable CeeCee Rafael. I find it hard to say no to that woman, myself."

"*Hard?* Try *impossible*, thanks to all the publicity she's given my up-and-comers over the years. The feature she wrote about RCR in time for their debut release is what bought me my first house." My phone buzzes and I look down. "I've got to take another call, Len. Don't forget to text me how many tickets your daughter wants for the RCR concert. I'll make sure she and her friends get backstage to meet the band."

"Wow! Thank you. You're going to win me Father of the Year with this birthday present."

"Show me some mercy on my next bill, and we'll call it even." I disconnect the call and pick up with Isabel. "Well, if it isn't 'America's Sweetheart.'"

Isabel giggles. "Oh, you saw that interview, did you? Wasn't it amazing?"

"I wouldn't call the interview 'amazing,' no. The *headline* was amazing. That's the kind of nickname that'll stick. But the interview itself was only okay. You laid on the 'relatability' factor a bit thick. The photo spread was smokin' hot and on-brand, however, although I'd have told them to lay off the photoshop, especially on your face. You're not twenty-two anymore, but why would you want to be? Overall, though, I'd say the piece was a win. It was certainly well timed, considering the studio's big announcement last week. Congratulations on that, by the way. I've always said you've got superpowers, haven't I? And now, it's official."

"Holy fuck, Reed. A simple 'Yes, Isabel, the interview was amazing' would have sufficed."

"You want me to lie to you?"

"Absolutely."

I scoff. "Don't ask for my opinion if you don't want to hear it." I check my watch. "Why are you calling me? Aren't you filming pick-ups in Toronto?"

"I've got a few days off, so I flew into LA for a meeting with the studio head. Unfortunately, though, he had a family emergency while I was in the air and needed to reschedule. Which means, lucky you, I've just landed in LA with zero plans for the next thirty-six hours. Let's fuck like rabbits! I'm a horny bunny."

"Sorry, I'm booked solid between now and the break of dawn, when I'll be boarding a flight to The Big Apple."

"Break all your silly plans. It's been way too long and I miss you."

"I would if I could." I'm not sure that's a true statement, actually.

Isabel's voice turns stiff. "You've got a hot date?"

I look at my watch again. Shit. I need to end this call in exactly four minutes to make it to the stupid panel on time. "No, I don't have a hot date—not that it'd be any of your business, if I did. I've got an event at UCLA in a few minutes, and then I'm meeting a couple friends for dinner and drinks."

Isabel sighs with relief. "Perfect. Yes, I'll join you for dinner. Thanks for asking."

"Not this time."

"Oh, come on. Whoever your friends are, they'd be thrilled to break bread with 'America's Sweetheart.'"

"Nope. It's a Boy's Night Out. Maybe next time."

"Who are the friends?"

"Josh Faraday and another guy from college you don't know."

"Josh Faraday! He'd *love* to see me! Remember how much fun you, me, Jen, and Josh—"

"That's ancient history. Josh is happily married these days."

She gasps. "*Josh Faraday is married?*"

I look at my watch again. "Yup. He's married with children and living in Seattle. And I've got to hang up in three minutes to make my event."

"Wow, I thought for sure Josh would die a bachelor, the same as you."

"So did Josh. But the minute he met his crazy wife and her even crazier family, all he wanted to do was build a white picket fence with her. He's got two babies and another on the way and says he wants to fill a minivan. Josh is so happy these days, I'd hate him if I didn't love him so much."

Isabel scoffs, and I know she's aggravated to hear me use the word "love" in relation to Josh, when I've never once said it in relation to her. "Come see me after you're done with your friends," she says. "Whatever time it is. I don't care how late you come, as long as you do." She snickers. "And then make *me* come."

My stomach tightens. If I didn't know it before this call, I know it now: I've got no desire to hook up with Isabel again. And not just because I'm busy tonight. If I were as free as a bird tonight, I'd still say no. "If you're horny, call some aspiring model or actor," I say. "Fulfill your Mrs. Robinson fantasies."

Isabel scoffs. "I'm not horny for just anyone, Reed. I want *you*." Her tone becomes vulnerable. "I miss you."

Fuck. How did I let myself get into this situation with this woman, *again*? Drunkenly fucking her at that party in the Hamptons was a felony stupid thing to do, no matter how much she swore she could handle a no-strings arrangement.

I look at my watch again. "I have to go, or I'm gonna be late. Travel safe back to the land of Maple Syrup. And congrats again on the franchise deal. I love being able to say, 'I knew her when.'"

"*Wait*," Isabel says sharply. "I need to see you, if only for an hour. I won't take no for an answer, Reed."

I clench my jaw. Oh, how I hate that expression. If I want to say no to a request, then I'll say no. Unless, of course, the person asking me for something is my mother, sister, CeeCee, Josh, or Henn. Also, my housekeeper, Amalia. That woman can have anything she wants from me, too —although she'd never ask, so it's a moot point. Clearly, it's time to cut the cord, once and for all. "Isabel," I say calmly. "It's obvious this 'whenever we happen to be in the same city' arrangement isn't working out as well for you as you promised it would."

"I'm not allowed to miss you?"

"You're not, actually. I certainly don't miss you."

She inhales sharply. "Don't be mean."

"I'm not. I'm being honest. I have no ill will toward you. No desire to hurt you. But the truth is I don't think about you when I'm not in your presence. Which, literally, means I don't miss you. And, clearly, being missed is something you want and need."

"Yeah, I'm such a weirdo. Do you enjoy hurting me? Is that it? You get sick pleasure from being mean to me?"

"How am I being mean? You're literally *begging* me to fuck you. If you had an ounce of self-respect, you wouldn't be telling me you 'won't take no for an answer.' You'd be telling me to fuck off."

Isabel says nothing to that. But I can tell by her stilted breathing she's holding back tears.

I soften. "I'm not good for you, Isabel. Never have been. Let's walk away, once and for all, before you get hurt again, okay?"

"You want me to walk away before I get hurt?" she spits out. "Yeah, it's a bit too late for that, Reed."

I sigh. "I've got to go. Congrats on becoming a superhero."

"Are you getting back at me for hurting you? That was a million years ago, and we weren't even dating exclusively at the time."

"You didn't hurt me. Don't conflate my passionate desire to seek revenge against a punk-ass ingrate with a passionate desire for *you*."

She draws in a shocked breath.

"You're obviously looking for more than a sexual fling with me," I continue. "And that's not something that interests me. Not with you, not with anyone. It's nothing personal."

"Nothing personal?" she shouts. "Reed, I'm in love with you! I'm sorry if that's an inconvenient truth, but I can't help what I feel."

For a long moment, I look out the window of my sports car at the cement walls of the parking structure, feeling angry with myself for opening myself up to this drama again. And for what? Some drunken, nostalgic pussy at a party. "I can't fathom you're actually in love with me, like you're claiming. But if you are, then that's your misfortune, I guess."

"What the fuck is wrong with you?" Isabel whispers.

I can't help smiling at the question—the same one I've been asked by women my whole life. Shit, I've even asked it of myself plenty of times, too. Most memorably, when I stood next to Josh on a beach in Maui and watched him exchange marriage vows. And then again, when I stood next to Henny on my patio in the Hollywood Hills and watched him do the same. When I stood on a beach in the Bahamas and watched my baby sister, Violet, say "I do." And, most recently, when I sat in a castle in France and watched CeeCee exchange marriage vows with a French billionaire, certain her third time down the aisle would be the charm, even though she and her new husband weren't even planning to reside on the same continent after the nuptials. All those times, and others, too, as I've watched the people I care about promising their eternal love to one person, I've found myself wondering, if only fleetingly... *What the fuck is wrong with me?*

"This isn't goodbye," I say, my heart softening at the sound of Isabel's sniffling. "If you need a date to a red-carpet event and you can't find anyone who looks as good in a tux as I do, then call me. And it should go without saying, your secrets will always be safe with me. We started this climb together as kids, and I'll always have your back. But if you're genuinely in love with me, like you say, then it's time for you to move on. There's no happily ever after I can offer you, sweetheart. No ending to this story where I'm the prince and you're my pretty princess, and we ride off together into the sunset on a white horse."

Isabel sniffles. "You're selling yourself short. You could be the prince, if you'd let yourself."

"I've gotta go. It's time for me to 'give back' to some college kiddies, all of whom are almost certainly plotting to ambush me with their music demos afterwards."

"Reed."

"I'm sure I'll see you at all the parties during awards season. And when I do, don't worry, I'll always make sure everyone thinks you're my 'one that got away.' Not the other way around."

"Reed. *Stop*. Please. You can't just—"

Click.

Oh, yes I can.

FOUR
REED

Ten years ago

I pick up my cell phone... and then immediately put it back down on my desk, my pulse pounding. I look around my garage, at the large cardboard boxes stacked against the walls, all of them filled with merch samples for RCR's upcoming debut tour. All of them requiring my approval by tomorrow. And all of them reminding me I'm going to be up shit creek if this massive gamble doesn't pan out.

I glance at the notepad on my desk, its pages covered with the furious editing notes I've scrawled for the director of RCR's debut music video. I glance at the documents stacked on my desk—licensing deals I've been chasing down for all three of my bands for the past four months. But, mostly, for Red Card Riot, the band I'm betting the farm will put my fledgling label on the map when their album debuts in two months.

Yeah, I've got to make this call. *Go big, or go home.*

"Majestic Maids," a female voice says, answering my call.

My heart pounds even harder. "Is this Francesca?"

"Yes. How may I help you?"

"I'd like to book an escort for later this month—for an important event."

"We're a cleaning service, sir. Not an escort service."

I tell her the name of the guy who referred me, a star midfielder for the LA Galaxy whom I met last month at one of Josh's raging parties, and the woman quickly changes her tune.

"To whom am I speaking?" she asks, her voice suddenly light and bright.

"Reed."

"Your last name, please?"

I pause, nerves tightening my belly. Am I being reckless here? It's technically illegal. But, oh well. I've come this far. Stolen from Peter to pay Paul for months now. I'm so close now, I can taste it. Which means now isn't the time to start playing it safe. I mean, come on. If a star soccer player and his teammates, plus a whole bunch of his famous friends, can trust this woman to be discreet, then I can, too.

"Rivers," I say, my tone surprisingly calm, despite the thundering of my heart.

"Hello, Mr. Rivers. I'm glad you called. When and where is your event?"

"The twenty-first, at Greystone Mansion in Beverly Hills. It's a black-tie event, so my date will need to rock a designer gown. Something that makes her look like ten million bucks."

"Not a problem. Tell me about the kind of woman you're envisioning. What type are you most attracted to?"

"Curvy brunettes always turn my head the most," I admit. "Even more than that, though, it's women with lots of confidence and sass. Actually, though, in this instance, sass maybe wouldn't be such a good idea. I don't think what personally attracts me is relevant here. For this event, the woman needs to be what *other* people covet. Someone who looks like she could walk a Victoria's Secret runway. You know, the kind of woman who looks like she could get any man she wants."

"And yet, she's chosen *you*. And what about later that night, after the event? Would you like to spend time with her, in private—perhaps enjoy some intimate, one-on-one time? It would be a good idea to choose someone you're personally attracted to, in case you'd like to leave yourself that option."

I lean back in my leather chair and gaze up at the ceiling of my garage. At my surfboards and snowboards and kayak resting above the wooden rafters. If everything goes according to plan on the twenty-first, if I find a way to meet CeeCee Rafael at that party and pique her interest in RCR enough to secure a well-timed mention in *Rock 'n' Roll*, it'll be a whole new ballgame for me. I'll finally be able to move my operations into an actual office space—hopefully, that amazing one on Sunset Boulevard. I'll be able to hire a couple full-time staffers. Maybe even buy myself a condo, if I catch a few other lucky breaks. Yeah, if I hit a grand slam at the party, then I'll surely be in the mood to celebrate with at least a BJ from my smoking hot escort. On the other hand, though, if things *don't* turn out the way I'm hoping, if I leave that mansion on the twenty-first in the same position I'm in now—crossing my fingers and toes I've done enough to squeak RCR onto the bottom rung of the fucking alternative rock chart, then I'll surely want to be alone after the party.

"I'll play it by ear on hiring my date for 'intimate services' after the party," I reply. "I want to be certain there's sufficient chemistry between us to move forward on that."

The woman snorts, like there being a lack of sexual chemistry is a ridiculous notion.

"Look, I'm not calling because I can't get laid," I say, annoyance flashing through me. "I can. And by exceptionally beautiful women. I'm calling because this is going to be a critical work event for me, possibly life-changing, and I won't have the time or bandwidth to deal with a date who's pissed at me for God knows what. For not paying enough attention to her. For not introducing her around or trying to help her career. I want someone on my arm who understands I'm building a fucking empire here—a *brand*. And that means I need to communicate my place in the hierarchy the second I walk through the fucking door."

"I understand, Mr. Rivers," she says soothingly. "I think you're brilliant to realize an exceptionally beautiful woman on your arm is a must-have status symbol in this town. But how about I tell you the pricing on intimate services, just in case?"

Without waiting for my reply, she quotes me a number for "unlimited services." It's a number I consider to be ludicrous, and tell her so. So, she offers to take twenty percent off her price, if I book now.

"That's still too high a price for something I can get for free on my own," I say. But the truth is, I simply can't afford that price tag, whether it's reasonable or not. Not now, I can't, before I know if I've secured a feature in *Rock 'n' Roll* for RCR.

"Mr. Rivers," Francesca says, like she's talking to a moron. "You want a girl who looks like she could walk a runway? Well, my girls actually *do* walk runways. Indeed, they're signed to the best modeling agencies in the world. And as far as you getting it 'for free' on your own... we both know that's not true. Nothing comes for free. One way or another, a man always pays for it. With my girls, however, the only thing you pay is what's been agreed upon in advance. There's simplicity in that, don't you think? Freedom. Honesty, in a way. Far more so than having to wine and dine a woman to get to the same result."

She's speaking my language now. But since I'm cash-poor, whether I agree with her philosophy or not, I reply, "I'll decide that night, once I know for sure if we've got chemistry."

"Suit yourself. I was just trying to save you twenty percent."

"Let's talk next steps," I say, switching gears. "I want to be able to hand-pick my date from *unedited* photos. Headshots *and* body shots. Absolutely no photoshop."

"Not a problem. Wire me a deposit, and I'll send you a link to a gallery."

"Is the deposit refundable, if I'm not happy with any of the options?"

"Of course. But, trust me, you'll be happy."

"Make sure my date knows she's not allowed to network for herself that night. There are going to be lots of influential people at this party—household-name celebrities and power brokers—and I don't want her trying to hustle for herself."

"When I call the girls to ask about their availability, I'll be clear about that."

"My date can say she's a model with such and such agency, if she's asked about her career. In fact, if all goes well, I'm sure some of the power brokers at the party will seek her out afterwards, for music videos and whatever. And that would be great. I genuinely hope she cashes in. Just not that night. That night, she's there for *me*."

"Of course. What's the event, if you don't mind me asking?"

"A birthday bash for the founder of *Rock 'n' Roll*."

"Oh, wow. Sounds like fun."

"A 'who's who' of the music industry will be there. It's going to be the party of the year in my industry. Even more so than Grammys after-parties."

"So, you're the 'Reed Rivers' of River Records, then? I've been googling you as we've been talking."

"Yeah, that's me."

"Do you look anything like the photo on your website?"

"Yeah. It's unedited. Taken two months ago."

She chuckles softly. "Well, then, I can see why you have no trouble attracting beautiful women on your own. You're a very handsome man, Mr. Rivers."

"Unfortunately, I attract beautiful women who have no idea what it takes to build a fucking empire from scratch. Beautiful women who require way more attention than I can possibly give them at this point in my life."

"Well, Mr. Rivers, you've come to the right place. I can assure you that whatever girl you choose will have no trouble understanding what you're trying to accomplish here—and enthusiastically playing her part to assist you. Indeed, after seeing your photo, I'm quite certain your date, whoever she is, will have no problem staring at you at the party, all night long, like you're the handsomest, most powerful man in the world, a sex god who just got finished fucking her with his huge dick minutes before you two walked through the door."

I chuckle. "Francesca, has anyone ever told you you're damned good at your job?"

"I've been doing this a long time, Mr. Rivers."

"I'll send you the deposit right away. I'm looking forward to seeing those photos."

FIVE
GEORGINA

Present day

After settling into a third-row seat of the packed lecture hall, I pull out my laptop and do the exact thing Alessandra commanded me *not* to do: I load a flash drive with her three best songs. Obviously, I'm going to focus the majority of my energy on charming CeeCee Rafael. But there's no way in hell I'm *not* going to have my stepsister's music at the ready for the record label guy, just in case.

After stuffing the loaded drive into my purse, I pull out my phone and google Reed Rivers, as Alessandra suggested. And, lo and behold, the photo that pops up on my phone makes my jaw clank to the floor. *Hot damn.* My stepsister made Reed sound like a chick magnet, and now I can see why. He isn't only a young, rich, powerful music mogul—all of which would be catnip enough for virtually any woman—he's also scorching hot by any standard of male beauty. The kind of sexy that makes even the smartest women turn as stupid as a box of rocks.

Reed's chocolate eyes are piercing and intense. His dark hair is stylishly mussed. And, damn, his cheekbones look like Michelangelo himself chiseled them from a hunk of perfectly tanned marble. Surely, if the music thing hadn't panned out for this hunk of gorgeousness, he could have made his living starring in cologne commercials. He's just that beautifully crafted.

I flip to the images option on my browser, thirsty to see more photos of this insanely hot creature, and quickly discover Reed's tattooed, muscled body is every bit as jaw-dropping as his face. Add "swimsuit model" to the list of potential careers for him in a parallel universe. Holy crap. From top to bottom, Reed Rivers is more than a chick magnet—he's a Taser gun. A crossbow. Even if he were a pauper without an ounce of power or clout, any red-blooded woman would tumble into this man's bed without a second thought, if only to experience one delicious, reckless night with a god among men.

My heart rate increasing, I click onto Reed's Wikipedia page and devour the basics. His record label, River Records, burst onto the music scene with Red Card Riot's debut album ten years ago. And ever since, it's churned out hit after hit, with an ever-increasing roster of top-notch bands and artists.

Along the way, smart man that he is, Reed's parlayed his success in music into other successful investments and businesses, as well—in real estate, tequila, nightclubs, restaurants, and more. The man has even successfully invested in some hit independent films. Apparently, whatever he touches turns to gold. Which, of course, is why he's earned the nickname "The Man with the Midas Touch."

I come to the "personal information" section of Reed's Wiki page and find out Reed is thirty-four years old, six-foot-three, and an exercise enthusiast. No surprise on that last thing, given his sculpted frame. Snowboarding, triathlons, jumping out of airplanes, surfing, scuba-diving, rock climbing, cycling, beach volleyball, basketball, kayaking... If it gets Reed's body moving and his heart pumping, he's all over it. And, lucky for the world, there are plenty of hot photos online of him doing it all. *Damn.*

Back on Reed's Wiki page, I learn he's never been married and has no children. And that, apparently, he likes it that way. "I'm not a married-with-kids kind of guy," Reed has been quoted as saying. "Being Uncle Reed to my baby sister's and best friends' kids is perfect for me."

I keep reading and discover a bit of shocking news: Reed's father, now deceased, was a renowned white-collar criminal who hanged himself in prison fifteen years ago. His surviving family consists of his mother, a paternal aunt, and a much-younger sister. No details supplied on any of them.

I glance at the empty stage to make sure I'm not missing CeeCee's grand entrance, and then eagerly return to my phone. I click on the "romantic relationships" tab of Reed's page, and discover he's been linked to a smattering of high-profile women, some of them instantly recognizable actresses and models. It seems the highly likeable model-turned-actress, Isabel Randolph, is in more photos with Reed than anyone else. Did adorable Isabel manage to tie Reed's hunky, playboy ass down longer than anybody else?

I google to find out, and immediately discover my hunch is right: Reed and Isabel had a two-year relationship that ended about six years ago. I search their names in the images tab and a cache of sexy photos of the pair pops up. In some of them, Reed and Isabel are dressed to kill for a night on the town. In others, they're dressed casually, or in ski clothes, or swim suits, always looking perfect.

In one particularly gorgeous shot, they're both tanned and dressed in white, walking through what looks like a small village in some oceanside paradise. And that's all my brain needs to conjure images of the sexy pair going at it *hard* in some beachfront vacation villa, the aquamarine ocean their backdrop as they fuck each other's brains out...

Suddenly, Isabel in my hot fantasy becomes *me*. Out of nowhere, I'm the lucky woman who's sweaty and moaning and getting fucked hard by Reed on some Greek island. I'm the one on my hands and knees, growling as he invades my body with his, over and over again...

Oh, holy hell. I'm seriously losing it. These days, I think about sex as much as magazine articles always say the average male thinks about it. Gah. Why'd Bryce have to turn out to be such a Cling-On? If only he'd played his cards right, if only he'd been the cocky football star I'd thought, it's fifty-fifty I would have been having hot, sweaty sex with him this week. Not on a Greek island, with an aquamarine ocean as our backdrop, but I'd take it, just the same.

Applause erupts around me, jerking me from my reverie. Quickly, I drop my phone into my lap and direct my attention to the stage, just in time to see my idol striding across it in a sleek pantsuit, right alongside

Mr. Hottie himself, Reed Rivers. Who, by the way, looks even more tantalizing in person than in his hunky photos. *Wow.*

CeeCee and Reed and the other panelists take seats onstage as a woman with a lovely smile approaches a lectern. Our host for the event welcomes the audience, introduces herself as the head of UCLA's music department, and proceeds to introduce each panelist. We meet a renowned songwriter, a composer for movies, a singer who apparently had a huge hit in the '90s, and a music supervisor who selects songs for TV and film. Finally, the moderator introduces CeeCee, and I whoop and clap far more vigorously than anyone around me.

"Maybe some of you have heard of CeeCee's little magazine?" the moderator says with a sly smile. "It's called... *Rock 'n' Roll?*" Everyone, including me, laughs and applauds. "And last but not least," the moderator says, beaming a huge smile at Mr. Panty-Melter on the far end. "Help me welcome a gentleman known in the music industry as 'The Man with the Midas Touch.' He's one of this university's most esteemed alums. The founder of River Records. *Reed Rivers.*"

The crowd cheers wildly, much more enthusiastically than they did for anyone else. And, in a flash, I know Alessandra was right: everyone here has a music demo in their pockets they're hoping to slip to Reed after the event.

The moderator says, "Reed founded his label eleven years ago, at the age of twenty-three, right after he'd obtained both a BA in business *and* an MBA from this fine university."

The crowd cheers at the mention of our beloved school.

"In an early interview, Reed said he founded River Records with two goals in mind: one, bringing 'stellar' music into the world, and, two, making a 'shit-ton of money' while accomplishing goal number one."

The room explodes with laughter and applause.

Chuckling with the crowd, the moderator adds, "I think it's fair to say 'mission accomplished' on both counts. Would you agree, Reed?"

Reed smiles. "So far, so good. But, to be clear, I'm not even close to done with either of my stated goals yet."

The moderator looks like she's swooning at that response, but after taking a few deep breaths, she manages to return to the audience with a professional demeanor. "Let's get started. I'll begin with you, Reed. Your label is known for being particularly selective about the artists you sign. Correct?"

"Correct."

"Why is that?"

"Because we don't stockpile our artists, the way other labels do. If River Records signs you, it means we're committed to putting our full faith and resources behind you. Most labels sign a hundred acts, hoping one will have a hit, almost by chance. But while they play the odds like bean counters, we shoot for the stars, each and every time. But, of course, the flipside of that philosophy is that we need to be highly selective at the front end."

"Have you ever experienced a miss, despite your best efforts?"

"We've had disappointments, sure. But a complete miss? No, not yet. Knock on wood."

He raps his knuckles against the side of his head, a move he's obviously not inventing—and, yet, every student in the audience laughs and swoons like they're seeing the maneuver for the first time. And I can't help thinking, *Poor Isabel didn't stand a chance.*

As the moderator asks Reed some follow up questions, I take a surreptitious photo of him, and quickly shoot it off to Alessandra. And, of course, within seconds, my stepsister sends me a gif of a nuclear explosion, with the caption: "MY OVARIES," making me chuckle out loud.

After putting my phone in my lap again, I return to the discussion, just in time to hear the moderator say, "Thank you so much, Reed. I think you've shown us all why every aspiring artist I know would give their left kidney to get signed by your label."

Reed leans back in his chair, the king of all he surveys. "Actually, our contracts require new artists to give their *right* kidney. I keep them in mason jars in my office and nibble on them whenever I'm low on protein bars."

Again, everyone in the room, including me, laughs and swoons at Reed's wit and charm.

"I stand corrected," the moderator says, her face aglow. She clears her throat. "Moving on."

And away we go. Question. Answer. Rinse and repeat. Sometimes, the moderator addresses the full panel. Other times, she talks to a specific panelist, like she did with Reed. But, through it all, nobody holds my attention like CeeCee and Reed. But mostly Reed, if I'm being honest, except for when CeeCee is the one speaking. And even then, I can't help sneaking peeks at Reed to see how he's reacting to whatever CeeCee is saying.

After about twenty minutes, while the moderator chats with the music composer, I find myself sneaking yet another peek at Reed—and then jolting like I've been electrocuted when I discover his dark, piercing eyes fixed firmly on me. My heart lurches as our gazes mingle, and then stampedes when he doesn't look away.

Am I imagining this staring contest? Am I nothing but a horny woman projecting her fantasies onto an incredibly successful and sexy man? Surely, a man of Reed's stature wouldn't notice some random nobody in a crowded lecture hall... Yeah, I decide, Reed must be staring blankly, letting his mind wander, perhaps to the woman he banged last night, and I happen to be in what *appears* to be his sightline.

And yet... it really seems like he's actively, and quite flirtatiously, checking me out. But how could that be? Yes, men frequently check me out. It's part of the reason I became a bartender—because I realized I could channel some of that male attention into tips. That, and my father would kill me if I became a stripper. But, still, I think I'm being ridiculous to think a man who dates supermodels and actresses and *literally* parties with rock stars would notice *me* in this situation.

Deciding to find out, once and for all, I drag my teeth suggestively over my lower lip, smile brightly, and then... *wink* at Reed. And, to my shock, Reed Rivers *immediately* winks back. In reply, my flirtatious smile morphs into a full, beaming, goofy one, which Reed returns in kind. Although, to be sure, Reed's full smile is anything but goofy.

Still smiling broadly at me, he dips his chin, as if to say, *Hello.*

So, I return his gesture. *Hello, Handsome.* I waggle my eyebrows, just to triple-check I'm not imagining this. And, to my sizzling delight, Reed sends me a return eyebrow waggle that makes me giggle. How is it possible his eyebrow waggle is actually sexy? So sexy, in fact, it sends arousal pooling between my legs.

"What do you think about that?" the moderator says. "Reed?"

Reed abruptly swivels his head.

"What advice would you give anyone dreaming of a career in music, Reed?"

"Oh. Uh." Reed clears his throat. "Yes. Well, to begin with, I'd say 'fake it 'til you make it.' Not original, I know, but still good advice. People in this industry don't want to be the *first* or the *last* to jump on a bandwagon. So, your job is to convince them they've personally discovered the next big thing—someone only the coolest of cool kids know about at the moment." He launches into explaining his point further, and I force myself to look away—at CeeCee, the moderator, the other panelists... until, finally, I allow myself another quick peek at him. And, to my thrill, he's staring at me again. This time, when our eyes meet, Reed leans forward and says, "My last piece of advice would be this. When opportunity knocks, say *yes*." He flashes me a naughty smile. "Actually, say yes, yes, yes, without apology or hesitation. You might only get one shot. No regrets."

Arousal zings through my body, reddening my cheeks and hardening my nipples. Without meaning to do it, I nod slowly, letting Reed know I've heard him loud and clear. That I'm ready to say yes, yes, yes to him, any time, any place. All he needs to do is ask.

Reed smirks at me one last time, before turning to look at the moderator. "And that's pretty much it, Angela."

As everyone applauds, the moderator thanks Reed for his comments, which she calls insightful, inspiring, and "oddly arousing." And then, with a laugh, she announces we've reached the end of the presentation and asks the panelists to hang around to answer students' questions. And through it all, Reed and I can't stop eyeball-fucking each other from across the lecture hall like our lives depend on it.

Suddenly, I become aware students around me have risen from their chairs and are working their way toward the aisles.

"Did you see Reed flirting with me?" a blonde in front of me says excitedly to her friend.

"With *you*?" her friend says. "He was looking at *me*."

Shit. Does every woman in this building, including me, think Reed has been flirting with them for the past hour? My heart in my throat, I jockey through the slow-moving crowd and make my way toward CeeCee, who's standing on the opposite side of the hall from Reed. When I reach the back of CeeCee's short line, which, thankfully, is only a few students deep, I peek at Reed's massive line... and then at him... and discover, to my thrill, his eyes are on mine *again*.

Without hesitation, Reed sends me a sexy little wink, followed by an eyebrow waggle. And I can't help smiling broadly at the gesture. Of course, I give him as good as he just gave to me, making him smile... and just that fast, I know we're both thinking the same thing: whenever he gets through his long line, he's going to come over here to talk to me. And whatever that man suggests, whatever he asks, wherever he suggests we go, I'm going to follow his explicit directions and say, without a moment's hesitation or apology: yes... yes... *yes*.

SIX
GEORGINA

"Georgie!" a female voice says, and when I peel my eyes off Reed's white-hot smolder at the far end of the lecture hall, my favorite professor—the one who taught two of my investigative journalism classes this year—is standing before me.

"Professor Schiff!" I say brightly. "What are you doing here?"

"I came to say hello to CeeCee. We went to school together." She indicates CeeCee's line, now only four students deep in front of me. "You're here to meet her?"

I nod. "I'm hoping to charm her into reading a couple of my writing samples."

"Brilliant! Are you hoping to write for *Rock 'n' Roll*?"

"I'd love that, of course. But my dream job would be writing for *Dig a Little Deeper*. It's CeeCee's newest magazine, devoted to investigative journalism and in-depth interviews."

"I know it well. You'd be perfect for that, Georgie."

My heart leaps. "Thank you so much. I don't have high hopes, unfortunately, thanks to my overall GPA being less than stellar. But a girl can try."

"But you're a gifted writer. You aced both my classes."

"Thank you. Yes, thankfully, my grades bounced back this past year.

But the first years of college were a bit rough on me, personally. Especially last year. And my grades suffered, unfortunately."

My professor's features contort with concern. "Do you mind me asking what happened?"

I pause, and then decide there's no choice but to tell her. "My dad was battling cancer the past couple of years. Last year, I was the one who took care of him, while still juggling a full-time course load and two part-time jobs."

"Oh, my gosh. I'm so sorry. Helping him was all on your shoulders?"

I nod. "He has some neighbors who've been great. But it was mostly me. It's just my dad and me. My mom passed away when I was nine, going on ten." I look down at my blue toenails, peeking out of my flip flops. "I probably should have taken last year off, or at least dropped down to a part-time course load—but we'd already paid my full-time tuition and housing, so... " I look up, forcing a smile. "The good news is, he's doing great now. And his sister recently moved in with him, to help out. So, it's all good."

"Aw, Georgie. I'm so sorry." She puts her hand on her heart. "I'm so glad he's doing well now."

"Thank you. Me, too. We're both super excited for me to graduate and move full steam ahead on my job search, if only I can convince potential employers to look past my mediocre GPA."

My professor looks thoughtful. "Have you considered applying for an unpaid internship? I know it'd be tough at first, what with student loans and all. But lots of companies, including CeeCee's, use unpaid internships as their initial proving ground for new hires."

My spirit sinks. "I'd love to be able to do that, but I can't afford it. I need a good paying job, not just for my own expenses and student loans, but to help my dad afford some expensive medicine he still needs to take."

My professor looks downright distraught. "You know what, Georgie? Wait here. I'm going to personally introduce you to CeeCee."

My heart leaps. "Really? Thank you!" But as she turns to leave, my heart lurches into my mouth. "Professor?"

She turns around.

"Please, don't tell CeeCee what I told you about my father. I want to get a shot at a job because of my writing abilities, not for sympathy."

My professor smiles kindly. "Of course. I'll tell her only that you're one of the brightest, loveliest, most talented, and passionate journalism students I've ever had the pleasure, and honor, of teaching. All of which will be true."

A lump rises in my throat. "Thank you."

With a little wink, my professor turns on her heel and strides to CeeCee's line. My skin buzzing with excitement, I watch her apologize to two students at the front before exuberantly hugging her old friend. The two women talk for quite some time. Long enough that I find myself glancing at Reed after a bit, to make sure he's still there.

When I spot Reed across the room, he's talking to a female student. A pretty redhead who's got her hand outstretched, like she's offering him something. Is that a music demo in her palm? I bet it is, just like Alessandra predicted. Whatever it is, Reed's clearly not interested in taking it from her—also, exactly as Alessandra predicted. God, I was so naïve.

"Georgina," my professor says, drawing my attention.

Oh my God. *It's CeeCee.* She's standing before me. Looking like the legend she is.

Brief introductions are made, after which I begin babbling like the fangirl I am. I tell CeeCee about my admiration for her, for her magazines and fashion sense and philanthropy and business acumen. About my love for investigative journalism and her latest magazine, especially. And when I'm done rambling, CeeCee looks charmed, not annoyed. So much so, she invites me to join her and Professor Schiff for coffee at the nearby campus place—the one where I first met Bryce, actually.

But just before our threesome reaches the double doors at the front of the hall, I can't help glancing over my shoulder once last time at Mr. Music Mogul. To my thrill, he's watching me intently. A lion tracking a gazelle. Or, rather, a rich, powerful man watching the nobody he assumed he was going to fuck, just because he felt like it, walking straight out the door without even saying hello to him.

With a wistful smile, I flash Reed a wink, letting him know I'm as disappointed as he is not to get to experience whatever deliciousness might have transpired between us. And then, I straighten up and march out the doors behind CeeCee and my professor, feeling enthralled I'm getting this amazing opportunity... but also, if I'm being honest, a little disappointed I'll never get the chance to say the words "yes, yes, yes!" to the man who instructed me to say them, whenever opportunity came knocking for me.

SEVEN
REED

"Honey, I'm home!" Josh hollers as we enter the crowded bar, and Henn and I laugh.

All three of us have fond memories of this place, but especially Josh, since he's the one who tended bar here in college, albeit briefly. Just long enough for Josh to realize he loved tending bar, but hated punching a clock. A few months into his first-ever stint as an hourly wage worker, Josh struck a deal with the bar owner: Josh could tend bar whenever he wanted, without notice, provided he paid for whatever drinks he poured—using only expensive top-shelf liquor—and generously tipped whichever bartender he'd screwed out of tips by showing up unannounced.

Some of the guys in our fraternity house razzed Josh for essentially paying to work. But I totally understood: Josh wanted the same thing I'd wanted when I'd paid that sorority girl to eat her pussy a few years before—all the pleasures of a job he thoroughly enjoyed, without any of the associated hassles or commitments. As far as I was concerned, Josh was a genius for striking that deal with the bar owner, Bernie. In fact, he was my fucking hero.

I nudge Josh's shoulder and motion to the pool table. "You and Henn get next game while I get our drinks."

"You bought dinner," Josh says. "I'm buying drinks."

"Fuck off, Faraday," I reply, already walking away. "I could buy dinner and drinks for three lifetimes, and still not repay you for everything you bankrolled in college."

When I arrive at the crowded bar, I elbow my way to an open spot at the far end... and promptly lose my shit. *It's her.* The sultry, sassy brunette from the music school event this afternoon. *She's the bartender.* And she's every bit as boner-inducing as she was this afternoon. More so, actually, now that she's dressed to maximize her curves—and, surely, her tips—in a low-cut tank top, push-up bra, and skin-tight jeans.

She's standing in profile to me at the moment, taking orders from a rowdy group of frat boys, all of whom plainly think she's as big a knockout as I do. And who wouldn't? She's a bombshell, this girl. A bodacious siren plucked straight out of a Fellini flick. Thick, dark hair. Full, tempting lips in the perfect shape of a bow. Eyes that blaze with confidence. Sass. *Charisma.* Her skin is olive. Her limbs long. And those curves! Jesus Christ. They're enough to make a careful man do some seriously reckless shit.

When she left the lecture hall with CeeCee without saying a word to me, despite all the winks and smiles and heated smolders we'd exchanged for a full hour, I was shocked. Also, impressed. But, mostly, *intrigued.* Was she a wannabe pop star playing a master game of chess by ditching me—gambling I'd track her down through CeeCee? Or had I pegged the girl all wrong, and she was merely CeeCee's new personal assistant or niece?

The latter scenario seemed like a long shot, given the nature of the event and the girl's pop-star good looks—not to mention her brazen flirting with me. Nobody her age would ever flirt *that* aggressively with me, just because. They always want something. But I had to know for sure. Hence, my decision to do the very thing she was most likely counting on: I resolved to call CeeCee tomorrow to track the bombshell down, even if it turned out she was a music student wannabe pop star who was decidedly off-limits to me.

It's funny. Dumbshit guys at parties always assume I fuck aspiring artists, the same way I snack on kale chips. All the time. Without a second thought. But that couldn't be further from the truth. In actuality, I don't touch anyone who's hoping to further her career by fucking or blowing me, no matter how attractive she might be. It's the same whether she's an aspiring artist, an artist I've already signed, or one of my employees. They're all off-limits to me. No exceptions.

See, what I've learned, after a few unfortunate missteps early on, is that even the hottest sex isn't worth risking the possible fall-out—the risk that the same woman who throws herself at me on Tuesday will claim I've used my power and influence inappropriately with her on Wednesday, once it's clear I'm not going to give her what she wants.

I mean, sure, I'll fuck models or actresses who want to use me *indirectly* to boost their clout or Instagram following or finagle an introduction to a powerful friend. That's the way of the world. But fucking a woman who thinks giving me a BJ will *directly* advance her career—whether that's getting her signed to my label, or assigned to a headlining slot on a tour, or getting a promotion at one of my companies? Nope. I won't touch that woman with a ten-foot pole. Ever.

Well, until today, apparently, when I saw this bartender and immediately started flirting with her, without knowing for sure if she was free and clear or not. And then, to top off my recklessness, started telling myself all sorts of things I never tell myself. Stuff like, *Rules are made to be broken.* And, *Maybe it wouldn't be the end of the world if I fucked a wannabe, just once...* All the same things I'm telling myself now, yet again, as I watch this siren mesmerize that pack of fraternity boys into handing over all their cash.

Holy shit, she's mouth-watering. If I were casting her in a music video, I'd make it a tribute to old, black-and-white Italian flicks. The video would take place on a vineyard. She'd be The Vineyard Owner's Daughter in a peasant dress with a low neckline. The sultry virgin bursting out of her dress, who comes out of her villa with a jug of water and a basket of grapes, just as a group of soldiers shows up demanding lodging...

"Can I get you something?"

I peel my eyes off the siren to find a male bartender standing before me, his eyes narrowed. He looks like a younger version of Henn. A wouldn't-hurt-a-fly kind of guy with a goatee, the same as my sweet best friend—although, unlike Henny, this dude has forearm tattoos. Clearly, the ink is his attempt at "edging up" his classic nerd-vibe. It's not a bad look for him, actually.

"I'll wait to order from her," I say, motioning to the object of my lust at the other end of the bar. "We met today on-campus. I'd like to say hello."

The guy flashes me a look of disdain that says, *You and every guy in this bar, douchebag.* But all he says is, "I'll let Georgina know."

Georgina. It's the perfect name for her—a name I'll enjoy growling into her ear as I fuck her raw, without mercy...

No, Reed.

Stop.

You're almost certainly not going to fuck this little college kiddie, with or without mercy, because she's almost certainly an off-limits wannabe. Not to mention, quite possibly, a fucking teenager. Although, come to think of it, if she works behind the bar, she's got to be at least twenty-one...

It doesn't matter, my brain says. *She was at an event for music students. Walk away.*

But I want her, my dick replies, rather forcefully.

Well, tough shit, my brain replies. *You can find out why she left with CeeCee today, simply to satisfy your curiosity, but that's it. After that, you're going to walk away and shoot pool with your best friends, and forget this gloriously endowed goddess with the most kissable lips you've ever seen exists.*

My dick laughs heartily at that. And so, I laugh, too. Out loud. Like a fucking lunatic.

The bartender whispers something into sultry Georgina's ear that makes her turn around. And when she spots me, a wide smile spreads across her sensuous mouth.

Returning her smile, I put my arms up like, *I guess it's fate, huh?*

She saunters over to me like she owns the joint, places her elbows onto the bar, and leans over, giving me a much-appreciated view of her pushed-up tits in her tank. "Well, well, well," she says. "Look what the cat dragged in. Did you follow me here, Mr. Rivers?"

Up close, she's mesmerizing. Irresistible. I swear, if this supernatural girl can sing a note, and maybe even if she can't, I'm going to launch her to the top of the pop charts, even if I have to buy stock in Auto-Tune to do it. "I wish I could take credit for this happy reunion," I say. "But this is pure coincidence..." I look down at Georgina's nametag, just for appearance's sake. "*Georgina.* Or should I call you Miss... ?"

"Ricci. But, no. Call me Georgina or Georgie." She extends her hand with full confidence, and when I slide my palm in hers, my skin ignites at the point of contact. *Lust.* It's palpable. Undeniable. Sending my heart rate skyrocketing and my dick tingling.

I want her, my dick shouts, deftly muting out my brain's objections.

"Hello, Georgina," I say, shaking her hand. "Georgie. And, please, call me... *Mr. Rivers.*"

She laughs. "Well, that hardly seems fair."

"Life isn't fair." I lean forward, a wide smile etched onto my face. "Although, sometimes, it can be pretty fucking awesome, when you least expect it."

She returns my smile, a gleam in her hazel eyes. "This truly is a coincidence?"

"I'm smart, but not clairvoyant. I was at dinner with friends, and then happened to stop in here. How could I possibly have known you work here?"

"You could have followed me. Or had me followed."

"Pretty sure that's what's known as stalking, sweetheart. Way beneath my pay grade."

"You sure about that? I'm getting a serious stalker vibe from you."

"Okay, full disclosure, I was going to call CeeCee tomorrow to gather intel about you, in order to track you down. So, maybe stalking isn't beneath me so much as your accusation is a day premature."

She giggles. "What would you have asked CeeCee about me?"

"Your name, to start with. Your age. I definitely would have asked if you're a music student."

She shakes her head. "Journalism. I'm graduating next week."

My dick cautiously jumps for joy. *She's not off-limits.* "Congratulations. Are you a musician on the side, maybe? A singer?"

"Nope. Just a writer. My passion is investigative journalism."

I'm losing my mind with relief. Euphoria. Lust. Even as the business side of my brain is slightly disappointed I won't have the chance to make her a star. "How old are you, if you don't mind me asking?"

"I'm turning twenty-two next month."

She just keeps getting better and better. "I'm relieved to know you're not a teenager," I admit. "The thought occurred to me at the panel, as I was flirting with you, that your age could very well end in the word 'teen.' Once I realized that, I was pretty disgusted with myself for continuing to flirt."

"Not disgusted enough to stop, apparently."

I chuckle. "True."

"So if I'd turned out to be nineteen, you would have hung up with CeeCee tomorrow, and not tracked me down?"

I pause, unsure. Hearing her say that out loud, it doesn't ring true to me, even though before today, I would have sworn I'd never be caught dead pursuing a teenager. But, come on, I saw Georgina today and brazenly came on to her for a full hour, even though I knew there was a good chance she was eighteen or nineteen... So can I honestly say I wouldn't have pursued her if it had turned out she wasn't old enough to order a beer?

But, still. There's no reason to say any of that out loud, and come off as a dirty old man. And so, I say, "If CeeCee had told me you were a teenager, then I'm pretty sure I wouldn't have tracked you down."

She laughs. "*Liar.* If I'd been nineteen, you'd have told yourself 'Hey, she's legal,' and then done exactly what you're doing right now. Whatever that is."

"*Whatever that is*? Oh, God. I've got to step up my game, if you don't know. Georgina, sweetheart, I'm hitting on you. With all my might."

She bites her luscious lower lip. "*Oh?* Good to know." She smiles. "I think it's interesting you think nineteen is too young for you, but twenty-one isn't. Explain that one to me."

"Oh, twenty-one is too young for me, too."

We both laugh.

"Actually, before this moment, I would have sworn I'd never hit on a twenty-one-year-old. Never say never, I guess."

She adjusts her elbows on the bar. "To what do you attribute this astonishing reversal of yours, Mr. Rivers?"

I motion to her, like the answer is self-explanatory, and then add, "It's easy for a man to draw imaginary lines in the sand before he knows Georgina Ricci exists in the world."

She blushes. "Aw, well. Don't beat yourself up too much about being a creeper. Age is just a number, anyway."

"I think you have to get to your late twenties to be able to say that with a straight face. Before then, you come off as naïve."

"Oh, I'm not naïve. Not in the slightest."

My dick tingles at the possible subtext of that statement. Does she mean that as code for something naughty? Is she trying to tell me she's a freak in the sheets? "I didn't mean to insult you. I just meant there's a lot of highly formative life experience a person acquires between the ages of eighteen and twenty-five."

"There's a lot of highly formative life experience a person acquires between the ages of zero to a hundred."

"Well, that's true."

"Speaking for myself, I've acquired an ocean of 'highly formative' life experience between the ages of ten and twenty—too much of it, to be honest. But that's life. If we're doing it right, then we're constantly learning and growing."

"True, again."

"Except when it comes to you, I guess. You're so smart, so much smarter than the rest of us, you're all done learning and growing, now that you're the wise old age of thirty-five."

Holy motherfuck. Just this fast, this sassy girl's got me tied and trussed like a pig over a spit. And I'm loving it. I lean forward, smiling. "First off, I'm only thirty-four. Don't rush me. And, believe me, just like everyone else, I'm still figuring plenty of stuff out."

"Which proves my point. *Age is just a number*." She lays her cheek in her palm. "You've honestly *never* dated someone my age?"

"Not since my early twenties. And, to be clear, I don't plan to date you, Georgina. Just *seduce* you."

Her eyebrows rise at my brazen comment, though she seems more amused by it than offended. "Points for honesty. Damn."

"I'm a big fan of honesty."

"When it suits you, apparently." She smirks. "I'm pretty sure you've already lied to me at least a couple times."

I shrug. "Things may come to those who wait, but only the things left by those who hustle."

"Ah, so you admit you're a hustler?"

"I do. Proudly."

She drags her teeth over her sensuous lower lip. "So, tell me, Mr. Wise Old Rivers, why don't you date—or, sorry, *seduce*—much younger women? Is it some sort of firm rule for you, or has it just sort of happened that way?"

Good God, she's relentless. And I fucking love it. "I haven't given it much thought. I don't tend to be in situations where I meet women your age, other than in a business context, which means they're not a good idea for me to pursue, no matter their age. And, also, if I'm being honest, I'm a sucker for a confident woman—and genuine confidence, in my experience, as opposed to youthful cockiness, or play-acting confidence in mommy's heels, usually takes a bit of time to develop."

Oh, I've pissed her off now. "'Play-acting in mommy's heels'? How condescending."

I chuckle. "You asked me a question, and I answered it honestly. You don't like honesty?"

"I like honesty. Just not *assholery*."

I laugh heartily. I think she might very well be perfect.

"Just a tip?" she says, twirling a lock of dark hair around her finger. "Don't look down your nose at me and treat me like I'm a stupid child, which I'm not, if you want to have any shot at 'seducing' me. I've got a bit of an allergy to assholes, I should warn you, and also a bit of a temper. And I don't tend to respond well in the face of condescension or assholery."

My breathing hitches at the blaze in her eyes. The flush in her cheeks. She's the sexiest little creature I've ever beheld. "Duly noted. I apologize. Condescending to you wasn't my intention."

"Well, shit, I hope not. If it was, that would make you absolutely terrible at seduction."

I can't help laughing my ass off. She's unleashing the kraken on me in a way that's making me smile from ear to ear.

"You want to know a secret, Mr. Rivers?" she says conspiratorially. "I truthfully can't wait to see you take your best shot at seducing me. Don't get me wrong; I haven't yet decided if I'm going to let you be successful. But I'm certainly up for watching you try."

Okay, who's the liar now? Georgina's red-hot desire to get absolutely desecrated by me has been written all over her face from the minute she winked at me in the lecture hall.

I lean forward, matching her posture. "Aw, Georgina. Don't bullshit a bullshitter. I'm going to be wildly successful at seducing you, and we both know it. In fact, when the time is right tonight, I'm going to invite you to come to my house. And we both know what you're going to say in reply when I do."

She flashes me a snarky look. "I have no idea what I'd say to an invitation like that. Maybe if I had more highly formative life experiences, it'd be a different story. But as it is, I'm too busy play-acting confidence in my mommy's heels to know what I think or feel or want."

She flashes me a spicy little look that says, *Take that, you condescending prick*, and I'm suddenly dizzy with my desire for her.

I bite my lip. "So, it's gonna be like that, huh?"

"You bet your ass it's gonna be like that."

A palpable current of electricity passes between us. Sexual desire that shoots straight into my cock. "All right, beautiful. We'll go around and around for a while before I extend my invitation. We'll play a pointless, but highly entertaining, game of cat and mouse, just for the fun of it. But, I promise you, when the game ends, you're gonna say yes to me."

She shrugs. "Who knows what I'll say?" She winks. "But I can't wait to find out."

I return her wink. "*Let the seduction begin.*"

EIGHT
REED

"Georgie!" the male bartender shouts from the other end of the bar, making her jerk backwards from our sexy conversation. "You need help over there?"

"No, I'm good!" She returns to me. "You've got to order something, or I'm gonna get in trouble."

I throw down a hundred, order a beer for me, Scotch for Josh, and a gin martini for Henn. "Keep the change, as long as you take your sweet time making that martini."

"You got it." She gets to work.

"You're not even going to *pretend* to check my ID?" I say teasingly. "Way to make a guy feel old, bartender."

She slides my beer across the bar. "You already told me you're thirty-four. Are you saying you're a liar?"

"I'm saying I *could* have been lying."

"Yeah, well, the woman at the panel said you graduated from UCLA a decade ago. So unless you're one of those baby-geniuses who graduates medical school at age ten, I'm thinking it's safe to assume you were telling the truth. Also, Wikipedia says you're thirty-four. And we all know Wikipedia is never wrong."

A stool opens up in front of where Georgina is currently pouring Josh's Scotch and I quickly snag it. "Ah, you googled me."

"I did. No shame in that. While I was sitting in the lecture hall, waiting for the start of the program. I'd heard your name for the first time while walking to the event, so I figured it would heighten my experience if I knew a little something about you in advance. I also devoured every photo of you I could find."

I chuckle. "Did you google all the panelists to 'heighten your experience,' or just me?"

"Just you. I'd heard you're smoking hot, and I wanted to see for myself."

"And?"

She slides Josh's Scotch toward me. "And you didn't disappoint."

I take a sip of my beer to hide my wide smile. This girl could teach a master class in sexy flirting. "After all the photos you 'devoured,' the real-life version of me didn't disappoint?"

"The real-life version of you made my ovaries vibrate."

Holy fuck. I can't believe it, but I feel myself blushing. When was the last time that happened to me? "If I haven't made it clear enough, I find you smoking hot, too. Seriously, you're absolutely stunning, Georgina."

She bats her eyelashes. "Thank you."

"If I'd seen you while waiting for the panel to start, and somehow knew your name, I would have sat there googling the shit out of you, too, including devouring every photo of you in existence online."

"Sorry to say, you would have been disappointed. I'm boring online. Not a single scandalous photo out there."

"No? Come on. There's got to be *something* scandalous out there. Maybe some naughty photos with a male stripper at a drunken twenty-first birthday party?"

She grabs a shaker for Henn's martini. "Nope. Your online presence is way more scandalous and naughty than mine."

"Uh oh. What photos of me did you see?" I gasp in mock horror. "You saw my crown jewels, didn't you?"

She freezes mid-shake on the shaker. "You're telling me there's a photo of your crown jewels out there, and I missed it? Shit on a shingle! I'm embarrassed to call myself an aspiring investigative journalist."

I chuckle. "No, no. I have no idea if anything like that exists. I'm just saying it *could*. I've jumped fully naked off more than a couple yachts and diving cliffs in my day. Gone surfing and kayaking and waterskiing buck naked while shitfaced. I even went snowboarding naked down a private bunny slope once, after losing a bet at a party. Almost froze my ass, dick, and nuts clean off."

She giggles.

"It wasn't a laughing matter at the time. Unfortunately, the shrinkage factor was off the charts."

She laughs even harder.

"After all the crazy stuff I've done," I say, "God only knows what photos of me could be out there. I haven't googled myself in a long time to find out, so I really don't know."

She slides Henn's martini onto the bar. "Why haven't you googled yourself in a while? Shouldn't a guy like you keep up with what the world is saying about you?"

I take a long swig of my beer. "I used to keep up with that stuff, back when I was first coming up. I considered myself a student of the fame industrial complex. The cult of celebrity. I was ahead of my time, well aware the secret to my success was positioning myself as an 'influencer.' But once I got to the top of the heap, I realized keeping up to date on what people think of me—or, rather, of the online avatar they *think* is me—is a colossal waste of time. I'm not real to them, so who gives a shit what they think?"

She bends over to grab something behind the bar, and, as she does, I peek at her outrageous cleavage. Goddamn, I can't wait to suck those incredible tits. That's the first thing I'm gonna do when I get her to my house: peel off that shirt and absolutely devour those—

Oh. She's straightened up again and is staring at me—fully aware I just got hopelessly lost in fantasies about her tits for a minute there.

"I looked at your Instagram," she says, running a rag across the bar. "Looks like your avatar is having a pretty exciting life."

"He is."

"Sadly, though, I saw no evidence he's gone naked-snowboarding recently."

I finish off my beer and shrug. "Partying is an important part of my job."

"Poor, poor Reed has to work *so* damned hard."

I laugh. "I'm not complaining. I have fun. But make no mistake about it: I really do work hard. Very hard. You might have read on my Wikipedia page, I've got a few businesses to run?"

"Honestly, I was too focused on drooling over photos of you in your swim trunks to read too much about what you do for a living. And it's a good thing I didn't waste my time reading about all that stuff, anyway, seeing as how you're only planning to 'seduce' me. Who gives a crap what either of us does, or likes, or dreams about, or feels passionately about, when the only endgame is you getting me into your bed, right?" With that, she slides a refilled beer glass in front of me, even though I didn't order it. "A gift from me, Mr. Rivers. Because I can only imagine how thirsty seduction makes a guy. Especially when he's trying to seduce a young, stupid thing like me who's running around in her mommy's heels, play-acting confidence." With that, she turns on her heel and strides to the other end of the bar to tend to another customer.

And I've never been more determined to make a woman say yes to me in my entire fucking life.

"You're still sitting here?" Georgina says, sidling up to me.

"I'm still sitting here," I reply. I toss two hundred bucks onto the bar in front of her, right next to the two untouched drinks I ordered for Josh and Henn mere minutes ago. "Let's make it three martinis this time, Georgina. All of them made extra slowly. Keep the change, like before, as long as you take your sweet time making my order."

"You got it." She scoops up the cash, thanks me, and gets to work.

"Can I ask a stupid question?" she asks. "Are you famous? I can't tell. You were the biggest star on the panel. And you're all over the internet, hanging out with rock stars and celebrities. In some photos, you've even got a bodyguard or two. And yet, here you are, at Bernie's Place on a Thursday night, with no bodyguards, acting like a regular dude. Well, a very well-dressed regular dude with an extremely nice watch."

I take a sip of the Scotch originally intended for Josh. "I have what I'd call 'situational fame.' People in the music industry know who I am. At music festivals, I have to roll with at least two bodyguards, so I don't get attacked by wannabes. But just living my life in the world, like tonight, I can hang out with no problem. It's the best of both worlds."

"Meaning you wouldn't want to be more famous, if you could?"

"Hell no. I've seen massive fame close up, with some of my artists and past girlfriends, and it's not all it's cracked up to be. That's what doomed a few of my relationships, actually. The woman being too famous, or wanting to be. It's a drug for some people. And, as we all know, drugs don't lead to a happy ending."

"*Fame* is the culprit in your failed relationships? You're sure about that?"

I chuckle. "Well, that and I can sometimes turn into a colossal prick when I get bored."

"I'm shocked."

"Plus, I'm generally what you'd label 'non-committal' when it comes to relationships in the first place, so that could have contributed to the demise of a few of my relationships, as well."

She frowns. "Ah, so, you're a cheater?"

"No. If I say I'm exclusive, then I am. It's just really, *really* hard to get me to say I'm exclusive."

She nods, apparently approving of that answer. "I'm the same way."

"You turn into a colossal prick when you get bored, too?"

She giggles and winks. "Only when provoked. No, I consider myself 'non-committal' at the moment, too. For the foreseeable future, anyway. While I'm trying to launch my budding journalism career, I've decided not to focus on anything or anyone else."

"Do you have a job lined up after graduation?"

"No, unfortunately." She secures the lid on a metal shaker. "That's why I went to that event today. To try to give CeeCee a couple of my writing samples. My dream job is writing for her latest magazine, *Dig a Little Deeper*."

"I'm familiar with it. I think you'd be great at that. You're obviously good at connecting with people. Drawing them out." *And wrapping them around your pretty little finger, I'm sure.*

"Thank you. Fingers crossed."

"Was it mission accomplished with CeeCee? Did she take your writing samples?"

"She did. I got lucky and bumped into a professor after the panel who introduced us, and then CeeCee invited me to coffee. That's why I left without saying a word to you—because when opportunity came knocking, I did exactly what you told me to do: I said, 'Yes, yes, yes!'"

I chuckle. "Well, fuck. When I instructed you to say those three magic words, I was hoping you'd be saying them to *me*—and under much more intimate circumstances."

She flushes. "What did you think when I left with CeeCee?"

"I was intrigued. I couldn't decide if you were CeeCee's new personal assistant or intern or niece, or if you were playing the world's most masterful game of chess with me."

She slides a martini in front of me. "With *you*? How could me leaving with CeeCee have anything to do with *you*?"

I shrug. "It was an event for music students, so, I assumed you had to be an aspiring pop star with a demo in your pocket, like everyone else in the building. I thought you'd seen my long line and decided you'd get far more traction out of leaving with CeeCee—and gambling on me tracking you down tomorrow—than staying and trying to compete for my attention."

She looks shocked. "Damn. That's quite a leap. When I left with CeeCee, I was sure I'd never see you again. I can't even imagine thinking two moves ahead like you've suggested."

Jesus, she's such a bullshitter. "Yeah, well, if you'd actually been a music student who wanted to use me for more than my hot body," I say, "then I guarantee you'd not only have played chess with me, you'd have been fucking Bobby Fischer."

"Who's that?"

I smile to myself. For a second there, I'd forgotten how young she is. "He's generally regarded as the best chess player who ever lived."

"Oh."

"After observing you, I've got no doubt you'd be fully capable of playing chess like him, if the need arose." I sip Josh's Scotch again. "Seriously, Georgina, you wouldn't believe the shit people do to get my attention. Nothing surprises me anymore." I take a sip of the martini she slides across the bar and suddenly realize she looks sincerely offended by something I've said. "Oh, come on. Really? Don't act like I've slandered you by calling you out, Little Miss Journalism Student Who Goes To A Music Event to Ambush CeeCee Rafael. You're a hustler, baby. Scrappy and relentless. I've seen the way you expertly hypnotize your customers, including me, into giving you big tips. Don't even try to pretend you're not fully capable of playing chess as masterfully as Bobby Fischer."

She blushes crimson, letting me know I've pegged her right.

"But it's all good, Georgie girl. I'm a chess-playing hustler, too. In fact, one of my mantras in life is 'All good things come to those who hustle.'" I raise my glass to her. "To being scrappy and relentless. To hustling and playing chess."

She slides my third martini in front of me, looking tentative. But after a moment, a delightful sort of "what the fuck" expression washes over her gorgeous features. She grabs one of the martinis and clinks my glass with it. "To playing chess." She grins. "Even more masterfully than Bobby Fischer."

NINE
GEORGINA

"You about done over here?" Marcus asks, appearing out of nowhere next to me. "We're slammed, Georgie. Now isn't the time to take an extra long break."

"Oh, I'm sorry. Mr. Rivers here just—"

"Ordered ten more drinks," Reed interjects. He pulls out his wallet, and places *another* Benjamin onto the bar—this one, for Marcus. "A little something for the extra load you've been carrying because I've monopolized Georgina's attention."

Marcus glares at the bill on the bar before returning to me. "You need help making his order?"

"No. They're all pretty simple drinks."

"And I'm in no rush," Reed supplies.

"I'll work like a bunny," I say. "Sorry I've been MIA."

"Here's another hundred for you, man," Reed says, placing another bill next to the first. "I didn't think about how me monopolizing Georgina was impacting your night. Hopefully, this will make up for it."

Marcus mutters something under his breath. But, ultimately, he scoops up the cash and shuffles away, looking thoroughly annoyed as he goes.

"Oh, God. It *killed* him to take that money from you," I say, laughing.

Reed resumes his bar stool. "And yet, he took it. Proving, once again, the accuracy of one of my favorite mantras: 'Everybody's got a price. To get what you want from someone, you just have to figure out what their price is, and bribe the shit out of them with it.'"

I scowl. "That's one of your favorite mantras? Jeez, Reed. That's dark."

"I'm wildly successful in a cut-throat industry. You expect my favorite mantras to be about rainbows and unicorns and singing 'Kumbaya'?"

I squint at him. Is it weird I'm not sure I like him, but I'm hella certain I want to fuck the living hell out of him? "Do you actually want another ten drinks, or was that just a ruse to get Marcus out of my hair?"

"Heck yeah, I want ten drinks. Let's give my buddies a magical mystery tour of beverages to choose from."

"You've got buddies here? This whole time I thought you were alone."

He turns around and directs my attention to two guys at the pool table: a hot male-model type who's cut of the same cloth as Reed, and a nerdy-hipster guy who looks like he could be his hot buddy's modeling agent. Reed returns to me, smiling. "Let's make my buddies ten of the most complicated, time-consuming assortment of drinks you can muster." He places three hundreds in front of me. "Your tip, on top of whatever the ten drinks cost, *if* it takes you at least twenty minutes to complete my order."

Whoa. That's quite a tip on top of what Reed's already paid me tonight. Thanks to him, I'm already having the best night of tips of my life, by far. And I'm grateful for it, of course, given the medical bills stacked on my father's kitchen counter. But I'm also wary. Does Reed think he's finding *my* "price" with these tips—and bribing me with it? If so, he's dead wrong about that. If I decide to go home with him tonight, or any night, it won't have anything to do with his financial generosity.

I get to work on filling Reed's ten-drink order, *slowly*, while he settles onto his bar stool and chats me up. About ten minutes in, when I slide the fifth drink of his order across the bar, Reed finally makes his move. "Hey, do you think you could get out of here a couple hours early?" he asks. "I'd really like to spend some time alone with you tonight, but I'm flying to New York first-thing tomorrow, and I'll be gone for a week. The thought of waiting that long to get you alone is torturing me."

Holy shit. My mind is racing and my heart pounding. I want to say yes, despite all the "good girl" reasons I probably shouldn't. And not simply for the chance to give him Alessandra's music in private, but because... holy hell, I want to have sex with this sexy, arrogant man! But, unfortunately, that's a moot point because I truly can't leave my shift early.

"Sorry, I can't leave early," I say, pouting. "I wish I could."

Reed's face perks up. "Is that true—you genuinely wish you could leave early and come home with me? Or did you say that simply to be polite?"

I bite my lip, realizing I've just given up the ghost. "I wasn't being polite," I admit. "I'd genuinely love to leave early and go to your house tonight, but I truly can't. I guess we'll just have to get together after you get back from New York. It's too bad, but unavoidable. I won't get out of here until around two thirty, and it sounds like you have to get to the airport pretty early tomorrow."

Reed's jaw muscles pulse. He takes a long gulp of one of the drinks I've laid before him and shakes his head.

"What time do you have to leave for the airport?" I ask hopefully, on the off-chance we could make tonight work.

"Five, at the very latest."

I grimace. "Yeah, tonight definitely won't work, then. We wouldn't get to your place till three, and then you'd have to shove me out the door at four thirty. No, thanks. I'm up for a meaningless good time with you tonight, no strings, but, still, that's way too big a wham-bam-thank-you-ma'am for me. At least for our first time." I slide another drink across the bar and hold my breath, hoping Reed will try to convince me I'm wrong. But, no, Reed remains unusually quiet, looking deep in thought.

"Are you going to New York for business or pleasure?" I ask, simply to break the awkward silence.

He takes a sip of his drink. "Both."

I force myself not to frown at that answer. *Both.* Surely, the personal "pleasure" part of Reed's trip will involve him hooking up with a gorgeous woman. Or two or three. Probably some glamorous model or actress. *Shit.* It's suddenly dawning on me: if I don't go home with Reed tonight, due to time constraints, and he then flies off to New York to party with rock stars and fuck supermodels this entire week, he's going to forget I ever existed. And where will that leave my lady-boner? With blue balls, that's what.

But, more importantly, what would that mean for Alessandra? If I miss out on sexy times with Reed, because I wasn't willing to subject myself to a lightning-fast one-night stand, I'll cry into my pillow at the lost opportunity for a night or two. But I'll live, and eventually find myself another hottie to screw. A hottie as sizzling as Reed? Not bloody likely. But, still. I'll survive. But if I miss out on the chance to quite possibly make my stepsister's lifelong dreams come true, simply because I didn't want to rush some no-strings sex with Reed, I'd never forgive myself.

Out of nowhere, Reed lets out a tormented sigh. "Okay, look, Georgie. There's no way in hell I can wait a full week to get you alone. I respect everything you've said about not wanting to rush things tonight. In fact, I couldn't agree more. You're not a woman I want to rush anything with, believe me. I want to be able to explore every nook and crevice of your body for hours and hours."

I blush. *Whoa.*

"But I wasn't kidding: waiting a week might physically kill me." He looks at a clock on the wall, so I turn to look, too. It reads a few minutes until eleven. Reed says, "What if you could get off tonight in an hour—at midnight? That would give us over four hours together. Still, not enough, but certainly better than the alternative. What if I could arrange that, and promise you won't piss anyone off by leaving early and won't miss out on a single dollar of tips. Would you say yes to doing that tonight—to being my naughty Cinderella at the stroke of midnight?"

He's rendered me speechless. Confused. Frozen. *Turned on.*

Smiling like a shark smelling blood, Reed leans forward. "If I could arrange all that at the stroke of midnight, my sexy Cinderella, would you say yes? Would you say yes to letting me take you to my house to do every filthy fucking thing imaginable to your gorgeous body for four non-stop hours?"

Hell yes. That's what I'm thinking. *Hell to the freaking yes, Reed Rivers. Do all the filthy things to me. Bring it.* But that's not what I say. No, somehow, I manage to keep a straight face and reply, "No, I don't think I'd say yes to an offer like that." Much to my delight, Reed's face falls. Which is when I lean forward, lick my lips, and say, "You should already know me better than that by now. If given an offer like that, then I'd follow your explicit instructions from the lecture. I'd say exactly the thing you told me to say to you, whenever opportunity came knocking. I wouldn't say yes to you, Mr. Rivers." I wink. "I'd say, 'Yes... yes... *yes*.'"

TEN
REED

As Georgina walks away to process my credit card, Josh's unexpected voice at my shoulder jolts me. "What the hell happened to you?" he says. He elbows his way to an open spot at the bar next to me. "You were supposed to be getting us drinks, dumbass."

"And I did exactly that." I motion to the astonishing array of beverages before us on the bar. "Take your pick, my friend. They're all ours."

Josh laughs. "What the fuck?"

"Take a look at the bartender and all will become clear."

Josh glances to where I've indicated and immediately rolls his eyes. "I should have known."

"It was the only way I could get her to stand here talking to me for more than two minutes."

Josh surveys the concoctions in front of us. "What's what? It's like a box of chocolates."

"Yeah, you kind of have to taste them to figure it out."

He picks up a martini glass. "This looks safe."

"Since when are you 'safe'?"

"Since I've been waiting for a drink for fifty fucking years and I'm thirsty. Is this gin or vodka?"

"No idea."

He takes a sip. "Gin. And it's good." He takes several gulps. "You've seriously sat here flirting with her this whole time?"

"No, not this whole time. Before this stool opened up, I *stood* here flirting with her."

He glances at Georgina again. "She looks exactly like T-Rod when she first started working for me. I'm assuming that's a big part of her allure for you?"

T-Rod. It's a reference to Theresa Rodriguez, Josh's longtime personal assistant who's now a part-owner with Josh and T-Rod's husband on a chain of bars. A woman I've wanted to fuck since I first saw her ten years ago, when she was a twenty-one-year-old college grad and I was a twenty-four-year-old founder of a brand-new record label. And he's absolutely right: Georgina looks strikingly like her, although I hadn't made the connection until Josh pointed it out.

"She could be T-Rod's little sister," Josh says. "Emphasis on the word *little*. How old is she?"

"Almost twenty-two."

"Cradle-robber."

Smiling, I bring my glass to my lips. "She can vote, get a tattoo, buy cigarettes and liquor in all fifty states and weed in Washington and California. What more does a person need to be considered a full-fledged adult, other than all that?"

"Well, for starters, she could live in something other than student housing."

"If she can join the military and get permanently inked without her parents' consent, that's good enough for me. She's an adult."

"Keep telling yourself that, old man, if it helps you sleep at night."

"Weirdly enough, 'sleep' isn't the thing that keeps popping into my head whenever I look at her."

Josh drains the rest of his gin martini. "Is she a spitfire, too—just like T-Rod? How close a match is this, you fucking sicko wack job?"

"Yeah, she's a spitfire. She's already bitch-slapped me pretty good a few times. I deserved it, by the way."

"Of course, you did." He rolls his eyes. "You're so predictable. Whenever you hear the word no, in any context, you do whatever it takes to get to yes." He smirks. "Even if it means finding an uncanny double for the one woman in the world you wanted desperately but couldn't have."

Is he right about that? Have I been losing my mind over Georgina because she subconsciously reminds me of T-Rod—and I've got a score to settle? Or do I simply have a type—and Georgina is the most glorious version of it I've ever beheld in my entire life?

Unfortunately, "no" was the final answer in regards to my desire to fuck T-Rod. She's the Argentinian who got away, and always will be. Not emotionally, of course. I barely know the woman. But, God, how I've always wanted to experience her. And now, sadly, thanks to the rock on her finger and the babies who call her mommy, I never will.

My fascination with Theresa—you might even call it a low-key obsession—started the minute I met her. She was the highly organized, straight-laced twenty-one-year-old sent to Josh by a temp agency. And the minute I saw her, I wanted her. In fact, when I first saw T-Rod, I distinctly remember feeling like a nuclear lust-bomb had gone off inside me. The same thing I felt when I saw Georgina today.

Georgina.

Oh, God.

With T-Rod, it wasn't meant to be. Josh proclaimed her off-limits out of the gate—and not just for me, but for himself, too, and for all his friends—and by the time I decided to disregard his stupid proclamation, T-Rod's future husband was in the picture and my window of opportunity had decidedly slammed shut. But, this time, with sexy Georgina, she's not Josh's employee. Not his honorary little sister. And there's no would-be future-husband cockblocker slamming the door in my face. No, this time, with Georgina, it's smooth sailing for me to get to yes, yes, yes... In fact, there's not a doubt in my mind I'll be sinking myself inside her tonight—blissfully riding her, and myself, to four hours of heaven tonight.

"Aren't you about a decade too young to be having a midlife crisis?" Josh says, pulling me out of my reverie.

"Actually, my brain keeps saying that exact same thing. But, apparently, it seems other parts of my anatomy are running the show."

"Just be careful. The young ones fall hard." He snickers. "Probably because their brains aren't fully developed yet."

"Fuck you."

"Seriously, though. Tread softly, Rivers. I'm sure she's got huge stars in her eyes when she looks at you. You're gonna be able to manipulate her way too easily, so don't."

"She doesn't seem starry-eyed or manipulatable at all. I saw her earlier today, at that panel thing, sitting in the audience. I flirted my ass off from across the room for an hour and made it clear I wanted her to hang around afterwards and wait for me to get through my line, but she left anyway. I think that's what I like most about her—that she's willing to walk away. So rare these days."

Josh scoffs. "Sure, *that's* what you like most about her, you sick fuck. Clearly."

He indicates with his chin, where, at this moment, Georgina is bending down to grab something off a low shelf, gifting us with an insane view of her ass.

"Well, that and a few other things," I concede.

Josh laughs and sips his drink. "Is she a music student?"

"No. At least, I don't think so. She claims to be a journalism student, graduating next week. She said she went to that event today to meet CeeCee."

"She *claims*? She *said*?"

"I just think there's probably more to the story than that."

"Careful, Reed. Your paranoia is showing."

"I dunno, man. My gut keeps telling me she's got an agenda. Maybe she's a model on the side, and she's got her sights set on starring in RCR's next video. Or she's a dancer who'd ditch her big journalistic dreams in a heartbeat to back up Aloha on her next tour. I have no idea. All I know is, when I saw her at that event today, she zeroed in on me awfully fast, and came on like gangbusters. She's way too confident, and way too flirtatious with me, not to have an angle."

Josh shakes his head. "*She* zeroed in on *you*? Are you sure it wasn't the other way around, player?"

I shrug. "No, I'm not sure. That's my point. I'm usually sure when I'm the hunter, versus the hunted. With this girl, I don't know which way is up—who's got the upper hand. Who's got the bow and arrow. She's giving me whiplash in the best possible way."

Josh rolls his eyes. "Then enjoy it. No need to analyze it."

I sip my drink. "Oh, I'm enjoying it. Tremendously. But, still, my gut feels like she's got something up her sleeve."

Josh shrugs. "Maybe she thinks you could put in a good word for her with CeeCee."

I sip my drink. "Yeah, that could be it."

"If it's anything at all. Maybe, just maybe, she's a twenty-one-year-old journalism major who went to an event to meet CeeCee and unwittingly hooked a huge marlin on her line, when she hadn't even gone there to go marlin fishing. Maybe she's elated to catch the eye of a rich baller, who's not half-bad looking, who can take her backstage to meet Red Card Riot or Aloha Carmichael or 2Real or 22 Goats, any time he wants. Not to mention, take her to the best parties in town. And the best restaurants. Or to Paris on a whim. You're an exciting guy, Reed. To any woman. But especially to a kid like her." He claps my shoulder. "Stop being so fucking cynical. Not every woman in Los Angeles is looking to exploit you for professional gain. Some of them want to exploit you for your money, hot body, access to parties and private aircraft, and backstage passes."

I laugh. "You've gone soft on me, Faraday. Before Kat, you were even more paranoid than me about women's ulterior motives. You were a gold medal athlete in the sport of sniffing out gold diggers. We were brothers in paranoid arms, remember?"

"Yeah, before Kat, I was a paranoid asshat who didn't know the true meaning of happiness and wouldn't have known unconditional love if it bit me in the ass. So don't make my paranoia sound more glamorous than it was."

"Oh, for the love of fuck. Not this again. You swore at Henny's wedding you'd never again torture me with another speech about Kat 'saving you from—'"

"Thanks again for the generous tip, Mr. Rivers."

It's Georgina, standing before us with my credit card and receipt.

I smile and take my card. "You earned it." I motion to Josh. "Georgina, this is my best friend, Josh Faraday. Josh, this is Georgina Ricci. Bartendress extraordinaire. Aspiring journalist. Fellow UCLA alum, as of next week. Hustler. Chess enthusiast. Full-grown adult."

Josh laughs. "Hi, Georgina."

"Hi, Josh. Nice to meet you. And, for the record, I have no idea how to play chess."

Josh indicates the mess of drinks in front of us. "Looks like you know how to make drinks, though."

"I fake it pretty well. Reed figured out a clever way for us to hang out during a busy Thursday-night shift."

"That's Reed for you," Josh says. "The Man with the Plan."

"Oh? Wikipedia says he's The Man with the Midas Touch. Gasp. Is Wiki *wrong*?"

Josh chuckles. "No, he's that, too." He bats my shoulder. "Come shoot pool with us whenever you're done chatting up the bartender, brother. Take your time."

I open my mouth to tell Josh I'll follow him in two seconds, just as soon as I say a proper goodbye to the lovely bartender, when a female voice shrieking my name behind me splits my eardrums. It's a voice I don't recognize. Not at all. But I know, instinctually, it's attached to someone I'm going to loathe, whoever the fuck she is.

ELEVEN
REED

The woman shrieking my name is, indeed, a stranger to me. A young, blonde, high-strung one with a flash drive in her hand. After shrieking my name, she launches into an elevator pitch about her music, saying all the same things I've heard a million times before. She's a UCLA music student who saw me at today's event, she says. And, surprise, surprise, she's the next Adele.

"I don't accept unsolicited submissions," I say, putting up my palm. "No exceptions. And just a tip, Courtney. Don't compare yourself to Adele. Nobody is 'the next Adele.' You sound like a fucking amateur when you say that. Also—"

"Excuse me," Georgina says, and off she goes to the other end of the bar.

Fuck.

I'd forgotten Georgina was standing there, watching this entire exchange. Fuck! From Georgina's tone and body language, it's clear she thinks I'm being too harsh with this girl. But what am I supposed to do? Sit here smiling every time someone ambushes me during a relaxed night with friends? And more to the point, when I'm hitting on the hot-as-fuck bartender? If this girl hadn't bombarded me, I would have had a tantalizing "see you later, Cinderella" moment with Georgina. I'd have walked away from her on my own terms, leaving her wanting more. As it is, though, this girl is in my personal space, elevator-pitching me, while Georgina is standing ten feet away, looking upset.

"Enough," I say sharply to the blonde, cutting off her rambling. "When I told you I don't accept unsolicited demos a minute ago, that was your cue to fuck off."

The girl's mouth hangs open, just as Josh shifts his weight next to me, letting me know he thinks that was too harsh.

But fuck it. What this girl and Josh and Georgina don't understand —what *nobody* could understand, unless they've walked a mile in my shoes—is that I'm not on this earth to give out participation medals. I'm here to find and disseminate rare musical greatness, while also living my best life. And guess what? Pretending to give a shit every time some wannabe ambushes me with a demo isn't living my goddamned best fucking life!

I'm pissed as hell this blonde torpedoed my "see you later" with Georgina. And in the process quite possibly outed me to Georgina as the asshole that I am. But those aren't the main reasons I just told her to fuck off. In truth, the far less prickish reason for my behavior is that I'm helping this kid out. Teaching her something. If she truly wants to make it in music, she's going to encounter assholes far worse than me. On a daily basis, she's going to discover nobody will hold her fucking hand in this business. Not even if she's "the next Adele." Which she's *not*.

I glance at Georgina at the far end of the bar, making sure she's not overhearing anything, and to my relief, she's busy serving a customer. "Courtney," I say, "I'm doing you a favor here by not sugarcoating anything. Music is a brutal business, filled with savage, endless rejections that are going to crush your soul and disembowel your spirit and make you question your talent on a daily basis. And, to be perfectly honest, I can already see in your eyes you're not built to withstand any of that. Do you honestly think you are? Tell the truth. Swear on a stack of bibles you're up for that kind of abuse."

It's a test. If this kid caves, then my instinct about her is right: she'll never make it in the cruel world of music. But if she tells me to fuck off, if she says I'm wrong about her, and that she's going to hustle until her dying breath to prove me wrong, then, hell, maybe I've misjudged her. Maybe, if she pushes back like that, today will be her lucky day and I'll do something I never do: listen to her stupid fucking demo.

But, nope. Courtney doesn't push back. In fact, she does exactly what I'm expecting: she crumples, right before my eyes. "Sorry to... ," she murmurs, before scooping up her flash drive and sprinting away, tears pooling in her eyes.

"Jesus, Reed," Josh says. "That was a bit much."

"No, it wasn't." I pick up a mystery drink and take a long sip. "An Old Fashioned. Nice."

"Seriously, man. That was brutal."

"Yeah, well, tough shit. I can't go anywhere these days without someone trying to convince me they're the next Adele, Beyoncé, Laila, or Aloha. Or, if they're in a band, then they're the next Red Card Riot or 22 Goats. And guess what? *They never are.* Can I afford to waste five minutes, now and again, pretending to give a shit when someone approaches me with stars in their eyes? Maybe, though I wouldn't be happy about it. But, Josh, this shit happens ten times a day, every day. Am I supposed to waste a full *hour* out of every twenty-four on this shit? I bet even your mother-in-law, the nicest person I know, would tell me I'm well within my rights to shut this kind of shit down."

Josh sips a martini. "I strongly doubt my mother-in-law would be okay with you telling a young college student with stars in her eyes to fuck off."

My stomach clenches. "Okay, well. Maybe that one thing was a bit harsh. Do me a favor and don't tell your mother-in-law I said that, okay?"

Josh laughs. "Look, I get it. I can't imagine how annoying it would be to get bombarded like that all the time. I'm just saying there are other ways to say what you did that aren't going to scar the kid for life."

"If me telling her to fuck off scars her for life, then she shouldn't even think of trying to make it in music."

Josh sighs. "Whatever. Don't mind me. I fully admit I've turned into a huge softie these days. You should see how Gracie has me wrapped around her little finger. If Little G cries a single tear, I'm wrecked. Kat's gotta play bad cop with her all the time, because I'm too big a pussy to do it." He chuckles. "That kid is so damned cute. Same with Jack."

I take a sip of my drink, and say nothing. Truthfully, I don't think I'm *that* different from Josh. Tears wreck me, too, but only when they're shed by someone I love, not a stranger in a bar. For fuck's sake, I've spent my entire life wiping my mother's tears, and where is she now? In Scarsdale, in the finest mental facility money can buy, painting with outrageously expensive paints I've imported for her from France. And all of it, to keep her tears away.

And when my baby sister, Violet, got her heart smashed by her teenage love, and her tears wouldn't stop flowing, what did I do? Well, right after threatening to kill the bastard who broke her heart, I packed my sister off to the best college money could buy, three thousand miles away from the guy she couldn't seem to break away from on her own. All to keep her tears away.

And when my housekeeper, Amalia, cried for the first and only time in my presence—when that sweet woman broke down four years ago at my kitchen table and confessed her brother needed surgery and couldn't afford it and she was terrified of losing him—I not only wound up paying for the brother's *four* surgeries, I paid off his apartment lease for two years, too. All to keep sweet Amalia's tears away.

But some random chick in a bar cries because, waah, waah, the music industry is so hard? Because she's got a dream and I'm not rolling out the red carpet for her? Yeah, well, fuck her. I had a dream, too. And I mortgaged my soul, heart, blood, sweat, and tears to make my dream happen. I hustled and scrambled. And, yeah, I lied, too, on occasion, whenever truly necessary. But, most of all, I never gave up, no matter how many people told me I was crazy. No matter how many people said making money in music was impossible these days, thanks to streaming and illegal downloading and the new "singles instead of albums" culture. And now, here I am, laughing at all the naysayers, all the way to the bank.

Suddenly, I'm pinged with the thought of how supportive and awesome Josh and Henn have always been, which, of course, makes me curious about Henn's whereabouts through all this. I turn around and spot him at the pool table, happily playing a game of partners pool with three strangers. It's so fucking Henn, I can't help smiling about it.

"Come on," I say to Josh. "Grab as many of these drinks as you can carry, and let's shoot some pool. I'm in the mood to kick some ass."

"Well, you're not gonna kick mine. I've been sinking balls like a pro since we got here."

"Well, of course, I didn't mean *your* ass, dumbass. I meant *Henny's*. Come on."

As I start wrangling glasses off the bar, my gaze finds Georgina's on the other end of the bar. Instantly, my blood flash-boils at the way she's looking at me—like she wants to suck my dick. I smile, and Georgina looks away, her face blushing crimson. And, just this fast, I know a certain something about Little Miss Georgina Ricci... I'm not sure how much of my exchange with the blonde Georgina overheard, but I'm pretty sure it was enough for her to realize I'm maybe more of an asshole than she'd previously thought... Which is okay. Because, based on the heated look Georgina just flashed me before looking away, she very much *likes* assholes. Oh yeah, based on that scorching hot smolder, Little Miss Sexy-as-Fuck Georgina Ricci likes assholes... *a whole fucking lot.*

TWELVE
GEORGINA

I put my phone down and sneak another peek at Reed across the crowded bar. For the past forty-five minutes, while I've been busy working, he's been playing pool with his two buddies. And looking scrumptious while he does. I shouldn't feel this attracted to the guy. Not when I've got a strong hunch he's actually a big ol' prick. A charming one, for sure. A sexy one. But a prick nonetheless. And yet, I can't help myself. My attraction to him isn't admirable. But it's primal and raw and, apparently, not going to subside until I scratch my freaking itch.

A customer flags me down, and I peel my eyes off Reed's hard ass to tend to him. When I'm done, I glance at Reed again, salivate over his ass for a bit—also, his forearms, biceps, and profile—and then grab my phone to find out if Alessandra has replied to my most recent text. She has.

Alessandra: It's not RR's fault that girl cried. All he said is he doesn't accept unsolicited demos. Which, btw, comes as no surprise to me. (I told you so.)

Me: That's all I HEARD him say to her. After I walked away, he said a lot more I couldn't hear. And, whatever it was, it made her run away crying. Is that what he's going to do to me when I give him your demo? Make me cry?

Alessandra: Not if he wants to have sex with you, which he obviously does.

Me: He should be nice to people, whether he wants to sleep with them or not.

Alessandra: He can't take every demo shoved at him, G. He'd suffocate underneath an avalanche of plastic.

Me: Well, I'm going to make him take yours, if it's the last thing I do. The only question is… WHEN should I bring it up? Tonight? And if so, before or after we have sex? Or should I gamble that I'll see him when he gets back from NYC and do it then? Gaaaah!!! DECISIONS, DECISIONS!!!

Alessandra: Follow your gut. As long as you promise not to prostitute yourself to help me, I'm happy.

Me: Dude. If you could see his ass right now, you'd know my desire to sleep with RR has absolutely nothing to do with you and your demo.

It's the truth. In fact, having Alessandra's demo in my purse has become the bane of my existence. An albatross around my neck. Although, of course, I'd never tell that to Alessandra. My phone buzzes again, and I look down.

Alessandra: Send me an ass photo, please.

Chuckling, I take yet *another* surreptitious photo of Reed, this one while he's bending over the pool table, and send it off to my stepsister. And then I glance at the clock. It's two minutes until midnight. Holy crap. Is Reed *really* planning to do something at midnight, like he said before? He did call me Cinderella, after all, but that was almost an hour ago… My phone buzzes again.

Alessandra: Dat ass! OMG!
Me: I know. I've been wiping drool off my chin all

night. Hey, why aren't you sleeping? It's almost 3:00 there.

Alessandra: I couldn't sleep now if my life depended on it. I'm dying to see what's going to happen at midnight, Cinderella.

Me: Probably nothing, considering RR is no Prince Charming.

"Georgie," a male voice says, making me look up from my phone. It's Bernie, the owner of the bar... accompanied by none other than Reed and Reed's two friends.

"Oh, hi," I say lamely. I glance at the clock. Midnight on the button. "I didn't know you were coming into the bar tonight, Bernie."

Bernie claps Josh on his shoulder. "I wasn't planning on it, but then I got a call from this guy. Hey, Marcus! Come here!"

As we await Marcus, I glance at Reed, and the look of molten lust on his face sends arousal whooshing between my legs.

"What's up?" Marcus says.

Bernie introduces Reed and his friends, and explains that Josh used to work here many moons ago. "Reed wants to see Josh behind the bar again, for old time's sake. So, he's offered to pay for everyone's drinks until closing—at double our usual prices, just in case Josh is rusty." Bernie grins at Marcus and me. "He's going to tip each of you four hundred bucks, since you're both unexpectedly getting the boot for the rest of the night."

"The boot?" Marcus asks.

"You're off the clock," Bernie says. "Stick around and play pool or go home. Whatever you want. You're getting paid *not* to work."

"Wow, that's generous," I say, my eyes locked with Reed's. Holy hell, he's looking at me like I'm a sizzling steak on a plate, and he's a man with a fork and sharp knife. I keep my tone prim and proper. "Thank you, Mr. Rivers."

Reed smirks. "My pleasure, Georgina."

Bernie nudges Josh's arm. "I'll work alongside you, in case you've lost a step since your glory days. Come on."

"Lost a step?" Josh says playfully, following Bernie behind the bar. "I'm still in my prime, old man."

Laughing, the two men shoo Marcus and me out of the well, while Reed's other friend, the nerdy one, takes a stool. And, suddenly, I find myself standing on the customers' side of the bar with Marcus and Reed. Which isn't awkward at all.

Marcus looks suspicious as he assesses Reed. "I assume you did this because you're trying to impress Georgie."

"Marcus!" I say, shocked.

Marcus looks at me, his eyes blazing. "He's been ogling you all night, Georgie. Even when he's supposedly been playing pool, he hasn't stopped peeking at you."

My body zings with arousal, which is probably not the result Marcus was going for. Well, well, well. As I've been covertly ogling Reed from across the bar, he's been covertly ogling me?

Marcus turns to Reed. "I don't know who you are, but Georgina isn't going to fall at your feet, just because you're tossing out hundred-dollar bills like candy. Georgie's smart. *Special*. She's worth a hundred of the women you're probably used to picking up in bars by flashing your money clip."

"Marcus, stop," I say, putting my hand on his forearm. "I appreciate you looking out for me, but I don't need your protection this time. Truthfully, I've been ogling Reed all night, too. And not because of his money clip, but because we had great chemistry when we talked."

Marcus looks crestfallen. A knight toppled from his horse. The good guy, once again, *not* getting the girl.

My heart aching for Marcus, I turn to Reed. "Marcus is right about one thing, though. Your penchant for throwing around hundred-dollar bills is a bit much. Thank you for your generosity tonight. We both appreciate it. But if you keep throwing big money at me, I'm going to start wondering if you think I'm a stripper, rather than a bartender—which isn't something I want to be wondering."

Reed bites back a smile. "Sorry if I've offended you. Money was really tight for me in college. I waited tables and counted my lucky stars whenever I got a big tip. I just wanted to pay it forward."

Oh.

Well.

That was a pretty nice response.

And now I feel like an ungrateful bitch.

"Oh, yeah, thank you again," I say lamely. "Like I said, Marcus and I both appreciate your generosity a lot." I glare at Marcus, feeling annoyed he pushed me into making that embarrassing speech. "Right, Marcus? Reed has been incredibly generous, and we both appreciate it."

Marcus presses his lips together, clearly pissed.

I pat Marcus's shoulder. "I'm good, okay? I'm going to head off to enjoy this unexpected time off now. You should do the same."

Marcus looks heartbroken, but, after visibly recalibrating, he tells me to have a good time and stalks away with his big tips and unexpected two hours off.

"Are you two more than friends?" Reed asks.

"No."

"Much to his disappointment, I'm sure." He rubs his hands together. "But enough about him. Are you ready to head to my castle now, Cinderella? The clock has struck midnight, and your carriage—"

"Georgie!"

Oh, for the love of fuck, what now?

I turn around and palm my forehead. It's Bryce McKellar. The football star and Cling-on. The momma's boy who supposedly started believing in love at first sight when he saw me. He's here. And striding toward me with a bright smile on his face.

"Bryce," I gasp out, my heart rate spiking. "What are you doing here?"

Bryce hugs my stiff body. "You said you were working tonight, so I came by to say hi. I thought we could hang out when you get off."

I bristle. Bryce already asked me to hang out after work tonight, when I bumped into him on-campus, and I told him it wasn't going to work out. *But he came here, anyway?*

Bryce motions vaguely behind him. "I'm here with some teammates, so don't mind me until then. I can see you're busy... " His eyes drift to Reed and light up. "Hey, you're Reed Rivers!"

"And you're Bryce McKellar," Reed replies smoothly, extending his hand. "I've got season tickets. Congrats on last season. I can't wait for this upcoming one."

"Thanks. *Wow*. My sister is obsessed with you, man. What a trip."

"Your sister's a musician?"

"An amazing singer-songwriter. She plays piano. She's two years younger than me—going to USC, actually."

"Oh no. Yours is a house divided."

Bryce chuckles. "Yeah, she's a filthy traitor. But we still love her. Just barely, though." He chuckles. "Hey, how can I get my sister's music to you? You'd go crazy for it. She's the next Beyoncé."

"Unfortunately, I don't accept unsolicited demos, Bryce. No exceptions. But, as a favor to you, and only you, so don't tell anyone, I'll check out your sister's Instagram when I get a free minute."

"Really? Wow. Thanks!"

"Your sister's music is posted there?"

"Yeah. She always posts her stuff there."

Bryce tells Reed his sister's handle while Reed makes a note on his phone. And then, Reed shakes Bryce's hand and says, "Now, if you'll excuse me, I've got a hot date with a gorgeous woman."

"So do I, as a matter of fact," Bryce replies, winking at me. "It's been great meeting you."

"You, too. Kick ass next season."

"I will."

There's a beat. During which I feel like I'm going to pass out. Or barf. Or both. And then, both men say, "Georgina?" at the exact same time—a strange turn of events that would be comical, if it weren't so damned mortifying.

Of course, it's Reed, the man used to being king of the world on a whole other level than Bryce, who fills the awkward beat. Reed says, "Are you ready for our midnight date, my beautiful Cinderella?"

At Reed's comment, Bryce's face falls, full understanding crashing down on him—and I have to press my lips together to keep from giggling at his cartoonish expression. Not because I'm taking any pleasure in this awkward, embarrassing moment. But because it's now clear Bryce assumed I'd been taking Reed's drink order when he first walked up, not getting ready to head to Reed's house to bone him. And seeing him figure things out is genuinely amusing to me. But, also, simultaneously, rather unpleasant.

"I need a minute," I say to Reed. "Bryce? Can we chat for a second?"

Bryce looks like a deer in headlights. But he nods and follows me to a corner.

"I'm sorry," I blurt, before Bryce can speak. "I didn't know you were coming tonight. And I didn't know Reed would be here, either. I had no intention of humiliating you."

"You said you'd be getting off work at two thirty," he says dumbly. "It's only midnight."

"I wasn't lying," I say. "Without my knowledge, Reed arranged with my boss to get me off a couple hours early."

"*What?*"

I flinch at his sharp tone. If I felt like giggling at his reaction earlier, I don't now, as his shock seems to be morphing into anger before my eyes.

"I met Reed earlier today," I say, my heart pounding. "At that event I was running to when we bumped into each other. But that doesn't matter. Even if I hadn't met him, I was going to call you tomorrow to tell you I don't think we're compatible."

"*Not compatible?*" Bryce says, like I've just said I think the world is flat. "But... we've got amazing chemistry. I told you—you're stone-cold wife material."

"But, see. That's the thing. I'm not. I mean, I might be one day. But not now. I'm not looking for a relationship, Bryce. And it's clear to me you are."

He looks disgusted as it dawns on him: *if she's not looking for a relationship, then she must be headed off with Mr. Music Mogul for a meaningless night of fun... which therefore means she's not even close to the wife-material kind of girl I thought she was.* "But isn't he, like... forty?" he blurts.

My jaw sets. "He's thirty-four."

"What the hell, Georgie? I know he's rich and connected and all that, but—"

"I don't care about Reed's money or connections. And screw you for implying that. We've got chemistry, plain and simple." God, I hope I'm telling the truth about that. Is it possible I'm being blinded by Reed's power and money and the fact that he has the ability to make Alessandra's dreams come true? I don't *think* that stuff is what's attracting me, and making me look past some kind of dickish comments, but I can't deny Reed's star power is part of his appeal. But only because he's so confident and sure of himself. I mean, if Reed weren't "Reed Rivers," but equally confident and commanding, I'm sure I'd still be willing to traipse off to his house tonight, for what's almost assuredly going to be the best sex of my life. Wouldn't I?

"Yeah, well, we have great chemistry, too," Bryce says. "And I'm not forty fucking years old."

"Okay, this is pointless. Like I said, I never intended to humiliate you. I'm sorry if I've wasted your time or embarrassed you. I've got to go now."

"With *him*?" Bryce grabs my arm to keep me from leaving, his dark eyes on fire. "He's not going to give a shit about you after tonight, Georgie."

Before the "fuck you" in my throat escapes my mouth, Reed appears at my side, anger wafting off his muscled frame. "*Release*," he says sharply, like he's a dog trainer ordering the obedience of his pit bull. "*Now.*"

Instantly, Bryce obeys Reed, like a good doggie. But in one final show of defiance, he leans into my ear, right in front of Reed, and whispers, "I can do casual, if that's what you want. I just didn't think a girl like you would want that."

I don't acknowledge Bryce's insulting comment. Or his implication that "wife material" girls can't enjoy casual hook-ups, just like anyone else.

Reed's dark eyes are hard and his jaw clenched. He puts out his arm to me. "Ready, Cinderella?" He levels Bryce with a glare that makes my spine tingle. "It's time to go."

Relieved, I take Reed's arm. "I'm ready, *Prince Charming*."

I meant that last thing as a joke, of course. And Reed's smirk tells me he's taking it that way. Clearly, this man is nobody's Prince Charming. Least of all mine. Indeed, if there's such a thing as Prince Charming for anyone but my mother, I can't imagine he'd be a guy who brazenly cops to having no interest in doing anything but "seducing" women.

After I've linked my arm with Reed's, he puts out his free hand to Bryce, daring him not to shake it—daring Bryce to snub him because he's feeling territorial about a girl he barely knows—and thereby mess up his sister's chances at possible musical stardom.

For a second, Bryce stares at Reed's extended hand, but, quickly, he forces a smile and takes it. "No harm meant, man. It was just a misunderstanding."

"Totally understand. Have a great night."

"Thanks again for looking at my sister's Instagram."

"You bet," Reed says. "I'm looking forward to it." With that, Reed unlinks our arms so he can slide his strong arm around my shoulders, before confidently guiding me toward the front door.

As I walk with Reed, I feel swept away. Like I'm physically swooning. I inhale the scent of Reed's cologne, as well as his confidence. I register the strength and hardness of his fit body. The urgency and command of his grip on me. All combined, I'm feeling physically intoxicated by Reed in this moment, in the best possible way.

"Have you slept with him?" Reed says, when we're out of Bryce's earshot.

"That's none of your business." Okay, I can't help myself. "But, no, I haven't. Get this. Bryce and I haven't even *kissed*."

Reed chuckles. "Well, damn. He's awfully wound up about a girl he's never even kissed. Although, in the guy's defense, I could say the same thing about myself."

Butterflies release into my stomach. "Thank you. That's a nice thing to say."

"I'm a nice guy."

I snort. "That remains to be seen."

Reed chuckles. "I knew I liked you, Georgina. You don't pull any punches."

"Honestly, Reed, I still haven't decided if I like you. You're a bit of a mixed bag for me at the moment. But I'm most certainly attracted to you physically."

Reed shrugs. "Works for me. Like me or loathe me. It's all good. Just as long as you want to fuck me." He winks. "In fact, in my experience, it's often the ones who hate my guts the most who enjoy fucking me the most."

I say nothing. Because I've got a hunch he's right about that. I mean, look at me. I'm still peeved at the condescending way he spoke to me when he first walked up. More than a little wary about the way he treated that blonde girl. Not impressed by the way he looked at Marcus like he was dirt on the bottom of his shoe. And not certain if I was impressed or repelled by the way Reed took such obvious pleasure in cutting off Bryce's golden balls, and then dangling Bryce's sister's Instagram page in front of Bryce's face to keep him in line.

But even if the jury is still out on Reed's likeability—whether I ultimately decide I like him or loathe him, as Reed said—he's absolutely right: there's no doubt in my mind I want to fuck him like my life depends on it. More so, in fact, than I've wanted to fuck anyone in the four years since I started having sex.

Reed draws me into his muscled frame even closer, and whispers, "What'd you do to that boy, Georgie? Tell me the truth, as a cautionary tale."

"I did nothing, I swear. We met on campus. Talked and texted a few times. And that's it. For some reason, he seems to think it was love at first sight for us."

"No."

"Or so he said." I scoff. "Talk about a lady-boner-killer."

Reed smiles. "You don't believe in love at first sight, Cinderella?"

"No, Prince Charming, I don't. I frankly think the entire idea is ludicrous. But Bryce believes in it. Unless he was only saying that to me because he thought it was what I wanted to hear. Which would then make him horrifically bad at reading a girl's signals."

"Naw, he was being straight with you," Reed says. "Despite everything he's got going for him on the playing field, that kid's got zero game."

"And yet, he was willing to throw his supposedly instant love for me under the bus, to get you to listen to his sister's music. Love, zero. Ambition, one."

"Like I said before: everyone's got a price. You've just got to figure out what it is, and bribe them with it."

"I don't have a price."

He smirks.

"I don't."

He pats my head. "Okay, Georgie girl. You're the only person on Earth without a price." He chuckles. "It's times like this I'm reminded just how young you really are." He opens the door for me. "The truth is, sweetheart, if you think you can't be bought, that only means nobody's been smart enough to figure out your price yet."

THIRTEEN
REED

The cool night air envelops Georgina and me as the door of Bernie's Place closes behind us. I'm buzzing. Off-kilter. Feverishly lit up with my hunger for this woman's flesh—with my desire to explore and devour every inch of her, to breach her borders and push her boundaries—to claim her, conquer her, *ruin* her—until she's begging for mercy and crying tears of euphoria.

Only a few feet outside of the bar, a tsunami of lust washes over me. So much so, I stop walking, pin Georgina against the building's façade, and do the thing I've been aching to do since I first laid eyes on her: I press my hungry mouth to hers. And when she parts her lips and invites me inside with a soft and sexy moan, when my tongue enters her mouth and tangles with hers, when her body unmistakably bursts into white-hot flames against mine, I lose my fucking mind. Instantly, I'm a flaming pyre of greed and need. So overwhelmed with hunger for her, I can't remember my own name. Has a simple kiss ignited my body like this before? If so, I don't remember it.

My phone buzzes with an incoming text in my pocket, but I ignore it. Surely, it's Isabel again, insisting I call her. The same way she's been doing all night. But everything I needed to say to her, I said this afternoon. And even if I hadn't, nobody but Georgina exists anymore. Not in this moment. Right now, the entire world is Georgina and me, and nobody else.

I deepen my voracious kiss, my tongue demonstrating how my body is going to move inside hers when I get her into my bed, and she responds enthusiastically in kind, kissing me with as much passion and energy as I'm showing her. In short order, I'm so aroused, I can barely breathe. I push myself between her legs, yearning to burrow my throbbing cock inside her, and she moans her invitation for me to continue my assault. And so, I do. I press myself against her center, *hard,* still kissing her, yearning to massage that magical, delicious bundle of nerves that's going to drive her fucking wild when I get to it with my tongue, and Georgina slides her arms around my neck and grinds herself against my hard dick, making me even more desperate to sink myself inside her.

As our kiss continues, every atom inside me explodes into a fierce, unquenchable fire ball. Gasping for air, I grab Georgina's thigh and hoist it up, opening her to me like a blooming flower, and she shudders and grips my shoulder ferociously, like she's hanging on for dear life. We're a raging inferno now, Georgina and me. Both of us combustible in a way I haven't felt in a very long time. If ever.

Panting, I disengage from our kiss. But only because I'm acutely aware it's not nearly enough. *I want more.* And I can't get it on a sidewalk.

"We're fire," I murmur, brushing my lips against her soft cheek. "I can't wait to get you naked and kiss your pussy, just like that."

Her chest heaves. "Oh, God."

I kiss her again, simply because I can't resist, even though I know I'm only wasting our precious time at this point. And then, after we've forced ourselves apart again, we clasp hands and begin striding up the sidewalk like we're walking on air.

"Where are we going?" Georgina asks breathlessly.

"To a campus parking structure a few blocks away, to get my car, which will take us to my house in the Hollywood Hills, where I'm going to strip you naked and fuck you like you've never been fucked before, for four straight hours, without a break, right up until the last nanosecond before I need to leave for the airport."

She says nothing. But her gorgeous hazel eyes tell me she's in favor of that plan.

We talk logistics. I ask if her car is parked somewhere around here. She says, no, she doesn't own a car. That she always walks to work, or takes the campus shuttle, and then Ubers home.

"If there's time later, I'll drive you home on my way to the airport," I offer. "If not, I'll call a car for you. I apologize, in advance, if I have to call a car. I'd prefer to drive you, of course."

"It's all good. Whatever we need to do to maximize our time together, that's what I want to do."

I flash her a wicked smile. "Have I mentioned I like you, Georgina Ricci?"

"You have." And that's it. She notably doesn't return my compliment. Which, frankly, turns me on even more. The last thing I need is for this firecracker of a woman to kiss my ass. Unless, of course, she's going to do it literally.

We walk in silence for a moment, electricity coursing between our hands, until Georgina says, "What did you say to that girl at the bar after I walked away? She looked upset."

"I told her I wouldn't take her demo."

"I heard that part. What did you say after that—after I walked away?"

"Nothing really. I told her music is a tough business. That she shouldn't compare herself to Adele." I shrug. "Some people don't handle rejection well." I pause. "Also, I told her to fuck off. But I did it nicely."

She looks shocked. "There's no 'nice' way to tell someone to fuck off. No wonder she cried."

"Josh said the same thing. But here's the thing, Georgie. I get bombarded by wannabes all the time. Occasionally, I snap. So sue me." I snort. "Which also happens to me all the time, by the way."

She's quiet for a long moment as we continue walking toward campus, past storefronts and restaurants. And for a moment, I'm worried I've blown it. Scared her away. Miscalculated. Finally, she says, "You *never* take unsolicited demos—from *anyone*?"

"Correct."

"*Never*?"

"Never."

"*No* exceptions?"

I look at her, trying to read her. Does she have a demo for me, despite all her protestations earlier about her lack of musical ambitions? Is that it? "That's right. No exceptions."

"How'd you find Red Card Riot?"

"Someone I trusted told me about them."

"22 Goats?"

"Someone I trusted."

"Laila Fitzgerald?"

"One of my scouts found her and presented her to me. Same with 2Real. A scout stumbled across him on YouTube. And with Aloha, her former bodyguard had started working for me, and told me she was looking to switch labels. See? Not an unsolicited demo in the bunch."

"And yet, you agreed to listen to Bryce's sister's music."

"On her public Instagram page, you might recall."

"Isn't that the same thing, in the end?"

"No. An Instagram account is out there for anyone to see. It hasn't been curated specifically for me. Usually, the stuff there is pretty raw and not overly produced. Also, when I'm not physically taking something handed to me, it sets up lower expectations. It's less of a 'promise' by me to listen or follow up, and more of a casual, 'I'll take a look.'"

"Why were you willing to check out Bryce's sister's music at all, though, but not that blonde girl's? Was it yet another perk of Bryce being a football star?"

We're walking hand-in-hand up the darkened sidewalk at a good clip now, both of us like horses sensing the barn is close. I'm bursting to touch Georgina. To run my hands and mouth all over her. I grip her hand more tightly in mine at the thought. "It was partly about Bryce being a football star," I admit. "But not in the way you think. Mostly, I wanted to neutralize Bryce when it came to you, as quickly and efficiently as possible."

"'Neutralize' him?"

I smile at Georgina—at her inquisitive, gorgeous face. "When Bryce first walked up, I didn't know what the situation was between you. For all I knew, you two were fucking, or maybe even in love."

She scoffs. "Uh, no. If I'd been in love with Bryce, or anyone else, I would never have so much as flirted with you."

I shrug. "Either way, I felt the need to neutralize him—to unequivocally get him out of my way. And what better way to do that than to show you, right out of the box, he can be bought—that he'd kick you to the curb in a heartbeat for the mere *chance* of getting his sister signed to my label?"

"You thought Bryce would choose his sister's music career over *me*, the great love of his life?"

"I had no idea. But I sure as hell hoped so. Which is why I said I'd check out his sister's Instagram. And, lo and behold, I found the guy's price on the first try. That's actually one of my favorite games. Figuring out someone's price and bribing them with it: watching with glee as they pick my offered bribe over something else they'd normally choose. Something they *should* choose, but don't because what I've offered is just too tempting. It never ceases to amuse me how easily people can be bought."

She shoots me a look of disdain. "One of your favorite games is playing the devil on someone's shoulder?"

"That's a great way of describing it. Yeah, most definitely."

"But you have other favorite games, too?"

I chuckle, but say nothing. Oh, little Georgina. You'll learn soon enough about my other favorite games.

For a long moment, we walk in near silence, the only sounds coming from the occasional car driving by and our brisk footfalls on the cement sidewalk.

Finally, Georgina says, "You said Bryce's status as a football star also figured in, although not like I think? What did you mean by that?"

I chuckle. "Man, you really picked the right major, didn't you?"

She makes an adorable face. "Sorry. When something fascinates me, I can't help asking a million questions."

She looks earnest and adorable right now. Beyond beautiful. Which makes me feel bad I suspected she was lying to me earlier about not wanting to be a pop star. Maybe Josh was right. Maybe Georgina is nothing but fascinated by me. Maybe she wants nothing but a hot night of sex with a baller. And who could blame her for that?

"Don't apologize," I say, just as we reach the parking structure. "I meant that as a compliment." We come to a stop in front of the elevator. I press the call button. "To answer your question about how Bryce's football-star status played into my thinking, I'd rather show you than tell you." The elevator doors open, and I lead her inside the box. "Do me a favor and call up Bryce's sister's Instagram, baby. I'm gonna teach you how to be a music scout for me."

FOURTEEN
GEORGINA

After getting Bryce's sister's Instagram handle from Reed, I call up her page on my phone—trying desperately, as I do, not to let on that I'm a hair's breadth away from having a nervous breakdown. All night long, I've been filled with anxiety about how and when to tell Reed about Alessandra's music. And now, he wants to teach me how to be a "music scout"? Good lord, if I can't find a natural opening to mention Alessandra now, then I'm officially hopeless.

Shit. I feel like the stakes are higher now than ever. After that scorching hot, best-kiss-of-my-life kiss with Reed in front of Bernie's Place, I'm especially determined not to blow my chance to have sex with him tonight. But I can't help worrying Reed is going to feel betrayed when I finally pull out that flash drive. Will he think Alessandra's demo was my singular motivation this whole time? Will he view it as proof that I am, indeed, Bobby Fischer? Or has that amazing kiss worked the same kind of magical swooning spell on him that it worked on me, such that he'll be nothing but sweet and receptive when I finally pull out Alessandra's music? In short, I'm wondering if Alessandra's demo will provoke the same kind of benevolence Reed showed to Bryce... or the kind of wrath he showed to that cute little blonde at the bar.

"Well?" Reed says. "Did you find the sister's account?"

"Uh, yeah." I survey the endless selfies on Bryce's sister's page. "She's really pretty. She looks like Aloha Carmichael."

I show Reed my screen, and he nods his agreement.

"Okay, so, that's strike one against her."

"*Against* her?" My stomach drops. "I meant she looks like Aloha as a compliment."

The elevator doors open on the fourth floor of the structure, and we step out into the near-empty garage.

"I'm parked over here," Reed says, pulling me to the right.

My heart is thundering. "Reed, Aloha is gorgeous and one of the biggest stars on the planet, as you well know. How could looking like her be anything but a good thing?"

"Think, Music Scout. Why would I want to sign Aloha Two-Point-Oh, when the original is already one of my biggest earning stars? I owe it to Aloha to put all my Aloha-shaped eggs into *Aloha's* basket, not the poor man's version of her. There's only so much Aloha-style marketing and songs to go around. I would never want to dilute Aloha's market share."

I'm dumbstruck. I open and close my mouth, not sure how to respond. Now I *really* don't know what to tell him about Alessandra. Whenever I tell anyone about her, I always say she sounds like the lovechild of Adele and Laila Fitzgerald. But Reed is saying that would be a *bad* thing?

"But, still, Music Scout," Reed continues, "we'll press on. She's not 'out' after only one strike. There could be other factors weighing in her favor. Next up, tell me about her numbers. How many followers?"

I look down. "Almost ten thousand. That's good, right?"

"Is it? You tell me, Music Scout."

"Yeah, ten thousand seems like a whole lot to me."

Reed shakes his head. "Nope. It's not impressive. In fact, it's anemic and highly *un*-impressive."

Well, fuck. My stomach is churning now. Alessandra barely has a thousand followers. If this girl's following is anemic and unimpressive, what's Alessandra's? Pathetic? *Laughable?*

Reed says, "But that's not the end of the road for this girl, either, Music Scout. If those ten thousand followers are actual people—not bots or ghosts set up to make her look good—if it turns out they're genuine, enthusiastic, and highly interactive fans—then that's something to consider."

"How do we know if they're real or not?"

"You'd have to audit her account. Look at the interactions on each photo and video. Click on the profiles of the interactive ones and see if they come off like real people with real lives, or fake accounts. Once you start looking closely, you can usually tell fairly easily."

I make a move to swipe at my screen, like I'm going to get started on what he's just instructed, but Reed stops me with a gentle touch.

"Not now, Music Scout. I'm just educating you, for later. That job could take a while, so we'll put it on the back burner for now. There's no point wasting our time on auditing her followers if she's got no talent. Or if she's got talent, but she's not a good fit for us. For now, we'll put a pin in that, say she looks *meh* on numbers, certainly not great, but there could be extenuating circumstances that will give her more of a platform in the future than the average bear."

Reed stops walking, and I follow suit, right in front of a breathtaking, gleaming black sports car. It's the kind you'd see on an actual racetrack, or in a spy movie. And, suddenly, I realize... *this is Reed's ride*. As in, the car he drove to get here today. On actual city streets. Holy shit.

"This is your *car*?" I blurt lamely.

Reed smiles. "One of them." He presses a button to unlock it, and a gentle chirp echoes throughout the empty cement structure.

"What is it?" I ask, slack-jawed.

"A Bugatti Chiron."

"A Bugatti... ?"

"*Chiron*. They vastly improved the Veyron with this model. It's got exponentially more pick-up."

"Well, thank God for that. I always say the Vey-whatever was a piece of shit."

He snorts.

"It's gorgeous," I say, in genuine awe. "A work of art."

"It is." He assesses his baby for a long beat. "If I didn't already have a hard-on because of you, Georgie, I'd have a hard-on looking at this car. I've got a thing for fast cars."

"And fast women," I say, like we're in a poorly written action movie.

Because, come on, who could resist inserting that cheeseball line into this surreal moment, in front of *this* car?

Luckily, Reed gets my offbeat humor, apparently, because he laughs at my stupid joke as he leads me around to the passenger side. But just when I think he's going to open the door for me, he slides his palm onto my cheek, pins me against his gorgeous car, presses his hard-on into my clit, and kisses me deeply—this time, with even more heat and greed than the last time. And, once again, I'm instantly ravenous for him. My heart exploding, I slide my arms around his neck and grip his hair and kiss him the same way I'm going to fuck him at his house: without holding back.

"You drive me crazy," Reed whispers into my lips. "I can't resist you."

"Please don't."

His burning eyes scan my face for a long, heated, delicious beat. "Damn, you're gorgeous, Georgie."

I take a deep, steadying breath. "Damn, you're... mildly attractive, Reed."

He laughs—and so do I. Because, as we both know, Reed Rivers is drop dead gorgeous. His features aren't objectively perfect, by any stretch, in terms of symmetry. But the way they come together, the way his face is animated by his intelligence and wit and charm and *confidence*... the overall package of him is like catnip to this particular kitty. And I've got to think any other kitty who happens to cross his swaggering, strutting path.

After one more kiss, Reed opens the passenger door for me, gets me situated in the luxurious leather seat, and shuts me in with a soft click. And the minute I'm alone in Reed's car, as Reed makes his way around the back to his door, I quickly google the car name he mentioned... and then gasp at the crazy words on my screen: *Bugatti Chiron. One of the fastest cars ever manufactured. Approximately 45 units sold worldwide per year. Price tag: $2.9 million.*

Holy crap! I'm sitting in a car worth three million bucks? I suddenly feel faint.

I swear I'm not going home with Reed because of his money. But, holy crap, it's not every day a girl sits inside a three-million-dollar machine. For God's sake, I've never been inside a three-million-dollar *house,* let alone a three-million-dollar *car.* Suddenly, I feel nervous to move a muscle inside this car. To breathe. What if I spontaneously combust—or barf or pee? The driver's side door opens and Reed slides into his seat. "Have you been dutifully scouring the girl's page to find a video for me, Music Scout?"

"Uh. No. But I will." I flip back to Instagram, my heart pounding in my chest.

"Here. Plug in," Reed says, holding up a cord. "We'll listen to her through my speakers."

My hands shaking, I plug my phone into Reed's offered cord.

"You okay?" Reed asks.

I wipe the flop-sweat off my forehead. "Yeah, I'm great."

But I'm a liar. I'm not "great." I'm feeling a bit sick, actually. Being in this car has made me realize just how successful Reed is. How big a deal it is that I've not only got his undivided attention, but we're *organically* talking about discovering new music, thanks to Bryce. What if I blow this chance for Alessandra? I can't do that. Not even for one night of the best sex in my life.

Reed starts his car, and its expensive engine purrs like a kitten. "Listen to that," he says lovingly. "Beautiful."

"Yeah, beautiful. At least, I think so. Honestly, I wouldn't know. I grew up driving my dad's 2004 Volvo, and I haven't needed a car of my own since I've been in school."

Reed chuckles. "I feel you. In college, I drove a '95 Honda Accord with a transmission that slipped and a passenger window that wouldn't roll down."

I chuckle, and he does, too. And, just like that, something passes between us. Something real. And sweet, believe it or not. Something that makes both of us smile like school kids with mutual crushes on a playground.

"Okay, cue something up already, Music Scout," Reed barks playfully, backing his glorious car out of its parking spot. "I've wasted enough time on this girl. I'll give her one more minute of my precious time, and then I'm going to focus on nothing but *you* until I have to drag my sorry ass to the airport."

"Okay, I'm looking... " I look up from my phone. "Actually, can I ask a quick question? What did you mean when you said 'extenuating circumstances'?"

We're headed down a ramp toward the garage exit now, but Reed glances away from the windshield to look at me quizzically. Clearly, he has no idea what I'm talking about.

"You said her Instagram followers aren't impressive, but there might be 'extenuating circumstances' to give her more of a future platform than the average bear?"

"Oh. Yeah." He turns out of the garage and we take off smoothly into the night. "This is what I mean about Bryce's football-star status coming into play. Assuming Bryce doesn't get injured this coming season, he'll almost certainly get drafted pretty high, and then quite possibly play in the NFL. Which means there's potential for him to have a huge, national platform in coming years, if he doesn't fuck it up. And you know who he'll almost certainly feature on his social media? His baby sister, the wannabe pop star. So, even if his sister's numbers aren't all that great now, she's got huge growth potential. Plus, she's young. Even putting her brother aside, I always keep in mind the young ones almost always need time to grow and develop."

I sigh with relief. Alessandra's nineteen. Would Reed consider Alessandra the kind of "young" artist he'd give a chance to grow and develop? "Interesting," I manage to say, even though my heart is crashing. "So, let's say a singer-songwriter has, I don't know, a thousand followers, and they're, say, nineteen… Then it's not totally impossible for you to want to sign them?"

"There are lots of factors to consider. That's precisely what I'm trying to teach you, Music Scout. In the end, it all hinges on talent." He smiles. "Unless, of course, the wannabe happens to look like you. I swear, I could Auto-Tune the shit out of you and make a mint. In fact, I think that'd be a fun experiment. You wanna try it?"

I laugh. "No, thanks."

"Worth a shot."

I bite my lip, trying to decide how far to push my luck. "So, um, a nineteen-year-old with a small social media following, but amazing talent, would still have a chance?"

Reed's smile fades. He turns away from the road and looks at me for a long beat with hard eyes, like he can read my damned mind. And I know I've messed up. Pushed too hard. Made him suspicious of me. But just as I'm about to throw my palms over my face and confess my sins, Reed returns his attention to the road and says, "That's exactly right, Music Scout. Nothing's impossible, if the artist's talent is mind-blowing enough. Now, to be clear, I'd strongly prefer a potential artist have a shit-ton more followers than a thousand. I mean, in this day and age, if they don't have at least 5k, then what the fuck is wrong with them? Are they stupid? Addled with crippling anxiety? See, the thing to understand is that the music industry is a *business*. You can't sit alone in your room, writing songs for yourself, and not sharing them with the world. I mean, you can, but that's what's called a *hobby*. The *business* side of music is about *selling* that music. Which means you have to *play* your songs for other people and get them to connect with the music and you—which then makes them want to *buy* the songs, or a ticket to your show. The *business* side of music is about *moving* people with your *art*—or, at least, your *charisma*. One way or another, it's about making people *feel* and *connect*. But not for art's sake. But because, in the end, you want them to *buy*. And that means every artist today, whether they're at the top of the game, or just getting started, is a salesperson, in addition to being an artist. If they can't hang with that, then they're not going to succeed. Not with me, or anyone else, and I don't want them—unless, of course, they look like you and/or hit me like a ton of bricks like Laila or 2Real or Red Card Riot or 22 Goats."

Fuck! This is *so* not good. Alessandra's voice is sensational. Her songs incredible. But she'd be the last person in the world to try to convince anyone of either. In fact, I think it's safe to say Alessandra is the worst salesperson who ever lived, when it comes to selling herself. Hence, the reason I'm such a vocal cheerleader for her. If I don't scream from the top of every rooftop about my stepsister, then who will?

"As an example," Reed says, apparently unaware I'm on the verge of having a panic attack mere inches away. "Let's say an artist has strong content, but for whatever reason, I'm on the fence about them. Maybe I love their sound, but I'm concerned they're too niche for the mainstream market. Or, maybe, I'm concerned they lack X factor as a performer. Well, in a case like that, a strong social media presence with diehard fans, even if their following is relatively small, like Bryce's sister's, might tip me over the edge to sign them, because that will convince me they've got what it takes to attract an audience. Plus, I can use their current fans as a test group. I can tailor marketing and branding to include whatever's been working for them, and expand on it." He shrugs. "If there's one thing I've learned in this business—in life, really—it's that the cult of personality—the 'cool kid industrial complex'—is very real and very powerful and should be exploited at every turn. The influencer culture is exactly what made the fiasco of the Fyre Festival possible. Did you see either of those documentaries, by the way? On the Fyre Festival? I was totally obsessed."

"Yeah, I watched them both. I was obsessed, too. I watched them back to back."

"Me, too," he says. "Which one did you like better?"

"The Netflix one, I think?"

He opens his mouth to respond, but I speak first.

"One more question, though. If that's okay."

Reed's jaw tightens. Ever so briefly. But he looks away from the road and smiles at me. "Sure thing. *Investigate* to your heart's content, Madame Journalist."

My stomach clenches. My gut is telling me to drop this topic and loop back to it later, maybe after we've talked about the Fyre Festival at length—but I'm so close now to gathering the courage needed to mention Alessandra, I simply can't leave it alone. "What if an artist is wildly talented, but super shy?" I ask. "What if she, or he, has virtually no social media presence, but their talent is out of this world? Would you still consider signing them?"

Reed shifts his hands on his steering wheel. "That's an exceptionally rare scenario. But, yes, on the rare occasion when I've been struck by lightning, I've signed the person, or band, on the spot, with no consideration whatsoever of their following." His jaw muscles pulsing, Reed shifts his car into high gear as we race down a long straightaway on Wilshire Boulevard. "Any other questions, Music Scout, or are you ready to play me something from Bryce's sister now?"

"Oh. Yeah. Sorry." I fumble with my phone. I wish Reed could see Alessandra perform in person, so he could experience the way her live vocals burrow into a person's soul. The way she evokes emotion with the subtlest of inflections. "Okay, I've found a video of Bryce's sister at a piano."

"Play it. I want to get this over with already."

My hand trembling, I cue the video, and two seconds later, the sounds of simple piano chords fill Reed's car, followed by... a beautiful voice. A breathtaking, soulful one that instantly sends shivers racing across my flesh. Oh, God. This girl is amazing!

"Okay, turn it off," Reed says, even before the girl has reached her first chorus. "I've heard enough."

My heart is galloping. "Enough to know you want to sign her?"

"Enough to know I don't. Turn it off, please. I'd prefer silence, so we can talk."

My lips smashed tightly together, I comply with his request, and the car becomes silent, except for the sounds made by Reed's fancy car.

"You barely listened to her," I finally say.

"I listened twice as long as I normally would, to give my new music scout plenty of time to make her assessment."

"Well, my assessment is she's *amazing* and you should have listened some more."

"She's got talent. No doubt about that. But she's not a fit for River Records. Best of luck to her. *Next.*"

I can't believe it. Is he crazy? Deaf? She was soulful and moving. Lovely. Granted, the song she was singing might not be the stuff of global smashdom, but, surely, Reed heard enough to want to listen to another song.

"You thought she was lightning in a bottle?" Reed asks.

"I thought she was *possibly* lightning in a bottle. Enough to keep listening, to find out for sure."

He shifts his car. "And that's why you're a journalism major, and I'm me."

I repress the urge to flip him off and look out the passenger side window. Crap. If he didn't give this girl the time of day, then how long will he listen to my sweet Alessandra pouring her heart out?

"Georgina, she's a second-rate Laila Fitzgerald," Reed says. "And I've already got the original."

I bite my tongue, too pissed and flabbergasted to respond. I know it's irrational, but I'm feeling vicariously crushed for this girl—which, in turn, makes me feel crushed for Alessandra.

"Are you familiar with Laila Fitzgerald?" Reed prompts.

I roll my eyes. "Of course."

"And you didn't hear the similarity? The way she copied Laila's inflection? Georgina, she was literally *copying* Laila. She doesn't have a sound of her own. Doesn't know who she is. That makes her a hard pass for me. *Next.*"

And the hits just keep on coming. Alessandra doesn't *try* to sound like Adele or Laila! She's been singing the same way since she was little! Is Reed saying Alessandra wouldn't be a legitimate prospect for him simply because she sounds like a combination of two fabulously successful artists?

"What's wrong?" Reed says. And when I look at him, he's doing that thing again. Staring at me like he can read my mind.

"Nothing," I say, but even as I say it, I know my tone is less than convincing.

Reed sighs. "Look, I'm sorry if you feel sorry for this girl. But move on. She won the lottery that I listened to her at all. I have a team of people I pay a lot of money to scout bands and artists for me, and then present their findings to me at weekly meetings. And you know why? Because I'm too busy and impatient to get eyeballs deep in this shit myself. I'm sorry if the reality of the music business seems harsh and heartless to you, but I know my business. And not only that, I have only one life to live, and finite hours in each day, and I can't waste valuable minutes on anything, let alone aspiring singer-songwriters who I know within seconds aren't going to be a fit. I know within the first ten seconds of a song if someone has a glimmer of a chance to make it onto my roster. The minute I know they *don't*, then I move on. Life is too fucking short to do otherwise. Do you understand?"

"Yes," I say softly, feeling like I'm being physically crushed by the weight of the music demo sitting in my purse. Why, oh why, did I have to have that damned thing in my purse tonight? This night would have been so much more fun, so carefree and sexy and glorious, if I had nothing on my mind but Reed's smoking hot body right now.

Reed pulls onto a side street, where we twist and turn in silence for a bit, until finally coming to a stop in front of a large metal gate. Reed pushes a button and the gate begins sliding slowly open. Silently, he drives through the gate and down a driveway, until parking at the top of a circular drive in front of an extremely large house nestled into the slope of a hill.

Reed turns off his fancy car's engine and turns to me, his brown eyes blazing. "For the love of fuck, just ask me already, Georgina. Let's get it out of the way, whatever it is, so we can move past it and have a great time together."

My heart stops. "Ask you what?"

"Whatever the fuck it is you've been scheming and plotting to ask me this entire car ride. Probably from the second you winked at me in the lecture hall, if I were a betting man." His eyes harden. *"Which I am."*

Words won't form. I'm a deer in headlights. A thief caught with her hand on a combination lock. *Shit.*

"You want me to listen to a song, I assume?" he says, letting his hand drop from his steering wheel with exasperation. "'Someone' who doesn't have a big social media following?"

He's taken the air out of my lungs. Sent my heart rate galloping. I nod slowly, my cheeks burning. "I'm sorry."

"Is this 'someone' you, Georgina?"

"No."

He looks unconvinced.

"It's my stepsister, Alessandra. Well, my former stepsister. Her mom married my dad when I was eleven and she was nine, but they divorced a year later." I take a deep breath. "She's *so* talented, Reed. A true artist. I'd be thrilled and grateful if you'd, please..." I swallow hard. *Shit.* "Take a quick listen to her music and tell me what you think."

A small puff of air escapes Reed's nose. He shakes his head and looks out his driver's side window. "I knew it," he mutters. "It never fails."

I'm horrified. "Wait. No. You think Alessandra is the *reason* I came here with you tonight? She's not."

Reed swivels his head to look at me, his face nonverbally communicating he thinks I'm a fucking liar.

"Reed, I'm here because I'm genuinely attracted to you."

He bites back a scoff. "Do you just so happen to have Alessandra's music demo with you right now, Georgie, or do you want me to check out her Instagram page?"

Oh, fuck. "I... I have her music demo."

His chest heaves. "Wow. What a coincidence. Do you carry it around with you, everywhere you go?"

I feel tears threaten, but I stuff them down.

"Did you have it earlier today, when you went to the event to 'meet CeeCee,' and our eyes met, and *you* winked at *me*? Did you have your stepsister's music demo then, Georgina?"

I can't move. Or breathe. I've never felt so cornered in my life. So misunderstood... and, yet, so *guilty*.

Reed leans toward me, overwhelming me with his intensity. "Did you walk into that lecture hall today, hoping to give me that flash drive, Georgina? Tell me the fucking truth."

I open and close my mouth. And then slowly nod. "But it's not what you think. I genuinely went there to meet CeeCee, like I said, but since I knew you were going to be there, I *also*—"

He waves me off. "It's fine. I get it. You were multi-tasking. Killing two birds with one stone, right?"

My breathing is labored. I'm physically squirming in my seat. "Exactly. I didn't lie to you, Reed. I flirted with you only because I'm attracted to you. Not because of the demo."

He looks out the window again. "It doesn't matter, either way. Don't worry about it. I knew you were gaming me this whole time, so it's not like this changes anything. Frankly, it's par for the course for me, and a huge relief to finally have my hunch confirmed."

"Reed, listen to me. I haven't been 'gaming' you—"

He returns to me and his face is calm. Like he's wearing a Reed Rivers mask now. "It's okay, Georgina. I strongly prefer knowing someone wants something from me, rather than having to suffer through the exhaustion of them pretending they don't. God, I hate having to play along when they pretend they've never heard of me or any of my artists. To be honest, I don't have a problem with you letting me do filthy things to your body for four hours in exchange for me listening to your stepsister's demo. In fact, I think that's a fair trade-off. If you want to know the truth, one of my kinks is that I sometimes like to treat myself to a bargained-for exchange, just for the simplicity of it. The thing is, though, if I'm gonna pay for sex, whether with money or some other form of currency, I like *knowing* that's what I'm doing, rather than having a woman lie to my fucking face about it."

I'm livid. Beyond offended. In a flash, rage surges inside me, supplanting the arousal I've been feeling up to this horrifying moment. "You're calling me a whore," I say through gritted teeth, and to my shock, he doesn't correct me. He simply raises his eyebrows and tilts his head, as if to say, *If the shoe fits...*

And that makes me even angrier. "You asshole!" I seethe. "I wasn't going to sleep with you in *exchange* for you listening to Alessandra's music! They were two separate things!"

Reed flashes me yet another nasty look, conveying his disbelief.

"Fuck you," I spit out, the Italian in my blood taking over. "How dare you imply I'm willing to whore myself out to get something for Alessandra. How dare you!"

He chuckles. "How dare I? Save your indignation for your next performance, Georgina. The jig is up. You want something from me. I want something from you. There's no need to scream and act outraged about any of it. Let's talk like rational adults about the terms of this exchange and put this deal... to *bed*." He winks.

My jaw thuds to the floor of the car, even as my heart explodes with rage. "Asshole!" I unfasten my seatbelt with frantic fingers, swing open my door, and stomp away from Reed's fancy car, pulling up the Uber app on my phone as I go.

"Where the fuck do you think you're going?" Reed says, marching after me.

"Home. Call me crazy, but my lady-boner sags to my knees when an arrogant, self-entitled prick-asshole calls me a fucking whore."

"Sweetheart, trust me, if I fuck you hard enough while calling you that, you're gonna come harder than you ever have."

I whirl around, intending to slap him, but he grabs my arm and laughs. The bastard *laughs*.

"Fuck. You," I spit out, wrenching my arm from his grasp. "I wouldn't sleep with you now if you were the last man on earth!"

We're just inside the metal entrance gate of his driveway now, standing in the foggy darkness near a streetlamp. And, in this moment, I've never hated anyone as much as I hate Reed fucking Rivers.

"Stop being so dramatic," he says. "Nothing's changed. I admit I was thrown for a loop for a split-second, but I still want to fuck you. The only difference now is I'm aware I've been your mark all along. Well, bravo, Georgina. Well played. But like I said, that's not a deal-breaker for me. I just like knowing the price list in advance, that's all." He looks me up and down. "The menu of options, shall we say, of what I'm getting in exchange for giving this stepsister's music a listen."

I ball my fists, forcing myself not to punch his smug face. "I'm not being *dramatic*," I shout. "I'm disgusted and enraged at you because you're a pig and a jerk who's treating me like a *whore*. Because I've suddenly realized: *I hate you*."

He laughs. "You *hate* me? And you're not being dramatic? Okay." He leans his broad shoulder against the post of the iron fence, and then puts a languid hand in his pocket. "Let me remind you: you're the one who's had an ulterior motive this whole time, as you've been winking at me, and kissing me, and pushing your tits at me at all the right angles, and—"

"Fuck off, Reed!" I shout. "Fuck off and *die*, you arrogant, rude, self-entitled piece of shit."

"Oh, my, my, my. And *I'm* the asshole here? Nice language, Georgina. Tsk, tsk."

I palm my cheek in mock horror. "Oh, no, did I hurt your sensitive ears with my filthy mouth, Mr. Rivers? Or does this cut even deeper than that?" I add my other palm to my face. "Oh, no. Did I hurt your actual *feelings*? This whole time, were you thinking I might *actually* be your Cinderella, and you might *actually* be my Prince Charming? Do you, like Bryce, believe in love at first sight?" I put my hands on my hips and narrow my eyes. "Or is it simply that this is the first time you can't have what you want, and it's killing you? That's what's got you so worked up, isn't it—knowing you're *never, ever* gonna fuck this epicness?" I motion to my body. "Too bad, sweetheart, because I promise I would have been the best you've ever had."

His nostrils flare. His chest heaves. And thanks to the massive boner straining inside his pants, there's no question my punch has landed. "Okay, enough," he says. "Stop acting like a petulant child and come inside. It's cold out here and you're pissing me off."

"Sucks to be you, I guess. I've already called an Uber."

"Cancel it. We're going inside now. I'm gonna listen to one of your stepsister's songs—*one*—but only if you promise not to have a fucking tantrum if I tell you she's not a fit. And then, in exchange for me listening to that *one* song, we're going straight to my bedroom, where I'm gonna rip off those clothes, tie you to my bed posts, and fuck you like you've never been fucked before. So hard, you'll be seeing stars. So well, you'll be crying for mercy and coming harder than you knew was possible."

He's going to tie me to his bed posts? My traitorous clit pulses sharply at the imagery. But, still, in my white-hot rage, I stay the course. "You're not gonna do any of that," I spit out. "And you wanna know why? *Because I don't fuck assholes.*"

Reed's eyes are on fire, his indignation from a moment ago now replaced by white-hot lust. "Come inside and play me the goddamned fucking song, Georgie, so I can fuck your brains out, for both our benefits. We don't have all night and I'm losing my fucking mind over you. Not to mention my fucking patience, too."

I scoff. "I'm not going inside with you. And I'm not going to play my stepsister's music for you, either, because you don't deserve to hear it."

He sighs and looks at his watch. "Can we fast-forward this part, please? Unfortunately, I'm flying commercial and can't delay my flight."

I look down at my phone. "My Uber is one minute away. The longest minute of my life."

"Cancel it," he commands. "For the love of fuck, you've come this far. Use your head, Georgina. The chess game is over. I said *yes* to listening to a song." He sighs. "Fine. If you cancel the Uber and come inside right now, I'll listen to *two* songs."

"Oh, you're *begging* me now? Negotiating against yourself? How delicious. Well, beg all you want, Mr. Big Shit. The answer is still no. Because no matter how great Alessandra is—and trust me, she *is* great—you're going to say she sucks, just to push my buttons. That's clear to me now. You're a Defcon one level button-pusher, Reed Rivers. I realize that now. And I'm not willing to play your stupid game of chess."

He drags a palm over his stubbled face, looking tormented. "Sweetheart, stop acting like a bratty little child. You're out of control. I'll listen and give my honest opinion, good or bad. I promise, I'm fully capable of separating business and pleasure. *Because I'm an adult.*"

Rage rises inside me again at his obvious implication: *that I'm not.*

"If your stepsister is a fit, then I'll say so. Of course, I will. Because that would benefit me." He smirks. "Although, in the interest of transparency, I should probably admit pushing your buttons is rapidly becoming my new favorite game."

I let out a primal shriek of rage that makes Reed laugh, which only pisses me off more. "Stop being so goddamned condescending!" I shout. "This isn't a joke. This is my stepsister's *life*. Her dream. And you're making a mockery of it. Plus, you've repeatedly impugned my character!"

Reed's eyebrows shoot up at my dramatic last comment, and, I must admit, I think maybe my word choice and intonation were both a little over-the-top. But, whatever. I'm so fucking angry, I press on, letting myself feel whatever I feel and say whatever angry, babbling, bizarre thing pops into my head. "You're not the only 'adult' who can separate business and pleasure, Reed. Yes, I went to that event with Alessandra's demo in my pocket. That was the business side of things for me. And, yes, I planned to give it to you, if the opportunity fell into my lap. And, yes, maybe I flirted with you a little more aggressively than I normally would have, at first, simply because I was so shocked and excited when I realized I'd caught your eye. But guess what is also the truth? The *pleasure* part of this equation for me. Namely that, by the time I served you that tenth drink, I wanted you, Reed. I wanted to come home with you, and let you do literally anything you wanted to me, for no other reason than I wanted to experience the pleasure of it."

"Liar," Reed says. But before I can smack him, he adds, "You knew you wanted to fuck me by the *third* drink."

I know he's trying to calm me down with humor. But it's too late for that. The man basically called me a whore. There's no coming back from that. "Maybe even the first," I say. "But now? Congratulations. I wouldn't fuck you if you paid me."

"Interesting choice of words."

I grit my teeth. "It was a figure of speech. I meant I wouldn't fuck you if you were the last man on earth. Is that clear enough for you?"

He sighs. "Okay, it's time for you to stop acting like the hotheaded, impetuous twenty-one-year-old you are, and come inside. It's cold out here, and I'm hard as a rock for you. Let me bribe you, sexy Georgina. I promise you'll like giving me your end of the bargain."

My traitorous clit pulses again. This time, thanks to the look of molten lust on Reed's face. There's no way I'd say yes to him, obviously

—let alone yes, yes, yes. But I can't deny my body wants to, even in the midst of my mind's rage and disgust.

But before I've said a word, I'm saved by the bell. Or, rather, by the blinding headlights of my Uber shining onto Reed's chiseled face.

"Perfect timing," I say smugly, turning away from Reed. "*Ciao, stronzo.*"

I wave to the driver on the other side of the gate to let him know I'm coming, but Reed grabs my shoulder.

"Tell him to leave," Reed commands, his voice brimming with intensity. "Come inside with me and play me the demo. Let me show you what your body can do, Georgie."

I whirl back around. "I already know what my body can do. You wanna see?" Glowering at him, I flip him the bird with both hands. "Pretty cool, huh?"

Reed leans against the gatepost and chuckles. "Wow. Tell me how you really feel about me, baby."

"There aren't enough middle fingers in the world to tell you how I really feel about you, *baby.*"

He grimaces playfully. "So heartless."

"It was never my 'heart' that felt attracted to you, so it's not a big loss."

"Tsk. So rude. You'll catch more flies with honey. Didn't your momma ever teach you that?"

No, she didn't, asshole, because my mother is fucking dead. But if she were here, there's no doubt in my mind my fiery, fabulous badass of a mother would be applauding me for flipping you off, ya big dick. In fact, she'd be flipping you off, right along with me. I don't say any of that to Reed, of course, but it's sure as hell what I'm thinking.

Wordlessly, I turn around and inspect the metal gate, my anger at an all-time high. First, this arrogant piece of shit tells me I'm "play-acting confidence in my mother's heels," and then he tells me my momma should have taught me to play nice in the face of flaming assholery? Well, fuck that. And fuck *him*. "How do I get through?" I yell, pounding on the iron gate with my palm. "Help me out of here or I'm gonna climb over this gate and fall on my ass, and then sue *your* ass for negligence and false imprisonment!"

Calmly, Reed slides a key into a lock on a pedestrian side gate, and I stomp through the opening without so much as a thank you. But when I reach the other side, I realize I can't actually storm off without trying one last-gasp attempt at helping Alessandra. Even though, obviously, anything I say to Reed at this point will fall on deaf ears.

I turn around. "My stepsister's name is Alessandra Tennison. Her Instagram handle is *TheRealAllyT*. She barely has any followers and no brother destined for the NFL. She's just a shy, sweet, incredibly talented nineteen-year-old who's finishing her sophomore year at The Berklee College of Music in Boston. Her father died a week after her eighth birthday, after going out for an early-morning jog and getting mowed down by a texting driver. And her happiness, her dreams, mean everything to me. A shit-ton more than any one-night stand with a manipulative, arrogant asshole." With that, I whirl around, march to my Uber, and throw myself into the backseat.

"Georgina?" the driver says, per safety protocol.

"Yes. Please, go."

As the car takes off, I steal one last look at Reed. He's standing on the other side of his slatted gate, one of his forearms laid flush against it, and his forehead resting on his arm. His eyes are two hot coals, smoldering in the dim light of the nearby streetlamp. His dick is plainly bulging behind his pants. As hard as a rock, like he said earlier. And for a fleeting moment, I'm a bit pissed at my values, not to mention my Italian temper, for making me miss out on what was almost certainly going to be the hottest hate-sex of my life. *He was planning to tie me to his bed posts?* Holy hell.

As I stare at Reed from the backseat of the departing Uber, seriously questioning my life choices, my temper, and my penchant for sometimes missing the forest for the trees, Reed shoots me a clipped wave in farewell, his cocky body language shouting, *It's your loss, baby!* And that pisses me off, all over again. Without a thought in my head, I raise both middle fingers into the air out the back window before turning around and taking several deep, shaky breaths... before, finally, letting the anger and embarrassment I've been holding back seep out of me in the form of big, soggy tears.

FIFTEEN
REED

"Reed!" CeeCee says brightly, picking up my call. "How's my favorite music mogul?"

"Fantastic, thanks. I just landed in New York, and I'm on my way to meet up with the Goats at their hotel."

"Oh, how I love the adorable Goats! Tell them I said hello."

"I will. They're kicking off *Good Morning America's* summer concert series on Monday."

"How wonderful."

"What about you, CeeCee? What's my favorite media mogul-*ess* up to this week?"

"Well, sadly, I'm not in New York escorting 22 Goats to *Good Morning America*. You've got me beat there. But I've got a few exciting things lined up before I'm scheduled to jet off to meet my darling Francois in Bali."

"Oh, God, I love Bali. Where are you staying?"

She tells me about her trip's itinerary for a bit and then says, "Thank you again for yesterday. Angela was thrilled with the lineup of the panel—particularly, that she was able to snag a superstar like you as the event headliner."

"I wasn't the headliner. *You* were. I was just another panelist."

"Ha! Don't attempt false modesty with me. I didn't have a line out the door afterwards. Did all those students want to ask you questions about the music industry, or did they just want to flirt with you?"

"Actually, most of them wanted to give me their music demos."

"Of course, they did. And... ? Did you discover anyone particularly intriguing?"

My stomach clenches. Did CeeCee notice me losing my shit over Georgina? Is she fucking with me by asking me that? "No, not really," I say, my heart pounding. "I don't accept unsolicited demos, as you know."

"Yes, and I think that's wise. If word got out you did, you'd need bodyguards twenty-four-seven, not just at music festivals. All the more reason I'm grateful you were willing to subject yourself to the onslaught yesterday."

"It was my pleasure. Anything for you."

"Aw, thank you. That's wonderful to hear because, actually, there's something else I'd like you to do for me: give me an in-depth interview for *Dig a Little Deeper*."

I chuckle. "Not this again. Anything but *that*."

"Why are you being so stubborn about this?"

"Why are *you*? Surely, you've got A-listers lined up around the block, wanting to get featured in your new magazine. Why do you keep coming after me?"

"Because everyone else has already been profiled a thousand times. You, on the other hand, are a glamorous man of mystery. You're enigmatic, Reed. Inscrutable. We can all see you're living an enviable life, or so it seems, but what's behind the curtain? What does it take to keep all those plates spinning? And how much has your past influenced your current success? The world knows, generally speaking, you've had to overcome a lot to get where you are, and yet, you've never once been interviewed about any of it."

And I never will, I think.

"Come on, Reed. You never let anyone peel back the layers of your onion. Let me be the first."

"I'm quite content being an unpeeled onion. But, thanks."

"I'm envisioning a cover story, honey. An up-close headshot on the cover with those gorgeous eyes of yours, front and center, staring into the reader's soul... It'd be an interview bursting with my admiration and love for you. I'd show you as the inspiration you are."

"I'm not an inspiration."

"Yes, you are. And yet, nobody knows it because you always seem so polished. Let down your guard a little bit, and I promise it'll be the best interview of your life."

"CeeCee, nobody needs to know the nuts and bolts of me. How hard I've worked to get here. What I've overcome. Let them think I walk on water and bathe in Evian and shit diamonds and fuck supermodels every second of my golden life. *That's* my brand—which, by the way, I've meticulously cultivated in order to sell a shit-ton of music over the years."

CeeCee sighs with disappointment. "I think an in-depth interview would be even better for your 'brand.' I truly do. It'd be a win-win."

"I'm sorry," I say. "It pains me to say no to you about anything, love. In some ways, you've been more of a mother to me than my own. But—"

"Now, see! That's exactly the kind of thing I want to talk to you about in an interview! You've never said anything like that to me before. And now I'm dying to know what you mean."

I look out the car window at the bustling streets of Manhattan. "I'd be happy to tell you over drinks some time. *Off* the record."

"I'll hold you to that. So, what can I do for you, my dear?"

"Nothing."

"You called *me*, remember?"

"Oh. Yeah. I just called to tell you how much I enjoyed doing the panel, despite all the griping and bitching I did this past week about having to do it."

"Aw, I'm so glad."

"Icing on the cake, I wound up chatting with your friend, Angela, about being an expert witness on this stupid copyright infringement lawsuit I've got to defend, and she just now emailed Leonard and said she's reviewed the case in detail and she's happy to do it."

"Fantastic! You'll love Angela. Your jury is going to adore her."

"The case won't get to a jury. Some moron-band nobody has ever heard of is claiming Red Card Riot stole a chord progression that can be found in everything from Mozart to Bruno Mars."

CeeCee scoffs. "God, I hate people."

"I would have told you all about it yesterday, but you took off without so much as a quick goodbye."

"Sorry. You were being mobbed by kiddies, and I only had a short window to grab a coffee with an old friend."

Bingo. Finally, we get to the good stuff. "Oh yeah? Who?"

"Gilda Schiff. An old friend from college. She's a journalism professor at UCLA."

My heart is suddenly thrumming. "Hmm. The woman I saw you leaving with looked a bit younger than an 'old college friend.'"

"Oh, your eagle eye noticed that gorgeous creature who left with Gilda and me, did it, all the way from across that huge lecture hall?" She chuckles. "The college kiddie with us was one of Gilda's journalism students. Apparently, she had the bright idea to attend a music school event to meet me and try to land herself a writing job."

"With *Rock 'n' Roll*?"

"No. Georgina has her sights set on *Dig a Little Deeper,* though she said she'd take any opportunity."

My heart rate increases, yet again, just hearing Georgina's name. In a torrent, I'm suddenly remembering Georgina's "greatest hits" from last night. Our amazing kisses. The way her tits peeked out of her tank. The way her hazel eyes flashed with homicidal rage when she told me off in front of my house, making me hard as a rock. And, finally, the way she hurled herself into that Uber, and then flipped me off with both hands as her car peeled away. And all of it, despite the fact that anyone else would have stayed and kissed my ass—not to mention, come inside and sucked my dick—to advance her stepsister's cause.

I clear my throat, my breathing shallow. "So, are you going to hire her?" I ask, trying to sound as nonchalant as possible. "I gotta think her worming her way into meeting you at a music school event is a point in her favor. It shows she's capable of thinking outside the box, don't you think?"

"Oh, absolutely. And being able to think outside the box wasn't the only point in this young woman's favor."

You can say that again.

"She's a treasure, Reed. An absolute gem. Funny and engaging. Charismatic and confident. An excellent writer, too. I just finished reading her writing samples, and I was duly impressed."

My eyebrows rise. I didn't see that one coming, I'm ashamed to admit. Gorgeous, witty, magnetic, sexy, curvaceous Georgina is also an excellent writer? Well, I'll be damned.

CeeCee continues. "She's still a bit green, of course. Definitely needs some real-world experience. But with some guidance, I think she's got potential to become a top-notch journalist."

My heart is crashing in my ears. Holy fuck, I want this for Georgina. "It sounds like the event was a win for us both, then. I found myself an expert witness for a frivolous lawsuit, and you found yourself a newbie journalist to hire."

"Actually, no, I don't think it's going to work out for me to hire her, I'm sad to say."

My heart stops. *No.* "Why not? From the way you've been talking about this girl, it seems like hiring her is a no-brainer."

"It would be, if only I had the right position for her. But, unfortunately, I don't."

I take a deep breath to make sure my voice doesn't sound over-eager. "Surely, you could move things around to make a spot for her. Good talent is hard to find."

"The problem is we don't hire kids straight out of college for *Dig a Little Deeper*. Only seasoned professionals. And at *Rock 'n' Roll*, which she said wasn't her first choice, anyway, writers with no experience are required to funnel through an unpaid, three-month internship as a proving ground before we even think of offering them a paid position on the writing staff."

Another deep breath. "Okay, so, offer her an unpaid internship at *Rock 'n' Roll*. Let her hone her chops and earn her way to a paid gig."

"Why are you fighting so hard for this girl? In fact, why are you even wasting your time talking to me about her at all? Normally, you'd have brushed this topic aside faster than a sneeze."

"No, I wouldn't."

"You absolutely would. Is it because she's so beautiful? Or didn't you happen to notice that with your eagle eye from across the lecture hall?"

Shit. "I didn't notice that, actually. I only saw her from the back." *Fuck.* "Maybe yesterday's panel inspired me to want to give back."

"Uh huh."

I audibly shrug, hoping it sounds authentic. "Maybe yesterday's event made me remember what it was like when I was first starting out, and every bit of mentorship meant so much to me. Especially yours."

"Mmm hmm. What aren't you telling me, Reed?"

"Nothing. I'm just trying to help a young woman with a dream, out of the goodness of my heart—thereby helping my dear friend. You said she's got something special, and I want you to have the best people on your staff because I love you so much."

She laughs. "Wait. There's *goodness* in your heart?"

"That's what you took from everything I just said to you?"

She laughs again.

"Hell yeah, there's goodness in my heart," I mutter defensively. "It's just hard to notice because it's hidden underneath so many mysterious, enigmatic 'layers' of my onion."

She hoots with laughter.

"Seriously, Ceece, you should hear the way you've been talking about this girl. You're obviously smitten with her."

"Oh, I am. She was exceptional, Reed. The brightest, most charming and charismatic newbie I've met in a long time. Maybe, ever. I sat across the table from her in that coffee place and thought, 'Anyone this girl interviews wouldn't stand a chance. She'd get them to spill *all* their secrets in the first five minutes.'"

I smile to myself. Truer words were never spoken. "Well, there you go," I say breezily. "Don't let someone like that get away."

CeeCee sighs. "The thing is, I'd feel like an asshole offering Georgina an unpaid internship. After Georgina left the coffee place, my friend, Gilda, told me Georgina's father recently battled cancer, and Georgina needs a paid position after graduation to help him afford some expensive medication he still needs to take."

My stomach drops into my toes at this unexpected revelation.

"Under the circumstances," CeeCee continues, "I'd feel terrible offering Georgina an unpaid internship. Actually, I was thinking of picking up the phone and trying to help her get a paid position somewhere else."

"What? You can't do that. Break your rules and hire this girl for pay, CeeCee."

"I can't. My hands are tied. If I make an exception for Georgina and let her bypass the internship program, my staff would flood me with résumés, insisting their best friends and nephews should get the same treatment."

"It's your company. Surely, you can make an exception, just this once."

I hear a slapping noise. Like CeeCee's just slammed her palms onto her desk. "Okay, Reed. That's it. What the fuck aren't you telling me?"

My heart stops. "Nothing. You just seem particularly moved by this girl, and I don't want you regretting your decision later. To be honest, I'm moved by her, too—by this thing with her father. I know what it's like to want to do whatever it takes to help a parent in need."

CeeCee is quiet for a moment in the face of my unexpected comment. I never talk about my mother. And now, in this one conversation, I've referred to her *twice*. Surely, CeeCee thinks the sky is falling.

"I really *was* moved by Georgina," CeeCee says wistfully. "Even before I found out about how she helps her father. She was truly lovely, Reed. A diamond in the rough. Plus—and I probably shouldn't admit this, but—the fact that she's so gorgeous and sexy would make her hugely effective if I were to assign her to interview musicians for *Rock 'n' Roll*. I know it sounds sexist, and maybe a little underhanded of me, but the fact remains that interview subjects, especially male musicians, tend to open up like steamed clams with really stunning interviewers, as I'm sure you've noticed yourself over the years."

I chuckle. "Why do you think I've always opened up the most with *you*?"

She snorts. "Always, such a charmer. Seriously, though, without even realizing what they're doing, horny musicians always turn themselves inside out, trying to impress the really gorgeous ones, which never fails to translate into interview gold."

I pause for a moment. Long enough to make it seem like I'm weighing what I'm about to say. "I tell you what, CeeCee. I'm going to give you a gift, because I love you and also want to help this girl. I'm going to make a six-figure donation to one of your favorite cancer charities—the one that supports family members of those affected by cancer. They can use part of my donation to set up a grant for this Georgina of yours—the equivalent of three months' salary, plus whatever might be needed to pay for this expensive medicine her father needs. That way, you can officially hire Georgina for the usual *unpaid* internship, as far as your payroll department and other employees are concerned, but she'll actually get paid on the sly. *Boom.* Georgina and her father win. You win. *Rock 'n' Roll* wins. Everybody wins."

"Everybody wins but *you*. Why would you do this?"

"Because I'm a good guy. Because I love you. But, mostly, because you said she'd be particularly good at interviewing musicians and that gives me an excellent idea."

"Ha! I knew there had to be a catch."

"What would you say if, in exchange for my generous donation to one of your favorite charities, *Rock 'n' Roll* does a special 'River Records issue,' featuring nothing but my artists?"

"I'm so relieved to find out you have an ulterior motive for your generosity. For a second there, I felt extremely disoriented."

"My motive isn't *ulterior*. It's *parallel*. Yes, I want to get something out of this, but I *also* want to do good. For you and this 'diamond in the rough.' Seriously, what's the downside of my proposal? It's a no-brainer."

CeeCee is quiet. Thinking. Processing. Trying to figure out what she's missing here. Why I'm bending over backwards.

"I'll roll out the red carpet for this girl," I say. "She'll have full access to everyone on my roster, all at once. I've never done anything like this before, and I'd only ever do it for you."

"It wouldn't just be her," CeeCee says, and, instantly, I know I've got her. "I'd have to assign several people to the issue. Plus, I'm sure I'd write a few pieces, too."

I smile broadly. "Whatever you want, as long as the newbie works on nothing but the River Records issue during her summer internship."

"Why?" CeeCee asks, her tone instantly suspicious.

"Because I'm paying her fucking salary, that's why."

"Oh."

CeeCee is quiet for a long moment. And I don't blame her. It's highly unlike me to bend over backwards to help a stranger. But not outside the realm of possibility, I'd think, considering all the benefits that will flow to both CeeCee and me from this arrangement. Obviously, I've omitted to tell CeeCee the foremost benefit that will flow to me. My top reason for doing this. Namely, that this arrangement will undoubtedly lead to me fucking Georgina at some point during the summer—which, in this moment, is something I want for myself more than I want my next breath. Certainly, more than I want the two hundred grand I'm planning to donate to CeeCee's cancer charity. But, so what if I haven't told CeeCee that part? Omitting that *one* particular nugget of information doesn't make what I *have* mentioned any less true.

"Okay," CeeCee says. "I'll agree to the special issue—"

"Wonderful."

"*On one condition.*"

I hold my breath.

"It absolutely *must* include a full-length interview of *you*."

I exhale with frustration. "CeeCee."

"We can't do a River Records issue without an interview of Reed Rivers. It can be a simple two-pager, if you like, but an interview of you is non-negotiable."

Again, I look out the window of my limo, just in time to see the bushy trees of Central Park coming into view. "All right," I concede. "I'll sit down for a basic *one*-pager, including a five-by-seven photo of me to take up space."

"A *two*-pager, including a three-by-five photo. That's my final offer."

Fuck. I say nothing for a moment, mulling my options.

"A two-pager can't, by its very nature, be as in-depth as the five-pager I've been dying to do for *Dig a Little Deeper*. Plus, don't forget, this would be for *Rock 'n' Roll*, so it will be fluff. Mostly."

"So, it'll be like the 'Man with the Midas Touch' interview?"

I can practically hear her devious smile. "No, it'll be meatier than that. For God's sake, Reed, for that one, the only really personal thing you said was you're not interested in marriage or children. I'll need a lot more than that for a River Records special issue. But, still, yes, the piece will, by necessity, be *basically* on-brand for *Rock 'n' Roll*."

I roll my eyes at my predicament, even though CeeCee isn't here to see it. "Okay. Fine. A two-pager. But it's not going to 'peel back the layers' of my onion too far. I'll give a little something more than last time, but my deepest layers will stay firmly unpeeled."

"Deal. We'll peel back only *one* layer of your onion."

My driver honks his horn and screams at a yellow taxi that's stopped immediately in front of us to let its passengers out.

"Ah, New York," CeeCee says. "I can hear it from here."

I chuckle. "There's no place quite like it. So, will this Georgina of yours interview me for this onion-peeling interview?"

"Do you *want* Georgina to be the one to interview you?"

I pause long enough to make it seem like I'm genuinely considering the question. "Yeah, that's probably a good idea. She might bring a fresh perspective and voice a more seasoned writer wouldn't. Plus, you already interviewed me for that 'Midas Touch' piece. Might be fun to switch things up."

"I agree. I was actually going to suggest she do it. I've got a hunch she's going to be particularly talented at peeling back your layers, my dear."

Another wave of paranoia washes over me. Seriously now, did CeeCee notice me losing my shit over Georgina—and she's been fucking with me this whole conversation? "Just make sure she knows she's only allowed to peel back *one* layer of the onion," I say, hoping my voice sounds playful and calm. "No additional layers shall be peeled during the course of this interview."

"I'll be sure to tell her. No worries, sweetie. Hey, would you be willing to give Georgina a work station at River Records for the summer—just for ease of access?"

Ease of access. Oh, God. I've got such a dirty mind. Upon hearing those words in reference to Georgina, my brain can't help but imagine myself opening Georgina's olive thighs and sinking myself deep inside her—getting to feel the Nirvana I've been waiting ten fucking years to feel, ever since I first laid eyes on Georgina's double a decade ago and felt an urgent, animalistic desire to fuck the living hell out of her.

"Reed?"

"Yes. A work station for Georgina would be fine with me. Talk to Owen about it. Just as long as we're clear that she's *your* employee. Not mine. I don't want my artists thinking this girl is a shill for our marketing department. It's important they know she's a *bona fide* reporter for *Rock 'n' Roll*, interviewing them for an important special issue. *You're* her boss. Not me. I want them to take her seriously."

"Of course, Reed. So do I. You know I'd never allow my magazine to be used as a propaganda arm of your label. This issue is going to have journalistic integrity, even if it happens to work to your label's and artists' extreme advantage, as much as it works to mine." She clucks her tongue. "Oh goodness, my mind is already racing with a thousand ideas. When will you be back from New York? Let's have dinner."

"Not before you head off to Bali, unfortunately. We'll have to do it when you get back. In the meantime, feel free to call Owen to arrange logistics and scheduling. Let's get this special issue cooking with gas."

"Fabulous. Georgina mentioned she's graduating on the twenty-second. So I'll get her on-boarded the very next day, right before I head off to Bali."

My limo stops in front of the Ritz Carlton, right across from the Park, and a doorman in white gloves promptly opens my car door. "I've made it to the Goats' hotel. I gotta hang up."

"Bags, sir?" the doorman says, and I motion to the trunk before striding toward the double doors of the hotel lobby.

"Have fun in Bali," I say. "Say *bonjour* to Francois for me."

"I will. I'll call the cancer charity now, right after we hang up, and email you the info for the donation. Oh, and, Reed. One more thing."

I stop walking, just inside the doors of the hotel, my heart pounding. Is this it? Is she going to tell me she's sniffed me out?

"Let's make sure all the horny musicians on your roster treat this young woman with respect and professionalism, okay?"

I sigh with relief.

"I know you didn't get a good look at her as she was walking out of the lecture hall, but, trust me, she's stunning. And as we both know, musicians aren't always the most restrained members of the male species when it comes to beautiful women."

I smile to myself. *The same could be said of music executives.* "Don't worry," I say. "Owen and I will make it clear to everyone: the newbie reporter is off-limits."

"Thank you. Georgina has worked her way through school as a bartender, so I'm sure she's quite adept at fending off horny heathens. But, still, it never hurts to remind everyone she's there to do a job, and not to get hit on right and left."

My blood simmers at the thought of any of my guys making a move on Georgina. But a couple of them, in particular. "We're on the same page," I say through clenched teeth. "I promise, CeeCee, if any of my guys hit on your summer intern, they're going to have to answer to *me*. And, I guarantee, it won't be pretty."

SIXTEEN

GEORGINA

"He was such an asshole!" I say to Alessandra. And, of course, I'm talking about Reed.

It's my graduation party. A few hours ago, while clad in a traditional cap and gown, I accepted my diploma, posed for a smiling photo, and became the first person in my family to graduate from college. And now, my small extended family and a few longtime family friends have gathered in my father's two-bedroom condo in the Valley to celebrate.

At the moment, Alessandra and I are standing in Dad's small kitchen by ourselves, sent in here by Aunt Marjorie to slice up the cake. But since this is Ally and me we're talking about, we've long since forgotten our assigned task, and we're doing nothing but gabbing, gossiping, and laughing together. All the things we always do when we get together, whether in person or on our phones—but especially in person. And especially when it's been months since we've been together in the flesh.

Alessandra leans her slender hip against the counter, her blue eyes shining. The late-afternoon sunlight streaking through the kitchen window is bringing out the auburn highlights in her dark, curly mop and highlighting her glorious freckles. Her smile is as sincere and warm as ever. Her lavender aura every bit as peaceful and serene as usual—every bit as much as my blazing-red aura is fiery and passionate.

"Maybe you hurt Reed's feelings and he was just, you know, lashing out as a defense mechanism," Alessandra says, causing me to snort-laugh. "I'm serious," she persists. "From what you've described of your chemistry with him, and the crazy fireworks that went off for you when you kissed... I don't know, honey, maybe you're underestimating the fireworks that went off for *him*."

Again, I snort.

But Alessandra won't let it go. "Even if Reed's rich and powerful and older, and used to banging supermodels—"

"Actresses, mainly, I think. Probably models, too. But actresses and daughters of famous people seem to be in most of the photos with him."

"Okay, whatever. My point is Reed is still a man. And men fall for you, Georgie. That's a fact. It's your superpower."

I scoff. "Men want to have *sex* with me."

"Only because you push them away emotionally, so they'll take whatever they can get."

The image of Shawn's phone screen that fateful morning pings my brain. The memory of how I stumbled across those sickening strings of texts and photos—the exchanges between Shawn and several women that made it painfully clear he'd been running around on me for quite some time, with multiple women, when I'd been nothing but faithful and supportive. And, worst of all, he'd done it all while my life was falling apart and I needed his love and support and faithfulness the most. I feel a deep ache remembering my hot tears I shed that horrible morning... and then a glint of pride, even though I probably shouldn't, thinking about that bad thing I did when my tears turned to fury.

"I haven't *always* pushed men away emotionally," I say. I run my fingertip through a blob of icing on the corner of the cake and slide my finger into my mouth.

Alessandra sighs sympathetically. "I know, honey. I'm just saying maybe it hurt Reed's feelings, more than you realize, when he found out you had an agenda the whole time, so he acted like a dick to mask his hurt feelings."

I put my palm up. "Okay, you gotta stop now. You're crediting Reed with way too much humanity. The man thinks he's a god among men, the immortal ruler of everything he surveys, and he was simply pissed I wasn't falling at his feet like all the other mortal girls. I didn't hurt his feelings, if he has them. Did I bruise his ego? Probably. But that's it. Feelings weren't involved for either of us. He made it clear from the start he wanted to bring me to his house for nothing but sex, and I made it clear I was super down for that plan. The End."

Alessandra pops a bite of cake into her mouth. "Don't sell yourself short, Georgie. You have a way of making people *feel* something. It's your gift. The gift of genuine, and often instant, connection."

I shake my head. "Not this time. If you met Reed, you'd understand. He's unapologetically on the prowl. He flat-out said he didn't want to 'date' me, only 'seduce' me." *And tie me to his bed posts.*

"He actually used the word 'seduce'?" Alessandra asks.

"He sure did."

She chuckles. "Wow. Was he wearing a suit with a skinny tie and holding a gimlet when he said it?"

We both giggle at the old-school imagery. But, if I'm being honest, my laughter is tinged with wistfulness. Regret. Yearning. Because, damn, Reed rocked that old-school, sexy word—*seduce*—like nobody's business.

"The crazy part is," I say, "Reed didn't sound like he was doing a *Madmen* parody when he said it. Somehow, it came across as nothing but hot." I bite my lip. "Actually, after being subjected to so many drunk fuckboys and their fumbling attempts at hitting on me, it was thrilling to have such a suave older man come on to me like some kind of old-school movie star." I sigh at the sudden flood of memories wracking my brain. The cocky look on Reed's face when he said he didn't plan to date me. The way he called me Cinderella. And, of course, our amazing kisses... Oh. I suddenly realize Alessandra is staring at me, her eyebrow arched. "What?"

My stepsister flashes me a snarky look. "If you could see your face right now... Georgie, you don't hate Reed. You still totally want to screw him!"

"No, I hate him with the fiery passion of an erupting volcano... *and* I still totally want to screw him."

We both burst out laughing.

"But don't mistake hate-lust for genuine feelings," I add. "Not on my end, and certainly not on his. He flat-out said he's 'non-committal' about relationships. Which, by the way, is a lovely way of saying he's a commitment-phobe. Which is great with me, of course. I told him, 'Hey, you're non-committal? Cool, dude, because so am I.'"

"That you are." She takes another bite of cake and snickers. "Sounds like you two are exactly each other's types, huh? Or, at least, Reed is yours: emotionally unavailable and smoking hot."

Sighing, I pick up a fork and steal a bite of cake off Alessandra's plate. Because, really, what can I say to that accusation? Reed is, indeed, precisely my type. The most perfect example of it I've ever encountered. A glittering paragon of suave, cocky, unattainable male perfection, with a side of assholery, like nothing I've encountered before. "I'm sorry, Ally. I can't believe I screwed things up so badly for both of us. I wish I'd handled things differently that night. For both our sakes."

"It's that Italian temper of yours," she says, rolling her eyes. "Getting you into trouble, once again."

"I know. I'm sorry."

"I'm kidding. You have nothing to apologize for, especially not to *me*. If Reed was rude and disrespectful to you, then I'm thrilled you told him off. Never think you have to take shit from any man, even a rich and powerful one, especially not to help *me*. My time to shine will come soon enough, baby girl. I know it. And when it does, I won't take crap from anyone. And I certainly won't prostitute out my beloved sister-from-another-mister to get ahead."

Oh, my heart. If I didn't already love this beautiful girl, I would have fallen head over heels in love with her now.

I look out the window of my father's small kitchen at the cloudless blue sky, trying to gather my thoughts. Ever since I got home from Reed's the other night, I've felt a powerful ache growing inside me. An overwhelming sense of regret gathering steam. And now, I can't help wishing I could rewind the clock and do things differently that night. "The thing is... " I say. "It's not like, before Reed implied I was a whore, I'd thought he was my Prince Charming. It's not like the horrible things he said to me outside his house shattered my illusions about him."

I look down at my hands, feeling my cheeks redden with shame. I'm not proud of myself for wishing I could rewind the clock and follow Reed into his house that night—where I'd then let him tie me up and fuck me like an animal for four hours straight, in exchange for him listening to Alessandra's demo. But, if I'm being honest, that's exactly what I've been wishing these past few days, now that I've had some time to reflect.

"What are you saying?" Alessandra asks, her eyebrow arched.

"I'm saying... Reed already had a horrible opinion of me that I wasn't going to shake, no matter what I said or did. So, in that case, why did I even bother trying to convince him my intentions were pure? I should have kept my eye on the prize and done exactly what he expected of me—fucked him as payment for him listening to the demo. At least, that way, we both would have gotten what we wanted out of him."

Alessandra smiles. "Actually, Georgie, it sounds to me like you did the *one* thing you could have done to change Reed's mind about you. Plus, bonus points, you did it in style—with your two middle fingers raised to the sky. So classic."

I giggle. "You should have seen the look on Reed's face as I was driving away. He was so fucking pissed at me."

"Hey, ladies." It's my father, coming into the kitchen. And his voice makes us girls both straighten up. Dad strides across the small kitchen and puts his arm around my shoulders. "Aunt Marjorie sent me in here to ask about the cake. She suspects you two girls have gotten to chatting and completely forgotten why you came in here."

Alessandra and I giggle and nod.

"Guilty as charged," Alessandra says.

Rolling his eyes, Dad picks up a knife and begins cutting the cake for us. "Ally, would you mind distributing slices to everyone? There's something I want to talk to Georgie about."

"You betcha, Pops," Alessandra says.

The three of us load cake slices onto a tray for Alessandra, who then breezes into the living room to expertly deliver them like the part-time waitress she is.

When Alessandra is gone, Dad turns to me and smiles proudly, his eyes instantly moistening. He places his hands on my shoulders, a sure sign an emotional speech is coming. It's not a rare occurrence with my father—watching him become overcome with emotion. He's always worn his tender heart on his sleeve, my Dad. It's the thing I love most about him.

"You're my pride and joy, Georgie," he says, tears threatening. "You know that, right?"

"I do, Daddy. Thank you for always telling me that. And for doing without so much, for so long, so I could get a college education."

"It's what Mommy and I both wanted for you. We wanted you to be able to make a living doing something you feel passionately about."

My eyes are glistening now, along with Dad's. God, I wish my mother were here to witness this proud and happy day.

Dad reaches into his pocket and pulls out a small box. And, instantly, I know what's inside. My mother's wedding ring. Instantly, I hurl myself into my father's arms and burst into tears. And so, of course, my emotional, tenderhearted father cries along with me.

"You always said you'd give it to me on my wedding day," I mumble into Dad's shoulder.

"I realized your mother would want you to have it today," he whispers into my hair. "She came to me in a dream last night and told me to give it to you. She said, 'Georgie doesn't need a man to make us proud. She's already the woman we've raised her to be.'"

I sniffle. "That sounds just like Mommy."

Dad pulls back from our hug and wipes his eyes. "You know I'm hoping you'll have a family of your own one day, but only because I want you to experience the kind of love story I had with your mother. I want you to experience the kind of unconditional love I feel for you, Georgie."

"I know, Daddy. I love you, too."

"But that doesn't mean you need to get married or have babies to make me and your mother proud, or to be the woman we dreamed you'd grow up to be. Without going to college myself, I didn't fully understand how proud I'd feel today. How amazing it would feel to watch you—" He presses his lips together, too choked up to continue. Which makes me choke up, as well. And for a moment, we're both silently swallowing air and wiping our eyes.

Finally, Dad gathers himself enough to open the box, and I gasp at the sight of the diamond-encrusted ring inside, the one I remember my mother always wearing with such pride on her lovely hand. Beaming with his love for me, my father says, "*Amorina*, today, you're exactly the woman your mother and I always dreamed you'd be. Wear this ring, and let it always remind you of that."

I slide the ring onto the ring finger of my right hand, but it's too big. I try my middle finger next, and smile when it's a perfect fit. "Isn't it pretty?" I say, holding up my newly decorated hand. "Now, I'll look like a queen whenever I flip someone off."

"*Georgie.*"

I giggle. "Aw, come on, Dad. You know it's perfect Mommy's ring fits my middle finger, instead of my ring finger. We both know I'll get far more use out of it this way."

Dad sighs. "You're still sure you 'never' want to get married?"

I purse my lips, considering. "No, I think I'm over that. I only felt that way right after your divorce from Paula. But only because you and Paula made marriage look like an exceedingly stupid thing for anyone to do."

Dad rolls his eyes. "That's an understatement."

"I think nowadays I'm open to *maybe* getting married one day. Just not until I've gotten my career going. And certainly not before age thirty. I only want one kid, though, so I don't need to be in any rush."

Dad looks satisfied. Maybe even relieved. And I totally get it. It's not that my father believes marriage and babies is the only endgame for a woman. Not at all. He's a traditional guy in some ways, but not about that. No, I think in addition to him wanting me to experience a love like he had with my mother, and the love he has for me, he simply wants to feel confident I'll be safe and protected, and loved unconditionally, my whole life, even after he's gone, whether his departure from this earthly life comes way sooner than either of us would want, or, God willing, decades from now.

Dad takes my hand and gazes at it, perhaps thinking about the happy day, so many years ago, he married a nineteen-year-old spitfire who, tragically, wound up leaving this earth far too soon. He says, "She's smiling down on you right now, you know."

"I know," I say. "I can feel her. She's smiling down on you, too, Daddy. *Always.*"

I put my palm on my father's face, letting my mother's ring brush his stubbled cheek, and then kiss his other cheek tenderly.

I'm not lying about my mother *always* smiling down on him, by the way. Even when Dad stupidly married Paula, in the midst of his grief, I know my kind-hearted mother was in heaven, cheering him on. Wanting him to find love again. Wanting him to feel joy after so much sorrow. True, it wasn't true love for Dad and Paula, to put it mildly, but I'm positive my mother didn't hold it against my brokenhearted father for blindly stumbling through his pain in that way.

"Don't worry about me, Daddy," I whisper. "I'll always be okay. I'm a fighter. A *hustler*."

He chuckles. "A *hustler*?"

I wink. "All good things come to those who hustle." My phone buzzes in my pocket. I pull it out, check the screen, and whoop. "This is the call I've been waiting for, Daddy! Oh my God!"

"I'll give you some privacy," Dad says excitedly. He beelines for the door of the kitchen. "Good luck!"

When he's gone, I hastily answer the call, my hands shaking and my heart thrumming in my chest. "Hello, this is Georgina."

"Hi, Georgina," a woman says. "This is Margot, CeeCee Rafael's personal assistant."

Oh my God! *This is it.* The call I've been waiting for since I walked out of that coffee date with CeeCee. I collapse into a kitchen chair, praying this woman is calling with happy news.

"Hello, Margot. How are you?"

"Couldn't be better. CeeCee was wondering if you might be able to come to the office tomorrow morning at ten? Sorry for the late notice, but she's traveling internationally the following day, and she wants to personally give you some great news. It's about a job opportunity she has for you. I think you'll be pleased."

I squeal, making Margot chuckle. But before Margot responds to my exuberance, a male voice in the background on her end says something to her. "I'm sorry, Georgina, can you hold for a minute? So sorry."

"Sure."

And she's gone, leaving me on hold listening to Katy Perry tell me I'm a firework.

Okay, Georgie, I say to myself. *Don't get too excited. You might have to turn down whatever CeeCee offers you.*

Sadly, it's the truth. I've done my research, and therefore know *Rock 'n' Roll* never hires recent college grads for paid positions. Indeed, there's a mandatory *unpaid* three-month internship for college grads, which the company uses as a proving ground. If it weren't for Dad's medical expenses, I'd take anything offered to me, whether paid or not. Anything to get my foot in the door. Hell, I'd be this assistant's unpaid assistant, if that's what was offered to me. But the reality remains, I can't afford to take an *unpaid* job, for more than a few weeks, given Dad's situation.

Of course, Dad always says it's not my job to take care of him financially. "I'll be able to pick up carpentry work again any day now," he always says. But that seems like a gigantic stretch to me, given the lasting side effects Dad has been experiencing from his treatments.

Dad also likes to say he could sell the condo, if worse came to worst. But on that score, Dad's equally full of shit. I've seen Dad's bank statements. I know he's upside down on this place—meaning any profit he might make from selling it would go straight to the bank.

"I'm back," CeeCee's assistant says. "Sorry about that. So, does ten o'clock tomorrow work for you?"

"Yes. It's perfect. Thank you."

"Please, don't be late," the woman says. "CeeCee's schedule is jam-packed tomorrow, since she's headed to Bali the following day. She's moving things around to squeeze you in, simply because she's so excited to talk to you in person about the job offer."

My heart leaps, even though my brain knows it probably shouldn't. "I'll make sure to get there fifteen minutes early."

The woman gives me the address for tomorrow's meeting, plus some parking instructions, and then signs off by saying, "Don't be nervous, okay? I think you're going to be extremely happy with what CeeCee offers you."

SEVENTEEN
GEORGINA

Oh. My. Freaking. God.

I can't believe my ears.

I'm sitting across from CeeCee in her luxurious office. CeeCee is seated in a white leather chair at an expansive glass desk, looking like a baller in a black pant suit and badass earrings, while I'm sitting across from her in my only pencil skirt, trying not to shriek uncontrollably at what she just said. Holy fucking crap, CeeCee Rafael wants to hire me for a *paid* internship at *Rock 'n' Roll*!

"I know you had your heart set on *Dig a Little Deeper*," CeeCee says, leaning back into her beautiful throne. "But if this internship goes well during the summer, who knows where it could lead."

I babble stupidly for much too long about my euphoria and gratitude. About dreams coming true. I ask if there's someone at the cancer charity I can thank for the grant CeeCee has unexpectedly arranged for me, and, holy fuck, for my father's medication, too, and she tells me, nope, she'll forward my effusive thanks to the powers that be.

Handing me a tissue for my tears, CeeCee says, "I hope you're not upset at Gilda—Professor Schiff—for mentioning your father's illness to me. She only told me so that I could think outside the box in terms of arranging payment for you."

Again, I babble into my tissue, using far too many words to say, in essence, I'm so, so grateful, to CeeCee and Professor Schiff and the amazing cancer charity.

CeeCee clasps her manicured hands and places them on her glass desk. "So, do you want to hear about your assignment for the next three months, my dear?"

I wipe my eyes one last time and put the tissue into my lap. "Oh my gosh. *Yes.*"

CeeCee flashes me an excited smile. "For the next three months, Georgina, you're going to be working *exclusively* on a singular, exciting project." She pauses for effect. "A special issue of *Rock 'n' Roll* devoted solely to the artists and inner workings of one record label... River Records!"

My jaw drops along with my stomach. *No.* This can't be happening. The best news of my life has just turned into the worst. CeeCee is hiring me to work exclusively on an issue devoted to Reed River's label... for the next *three* months? It's a catastrophe!

"Don't worry, you won't be the only one writing for this issue," CeeCee says, apparently misreading the look of panic on my face. "I'm also assigning a couple of seasoned writers, too, who'll contribute content and also mentor you. Plus, I'll write a few pieces for the issue, too. But, make no mistake about it, Georgie, your job is to interview the shit out of as many River Records artists as you can personally manage throughout the summer and turn those interviews into fresh, fun, original content. I want you to think outside the box and really run with it."

Holy fucking hell. My mind is racing with thoughts, all of them centering on Reed fucking Rivers. Does he know CeeCee has assigned me, the woman who double-flipped him off the last time he saw her, to this special issue? If he doesn't already know, will he get me kicked off the project the minute he finds out?

For several minutes, CeeCee details her vision for the issue. And, slowly, despite my panic about Reed, I begin to feel swept away by the excitement of it all. We brainstorm ideas for a bit, our mutual enthusiasm mounting. And, finally, CeeCee says, "And, of course, what would a special issue about River Records be without an in-depth, featured interview of the man at the helm of it all, Reed Rivers?"

And there it is. The two little words I've been dreading since CeeCee first told me about this assignment: *Reed Rivers.* If Reed doesn't know about me being assigned to the project, he's going to find out soon enough. And when he does, will he pick up the phone and tell CeeCee to send someone else—someone who didn't tell him to fuck off and die, and then peel out in an Uber while he stood in front of his house with a raging boner poking the front of his pants?

"Is something wrong, Georgina?" CeeCee asks.

I shake my head. "No. I'm just feeling a little woozy due to excitement. This is a doozy of an opportunity, CeeCee. A doozy with a capital 'oozy.'"

CeeCee giggles. "Yes, it is."

"Um. Out of curiosity," I say, "how much of this idea has been cleared with Mr. Rivers?"

"All of it. Nothing happens at River Records without Reed clearing it. You'll find that out soon enough. He's extremely hands-on."

Hands-on. In a flash, my body remembers what it felt like to have Reed's greedy hands on me as he kissed me. I'm suddenly remembering the scent of his cologne. The delicious roughness of his stubble. The death grip of his palms on my ass that made me delirious with arousal... *He wanted to tie me to his bed posts.* My cheeks hot, I clear my throat. "So, he's already agreed to do the interview... with me?"

"He has."

"But I mean... with *me*, specifically?"

CeeCee tilts her head like Scooby Doo sniffing out a snack.

"I mean, does he know I'm a newbie?" I add quickly. "Does he know I'm straight out of journalism school, with no experience?"

CeeCee nods. "Yes, Reed and I talked about that very thing, and he smartly recognized, as do I, that you'll bring a fresh, exciting energy and voice to the project." She smiles kindly. "Don't be nervous, Georgina. I'm sure, after seeing Reed on that panel, you're a bit intimidated. And I don't blame you. He's incredibly successful and confident. And his communication style is blunt and unapologetic, to say the least. But he's a very good friend of mine, and I can honestly say he's a sweetheart underneath all that swagger. Plus, he trusts my judgment. And I've told him I've got a lot of faith in you."

A shudder of nerves sweeps through me. "I hope I'm able to prove you right."

"You will. It was when you talked about bartending during our coffee date that I knew you'd be a fantastic interviewer. Like I told you then, bartending is just another form of what a journalist does. As a bartender, you've honed the art of talking to people. Listening to them. Making connections in a short amount of time and getting them to open up. Now, you'll be taking those skills and simply putting the experience down on paper—which your writing samples, and Gilda's high praise of you, lead me to believe you'll be able to do with ease."

"Thank you so much. I didn't really think of bartending being related to journalism in that way. But I think you're right."

"Of course, I am." She leans forward conspiratorially. "I'm most excited to see how you're going to handle Reed's interview. I have a strong feeling he'll be uncharacteristically chatty with you."

I press my lips together, suddenly feeling sick. Shit. Is this my cue to come clean? To confess to CeeCee that Reed likely won't be uncharacteristically chatty with me, because, surprise, the last time I saw the man, I kissed the hell out of him, rubbed my aching clit against his huge dick like a cat in heat… and then left him standing at his front gate with not only blue balls, but, almost certainly, a firm desire to never lay eyes on me again?

"I feel like I should tell you something," CeeCee says, taking the words right out of my mouth. She leans back into her chair again. "For the past two years, ever since I first conceived of launching *Dig a Little Deeper,* I've been begging Reed to give me a full-length, in-depth interview for that magazine. But he's always said no." She steeples her manicured fingers. "You might not know this, but Reed's father was a notorious white collar criminal who killed himself in prison when Reed was nineteen or twenty. His father's case was extremely high profile. All over the news. And yet, Reed never, ever talks about it. Certainly not publicly, anyway. And not with me, despite the fact that I've known him ten years. And yet, I think that's the one thing the world would be *most* fascinated to hear him talk about."

I swallow hard. "Yeah, I think I read something about that on Reed's Wikipedia page."

Shit. I clamp my mouth shut, instantly regretting I let it slip I've already read up on Reed. But, thankfully, CeeCee doesn't seem to notice my blunder.

Without missing a beat, CeeCee says, "Of course, the friend in me would never push Reed to talk about his father, if he doesn't wish to do so. But the journalist in me wants you to be aware of the existence of this dynamic, just in case it happens to come up. If, by some chance, Reed slowly opens up with you throughout the summer, and you get the chance to expand the scope of your initial interview—to 'dig a little deeper,' shall we say, beyond what we'd normally expect to write about in *Rock 'n' Roll*—then I want you to run with it, without hesitation."

I process CeeCee's words for a moment. "Are you saying if I'm successful in getting a really in-depth interview of Reed, you'll publish it in *Dig a Little Deeper,* instead of *Rock 'n' Roll?*"

CeeCee shrugs. "I'm saying I'm open to the idea. Of course, I've got no interest in tricking Reed. That should go without saying. He's my friend and I love him. What I'm saying, however, is that, if it turns out Reed is responding well to you, and you see an opportunity to go more in-depth with him than originally thought—with his consent, of course—then I want you to seize that chance."

I bite my lip, my mind whirring and clacking. "If I do get something amazing out of Reed, something that knocks your socks off, and you wind up publishing it in *Dig a Little Deeper*... would you hire me for that magazine?"

CeeCee shrugs nonchalantly, but I can tell by the twinkle in her eye, I've asked the exact right question. "I can't answer that without reading the piece first." She weaves her fingers together. "But, yes, of course, I'm open to the *possibility* of hiring you at *Dig a Little Deeper* after your summer internship, *if* you prove to me you've got the chops for it."

I'm lightheaded. Dizzy. Overwhelmed with ambition and excitement. "I'm going to knock this out of the park, CeeCee. You'll see."

She chuckles. "Darling, I truly believe you will."

We talk about the logistics of my job for a bit. The fact that some guy named Owen, and not Reed, will be my contact at the label—which, admittedly, calms my nerves about the whole thing.

Finally, CeeCee says, "Okay, let's talk turkey about the animals in the zoo for a bit, shall we?"

"The animals... ?"

"The musicians you're going to be interacting with on a daily basis, and partying with, and making friends with, all summer long. Because that's what always happens with musicians. They invite the writers to party with them, and peek into their lives, even if it's just for one crazy day. And, of course, you'll always say yes to any invitation, because the best interviews happen off-the-cuff, in the moment, when you're a part of *their* lives."

I nod.

"The downside of all that, of course, is that, sometimes, they forget you're there to do a job, rather than be their groupie."

"Ah."

"I'm sure this won't come as a shock to you, Georgie, but musicians, especially ones of the male variety, aren't known for being particularly restrained around women, especially exceptionally attractive women, like you."

I blush. "Thank you."

She leans forward in her chair. "Don't take any shit from them, Georgina. You're not a sex object. You're a professional journalist for an esteemed magazine. Party with them. Have a blast. Be their friend. But never forget they need you as much as you need them. That's how this machine works. It's symbiotic. The musicians make the music, yes, but they'd be nothing without their fans. And they need *publicity* to get and keep their fans. They need *mystique* and validation, which my magazine provides to them better than anyone else. You're every bit as powerful as they are, Georgie, I promise you that. You got that?"

"Yes, ma'am." I flex my arm muscle, and she chuckles.

"I've made it clear to Owen you're to be treated with professionalism and respect, by *everyone*. I don't care how big a star any particular guy might be, if someone hits on you and makes you feel uncomfortable, then you're to go straight to Owen or to me, and we'll set the brute straight, without a moment's hesitation. You understand?"

"I do. Perfectly. Thank you so much for looking out for me. But don't worry. I was a bartender, remember? And a waitress before that. I've handled 'animals at the zoo' many times, and still managed to walk away with great tips."

"You see? I told you bartending was a perfect training ground." She picks up a pen and fidgets with it. "Any questions, my love? I've got to run off to a meeting in five."

I bite my lip, weighing the pros and cons of asking the question on the tip of my tongue, and finally decide it's going to be a long summer, if

I don't ask it. "Yeah, just one question." I clear my throat. "What if I'm partying with someone and having a blast and befriending them, like you've told me is smart to do... and what if someone flirts with me, or hits on me... and I actually *like* it? *A lot.* What happens then?" My cheeks bloom with embarrassment. "I mean, I don't want to do anything unprofessional. Or cross any forbidden lines. It's just that... if I find someone insanely attractive, and I'm single, and so are they, am I allowed to make it clear I *like* being hit on by this particular person, or would that be considered unprofessional and a big no-no?"

Thankfully, CeeCee doesn't look the least bit shocked or appalled by my question. Only amused. Indeed, so much so, she's smiling from ear to ear. "Have I mentioned I really like you, Georgina?" She laughs heartily. "Sweetie, go for it. Insanely hot men grow on trees in the music industry, and you can always do whatever the hell you want with them, just as long as it's what *you* want to do, for *you*, and not because you think it's required for the job." She smiles slyly. "To be honest, I can't even count the number of times I've slept with a musician I met on the job. And some of them were huge household names, too." She winks. "This was all long before I met my beloved Francois, of course. But, whew! I've definitely had my fun out in the field. And I don't regret a single minute of it." CeeCee makes a big show of looking right, and then left, as if she's about to tell me a secret in a crowded room. She leans forward, a naughty expression on her face. "In fact, I've conducted some of my most 'probing' interviews while lying buck naked next to my interview subject... in bed."

My jaw hangs open, practically clanking onto CeeCee's glass desk, and she giggles uproariously at my expression.

"Have fun, Georgie," she says, smiling brightly. "As long as you never lose sight of the fact that you're there to get me lots of compelling and fresh content for *Rock 'n' Roll*—and, perhaps, something spectacular for *Dig a Little Deeper*, too, if the stars are aligned. As long as you do that, then whatever else you might do along the way, simply because you're young and gorgeous and you only live once, is your own goddamned business."

EIGHTEEN
REED

As my driver takes us down the long, tree-lined driveway of my mother's facility, I look out the car window and let my mind drift. Not surprisingly, it lands on Georgina. *Again.* The same way it's been doing this entire past week. Once again, I find myself thinking about Georgina's flushed cheeks as she told me off in front of my house. And then her flashing hazel eyes, and raised middle fingers, as she drove away in that Uber.

I can't believe that crazy woman ditched my ass, even though she *knew* it was in her stepsister's best interest for her to stay and kiss it. Not to mention, for her to come inside and suck my dick. And yet, hotheaded, sassy, glorious Georgina Ricci got into the backseat of that car and left me in her dust, her two middle fingers riding sky-high, and her integrity firmly intact. *And I haven't stopped thinking about her since.*

"Mr. Rivers?"

I blink and realize we've arrived at the front of the mental facility—a posh place in Scarsdale, an affluent town about forty-five minutes outside the City, that boasts a "bed and breakfast"-type vibe for its patients. I check my watch while unlatching my seatbelt. "This is going to be a quick visit this time, Tony. So don't drive off to buy a pack of cigs or anything. I want you here when I come out, ready to haul ass to La Guardia."

"I'll be here."

Inside the lobby, I show my identification to the attendant, per protocol, even though everyone knows me. After signing the log, I leaf through the past few weeks of signatures, making sure my mother's best friend since childhood, Roseanne, has visited as frequently as our contract requires. With relief, I discern Roseanne has, indeed, held up her end of our bargain. And also that my saint of a little sister visited yesterday with my little nephew in tow, exactly as she told me she was planning to do as the three of us strolled through the Central Park Zoo earlier this week.

"You don't have to visit my mother," I said to my sister in front of the elephant enclosure. "She's never even acknowledged your existence. Fuck her."

"*Reed*," Violet chastised. "Don't say that about your mother."

"I'm just saying you owe her nothing."

"It's not about me *owing* something to her. It's about me doing something nice for a lonely lady in a mental hospital. I often do what I can to brighten the day of a perfect stranger, so why not your mother? You've mentioned several times she doesn't get a lot of visitors, only you and that 'friend' of hers you have to pay. And you've also mentioned she never stopped loving our prick-ass father, despite their nasty divorce and everything else."

"She was always his doormat. I don't know if you can rightly call that 'love.'"

"Well, either way, I think it might be nice for a lonely lady to get to see a cute little baby who has her ex-husband's DNA inside him. The same DNA as her own beloved son. Maybe seeing my baby will remind her of happier times in her own life."

I felt a mix of emotions right then, during that conversation with my sister in front of the elephants. First off, I felt shame at my secret knowledge that the words "beloved son" probably didn't apply to me, at least if you were to ask my mother. But, mostly, I felt awed by my sister's selflessness. Not that I should have been surprised, really, since compassion is her defining characteristic. But, still, as I stood there with Violet8 and my sweet little nephew, watching an elephant dunk its thick trunk into a trough of water, I had this distinct thought: *How the hell does this girl have Terrence Rivers' DNA inside her, the same as me, and yet, unlike me, she doesn't have a single asshole bone in her body?*

I close the facility's logbook, having finished my inspection of it, and return it to the attendant at the front desk. And then, I make my way down the familiar hallway toward Mom's room—the biggest one at the facility, with the best view of the garden. But when I poke my head inside Mom's room, she isn't there.

I turn to leave, figuring Mom must be at yoga, or perhaps painting in a hidden corner of the garden, when a canvas by the window catches my eye. I walk toward the easel, bracing myself for my inevitable exasperation when I survey it, and audibly groan when I make out the details of the scene depicted. *Fuck*. It's yet another happy family portrait. *And I want to smash it against the fucking wall.*

To an outside observer, this painting, like all the others, would likely seem like nothing but a pleasant idyll. A lovely tribute to family. And if it were a one-off, or a two-off, or even a hundred-off, I'd probably agree. In reality, though, as I know too well, this painting is actually anything but a pleasant idyll. No, it's a physical manifestation of my mother's unwell, hyper-fixated mind. Evidence of what doctors call my mother's "perseveration."

In short, my mother's got an obsessive compulsion that prompts her to pick up a paintbrush, every week of her life, and paint yet another iteration of this exact scene, with only a few small variations and variables, over and over and *over* again.

Indeed, no matter how many times her doctors, therapists, "best friend," or I encourage my mother to, please, *please*, paint something else —*anything else*, for the love of fuck—Eleanor Rivers always paints the same thing. An idyllic depiction of her family at rest or play, enjoying some pleasant sunshine without a care in the world.

This time, Mom's portrait depicts a late-afternoon family picnic in a park surrounded by gorgeous cherry blossoms. As usual, Mom's painted herself as a young mother. This time, Mom's avatar is seated on a red blanket with her two small sons: my older brother, Oliver, who's holding an ice cream cone and looks to be about seven or eight, and me, holding a lollipop, looking to be around five or six.

Mom always paints Oliver the same way—looking like he's around eight years old—even though, in reality, he drowned in our backyard swimming pool at age four, when I was two. Mom also gives Oliver some sort of treat in every painting. An ice cream cone, as with this one. A piece of candy. A shiny new toy. A puppy. A kite. A kitten. A butterfly net. Apparently, one of Mom's greatest pleasures is showering her ill-fated older son, in paintings, with all the little gifts she never got to give him in real life.

Scattered around Mom and her two happy sons are Mom's three younger sisters and mother, all of them clad in merry, pastel dresses, and all of them gaily spinning cartwheels and jumping rope... even though, in real life, tragically, all four of them died in a horrific house fire when Mom was barely sixteen.

Mom had been babysitting a neighbor's three children at the time of the fire, mere blocks away. When word of the blaze got to Mom, she frantically sprinted home, hell-bent on hurtling herself inside the burning structure and saving everyone she loved so much from catastrophe. But, alas, by the time she got to the house, it was already abundantly clear it was too late. Four of the only five people my mother loved in this world were already gone.

As for the fifth person in this world my mother loved, her father, he was a traveling salesman on a trip at the time, marooned that fateful night with a flat tire about two hours away. Or, at least, that's what Charles Charpentier swore to investigators, when no witnesses could confirm his whereabouts, one way or another.

To this day, I think my mother mostly believes her father's version of events, which is why she always includes him in her happy family paintings. Including her father in her paintings is my mother's way of declaring to the world: Charles Charpentier's sole surviving child rejects the wicked rumors about him—the whispers that swirled around Scarsdale immediately after the fire, and then continued swirling endlessly, long after the man killed himself on the one-year anniversary of the tragedy.

According to my grandfather's doubters, Charles Charpentier was a compulsive gambler who'd arranged to burn down what he'd *thought* would be his empty house that fateful night, in order to collect insurance money and pay off his mountain of debts. To my mother, on the other hand, her father was a tragic figure who lost *almost* everything that horrible night, all at once... and, tragically for her, the only thing that remained, the man's eldest daughter, simply wasn't enough to keep him from putting that gun to his head and pulling the trigger.

Interestingly, Mom always places her father off to the side in every painting—as if he's watching his family's revelry from a distance, but not participating in it. I think Mom keeps her father at arm's length in this way, each and every time, because, in the deepest recesses of her unwell mind, she's not sure what to think about him. Consciously, she's decided to believe in his innocence. But, subconsciously, I'm guessing she's got her doubts. Perhaps she includes her father's figure in her paintings, in the first place, as a declaration of love and support for him... but she then feels compelled to set him apart, away from her beloved mother and sisters, as a show of loyalty to them... just in case, on the off-chance, the incessant whispers and gossip about her father were actually true.

"She's in the yoga room," a voice says. And when I turn around, it's one of the nurses. Tina. A middle-aged woman in blue scrubs who's worked here forever.

"Thanks," I say. "I'll look for her there."

Tina comes to a stop next to me, her eyes trained on Mom's canvas. "No grandma this time? Poor Grandma hardly ever makes the cut."

"Mom's grandmother should be grateful to make it into any of Mom's paintings. By all accounts, Grandma was a raving bitch."

Tina chuckles.

"My guess?" I say. "Grandma won't make it into a painting until Christmas."

"Christmas?" Tina says. "Dang it, I hope not. We've got a pool about when Grandma's going to make her next appearance, and I put my ten bucks on Thanksgiving. If Grandma shows up to eat turkey, I'll win a hundred bucks."

"Sorry, I wouldn't count on it, Tina. Apparently, Grandma hated my mother's cooking and told her so, repeatedly. So, I'm thinking the last thing Mom would want to do is give Grandma a seat at the Thanksgiving table, only to let her bitch about Mom's turkey being too dry."

"Shoot."

"But, hey, I guess it's *possible* Mom could paint Grandma at the Thanksgiving table, to let her rave about how *perfect* everything is.

Mom's been known to paint revisionist history a time or two. Or *forty-two billion*."

Tina points. "Who's the baby? I don't think I've seen him or her in one of your Mom's paintings before."

"I believe that's my nephew."

Tina grimaces, apparently assuming the baby must be deceased, if he's making an appearance in an Eleanor Rivers original.

"He's alive and well," I clarify quickly. "My sister brought him to visit yesterday for the first time."

"Oh, I was off yesterday." She peers at the tiny blonde figure as he plays with a red ball in the hinterlands of the grassy park. "Wow, one meeting with him and your mother's already put him into one of her paintings? He must have made quite an impression. It took me working here eight years before your mother finally made me an ice cream vendor in one of her paintings."

I shrug. "She's always loved babies. It's when they get to age seven or eight that she has no fucking clue what to do with them."

Tina flashes me a look of sympathy, before returning to the canvas. "Why do you think your nephew is way off in a corner like that, so far away from everyone else? I would have thought she'd at least let one of her sisters throw that ball to him."

"Your guess is as good as mine," I say. But I'm a liar. I know exactly why my mother has banished my nephew to a far corner: it's a sign of his paper-thin connection to "her" family. But why would I admit that to Tina? Especially when, like Tina said, the fact that Mom's included him at all, after only one visit, is a sign of progress, however small.

"She adores you, you know," Tina says. "She talks about you all the time."

I smile politely and shove my hand into the pocket of my jeans. But I know the truth. If my mother talks about me at all, it's only to brag about my money. The truth is, my mother isn't capable of loving me in the way other mothers love their children. But that's okay. She doesn't need to be capable of it. I've long since stopped hoping for, or expecting, motherly love from her. All that matters to me now is that she is, in fact, my mother, and that *I* love *her*. All that matters is she's on the short list of people I'd do anything for, protect until my dying breath, and love unconditionally, forevermore, whether she's capable of returning my devotion, or, shit, even simply *liking* me... or not.

NINETEEN
REED

In the yoga room, I discover Mom at the front of the class with her boyfriend, Lee—a paranoid schizophrenic who's so heavily medicated, I've never heard him say more than four words during any given visit. At the moment, the class, including Mom and Lee, are attempting to do the Warrior Two pose, although what they're managing, to be generous, isn't exactly the stuff of yoga instructional videos.

"Reed is here," the instructor says to Mom, making her turn around. And when Mom sees me standing in the doorway, she claps, rises from her pose, and makes her way over to me.

When Mom arrives, I squeeze her frail body into a tight hug and tell her I love her. She doesn't return the words, but that's not a surprise. She once told me those words aren't in her vocabulary, because whenever she says them, someone dies. So, really, I suppose I should consider my mother's refusal to tell her only living son she loves him a gift. She's merely trying to save her son from dying, after all. And there's nothing wrong with that.

"I can't stay long today, Mom," I say. "I have to catch a flight back to LA for a concert. For work."

For Georgina.

Again, the force of nature that is Georgina Ricci flashes across my mind. I imagine her showing up backstage tonight at the RCR concert, excited to begin her first day on the job with a press pass around her neck... and then being greeted at the backstage door by... *me*. Oh, God, I can't wait for that delicious moment when our eyes meet again. When she realizes she's got to play nice with me, whether she likes it or not. In truth, I've been obsessing about it all week long.

"LA," Mom says with disdain. "I never should have let Terrence convince me to leave my family here in Scarsdale to move to LA. That was the beginning of the end for me."

I take a deep breath and bite my tongue. Mom says something like this every time I visit, and it's a whole lot of crazy. First, let's be real here: the fire was the beginning of the end for her. Doesn't she realize her family perished long before she even met Terrence Rivers? Which means my father didn't "convince" her to leave her family, or anyone else, to move to Los Angeles. Actually, as far as I understand it, my thirty-five-year-old father convinced his deeply troubled, but stunningly beautiful, pregnant nineteen-year-old bride to leave Scarsdale, in the hopes she'd be able to leave her traumas far behind, and embrace the new life growing inside her. To begin a new chapter, in a new place, with a new husband.

Or, shit, maybe Mom is simply acknowledging she would have preferred to stay in Scarsdale forever, with the ghosts of her dead family, than move to California and become the mother and wife, and then, unhinged ex-wife, she ultimately became.

Either way, the comment annoys me whenever Mom makes it, because it's my mother's dead family that presently ties her to this facility in Scarsdale. And that's a huge fucking inconvenience for me. I've begged Mom, more times than I can count, to let me move her to an even better facility in Malibu—a place right on the cliffs overlooking the glittering Pacific Ocean. But, no. She won't do it. No matter what I say or do, or how many brochures of the Malibu facility I show her, Mom says she won't leave her "family," ever again. Plus, she steadfastly refuses to leave Lee, her "boyfriend," so, it's a double non-starter. Of course, I've offered to move Lee to Malibu, along with her, on my fucking dime, by the way—which wouldn't be cheap—but she always says Lee won't leave his brother, who apparently lives in the City. A fact she's apparently been able to extract from a man so medicated, he constantly drools down his chin and says not more than six words a day.

"You have to stay for lunch," Mom says brightly to me. "They're serving chicken pot pies. Your favorite."

They're not my favorite. In fact, I rarely eat carbs. "Maybe next time," I say. "I've got to keep this visit short, like I said."

Mom frowns. "Your last visit was short, too."

"No. Last time, I spent the entire day with you. We watched *Jeopardy* and played Scrabble. Remember?"

She shakes her head. "No. Last time, you had to leave because of some awards show."

Oh my fucking God. The Grammys thing was *months* ago. During my most recent visit, Mom had a terrible meltdown, so I stayed the entire day with her, holding her hand. Listening to her talk. Trying, and failing, to make her smile. And then, finally, when she calmed down, we watched *Jeopardy* and played fucking Scrabble. And, by the way, I did all of this, even though I had so much on my plate at work, I hadn't slept more than three hours a night in a week.

And while I'm cataloging recent visits in my mind, the visit before the most recent one was a long one, too. During which, as I recall, I joined Mom's yoga class, let her win in checkers, *and* listened to her read mind-numbing poetry by Sylvia Plath. But, of course, Mom doesn't remember my last two extra-long visits. All she remembers is the time, months ago, I had to make it quick because Grammy nominations had just been announced, and my artists had collectively received more nominations than ever before—and I had to blow out of here to manage the happy chaos of my life.

"Come," Mom says, putting out her hand. "I want to show you my painting."

I take her hand and let her lead me to her room, and then "ooh" and "aah" as she shows me the picnic I've already seen.

Simply to make conversation, I ask, "Once you finish filling in the grass and trees, will it be complete? Or is there something else you're planning to add, after that?"

Shit. Tears instantly well in Mom's eyes. "I can't finish the grass and trees because I'm out of the right color green!" she blurts. "And the only place they sell it is Sennelier!"

And that's it. She melts down. Which is so fucking crazy, I can't stand it. Sennelier isn't Mars, for fuck's sake. It's a renowned art store in

Paris, with an easy-to-navigate online store—the place I order all Mom's uber-expensive art supplies. And yet, she's just said the name of the place like it's located in another dimension.

I grab a tissue off Mom's nightstand and hand it to her. "I'll order whatever you need online, Mom. There's no need to cry."

"How? You can't help me because you're going back to *California*."

I can't help chuckling at the way she just said "California," as if she'd said the word "Satan" in its place. "Mom. Take a chill pill, would you? I'll pay whatever it takes to get it here overnight. Come here. Watch this." I pull her sobbing frame to the bed and sit her down, the same way I've done countless times. Calmly, I get onto my phone and head to the French art store's website—a site I've already bookmarked for easy access—and then place an outrageously expensive order for rush delivery of every single shade of green in their store. "See? *Aucun problème, madame.* Whatever your heart desires, I'll always get it for you. No need for tears." I put my arm around her frail shoulders and hug her to me and she cries a river of tears—a torrent that obviously has nothing to do with her needing a few more tubes of green paint. As Mom's tears continue flowing, I covertly check my watch. *Fuck.* "I've got to go, Mom," I say, my stomach twisting. "I really can't miss my flight."

"Because you have to go to *California.*"

"Because I need to work."

"But you haven't had lunch yet."

"Next time. I'll eat on the plane."

She sits up and levels me with her dark, piercing eyes. "You're staying for lunch, Reed Charlemagne," she declares. "I won't take no for an answer."

I take a deep breath and bite my tongue. God, how I hate that fucking expression. She's said it my whole fucking life, as long as I can remember, and whenever I hear it, no matter the situation, the only thing I want to do is scream "No, no, no, motherfucker!" like a toddler with a very dirty mouth. But, because I'm an adult, and I really shouldn't call my mother a motherfucker, I take another deep breath, squash my instinct to rebel, and say, "I'll stay for a quick lunch. But no dessert. I've got to watch my girlish figure."

Sniffling, Mom wipes her eyes. "You don't have a girlish figure. You're a strong, muscular man. Just like your father."

"It was a joke, Mom. It's called *sarcasm*." I rise from the bed. "Stay put. I need to make a quick call to arrange a later flight, and then we'll head to the dining room."

"But you're coming back?"

"Yes, I'll be right back. I promise."

Pulling out my phone, I dip into the hallway.

"Howdy, boss," Owen says, answering my call.

"Change of plans, O. I need a new flight to LA, about an hour and a half later than the original one. Book me private, if necessary. I don't care how much it costs, just as long as I make it to the RCR concert before it starts."

"What's up?"

"My visit with my mother is taking a little longer than planned. We're going to enjoy chicken pot pies together."

"How lovely. My favorite."

"Believe me, I wish you could be here to take my place. So, listen. Since I won't make it to the arena as early as planned, you're going to have to be the one to greet the new *Rock 'n' Roll* reporter when she arrives."

"No problem. I met with her yesterday and showed her around the office. Her name is Georgina. She's great."

Georgina. In a flash, I'm flooded with images of her again. Those earth-quaking kisses. Her mouthwatering tits peeking up from her tank top. Her ass in those tight jeans when she bent over. And, of course, those blazing hazel eyes as she raised her middle fingers into the sky.

I clear my throat. "Personally escort her around backstage, okay? And do *not*, under any circumstances, leave her alone with Caleb. You got me? That's your top job. If you fuck that up, I swear to God, you're fired."

I can hear Owen smiling on his end of the line. As he well knows, there's virtually nothing he could do, or not do, to get canned by me. Which is why I feel comfortable threatening him with it all the time, but only to emphasize when a particular task is especially important.

"I got it, boss," he says. "Georgie gets no alone-time with Caleb."

"I can't emphasize this enough, O. Georgina is *exactly* Caleb's type and he just broke up with some airheaded supermodel, so he's gonna be especially on the prowl. A thousand bucks says he's gonna pounce on

Georgina the second he gets a clear shot. So, for the love of God, make damned sure he doesn't get a clear shot."

"So, you've seen Georgina, then?"

Shit. I remain mute, feeling like I've been caught red-handed.

"So... hmm," Owen says. "I'm sensing Georgina might not only be *Caleb's* exact type. Could it be she's also someone *else's* exact type, too...?"

I grimace sharply to myself at my implicit admission, but, nonetheless, forge ahead in a businesslike tone. "I'll be heading straight to the concert from the airport," I say evenly, "so be sure to tell the LA car service about the change in my itinerary."

"Will do, boss. No problem. Enjoy the chicken pot pie with your momma. I'll text you the new flight info. And don't worry, I'll make sure Georgina meets the entire band, all at once."

"Good. Don't fuck it up, O. Your job depends on it."

"Yes, sir."

After hanging up with Owen, I text the change of plans to my driver, Tony, out front, and then return to my mother's room. When I get there, I find my mother staring blankly out her window at the garden.

"Mom?"

She doesn't flinch.

I place my palm gently on her shoulder. "Ready to eat, Mom?"

She turns her head. "Who'd you call?"

"Owen."

"The gay man who works for you?"

"The gay, smart, loyal, reliable, funny, organized, creative man who works for me."

"I like that you have a gay male secretary."

"Owen's not my secretary. He defies traditional description."

"So do I."

I laugh. I meant that Owen's *job* defies traditional description, thanks to everything he does for me and the label. But Mom's retort was too funny—and accurate—to correct. "That's true, Mom. You most definitely defy traditional maternal description."

"Have I met Owen?"

"No. But guess what? His last name is French. *Boucher.*"

She gasps. "Butcher! He's from France?"

"Not Owen himself. But somewhere along the line, someone in Owen's family tree was French. He told me about it once, but I forget the details."

"Yet another reason for me to meet this man. My instinct tells me Owen Boucher and I would be kindred spirits. He's got a French butcher somewhere in his family tree and I've got a French carpenter in mine. We're soulmates."

"Owen's name is 'yet *another* reason' you're soulmates?" I say. "What's the first reason?"

"He's gay," she says matter-of-factly. "And I'm an artist. Artists and gay people always get along. We share a common understanding of what it means to be an *outsider* in this dark and lonely world."

I smooth a lock of her gray hair. "Maybe I should bring Owen the Butcher here to have chicken pot pies with Eleanor the Carpenter some time, eh? You two can sit in the garden and talk about art and sexuality and Sylvia Plath and being *outsiders* until your heart's content."

"And our French lineage."

"That, too."

"I'd like that." She frowns sharply. "Seeing as how my son hardly ever visits me because he's too busy going to rock concerts and awards shows in *California*."

I close my eyes and pray for strength from a God I don't believe in. "I visit as much as I can. If you'd let me move you to—"

"I'm not moving to Malibu, Reed. My home is here."

My gaze drifts to Mom's painting again. To my nephew on the outskirts of the grassy park—the first new "family" member she's ever painted. And it's enough to keep me from going completely mad. Barely, yes, but it is. "If I bring Owen to visit, will you promise to include him in your painting that week?"

Mom shrugs, as noncommittal as ever. And I know in my heart, even if I were to fly Owen to Scarsdale to have chicken pot pies with her, even if they were to have the best conversation in the world about art, sexuality, 'outsider-ism,' Sylvia Plath, and France—a torture I'd never subject Owen to, by the way, unless I were paying him a hefty bonus—she wouldn't paint him in that week's opus. Because he's not family, and she'd need *years* to shift gears enough to let an outsider, even an exceedingly pleasant gay one, intrude in her reality.

I also know something else as I stand here with Mom. A thought I quickly stuff down and push away the moment my brain conjures it: no matter how many "Owens" I might arrange for my mother to talk to, or what fancy French paints I might buy for her on rush delivery, none of it will ever be enough to make her love me. At least, not like most mothers love their children. Not the way she loved a certain four-year-old who never grew up to become imperfect in her eyes, who never grew up to remind her of his father, Terrence—a dashing, charismatic, broad-shouldered man who, many moons ago, promised to take care of and love a gorgeous, tempestuous teenager named Eleanor... but, instead, only wound up shattering her already broken heart.

TWENTY
REED

I slide into the backseat of the car picking me up from LAX and confirm with the driver he's taking me to RCR's concert at the Rose Bowl. Logistics sorted, I pull out my phone to answer the million and one unread emails and texts requiring my attention. But I can't concentrate on them for shit. Because... *Georgina.* Yet again, that woman has hijacked my thoughts. Only this time, now that my body senses it's once again in the same city as hers, that I'm mere minutes away from actually being in Georgina's glorious presence again, I literally can't think of anything but her.

If only I hadn't been a pussy and agreed to stay for lunch with my mother, I would have arrived at the stadium in plenty of time to personally greet Georgina when she arrived, her shiny new press pass around her neck. Damn. I really wanted to see the look of excitement and anticipation on her face in that moment, and then watch with amusement as her features instantly morphed into anxiety when she saw me and realized that, maybe, those double-birds she flipped me a week ago weren't such a good idea, after all. Oh, God, that moment was going to be such a turn-on for me. But thanks to those chicken pot pies, and my eternal soft spot for my mother, I missed it.

Plus, I've missed out on some other good stuff, too. For instance, being the one to show Georgina around backstage and introduce her to everyone. I very much wished to do that, not only to be helpful to Georgina, but to communicate to every fucker within a mile radius, especially a certain drummer for RCR, that Georgina is *mine*. Not to be touched. Not to be flirted with. Off-fucking-limits. *Mine, mine, mine.*

Plus, of course, I very much wanted to be able to pull Georgina aside, after initially letting her twist in the wind for a bit, to clear the air about the other night. After some reflection this past week, I've come to realize I *might* have overreacted a bit when I found out about her stepsister's musical aspirations. But I also think Georgina fucked up, too. Royally. And I'm interested to see if, after a week of her own reflecting, Georgina is ready to own up to her part in the way things blew up between us. Is she going to hold tight to her prior indignation with white knuckles, or admit she flew off the handle like a fucking lunatic and apologize to me, as she should? Frankly, I'm dying to know.

I'm going to fuck her, either way, of course, whether she doubles down on her "fuck you's" or has the good sense to start kissing my ass, now that she realizes it's in her best interests. But I'd be lying if I didn't admit I'm hoping to witness another round of fiery sass from feisty Georgina, just for the pure entertainment of it. Oh, and also because watching her fly off the handle makes me so fucking hard, it physically hurts.

"There's a VIP entrance at the back," I say to my driver as we approach the Rose Bowl's parking lot. And, five minutes later, he's pulling up to the restricted-access loading zone in the back. Sure enough, I spot Owen standing curbside, awaiting me as instructed. At the moment, he's staring at his phone while smoking a cigarette. Being punctual and reliable and humble and patient. You know, being Owen. "Right here," I say to the driver, while simultaneously shooting off a text to Owen: *Look up. I'm here.*

When Owen looks up, it's just in time to see me barreling out of the parked car and marching with urgency toward a large metal door.

"Tip the driver and get my luggage delivered to my house, would you?"

"Aye, aye, Captain."

"Where's Georgina?"

"Greenroom B. I left her in the care of a PA, talking to the entire band."

"All four of them?"

He nods. "Plus, Leonard and his daughter and a gaggle of her friends."

I breathe a sigh of relief. Caleb couldn't possibly make too much progress with Georgina in a crowd like that. "Perfect."

Leaving Owen behind to figure out my luggage and the driver's tip, I breeze past a security guard posted at the VIP door—who, lucky for him, lets me pass without stopping me for my ID—and then, once I'm inside the stadium, begin marching like a madman through familiar hallways toward a back elevator.

Georgina.

Goddammit. Now that I'm this close to her, I'm feeling consumed by a physical craving to kiss her again. Once I finally fuck her, I'm positive this mini-obsession that's been building inside me all week will quickly fade. But until then, it's here, baby. In full force. Like a raging boner that won't go away until it at least gets a hand job.

Nearing the greenroom, I hear female laughter, and my heart seizes.

Georgina.

I stop outside the doorway to catch my breath. Rake my fingers through my hair. Drag my palm over my stubble. And, finally, enter the room like I own the place. But, shit, I don't see Georgina anywhere. Fuck!

"Reed!" my attorney, Leonard, calls to me. And I'm instantly trapped. Fuck, fuck, fuck!

Still glancing around for Georgina, I greet Leonard, and then his euphoric teenage daughter, and her equally excited friends. I say quick hellos to the guys of Red Card Riot, and clench my jaw when I realize only three of the four are here: Dean, Emmitt, and Clay. *Caleb is nowhere to be found.*

On any other day, I'd be thrilled to find Caleb Baumgarten—the drummer the world knows as "C-Bomb"—absent from a room I'm standing in, thanks to a longstanding beef between us. But this one time, Caleb being MIA, when Georgina is also nowhere to be found, is evoking near-panic inside me.

"Where's Caleb?" I bark at Dean, the lead singer and guitarist.

"Whoa, chill, man," Dean says, laughing. "We've got plenty of time before showtime."

"Where is he?"

"He left a while ago with some newbie reporter for *Rock 'n' Roll.*" Dean flashes me a knowing look. "It's her first day on the job, so Caleb gallantly offered to take her for a little pre-show 'tour' of the backstage area."

Motherfucker. I knew Caleb would be all over Georgina like white on rice, sooner rather than later. But *this* fast? It's a fucking record, even for him.

I say my quick goodbyes to everyone, bark at a shocked production assistant to take extra-good care of Leonard and his daughter's party, and then I'm gone, out the door and racing down the cement hallway.

I poke my head through a series of doors, all while brushing off repeated requests for my attention. "Not now," I bark at whoever. "Ask Owen about that."

Finally, I hear it. The sound of Georgina's laughter. It's muffled. Coming from a distant dressing room. But it's most definitely her.

I pick up my pace. Burst through a door. And there they are. Georgina and Caleb. Sitting mere inches from each other, face to face. Georgina's on a couch, looking star-struck and flushed. Caleb looks like a bearded shark at feeding time, his jacked, tattooed body draped over an armchair, his green eyes on fire.

When I enter, the pair jolts in surprise. Georgina, God bless her, lurches back at my intrusion, her body conceding it's mine, even if her brain doesn't know it yet.

Caleb, on the other hand, smiles like a sniper and leans *toward* Georgina when he sees me, his ripped body staking its claim.

My gaze moves from Caleb's bearded smile to Georgina's panicked eyes. And when our gazes mingle, when Georgina's hazel eyes meet mine, I feel the same explosion of chemistry, fire, and attraction I felt between us in that lecture hall—and then again, even more so, at the bar. And, yet again, when we walked outside Bernie's Place, and I pinned her against the building and pushed my raging boner against her and kissed the living hell out of her, overwhelmed by the nuclear bomb exploding inside me—the powerful yearning I felt to claim, conquer, own, *desecrate.*

Georgina's chest heaves at the sight of me. And, instantly, I know the same forest fire raging inside me at the sight of her is burning out of control inside her, as well.

"Time to go," I bark at Caleb.

But Caleb only scoffs. "There's plenty of time before we hit. The opening band hasn't even—"

"You're missing an important VIP meet and greet."

Caleb waves his tattooed knuckles. "This is way more important than that. Georgie isn't a groupie, man. She's a writer for *Rock 'n' Roll*, assigned to do an interview of the band, and of me in particular. She's joining the tour this whole week, starting tonight, so we can hang out and she can do a really cool in-depth interview of me."

No.

Fuck no.

There's so much "fuck no" about everything Caleb just said, I can barely keep myself from hurtling my body across the room like a missile, wrapping my hands around his tattooed neck, and squeezing the life out of him. Did Owen approve everything Caleb just said? If so, he's fucking fired. For real, this time.

"Hi, Mr. Rivers," Georgina says, rising from the couch, her hand extended. "I'm Georgina Ricci from *Rock 'n' Roll*." She proudly holds up the press pass around her neck. "CeeCee told you about me, I hope? I'll be working exclusively on the River Records special issue. I'm really, really excited about it, Mr. Rivers."

Her eyes are pleading with me. Begging me not to throw her out, along with Caleb. And it suddenly occurs to me she has no idea how I fit into this new job opportunity of hers. Did I have a hand in her getting this assignment—or was it given to her against my will? Obviously, Georgina's wondering where we stand after the other night. Am I going to help her during this summer internship... or fucking torture her?

"I'm excited you're here, Georgina," I say warmly, attempting to put her at ease. I shake her hand and my flesh tingles at her touch. "CeeCee has said some great things about you. I'm excited about the special issue, and glad you're working on it."

Her shoulders soften, her expression conveying, *Well, that went a whole lot better than I feared it would.*

I peel my eyes off Georgina to glare at C-Bomb. "Time to go, Caleb.

Those VIPs were promised a photo op with the *full* band. Everyone's waiting on you."

He languidly pulls out a box of cigarettes. "They'll survive. I'm gonna chill here with Georgie until showtime. We need to chat a bit about ideas for my interview." He winks at Georgina. "It's gonna be sick."

I take a deep breath. "You're contractually obligated to show up for 'designated VIP meet and greets,' Caleb. And I'm hereby designating this one as a contractual obligation."

Caleb lights his cigarette and takes a long drag off it, his green eyes shooting daggers at me. But when it's clear I'm not going to budge, and that this could get a tad bit embarrassing for him in front of Georgina—because, come on, we both know I own his fucking ass at the end of the day—Caleb slowly rises from his chair and stretches his hulking frame. "Duty calls." He smiles wistfully at Georgina. "See you later."

"Have a great show," Georgina says. "Don't worry. We'll have plenty of time to talk this week."

"I'm throwing a party in my hotel suite after the show. Why don't you come and see how the band blows off steam after a show? Spoiler alert: there's alcohol involved."

She chuckles. "I'd love to. Thank you. Spoiler alert: I like alcohol. I bartended in college."

"Hey, yet another thing we have in common! You know how to make drinks, and I know how to drink 'em."

"*Hey.*"

He beams a huge smile at Georgina that makes me want to lurch over to him, take his stupid Mohawk in my fist, and slam his smug face, repeatedly, into the floor until it's a bloody pulp. But, somehow, I force myself to stand still, not moving a muscle. Not even breathing.

Caleb says, "I'll tell my PA to get your phone number during the show, so I can text you the info for the party. Are you staying at the Ritz, with all of us?"

Georgina blushes. "Oh, gosh, no. I'm booked at budget hotels this week. But never more than five miles from where you guys are staying, so it'll be easy for us to connect."

"Fuck that, dude. I'll book you a room at the Ritz tonight, on me, so you can party with us and only have to stumble a short way to your bed afterwards."

A puff of disdain escapes me involuntarily, and Caleb smiles, letting me know he's heard it, and is thoroughly enjoying having this exchange with Georgina in front of me.

"Wow... that's certainly not necessary... " Georgina says about the offered hotel room.

"I insist," Caleb says, ever the gallant fucking gentleman.

"Wow. Thank you. Okay."

"Caleb," I say sharply, a hair's breadth away from committing an extremely bloody form of murder. *"It's time for you to go."*

Caleb smirks, winks at Georgina, takes another long drag off his cigarette and finally saunters out the door, but not before turning at the doorframe and shooting me a quick, nonverbal "fuck you, bitch." Which, of course, I return in kind. Fucking punk-ass little bitch prick.

When Caleb is gone, I march to the door and close it behind him, breathing deeply to banish my homicidal thoughts. Finally, I turn to face Georgina—the woman who's relentlessly invaded my thoughts and dreams and masturbation fantasies this entire week. Damn, she looks even hotter than last week. As ripe as a peach.

Georgina fidgets under my intense, silent gaze, looking like she doesn't know if I want her to stay or go. If I want to kiss her or spank her or tell her to get the fuck out or to hop onto my cock. And so, I decide it's time to make things crystal clear to her. Right fucking now.

"Sit down, Georgie," I say sternly, my jaw clenched. "We need to have ourselves a little chat."

TWENTY-ONE
REED

As I cross the room toward Georgina, muted music from a distant part of the stadium begins wafting through the walls of the small room—the sound of the opening band, kicking off their short set.

I unbutton my suit jacket and take the armchair across from Georgina. The one formerly occupied by Caleb. I place my ankle on my knee. And exhale. "Congratulations," I say calmly.

"On what?" Her gorgeous features are etched with anxiety. Obviously, she's wondering where things stand between us, given her fiery, early-morning exit from the front of my house a week ago.

"On the new job," I say. "And your graduation. I presume you graduated last week, as planned?"

She nods. "I'm officially a UCLA alum. Go, Bruins. I'm actually the first college grad in my family. My dad couldn't stop crying." She presses her lips together, like she's forcibly keeping herself from rambling further.

I can't help but smile at her adorableness. "That's awesome," I say. "I'm sure your parents are insanely proud of you."

Something flickers across her pretty face that makes me question my words. Have I just unwittingly highlighted the age gap between us—come off like a friend of her father's? Or could it be her parents *aren't* proud of her, for some reason? I can't imagine that's the case, but I suppose it's possible they wanted her to study something other than journalism?

When I don't speak for a long moment, but instead opt to stare her down and revel in her obvious anxiety, Georgina puts her hands into her lap, like she doesn't know what to do with them. She bites her lower lip. Fidgets. And then, "How was New York?"

"Busy, productive, fun, exhausting, and highly lucrative."

"Oh. That sounds good."

"It was. Very good."

I fall silent again, enjoying the way my silence turns her breathing shallow. The way it brings a flush to her cheeks and cleavage. Yeah, I'm being a bastard. Making her sweat, simply to amuse myself. Well, and also to punish her a tiny bit for the way she double-flipped me off. For fuck's sake, Georgina was the one with a music demo in her pocket. Not me. She was the one with a hidden agenda. And yet, she had the audacity to flip *me* off and screech away in an Uber, leaving me standing there, after I'd stooped to *begging* her to come inside? When was the last time I begged anyone for anything? And yet, Georgina made me do it, just that fucking fast. Well, never again. That's for fucking sure.

"So you wanted to have a little chat... ?" she prompts, her voice tight.

I pick at a piece of lint on my suit jacket. "Yes." I pause again, for dramatic effect. "This plan for you to join RCR on tour this coming week?"

She nods.

"It's the first I'm hearing about it, and I don't approve. You'll have to find something else to do this week. Tagging along on RCR's tour is off."

"*What?*" she blurts. For a moment, she gapes like a fish on a line, before shouting, "You can't do that, Reed!"

"I just did."

"CeeCee cleared the whole thing with Owen! Owen helped arrange it!"

"And Owen works for *me*. Well, he used to. If he arranged that shit show of an idea, then he's fired."

She turns pale.

"I'm joking. Owen is bulletproof. Ask anyone."

"Reed, you can't call everything off. CeeCee is excited about the idea, and so am I. And so is the band. Just now, when I was talking to all four of them about it in the greenroom, they said—"

"I don't give a flying fuck what the band said. The plan wasn't cleared through me. And I don't like it. I think it's an unoriginal, tired idea that's already been done a thousand times. Ever seen *Almost Famous*?"

She's flabbergasted. "Well, granted, we might not be inventing the wheel here, but who cares? Readers will eat it up. What fan wouldn't want to tag along with RCR on tour, through me? It's every music lover's fantasy. A once-in-a-lifetime chance to peek behind the—"

"Stop trying to sell me. It's dead. Move on."

She consciously shuts her gaping mouth. "But... Reed, I've got hotel rooms booked for the entire week!"

Oh, Georgina. I resist the urge to chuckle at her indignation. Her naiveté. As if the tragedy of a few unused hotel rooms would stop the world spinning on its axis. If I'd forgotten Georgina is only twenty-one, I was just now reminded of it. "Hotel room reservations are almost always refundable," I say calmly to my little kitten, trying not to smile at her lack of real-world experience. "And if not, then I'll reimburse *Rock 'n' Roll* for any expense, seeing as how the rooms were booked after coordination with Owen. Who, to be clear, will be out of a job after this, I promise you that."

Again, she looks pained.

"Kidding again. Get used to it. It's a running joke."

Georgina rubs her face, distraught. And, for a moment, I feel kind of sorry for the poor little thing. She looks like a possum caught in an iron trap. Like a little lamb being carted off to slaughter. But, to my surprise, after a few deep breaths, she visibly gathers her strength and straps on her warrior's armor. Suddenly, the simpering twenty-one-year-old vanishes, supplanted by the same fierce superhero I witnessed in front of my house the other night.

Georgina's eyes are sharp now. Her nostrils flaring. After one more deep breath, she puffs out her spectacular chest and lets me have it. "I won't let you do this," she says, her eyes ablaze. "CeeCee made it *very* clear to me *she's* my boss, not *you*. She also said you explicitly agreed we're not churning out propaganda for River Records here—we're independent *journalists*. You've expressly agreed CeeCee's got full editorial control, and CeeCee, my *boss*, has decided I'm touring with RCR this entire week."

A faint smile lifts the corners of Georgina's indignant mouth, like she thinks she's dealt me a death blow with her little speech. And, once again, I find myself fighting not to smile. Holy shit, she's fucking adorable. Irresistible. Feisty. Glorious. Oh, how I wish she could sing, even a little bit. Because the girl's got star power in spades, in a way truckloads of wannabe actresses and models and pop stars would kill for. "Everything you've said is exactly right," I reply. "Especially the part about you being *CeeCee's* employee, not mine. In fact, I wouldn't have agreed to this arrangement if it created any kind of employer-employee relationship between you and me." I lean forward, my eyes on fire. "And do you know *why* I didn't want you as my employee, little Georgina?"

Her chest rises sharply. Her nostrils flare again. She shakes her head.

I smile. *"Because I never fuck my own employees."*

Georgina's lips part with surprise at my obvious implication, left unsaid: *but I have no problem fucking one of CeeCee's*.

"Well, news flash," she says, narrowing her eyes. "You're not going to fuck me, either, no matter whose employee I am." She leans forward, cutting the distance between us in half. "And do you know *why* you're not going to fuck me, Mr. Rivers?" She's close enough for me to see the caramel flecks in her hazel eyes. To smell her shampoo and moisturizer and toothpaste. *"Because. I. Don't. Fuck. Assholes."*

I can't help smirking at her bald-faced lie. "Well, so much for you fucking C-Bomb, then. That's a relief."

She clenches her jaw, clearly annoyed, but says nothing.

I cock my head. "So, that's your clever way of telling me, yet again, that *I'm* an asshole?"

"Seems like a logical deduction to make from what I just said."

"Well, that's an interesting interpretation. Between the two of us, I think any reasonable person would say *you* acted like a far bigger asshole the other night than *me*."

Her eyebrows furrow sharply. "Are you high? You were a colossal dick to me, Reed."

"Oh, really? Huh. I didn't tell anyone to fuck off and die. And I'm certainly not the one who had a demo in my pocket the entire time we were flirting. Just a boner, which certainly doesn't qualify as a hidden agenda."

"Ha! You want to talk about hidden agendas?" she booms, her glorious temper rising and reddening her cheeks. "Every word out of your mouth that night was a lie, designed to get you into my panties. You think it's not a hidden agenda to pretend to give a rat's ass about what a woman says, to pretend to care about having a conversation with her, for the sole purpose of 'seducing' her? I know you're a hundred-and-five and all, but we kids these days call men like you 'fuckboys,' Reed. *And it's not a compliment.*"

"Getting you into my bed wasn't my *hidden* agenda, Georgina. It was my expressly stated goal. I explicitly told you, straight-up, I wasn't interested in dating you. Only seducing you. Maybe you 'kids' today aren't familiar with the art of seduction, so let me translate for you. The entire purpose of it is getting to the *fucking* part. So, please, enlighten me. Tell me, what was I hiding from you that night? Name one fucking thing."

She opens and closes her mouth, at a loss for words.

"I thought so," I say, leaning back in victory.

"Okay, Mr. Rivers. Listen up, you arrogant prick. I'm going to explain what happened the other night, *once*, without leaving anything out. And then I'm going to move on and never speak of this again, because I'm already sick to death of the stupid topic." She takes a deep breath, apparently trying to keep her temper under control, and every cell in my body strains with desire for her. "I wasn't using you that night, Reed. I was genuinely, sincerely, outrageously attracted to you, from the first second I saw you. I assure you, I wanted to get 'seduced' by you, every bit as much as you wanted to seduce me. And, for the record, yes, I was fully aware 'seduction' was a euphemism for 'fucking.' Aware of and quite thrilled about it."

I'm breathing deeply. Trying not to let on how intoxicating she is to me—that she's already won me over, and then some.

"To be honest," Georgina continues, crossing her arms. "I bet I wanted to have sex with you, even more than you wanted to have it with me. Because, heck, you can have sex with anyone in the world—just by snapping your fingers, Mr. Big Shit Music Mogul. For you, banging some nobody student-bartender isn't a big deal. Just another Thursday night. But, for me, getting 'seduced' by Reed Rivers, going to his fancy house in his fancy car, was a *very* big deal. And before you call me a gold digger, I'm not. Why would I care about your money, when I was in it for nothing but one night of sex? But who wouldn't feel swept away by you and your glamorous life? You made me feel like I was in a movie. I haven't slept with that many guys in my life. And certainly never anyone as experienced and exciting and dashing as you. I'm not saying I gave a shit about you, personally, okay? Even as we were driving to your house, I wasn't sure I liked you. But one thing I was positive about: I sure as hell wanted you to do filthy things to me—with absolutely no strings attached, I might add—simply for the fun of it."

Every word out of her mouth has been music to my ears. And to my cock. And not a huge surprise, to be honest. Of course, Georgina sincerely wanted to fuck me that night—for all the reasons she just set forth. She's a journalism student, after all, not an aspiring starlet—a whole different breed of woman than the ones I'm used to encountering. Plus, even the best actress in the world couldn't have faked Georgina's reaction when we kissed. The way she bucked and jolted into me, and then kissed me back with a passion that took my breath away—like she was drowning and I was oxygen. Or, fuck, maybe it was the other way around, and she was the oxygen. Either way, Georgina's passion that night reflected back to me everything I was feeling in that moment—like every atom in my body had been doused in lighter fluid, and then set ablaze by the torch that was Georgina Ricci.

Which is probably why... maybe... now that I'm thinking about it... I reacted the way I did when I first found out about the demo. For a split-second there, I irrationally thought maybe Georgina *had* been the world's best actress, and that she'd played me expertly the whole time, even during our nuclear-bomb of a kiss. And I didn't like how that made me feel. But now... now that I've had time to process and reflect, now that I'm seeing the earnestness in her eyes, I know for certain she's telling me the truth. Of course, she is. Which means I really was an asshole that night. But realizing I was an asshole doesn't mean she wasn't one, too. And it certainly doesn't mean I'm inclined to let her off the hook. Not yet, anyway.

"So, you expect me to believe it was pure coincidence you had your stepsister's music demo in your pocket that night?" I ask.

Georgina rolls her eyes. "Will you stop being a stubborn dickhead for a second and just listen to me? Holy hell, you're even more stubborn than me."

I bite back a smile.

"I'd never heard of you before the event. On my walk there, Alessandra told me about you during a phone call. So, because I *love* my stepsister, and always want her dreams to come true, I loaded a flash drive with her best songs the minute I got to the lecture hall, just in case the chance to hand it to you fell into my lap. Wouldn't you have done the same thing for someone you love? God, I hope so... or else you're an even bigger dickhead than I think you are."

This time, a huge smile spreads across my face. When was the last time anyone spoke to me like this? T-Rod, I'm pretty sure. In Maui, several years ago during Josh's wedding week. Anyone since? I truly don't think so.

"The truth is, having that demo in my purse the whole time we were talking at the bar turned out to be an albatross around my neck. Of course, I wanted to come through for Alessandra, but I didn't want that demo to screw up my own chances of getting 'seduced.' Which, yes, I fully realize, is exactly what wound up happening. The bottom line is I wanted to have sex with you, Reed, because you made my ovaries vibrate. Was I *also* hoping you might be willing to take a few minutes of your precious time to listen to my stepsister's songs? Yes. So sue me. But, I swear to God, my desire to help Alessandra wasn't a 'hidden agenda.' It was an agenda that ran *concurrently* with my own."

I smile. How could I not? I'm the guy who's paid money to a cancer charity to get this girl here, after all, because I want to fuck her so badly. But *also* because of some other motivations that run *concurrently* with my desire to fuck her. Things like my genuine desire to help Georgina and her father, and to get CeeCee a promising new employee, and my artists some great publicity. But, yeah... mostly, because I want to fuck Georgina. "Thank you for explaining all that to me," I say. "For what it's worth, while I was making your ovaries vibrate, you were making my balls vibrate."

She can't help smiling at that. "Thank God for small mercies."

"Look, I admit I gave you a bit of a harder time the other night than you rightly deserved. And for that, I sincerely apologize."

She looks shell-shocked. And then deeply pleased. "Thank you. I accept your apology."

There's a beat, during which the opening band hits the last, crashing drumbeat of their short set.

"What about you?" I say.

"What about me... what?"

"What do you apologize for?"

She pulls a face that says, *Not a goddamned thing.*

"You don't think you have anything to apologize for?"

She twists her mouth. And then says, begrudgingly, "I'm sorry I double-flipped you off. It was rude of me. One middle finger would have sufficed. This one. With my new pretty ring on it."

She flips me off, singularly, and I can't help chuckling, despite myself.

She shakes her head and exhales. "Okay, yes, I *maybe* went off the rails a teeny-tiny bit. But, honestly, I'm proud of myself for telling you off and leaving when I did. I chose my integrity over my libido. If choosing my integrity over sex with a smoking hot asshole isn't 'adulting,' then I don't know what is."

"Mmm hmm. Because you never, ever fuck assholes."

"Correct."

"Not even the smoking hot ones."

"Correct again."

Chuckling, I shake my head. "You're such a liar, Georgina Ricci. And a terrible one, at that. I'd bet anything, literally anything, you *only* fuck smoking hot assholes. In fact, I'd bet a million bucks you'd rather fuck an exciting, smoking hot, bad-boy asshole, than some nice, boring, God-fearing *football star* with a Captain America smile any day of the week."

She rolls her eyes, plainly annoyed I've invoked Bryce McKellar to make my point. But then she makes a face that tacitly admits I've pegged her exactly right. Yep. This girl is a fireball who's hopelessly attracted to assholes like me, the ones who throw lighter fluid on her flames, whether she likes it about herself or not.

A genuine affection for her rises up inside me, an attraction to her feisty, flawed, adorableness. And I suddenly can't help smiling at her from ear to ear. To my surprise, she returns the gesture, flashing me the most genuine smile she's graced me with since we chatted at the bar... and, just that fast, something passes between us. Respect. Understanding. Georgina knows I see through her hotheaded, drama-loving bullshit, and I know she sees through my button-pushing, keep-you-at-distance bullshit. We're the same, Georgina and me. Two bullshitters, buried beneath hardened outer layers. Two people who recognize themselves in the other. At least, in this moment, it sure feels like we do.

In a distant part of the stadium, the crowd roars, signaling Red Card Riot has just walked onstage. And a few seconds after that, we hear the band launch into the first song of the night—an instantly recognizable, global smash off their second album called "Ready or Not."

"Well, that's my cue," Georgina says, popping off the couch. "Good chat, Mr. Rivers. When I get back from touring with RCR at the end of the week, I'll call to schedule your interview."

"Sit down, Georgina."

She freezes.

"I said sit the fuck *down*. You're not going on tour, and we're not even close to finished with our little chat."

TWENTY-TWO
REED

Georgina sits back down on the couch, looking like a petulant teenager who's just been grounded from going to a concert with her girlfriends. "Come on, Reed. This tour is my best chance to get an amazing interview out of C-Bomb."

I can't believe my ears. "You still think you're interviewing C-Bomb?" I say, barely containing my disdainful chuckle. "Sweetheart, no. That's off, too. *Obviously*."

"*What?* No!"

"You can interview the full band, if you like, *after* they return from tour in a month. I'll set that up for you. But the mini-tour *and* the one-on-one with C-Bomb are both off."

Georgina balls her hands into fists of frustration and bangs her thighs, morphing from a grounded teenager into a toddler being denied an ice cream cone. "But CeeCee specifically assigned me to interview C-Bomb, as my top priority. She said everyone always interviews the frontmen of bands, like Dean, and never the drummers. She said C-Bomb, with his bad-boy persona and muscles and beard and crazy hair, will make an eye-catching cover boy and sell a shit-ton of magazines. She said you'd *love* the idea!"

I'm floored. None of what she just said makes any sense. CeeCee knows I loathe C-Bomb with the force of a thousand suns. And yet, she told Georgina I'd "love" the idea of him being a featured interview in the issue—and our fucking *cover* boy? Ha! I can't fathom a more ludicrous statement. So, why the fuck did CeeCee say any of it? Why did she send Georgina straight to C-Bomb, on day one, as her "top priority," when she had to know I'd nix the idea from jump street? I blink rapidly, trying to reboot the faltering computer in my brain. "CeeCee said I'd 'love' the idea of you interviewing C-Bomb?" I ask slowly, simply because it's so preposterous, I'm not sure I heard her correctly.

Georgina nods furiously. "And, don't forget, you agreed to give CeeCee full editorial control, so really, it's up to CeeCee whether I interview C-Bomb, not you. And CeeCee says *yes*."

I scoff at the ridiculous notion. "CeeCee has full editorial control regarding the artists I make available to her. But, see, since I own every band and artist on my label, *I* decide who's made available. And I'm not making RCR available to you until they get back from tour—and, even then, not as individuals, only as a full band."

Oh, she's livid now. "But, why?" she booms, her eyes bulging. "Why, why, *why* are you doing this to me?"

"I'm not doing anything to *you*. I'm protecting my brand. The tour idea isn't original or fresh enough. And C-Bomb isn't a good interview subject or representative of his band or my label, as an individual. My job is to sell RCR's upcoming album. And to do that, I want Dean's blue eyes front and center, because *Dean* is the one who sells records and tickets and posters for walls."

"So does C-Bomb! He was *literally* on my wall when I was a teenager, Reed! And he hasn't been interviewed a fraction as much as Dean."

My heart is galloping. Georgina's confession that she had Caleb on her teenage wall is driving me fucking crazy—and most definitely having the exact opposite effect she's intending. But somehow, I manage to keep my voice calm and professional as I say, "I don't want an interview of C-Bomb for sound business reasons. Conversation over."

Georgina grunts in frustration. "Lies, lies, lies! Stop bullshitting me, Reed. You don't want me going on tour with RCR, or talking to C-Bomb, because you think he'll make a move on me!"

"No." I lean forward, my eyes blazing every bit as much as hers. "I don't want you going on tour with RCR, and talking to C-Bomb, because I *know* he'll make a move on you."

Fuck.

Why'd I say that?

At my confession, Georgina leaps up and points at me in the armchair. "I knew it. Ha!" She crosses her arms. "Well, so what if he does? You and I aren't dating. In fact, you've made it clear you've got no intention of *ever* dating me. Which means you get no say on who, besides you, gets to try to *seduce* me. I'm an adult, Reed. And so is Caleb. You might own Caleb's *band*. But you don't own Caleb, the *man*. And you sure as hell don't own *me*."

My body feels like it's short-circuiting. I'm feeling so jealous, so possessive, so turned on by the fire in her eyes, I can't think straight. Did Georgina have sexual fantasies about Caleb as a teenager? Did she practice kissing her pillow, while pretending it was Caleb? "Caleb can't have you," I say evenly, my heart raging in my ears. "Nobody on my roster can have you. In fact, nobody on planet Earth can have you, until this thing between us has run its course."

She stares for a long beat, flabbergasted. And then throws her head back and bursts out laughing. "The ramblings of a madman. Nobody on *Earth* can have me until you've grown tired of me and thrown me away? Gosh, what a lovely offer, Mr. Rivers. But, no, thanks. You don't get to have me. You don't get to plant your flag in me vis-à-vis the entire fucking *world*. And you most certainly don't get to screw with my job, just because you want to fuck me and I've turned you down. That's illegal, you know. I've got rights. Or haven't you been following the news lately? That kind of shit isn't allowed anymore, Reed.'"

Oh, Jesus fucking Christ. "Georgina, I have no intention of screwing with your job. On the contrary, I only want to help you do it. I want this special issue to be a grand slam, every bit as much as you do. But don't, even for a minute, forget your *job* is to write about *my* artists. You're in *my* house now, Georgina, which means you're going to play by *my* rules, whether I want to fuck you or not. Which, to be clear, I do. Very much. I don't deny that. But that fact doesn't change the fact that you'll toe the line when it comes to my artists. And not just you. Anyone who wants to interview my artists, whether they're from *Rock 'n' Roll* or any other publication, whether I want to fuck them or not, always, *always* plays by my rules in my house. No exceptions, not even for you."

She puts her hands on her hips. "God, you're so full of shit. There's no 'sound' business reason for you to put the kibosh on the C-Bomb interview. You're feeling jealous and territorial. Plain and simple. You might as well have pissed on my leg when you walked in here and found me with him, you looked so freaking jealous."

She's absolutely right. But there's no way in hell I'd ever admit that. "Find something else to write about this week," I say. "I'm done talking about this."

Georgina lets out an exasperated sigh and sits back down on the couch. "Reed, listen to me. I need this tour. CeeCee said she'll consider everything I write this summer as an audition for me to write for *Dig a Little Deeper*." Emotion threatens at the mere thought of it, but she swallows it. "I know I could get an *incredible* interview of Caleb, if only I had the chance to hang out with him for a full week."

"I have faith you'll find some other amazing person or topic to write about, if you put your mind to it."

She takes several deep, calming breaths. And then drags her palm down her face. "I didn't want to have to play the sympathy card here, but you leave me no choice. I was *really* counting on those free hotel rooms this week. Please don't mess that up for me because of petty jealousy. Please."

"What are you talking about?"

She tilts her head back and sinks into the sofa, her body melting in adorable surrender. "I had to vacate student housing on graduation day. My student loans are all used up, and I'm told I won't get my first paycheck for this job for about three weeks… " She sighs. "I've got, like, seven dollars to my name right now, so I was counting on a week with no expenses to get back on my feet. Before I got this job, I was going to move back home with my dad in the Valley, so I could help him with his expenses. But now that I'm going to be spending so much time in Hollywood, commuting like that won't work. I was hoping to take this week, with no expenses, to figure out a cheap living situation for the summer. Maybe a friend's couch. A room to rent."

My heart twists. It's so rare for Georgina to drop her tough-girl routine. But whenever she does, I find her all the more alluring. "I'll book you a hotel room for the summer—on me," I say simply. "Something within walking distance of my office."

She sits up. "Seriously?"

"Sure. I wish all life's problems were this easy to solve."

She's absolutely elated. She hops up like she wants to hug me, but abruptly sits back down, her cheeks flushing. "Thank you so much, Reed." She fans her blushing face. *"Thank you."*

My heart skips a beat at the look of pure joy on her face. "You're very welcome, Georgina."

In a heartbeat, the expression of joy on her face is replaced by one of skepticism. "Not to look a gift horse in the mouth, but why, exactly, are you doing this?"

"Because it makes sound business sense," I say, lying through my teeth. "You'll be able to maximize your time this way. Plus, you'll be relaxed and close by. All good things for the special issue, in the end."

Her skeptical smile turns absolutely breathtaking. "Liar," she says softly. But she's said the word playfully. Affectionately, even. And it sends a flock of butterflies whooshing into my stomach—which is a shock to me. I haven't felt the cliché of "butterflies" too many times in my life. And when I do, they usually feel foreign and strange to me. But, holy fuck, this time, I'm feeling them and thoroughly enjoying them.

"You ready to stop screaming at me and watch the rest of the concert with me?" I say. "We can watch from the wings." I rise, assuming her answer is yes, yes, yes... but quickly realize I've miscalculated. Georgina's not standing with me. Indeed, she's staying put and shaking her head.

"Fuck," I mutter, sitting back down. "Now what?"

Everybody's got a price.

I say it all the time and know it to be true. But something tells me Georgina Ricci's price ain't a free hotel room a few blocks away from River Records.

TWENTY-THREE
REED

"Seeing as how you won't let me go on tour or interview C-Bomb," Georgina says, her eyebrow arched, "you owe me something as good or better."

"I'll let you interview RCR and also Dean, individually."

"Not good enough. Dean's been interviewed a trillion times. He's so good at being interviewed by now, I'm sure I'll be able to chat with him for twenty minutes at the party tonight and walk away with an entire interview all sewn up."

I can't believe my ears. "You still think you're going to that party tonight? Georgina, obviously, that's off, too. Same as everything else."

She throws up her arms. "No!"

"Yes."

"But Caleb invited me!"

"And I'm uninviting you. I thought you understood the party being cancelled was part and parcel of everything else I've cancelled."

"Okay, that's it. The last straw. I quit." But she doesn't move. She just sits there, stewing. Thinking. *Strategizing.* Finally, she visibly lights up with an idea. "What if I took off my press pass and went to that party tonight as a civilian? Not as a reporter. Just as Caleb's personal guest. I could do that, and you couldn't say boo about it."

My heart rate spikes. *Fuck.* The clever girl's found herself a loophole. *Fuck me.*

Georgina smiles wickedly, and I know I've done a shitty job of maintaining a poker face. Indeed, whatever she just saw flicker across my face, it's egging her on.

"You know what?" she says, sitting up. "That's exactly what I'm going to do. Throw away my press pass and go to the party tonight as a civilian. And not only that, I'm going to throw away my press pass for the entire week, and start my job a week later than originally planned, and go on the tour, too. Why should I be an official reporter on the tour" —she levels me with her blazing eyes—"when I can be Caleb's... *groupie?*"

Oh, for the love of fuck. She's evil. A shark smelling blood. A demon.

Georgina licks her lips. "Band members are allowed to bring guests on their tours, right? I bet that's even stated in their contracts. So, fine, I'll just be Caleb's personal guest for the entire week and all my problems will be magically solved." She snaps her fingers. "Don't forget, C-Bomb offered to get me a hotel room at the Ritz tonight, on his dime, just to make things easier on me after the party. Wasn't that sweet of him? So, I'm thinking, maybe, if I ask him really sweetly to get me rooms in every city along the tour, he'll do it for me. Do you think he would? I bet he would." She drapes her arm across the back of the couch. "And if not, then, gosh, maybe he'll be willing to let me crash in his bed... every... single... night."

Oh, my fucking God, she's diabolical. Pure, unadulterated evil. A force of nature. A human asteroid hurtling toward my planet. How did I not see this coming? I'm normally brilliant at predicting my opponent's tactical maneuvers. But this time, I must admit, Georgina Ricci has outplayed me. I clench my jaw, forcing myself to keep a poker face. But, damn, this diabolical woman just laid down a royal flush to my two pairs and I'm losing my fucking mind.

"What was that groupie's name in *Almost Famous?*" she asks breezily.

I force myself to sound nonchalant. "Penny Lane."

"That's right. I bet I'd get a ton of great content for *Dig a Little Deeper,* if I pulled a Penny Lane this whole week with Caleb." She swipes her palm through the air in front of me, like she's imagining her name in lights. "'My Tantalizing Week as a Badass Drummer's Penny Lane.' By Georgina Ricci." She smiles wickedly at me and lowers her hand. "Gosh, with a scintillating title like that, I bet the article would fly off shelves. It'd probably be the best-selling issue of *Dig a Little Deeper* yet, doncha think?"

Oh, she's good. But, still, as I sit here staring at her, I'm starting to smell her panic. To make out the chinks in her armor that betray the panic bubbling frantically underneath all that gorgeous bravado. Her shallow breath. Flaring nostrils. The crimson in her cheeks. Ah, yes. Despite this little show she's putting on for me, gorgeous Georgina is actually terrified I won't call her bluff, but will, in fact, let her walk out that door to become C-Bomb's groupie this week. Now that I'm smelling her delicious fear, I'm positive she doesn't want to do it. Doesn't want to be his, whether she had his poster on her wall as a teen or not. *If* she did, at all. God only knows what this demon would be willing to say to fuck with me. But, no, either way, this girl is dying to be *mine* and nobody else's. I'm sure of that now, thanks to the way her heart is visibly crashing behind her incredible tits.

Should I let her twist in the wind a little bit longer? Let her panic boil over? Yes, I should. Unfortunately, though, I'm too worried I'm wrong about her not wanting to fuck Caleb to risk it. Taking a long, deep breath, I drape my elbow over the back of the armchair, matching her posture. "I'd strongly urge you against pursuing a 'Penny Lane' strategy with C-Bomb. You might get one scintillating article out of it, but you'd likely torpedo your career. It's a marathon, not a sprint, baby."

"Would an article like that torpedo C-Bomb's career?"

"Of course not. An article like that would add to his mythos as a sex god."

"That's sexist."

"Maybe so, but that's life. He's the drummer in a rock band, and you're a brand-new baby journalist who needs to be taken seriously."

She presses her lips together, conceding I've just scored a point in our game of table tennis. A point she's awfully glad I've scored, if I had to guess.

"Plus," I say, "is doing an end-run around me, the CEO of River Records, really in your best interests, long-term? Even if the other night had never happened between us, even if I had no designs on you for myself—which, to be clear, I do—do you honestly think it would be wise for a summer intern at *Rock 'n' Roll* to defy a direct order from the founder and CEO of the very label she's been assigned to write about? Tread carefully, Miss Ricci. Think about the full consequences of your actions. No more flying off the handle."

Her chest heaves. And her nostrils flare. And I know she's pretty much crapping her pants at her predicament—and the corner she's painted herself into. "All right," she says. "I'll put my Penny Lane piece on the back burner... *for now*. But only if you offer me something that's as good or better. Because there's no way in hell I'm going to call my boss, who isn't *you*, by the way, and say the assignment *she* gave me is off because, oh, gosh, the CEO of the label I'm assigned to write about wants to fuck me, and therefore doesn't want me to be alone with Caleb Baumgarten.'"

And... she's back. Guns blazing. Damn. I must admit, I'm proud of her for pulling that rabbit out of her hat at the eleventh hour. Deeply impressed, as a matter of fact. "That one-on-one interview of Dean?" I say. "It'll be a full-day thing at his compound in Malibu. In fact, if I ask him to, I'm sure he'll give you a tour of the place. Maybe even cook for you. Stir-fry, probably. That's his specialty. Plus, Dean loves to surf, so we could do a photo shoot of him on the beach with his board, and he could talk about how much inspiration he derives from the ocean. Surely, a clever girl like you could parlay all that into something deep and meaningful that CeeCee would run in *Dig a Little Deeper*."

Georgina sniffs like my offer is shit. But it's got to be tempting to her. Dean is a global rock star. A revered musician, songwriter, and heart-throb. And yet, he's not a famewhore, which means he doesn't do a whole lot of in-depth interviews—preferring, instead, to do a thousand and one superficial ones—only whatever publicity is minimally necessary to sell the band's latest release.

"You're not concerned I'm going to have sex with Dean if I spend the day with him at his compound in Malibu and eat his stir-fry and watch him surf?" she asks, her brow arched wickedly. "He's not too shabby to look at, if you haven't noticed."

"I'm not worried."

It's the truth. Dean's not a threat to me. For one thing, he's a good guy. Not an asshole, like Caleb. And if there's one thing I know about my Georgie girl, she likes herself a good asshole. Also, Dean's not on the prowl. He's been in love with the same girl his entire life—the girl he wrote his band's debut single about years ago—Shaynee—and she's recently re-entered his life. And, finally, even if Dean's heart weren't otherwise engaged, he's the kind of guy who'd respect an off-limits designation by the head of his fucking label, unlike Caleb. In short, the guy's not a threat to me, any way you slice it.

Georgie doesn't flinch. "Well, that's a lovely offer, Mr. Rivers. Thank you. I'll take you up on all that. But it's still not enough to keep me from calling CeeCee and ratting you out. If you want me to call my *boss* and tell her I'm not going to fulfill the assignment she gave me, because Reed Rivers wants to fuck me so badly, then you're going to have to give me more." She gazes at her manicured fingernails, as if she's suddenly bored as hell. "Frankly, Reed, if Dean is all you've got to 'bribe' me with, I'd just as soon throw my press pass into the trash and become C-Bomb's personal Penny Lane. I'm sure CeeCee wouldn't mind me starting my job one week later than originally discussed, to get a meaty article like that."

Exasperated, I lean back into my armchair. "All right, Meryl Streep. Cut the crap and just tell me your price. You've obviously got one in mind. Put your cards on the table and tell me what it is."

"Whatever do you mean?"

I lean forward sharply. "You know exactly what I mean."

"Ooooh. As in, 'Everybody's got a price'?"

"What's yours?"

A smug smile spreads across her gorgeous face. She leans forward, giving me a lovely view of her tits in her low-cut blouse. "My price? Well, Mr. Rivers, it's *you*, of course."

"Well, damn. That's an easy one, baby. Lock the door and bend over the back of that couch, and I'll give you every fucking inch of me."

Again, she doesn't flinch. "No, I want to *write* about you, Mr. Rivers. I want you to give me an in-depth interview, suitable for *Dig a Little Deeper*."

I burst out laughing. "No."

"*Yes.*"

"Didn't CeeCee tell you? She's already asked me to do that a hundred times, and... " I trail off.

CeeCee.

Of course.

Why didn't I figure this out sooner?

Georgina is CeeCee's unwitting pawn. CeeCee sent Georgina to Caleb, as her top priority, because she knew it would turn out exactly this way. CeeCee knew I'd get jealous and possessive and nix the idea... and that Georgina, clever girl that she is, would be smart enough to exploit my reaction and use it as leverage. Fucking CeeCee. I have to admit, the woman is brilliant, even though I'm pissed at her right now.

"An interview with me is already part of the deal for the special issue."

"Yes, I know, but I want you to give me something more in-depth—a wide-ranging interview that breaks new ground with you. Something covering both business and personal topics. Something on-brand for *Dig a Little Deeper*."

I scoff. "No."

Georgina rises and strides toward the door. "All right, then. Goodbye. I'm going on tour with Caleb, as his Penny Lane."

She's bluffing and I know it. There's no way in hell she could have felt what I did when we kissed and still want to fuck Caleb, or anyone else who isn't me, any more than I want to fuck anyone who isn't Georgina.

When I say nothing behind her, Georgina calls out over her shoulder, still striding toward the door, "I'll see you in a week, Mr. Rivers—that is, if Caleb hasn't fucked me to death by then."

Oh, Jesus Christ. I'm ninety-nine percent sure she's bluffing, but on the off-chance she's not... "Georgina!" I shout, much more loudly than I mean to say it. "*Stop.*"

She freezes at the door, her back to me.

I'm quaking. Flooded with adrenaline. Arousal. Jealousy. "I'll negotiate with you about the scope of my interview," I choke out. "But only if you don't walk through that door right now. If you walk out of here, you'll get absolutely nothing from me but a fluffy, bullshit interview that's barely suitable for *Rock 'n' Roll*."

She turns around slowly, and the minute I see her face, I know every cell in her body is sighing with relief. Obviously, she had no desire to walk out that door. Indeed, she was counting on me stopping her, exactly the way I did.

I'm expecting her to head back to the couch, but she doesn't. Instead, she takes a slow step toward the armchair—toward *me*—her hazel eyes on fire. "Here's an idea, Reed: How about you let me shadow you this whole week to see what your life is really like? If I can't tour with RCR, then I'll 'tour' your life. I'll observe you and interview you along the way, about whatever topics you're comfortable talking about." She's closing in on me, making my dick come alive with each step.

Without consciously telling my body to do it, I rise from my chair, my body drawn to Georgina's like steel to a magnet.

"You won't have to answer any question you don't want to," she purrs. "So, really, what's the risk to you in saying yes to this idea? I'll shadow you for a week, and then I'll write my piece, whatever it turns out to be, and take my chances as to whether CeeCee decides to publish it in *Rock 'n' Roll* or the other magazine. Either way, you're required to do an interview. Let's spend a week together and see what comes of it."

Georgina has reached me now. We're standing mere inches apart, our body heat mingling. I swallow hard. I have no desire to let anyone see how the sausage gets made in my world. On the other hand, though, Georgina is right. I can pick and choose the questions I answer. Control the narrative. And it certainly wouldn't be the worst thing in the world to have this woman tied to my hip for an entire week. By day two, at the latest, she'll surely be naked and spread eagle in my bed.

She looks up at me, her full lips wet and her hazel eyes sparkling. "I won't take no for an answer," she whispers. And for the first time in my life, the phrase doesn't make me want to scream "No, motherfucker!" It makes me want to whisper, "Yes, baby, yes. Whatever you want."

I extend my hand. "You've got yourself a deal. Well played."

Her face lights up with surprise. Joy. *Relief.* And, suddenly, she looks every bit the twenty-one-year-old newbie she is. "Seriously?"

I nod. "One week. You'll be my shadow. I'll be your interview subject. And we'll see what happens."

"Will you still get me a hotel room, so I won't have to commute from the Valley?"

I force myself not to smirk. If I get my way, Georgina won't be sleeping in a hotel room this coming week. She'll be lying next to me, naked, every fucking night. "Of course," I say, extending my hand again. "Do we have a deal, Madame Reporter? Can we finally agree to put this Penny Lane bullshit to rest?"

She stares at my extended hand without moving. And I can practically see the gears in her head turning. I lower my hand. Oh, for the love of fuck. *What now?*

She looks up and grimaces at me. "Sorry, I just realized there are two more things I have to ask for—"

"Georgie!"

"Before shaking on it."

"No."

"Two teeny-tiny things."

"No."

"And, then, I swear, we'll absolutely be able to put this deal"—she smiles adorably—"to bed."

TWENTY-FOUR
GEORGINA

Reed lowers his hand and plops onto the couch, looking highly annoyed with me. "Whatever else you're going to ask for, the answer is no. I'm done negotiating with you."

"But you haven't even heard what I—"

"It doesn't matter. Amateur hour at the poker table is over. Scoop up your chips and walk away while you still can, Miss Ricci. The deal we just negotiated is my final and best offer."

I sit in the armchair across from Reed, my heart racing. "Just listen to me."

He puts up his palm. "Tread carefully. Whatever you're going to ask for, make sure it's worth risking what I've already put on the table. Maybe, in response to whatever new things you demand, I'll demand something new, too. Something you don't want to give. Or, maybe, I'll start taking things *off* the table. Stuff you thought was already settled and done. Do you really want to risk that?"

Shit, he's intimidating. Confident and sexy and formidable beyond belief when he flips into his "music mogul businessman mode." But it can't be helped. Just before I shook Reed's hand, I realized I'd never forgive myself if I didn't get two more items sneaked into our deal. "Yeah, both things are worth it to me," I say confidently, even though I'm shitting a brick.

Reed scoffs, leans back on the couch, and motions like he's giving me the floor. "Let's hear it, then."

My stomach somersaults. I take a deep breath. "Okay. First off, about that party tonight—"

"No."

"*Listen.* I want *you* to take me there, Reed, in my official capacity as a writer for *Rock 'n' Roll,* solely to—"

"No."

"Listen! I want to observe how RCR lets off steam after a show. And I also want to break the ice with them for my future *group* interview of them and my solo stir-fried interview with Dean. Reed, come on. Readers would want to read about a star-struck fan getting to party with rock royalty, and you know it. It'd be a huge missed opportunity for me to not go. In fact, I'd even say it'd be a gross dereliction of duty if I *didn't* go, which *might* get me fired."

Reed's dark eyes are unmistakably *unimpressed*. Well, damn. I thought I was being pretty persuasive. But, okay, I'll try another tack.

"Reed, like I said, I had a RCR poster on my wall as a teenager. 'Shaynee' is one of my all-time favorite songs. My fourteen-year-old self would never forgive me if I missed this party. I know you party with rock stars all the freaking time. For you, it's as ho-hum as eating a bag of chips. But it'd be a once in a lifetime experience for me, and, selfishly, I *reallllly* don't want to miss out."

Reed exhales like he's painfully bored. "Are you finished? Have you now exhausted all your less than persuasive arguments regarding item number one?"

"Only if you're going to say yes. If not, I've got another ten minutes all cued up."

He can't resist smiling at that. "Okay, so, if I'm understanding this correctly, Little Miss Georgina Ricci is dying to party like a rock star, huh?"

"She is. But for professional purposes only."

Reed can't help chuckling. "All right, sweetheart. I tell you what I'll do. Actually, I was already contemplating doing this exact thing. I talked to Owen about this yesterday, as a matter of fact. A week from today, next Saturday, I'm going to throw a party at my house—a fucking awesome rager, celebrating the special issue. And you and the other writers assigned to the project will be my guests of honor."

I leap up from the armchair and squeal and jump around with glee.

"Every artist on my label who isn't on tour will be there, so they can meet you and the other writers. It'll be a chance to break the ice and brainstorm. And, of course, you'll have the chance to party like a rock star, exactly as your fourteen-year-old self would have wanted."

I can't stop jumping around, laughing and hooting like a maniac, and Reed can't stop laughing at my silly display.

"Are you drunk?" he asks, laughing.

"I feel like it!" I say, giggling. "Thank you!"

"I take it we've reached agreement on your item number one?"

"Yes!" I shriek, doing a stupid little twirl. "Thank you so much!" When I come out of my spin, I have the impulse to hug him, *again*, but jerk back sharply at the last second, same as last time, as if I'm saving myself from a burning pyre. For the love of fuck. I can't hug this sexy man. If I do, then I'll kiss him. And if I kiss him, then I'll fuck him—maybe even in this room. And if I fuck him, especially here, then I'll lose all my bargaining power on item number two—which, frankly, is the far more critical item for me to secure.

I stand stock still in front of Reed, my chest heaving from my little dance, to discover Reed's cheeks blazing red and a massive erection bulging behind his pants. Oh, God, that hard-on is making my mouth water. I want to rub myself against it... and then pull it out of its bondage and ride it like a pony.

But, no.

I have to remain strong.

I have to get through my second demand without folding like a beach chair, or I'll never again have a shred of bargaining power with him. That much is clear.

Out of nowhere, Reed clears his throat and abruptly strides across the room. "You want a beer, party animal?"

I plop onto the couch, my heart racing. "Sure. Thanks."

Reed's gorgeous body is poetry in motion as he glides across the room. His ass divine. He grabs two bottles from a mini-fridge, pops their caps, crosses the room again, and hands a cold bottle to me. To my surprise, he sits next to me on the couch this time, foregoing his armchair. And, as he settles into his seat, I can't help noticing his boner is gone.

Reed takes a long swig of his beer. "Just a heads up about the party," he says. "Red Card Riot won't be there. They'll still be on tour. But that's for the best, because I want to introduce you to 22 Goats, and they won't come if RCR is invited."

I tilt my head. "The 22 Goats guys don't like the RCR guys?"

"Wow. You don't follow celebrity gossip at all, do you?"

I shake my head.

"C-Bomb and Dax had a pretty big falling out. The other guys don't give a shit about any of it, but nobody in either band is willing to cross the picket line. They've gotta support their guy. It's how it works in a band."

I open my mouth to say, "I bet my stepsister, Alessandra, would know all about the beef between C-Bomb and Dax. She follows celebrity gossip religiously, especially when it comes to musicians." But, instantly, I shut my mouth, realizing I now need to add "item one-and-a-half" to my list of demands. Crap! I can't attend Reed's rock-star-studded party without bringing Alessandra as my plus-one. And not even as a ploy to get her signed to River Records. No, that's what my second item will address. But because Alessandra, the girl who attends a renowned music school and is obsessed with music and musicians, and always has been, deserves more than anyone I know—and far more than me—to party like a rock star with Reed's roster of world-renowned rock stars. "Hey, uh, before we leave item one for good... " I begin.

"Oh, for the love of fuck!" Reed blurts, throwing up his hand. "What now, Georgie?"

I press my palms together in prayer. "Can I *please* bring someone to the party, as my plus-one? I mean, not as a date or anything. Someone "

"Your stepsister?"

I nod sheepishly. "Not as a ploy to get her signed. She could stand in a corner and people-watch the entire night and never talk to you or anyone, and it would still be the best night of her life."

Reed swigs his beer, rolling his eyes. "She's a student at Berklee in Boston, you said?"

I nod effusively. "She just finished her second year last week. She's in LA for my graduation. Please, *please,* don't make that poor girl sit at her mother's house watching Netflix on a Saturday night while I'm at your house, partying like a rock star with 22 Goats."

Reed pauses. And then shocks me by saying, "Okay."

"Okay?"

"She can come."

Without meaning to do it, I leap onto his lap and straddle him. "Thank you!" I throw my arms around his neck and kiss his cheek. "Thank you, thank you, thank you!"

Instantly, Reed's erection hardens deliciously underneath me. "*On one condition*," he adds.

I freeze on top of him, panting... and wait.

"Neither of you will try, even once, to get me to listen to her music that night."

"I promise."

"I'll be off the clock, Georgie."

I nod enthusiastically. "I promise I'll control myself. And, don't worry, Alessandra would never try to sell herself to you, anyway. Not that night, or ever. She's painfully shy and the worst at tooting her own horn. Plus, I'm sure she'll be too star-struck that night to say two words to anyone but me."

Reed tilts his head back and exhales, annoyed with me. "Georgina, come on!"

"*What?*"

He lifts his head, still keeping his arms firmly planted at his sides. "Why would you tell me that about her? Think, sweetheart." He puts a palm on my cheek. "Use that amazing bean of yours, baby. At some point, you *are* going to try to sell me on her music, right? In fact, I'm guessing that's your item number two. And do you really think telling me she's 'painfully shy' is a good selling point for an artist you're trying to sell to me?"

My stomach drops. "Fuck." I slide off him and slink back to the armchair and curl my legs underneath me.

"Well, shit. I didn't mean to make you run away," he mutters.

"She comes alive onstage, Reed. She's only painfully shy whenever she doesn't have a guitar in her hands." I bite my lip. My nipples are rock hard and my clit throbbing from our unexpected contact a moment ago, and I'm finding it hard to think straight. "Actually, yeah, can we just move on to item number two now?"

"Sure. Did I guess right?"

I nod. "Did you happen to check out Alessandra's Instagram page, like I asked you to do the other night?"

Reed chuckles. "You didn't 'ask' me to check it out. You shrieked her handle at me, right before speeding off in an Uber, both middle fingers raised in the air. And, no, I didn't check her out. In fact, I forgot her handle two seconds after you screamed it at me. Call me crazy, but I don't tend to do favors for shrieking people who've passionately told me to fuck off and die." He subtly adjusts his hard dick in his pants, and the gesture zings me straight in the clit. *I want that.*

"Fair enough," I say. "But that's water under the bridge now, right? Now that we've both agreed we could have handled things better that night. Surely, now that we're friends again, you're feeling inclined to listen to her music now... to put our deal to *bed*?"

"Nope. I have zero desire whatsoever to listen to your stepsister's music. Especially not now that I know she's 'painfully shy.'" He shifts in his seat again, relieving his hard-on, and shoots me a smile that doesn't reach his eyes. "So, are you ready to shake on a deal now or what?"

"*No*. Reed, it would take mere minutes for you to listen to Alessandra's demo, and I'd be eternally grateful to you."

"You should already be eternally grateful to me. I'm letting you follow me around for a week, throwing a party for you, and letting you bring Alessandra as your guest to the party. Actually, you know what? Thanks to your lack of eternal gratitude for everything I've already agreed to give you, I'm thinking maybe I should start taking things *off* the table. Maybe we don't need a full week for our interview. Maybe we can get it done in five days. Yeah, that sounds good. Five days, it is."

"Reed, no."

"Hey, I warned you. Think hard before throwing in new, last-minute demands that might fuck up what you've already secured. You're about to learn an important, but basic, lesson in negotiations the hard way, Georgie. *Know when to cash in your chips and run like hell.* Actually, the more I think about it, I think we can do our interview in *four* days."

Fuck! I feel like I'm going to pass out. But I can't fail Alessandra now. If one of us is going to swerve, it's going to have to be Reed. "The three songs on her demo are about three minutes each," I sputter. "I'm asking for less than ten minutes of your time."

"We're down to three days now. Tick tock. Cash in your chips, baby."

I grit my teeth. "River Records would be lucky to sign Alessandra. Don't agree to listen to her demo for *me*. Listen for *you*."

"Two days." Reed shakes his head and taps his watch. "You're blowing it, Georgie."

What the fuck is wrong with him? One minute he's charming and sweet, and throwing me a party, and grinding his dick into me as I'm kissing his cheeks like crazy, and the next he's—

Oh.

I suddenly get it.

I know what Reed is doing. What he wants.

He wants me to bribe him.

To figure out his price.

Everyone's got one, right?

Well, then, I guess I'll just have to pull out the big guns, and figure out Reed's.

TWENTY-FIVE
REED

Georgina's entire demeanor shifts on a dime. Right before my eyes, she transforms from a panicked possum in a trap to a sultry *femme fatale*. She gets up from the armchair and straddles me on the couch, batting her eyelashes at me. She rubs her nose against mine. "All right, Mr. Rivers. Let's cut the crap. I'm ready to close this deal, sweetheart. You said everyone's got a price." She runs her finger across my cheekbone. "So, what's yours, honey?"

Hallelujah. "I don't have a price, Georgina."

She shoots me a snarky look, fully aware I'm throwing her own naïve words back at her. "How about this?" she purrs, her fingertip making its way to my ear. "You agree to listen to Alessandra's full demo—all three songs—and, in exchange, I'll give you a lap dance that lasts the same amount of time as you give Alessandra's music."

My cock is hard underneath her, my breathing shallow. But I force myself to keep a straight face and my hands on the couch cushions. I've come this far. I'm not going to cave until I get exactly what I want. I say, "Wasn't it you who told me to fuck off and die when I suggested this very sort of bargained-for exchange was your agenda from the start? And now, here you are, mere days later, surrendering your righteousness like an expired passport?"

She grinds herself into my steely bulge. "I've learned a few things about negotiation tactics since then. I've got a very good teacher."

Oh, fuck. I'm on the bitter cusp of throwing my arms around her and kissing the hell out of her sultry mouth. Which I absolutely can't let myself do, or else I'll surely cave and give the girl anything she wants.

"Lemme guess," I say, my chest heaving. "Has a certain hothead spent the entire past week regretting the way she flew off the handle the other night?"

"Maybe I've realized bribing you with something I want to give, anyway, would, in fact, be a win-win."

My cock is straining. Aching. More likely than not, dripping with my need for her. "Would this lap dance be performed in the nude?" I ask.

She looks shocked. "*No.* I'd perform it in this. Right here and now." She motions to her outfit—a short skirt and low-cut blouse. "After shaking on the deal, I'd give you a little show... " She nuzzles her nose against mine. "And then you'd listen to all three songs, right here and now, as well."

I shake my head. "For a *clothed* lap dance, I'd be willing to listen to *ten seconds* of the *first* song. But that's it." My tone is businesslike. Flat. Like we're two farmers negotiating the price of grain. But, inside, I'm a hurricane of pent-up sexual arousal. On the bitter edge of folding like bad poker hand.

"Ten seconds?" Georgina purrs, skimming her lips across my cheekbone. "That's an insult to lap dancers everywhere, Mr. Rivers. Or, at least, to this one."

I can barely breathe. "You saw me listen to Bryce's sister's music. Ten seconds is all I need—to assess a demo, to be clear. I need much, much longer than ten seconds to do something else."

She giggles. "Come on. A sexy lap dance ought to get me *at least* a full-song listen."

"Okay, time out for a second." I put both palms on her gorgeous face and her pouty lips part in surprise, begging me to kiss them. "Think, sweetheart. Why would you even want me to listen to a full song, even if you could get me to agree to that?"

She furrows her brow like she doesn't follow my logic.

"Imagine you get me to agree to a full-song listen. And then, imagine that, ten seconds in, I have the same reaction I had to Bryce's sister. Hard pass. If I know I'm not impressed after ten seconds of a song, would it really benefit Alessandra if I'm then obligated by the terms of our agreement to keep listening to the same fucking song that doesn't impress me for another three minutes?"

A light bulb goes off on Georgie's beautiful face. She gets it. "Ah."

I drop my hands and grip the couch cushion again, forcing myself not to interact. Not to grab her ass. Not to give in. Not to cave. "See?" I say. "You gotta think a couple moves ahead. Be careful what you ask for in a negotiation, because you don't want to screw yourself by unexpectedly getting exactly what you've asked for."

She slides her arms around my neck and my cock jolts. "But what if the song *isn't* a hard pass? What if you think an artist has potential? You wouldn't turn off a song after ten seconds in that case, would you?"

"No," I concede, barely able to breathe through my arousal.

"You'd continue listening to the entire song, right?"

I take a deep breath and collect myself. "Not necessarily. Sometimes, if I like someone's voice and style, but hate the song, I'll listen for about thirty seconds and then flip to another song, hoping the next one will click better for me."

She processes that. "Okay, so... " She skims her lips across my jawline. "How about I give you one *clothed* lap dance in exchange for you listening to the first thirty seconds of each of her three songs."

Georgina looks proud of herself for that suggestion. Hopeful. Fucking adorable. But I shake my head. "You gotta sweeten the pot more than that, Ricci. A clothed lap dance ain't nearly enough for three songs. What else you got to offer me?"

She twists her mouth. "Two lap dances? A clothed one... plus, a second one in my bra and undies."

Now, we're cooking with gas. "You're getting warmer." I can't help touching my palms to her back, and she shudders exquisitely at my touch. I say, "Would you do both lap dances here, in this room?"

Her breathing is labored. She's begun grinding herself into my hard-on, causing my cock to throb and strain. "No," she says. She skims her lips across my jawline. "I think we should do the bra-and-undies lap dance in my hotel room. Don't you? And I'll throw in a striptease, down to my bra and undies, too." She's panting now.

Grinding herself enthusiastically into my cock. Getting herself off. And I'm loving it.

"We'll do the striptease and lap dances at my house tonight," I say, skimming my lips across her soft cheek. Inhaling her scent. Craving her like I've never craved anyone in my life. "Not your hotel."

She nods effusively, her body grinding against mine, her lips a breath away from mine, begging to be kissed.

"And," I whisper, on the cusp of pressing my lips against hers, "you'll stay at my house this week, while you're 'shadowing' and 'interviewing' me. In one of my guestrooms, if you want. Or in my room, with me. Either way, you'll stay at my house this week."

She lets out the softest of moans as she continues rubbing herself against me. "I suppose it *would* be easier to follow you around, if I'm staying at your house."

I'm trembling with arousal. I whisper, "Say yes, Georgina."

"Yes."

I skim my lips against hers, desperate to breach her borders and claim her. "We've got a deal?" I say softly. "What do you say, baby?"

She grinds herself hard against me. Grabs either side of my head and grips my hair. She's breathing hard. Dry humping me like her life depends on it. "What do I say?" she murmurs breathlessly, her eyes half-mast. "I say 'Yes,' Mr. Rivers." She smiles. "Actually, no." Her eyes ignite. "I say, 'Yes... yes... *yesss*.'"

TWENTY-SIX
GEORGINA

With a low growl, Reed smashes his lips into mine. And, I swear, I almost come as his tongue slides inside my mouth. In short order, we're passionately kissing, both of us on fire. I clutch at him feverishly as I kiss him, grind myself against his steely hard-on beneath me, desperate for him.

"Consider this my first lap dance," I gasp into Reed's hungry lips. And in reply, he slides his strong hands down my back, straight to my ass cheeks, and grips me *hard*. Like I'm a life preserver and he's a drowning man. Like I'm a drug and he's the junkie. All of it, making my body jolt and writhe on top of him with pleasure.

I thought I remembered what it felt like to kiss this scorching hot, formidable, sexy asshole of a man. But I was wrong. Before this moment, I rated kisses in my head as good, great, and fire. But, now, I'm being forced to recalibrate as I realize the top rating possible for any kiss, for the rest of my days, won't be fire any longer. Forevermore, it will always be: *Reed Rivers*.

I can't get enough. And, clearly, Reed feels the same way. As he kisses me, he touches me voraciously. My cheeks. Neck. Hair. Ass. And with every touch of his fingertips, palms, lips, and tongue, every grind of his hard-on against my throbbing center, his body confesses the truth: he was never, ever going to let me walk out that door to hook up with Caleb.

No fucking way. My body is his, until this thing, whatever it is, has run its course. Exactly like he said.

As our kiss intensifies, Reed lifts my skirt, and I spread my thighs, giving him the access my body so forcefully craves.

I'm vaguely aware the crowd in the arena is roaring as RCR finishes playing a song. But then, the band launches into their next song—their huge smash hit, "Shaynee"—one of my all-time favorites—and I can't help gasping with added excitement.

"I'll take you to see the show another night," Reed growls hoarsely into my lips, apparently reading my body language. "You can pick the city, baby. I'll fly us wherever you want to go and we'll sit front-row center. But right now, you're staying right here. Right now, you're all mine, baby." With that, Reed's fingers breach the crotch of my cotton panties and slide deliciously inside me, making me moan. "You're so wet," he growls.

He begins stroking my aching clit with his slick fingers while simultaneously, with his other hand, lifting my shirt and pushing my bra off and away. When my breasts are freed from their entrapment... Reed leans back from kissing me to look at them. And what he sees, clearly, he likes a lot. With an animalistic growl, he leans in and devours me. Sucking. Licking. Reveling. Holy shit, he's freaking motorboating me! And all the while, he's continuing to finger-fuck me with zealous expertise.

A sound of pure pleasure lurches out of me. A sound no human has ever manufactured unless they're dying or coming hard. My eyes roll back into my head... my insides clench and warp in slow motion... my clit zings and aches with a tingling, zinging warning... and then... *Bam!* A rocket of bliss envelops me as my center and everything connected to it, including the deepest muscles of my core, begin clenching so hard, I'm seeing little white stars.

"Oh, God, Georgina," Reed says, his breathing labored. "You're so fucking incredible." He tilts his lap sharply, sliding me off him, sending me onto my back on the couch. His eyes on fire and his body quaking with lust, Reed yanks up my skirt, and begins peeling off my moistened undies. "I've wanted to taste you since the minute I saw you."

"Reed," I breathe, feeling swept away by my arousal.

"You want me to eat your pussy, baby?"

I nod profusely.

"Say it."

"Yes." I lick my lips, coming down from my orgasm. "Yes, yes, yes."

He tosses my undies behind him on the couch. "I'm going to eat your pussy better than it's ever been done, beautiful girl. You're going to come harder than you've ever come in your life."

I gasp, simply because, um, I just did. Does he mean he's going to make me come even harder than *that*? Holy shit.

With obvious enthusiasm, Reed grabs my thighs with his large hands, spreads me out before him, grabs my ass from underneath, and pulls my center into his waiting lips... where he then proceeds to eat and lick and nibble and suck and finger the living fuck out of me until I'm moaning like I've never moaned before.

It's a shocking whirlwind of pleasure. An overwhelming avalanche of stimulation. Nobody's ever performed oral on me quite like this before. With so much... expertise. Confidence. Enthusiasm. *Passion.* The pleasure, right out of the gate, is so extreme, so full-throttle, I'm not sure I can withstand it without losing control of myself, either physically, emotionally, or both...

I clutch at the couch cushion underneath me, feeling like I'm grasping at the last shreds of my self-control. Maybe even my sanity. And soon, the way Reed's licking and stroking, hitting all the right magical spots, over and over again, methodically, without reprieve or apology, is too much to bear.

"Oh, God," I choke out, coming like a wrecking ball.

Wave after wave of glorious pleasure slams into me. It's making my eyes roll back into my head and my entire body seize. Just like Reed promised, it's the best orgasm of my life. Holy crap.

Finally, when the pleasure subsides, I wipe at my face and realize, to my surprise, I'm more than dripping with sweat. *I'm crying.* Tears of euphoria. It's a first for me—bursting into tears at the moment of release. But, then, I've never in my life had an orgasm this powerful. This all-encompassing. This heavenly.

When Reed raises his head from my thighs, he looks drugged. Feral. His lips and chin are slathered in me. His dark eyes are burning with desire. At the sight of my sweaty, tear-stained face, a wicked smile spreads across his stunning face. "Good?"

"The best, ever." I wipe at my face. "Don't freak out I'm crying. I just lost control—"

"Georgie, it's totally natural. Believe me, it's the best feeling in the world for me to take you that high."

His understanding makes me relax and smile. "Oh, God, Reed, that was so fucking *good*. I've never felt anything that good in my life."

Reed runs his warm palms over my bare thighs, hiking my dress up even higher onto my belly. "There's a lot more where that came from, beautiful," he says. "When I fuck you, I'm gonna make you—"

Without warning, the door to the small room swings open, and a production assistant pokes her head in, making me jump like a cat on a hot tin roof and scramble feverishly to cover my bare breasts and thighs and crotch and—

"Oh my God!" the P.A. blurts, saying the words along with me. She turns her face away. "Caleb sent me to look for someone."

"I think you found her," Reed says calmly. "Wait in the hallway for a minute. I want to talk to you."

"No, I'll go and—"

"*Wait in the hallway for my signal*," Reed commands sharply. "I want to talk to you."

"Reed, no!" I whisper-shout. "Let her go. Please. Oh my fucking God."

For some reason, Reed's not freaking out like I am. In fact, he's as cool as a cucumber. He calmly hands me my underpants, and when I snatch them from him, shooting him daggers, he says, "She's already seen me camped between your naked legs with your pussy and tits hanging out. Pretending she didn't see won't make her un-see it."

"Fuck."

I get my undies on and pull myself together, trembling with embarrassment. Holy fuck! This is worst-case scenario for me. Getting caught with the big boss between my naked thighs with my wahoo and tits hanging out on the first day of my employment. I can't believe I let this happen. It's nothing short of a disaster for me.

At Reed's signal, the young woman sheepishly re-enters the room, her head pointedly turned away. "Sorry to bother you, Mr. Rivers."

"And Miss Ricci," Reed supplies, making me throw my palms over my face. "You can look at me. We're just sitting here, having a conversation."

She slowly turns her head to look at Reed. "Uh. Caleb sent me to find Miss Ricci, and get her phone number for... him. He said Miss Ricci is, uh, coming to tonight's after-party in his suite... as his... personal guest, and that I should, um, arrange a hotel room for Miss Ricci... at the Ritz... on the same floor as... Caleb's room?"

To my shock, Reed flashes me a beaming smile. A triumphant, elated one, like he's the heavy weight champ who just scored a knockout punch in a title fight. And, all of a sudden, I get why Reed called this poor girl back into the room and supplied my name and orchestrated this horrifically humiliating moment. *So he could spike the ball in the middle of Caleb's end zone.*

"Change of plans," Reed says coolly to the PA. "Tell Caleb I've decided Miss Ricci isn't attending his party tonight, after all. Not as his personal guest, or in her official capacity. And she's not joining the tour this coming week, either, or interviewing him individually. You can tell him I've nixed all of it for business reasons. But assure him, please, that Miss Ricci is working on a fresh, new angle for a full-band interview, which we'll lock down next month after they're back. This week, however, Miss Ricci will be working on a piece about me, as required by my arrangement with the head of *Rock 'n' Roll*."

The poor woman looks like she's going to keel over from stress. "Um," she says. "Yeah, I really don't think I can say all that to Caleb."

"Sure, you can," Reed says. "Tell him everything I just said, using my exact words. However, do not, under any circumstances, talk to anyone, including Caleb, about what you think you might have seen in this room when you first walked in. Whatever you thought you saw happening between Miss Ricci and me, you were mistaken. We were simply having a conversation."

The girl grimaces with discomfort. "I'd never say a word about anything. Because I didn't see anything besides two people talking. But, um, Mr. Rivers, would it be okay if *you* tell Caleb everything you said?" Her face is pleading. Vulnerable. Panicked. "Please? Because I don't think I can remember it all. And, also because... " She takes a deep, shuddering breath. "I think Caleb is going to get really pissed off when he hears all of that, and I really don't—"

"What's your name?"

"Amy O'Brien."

"Nice to meet you, Amy," Reed says. "You're traveling with the tour?"

She nods. "I'm assigned as Caleb's PA. Whatever he needs... " She looks at me and blushes. "I mean, as his gofer. You know. Not for... "

She clamps her lips shut, and again, I bury my face in my palms. Holy crap, this is a nightmare.

"Let me explain something to you, Amy," Reed says, his tone brimming with condescension. "I'm the reason you get a paycheck every two weeks. Not Caleb. I'm actually Caleb's boss. Did you know that?"

"Yes, sir."

"Which means, if you think about it, I'm *your* boss. And *that* means when I tell you to do something, then you're gonna fucking do it, unless, of course, there are extenuating circumstances. For instance, if you're feeling scared for your physical safety, you need only tell me that and all bets will be off. Are you feeling scared for your physical safety to go tell Caleb what I said, Amy?"

"Uh... " She sighs and shakes her head, obviously wishing she were feeling scared for her physical safety right about now.

"Is that a no?" Reed asks.

"That's a no." She grimaces, again telegraphing her fervent wish to feel physically threatened rather than have to traipse back to Caleb and tell him what Reed said.

"Do you have any *religious* objections to telling Caleb everything I just said?" Reed asks.

"No, sir."

"Is there any reason whatsoever you can't tell Caleb what I just said, other than the fact that you hate confrontation and conflict and maybe don't want to watch him have a tantrum?"

"Well, also, I can't really remember what you said. My brain is kind of freaking out right now, to be honest, Mr. Rivers."

"I understand. Listen carefully, Amy. I'll repeat it all for you." Slowly, Reed repeats everything he said earlier, and the poor girl nods and holds back tears the whole time. "Repeat it back to me, Amy O'Brien."

She does. Not well, but she manages.

"Good. And that's all you're going to say. If Caleb asks *why* Miss Ricci isn't going to the party, or *why* I've decided the tour and individual interview aren't happening, you'll say he can talk to me about it, if he wants clarification."

"Yes, sir."

"Amy, do you remember signing an NDA when you accepted this job?"

"Yes, sir."

"Do you understand what an NDA is?"

"It's a non-disclosure agreement."

"That's right. It means if you tell anyone about the private things you witness while on tour, you could not only get fired, but also sued for the money set forth in the liquidation clause of the contract. You understand that, right?"

She turns green. "Yes, sir. I won't say a word about anything to anyone, but what you told me to say."

"Good. Because if I hear so much as one word of gossip about Miss Ricci and me, I'll blame you. And I won't go easy on you, Amy. I'll not only fire you, but also sic my lawyer on you to get the full extent of our legal remedies."

Amy nods. She's physically trembling.

"You can go now, Amy. Good talk."

"Yes, sir. Thank you. Sorry."

And off she goes, looking like she's dragging herself to her own execution.

When she's gone, Reed turns to me, looking triumphant. Turned on. And ready to finish what we started before that poor, poor girl interrupted us.

But we're most definitely not on the same page. I feel sick. Panicky. Disgusted at what Reed just now put that poor girl through, even though I'm also selfishly grateful to him for protecting our secret with such relentlessness. But most of all, I feel angry with myself for putting myself in a position where it was so easy for me to get caught with my tits hanging out and my panties off and my thighs spread for Reed... on the first freaking night of my job! If I was going to fuck the big boss, why'd I do it *here*, where anyone could stumble upon us? Why didn't I at least lock the freaking door? When word gets out I'm fucking Reed, which it will, who's going to respect me? Absolutely nobody, that's who.

"Now, where were we?" Reed mutters, reaching for me like the past few minutes of torture didn't happen.

But he's delusional if he thinks I'm going to fuck him now. In this room. Or at all. In a flash, I feel gripped by the instinct to flee and never look back. My heart exploding, I stumble off the couch, muttering curses under my breath when I bang my knee, and then sprint, like a bug-eyed bat out of hell, straight out the door.

TWENTY-SEVEN
REED

I chase Georgina down the hallway and grab her arm, but she rips herself from my grasp. "I can't do this."

"Do *what*?"

She whirls around, her eyes panicked. *"Fuck the big boss."*

I hear footsteps nearby. People talking and laughing. So, I pull Georgina through a nearby door marked "Janitorial." And suddenly, we're standing mere inches apart in a large closet. I pull a cord to turn on a bulb, and then back Georgina into a shelf with my arms on either side of her. "I'm not your boss. We've already established that."

"You think that PA who saw you eating my pussy knows that?" she whispers frantically, looking near-hysterical. "Right now, that girl thinks I fucked you to get my job!" She rubs her forehead. "Oh, God. Everyone is going to think that same thing, Reed—the same thing everyone always thinks about me—that I get whatever jobs or opportunities, not based on merit or hard work, but thanks to nothing but my tits and ass—because some asshole in charge wants to fuck me!"

My stomach drops. *Shit.* "Okay, calm down," I say soothingly. "Nobody is going to find out anything, because that PA isn't going to say a word. You saw how I put the fear of God into her. Do you think I get off on bullying little PAs like that? No, of course, not. I did that for you. Because I knew you'd freak out, exactly like this."

"It's really important to me that everyone knows I got this job because CeeCee believes in me, Reed. Because she thinks I'm a good writer. And not because Reed Rivers wants to fuck me!"

Fuck, fuck, fuck. "Of course, sweetheart," I say soothingly. "All anyone has to do is talk to you for half a second to realize you're smart as hell and a total badass and absolutely deserve to be here."

"Oh, God." She palms her forehead. "*Caleb.* Once he finds out you've nixed the party and tour, he'll assume we're fucking. What else could he possibly conclude? And then he'll tell the rest of the RCR guys about us, and then my interview with the band, and with Dean individually, will be awkward and stilted and embarrassing, and everything I've dreamed about achieving in my life will be shot to hell—"

"Okay, stop. You're spiraling, Ricci. Pull your shit together." I put my palm on her cheek. "Nobody will ever know I've gotten into your cute little cotton panties. Will they *assume* that's what I *want* to do? Yes. But they would have assumed that, anyway, whether that PA walked in on us or not. Because, news flash, Georgie, I'm *me*—a guy who likes sex with beautiful women. And, news flash, baby, you're not only beautiful but sexy as fuck, too. So, *of course*, people are going to think there's a strong chance I want to fuck your brains out. But so does every other man who sees you, Georgie, not just me. It'd be weird if I *didn't* want to fuck you."

Georgie looks moderately appeased by that logic.

"Frankly, if guys on my roster, especially Caleb, think I'm aiming to fuck you, then that's fantastic. In fact, that's precisely what I want them to think."

"What? *Why?*"

My cock feels like it's going to explode from the excitement of Georgina's two incredible orgasms and the closeness of her heaving body in this cramped space. I take a deep breath. "If they think I'm hot for you, then they'll stay the fuck away. The guys on my roster know not to cross me. They've seen what happens when they do. I've got them well trained."

"What does that mean?"

"It means I've made it clear in the past I don't play nice when someone on my roster fucks a woman I'm already fucking or have set my sights on fucking."

Her eyebrows rise. "How have you made it clear? What happened?"

"It doesn't matter. All that matters is them knowing I want to fuck you, whether I've been successful in doing that or not. That's enough to make you off-limits to them."

I scowl. "I'm not your property, Reed. You can't call dibs on me like the front seat of a Chevy. I'm a professional journalist. Here to do a job and do it well. If I happen to be fucking you on the side, then that has nothing to do with my job. The two things are completely separate."

Holy shit. She's so fucking sexy when she's angry, I can't contain myself. I press myself into her so she can feel how hard she makes me. How badly I want to get inside her. "Of course, you're here to do a job. That's indisputable. And, of course, you're going to do your job well. Now, tell your brain to shut the fuck up, would you? You're overthinking this. *Nothing's changed.* The PA will say nothing but what I told her to say. Our deal is still in full force and effect—we're gonna have a fun week together at my house, during which you're gonna try to use sex as a weapon to pull more out of me for my interview than I ever thought possible, and I'm gonna let you think it's working like gangbusters so I can keep fucking you and eating your sweet pussy all week long. It'll be a great time had by all." I skim my nose along her jawline while pressing my cock into her center, and she rubs herself against my hard-on in reply. "Come on, baby. Use me for a good time. Use me to try to get yourself a job with *Dig a Little Deeper.* Use me to make all your dreams come true." I press myself even harder into her and bite her earlobe. "Use me however you want, Georgie, just as long as you let me use your body this entire week, starting right now. Baby, I've never been so turned on by anyone in my life, I swear to God, and I don't think I can survive the night if I don't get inside you right fucking now."

A little moan of arousal escapes her throat as she continues riding my straining bulge—until, finally, she throws her arms around me, turns her head, and smashes her mouth against mine.

Instantly, the second my lips meet Georgie's, a dam breaks inside me. A tsunami of arousal slams into me. Panting, I frantically unzip my pants as Georgina furiously pulls down her undies, whimpering with arousal as she does.

"I'm on the pill," she gasps out. It's a comment that only makes me realize I hadn't even thought about protection—which is so unlike me, so utterly out of character, I don't even know who I am right now. What spell has this sexy girl cast on me?

She pulls my hard cock out of my briefs, its head already dripping with the evidence of my blossoming addiction to her. Breathing hard, I grab her ass, pick her up roughly, slam her into a shelf, and impale her, thrusting hard into her until I'm balls-deep and growling with relief. Oh, God, she's perfect. Wet. Tight. Warm. *Bliss.* Just this fast, I'm losing my fucking mind.

Georgina moans my name as I growl hers and begin thrusting like an animal against the shelf. As I get into a groove, she digs her fingernails into my shoulders, making me jerk and moan. She bites my neck and begs me not to stop, making me feel like I'm going to pass out.

Her excitement is obviously mounting as I plow into her, over and over again. I'm spiraling. On the brink of exploding.

"Yes," she growls with each powerful thrust. "*Yes, yes, yes.*"

I'm delirious. On the cusp of complete ecstasy. But I hang on, not wanting to release before her. Thankfully, just when I think I can't hang on a second longer, just when I think I might not be able to stay *conscious* a second longer, Georgie comes, *hard*, throwing her head back into the shelf behind her and stiffening exquisitely in my arms as her muscles ripple and clench around my cock. Oh, for the love of all things holy. If there's a more sublime sensation in human existence, than the sensation of Georgina Ricci coming hard around my cock, I can't fathom it. It's a pleasure so intense, so all-consuming and addicting, I can't help coming, too. Which I do, so fucking hard, I'm momentarily paralyzed by the ecstasy shooting through my body, all of it culminating in flashes of blinding white and yellow light.

As I come down from my incredible orgasm, my heart is crashing seismically. My back is soaked in sweat. I place Georgina's feet on the ground, and she immediately tilts her glorious face up to mine for a kiss. Of course, I oblige her, devouring her mouth while raking my hands over her cheeks, neck, and hair. I can't get enough of this woman. This siren. She's my new drug. An addiction I couldn't possibly resist, even if my life depended on it.

When our mouths disengage, Georgina sighs happily. "That was fucking incredible."

I take a deep, shuddering breath, trying to calm my racing heart.

"When you came, that was as close to God as I've ever gotten in this lifetime. Holy shit, Georgie. That was fucking insane."

"I've never had an orgasm during intercourse before. It felt incredible."

I run my thumb over her plump lower lip. "Sweetheart, this is only the beginning. This week, oh my fucking God. I'm gonna show you what your body can do—things you didn't even realize were possible."

She bites her lip. "We're gonna have fun this week, aren't we?"

"Oh, Little Miss Georgina Ricci, you have no fucking idea."

After another deep kiss, we pull our disheveled clothes together, smooth out our frayed hair, and quickly agree to slip out of the closet separately, just in case—with Georgie leaving first.

"I'll meet you in Greenroom B in five," I say.

"See you there," she says flirtatiously. But as she grabs the doorknob, she turns to me, her beaming, wide smile snatching the air out of my lungs. "Thank you for everything, Reed."

My heart stops as paranoia flashes through me. Does she somehow know I'm the source of the cancer charity's grant? Has she figured me out? "I haven't done anything," I say lamely.

"Of course, you have. You've agreed to throw a party and let Alessandra come. You've agreed to listen to Alessandra's demo later tonight at your house. And you've agreed to keep an open mind about your interview—to let me at least *try* to get something suitable for *Dig a Little Deeper* out of you. I'd say you've already done a whole helluva lot."

Sighing with relief, I return her smile. "I only said that last thing so I could get into your pants. Don't get too excited."

Her smile widens. "Careful what you agree to in a negotiation, Mr. Rivers. After a full week of getting into my pants, I predict you're going to open up to me more than you ever thought possible."

I chuckle. "That's what I want you to think, sweetheart. Don't hold your breath on that."

"We'll see."

"I'm not one of the fraternity boys you're used to wrapping around your little finger for tips. As gorgeous as you are, I'm sure I'll be able to withstand your attempts to 'unpeel my onion' just fine."

"Challenge accepted." With that, she turns the knob, and off she goes... leaving me alone in a janitorial closet, with a body that's alive and pulsing in a way it's never been before, and a mind that's racing. How the hell am I going to spend an entire week fucking that gorgeous woman without breaking down and giving her every last thing her devious little heart desires?

Beautiful LIAR

USA Today and International Bestselling Author
Lauren Rowe

PLAYLIST

Music Playlist for *Beautiful Liar*

"A-YO"—Lady Gaga
"Cringe"—Matt Maeson
"Broken"--LovelyTheBand
"Girl is on My Mind"—The Black Keys
"She's Like Heroin to Me"—The Gun Club
"Obsession"—Animotion
"Waterfalls"—TLC
"Sweet but Psycho"—Ava Max
"My Addiction"—Adam French

TWENTY-EIGHT
GEORGINA

The iron gate in front of Reed's house comes into view in the car's headlights, and I smile to myself. *I can't believe this is my life.* I'm sitting next to Reed in the backseat of the black sedan that's driving us to Reed's house from the Red Card Riot show, and I'm losing my freaking mind. A mere nine days ago, I stood on the other side of that same iron gate, shrieking at Reed to let me out or I'd sue him for negligence and false imprisonment. And now, here I am, wanting nothing more than to get my horny ass back *inside* that damned gate, so Reed can take me to heaven again, the same way he did in that janitorial closet earlier tonight.

"Ah, the scene of the crime," Reed says playfully as the car approaches his house. He squeezes my hand, releasing an unexpected ripple of butterflies into my belly. "Are you, by any chance, feeling the sudden urge to double-flip me off—or perhaps sue me for 'negligence and false imprisonment'?"

I bat my eyelashes at him. "Now, why would I want to do that, when we buried the hatchet so deliciously earlier tonight?"

Reed leans forward and grazes his soft lips against my cheek. "And, oh, how amazing it felt to bury my hatchet inside you, Georgina Ricci. So damned good, I can't wait to bury it again and again, all week long—and even more *deliciously*."

My clit pulses at Reed's words and then throbs with yearning when Reed skims his lips across the length of my jawline. I turn my head, intending to crush my hungry lips against his, but it's not meant to be. The car has stopped, signaling we've arrived at our destination.

"Is there a code?" the driver says, referring to the gate, and Reed shoots me a heated smolder that says, *Hold that thought.*

"We'll just get out here," Reed tosses out.

After we pile out of the sedan together, Reed heads to the trunk to retrieve my suitcase—the one I packed thinking I'd be spending an exciting week on the road with rock royalty—while I head to the gate and stare slack-jawed through its metal slats at Reed's breathtaking house. After a moment, Reed appears at my side, wheeling my suitcase behind him. He unlocks a pedestrian gate and politely gestures for me to pass through first, which I do.

"Are you cold?" Reed asks as I walk by. "You're shaking."

I rub my upper arms. "Just excited. Also, nervous."

"Nervous?" He closes the gate behind us. "There's nothing to be nervous about, Georgie girl. I come in peace. For the next week, my home is yours."

Butterflies. They're not rippling inside me any longer. They're flapping up a damned storm.

"Thank you."

Inside the darkened house, Reed parks my suitcase and flips a switch, and I gasp at the magnificence illuminated before me. Reed's massive living room is fit for a modern-day king. Its ceilings aren't high—they're towering. Floor-to-ceiling windows announce the owner of this manor is literally, and figuratively, on top of the world. Dark wood and ironwork declare a masculine, powerful man resides in this castle. But colorful tiling and unexpected pops of decorative color—sapphire blues, ruby reds, royal purples—make it clear the powerful owner of this manor is a cultured gentleman who isn't afraid to take risks.

Reed motions to my bag at the front door. "Would you like me to bring your suitcase to my bedroom, or would you prefer to sleep in a guest room this week?"

Anticipation flickers across Reed's chiseled face. A flash of vulnerability, I'd even say—like he's momentarily possessed by the spirit of a teenager asking his crush to prom. But as fast as that vulnerability appears on Reed's handsome face, it vanishes again, supplanted by his usual confidence.

But there's no going back. I've caught a glimpse of what lies beneath Reed's usual swagger, however fleetingly—as if I'd gazed out the window of a speeding train and caught the briefest glimpse of a sparkling, silver lake through a thick blanket of pine trees—and, just this fast, I'm instantly hooked and want to see it again.

"I think I'd prefer to sleep in a guest room this week," I say. But I'm lying through my teeth. If I were telling the truth, I'd admit I want nothing more than to sleep next to Reed in his bed this week. But, unfortunately, my gut is telling me, rather forcefully, that carving out a safe space for me to take an occasional time out from Reed, and my thumping lust for him, will go a long way toward keeping me on-track to fulfill my higher purpose. I'm not only here to fulfill my carnal desires, after all. More importantly, I've got a job to do.

"Whatever makes you comfortable," Reed replies smoothly. But he can't hide the flash of disappointment that flickers across his face as he says it. This time, he's not a teenager asking his crush to prom. He's the boy who's just gotten flatly turned down.

I brush my fingertips against Reed's forearm. "Will you give me a tour?"

He clears his throat. "Of course." He turns and gestures to the expansive space. "This is my living room—the place you're going to party like a rock star this Saturday night."

"It's gorgeous."

"This room is the main reason I bought the house. I wanted a place where I could throw epic parties. And when I walked in here, I said to myself, *Bingo*."

"Why so many parties?"

"It's a big part of my business plan. Whenever one of my A-list artists kicks off a tour in LA, I throw their after-party here to celebrate and generate buzz for the tour. I also throw parties to celebrate award nominations and wins. Also, to celebrate whenever one of my artists' albums goes gold or platinum or diamond—which, thankfully, happens a lot these days. Plus, on top of all that, I allow certain charities to throw their annual fundraising galas here."

I look around the impressive space. "Do you ever throw parties here just for fun?"

"Sure. I've hosted bachelor parties and birthday parties. I even had a wedding here—for my best friend, Henn. You met him at the bar."

I nod. "That was sweet of you to let him have his wedding here. You're a good friend."

Reed shrugs. "Henn is a brother to me, and his wife, Hannah, is the best. It was my pleasure to do it for them."

Aw, damn. My heart just skipped a beat. "So, uh, what are some of the charities you've let use the place?"

Reed talks passionately for a bit about his favorite charities—one his sister is heavily involved with that helps kids with cancer, and another devoted to saving the planet. And as he speaks, I have the urge to do two things: one, jump his bones, just because he's yummy as hell, especially when he talks about making the world a better place. And, two, I'm dying to pull out my phone and record him speaking, or at least take furious notes, so I can quote him precisely when I eventually sit down to write my article. But I refrain, figuring Reed might clam up if he sees me pulling out my phone.

"And, of course," Reed says, "CeeCee's favorite charities always have an open invitation to throw their fundraisers here. When it comes to the indomitable CeeCee, my answer is almost always yes."

I shoot Reed a snarky side-eye. "Yeah, unless what CeeCee wants is an in-depth interview for *Dig a Little Deeper*."

Reed chuckles. "I said my answer is *almost* always yes. CeeCee knows she can have anything she wants from me, except *that*."

"Why is that, again?"

"Because the inner workings of my mind and life aren't anybody's fucking business."

I make a face that says, *Well, alrighty then*. And Reed smirks in reply before returning his attention to his expansive living room.

"It might seem like this house is too big for a bachelor to live here alone," he says. "But I've never once regretted buying this place."

Excitement about Saturday night's party ripples inside me. "I can't wait to see your house in action. Thank you so much for throwing the party, and for letting me invite Alessandra."

"No need to thank me. Like I said, I'm throwing the party for business reasons—because I've determined it will help you and the other writer assigned to the special issue bond with my musicians in a way that will elevate the end product."

I flash Reed a snarky look. "Sure, Reed. You not wanting me to party with C-Bomb this week didn't inspire your decision at all."

"Not at all." He matches my snarky expression. "Come on, Intrepid Reporter. There's a lot more to see." He takes two steps and tosses over his shoulder, "And, yes, you can take notes on your phone. But, please, don't record me speaking, unless I've expressly consented."

I stop walking, surprised he's read my mind so accurately, and Reed stops walking, too.

"Georgie, you've got the most expressive face I've ever seen, and I can already read it like a book." He crooks his finger. "Now, come, come, little kitty. I'll show you the whole house, anything you want to see. Just as long as the last stop is my bedroom upstairs."

TWENTY-NINE
GEORGINA

Reed leads me through several rooms on the ground floor of his impressive home, while I "ooh" and "aah" and take furious notes on my phone. He shows me a game room. A wine room. A home theater. We walk down a hallway and turn a corner and, suddenly, I'm standing in the most spectacular kitchen imaginable—a beautiful, sleek space that instantly makes me wish my mother were alive to see it.

"Do you cook?" I ask, running my palm over a sleek countertop.

"I cook breakfast pretty well. But, mostly, it's my housekeeper, Amalia, who cooks in here. Caterers, too."

"When is Amalia at the house, typically?"

"She stays overnight Monday through Thursday every week, unless I've told her to take off at five during any given week. Some weeks, I want complete privacy when I get home from work."

I open my mouth to suggest perhaps this coming week should be one of those weeks of extra privacy, but the clever man beats me to the punch.

"Yes, Georgina. Of course, I've already told Amalia to take off at five every day this week. I had no choice, once I found out you're a screamer. My house is big, but it's not big enough to contain Georgina Ricci's screams of ecstasy."

I swat his shoulder. "I've never screamed like that with anyone but you."

"Well, that's a given." He gestures for me to follow him. "The quicker we get through this tour, the quicker I'll get to hear you scream again."

He leads me through a set of French doors and around a corner, and, suddenly, we're standing on a serene patio, complete with water features, twinkling lights, and manicured bushes and flowers.

"Am I dead?" I ask, looking around the peaceful space. "Is this heaven?"

Reed chuckles. "That's what Henn's wife, Hannah, said when she first saw this patio. That's why I offered to host their wedding here—because Hannah loved it so much."

"I can't believe you let them have their wedding here. That was so generous."

Reed shrugs it off. "All I did was open my house and wallet, and Hannah and her wedding consultant did the rest."

"Wait, you *paid* for the wedding? I thought you meant you let them *use* your house for it—which, right there, would have been an incredibly generous thing to do."

Reed pulls a face like that's a ridiculous notion. "What kind of person says to his best friend, 'Sure, you can *use* my house to marry the love of your life,' but then doesn't foot the bill?"

"Um, plenty of people say that. And I'm sure it's very much appreciated."

Reed waves at the air. "Go big or go home, baby. It's one of my favorite mantras." He points to my phone playfully. "Write that down, Intrepid Reporter. 'Reed lives by the mantra, Go big or go home.'"

I roll my eyes. "I think I can remember you're a big fan of 'going big' without writing it down." I motion to our surroundings. "All I'll have to do is look around me this week to remember that fact."

"Suit yourself. I wouldn't design to tell a professional how to do her job." He flashes me a charming smile. "Ready to move on?"

"Lead on."

I follow Reed down a pathway, past a basketball court, and then past a beach-volleyball court, and a moment later, we're standing next to an elegant black-bottom swimming pool overlooking the twinkling lights of Los Angeles.

"This is spectacular," I say. "I love swimming—being weightless. If I lived here, I'd swim laps every day of my life. Or maybe, just come out here to float."

"Feel free to use the pool any time you like. It's heated."

"Thank you. I'll definitely take you up on that. Although, given that I didn't pack a swimsuit, I think I'll wait until after Amalia leaves each day. I wouldn't want to give the poor woman an unexpected view of my ass."

Reed arches his brow, his dirty thoughts etched all over his face. "As you wish. Full disclosure, though..." He gestures above us, to a second-story wall of windows. "That's my bedroom right there. If I hear a splash, I'm gonna head straight to my window, hoping to see an unexpected view of your ass."

"As you wish. As long as you join me after I've gotten my workout in."

"No need to swim as your work out. I work out every morning, first thing. I was assuming my shadow would join me."

"Oh, I love morning workouts. I taught some morning classes at the gym at UCLA."

"You *taught* classes?"

I nod. "Spin and Pilates."

He gestures to my body. "Well, that answers that question. Well, hell. If you like spin, you should try out my Peloton this week."

"Oh! I've always wanted to try one." I frown. "Except... shoot. I didn't pack my cycling shoes, any more than a swimsuit... probably because I *thought* I'd be on the road this week with one of my favorite bands."

Reed pulls out his phone, ignoring my snarky tone. "What's your shoe size, Ricci?"

"Oh. No. I didn't mean for you to—"

"I insist."

"I can't let you buy me cycling shoes, Reed."

"Tell me your damned shoe size, or I'll sic Amalia on you. And trust me, you don't want a determined Amalia on your ass."

Reluctantly, I tell Reed what he wants to know, and he places the order.

"Thank you. You're making me feel right at home."

"My home is yours." He drinks me in for a long beat, brazenly undressing me with his eyes. "How about we cut this tour short, and head straight to the last stop?"

"Nope," I say. "I want the full tour. Plus, don't pop a stiffy yet, dude. You're not getting into my pants again until you've fulfilled your end of our bargain."

He looks at me blankly.

"Alessandra's demo? You're required to listen to the first minute of all three songs."

"Aren't you forgetting a little something? Before I'm required to listen to a single song on that demo, you're required to give me two lap dances and a striptease."

I scoff. "I've already paid my debts to you, and then some. Letting you eat me out at the stadium was the equivalent of *five* stripteases. And the way you fucked me in that closet was the equivalent of *ten* lap dances. Plus, regardless, all bets were off the minute that PA walked in on us, and saw my tits and wahoo hanging out, and you camped between my legs with shiny lips. That was the most humiliating thing that's ever happened to me, Reed. I get a free pass for that."

Reed chuckles. "Fair enough. All right. I hereby release you from your debts, on one condition: I'll listen to the demo in bed—while lying next to you."

I raise my index finger. "If we're *on top* of the bed, yes. Not *in* it. And if we're fully clothed."

He chuckles. "On top of the bed, but in our pajamas."

I pause. "Agreed."

He winks. "Tricked ya. I sleep in the nude."

I giggle. "You've got to wear sweatpants, at least, or we'll get too distracted and never make it through the entire demo."

"I'll wear briefs. That's my final offer."

I roll my eyes. "Fine, but I'm wearing my actual pajamas."

He grins. "Always such a fierce negotiator. All right. Our contract is hereby amended. Sign here." He puts out his palm and I mime signing my name across it. And then, with a charming, seductive smile, he slides his hand in mine and leads me away from his swimming pool to continue the tour.

"And here I thought only guys with small dicks had a thing for sports cars," I say. "I couldn't have been more wrong."

We're standing in Reed's expansive garage, which is filled with not one, not two, not three, but *six* gleaming sports cars. As we've walked down the line of them, Reed has waxed poetic about all of them—although none more so than his Bugatti, parked at the far end. His pride and joy.

After Reed has finished telling me about his car collection, we come upon an elaborate shelving unit on the far end of the garage that's filled to bursting with outdoor-adventure and sporting equipment. I ask him a few questions about all of it, just to be thorough, and he talks enthusiastically about his love of fitness. I gesture to a surfboard, and he tells me a few stories. I gesture to a set of golf clubs and ask if he's a big golfer, expecting him to nonchalantly dazzle me with his prowess on the links. But to my surprise, Reed says he hates golf. "I'd actually rather get a root canal than spend a day golfing."

"Then why do you have a fancy set of clubs? Just in case you wake up one day with the nagging impulse to torture yourself?"

Surprisingly, the question elicits a contemplative expression from Reed. A deep furrow in his brow, followed by a deep exhale. "Okay, Intrepid Reporter," he says. "I'm going to throw you a bone, kid. I promised CeeCee I'd let you unpeel *one* layer of my onion during this interview. So, let's unpeel it now, and get it out of the way—like ripping off a Band-Aid. That way, we can relax the rest of the week with no stress."

"Sounds great," I say, even though I'm thinking, *Oh, honey, if you think I'm stopping at one layer unpeeled, then you don't know me at all.*

For a moment, Reed runs his fingertips over the gleaming head of a golf club, looking lost in thought. Finally, he says, "When I was growing up, my father was obsessed with golf. So, of course, since I idolized my father, I wanted to be obsessed with golf, too."

Holy crap. I didn't see that coming at all. I can't believe Reed is talking about his father, without any coaxing.

Reed says, "My father used to golf every weekend. And, of course, during the week, he was busy with work and his mistresses. Although I didn't know about that second thing until much later. All I knew was, if I wanted to spend time with my father, which I did, then I had to pick up golf and tag along with him on the weekends."

My pulse is thumping in my ears. My fingers feel like they're physically itching with the urge to take notes. But I stand still, holding my breath, afraid to do or say anything that might break this unexpected spell. I don't know what's prompted Reed to give me this scoop, and I don't want to do anything to make him change his mind.

"Finally, around age twelve, about a year before my father got arrested, I could finally hit from the back tees, where he teed off. And, man, he was so proud of that. In the clubhouse, my father would tell anyone who'd listen, 'My boy, Reed, is only twelve, and he's already hitting off the back tees!'" Reed looks wistful for a beat, before his face darkens. "And then, out of nowhere, the FBI raided our house at dawn one morning and dragged him away. Suddenly, his face was all over the news. The press was saying he was some kind of monster. But since I knew he was innocent, I kept playing golf every weekend by myself, so I'd continue making progress, and continue making him proud once the trial was over and he came home."

Oh, Reed. The look on his face is making my heart squeeze.

With a deep sigh, he frowns at his golf clubs like they're flipping him off. "Obviously, nothing worked out the way twelve-year-old Reed thought it would. The jury convicted my father on all counts. He got sentenced to one hundred sixty-seven years in federal prison. And, for the first time, I devoured all the articles about him. I learned about the mountain of evidence against him. And I realized the jury had gotten it right. My father had done all of it. He'd lied and cheated and stolen, over and over again, while pretending to be a pillar of the community." He sighs. "And, all of a sudden, I felt ashamed to be me. Ashamed of my name. I worried people would think I'm just like him. A liar and a thief." His dark eyes find mine. "And I sure as fuck didn't want to play fucking golf anymore."

My stomach clenches at the hardness in his eyes. "I'm so sorry for everything you've been through in your childhood, Reed."

"Everybody's got shit from their childhood. Terrence Rivers just happens to be mine." His Adam's apple bobs. He manages a thin smile. "All right, Intrepid Reporter. My onion has now officially been peeled, in accordance with my promise to CeeCee. How about I show you some memorabilia in my home office now?" He gestures to a side door. "From there, I'll show you the gym upstairs, your room... and, finally, mine."

THIRTY
REED

"This is so cool!" Georgie says, shoving her nose into a framed gold record on the wall. For the past ten minutes, I've been showing her various items of memorabilia in my home office, figuring it'll go into her article. And, as expected, she's been geeking out over all of it.

"That one was for RCR's debut," I explain, chuckling at Georgina's enthusiasm. "It was my first gold record, so I keep it here, rather than with the others at the office. When I got that first one, I didn't even have a full-time staff yet. River Records was just me, hustling my ass off. So I feel like it belongs here."

"You must be so damned proud of everything you've accomplished. Hell, *I'm* so damned proud of you."

I try not to smirk like an asshole at how adorable she is right now. So fresh-faced and excited. But, truly, in this moment, Georgie being "proud" of me is like a cute little house kitten congratulating the king of the jungle on a kill.

"Have I said something that amuses you?" she asks, resting her hand on her hip.

I pause. Shit. Apparently, this girl can read me like a book. "Only in the sense that I find your enthusiasm and adorableness slightly amusing."

"See, the thing is, though, when you look at me like I'm a silly little girl when I'm simply talking, it comes off as condescending—like you think I'm stupid or you're somehow better than me. I mean, yes, I realize you're wildly successful. But that doesn't make you an inherently better or smarter person than me."

Oh, for the love of fuck. "Georgie, I don't think you're silly or stupid whatsoever. On the contrary, I think you're wickedly smart. And I don't think I'm better than you, or anyone else. I mean, yes, of course, I think I'm better than ninety-nine percent of the world's population in terms of my business acumen, at least in my industry. And, yes, I *know* I'm better in bed than any man you'll ever sleep with in your entire life. But, other than those two areas, I'm fully aware I'm just a humble, ordinary guy making his way through life, as best he can."

She rolls her eyes. "There are many adjectives to describe you, Reed Rivers. But humble and ordinary aren't two of them."

I cross my arms over my chest, beaming a huge smile at her. "You know, Georgie, when you roll your eyes at me like that, when I'm simply trying to have a conversation with you, it comes off condescending. Like you think I'm silly and stupid and you're better than me."

"Good. I'm glad you've understood my body language to a tee."

I chuckle.

"But, don't worry, I only think I'm better than you when it comes to a few distinct things: brains, beauty, and emotional intelligence. Other than those three areas, I'm fully aware I'm just a girl—a silly, adorable girl, who's play-acting confidence in her mommy's heels and doing the best she can to make her way through life."

I shake my head. "You're never going to forget that 'mommy's heels' comment, are you?"

"Never. Brace yourself. You're going to hear it a lot this week."

"Lovely." I perch an ass cheek on the edge of my desk. "Look, if I come off as condescending or arrogant at times, it's only because... *I am.*"

She chuckles. "Well, points for honesty."

"I couldn't do what I do for a living, and have the success I've had, without sincerely believing I'm the best. But that doesn't mean I think I'm an inherently more valuable *human* than anyone else. In a lot of ways, I still feel like that same college kid who couldn't afford to fix the slipping transmission and busted window on his shitty-ass Honda."

"Well, that explains your six fancy sports cars."

"Seven, actually. My beloved Ferrari is in the shop."

"Oh, no. So sorry to hear that. Whatever will you do until your *seventh* sports car is returned safely to you?"

"Barely survive? Cry into my pillow every night? It'll be tough, but I'll soldier on."

"I'm sure the Bugatti will help get you through."

"Barely."

"So, what's wrong with your beloved Ferrari?"

"The front right fender got bashed in a couple weeks ago. It broke my damned heart."

"What happened?"

"It was the craziest thing. I was driving on Mulholland, taking a curve a bit too fast, when a tree jumped out into the middle of the road, right in front of me. Too quick to swerve."

I'm thinking she'll return my joking demeanor, but she looks concerned. "Were you hurt?"

I shift slightly on the edge of my desk. "No. But I can't say the same for the front right fender of my Ferrari. It was smashed up pretty badly."

Without warning, Georgina beelines to me at the edge of my desk, nudges her way between my thighs, and kisses me. I don't know what's prompted this sudden, urgent display of affection from her, but I don't question it. Without hesitation, I wrap my arms around her back and return her kiss with passion, every cell in my body exploding with desire for her.

Finally, when we break free from our passionate kiss, Georgie nuzzles her nose along my jawline and whispers, "I'm so glad you weren't hurt in that crash. The world would really miss having Reed Rivers in it."

Goosebumps erupt on my arms and neck. *Where did this come from?* "Hey, are you okay? I'm fine. Really."

She nods. "It just scares me to think everything can change in the blink of an eye. That someone as young and fit as you could have been gone, just like that." She snaps her fingers. "Sorry. Was that too dark?"

I smile sympathetically. I'm sure Georgina's thought a lot about mortality these last few years, with her father fighting for his life. Far more than most people her age would think about it. "No, it's a good reminder. I was cocky driving around that corner. Going way too fast. It was a good wake-up call for me that I'm not actually invincible."

She nods her approval and then resumes looking around the room. She looks at a framed magazine article—a *Forbes* "30 Under 30" piece featuring me. She runs her fingertips across the spines of the books on my shelf. Self-help, motivational, business, and fitness titles, mostly. And then she notices a small framed photo on my desk.

"Is this you?" she asks, picking up the frame.

It's my favorite photo from when I was a kid. The one shot from my childhood where my smile, and my mother's, too, seemed genuine and not put on for the camera. It's also the one shot I've got that includes both my mother and Amalia. Also, a shot from my one and only childhood birthday party—the one time in my life when my mother, still grieving Oliver, somehow pulled her shit together enough to do that thing all the other kindergartners' mothers had done that year for my classmates: she threw me a big birthday party with balloons and a cake and paper plates bearing images of my favorite cartoon. It never happened again. But, to this day, I remember how much fun I had at that once-in-a-lifetime party. How much fun Mom had, too. Truly, I felt like I'd died and gone to heaven that unique, carefree day with my mother and Amalia and the kids from school—the mysterious place my mother had always told me my big brother Oliver had gone to live.

"Yeah, that's me with my mother and Amalia. That shot was taken on my fifth birthday."

"Amalia, as in, your housekeeper, Amalia?" Georgina says in surprise. "I didn't realize you've known Amalia your entire life."

I gaze at the photo in Georgina's hand. "Amalia was already working for my family when I was born. She only stopped when my father went to prison, when I was thirteen."

For a split-second, the chaos of that time flickers through my mind. I remember the shock of it all. The early morning raid by the FBI that took my father away from me forever. The shock I felt at being ripped away from Amalia and sent to live with some distant relative I'd never met before, since Mom was already living in a facility by then, thanks to the stress of the custody battle a few years earlier.

"And when did Amalia come back into your life?" Georgina asks, still looking at the photo.

I clear my throat. "About ten years later. The minute I could afford to pay Amalia a salary, she was my first 'purchase.' Long before my first sports car. I think I hired Amalia right after I'd turned twenty-four?"

"Aw, that's so sweet, Reed. That makes my heart go pitter-pat." She returns the photo to its spot on my desk, her face aglow. "What a lucky little boy you were to have not *one*, but *two*, mothers growing up."

I try to return Georgina's easy smile, but I can't. The little boy in that photo wasn't lucky. Far from it. And he didn't have *two* mothers. He barely had one. But only because two halves make a whole. In truth, my mother has never been fully functional. Not like other kids' mothers. And nothing like the kickass, nurturing mothers I've observed as an adult, like Henn's mother and my sister's mother-in-law. Hence, the reason my father hired Amalia in the first place: to help my woefully ill-equipped mother with Oliver when he was born. And, as much as I love and appreciate Amalia, and can't imagine life without her, I can't honestly say she's a "whole" mother to me, either, simply because she's my employee. In reality, I pay her to mother me. I pay her to love me. I'm literally the woman's job. What would it be like to have a mother like Amalia who's not on my payroll? I can't even imagine it.

"You and your mother aren't close?" Georgina asks tentatively, apparently reacting to something she's seeing on my face.

Shit. Is this woman a mind reader? "No, we're close," I say. It's a knee-jerk reaction. I don't talk about my mother. She's an aspect of my life I don't share with anyone, other than the staff at her facility. But Georgina's looking at me like she's unconvinced. Like she saw *something* on my face that doesn't jibe with my words. My cheeks flush. "It's just that my mother lives on the East Coast, so I don't get to see her as much as I'd like."

"Oh," Georgina says. "That's too bad."

"Yeah, I visit her whenever I get to New York on business, though. Which I do about once or twice a month."

Georgina looks thrilled by that response. "Oh, I'm so glad you're able to visit your mother so much, Reed. Both for your benefit, and hers. What do you do with your mom when you visit her?"

Fucking hell. Seriously? How did our conversation about my music memorabilia and the *Forbes* "30 Under 30" list wind up *here*—with talking about my mother? And, more importantly, how do I steer it back to the stuff I actually want her to write about?

"Um... well. My mother and I do all sorts of things when I visit her. We play Scrabble. We watch *Jeopardy* and eat chicken pot pies. We do yoga."

"Yoga? You do *yoga* with your mom? Oh my gosh, Reed. *Swoon*."

I bite my lower lip. She's swooning over *that*? I can't help returning her beaming smile. Actually, she looks so damned cute right now, so over-the-top adorable, I'm momentarily forgetting to be annoyed by this topic. "Yeah. We do yoga. Play ping pong and gin rummy. My mom loves to paint, so she's always got her latest masterpiece to show me, too. Whatever Mom wants to do, I'm always there for it."

Georgina puts her hand on her heart and sighs like a Disney princess looking into a wishing well. "That's the sweetest thing I've ever heard in my life. I love that you're so close to your mother. It makes my heart hurt, it's so sweet." Georgina flashes me another beaming smile that makes my heart physically palpitate before she says, "My father always told me, 'If you want to know the measure of a man, look no further than the way he treats his mother.'"

I nod vaguely, not sure how to respond to that. If you ask me, the measure of a man is the empire he's built from dirt, with nothing but his blood, sweat, and tears. But okay. Tomato. Tomahto.

"You grew up in LA, right?" Georgina asks.

"Correct."

"Why did your mother move to the East Coast? Does she have family back there? Did she remarry?"

What the serious fuck? She's relentless. A dog with a meaty bone. "Uh, she... yeah, my mother grew up in Scarsdale, and has family back there. She's never remarried, but she does have a serious boyfriend. This guy named Lee. They live together."

"Oh, how saucy. Good for her." She laughs. "I think it's wonderful for your mother to have a companion later in life. Do you like Lee? Is he nice? Does he join in when you and Mom do yoga?"

Seriously, how the fuck am I talking about this with Georgina? I've had that same goddamned framed photo on my desk since I moved into this house five years ago, and nobody has ever noticed it or asked me about it. Not *once*. But in walks Georgina Ricci, the Intrepid Reporter, and in a matter of minutes, she's sniffed it out—and then pushed and pushed for more and more. I thought telling Georgina that story in the garage about my father and golf would more than satisfy her hunger for personal details. Is she going to be on my ass for stories like this about my life all week?

I want to say, "Enough about this. Moving on." But I'm positive that will only backfire on me. Spur her on more. Put her on the scent. So, instead, I say calmly, "Lee is a nice enough guy. He's really quiet, though, so it's hard to get to know him. But my mother loves him, and that's all that matters to me. And, yes, he occasionally joins in on yoga. But just barely."

Georgina giggles. "I love hearing you talk about your close relationship with your mother. Does she come visit you in California? I bet she's so proud of you and all you've accomplished."

Jesus Christ. When will this torture end? If Georgina loves mothers so much, maybe she should call up hers and have a nice, long chat, and leave mine alone. But there's no way I'm going to let Georgina know this is a sensitive topic for me. If I do, my gut tells me she'll only be *more* intrigued—which would make this one hell of a long week for me.

"My mother visits me occasionally," I lie. "I've actually offered to set her up in a place in Malibu, right on the beach, but she prefers living at her current place with Lee. Lee's got family in the City, apparently. Plus, he's got some health issues that prevent him from traveling, so they've decided to stay put in Scarsdale for the foreseeable future."

Georgina glides to me, wedges herself between my thighs, slides her arms around my neck, and nuzzles her nose against mine. "You want to hear something super kinky?"

"There's no need to ask me that question. My answer to it will always be a resounding yes."

She giggles. "The fact that you keep that photo on your desk, and visit your mom regularly—and do yoga and play Scrabble with her, and make her happiness your top priority..." She physically swoons in my arms with a heavy, happy, sexy sigh. "Oh, God, Reed. All of that *really* turns me on."

The butterflies in my stomach turn into a hard-on—one that's giving me instant amnesia about the annoyance I've been feeling about this topic. I slide my arms around Georgie and smile broadly at her. *"That's what turns you on? What kind of sick fuck are you, Georgina Ricci?"*

She giggles. "Maybe when you go back East on your next business trip, I could come with you to meet your mom? I'd love to chat with her about what you were like as a little boy."

Well, that's a nonstarter, obviously. But she feels so good in my arms, and smells so damned good, I find myself lying to her face. "Maybe. We'll have to see how scheduling works out."

Squealing, Georgina kisses my cheek, and then proceeds to lay soft kisses up and down my jawline that harden my thickening dick to steel. Her lips against my ear, she whispers, "I'm so glad I'm staying here with you, instead of at a hotel. Seeing you in your natural habitat has been a huge turn-on for me."

I turn my head and bring my mouth to hers, and when my tongue slides into her mouth, fireworks explode inside me. We kiss for several delicious minutes, our tongues dancing, our lips devouring, our bodies becoming more and more ravenous. Finally, when we disengage, Georgie looks as aroused as I feel.

"Come on, baby," I say, running my thumb over her bee-stung lower lip. "Let's take this house tour upstairs."

THIRTY-ONE
GEORGINA

Freshly showered and clad in a white tank top and soft, pink shorts with "Sassy Pants" on the ass, I knock on Reed's bedroom door.

"*Entrez*," his sexy voice calls from behind the door.

Clutching Alessandra's demo, I open the door and step inside the vast room... and gasp at the sensuous scene before me. As expected, Reed is wearing nothing but briefs. Sexy black ones, to be exact. But expecting him to be nearly naked, after previously seeing online photos of him in swim trunks, is a very different thing than seeing this god among men nearly naked in person. He's mouthwatering, this man. Scrumptious. Delicious. An erotic work of art.

He's lying atop his bed. Also, as expected. But this isn't any normal bed. It's a massive wood-carved four-poster that's, not surprisingly, fit for a king. Its frame is imposing and masculine. Its mattress covered in a ruby-red duvet and sumptuous pillows of gold, blue, and purple. If Henry VIII were alive today, he'd sleep in this bed.

And the cherry on top of this fantastical cake? Or, rather, the *mirror*? Reed's got one on his ceiling. A mirror. Directly above his porno-king bed. It's a feature that turns me on and amuses me in equal measure.

"Nice mirrored ceiling," I say, my tone bursting with snark as I walk across the room. "I didn't know that was an actual thing, except maybe in music videos and porn."

"Hey, don't knock it till you've tried it."

"I'm not. I'm *mocking* it before trying it."

He chuckles. "Trust me, little kitty. Watching yourself having sex is gonna get you off like crazy. It's like watching yourself in a live-action sex tape. So fucking hot." He pats the mattress next to him, his eyes blazing. "Come here, kitty-kitty."

I do as I'm told. I climb onto the bed next to him, still clutching the demo. But when he leans in to kiss me, I hold out the flash drive, sensing one kiss, and I'll quickly forget about the demo for the rest of the night. "I look forward to watching myself getting fucked by you in your mirrored ceiling *after* you listen to *this*. All three songs. A minute each. A deal's a deal."

Reed eyes the demo in my hand, but takes it, although he's looking at it with downright disdain.

My stomach flip-flops. "You promised, Reed."

"Yes, I know." He exhales. "But we need to set some ground rules. Before I listen, I need you to promise that, whatever my ultimate opinions on that demo might be, you're going to react calmly and with maturity."

I roll my eyes. "Remember that thing I said about you coming off as condescending at times? Yeah, well, this is one of those times."

"It needs to be said, Georgie. This is business for me. Nothing personal whatsoever. I want you to promise you won't react emotionally if things don't go as you're hoping. Whatever happens, I don't want this demo to get in the way of us having a great time tonight and during this entire week."

"I'm an adult, Reed. *Of course*, I know this is business for you. Whatever happens, I'll handle it calmly and in a mature fashion, and *without* letting my emotions run wild. Unless, of course, you fall head over heels for her, at which point I'm going to attack you with so much *wild* emotion, I might accidentally snuff the very life out of you. I apologize profusely in advance, if I wind up ending your life out of pure, unadulterated joy." I giggle, but he remains steadfast and serious. Which makes my stomach somersault again. "Reed, all of this is a moot point. I'm *positive* you're going to absolutely love what you hear. But, in the event you're on the fence, I promise to hear you out and respect whatever you say, as long as you're being honest with me."

"Of course I'll be honest. One hundred percent honest."

My stomach seizes with nerves. All my bravado leaves me. Holy shit. *This is it.* I'm ninety-nine percent certain Reed will love Alessandra... but what if he doesn't? I can't fathom having to call Alessandra and tell her Reed finally listened... and wasn't impressed. Making that call would break my heart. But there's no going back now.

"I'm ready," I say. "Go ahead."

Nodding, Reed pushes the flash drive into the side of his laptop. And a moment later, there she is. Alessandra. In a video. Sitting in a small studio, strumming her guitar, and singing from the depths of her soul.

I hold my breath. Wring my hands. And watch Reed as he watches Alessandra's video. I think I'm pretty good at reading him, but he's completely unreadable to me now. Indeed, just this fast, he's flipped into full-throttle business mode, despite the fact that we're lying together, almost naked, on top of his bed. Indeed, just this fast, we might as well be sitting across from each other at his desk at River Records.

I peek at the counter at the bottom of the video and my spirit cautiously surges. Reed's now watched Alessandra's video a solid forty seconds longer than he listened to Bryce's sister! That's got to be a good sign, right? But I've no sooner made that observation than Reed pauses the video.

"Okay," he says, his voice devoid of emotion. "Which file do you want me to play next?"

Shit. Fuck. He stopped Ally's video at exactly the one-minute mark —precisely the length of time he'd promised to listen. If he loved her, wouldn't he listen longer, despite what he promised? "That one." I point to his screen. "It's an audio file. No video. But her voice on this one is especially—"

"We'll let the song speak for itself," he says bluntly. "The time to try to charm and sell me is over, Georgie."

Holy fuck. I shoot him a look that says, *Well, shit. No need to be rude about it.* But he's not looking at me. Indeed, without so much as a glance at me, Reed clicks on the file I've indicated. And, once again, Alessandra's voice is wafting from his laptop speaker.

It's rinse and repeat. Reed listens, stoned-faced and impassive, for exactly one minute, before pausing the song and moving on to the third file. Another audio file. Which he then listens to for exactly one minute, without giving away a damned thing.

And that's it.

The room is filled with nothing but the sound of my anxious breathing now. Reed has listened to all three songs on Alessandra's demo, as promised. And he's right: the time for scheming and negotiating and flirting and middle fingers raised to the sky is over. Alessandra's music must now speak for itself, without any help from me. I let out a slow exhale, feeling nervous and frayed.

Reed slowly closes his laptop. He purses his lips. And, finally, looks at me, his dark eyes intense and giving nothing away. "She's talented," he says matter-of-factly. "She's got good vocal control. A nice texture to her voice. There's no doubt she deserved her spot at Berklee."

I nod, feeling like I'm going to pass out.

"One day, when she figures out who she is as an artist, as a person, I'm sure she'll blossom. But, as things stand now, she's not there yet. Not even close, if I'm being honest. I'm sorry, Georgie. She's a pass for me."

It's worst-case scenario. Way worse than I could have imagined. A truly gut-wrenching disappointment. Without meaning to do it, I whimper and then clutch Reed's arm with urgency.

"If you saw Alessandra perform live, I know you'd be able to see how special—"

"No, Georgie. Don't. It's over. I'm not on the fence about her. Not in the least. She's not for me."

I can't believe my ears. I feel physically sick. Like the room is spinning. "But... when you listened to Bryce's sister, you said young artists always need room to grow and develop." Tears begin welling in my eyes, unbidden, despite my fervent desire to keep my eyes dry as a bone. "Ally just needs a little professional guidance. If she could get some coaching to help boost her confidence, I know—"

"Georgie, stop. Please. My answer is no."

I blink and the tears welled in my eyes squirt down my cheeks.

"Aw, Georgie. I knew this would happen." He reaches out to wipe my cheek with this thumb, but I jerk my face away, too ashamed at myself for crying in front of him, for doing exactly what I promised I wouldn't do, to let him comfort me. Actually, he's the last person I want comforting me right now. I hate that I'm reacting like this. In fact, I'm livid with myself for it.

But when I jerk away from Reed, it's immediately clear he's misinterpreting my body language. He doesn't know I'm angry with myself. He thinks I'm punishing *him*. Taking my proverbial ball from the playground after not being chosen for a team and marching home.

"So predictable," he says, his tone turning acidic on a dime. "I don't get to touch the merchandise if I didn't pay your *price?*"

I'm shocked. Disgusted. *Pissed.*

Shaking his head, Reed retracts his hand from me and says, his voice low and intense, "Yes, Georgina. I told you young artists often need time to grow and develop. You might recall, however, that I made that comment when I *thought* we were having a conversation about music scouting *in general*. When I didn't have a clue we were *actually* talking about your stepsister, specifically. If I'd been privy to that information, then I would have clarified that, yes, I'm willing to help a young, wild bucking bronco of an artist learn to rein him or herself in a bit. To control their wildness. There's nothing better than barely contained chaos. But what I'm not willing to do, Georgina, *ever*, is try to coax a painfully shy pony who's afraid of her own shadow to poke her goddamned head out of the barn and take a fucking risk."

I gasp. *Asshole.*

"Life is too fucking short to try to coax someone out of their shell."

I'm aghast. Flooded with a whole bunch of emotions. Anger. Shock. Regret. Disappointment. Embarrassment. But, yeah, mostly...*rage*. At Reed, for being a dick right now. He doesn't want to sign Alessandra? Okay. Fine. No need to be a prick about it.

I know this is business to him, but I'm lying next to him on his bed in my pajamas, while he's nearly naked. It's not like we're sitting across from each other at his office! It's not like I'm some stranger off the street, like that poor girl who asked him to listen to her demo at the bar—but he's treating me exactly like her! After fucking me—after eating me out—am I seriously *no* different to him than that poor girl at the bar? Would it kill him to soften his rejection, just this once, so as not to decimate me?

But I'm equally mad at myself, as well, for being stupid enough to say the words "painfully shy" to Reed about Alessandra the other night.

Obviously, I doomed my poor stepsister in Reed's eyes before he'd even heard her first note. Why was I so stupid?

Reed exhales. "Look, I know this is disappointing to you, but that's life. You promised you'd handle my opinion maturely, and that's exactly what I expect you to do."

Adrenaline surging inside my veins, I leap up from the bed and barrel toward the door. If I don't extract myself from this situation for a bit to cool down, I'll surely say something I'll regret.

"Goddammit," Reed barks from behind me. "Don't be so dramatic, Georgie. You promised you wouldn't let my opinion affect our time together."

I whirl around at the door. "Okay, first off, I'm not being *dramatic*, Reed. This isn't an act, designed to get a reaction out of you. I'm sincerely, genuinely crushed and in need of a minute to process my overwhelming and unexpected emotions." I'm shaking. Flailing. "Gee, I'm so sorry if my pesky emotions are screwing up your plan to get laid tonight, but that's life. Yes, it's true I said I wouldn't let your opinion affect our time together, but that was before I knew you'd talk to me like you're *entitled* to my body. You're *not*. You don't want to sign my stepsister to River Records? Fine. Whatever. Your opinion is obviously wrong and stupid, but you're entitled to it. But there's no excuse for you to be a flaming prick about it, especially when I'm sitting next to you barely clothed."

He throws up his hands. "Oh, for the love of fuck. You're going to make this about me, when you're the one who wouldn't let me touch you because I didn't give you what you wanted."

"You don't know what you're talking about. Not everything is about you."

"I'm running a for-profit record label in a cutthroat industry, Georgie. Not the Make-A-Wish Foundation."

I flip him off with my right hand—with the middle finger wearing my mother's wedding ring. And I truly believe she's cheering me on from heaven for doing it.

"So mature," he says. "And so predictable."

"Oh, I'm sorry. Was that too 'dramatic'?" I say mockingly. "Am I play-acting in my mommy's heels? Well, guess what, Reed? I wish I were play-acting in my mommy's heels. Unfortunately, I haven't had the pleasure of wearing my mommy's heels, whether to play-act in them, or just dress up for a special night out, since I was nine. Which is when she died in a car accident. So, don't say a fucking word about my mommy's heels ever again!"

He's stricken. Pained. Full of regret. "Oh, Georgie. I had no idea."

"And then my father married Alessandra's mother, and it felt like my mother had died a second time." I wipe my eyes, but it's no use. I'm a hot mess. "I was so full of rage about the wedding, Reed. Crushed. Confused. Betrayed. But Alessandra was sweet about it, even though *her* father had just died. She had every reason to be as angry as I was. She had every reason to lash out, the way I did. But, see, that's not Alessandra Tennison. Whereas I've always lashed *out* when I'm hurt, she's always lashed *in*. Yes, I'm too quick to flip someone off. I own that. But at least, I get it out. That poor girl has struggled her whole life with anxiety and self-doubt and crippling shyness. But she's come so far. She went to that audition for Berklee and *nailed* it. She's come so far out of her shell, you have no idea. And do you know why? *Because of her music.* So, yes, she might still be a sweet little pony who's afraid of her own shadow sometimes. But she's well worth the time and effort to lead her out of the barn. I know, because for years, I was the only person she played her songs for. The only one. She knew I was going through so much, and she'd sing those songs to me and make me feel better. She was my angel. And all I wanted was for something wonderful to happen for her. I just wanted to pay her back for all she's given to me, through her music, and her love, and kind heart, over the years."

"Georgie," Reed says. He gets up from the bed, clearly intending to comfort me.

But I hold up my palm. "Stop."

He stops in the middle of the room, mere feet away from me, his bare chest heaving.

"I get that you couldn't possibly love Alessandra's music the way I do. And I know in your world nobody gets a gold star for progress, only results. But that doesn't mean I don't feel crushed in this moment, to hear your brutally honest opinion. It doesn't mean I'm not allowed to feel whatever I honestly feel, and give myself time to process it and try to move past it. I'm sorry you're not getting laid tonight, like you planned. Like you think you're *owed*. But you should know I'm not withholding my body from you because you didn't give me the result I wanted on the demo. I'm not a spoiled brat. And I'm not a whore. I'm withholding my body from you because I'm pissed at the way you spoke to me. The way you assumed I'm so quick to trade on my body." I take a deep breath. "Now, I'm going to my room to be alone for the rest of the night, to process my emotions and anger, because, if I don't, I'm going to say something I regret. Or, quite possibly, punch you in the face." With that, I swing open Reed's door with gusto, tossing over my shoulder, "See you in the morning, Mr. Rivers. *But only because you're my fucking job.*"

THIRTY-TWO
REED

After Georgina slams my bedroom door shut behind her, I stride to it, every fiber in my body urgently wanting to fling it open and follow her. But I stop myself. Indeed, I stand at the door and press my forehead against it and force myself to stay put.

Goddammit. Why did Georgie have to push so hard about that demo? I knew listening to it would lead to nothing good. *I could feel it in my bones.* But she pushed and pushed. And now, here we are.

Doesn't she know I went in wanting to love Alessandra's music? Doesn't she know nothing would have given me greater pleasure? But I had to be honest. Brutally honest. I'll lie and fudge a little about certain things. But not about my professional judgment. Not for friends or family or anyone else. Not even for the most electrifying girl I've ever met in my life.

Fuck. I thought I'd be tying sexy Georgina's limbs to my bedposts tonight, and then fucking her to bliss like she's never been fucked before. Not making her hate my guts. Yeah, making Georgina storm out of my bedroom tonight most definitely wasn't the plan. Neither was making her cry.

For the love of fuck, how was I supposed to know about Georgina's mother? Somewhere in my brain, I vaguely remember Georgina saying something about Alessandra losing her father as a kid... I think? But

Georgie's never said a word about her own mother. How was I supposed to know Georgina's grief about her mother, and her love for Alessandra, and for Alessandra's music, are all tied up together inside her? I mean, if I'd known that, it wouldn't have changed my opinion in any way. It wouldn't have changed the ultimate result. But *maybe* I would have phrased things slightly differently. With a touch more, I don't know, gentleness? Am I even capable of doing that, though? I sincerely don't know.

Shit!

I want so badly to march into Georgina's room and explain myself. Or maybe, just try to comfort her. But I know I can't. Georgina said she wants to be alone, and I can't chase her. Long before she stormed out, when she was perfectly calm earlier, she requested a separate room, much to my dismay. Which means she didn't want me the way I want her, even before this latest fiasco.

Sighing, I straighten up from the door, drag my exhausted ass back to bed, and turn off my lamp. God, I'm exhausted. This has been a long damned day. I close my eyes and command my body to sleep. But, soon, it's clear my body isn't going to obey. I'm way too wound up.

Muttering expletives, I grab my laptop and click into a licensing agreement requiring my review. But I can't concentrate. Because... *Georgina.*

Goddammit! I knew she'd fly off the handle about the demo. I knew it, without a doubt. Because underneath all that beauty beats the heart of a fucking psycho. There. I said it. She's beautiful and sexy and smart and funny. And the most exciting woman I've ever met. But all that comes with a price. Namely, that she's also a fucking psycho.

I sit up in bed and drag a palm over my face. God, she's sexy as hell when her psycho peeks out. I shouldn't get turned on by her flashes of anger the way I do, but, oh, God, I do. So fucking much.

I sit up, grab my phone, and text Owen: *You up?*

Two seconds later, I get his reply: *No, I'm asleep.*

Calling now.

Oh, yay.

Of course, Owen dutifully picks up after one ring. Because he's Owen.

"Hello, boss," he says. "How lovely to hear from you at midnight after I worked all day and night."

"Yeah, don't you mean after you fucked up? You're the one who let Georgina out of your sight, just long enough for C-Bomb to get her alone."

"I let Georgina out of my sight because she was with Leonard and his daughter, and you texted me a *demand* to meet you outside the VIP door."

"Okay, we're wasting time. Moving on. I need a favor."

I explain what I want and Owen tells me what I'm asking for might as well be the moon and the stars, thanks to the short turnaround time I'm demanding.

"If anyone can work a miracle, it's you," I say.

Owen mutters something under his breath.

"I'll pay triple market price," I toss out. "I don't care how you make it happen. Just do it."

He sighs. "Okay, I'm sure I know someone who knows someone who can help me. I'll see what I can do. No promises, though."

I smile to myself. When Owen Boucher says he'll "see what he can do," the task is as good as done.

"So, based on this 'favor,' I'm assuming Georgina's interview of you is either going very, very well... or you've somehow *really* pissed her off?"

I roll my eyes to myself. Fucking Owen. Nothing gets past him. "It's door number two, unfortunately. She's in my guestroom down the hall at the moment, trying to resist her stated desire to 'punch me in the face.'"

Owen chuckles. "Oh my. What did you do, Reed? And is it wrong I'd kind of like to see her follow through with that threat?"

"I did something monstrous." I flap my lips together. "I didn't sugarcoat my opinion regarding her stepsister's music demo."

"Oh, the horror."

"I know."

"Were you harsh about it?"

"No, I was honest."

"You were harsh."

"No. Well, maybe a little bit. I got pissed for a second there, so maybe I didn't word things as nicely as I should have."

He chuckles. "Was she already planning to sleep in the guestroom before you listened to the demo, or is she freezing you out *because* of the demo?"

"She was already planning to sleep there."

"Well, that's good, right? At least, you know she already hated you, even before you pissed her off."

"There was never any question she'd sleep in a guest room," I lie. "Georgie and I have a purely professional relationship, Owen."

"Oh, really? Then why wasn't I allowed to let C-Bomb get her alone?"

"Which you fucked up."

"And why am I moving heaven and earth to arrange that delivery for first-thing tomorrow morning?"

"For your information, I had the idea to give Georgie this present hours before she wanted to punch me in the face. I just didn't get around to asking you to arrange it before now."

"Uh huh."

"I can give a gift to a woman I'm not romantically interested in. Look how many gifts I've given to CeeCee over the years, to celebrate a birthday or whatever accomplishment."

"CeeCee isn't a twenty-something-year-old fireball who's built like a brick house. And CeeCee isn't staying at your house for a full week, at your invitation, when a hotel would have been perfectly convenient. And CeeCee isn't a woman you won't let tour with RCR, or party with C-Bomb, even though both things would have made for an awesome article, and you know it. Should I go on, or are you going to cut the bullshit?"

"No, don't go on. In fact, shut the fuck up."

He chuckles.

"I'm already cranky, thanks to Georgie hating me and wanting to punch me. Why are you actively piling on?"

Owen laughs uproariously. "Wow, she's really gotten under your skin, hasn't she? Good for her."

I drag my palm over my stubble and say nothing. Because, what is there to say? It's obviously true: Georgina has gotten under my skin. In fact, I think she's done a whole lot more than that, not that I'd admit it to Owen. I'm pretty sure, just this fast, the girl has infiltrated my bloodstream. How the hell did Georgie do that? I've had all my usual guards and defenses up... But, somehow, she keeps finding ways to slither around and through and over them, like they're not even there.

"I've gotta go," Owen declares. "My cranky boss wants something unreasonable, so I've got to move heaven and earth to make it happen. I wouldn't want to get fired."

"You're lucky I didn't fire you tonight, after I found Georgie with C-Bomb."

"I'm counting my lucky stars. I'll call you if I manage to get a delivery scheduled. So leave your ringer on."

I smile broadly. "Thanks, O."

"Just think of me as your personal genie in a bottle."

"Oh, I already do."

We hang up, and I force myself to open up that licensing agreement from before. But I've barely made it through two paragraphs when I hear a splash outside my window that makes every hair on my body stand on end and my skin tingle with anticipation.

I scramble to my floor-to-ceiling windows on the opposite side of the room, and my heart leaps and bounds, every bit as much as my cock twitches. It's Georgina. Swimming laps in the moonlight. Giving me a glorious view of her naked backside.

THIRTY-THREE
REED

My cock is hard as steel and pulsing as I watch Georgina's naked form swimming laps two stories below. Back and forth across the length of my moonlit pool, she goes, her toned legs and arms working furiously. Back and forth she goes, torturing me. Have I ever seen a more perfect ass? I'm certain I haven't. I'm physically aching to bite that ass. To lick it and fuck it. I lean my forehead against the window, breathing hard. Feeling consumed with lust. Yeah, she hates me right now. But, even so, she obviously came outside to give me a show. Which means hating me isn't keeping her from wanting me. Unless, of course, she only came out here to torture me—to dangle what I can't have in front of me. Which, knowing her, is probably the case.

After a while, Georgina stops in the middle of the pool, flips over, and floats on her back. And I'm gone. Jolted with carnal, unadulterated, white-hot lust and desire like nothing I've felt before. I saw swaths and peeks and segments of her gorgeous body earlier tonight at the stadium, but this is the first time I'm seeing her fully nude, all at once, although the dark water lapping at her sides is doing its damnedest to impede my view. And, good lord, she's a wet dream. A goddess. The most beautiful creature I've ever beheld in my life, without a doubt.

My eyes trained on Georgina, I slowly pull my briefs off, freeing my straining cock, and toss them onto the floor. My breathing heavy and tortured, I bound over to my nightstand, open the top drawer, and quickly sift through the accoutrements I keep there—soft cuffs, cords, and various vibrating toys—until I locate a bottle of lube.

After briskly wetting my palm, I return to the window. And with my forehead pressed against the glass, and my eyes trained on Georgina's floating form below, I grip myself and get to work. I move my palm slowly, not wanting to get myself off too rapidly. But that's easier said than done, when your visual is Georgina Ricci floating naked in a moonlit swimming pool.

All too fast, I'm hurtling toward release. I feel my balls tightening. Tingles shooting through my core and cock and balls. I lay my free palm flush against the window, to the side of my forehead, and give myself permission to lose it. But just before I come, Georgina opens her eyes, turns her head, and looks straight at me, shocking the hell out of me and stopping my hand mid-pump.

There's a split-second pause, where neither of us reacts.

I'm a thief. She's a cop with a flashlight.

And then... Georgina smiles. And, thankfully, it's a bold, brazenly sensuous smile. A smile that tells me she likes what she sees. *A lot.*

My eyes locked with Georgina's, I resume my work—this time, far more slowly than before, just in case Georgina gets the bright idea to join me.

Biting her lip, Georgina glides to the side of the pool, hoists herself onto the ledge, and stands underneath my window—giving me my first wholly unimpeded view of her naked body. And she's glorious. Her curves are an hourglass in the moonlight. Her nipples erect. Her wet hair is slicked back, showcasing her high cheekbones and full lips. She's a goddess. A fantasy come to life. And... Oh, God, I think I'm gonna come.

Condensation begins pooling on the glass in front of my face. I'm a caged lion, an unruly beast trapped behind glass, being teased with a slab of meat. Oh, fuck, I'd pay her any amount of money if she'd come to me now and suck my dick. If only she'd get her hot ass up here and let me touch and lick every square inch of her and then fuck her every which way.

"Touch yourself," I mouth to her. And then again. And again. And again. Until, finally, her face lights up with understanding. Her body trembling with arousal, she sits on the ground, spreads her smooth legs wide, and touches herself, right where I'm dying to lick her.

Oh, God, this is so fucking hot.

With a loud groan, I lick at the glass, wishing my tongue were licking her sweet pussy. And that does it for her, apparently. Her eyes roll back into her head, her body stiffens and then quakes with her orgasm.

As my balls tighten and ripple, I grip my cock and aim it right at her tits, and, two seconds later, I'm streaking the glass with the physical evidence of my need. When the deed is done, and my painting complete, I press both palms against the glass, yearning to touch her. It's a good thing I don't do coke anymore. Because, I swear to God, if I were high on blow in this moment, I'd grab that armchair from the corner, crash it into this window, and leap through the jagged, gaping hole to get to her naked body two floors below. Which, obviously, wouldn't be good.

"Come to me," I mouth.

And she immediately responds by rising to her feet, her tits aimed right at me, and lapping at the air with the full length of her tongue, like she's licking up every last drop of my cum off the window.

"Oh, Jesus Christ," I murmur, every cell in my body exploding with desire. *"Come. Here. Right. Now."*

A naughty smile breaks free across her sultry face, telling me she's understood my command perfectly. To my thrill, she moves from her spot... but not to come to me, as instructed. No. Georgina is having too much fun torturing me to do that. She grabs a towel off a nearby lounger and returns to her spot, which is where she begins drying herself off, for my benefit. Slowly, Georgina towels off her arms and shoulders. Slowly, Georgina dries off her perfect tits and stomach and pussy. And, finally, with a little wink, she turns around, bends completely over—thereby giving me a view that nearly gives me a heart attack—and *slowly* proceeds to towel off her feet and shins and calves.

"Oh my God, you evil woman," I whisper, pressing my forehead against the glass. "You're the devil."

Her task complete, she straightens up and turns around to face me again, her tits pushed forward and her nipples erect. And then, with a little swish of her hips, she strides across the patio toward the French doors... and disappears from my line of sight.

My heart crashing with anticipation, I race to my bedroom door and press my ear against it, awaiting the sound of her footsteps in the hallway. She's got to be coming to me now, right? She wouldn't be so cruel as to leave me alone tonight after *that*.

Finally, after what feels like half my lifetime, I hear movement in the hallway. But the sound stops before it gets to my door. Is Georgina standing at the far end of the hallway, deciding whether to come all the way to the end, to my room? Or is she summoning the resolve to head to her own room, just to emphasize her point that, although she's staying here with me, she's far from a sure thing?

Yeah, I know exactly what's going on inside that glorious, devious mind of hers. She's standing at the end of the hallway, deciding which she wants more in this moment: to fuck me... or punish me?

I spear my fingertips into the door, wishing I could physically claw my way through the wood to get to her. Frankly, I'd wear my fingers down to bloody stumps to get to her, if I thought it would convince her to come to my bed tonight. I'd open a vein and give her every last drop of my blood, if it would mean she'd open her thighs to me tonight. I'd pay her any amount of money. The only two things I won't do? Lie about that fucking demo. Or beg. I begged her once, that very first night, right before she double-flipped me off and peeled away in an Uber. And I swear to God, I'll never do it again.

There's movement in the hallway again. Footsteps, as plain as day. I hold my breath and wait. And pray. But the brief footsteps are followed by the distinct sound of a door opening and closing at the other end of the hall. And that's that. The house is silent now. Apparently, Georgina decided she'd rather punish me, than fuck me, tonight.

THIRTY-FOUR
REED

At a quarter past eight, wearing cycling shorts and nothing else, I greet two deliverymen at my front door, lead them upstairs, and direct them where to unpack their big box. Most mornings, I get up quite a bit earlier than this to fit in my workout, but after yesterday's marathon day that began in Manhattan and ended with me jizzing against my bedroom window, I fell into a deep slumber until about twenty minutes ago—which was when Owen called and woke me up with the news that my delivery was about twenty minutes away.

I rap on Georgina's closed door. "Wake up, Bobby Fischer," I call out. "Rise and shine." Georgina moans softly behind the door, sending arousal streaking through me. Because, apparently, any moan from this girl, no matter the context, registers as something sexual to my brain. "Wake up, Georgie girl." I knock again. "Even if you hate my guts, you're going to be my shadow today. And right now, I'm heading into my gym for a workout."

"I'm up," she croaks out. "Just give me twenty minutes."

"You've got five. Throw on workout clothes and meet me in the gym."

In the gym, I do core blasters and plyometrics for a full twenty minutes before Georgina finally appears, her form-fitting short-shorts and sport bra instantly making me forgive her completely for keeping me waiting so long.

"Sorry, I..." she begins. But the second she notices a second Peloton bike set up next to mine, her words trail off. She rushes to the sleek stationary bike and grips its handlebars, like she's confirming it's not a figment of her imagination. "This wasn't here last night during the tour! How did this get here?"

I smile. "You said you wanted to try one. So, I decided to get you one. This way, we can ride together."

Her jaw hits the floor. "This is for *me*?"

I chuckle at her adorable expression. "Yes. It's my gift to you, with an assist from Owen. I know you don't have a place of your own yet, so I'll have it delivered to your father's place after this week, if you like. If not, you can leave it here as long as you need, until you get a place of your own with enough room for it."

"Thank you!" With an effusive squeal, she breaks into an effervescent happy-dance—a sexy, jiggling display that makes me want to give her a month's worth of exercise equipment, if it will guarantee I'll get this same reaction every time.

"I've only got one request," I say. "I'd like you to be my personal spin instructor this week."

"Hell yeah! With pleasure!" She shakes her ass with glee... but then freezes. "Shoot. I don't have any—"

"Shoes?" I point to a shoe box on the floor next to her bike. "Put on your new shoes, saddle up, and let's sweat."

Like a kid on Christmas, Georgina tears into the shoe box while I get my own cycling shoes on, and soon, we're both clicked into our pedals and ready to begin.

"Let's get warmed up," she says, and we both begin pedaling at a fairly easy pace. "So, how hard do you want to work this morning?"

"A ten out of ten," I reply, without hesitation. "Annihilate me."

Georgina snickers. "Careful what you wish for. I taught advanced spin for the past two years. I'm pretty good at this, if I do say so myself."

"Hit me with your best shot, Ricci. Make me pay."

"There is a God."

She cues up a thumping playlist, barks at me to gear my bike up to twenty-two, and then proceeds to lead me in a solid hour's worth of torturous sprints and savage climbs and relentless anaerobic drills that leave us both gulping for air and dripping with sweat. Well, correction: we're both dripping with sweat, but I'm the only one gulping for air. Somehow, Georgina's not only performing every drill and maneuver alongside me, she's *also* barking nonstop orders at me in a clear, smooth voice—something I couldn't pull off right now, if I tried.

Finally, Georgina declares our private spin class over, and I crumple over my handlebars in relief.

She giggles. "Wimp."

"You're the devil... The devil with perfect tits."

She laughs. "Of course the devil has perfect tits. How else do you think she gets stupid mortals to sell their souls to her? Now, pedal at a ten for a few minutes to get your heart rate down, Old Man. And then I'll lead you through some stretching on the floor."

Gratefully, I gear down as instructed, and slow my pedaling to an easy, cool-down pace.

"Seriously impressive, Georgie."

"Back at you. You kept up with me the whole time."

"Yeah, but I wasn't *also* barking orders the whole time. I'm only the Fred Astaire of spin. You're the Ginger Rogers."

She looks at me blankly, and, immediately, I know she's as clueless about Fred and Ginger as she was about Bobby Fischer.

I flick the end of my towel at her in mock annoyance. "Are you *trying* to constantly remind me how young you are?"

"No. Just how old you are."

I laugh. "Would it kill you to *occasionally* know one of my pop culture references?"

"Would it kill you to *occasionally* make a pop culture reference that someone under fifty would know?"

"Everyone knows about Fred Astaire and Ginger Rogers. They're way before my time, too. They've transcended their era to become cultural icons. You should know about them for your writing."

"Okay, Obi Wan Kenobi. Educate me."

I give Georgina a quick primer on Fred and Ginger as we continue pedaling slowly, including the fact that, in modern times, Ginger is generally credited with being the bigger badass of the duo. "And you want to know *why* everyone says Ginger was the bigger badass?" I pause for effect. "Because Ginger did everything Fred did... only backwards and in high heels."

Georgina laughs uproariously, without holding back in the slightest. And that's when I know she's truly ready to move on from the crushing disappointment of last night. Yeah, I'm sure she's still hugely disappointed things didn't work out the way she'd hoped, simply because she loves her stepsister and wants the world for her. But thanks to the belly laugh Georgina is gracing me with, I know for certain she's ready to put last night's fiasco behind us. And I couldn't be more relieved about it.

After a little more chatting, Georgie orders me off my bike, and begins leading me in some stretches on the floor. But a few minutes in, as Georgie is leaning over one of her legs, she shocks the hell out of me by whispering three little words I never expected to drop from her sultry mouth in a million years.

"I'm sorry, Reed."

At the sound of her whispered apology, I don't flinch, even though I feel like I need the crash cart. "Sorry, did you say something?"

She clears her throat. Exhales. "I said I'm sorry. About last night. For how emotional I was." She winces. "And for flipping you off."

"It's okay. I kinda like it when you flip me off."

She leans against her bike. "I couldn't sleep last night for hours after I came back up from the pool, so I had plenty of time to think. And I realized you gave me your honest, professional opinion. And no matter how wrong and stupid it was, I should have respected it." She shrugs. "I had a tantrum. Plain and simple. And I'm sorry."

Holy shit. Who the hell is this humble, contrite woman before me? I don't recognize her, except for the part where she called my opinion wrong and stupid. Whoever she is, she's making my heart squeeze, every bit as much as the fiery, tempestuous, bird-flipping version of her makes my pulse race.

"I understand why you got so emotional," I say. "You love your stepsister and want the best for her. Plus, obviously, your feelings regarding Alessandra are tied up with your feelings about other things, too." I touch her shoulder. "I'm deeply sorry about your mother, Georgie."

"Thank you." She pauses. "Honestly, until I started melting down like a lunatic last night, I didn't even realize how interconnected certain things are inside me. But, regardless, I shouldn't have freaked out on you.

That was crazy-pants and bananas and unfair to you, and I promise I'll try never to do it again. No promises, but I really will try."

Oh, my heart. "Hey, lose your fucking mind, if you need to, baby. Let your freak flag fly. I certainly didn't help matters with some of my harsh word choices. When it comes to doling out my professional opinions, I'm used to being brutally honest, without a filter. But I should have appreciated the unique context a bit more. I'm sure it was confusing to you to have me turn into Business Reed on you, while we were lying in bed together in our underwear."

She flashes me a crooked smile that tells me she appreciates my concession. "So, we're good, then?"

Every atom in my body sighs with relief. "We're good." I open my mouth, as if to say more, but close it.

"But... ?" she prompts.

"Before I let this moment pass, I just want to address something. At the stadium last night, you said you hoped I'd want to help someone I love, the same way you wanted to help Alessandra. You said if I don't have that same impulse regarding the people I love, then I'm an even bigger dickhead than you thought."

She grimaces. "Sorry. Wow. I really do fly off the handle sometimes, don't I?"

I chuckle. "No need to apologize. I'm only bringing it up because I want you to know that I *do* have that impulse, Georgina. I won't compromise my business judgment for anyone—as you've learned firsthand—but, other than that, I truly would do anything for the short list of people I love."

Her face softens. She touches my hand. "I don't doubt that for a minute, Reed."

"You don't?"

"No."

I sigh with relief. "I'm so glad."

She takes a long sip of water. "Let's keep stretching."

We hit the floor and she directs me into a runner's lunge.

"So, tell me," she says, bending over her bent front leg. "Who's on this 'short list' of people you love—the ones you'd do anything for?"

And there she is. The Intrepid Reporter has re-entered the building. But it's an innocuous question. One I don't mind answering, actually.

So, I do. "Well, my family, of course. My mother, sister, nephew, and brother-in-law. Also, Josh and Henn. I consider them family. Their wives and babies, too. CeeCee, as well."

"CeeCee said the same thing about you. She said she loves you."

"She did?"

"Yep. She said she loves you and would never want to trick or trap you in relation to your interview."

I nod, feeling touched. "I love CeeCee, too. She gave me my first big break and changed my life. I'll be grateful to her forever."

Georgina instructs me to sit on my ass for a new stretch, and I comply.

"How did you and CeeCee meet?" she asks.

"I crashed CeeCee's black-tie birthday party. I knew a guy who knew a guy working the door, so I bribed my way onto the list, rented an Armani tux and a limo, and then waltzed into the party like I was the goddamned guest of honor."

She giggles.

"It was the embodiment of 'fake it till you make it.' I even posed for photographers on the red carpet outside, like they were all there for me."

We laugh together.

"So, what'd you say to CeeCee that made her want to give you that first big break?"

"Nothing particularly ingenious. I told her about Red Card Riot, and I guess my genuine passion was evident. She said, 'Send me the album and I'll give it a listen.' And the rest is history. I think the main thing was we just genuinely liked each other. There was an instant connection."

"I felt that with her, too," Georgie says. "When I had coffee with her, I immediately felt like I'd known her for years."

"Yeah, CeeCee has that effect on people. So do you."

She blushes. "Thank you." She draws her knees up to her chest. "So, is that everyone on your short list?"

I pause to consider. "No, I'd put Amalia on the short list, too. Also, Owen. I'd take a bullet for Owen, but, for the love of all things holy, don't put that into your article, or he'll demand a massive raise."

Georgina looks surprised. "Oh. I wasn't thinking about the article. I'm just enjoying getting to know you."

Oh, Georgina. She's such a liar. A beautiful one. But a liar nonetheless. "Isn't everything we talk about this week fair game for your article?" I ask. "Are you saying this conversation is off the record?"

She ponders that. Or pretends to, anyway. "No, I can't promise that. I guess I was just thinking I'd get to know you this week, organically, and have faith the article will take care of itself."

I take a sip of water. "Sorry, I don't think that approach is going to work for me. At the end of this, I don't want to open the special issue and read something I thought I'd said to you during a private, intimate moment, like during pillow talk or whatever. If you really want to get to know me, then I'm going to need the ability to designate certain conversations as off-limits."

She sighs. "Aw, Reed. So sure everyone is out to get you." She crawls like a cat across the floor, opens my bent legs, and crawls between them onto her knees. She shoves her gorgeous face into mine. She's so close, I can see every pore in her smooth, olive skin. The gold flecks in her hazel eyes. She puts her hands on my cheeks. "Reed Rivers, I hereby promise I'm not here to trick or trap you. I'm here to get to know you and use whatever I learn to write an amazing article about an amazing man that will blow you, and everyone who reads it, away."

I shake my head. "Georgie, you have to understand, I haven't read a single interview or article about me that got everything exactly right. There's always something that gets lost in translation. Every time."

"Well, that sucks." She twists her mouth, considering. "All right. Here's what we'll do. You'll promise that anything you say to me this week, and whatever I might observe, will be fair game for me to *write* about." She puts her fingertip to my lips, silencing me. "But *I* promise to let you see my article before showing it to anyone else, even CeeCee. And if there's *anything* you don't want in there, anything I've gotten wrong or you don't particularly like, then I'll take it out. It's as simple as that."

I squint. "What's the catch?"

"There isn't one. This way, you'll feel free to say whatever you want around me, no matter how stupid or arrogant or condescending it might be." She winks playfully. "And you won't have to worry it might make you look bad later." She slides her arms around my neck and kisses my cheek. "Now you have no excuse not to let down your guard with me."

Let down your guard. I can't believe it. Normally, when a woman says this sort of thing to me, I get hives. Or feel the urge to run away. Or shut down. But hearing those words from Georgina, I'm feeling nothing but excited and turned on.

"My only request?" she says. "When you read my ultimate article, just remember I'm not out to get you. Give it a chance. Please."

I pause. "You've got yourself a deal." I kiss her, and, just like that, those damned butterflies are going to town inside my belly again. Rippling and flapping like crazy. I smile. "Now that we've got that figured out, let's celebrate."

She motions to the massive bulge behind my shorts. "Gee. Do you have a particular kind of celebration in mind, Mr. Rivers?"

"As a matter of fact, I do." I grin wickedly. "You mentioned you like being weightless..."

"Oooh, after last night's torture, you're dying to fuck me in your pool, aren't you? I'm definitely in favor of that."

"Yes, but another time. I've got something else in mind right now." I jut my chin over her shoulder, toward a harness hanging from the ceiling in a corner. "I was thinking you should slide into that contraption right there and let me fuck you into oblivion."

She turns around to look where I've indicated. "What is that thing? Some sort of yoga swing?"

I stand and pull her up. "No, little kitty. It's my sex swing."

Her eyebrows ride up.

"And, I promise, you're going to love it."

THIRTY-FIVE
REED

I'm naked and hard as a rock, standing before Georgina's naked, suspended body. Her thighs, calves, back, and ass are supported by the hanging straps of the swing. And, thanks to my meticulous adjustments, her hips are now positioned at the precise height and angle to ensure maximum G-spot stimulation with every thrust. Which means, before I'm done with her, Georgina is going to get a huge, wet, and incredibly pleasurable surprise. An orgasm like nothing she's experienced before. And I can't wait.

I take a deep breath to control my spiraling excitement. "Lean back and relax," I coo, trying to keep my voice soothing and calm, even though my cock is already seeping with wetness.

Georgina leans back and visibly melts into the harness. "*Whoa.* This is wild."

"Comfortable?"

"Very. Although I've never felt more like a fly in a web."

I make another minor adjustment. "You're not a fly in a web, sweetheart. You're a butterfly in a net."

"Oh, well, that's so much better."

I stroke her thigh and she shudders with anticipation.

"It is. The spider only wants to destroy the fly. But the butterfly hunter wants to *possess* and *admire* the beautiful butterfly."

"Yeah, and then tack its wings to paper and enclose it in an airtight frame."

"The price of beauty, baby." My cock straining and wet, I open her thighs and stroke her slit gently. "You're about to discover there's incredible freedom that flows from being trapped like a butterfly in a net. When there's no option but to lean back and surrender to the pleasure, when there's nowhere to go, mentally or physically, when you can't pull away from the intensity of the pleasure you're experiencing, you're forced to let go completely and surrender. And it's in that moment of complete surrender that you're finally able to experience a new level of pleasure you had no idea existed."

I begin massaging her clit now, manipulating it firmly, back and forth, and she sighs and coos and sinks deeper into the harness.

"Take deep breaths, in and out," I instruct. "That's it. Relax. Don't fight the pleasure. There's nowhere to go. So, you might as well embrace it."

I kneel between her suspended thighs, and get to work on her with my tongue and fingers, and, in no time at all, she's rocking and jolting in the swing with a powerful orgasm.

Even before she's come down from her climax, I rise and plunge myself inside her, and Georgina growls ravenously at my delicious invasion. My hands firmly on her hips, I thrust in and out, hard, over and over again, the head of my cock slamming her G-spot without fail. Methodically. Precisely. Mercilessly. And, clearly, she's rapidly losing her mind.

But I don't let up.

Not for a second.

I pound her rhythmically, with no variation, until she's growling and begging me not to stop. I keep fucking her when her eyes roll back into her head. And when she lets out a long, animalistic growl. I fuck her when she's so wet, each thrust elicits a sloshing noise. And when her innermost muscles begin clenching and unclenching in delicious, rhythmic waves around me. I don't let up on beautiful Georgina's G-spot, even when it's clear she's been reduced to a feral animal. When her body goes slack and her head lolls to the side and the only sounds out of her sensuous mouth are groans and growls, peppered with my name and shrieks of "yes."

I fuck Georgina Ricci until she can't imagine fucking anyone else, ever again. Until *I* can't imagine fucking anyone else. Until we're both sweating and moaning and quaking and on the cusp of literal exhaustion.

I fuck her until, finally, I reach the finish line—the moment when Georgina lets out a scream of ecstasy that's so primal, so tortured, I know it can only mean I've finally hit the motherlode. Two seconds later, every muscle of hers surrounding my cock tightens like a vise around me. She throws her head back into the swing... and creams around my cock. Clearly, she's having the orgasm of her life. A wet, all-body climax that will change the way she thinks of sex—and her body—forever.

At the sensation of the warm liquid squirting from Georgina's body all over mine, I feel the most intense pleasure I've ever experienced, hands down. It's better than any drug—which isn't a figure of speech. My eyelids flutter at the injection of Georgina's drug into my vein. My eyes roll back. And I come inside her with the force of a rocket. Like I'm seeing God. Like I'm immortal.

As I come down, I crumple over her, quaking and sputtering. And she grips my sweaty hair and babbles incoherently about how amazing that was.

When I've caught my breath, I lift my head and gaze at Georgie's gorgeous face, and what I see there is sheer perfection: my own bliss reflected back at me. I'm on fire. High like never before. I pull her up, cradle her back, and devour her full lips with unfettered passion.

"Did you see what happened to me?" she sputters. "Oh my God, Reed. That's never happened to me before."

In reply, I kneel between her legs and begin licking up my sweet trophy. And she coos and sighs and laughs through it all.

"Oh, God, Reed. You're amazing. That was beyond incredible."

I smile and say nothing. What is there to say? I've done exactly what I set out to do. I've shown her what her body can do. *But only with me.*

She's an addict now.

Newly created.

A junkie hooked on a powerful drug. And that powerful drug... is *me*.

THIRTY-SIX
GEORGINA

Freshly showered, I bop into Reed's kitchen to find him standing at his stove, dressed like a baller, and listening to blaring music. I wrap myself around his free arm, inhale the faint scent of his musky cologne, and swoon from the depths of my soul.

"A man who cooks me breakfast?" I purr. "I can't think of anything sexier. Well, yes, I can: a man who cooks me breakfast *after* giving me supernatural orgasms in a sex swing."

"Oh, you think you're getting some of this?" he teases, indicating the food he's stirring in his pan. "Fend for yourself, Ricci. This is all for me."

I giggle like a fool.

"Someone's in a good mood."

"What the hell did you do to me? I feel *high*."

He kisses the top of my head. "That tends to happen after a girl has the best orgasm of her life."

"*By far.*" I inhale deeply again. "God, that smells amazing. What is it?"

"Scrambled eggs with turkey chorizo, onions, jalapeños, and spinach."

I give his arm a little squeeze. "I meant your cologne, Tiger. But breakfast smells amazing, too."

"Did you do a couple shots of tequila before coming down here?"

"Nope. I did a couple shots of Reed Rivers. I'm punch drunk on nothing but you, sexy man." I give his ass cheek a playful little pinch. "Knowing I'm going to get to be a butterfly caught in your net all week long is making me giddy."

Reed turns off the burner and reaches for a pepper shaker. "Don't get too attached to the sex swing. I get bored easily. I like mixing things up."

"Yes, I've stalked you online, remember? I'm well aware you get bored easily and like mixing things up." It's a reference to the many different women photographed on Reed's arm, as I'm sure he realizes—and I instantly regret saying it. Yes, I've kept my tone flirty. But it doesn't take a PhD in psychology to know the comment is borne of insecurity, an uncertainty about the rules of engagement here. After the life-changing sex we just had, I can't help wanting Reed all to myself. Is that an unreasonable expectation?

Reed puts down his spatula and grabs my shoulders gently. "Georgina, don't go psycho on me, okay? I meant I'm going to be mixing things up with *you,* and only you. The mere thought of you kissing another man while you're working on the special issue makes me want to commit murder."

I'm tentatively elated. But I can't help noticing Reed didn't make that last comment mutual. "And what will you be doing while I'm kissing only you for the entire summer? While I'm working on the special issue, will you be all mine, every bit as much as I'm all yours?"

He looks stern. "Georgina, I told you, quite clearly, the first night we met at the bar: it takes *a lot* to get me to agree to exclusivity."

I press my lips together, and he bursts out laughing at the expression on my face.

"Georgina, of course, it goes both ways! Yes, it takes a lot to get me to agree to exclusivity. But, baby, to put it mildly, you're... *a lot.*"

I giggle and throw my arms around his neck. "This is going to be so fun."

He kisses my cheek enthusiastically. "What your body did in the swing this morning was just the beginning. Oh my God. I'm gonna have so much fun with you."

He kisses me again before we reluctantly disengage from our embrace.

"I've instructed Owen to clear my calendar of all nighttime engagements this entire week," he says. "So I can focus all my attention on you."

I blush. "Thank you."

"Don't thank me. There's no place I'd rather be, every night this week, than with my butterfly, showing her all the amazing things her body can do."

I kiss him enthusiastically, and he squeezes my ass with equal fervor, making me squeal. But, finally, it's time to eat. Reed turns off the blaring music, grabs two plates, and divides the contents of his pan, and then we sit down at a small table in the corner of the kitchen to devour our feast.

After complimenting the meal, I ask, "So, what's on your schedule today, Music Mogul?"

"A meeting at my attorney's office, followed by my weekly Monday afternoon meeting with my team."

"Is your attorney that guy I met with his teenage daughter last night at the concert?"

"Yep. Leonard Schwartz. We've got some stuff to go over regarding a frivolous lawsuit." He tells me briefly about the lawsuit—basically, that some band has claimed Red Card Riot stole their song, based on a common chord progression that can be found in a million other songs.

"Can I come to the meeting with Leonard?" I ask. "I'd love to ask him about you."

He chuckles. "Sure. You might have to leave the meeting at some point, if we're going to talk about something that's attorney-client privileged. But you can certainly join the meeting at the beginning to interview Leonard."

"Great. I want to get an overview of what it takes, from a legal perspective, to run your empire."

"Knock yourself out."

We eat and talk, falling into easy, comfortable conversation. In response to my questions, Reed tells me a bit more about the copyright infringement lawsuit and I agree it sounds incredibly stupid.

"I took a class called Journalism and the Justice System this past year," I say. "It covered the intersection between journalism and the law. Like, how to report on trials and court cases and stuff. I learned so much.

My professor said ninety percent of all lawsuits wind up settling—that only about ten percent of court cases ever go to trial."

"Those are probably national statistics," Reed says. "I think the rate of settlement is even higher in California, where litigation is like breathing. Either way, those numbers would be reversed for me. I wind up settling only five to ten percent of the cases filed against my various companies, and fighting the rest with everything I've got."

"Why are your numbers so upside-down like that?"

"Most companies think of settling cases as a cost of doing business. They've determined they'll spend less money on a settlement than on protracted legal fees. Or, they're risk averse and scared to death of losing, so they pay out."

"But you don't think that way?"

He shrugs. "I have a different philosophy. I can't stand legalized extortion, so I only settle when I'm sure a case has merit. Or, at least, when I think a *jury* will think a case has merit. Yes, I might pay a ton in attorneys' fees to fight a case, but it's worth it to me, so I can sleep at night." He takes a sip of his cappuccino. "Plus, I firmly believe the long-term deterrence value is worth something, though I can't prove that. You can't prove the cases *not* filed against you because you've scared away unscrupulous plaintiffs' attorneys with your big swinging dick."

I laugh.

"If someone has a legitimate beef with me, fine. Let them bring it, and I'll settle the case like a man. Otherwise, they'd better brace themselves for a long, hard fight, that will ultimately lead to their resounding disembowelment."

I grimace. "Yikes."

"But enough about all that. Tell me about you, Georgie."

"What would you like to know?"

To my surprise, Reed launches into asking me a bunch of questions. He asks how I knew I wanted to pursue journalism. And then about my family and childhood. And, finally, about my mother and father. And to my surprise, he seems genuinely interested in my answers.

"You took it really hard when your dad remarried, huh?" he says.

I nod. "But when my father got cancer, I knew I had to let it go. Life is short, you know? I realized I love him with all my heart, unconditionally, and that's that. All that matters to me now is making sure my father stays cancer-free and keeps a roof over his head." I smile at Reed through my lashes. "Which is why I'm so grateful to you and CeeCee, for everything you've both done for my father and me."

Reed stiffens. "I haven't done anything. It was all CeeCee. She hired you. She's your boss."

I tilt my head. Shawn always made the exact same face Reed is making now, whenever I told him he was acting kind of weird and suspicious. "No, you've been amazing, Reed. You're letting me stay here this whole week, expense-free, remember? And you've also said you'll give me a hotel room after this week, too. Which means I'll be able to give almost all my salary to my father this whole summer, to help him try to catch up on his mortgage payments. And on top of all that, you're also throwing a party to end all parties on Saturday night *and* letting Alessandra come with me. I'd say all of that is a whole lot more than nothing. I was just saying I'm grateful."

Reed runs his finger down the handle of his fork. "Your father is behind on his mortgage payments?"

I blush. Why did I admit that? "I shouldn't have mentioned that to you. It makes me sound ungrateful for everything you and CeeCee have—"

"It's fine, Georgie. Tell me what's going on. He's behind on his payments?"

I press my lips together. I can't believe I let that slip.

He grabs my hand. "Did your father get behind when he got sick?"

I exhale and nod. "He hasn't returned to work since he was sick. He's a carpenter by trade, and chemo left him with some problems with his hands. But it'll be okay. I'm going to give him as much of the grant money as I can. It won't solve the problem completely, but it should buy him some time until we figure out what else we can do."

Reed rubs his forehead. But before he says a word, an older woman walks into the kitchen—a woman I immediately recognize from the photo on Reed's desk as Amalia. His housekeeper and second mother. Reed gets up and hugs Amalia in greeting, and then turns to me.

"Georgie, this is Amalia Vaccaro, my housekeeper. Amalia, this is Georgina Ricci. She'll be staying here for the summer."

My heart stops. Did Reed just say I'll be staying here... for the *summer*? When did I agree to that?

Reed continues, "I've put Georgie in the blue room upstairs. Make sure she's got everything she needs to feel at home, please."

"Of course. Hello, Georgina. Nice to meet you."

"And you." I stand and shake Amalia's hand, my mind racing about Reed's shocking comment.

"Please let me know if there's anything I can do to make your stay more comfortable this summer," Amalia says.

"Oh. Uh. Thank you. But I'm good. Just getting to stay here at all is a dream come true. It's a beautiful house."

"Yes, it is."

I look at Reed. "I'm so excited to stay for the summer. It's so much nicer here than any hotel."

Reed's handsome face breaks into a wide smile at my implicit acceptance of his invitation. Beaming a huge smile at me, he says, "Georgie, I just realized your bag isn't nearly big enough to hold everything you'll need this summer. I know you need a bathing suit. Probably some more workout gear. What else do you need?"

I'm buzzing. Tingling. Breathless. "No, no. I'm fine. If I need anything, there's a Target—"

"No, no, I insist. Amalia, do me a favor and give Georgie the house credit card for a shopping spree. Also, let's make her feel at home. Stock up on her favorite snacks and toiletries."

"Of course."

"Reed, I truly don't need anything."

"Georgina. You're staying for the summer. Not a week or a month. You need to feel completely at home. Which means we're going to make sure you have whatever your little heart desires." He winks. "Whether you like it or not."

THIRTY-SEVEN
GEORGINA

Reed heads to his home office to make a few calls before it's time to leave for his attorney's office, so I hang back in the kitchen to help Amalia clean up from breakfast. In part, because I genuinely want to be helpful. Reed and I made the mess, after all, and I'd be embarrassed to leave it for someone else to deal with. But, also, because I'm dying to talk to Amalia about Reed. What was Reed like as a little boy? What is he like as an adult boss? And, also, what can Amalia tell me about Reed's relationship with his mother? I can't yet envision all the themes of my eventual article, but Reed's lovely relationship with his mother brings a whole new depth to him that people never see, and I'm thinking maybe I'll use it as a touchstone in my article... if, indeed, it's everything Reed said it was. I was probably imagining it, but I thought I noticed a strange tightness in Reed's demeanor, just for a moment, when he was telling me about his mother's happy life in Scarsdale last night. And I'm curious to know if Amalia might be able to shed any light on the topic for me.

Amalia and I are standing side by side at the sink. She's the washer in yellow rubber gloves. I'm the dryer, holding a towel.

"When we're done here, how about we make your list?" Amalia says, her tone as warm and maternal as her body language.

"I'm sorry... My list?"

She hands me a cutting board to dry. "The list of whatever you'd like to have in the house during your stay. Your favorite foods and snacks and toiletries. Like Reed said."

"Oh, that." I wave at the air. "Thank you so much, but I don't need anything."

Amalia smiles like I've said something amusing. "Reed was very clear. He won't accept 'Georgina said she doesn't need anything' as an answer from me, I'm afraid."

I protest. She insists. So, I say, "How about you do for me whatever stuff you normally do in situations like this?"

She looks at me blankly. "In situations like what?"

I take the pan Amalia hands me. "You know, whenever Reed has a house guest for an extended period. He mentioned he sometimes invites bands to stay here for weeks, even months, at a time, right?"

"Well, yes. But he's never once asked me to roll out the red carpet for a band the way he did for you. Quite the opposite." She chuckles. "When it comes to musicians staying here, Reed pretty much always says, 'They'll take what I give them and like it.'"

I chuckle with her. "That sounds like him."

"Yes, it does. Which makes what he said about you all the more remarkable." She stops scrubbing the plate in her hand and looks at me. "Honestly, this is uncharted territory for me. Reed has never once asked a woman to stay here with him for an extended period. And he's certainly never asked me to roll out the red carpet for one."

My lips part in surprise.

"Oh, goodness. I hope I'm not out of line telling you that," Amalia says.

"No. Not at all." My heart resumes beating again. "Thank you for telling me. It's a wonderful thing to know."

"You've obviously made quite an impression on him." She flashes a sweet smile. "And I can certainly see why."

Color rises in my cheeks. "Thank you. Reed has made quite an impression on me, too."

Amalia clearly likes that answer. Smiling, she resumes her work at the sink. "What do you do, Georgina? Are you in the entertainment industry? An actress or model?"

"Oh, no. I'm journalist." My soul swells with pride to be able to say that sentence. "I write for *Rock 'n' Roll*. The magazine about music?"

"Yes, I know it. How wonderful."

"I'm working hard to get onto the writing staff of this other magazine owned by the same company, a publication devoted to in-depth interviews and investigative journalism."

"Oh, how exciting. Good luck."

Imposter syndrome suddenly hits me hard. "Actually, I should clarify: I'm only a summer intern at *Rock 'n' Roll*. I just graduated from UCLA, and this is my first real job. But I'm going to work very hard, and do everything in my power to nab a permanent writing position after the summer."

Amalia hands me a plate to dry. "I have no doubt you'll get whatever position you desire."

Oh, God. Is Amalia putting two and two together right now—piecing together the facts that I'm a *summer* intern at *Rock 'n' Roll*, a *music* magazine, and, huh, what a coincidence, I'm also staying with Reed, the head of a *music* label, for the entire *summer*? Crap. When I said I was going to do "everything" in my power to nab a permanent position, did Amalia secretly snicker to herself and think, *Everything, including Reed.*

"The magazine assigned me to do an in-depth interview of Reed," I blurt, feeling the need to make it clear to Amalia I got my job because of my writing skills—and not because of any help from Reed. "I'll be following Reed around and writing about him for my article, so he invited me to stay here for the summer to make things more convenient."

She smiles kindly. "Well, that makes perfect sense." She peels off her yellow rubber gloves. "I hope everything works out for you and your career, exactly as you're hoping, Georgie. May I call you Georgie?"

"Yes, I love being called that."

Shit. Now, I feel like I went overboard making Reed and me seem like nothing but interviewer and interviewee. Clearly, she knows there's more to it than that, seeing as how Reed has invited me to stay here for the entire summer, and he's *never* done that before. I don't want her to think I'm a liar.

"But, you know, besides the interview, Reed and I have also clicked personally," I say quickly. "He's been so sweet."

"I'm so glad," she says. And there's no judgment whatsoever in her tone. She puts her sponge and gloves and dishwashing soap away, and moves to the refrigerator. Which is where she begins pulling out ingredients and putting them onto the island. "Don't feel like you have to stay here with me, Georgie. I love the company, but I'm sure you're very busy."

"I'm not, actually. I'm just waiting for Reed to finish his calls. What's all this for?" I motion to the items she's placing on the island.

"I'm making a big pot of Reed's favorite chicken tortilla soup for dinner tonight. He asked me to make 'dinner for two.'"

I blush at the knowing look in her eye. She's sweet and nonjudgmental, but she's no fool. She knows exactly what's going on between Reed and me. Of course.

"Would you like some help making the soup?" I ask, my pulse pounding. "I'm a terrible cook—the absolute worst—so don't get too excited about my offer. But I can certainly help chop vegetables, if you don't mind a random finger in with your chopped onions."

She laughs. "No fingers, please. And, yes, I'd love your help." She grabs a cutting board and knife for me, and hands me an apron. "Reed likes this particular recipe because my version is filled with super foods. He's usually quite strict about what he eats. Fitness and nutrition are passions for him."

"Yes, he's mentioned that. Not that he needed to say it out loud. His body makes it pretty clear he takes excellent care of himself." I press my lips together again. What the hell is wrong with me? This is Reed's second mother, and I've just implied I've seen him naked? Seriously, I know I grew up without a mother, but this is ridiculous.

Thankfully, though, Amalia seems unfazed by my stumbling. In fact, she seems nothing but charmed—the same way CeeCee was when we had coffee together after the panel discussion.

Without missing a beat, she gives me some instruction, including showing me how to make a claw with my left hand while chopping so I don't cut off my fingers, and then puts me to work. And, in short order, I'm a regular sous chef, chopping away at vegetables while Amalia sautées onions at a burner across from me.

As we work at our stations, we chat easily, and Amalia's maternal demeanor calms me, reassuring me with each passing minute she's not judging me for having a fling with her much older, and powerful, boss. Amalia asks me questions, and, soon, I'm telling her about my life—my schooling and family. And I return the favor, drawing her out by asking her questions about her large family, which, it turns out, includes lots of beloved grandchildren.

Finally, about twenty minutes into our conversation, I feel comfortable enough to broach my primary topic of interest.

"So, Reed tells me you've known him his whole life?"

"Yes, I was there when they brought tiny little Reed Charlemagne Rivers home from the hospital, looking as sweet as can be." She chuckles. "He's not tiny anymore, obviously, but he's still as sweet as can be."

Yes, he is, I think. Followed immediately by, *Wow, what a difference a day makes.* Because, as late as yesterday, I never would have believed anyone would describe Reed Rivers as "sweet." But here I am, thinking that word describes him perfectly, after the whirlwind of the past twenty-four hours. Indeed, just this fast, I'm thinking there might be even more sweetness to Reed than I've seen. More than I ever thought possible.

But back to work.

I've got a job to do.

And I'm pretty sure Amalia, who's known Reed his entire life, is the perfect person to give me insight into this fiercely private man.

I say, "It's clear Reed feels exactly the same way about you, Amalia —that you're sweet as can be. Just this morning, he was telling me about his family, and he explicitly said he considers you a member of his family."

She stops what she's doing and looks at me, floored. "Reed said that?"

"He did. In fact, he said he loves you. And that he missed you so much after his father went to prison, when he was thirteen, he hired you as an adult, ten years later, the minute he was financially able to swing it. He said having you back in his life was so important to him, he hired you even before he bought his first sports car."

Okay, yes, I'm extrapolating and expanding ever so slightly from the actual words Reed said. But why else would Reed have hired Amalia the moment he was able to do so, even before buying a sports car, if he hadn't missed her terribly after she'd stopped working for his family—which Reed did explicitly say, coincided with his father going to prison?

From Amalia's body language, it's clear she's blown away by what I've said. Indeed, if I blew on her, she'd tip over. She leans her hip against the island and puts her hand on her heart.

"It means the world to me to hear Reed said all of that. Thank you so much for telling me this, Georgie."

"You're welcome." My heart skips a beat. It's been a long time since I've hung out in a kitchen with a kind, older woman, and helped her cook a meal. The experience is causing my heart to flutter like crazy. "Reed actually referred to you as his second mother." Am I fibbing? Did Reed say that, or did I? I can't recall. But either way, even if I was the one who said it, Reed certainly didn't correct me. And he *did* say he loves Amalia, and a photo of his mother and Amalia is one of the few personal shots in the house… So, I think it's safe to say I haven't told a lie.

"I love that sweet man so much," Amalia says, more to herself than to me. For a moment, she looks lost in thought. But then she shakes off her reverie, sighs, and smiles. "I'm frankly quite surprised Reed said all this to you. Especially, the part about me being with his family until Mr. Rivers went to prison. Reed is an extremely private person. Especially about his father, and his childhood. I think he doesn't like being reminded of anything unpleasant. He prefers not to think about it."

My heart is galloping. I have a feeling, if I handle this conversation right, I'll walk away with a goldmine of insight into parts of Reed he never shows the world. And I won't have to pull it out of Reed to get it. "Reed actually told me a very poignant story about his father last night in the garage. A story about how Reed used to golf with his father every weekend. The point of the story was to explain to me how devastated Reed was when he realized his father had actually committed the crimes he'd been accused of. So much so, he doesn't play golf now, because it brings up too many bad memories."

Amalia's jaw drops. Quickly, she looks down—and there's no doubt she's getting a grip on her emotions. When she looks up again, she looks pale. "I wish so badly I could have done more for Reed after his father went to prison. But there was only so much I could do."

"Oh, of course, Amalia. I'm sure Reed knows that. From what he said, you've been a very calming, nurturing presence for him his whole life."

Again, she looks shocked. "Wow. Reed really *has* shared a lot with you about his life, hasn't he?"

"Well, I have been assigned to write an in-depth article about him. But even more than that, we've really clicked, maybe because I've shared things about my life with him, too. I told him about my mother, who died when I was nine, and that's something I never, ever talk about with anyone. The same as Reed, I'm a person who prefers not to talk too much about things that make me sad."

"Oh, honey. I'm so sorry about your mother."

"Thank you. I think me opening up about that made Reed feel comfortable to do the same with me."

"Well, that makes a lot of sense. You and Reed have a shared experience. I mean, it's not the exact same thing, but both of you did lose your mothers at the exact same age."

I'm stumped. Reed lost his mother at nine? "Right," I say, like I know exactly what Amalia is talking about... even though, in truth, I haven't a clue. If Reed lost his mother at age nine, then who's the mother happily doing yoga and painting in Scarsdale with her boyfriend, Lee? Also, if Reed lost his mother at nine, why on earth didn't he mention that fact to me after I told him about *my* mother? I mean, not last night, when I was screaming at him like a freaking maniac. But this morning, during our amazing, intimate conversation in the gym, when we were both so open and apologetic and kind?

I'm thoroughly confused.

Did Reed's biological mother die when he was nine, and then his Dad somehow remarried before being shipped off to prison, and the woman in Scarsdale is actually his *stepmother*—a woman Reed always thinks of as his mother? That could be it. But, damn, if that's the case, Reed's father got married after the death of his wife awfully fast. As quickly as my own father did. Which, again, I would have expected Reed to mention when I was telling him about my father and Paula.

My head teeming with thoughts, I chop some carrots for a long moment, and finally cast out my fishing rod. "I'm so proud of Reed for all he's accomplished in his life," I say, "especially after everything he went through as a child."

"Oh, yes. I'm enormously proud of him for that, too. It breaks my heart, just thinking about everything he went through. But he's come out the other side and made all his dreams come true, while still retaining his kind heart. That's the best thing of all, if you ask me—that he's as kind and generous and sweet as ever, despite all his success."

Okay, who the fuck is Amalia talking about? I mean, yes, Reed has been enormously generous and sweet with me, but Amalia is making him out to be a saint.

"He really is so generous and sweet," I agree. "I mean, he didn't simply let Henn throw his wedding here. He paid for everything."

"Oh, I know. But that's Reed. If he cares about you, he'll move heaven and earth to make you happy."

"So I'm discovering. You know what I think? Reed is terribly misunderstood by people who don't know him well."

She stops what she's doing on a dime. "Oh my gosh, yes, he is! I'm so glad you understand that about him, Georgina, so you can show the world the *real* Reed in your article. So many people don't see his heart. They think he's only a shrewd businessman. But he's so much more than that."

"That's what I like about Reed most. That he's got so many layers."

Amalia nods enthusiastically.

And we both fall silent for a moment.

Finally, Amalia says, "To be honest, it shattered me to watch poor Reed's world come crashing down the way it did."

I continue chopping methodically, even though my mind is reeling. Is that a reference to Reed's father's arrest and conviction? Or a reference to whatever happened to Reed's mother when he was nine? "Yeah, from what Reed told me," I say, "it seems like everything was extremely difficult for him." What "everything" am I talking about? Honestly, I have no idea.

"I just felt so powerless to do anything to help him," Amalia laments. "And then his father was arrested, only a few short years later, and I thought, 'Oh my gosh. How much can that poor boy take?'"

"You did everything you could," I say vaguely, even though I still don't have a clue what we're talking about. "Reed knows that."

Amalia exhales deeply and stops what she's doing at the stove, so I stop chopping and give her my undivided attention.

"I tried to take him in when his father went to prison," she says. "But the judge said I wasn't a relative, so I couldn't have him. It broke my heart to watch him get sent to live with some distant relative he barely knew, rather than with me. I wanted to be the one to take him because I loved him like my own. I truly did." She wipes her eyes with her apron. "I still do."

Well, this is new information. When Reed's father was arrested, Reed was sent to live with a distant relative? Why? Where was Reed's mother... or his stepmother, if that's who the happy woman in Scarsdale is? Oh, God, I'm so confused. I move around to Amalia on the other side of the island, and put my hand on her shoulder reassuringly. "I'm sure Reed knows you did your best, Amalia."

Amalia shakes her head. "I cried when I couldn't get custody of him. I cried for myself and for Reed, and for his poor mother, too. Of course, I would have preferred his mother could have taken care of him, but that simply wasn't possible. Truly, it was just a tragedy, all around, for all of us."

"Yes, but you wouldn't be here with Reed now, all these years later, if he felt anything but love and gratitude toward you."

"Thank you. I only want the best for him."

"Of course, you do. I think that's what Reed appreciates about his relationship with you. How uncomplicated it is. When he told me about his mother... and her life in Scarsdale..." I trail off, not sure how to complete the sentence. What the hell are we talking about?

"Yes, I know Reed wishes she'd agree to transfer to the facility in Malibu. But she won't leave the one in Scarsdale."

And there it is. Finally. The truth. The word that explains that tightness I thought I saw on Reed's face last night when he talked about his mother's happy, perfect life in Scarsdale with her boyfriend, Lee. *Facility*. As in *mental* facility?

"Yes, exactly," I say calmly, even though my synapses are exploding. "He said he gets out there to visit as much as he can, but I'm sure it would be easier if she'd transfer to the facility in Malibu."

"Of course, it would. I'm sure it hurts Reed, more than he lets on, that she won't move to a facility closer to him, so he can spend more time with her and take care of her the way he wants to do." She looks toward the door of the kitchen, and then back at me. "I'm not surprised Eleanor won't move closer, honestly. She never put her boys first, right from the start. That was the hardest thing for me to watch, as their nanny. A mother should *always* put her children first, whether she's got a nanny or not."

Holy fuck burgers. My brain is whirring and clacking now, deftly processing the shreds of new information Amalia just supplied to me. *Eleanor*. Note to self: gather every bit of information you can on Eleanor Rivers of Scarsdale. *Boys*. Plural. Amalia said Eleanor never put the *boys* first. And that Amalia was "their" nanny. But Reed didn't mention he has a brother. Only a sister. And I don't think Wikipedia mentioned a brother.

I put down my knife, every molecule of my skin buzzing. "Hey, Amalia. I'm sorry. I just remembered I have to research something for one of the articles I'm writing. I'm sorry to ditch my duties as your sous chef, but—"

"Go, go. This is my job, not yours. Thank you for the conversation. I've wanted to talk to someone about these things for a very long time." She smiles kindly. "You're absolutely lovely, Georgie. It's no wonder Reed is so taken with you."

My heart squeezes. "Thank you. It's no wonder Reed loves you so much. I'm looking forward to cooking and chatting with you a lot this summer."

Amalia's face lights up. "I have some wonderful recipes I'd be happy to teach you."

"I'd love that." I hug Amalia goodbye, and then sprint upstairs to my room, where I flip open my laptop and hop online. Obviously, there's a whole lot about Reed's life he doesn't want to talk about. Which is perfectly fine. But that's not going to stop me from digging a little deeper... to try to get to know the man *behind* The Man with the Midas Touch... whether he wants me to... or not.

THIRTY-EIGHT
REED

I lean back in my chair, my phone pressed against my ear, looking out the window of my home office.

"Hi, boss," Owen says, answering my call. "Did the bike arrive?"

"It did. Right on time. Thank you."

"Did she like it?"

"She went apeshit for it." I smile to myself, remembering Georgie's jiggling happy dance this morning when she found out that second Peloton bike was hers. "Actually, her reaction made me want to give her even more gifts, just to see her lose her shit like that again and again. I was thinking of maybe getting her a car. I'd want to get her something cute and fun and reliable—a little convertible, maybe—but nothing too crazy in terms of pricing."

Owen pauses. "So, his and hers Bugattis are out of the question, then?"

I ignore the obvious snark. "I want something to bowl her over, but not something that will make me look like a madman. If the car is too extravagant, she'll think it implies some sort of commitment past the summer. And that wouldn't be good."

"As opposed to a commitment *within* the summer?"

"Oh. Yeah. Change of plans. Georgina's not staying at my house for a week anymore. I asked her this morning to stay for the entire summer, and she said yes."

He's quiet for a moment. And then, "Wow. That's quite a 'purely professional relationship' you're having with her, Reed."

I smile to myself. "Just do some research for me on cute little convertibles, would you? Tell me what you recommend."

"I already know exactly what I recommend: lay off the blow, Reed."

"I'm not high, Owen. At least, not on coke. Georgina doesn't own a car. Not even a shitty one. Who the hell doesn't own a car in LA? She needs one."

"You don't think maybe *any* car would be too extravagant a gift that makes you look like a madman? It's still *really* early days, Reed."

My spirit falls. I say nothing.

"You gave her a Peloton on day one. Maybe that's enough for now?"

My heart is thundering. He's right. I've let myself get swept away. I'm moving way too fast and I need to slow down. "A Pilates machine, then. She said she taught spin *and* Pilates classes. I don't know anything about Pilates. Isn't there a machine for that?"

"Yes, it's called a reformer. But, Reed. I'm not kidding this time. Do I need to call Promises and see if they've got a bed for you? Are you back on the blow?"

"I don't need rehab, Owen. I'm fine. I'm just... "

In a flash, my mind wanders to Georgie. In rapid-fire succession, I see her happy dance again. And then her floating naked in my moonlit pool. I see her standing naked underneath my bedroom window. And the look on her face when that orgasm in the sex swing shattered her. And, finally, I see the beautiful look of contrition on her face when she apologized to me this morning. The look that grabbed my heart in its iron fist.

And it suddenly occurs to me...

Holy shit.

Georgina isn't the one who's the junkie here. *She's the drug!*

"Reed?" Owen says. "You're just... what?"

I scrub my palm over my stubble. "Fucked." I shake it off. "Moving on. No car. Look into Pilates machines for me, okay? Now, tell me about the party. You've got everything cooking?"

Owen rattles off a brief update. He tells me invitations went out an hour ago. And that everyone who's not on tour knows it's mandatory they come. He says, "And I got your note about us having a stage filled with musical instruments, in addition to a DJ—so musicians can hop up there in random combinations and jam together. Great idea."

I thank him and give him my notes for Watch Party's upcoming album, which I finished listening to this morning while making breakfast, and we end the call.

After disconnecting with Owen, I get a text from Henn, telling me he just heard about the party on Saturday. But rather than text him back, I decide to call him, since I've got a few minutes before I have to head out to my meeting with Leonard.

"Hello, brother," Henn says. "What's up?"

"Nothing much. I'm busy conquering the world. You?"

"Oh, I'm just, you know, living the thug life. Hannah had a big project due at work and the nanny called in sick, so I'm trying to bang out some code for a client while Hazel is taking her morning nap. She's in her crib right now, sleeping butts-up coconut."

I chuckle. "I'm afraid to ask."

"That's what Hannah calls it when Hazel's sleeping with her bottom straight in the air. She smashes her cheek into the mattress and curls her little legs up underneath her, and points her butt straight up. It's the cutest thing I've ever seen."

"Send me a pic."

"Reed, Hazel is my *baby*."

I laugh. "I want to see."

"Are you drunk?"

"I'm just in a good mood. Now, send me a fucking photo of your baby doing butts up coconut before I beat your scrawny ass. My time is valuable, man. I don't beg."

He laughs.

My phone pings.

"I sent it."

"Aw. You're right. That *is* adorable."

"I can't get enough. I've got like nine hundred photos of the same basic shot on my phone." He chuckles happily. "But, surely, you didn't call to hear me gush about Hazel. I'm guessing you're calling about your party? I RSVP'd right before you called. It's perfect timing. Hannah's mom and my parents were already coming into town for the weekend for Hazel's birthday party on Sunday, so we've got overnight babysitting. Same with Josh and Kat."

"Oh, you've talked to Josh? He's coming, for sure?"

"Yeah, he texted both of us. You didn't see? He and Kat changed their flight to come to LA on Friday now."

"Awesome. You guys will have to pre-party at my house on Saturday afternoon."

"Count us in." He pauses. "So, you haven't said a word about Hazel's birthday party being the next day."

"Yeah, I totally forgot about that. Does it start before two?"

"No. It starts at three."

"And you'll be serving booze, I hope—preferably Bloody Marys?"

"Yes, to booze. I'll add Bloody Marys to the menu, specifically."

"Then I'll be there."

Henn pauses. "That's it? You're not going to complain the guest of honor has no idea it's her fucking birthday? Or that we'll be partying till dawn at your place, and that getting up for a baby's birthday party the next day is the last thing you want to do?"

I laugh. "Nope. I'm looking forward to Hazel's birthday bash. My party will be one for the record books, but it'll be crazy and hectic. It'll be nice to hang out with everyone the next day in a chill environment where we can actually talk. Just don't let me down on those Bloody Marys, and we're good."

"Wow. You're in a shockingly good mood."

I can't help smiling from ear to ear. "Yes, I am."

"Is there a specific reason?"

My smile broadens. I bite my lower lip. "Remember that hot bartender from Bernie's the other night?"

"No. Remind me what she looks like."

He's being sarcastic. Georgina is unforgettable.

"She's here. She stayed the night."

"*No.*"

"Yep."

He makes a sound like he's blown away. "Well, that's a twist I didn't see coming. I thought you said she hated your guts. You said she told you to fuck off and die in front of your gate and then took off in an Uber."

"She did." I chuckle. "But I happened to see her at the RCR show last night, and one thing led to another... And now she's here. I just made her breakfast, Henny."

"She's *breakfast-worthy*?" He whistles. "Wow. That was fast. Okay, back up. How did you 'happen' to run into her at the RCR concert? You pulled strings, didn't you? You made her think she'd won backstage tickets in a contest or something."

I smirk to myself. "You think I'm so Machiavellian, so sneaky and diabolical, I'd pull strings behind the scenes to create a situation where I could have a second bite at the apple with a woman who'd rejected me, without her even realizing I'd played God?"

"That's precisely what I think of you."

"Well, you're absolutely right. Thank you for knowing me so well."

I tell Henn the whole story. Georgina's internship, and how it came about. I tell him about the grant and that Georgina has no idea I'm the one who funded it. And, finally, I tell him about the interview I had to throw into the pot to get CeeCee to agree to doing the special issue.

"Wow, that's going to be one hell of a thorough interview when she's through with you," Henn says. "Considering she's got the entire summer to gather information."

"Yeah, especially since Georgina will be staying here at my place the entire summer."

"You're shitting me."

"Nope. I invited her this morning. And she said yes."

He's quiet for a beat. "I'm sorry. Could you hand the phone back to Reed, please?"

I laugh. "I know. It's crazy."

"You invited her for the summer... for the article?"

Anxiety flashes through me. Did I jump the gun? Inviting Georgie for the whole summer was a spur of the minute decision. Seeing her with Amalia, for some reason... it felt so natural and right. Plus, I knew she'd be in my life throughout the summer, regardless, working on the special issue... And, suddenly, I couldn't stand the thought of Georgina staying in a hotel throughout the summer, when she could be under my roof... "No, I asked her to stay for purely personal reasons," I admit.

"That's awesome, Reed. Wow. Plus, the incidental benefit is her interview of you is going to be amazing."

"I'm sure it will be. Unfortunately for Georgie, however, most of what she writes won't see the light of day."

"What do you mean?"

"Georgie made a rookie error. She gave me full editorial control over whatever she ultimately writes about me. Of course, I'll green light some of it. Whatever's on-brand for *Rock 'n' Roll,* plus a little extra something to give her an exclusive scoop. But beyond that, whatever she might write about my childhood and my family, that shit is coming out."

He sighs. "I know you hate talking about that stuff. But I think you should keep an open mind here, Reed. You never know. You might really like her article. The truth shall set you free, my brother."

"My truth is nobody's fucking business, Henn."

He sighs. "Yeah, I know. But let's think this through for a minute. Imagine she works all summer long on some epic article about you, something she's really proud of and excited to submit to her boss, and you nix ninety percent of it. She'll be crushed. Not to mention she'll hate you."

"She's the one who fucked up and gave me full editorial control. It'll be a life lesson for her."

"A life lesson about not trusting the asshole she's slept with all summer? Reed, implicit in your agreement with her was that she can trust you with her baby. She trusts that you'll give due consideration to whatever she ultimately writes."

I say nothing.

"I'm just saying you sound like you're walking on air today. You made her breakfast, for fuck's sake, and invited her to stay for the summer, just for the fun of it. And you're not even grouchy about Hazel's birthday party on Sunday. Whatever spell she's cast on you, don't fuck it up by sending her on a wild goose chase this entire summer that will end in her hating you."

He's right.

Georgina's going to hate me at the end of this.

Fuck.

My mind is racing. Calculating. Seeking a solution. And, finally, I've got it. Georgina can't hate me if I've already given her something even *better* than an in-depth interview of *me*. Something that equally accomplishes her goal. At the end of the day, Georgie doesn't even want an interview of me, specifically. She wants to impress CeeCee enough to get hired onto the writing staff of *Dig a Little Deeper*, and my interview is merely a means to an end. Which means I know exactly what to do.

"She won't hate me if I get her an even better interview than mine," I say. "All I've got to do is get her an A-list interview, with someone way better than me, and all will be forgiven."

"I'm not sure it works that way."

"Sure, it does. I've invited a shit-ton of A-listers to my party on Saturday, and I'll tell Owen to invite a shit-ton more. I'll introduce Georgie around on Saturday night, and see who she clicks with and make it happen for her." I smile. "This is actually a great plan. Georgie clicks with everyone she meets. It's like the girl has magical powers. She'll have her pick of the litter on Saturday night."

"If you say so," Henn says half-heartedly.

An idea pings me. "But it certainly wouldn't hurt to get myself some insurance—some proverbial belts and suspenders. I need a favor, Henny."

I tell Henn about Georgie's father—specifically, about his recent cancer battle and the financial troubles he's having because of it. "So, will you do me a favor and hack his bank or whatever, and find out how much he owes on his condo? And while you're at it, you might as well find out how much Georgina owes in student loans. Just find out Georgie's and her father's complete financial situations for me, if you would."

The line is silent.

"Are you still there?"

"Yeah, I'm here," Henn says.

"Can you do all that for me?"

"It should be easy to do. But *why*, exactly, do you want to know this stuff?"

"Just in case I want to play Fairy Godfather at some point."

"In other words, you're worried you're going to piss her off with the article, so you want to have her 'price' ready to go, just in case?"

I frown. My two best friends know me, inside and out. It's a blessing and a curse.

"Reed, listen to me," Henn says. "In all the time I've known you, I've never once heard you sound this jacked up about a woman. You sound like I did when I met Hannah—like you've been struck by a lightning bolt."

I roll my eyes. It's the stupidest thing I've ever heard in my life.

Henn says, "For fuck's sake, Reed, if you break her trust, you won't be able to buy your way out of it. Instead, how about *not* doing anything to make her hate you? How about opening up and telling her about your life and letting her write the article and get to know you. How about enjoying the summer with an open mind and seeing where that takes you. Take a chance on this girl. Take a chance on what might happen if you let down your guard a bit."

"Are you done?"

He sighs. "Yes."

"Thank you for the TED Talk, Peter. It was inspiring. But let me remind you, she's writing an article about me. She's not here to 'get to know me' in a vacuum. She's a shark, this girl. It's my favorite thing about her. Don't get me wrong. But we're not just two people shacking up. She wants something from me. So, 'letting down my guard' completely, as you've suggested, would be a felony stupid thing for me to do."

He sighs. "If you say so."

"I do. So, will you get me the financials I've asked for, or not?"

"Of course, I will. Just send me the names and whatever information, and I'll get it to you in a couple days."

"Thank you. I'll send you a text after we hang up."

"So, will you be bringing this breakfast-worthy girl with you on Sunday to Hazel's party?"

To my surprise, my heart leaps at the idea. I never bring dates to personal events with my good friends. Hardly ever to work events, either. And yet, here I am, eager to bring Georgina to my best friend's house and introduce her to pretty much everyone I care about, all in one fell swoop... Indeed, I can't wait to sit back and smile with amusement as Georgina casts her uniquely powerful spell on every last one of them.

"Yeah, I'll bring her," I say, trying to sound nonchalant.

But Henn's not a fool. He knows this is totally outside the box for me. "Holy shit, Reed," he says. Which is exactly what I was expecting him to say. But then, he goes on to say something I'm not. "For a smart man, you're dumb as dirt sometimes."

"Huh?"

"Don't fuck this up!" he booms. "Be completely honest with this girl. Let her know the real you. In fact, why all the secrecy about you funding her grant? Tell her so she knows what a generous guy you are. I'm sure she'll be thrilled to find out you're the reason her internship is a paid one."

"Are you insane? Henn, when I came up with the idea to donate to the cancer charity, my main motivation was to arrange things behind the scenes so I could get her into bed. You think she won't realize that in two seconds flat? The last thing I need is for her to doubt she got her job on her merits. Which she totally did, by the way. CeeCee was going to hire her, regardless."

"You truly don't think Georgina would be grateful to you for helping her?"

My stomach clenches fiercely. "She's proud, Henn. It means the world to her to be a 'professional writer.' I don't want her to doubt herself."

"But if she finds out you're the source of the grant, later, it'll be ten times worse than if you'd told her on your own, up front. You *not* telling her makes it seem like you did something nefarious and creepy, rather than something generous and kind."

"She won't find out."

"Well, if she does, paying off her dad's mortgage and her student loans won't fix the problem. Trust can't be bought."

I respect Henn's mind more than anyone's, probably. He's a literal genius—the smartest guy I've ever met. But this time, he's dead wrong. "I'm not telling Georgina jack shit about the grant, and she won't find out about it on her own. But, on the off-chance she does, then she'll forgive me because, by then, I'll have gotten her an A-list interview with someone even better than me *and* I'll have the information I need to immediately pay off her debts in full, too." I look at my watch. "I can't talk about this anymore with you. I've got to head to a meeting at my attorney's office. Thanks for getting me that info. I'll text you and everyone about a pre-party on Saturday."

"Hey, Reed. I really think—"

"Drop it, Henn. I've got this. I'll see you on Saturday. Thanks for the favor. Bye."

THIRTY-NINE
GEORGINA

Have you ever met some regular, nice person, and instantly connected with them in a genuine, easy way... only to find out *later* that regular, nice person was actually a big wig? Someone who would have intimidated the heck out of you, if only you'd known? But by then it was too late to feel intimidated. The easy friendship was already formed. The connection made.

Well, that's what happened when I met Reed's longtime attorney, Leonard. When I encountered him backstage at the RCR concert last night, he was a sweet older dude in jeans and a Red Card Riot T-shirt who was geeking out over watching his teenage daughter and her friends meet the band. But now that I'm sitting across from Leonard in his sleek office, and I can see the impressive diplomas and framed magazine covers and awards on his walls, I'm realizing he's actually a big wig. But it's too late now for me to feel intimidated, because all I see when I look into his smiling face is the sweet, kind dude in jeans and a Red Card Riot T-shirt from last night.

It's a lucky thing for me, actually. It's meant I've been able to dive right into deftly interviewing Leonard about the legal services his firm provides Reed and Reed's various businesses, without feeling hampered by nerves.

Unfortunately, though, all good things must come to an end. When the expert witness Reed and Leonard have been waiting on finally arrives, apologizing profusely for her delay due to traffic, it's time for me to head out and leave the trio to their meeting. She's the same woman who moderated the panel discussion the other day, though—the dean of UCLA's music school—so, before heading out the door, I mention I was in attendance at the panel and thoroughly enjoyed it.

"Oh, are you a music student?" she asks.

"No, I just graduated with a degree in journalism."

Reed pipes in. "Georgie is interning for *Rock 'n' Roll*. She's been assigned to write an in-depth article about me, so she's shadowing me this entire week. I've been told she's a brilliant writer. One to watch."

Goosebumps erupt on my skin, thanks to Reed's amazing words about me, and his tone while saying them. Oh my gosh. Everything Reed just said makes me want to jump his bones the moment we walk through his front door later tonight!

The woman asks me some polite questions about my internship, which I answer, but, soon, it's clear I should run along to let them get to work.

"If you'd like a quiet place to work while you wait for Reed, I can set you up in a conference room," Leonard offers.

"No, thank you," I say. "I think I'll head to a coffee place nearby and plan to come back here . . .?"

"In a couple hours or so," Leonard supplies.

"Perfect. Thank you for all the helpful information, Leonard. It was invaluable to me."

"It was my genuine pleasure, Georgina. Your questions were thoughtful and full of insight."

I blush. "Thank you. Please say hello to McKenzie and her adorable friends for me."

"I will."

I look at Reed and my heart skips a beat at the twinkle in his brown eyes. "Thank you for letting me tag along today. It's been so helpful."

"My pleasure, Georgina. I was also impressed with the questions you asked. CeeCee told me you're one of the most promising newbies she's ever had the pleasure to hire—if not the most promising. And I can see why."

Biting back a massive smile, I grab my laptop, say my last goodbyes, and head out the door. But I'm not going to a coffee place, like I said. I'm heading straight to the courthouse a few blocks away to do a little research. From what Leonard just explained to me about Reed's legal affairs, combined with something Reed said to me last night, I've got a strong hunch there's a damned good story out there, waiting to be uncovered by the right journalist. I just have to be smart enough, and scrappy enough, to be the one to find it.

FORTY
GEORGINA

While sitting on the courthouse steps with a fish taco, I read the lengthy printout I obtained a few minutes ago from a court clerk inside. Specifically, it's a list of every lawsuit filed against Reed and his various companies over the past ten years.

The list includes the following basic information about each lawsuit, without providing any details about the facts or specific claims asserted: the plaintiff's name, the defendants' names, and the general nature of claims asserted—for example, personal injury, breach of contract, wrongful termination, copyright infringement, etcetera. And, finally, the printout notes the ultimate disposition of the case. For instance, sometimes, judgment was granted, or the case dismissed, by the judge on a motion filed by one of the parties. Occasionally, some of the cases went all the way to trial. And, in rare instances, a given case was dismissed after the parties had reached a confidential settlement.

Of course, it's only the last category of cases that interest me, the ones Reed, or his particular company, settled, seeing as how Reed told me last night he only settles a case when he believes it has merit. Or, at least, when he thinks a jury would think so.

I pull a yellow highlighter from my computer bag and go down the "ultimate disposition" column, marking all the settled cases. But when I go back up to the top and begin going through my yellow markings, I realize this isn't the right approach. My search criteria was too broad, resulting in a list of crap I don't care about in the slightest. A slip-and-fall lawsuit filed against one of Reed's nightclubs, for instance. Another slip-and-fall against Reed's real estate holding company, regarding one of his apartment buildings. A lawsuit filed by a guy against the partnership that owns a nightclub Reed co-owns, claiming the guy didn't get paid his accrued overtime.

Snooze.

Frankly, I don't know what I'm looking for here. But my gut tells me to keep looking . . .

I pull the cap off a green highlighter pen this time, and decide to go down a different column on the printout. This time, I look at only the yellow-marked cases—the ones Reed's settled—but mark in green only the ones filed against River Records, specifically, as opposed to one of Reed's many other businesses. And, lo and behold, when I reach the end of the list this time, and I look at the intersection of my yellow and green markings, I discover the entire universe of cases now only numbers three:

First, a lawsuit filed nine years ago by "ALM Business Properties" against Reed, personally, and River Records, alleging breach of lease. That doesn't sound particularly sexy to me, but I decide to get a copy of it from the court clerk, nonetheless. Why not?

Second, a lawsuit filed eight years ago by someone named Stephanie Moreland against Reed, personally, and River Records, alleging wrongful termination, breach of contract, and sexual harassment. *Whoa.* Sexual harassment? Yeah, I'm definitely getting a copy of that one.

And, third, a lawsuit filed six years ago by a guy named Troy Eklund against Reed, personally, and River Records, alleging breach of contract, breach of the implied covenant of good faith and fair dealing, fraud, and assault. Another *whoa.* Fraud? Assault? Definitely another set of documents to order from the court clerk.

I scan the printout one more time, just to be thorough, and then shove my green and yellow highlighters back into my computer bag, throw away the empty wrapper from my delicious fish taco, and race into the courthouse. After making it through security at the front door, and then waiting in line at the clerk's office, I finally make it to the counter, coincidentally, getting the same guy who helped me with the printout earlier.

"Hello again," he says, shooting me a wide smile.

"Hello there. I've been through the list you gave me and figured out which lawsuits I'd like to copy." I plop the printout onto the counter between us. "The good news for me is that I only need three lawsuits on this huge list."

"Easy peasy. I'll have copies delivered to you in three to five hours. Just fill this out." He slides a form across the counter to me.

I bite my lip. "Is there any way I could get those records from you now—like, within the next hour?" I lean forward and flash him my most charming smile. "It'd be a huge help to me. My boss said she wants this stuff 'right away.' And it's my first week on the job, so I'd really like to impress her."

The guy's eyes flicker to my chest, ever so briefly, before drifting back to my face. "Yeah, okay. But just this once. Don't tell anyone I bumped you to the front of the queue, okay?"

"I promise. Thank you so much." I look at his nametag. "*Charles*. I'm grateful."

I read off the case numbers of all three cases, and Charles inputs them into his computer.

"You're in luck. All three cases are here in this building, in storage," he says. "I'll just have to go into the records room to grab whatever is there and make copies. It shouldn't take me more than thirty minutes or so, depending on how many documents are in each file."

"Wow. You're a life-saver."

He turns to go.

"Actually, before you go. While I'm waiting, I'd love to look at another printout. This time, regarding all the lawsuits filed against a different defendant."

"Sure." He returns to his keyboard. "What's the defendant's name?"

"Eleanor Charpentier Rivers."

It was easy to locate Reed's mother online this morning. Eleanor Rivers of Scarsdale, New York, whose address matches up with a high-end mental facility in the heart of the posh community. But, other than Eleanor's full name and address, and a passing reference to her name in a few of the articles written about Reed's father, I wasn't able to learn any details about the woman.

"Spelling on Charpentier?" Charles says.

I spell the name for him, and he clacks on his keyboard.

"It looks like there's only one lawsuit naming Eleanor Rivers or Eleanor Charpentier Rivers as a defendant or respondent. A 'Dissolution of Marriage and Custody of Minor Child' case, filed by one Terrence Rivers."

My heart lurches into my mouth. "Would you add that to my copy order, please? I'd like everything in that case file."

"Sorry, no can do," Charles says. "Family law cases are a different animal, stored separately. But since this one was from over ten years ago, I doubt they'd even have it on-site anymore. Plus, since the case involved the custody of a minor child, I'm sure the records would be sealed, anyway."

"Shoot. I really want to read that one."

Charles shrugs. "Sorry."

I twist my mouth, thinking back to what I learned in school. Specifically, a class called Journalism and the Justice System. "Do you think maybe there's some roundabout way I could get my hands on it? Like, some motion or deposition that might at least refer to it or summarize it?"

Charles considers my question for a long beat before his face lights up. "Hold on. I've got an idea." He clacks on his computer keyboard, and then smiles like a Cheshire cat. "Bingo. I searched for any case involving Eleanor Rivers, even if she was the *plaintiff*, and hit pay dirt. A year after the dissolution and custody dispute, Eleanor sued her divorce attorney for malpractice."

I look at Charles blankly, not understanding how this information helps my cause.

Charles smirks. "It means you're in luck. Apparently, Eleanor didn't like the result of her divorce and custody battle, and thought her attorney in that case botched the job. So she sued her for malpractice. It's not guaranteed you'll get *all* the details of the underlying divorce and custody dispute by reading the malpractice lawsuit that came a year later, but I'm guessing you'll at least get the gist."

"*Oh*," I say, a lightbulb going off. "Because, in order to explain how her attorney messed up in the divorce case, Eleanor would have had to summarize that underlying case?"

"Exactly." He clacks on his keyboard for a moment. "Okay, the malpractice lawsuit is something I can get for you. It's general civil litigation, not family law. But it was filed twenty-two years ago, so you'll have to fill out a form for that one, so it can be retrieved from the archives or microfiche, or whatever. You'll probably have the documents in about a week or so."

I'm giddy. "Thank you so much, Charles. Oh my gosh. You're a rock star."

I fill out the form he gives me, listing the address for delivery of the documents as the offices of *Rock 'n' Roll*—not River Records—even though Owen has kindly set me up with a cubicle down the hallway from him. I don't know what, of interest, I'm going to find in Eleanor Rivers' twenty-two-year-old malpractice lawsuit, if anything. But, whatever is in that file, I sure as hell don't want Reed walking in on me in my cubicle and discovering that I'm reading it.

"Thank you again for all your help, Charles. You're the best."

"No problem. I'll be back in a jiffy."

When Charles leaves, I take a rickety chair in a corner, pull out my laptop, and make furious notes. But a few minutes into my note-taking, I get a phone call from Reed.

"Why, hello there, Mr. Rivers," I say.

"Hello there, Miss Ricci. My meeting just ended. Where are you?"

My stomach tightens. "At a coffee place."

"Which one? I'll pick you up."

I glance at the empty spot at the counter, where there's still no sign of Charles. "Actually, um, the writer assigned as my mentor at *Rock 'n' Roll*—this woman named Zasu—happens to be downtown, so I'm going to hook up with her for a bit. I'll grab an Uber after that and meet you at your house."

"I can hang around and do some work in a conference room at Leonard's, if you won't be too long. I know you're excited to sit in on my weekly team meeting."

"Oh, I am. Will you be having another weekly meeting next Monday?"

"Yes. But won't that fall outside the week you've earmarked for shadowing me? Are you sure you want to keep following me around after your obligatory week is up?"

Reed's tone is flirty and fun, so I throw back more of the same.

"Hey, whatever it takes to write the best possible article about you, I'm willing to make the sacrifice. Although, to be clear, an extra day of following you around will be a *huge* sacrifice."

I can hear his smile across the phone line. "The Intrepid Reporter strikes again."

My stomach somersaults. I look around the clerk's office, feeling guilty as hell. But why? I'm not doing anything wrong I'm only doing exactly what I was hired to do: *dig a little deeper*. Exactly what Reed *knows* I was hired to do. I mean, come on, as fun as this surprising romance with Reed is, it's not like it will lead to anything serious. It's fun, yes. So fun, it should be illegal. But I can't let it sidetrack me from my higher purpose, which is writing the most kickass article I can, and getting myself my dream job.

"I think I'll catch the weekly meeting next week," I say. "And meet you back at your house later, after I'm done with my work."

"Okay. Work hard. Play hard. And I'll do the same." He chuckles. "Although, I must admit, I'm gonna have a bitch of a time trying to get you off my mind during my weekly meeting. I could barely do it during my meeting with Leonard and the expert witness."

My heart skips a beat. He's so freaking yummy, I can barely stand it. "Yeah, I can honestly say I've been thinking about you, pretty much nonstop, since I left Leonard's office. How was the meeting with the expert, by the way?"

"Couldn't have gone better. She agrees the copyright infringement lawsuit is total and complete bullshit—nothing but a meritless money-grab by an unscrupulous plaintiffs' lawyer."

"Oh, that's great news."

"It is. I already knew the lawsuit is bullshit. But the legal system is such a crap shoot sometimes. It's nice to hear an expert confirm what I already know."

"I bet. You've been sued a lot, huh?"

"Oh, God, Georgie. So many times, I've lost count. It would boggle your mind if you saw an actual list of all the times one of my companies has been sued for one thing or another over the years."

I look down at the printout of lawsuits that's coincidentally sitting on my lap at this very moment, and my stomach tightens again. Why do I feel like I'm doing something terribly wrong by having this printout? Why do I feel like I'm doing something disloyal by being here at all, and not telling Reed about it? Truly, I need to take a chill pill, keep my eye on the prize, and my mouth shut—at least, for now, until I know what's in the documents I've ordered. For all I know, I'll read the entire stack and think, *Yeah, so what?*

"Hey, maybe I should come to the coffee place and meet this other reporter," Reed says. "I could reschedule my team meeting..."

"No!" I take a deep breath. "Don't do that. Just go about your normal life. I don't want to be a disruption."

He chuckles. "Well, it's too late for that. You've already knocked my world off its axis, Georgina."

My breathing halts. "You've knocked my world off its axis too," I whisper. I cup my hand to the phone, so nobody else waiting in the clerk's office will overhear me. "I feel addicted to you, Reed. So horny for you, I think I might be losing my mind."

He lets out a slow exhale. "Amalia's leaving at five today. Be at my house at five-oh-one."

"I'll be there. I can't wait to be alone with you again. Now that I'm hearing your voice again, I'm physically craving you."

His breathing has become audible. "I can't wait to make you scream again. I can't stop thinking about the way it felt to fuck you in my swing."

"Georgina?" a male voice says, and I abruptly swivel my head toward the counter, bug-eyed, like a thief caught with two bags of money. Charles, the clerk, is approaching the counter.

"I've got to go," I blurt to Reed. "The... barista just called my name for my coffee order. I'll see you at five-oh-one."

"Don't be late."

"I won't."

My heart racing, I hang up, feeling like an asshole, a liar, a scumbag for lying to Reed, and stride to the counter. "Wow, that was fast. Thank you."

Charles puts a large cardboard box onto the counter between us. Its side is imprinted with the words *Courthouse Copy Service*. "This is everything," he says. "There weren't a lot of documents in each file. Just the plaintiff's complaint, the defendant's answer, and a notice of settlement."

"Perfect." I pay for the copies and reach for the box, but Charles doesn't let go of it. "Why don't I carry this to your car for you? It's kind of heavy."

"I'm strong. I can handle it. Plus, I don't have a car. But, thanks."

"Well, how about we grab a coffee, then? I'm due for my break."

Shit. Seriously? I don't have time for this. "Thanks for the kind offer. But I've actually got a boyfriend, so..." I physically yank the box from Charles' grasp. "Thank you so much for expediting this for me. You're a prince. Bye now. Have a great day." And off I go, as fast as my legs will carry me, while lugging a pretty heavy cardboard box.

When I get outside, I put the box down and pull out my phone. "Siri, where is the nearest coffee place?"

"I think I've found what you're looking for," Siri replies, showing me several nearby choices. I pick one, rest the box of legal documents onto my hip, and head off, excited to find a quiet spot where I can sip an iced coffee and devour as much of the contents of this box as possible before heading to Reed's house... where, God willing, he'll take me to heaven again, the same way he did in his swing this morning... only, this time, perhaps while tied to the four posters of his bed.

FORTY-ONE
REED

Me: Where the hell are you, butterfly? It's 5:18 and my net is rock hard and ready to capture you (so I can thereafter tack your wings to paper and enclose you in an airtight frame).

Georgina: So sorry! I lost track of time reading something at a coffee place downtown, and then got stuck in traffic. My navigation app estimates arrival time of 5:49. Don't you dare touch your butterfly net before then. Save yourself for me.

Me: I'll stay locked and loaded for you, baby. Gate code 874593. I'll be in my bedroom.

Georgina: Can't wait. PS I'm starving. Is there food?

Me: Amalia's soup.

Georgina: Oh yeah! So excited. Don't eat without me! XO

Me: Of course not. See you soon. XO

Smiling like a goof, I toss my phone onto my mattress next to me. For the love of fuck, I just texted her "XO." I've only ever texted that sardonically to Josh. What is this girl doing to me?

My phone on the bed next to me rings, drawing me from my thoughts, and when I glance at the screen, I see it's Isabel calling me. Fuck. She's been calling me all day, without ever leaving a voicemail. Sighing, I pick up my phone.

"Hi, Isabel."

"Finally!" she shouts. "I've been trying to call you all day. Why haven't you picked up?"

"I've been in meetings. Why didn't you send a text or leave a voicemail?"

"Because what I've got to say has to be said in an actual conversation."

My heart stops. *No.* In a flash, my brain hurtles back to that drunken night in the Hamptons. How long ago was that? I wore a condom that night, didn't I? I'm positive I did... Oh, God, *please* tell me I wore a condom... and that it didn't break.

"I'm getting married," Isabel declares, and every hair on my body wilts in relief.

"Did you just sigh with relief?" Isabel shouts, going from zero to sixty on a dime.

"I sighed, but it was with happiness for you. So, who's the lucky guy?"

"Seriously?"

"What?"

"I call you, out of the blue, to say I'm getting married, and *that's* your reaction? *I'm happy for you, Isabel, who's the lucky guy?*"

I chuckle. "How should I have reacted? I know you've always wanted to get married."

"To you, dumbass!"

"Well, we both know that was never going to happen, so it's good you've found your Plan B. Now, are you going to identify the lucky man you're going to pledge yourself to for eternity, or not?"

She pauses for a long beat, before saying, "It's Howard."

"*Devlin?*"

"Obviously, Reed."

Holy fuck. Even lying here on my bed alone, I make a face like I've just swallowed a bite of rancid yogurt. Howard Devlin is a sixty-something-year-old blow-hard billionaire movie producer/studio head who thinks his shit doesn't stink. He's always had an obsession with Isabel. That's not a secret. Ever since she first met him at her first big audition. But she's never given him the time of day. And now, suddenly, she's agreed to marry him? It was Howard's studio that signed Isabel to her four-movie deal a couple weeks ago. Did Howard make this engagement a condition of the deal? Is this a PR stunt? It's got to be. Isabel can't possibly love him. And she certainly doesn't need his money. She'll probably net upwards of fifty million by the time those four pictures are done, assuming they hit as big as hoped. Was fifty million Isabel's price to slip a ring on her finger? Or did Howard sweeten the pot, on top of that, to coax her into saying yes to his proposal?

"I didn't want you to find out online," Isabel says. "I'm going to post a photo of Howard and me tomorrow, with my rock on full display."

"You're making it 'Gram official, huh? Wow. This is serious."

"I want you to comment on the post. It's important people see we're still good friends, and you've got no hard feelings about me dumping you and moving on."

I chuckle. She didn't dump me. And I definitely don't have hard feelings. But what I say is, "Fine with me."

She sighs. "Thanks."

Oh, shit. I shouldn't do it. I don't give a fuck what she does. But that "thanks" sounded so damned defeated, I can't resist. "Are you okay, Isabel?"

"Of course, I'm okay. I just got engaged. I'm on Cloud Nine."

She sounds resigned. Detached. Just plain sad. But, unfortunately, I'm not the guy who can make her happy. Surely, Howard Devlin isn't, either. I'm not sure anyone could make Isabel happy, actually. Her online avatar is the happiest woman alive. But the real Isabel? She's got a gaping hole in her soul she's never been able to fill—though, God bless her, she keeps trying.

"So, Gary said you're throwing a party on Saturday night," she says, referring to Gary Pembroke, her agent, the top guy at the top talent agency in Hollywood. A guy who represents the highest echelon of A-listers, some of whom have already RSVP'd for my party.

"Yeah, my entire roster will be there, other than RCR and a couple others. Plus, a pretty impressive crowd from your world will be there, too."

"Yeah, Gary said it's going to be the coolest party of the year."

Well, clearly, she's trolling for an invitation. Which isn't going to happen. Hell no. Indeed, I open my mouth to say as much, when an idea slams me. *Georgina.* I bet she'd give her right arm to interview Isabel for *Dig a Little Deeper*! In fact, I bet Georgina would pick the world's current "It Girl" as an interview subject over me, any day of the week, if she were forced to choose only one of us. Granted, CeeCee sent Georgie to peel *my* onion, but I can't imagine CeeCee would complain if Georgina came back, instead, with an in-depth interview of the world's biggest movie star!

The only problem with this plan? Isabel's a notoriously wooden interview subject. She's renowned in the industry for giving great sound-bites—which is a skill in itself—but, otherwise, giving rote, formulaic interviews filled mostly with PR talking points. It's actually a fantastic thing when Isabel's on a press junket, where she's tasked with answering the same questions over and over to plug her latest movie. Or on a talk show, where the goal is being superficial and fun. But ask the woman to let down her guard and provide thoughtful, honest answers to less predictable questions, and she's a fucking train wreck.

But, still, I think this idea is worth a shot. I can't imagine a better "get" for Georgina than somehow managing an exclusive, in-depth interview of Isabel Randolph. Talk about something that will take the sting out of Georgina's disappointment at the end of the summer, if I wind up nixing most of her article about me. Of course, I'm not stupid. I'm only willing to invite Isabel to the party—a party attended by Georgina—if Isabel will be bringing the great love of her life as her plus-one, to ensure Isabel isn't all over me like a cheap suit.

"Hey, why don't you and Howard come to the party on Saturday?" I suggest. "If you want buzz about the engagement, then this party is the perfect place to get it. Photos of you two partying with rock stars and Hollywood A-listers will go a lot more viral than an Instagram post."

"Oh, that'd be great. Thanks."

I decide to give myself a bit of insurance that Isabel will actually show up to the party *with* Howard. "I'll even say a toast to you and Howard."

"Oh, that would be awesome. Thank you."

"You know what? I just got a great idea for an invaluable PR opportunity for you. Are you familiar with the magazine, *Dig a Little Deeper?*"

"Yeah. My PR woman keeps trying to nab a cover feature for me in that one, but no dice. Apparently, I'm not 'forthcoming enough' for the kinds of interviews they feature, especially for the cover slot."

"Did you know *Dig a Little Deeper* and *Rock 'n' Roll* were both founded by CeeCee Rafael?"

Isabel gasps. "Oh! Will CeeCee be at the party? I'd love to chat her up and convince her to give me that cover slot."

"No, CeeCee won't be there. She's out of the country this week. But just the other day, CeeCee told me, in confidence, she's considering a 'Women in Hollywood' special issue of *Dig a Little Deeper*." It's bullshit, but sometimes, the end justifies the means. "Don't tell her I told you about this, Isabel. CeeCee hasn't fully decided to do it yet. If she does, though, she said she's leaning toward putting Gabrielle LeMonde on the cover."

"Gabrielle?" She scoffs. "That's so inside the box. Yes, Gabrielle has three Oscars. But she's never secured a four-picture deal like mine. Nobody has. I'm a trailblazer, Reed."

"I couldn't agree more. That's exactly why I brought it up. You should be on that cover."

"Damn straight."

"This is confidential, too, but I happen to know CeeCee has assigned *one* of the two *Rock 'n' Roll* writers coming to the party, CeeCee's personal favorite, to gather content for *Dig a Little Deeper*. How about I introduce you to her, and you can charm the hell out of her —so much so, she wants to do an in-depth interview of you she could submit to CeeCee? If the interview is kick-ass enough, I'm sure CeeCee would want it as her cover feature for a 'Women in Hollywood' issue."

Isabel squeals. "I love it!"

"Apparently, this writer is some sort of phenom. Fresh out of college, and yet CeeCee said she's the best writer she's ever hired. I'm positive she'll be able to cook up something spectacular with you."

Isabel starts babbling about how excited she is. But as she talks, I hear Georgina's footsteps in the hallway—and, instantly, just knowing Georgina is in the house is making my dick buzz like a neon hotel *Vacancy* sign that's just been flipped on

"Hey, I've got to go, Isabel. I'll see you and Howard on Saturday."

"Thank you so much for always having my back, Reed. When push comes to shove, you're the one person—"

"You bet. I gotta go."

"Hang on. Are you planning to have a pre-party at your place before the party? I'd love to—"

"Nope. No pre-party. I'll see you at the party. Owen will text you. Congrats on your engagement."

Click.

FORTY-TWO
REED

I fling open my bedroom door after hanging up with Isabel, bursting at the seams to see Georgina. But she's not in the hallway. Shit. Did I imagine her footfalls a moment ago?

But I've no sooner had the thought than Georgina emerges from her bedroom door. When she sees me, her face lights up. Squealing, she barrels toward me, leaps into my arms, and wraps herself around me like a monkey in a tree.

And that's it. Without delay, we're a frenzied blur of lips and tongues and hungry, groping hands. I clutch her ass, kneading it frantically, as she grips my neck and hair and grinds her center against my aching bulge behind my pants.

Still devouring her, I turn around and bump and thump my way through my bedroom doorway, somehow making it across my room and to my bed without toppling over or sending a lamp crashing down.

Like a man possessed, I lay Georgie down on my bed and begin frantically peeling off her clothes and mine, while she gasps and purrs and goads me on. When we're both naked, I open her smooth, trembling thighs, crawl between them, and begin eating her with unbridled enthusiasm.

When I glance at her face, I find her looking enraptured... but with her eyes closed.

"Look in the mirror," I say. "Watch me eat you."

Her eyes flick open and train on the ceiling above us, and I get back to work, even more turned on to know she's watching me. And soon, she's losing her mind. Writhing, moaning, clawing at the bed. Until... *bliss*. I'm gifted with a screaming climax from Georgie that makes me dizzy with arousal. Panting, I crawl up the length of her writhing torso, place her thighs on my shoulders, and plunge myself deep inside her.

My thrusts are hard. Animalistic. Deep.

And Georgina responds by digging her nails into my forearms, screaming my name, and finally, coming hard. Not surprisingly, when I feel her innermost muscles constricting—milking me ferociously—it's more than I can withstand. With a loud groan, I release along with her, blurting her name like a prayer. I feel dizzy with my pleasure. Momentarily blinded by it. Blissed out like I've mainlined a brick of cocaine.

When we finally come down, I heave myself onto my back next to Georgina, trying to catch my breath, and she gasps at the air alongside me.

"That was amazing," she says.

"I told you not to knock the mirror till you tried it."

She smiles. "You have the most gorgeous ass."

"You have the most gorgeous everything."

I stroke her arm. "I've got some great news to tell you. Isabel Randolph called me today."

Georgina stiffens.

"*To tell me she's engaged*," I quickly add.

Georgina lifts her head and looks at me, but says nothing.

"To this guy named Howard Devlin. He's one of the most powerful movie producers in Hollywood. He actually owns a studio." I tell her a bit about Howard and the mega-successful studio he owns, concluding with, "His studio churns out blockbuster hits and Academy Award contenders, in equal measure. The guy can't miss."

"So, what you're saying is he's the Reed Rivers of the movie industry?"

I chuckle. "The reason I brought it up is that, while Isabel and I were talking about her happy news, I got an idea. What if you interviewed Isabel for *Dig a Little Deeper*? You know, in-depth, as one of the 'audition' pieces you submit to CeeCee?"

Georgina gasps. "Oh my God. I would love to do that! Do you think she'd say yes?"

"If you meet her and charm the hell out of her, I sure do. Which is why I invited Isabel and her new fiancé to the party on Saturday night. I figured it would be the perfect opportunity for you to get her to say yes to an in-depth interview."

Georgina bolts to a sitting position in the bed. Apparently, she's too excited about this idea to remain horizontal. "So, Isabel said she'd come to the party?"

"Yup. She also said she's excited to meet you and talk about a potential interview."

Georgina squeals. "You've already floated a possible interview with me?"

"Yep. To be clear, it's not a sure thing. You're going to have to convince her you've got the chops to write something worth her investment of time and image. And even if she winds up giving you an interview, you're going to have to finesse her to get something that will be on-brand for *Dig a Little Deeper*. For all her social media presence, Isabel is actually an extremely guarded person. Very curated, if you know what I mean. Too image-conscious for her own good. But if anyone can break down Isabel's walls and peel her onion, it's you, Georgina Ricci."

Elation washes over Georgina's face, followed immediately by determination. "By God, I'm going to make this happen."

I chuckle. "I don't doubt that for a minute. The way you handled Leonard today blew me away. If today had been a music demo, I would have signed you on the spot."

She leans down and kisses me. "Thank you for saying that."

"It's the truth."

"And thank you for trying to arrange this incredible opportunity for me. I can't believe it."

"You're welcome. I cracked the door open for you, baby. Now, kick that fucker wide open."

"Oh, I will." She bites her lower lip for a moment, her mind visibly teeming with thoughts. "Are you surprised she's getting married?"

"Yes and no. It's sudden. But she's always wanted to get married."

Her eyes narrow. "How do you feel about it?"

"About her getting married? I'm happy for her. Of course."

"No, but I mean... aren't you a tiny bit upset?"

"About...?"

"Isabel getting married."

I pull a face like that's an asinine comment. "Not at all."

She stares at me for a beat, like she's a psychic, trying to read my mind. And then, "You know that feeling when someone is driving away, and you suddenly realize you forgot to tell them something important? So you yell and wave at the car and maybe run after it down the street, but they don't see you... and then, the car is gone? You don't feel the tiniest bit like that?"

I smirk. "Is that your clever way of asking me if I feel like Isabel is my 'one that got away'?"

She looks like she's holding her breath.

I grab her hand. "Georgina, no. Isabel and I are more like brother and sister than exes at this point. I still care about her as a person, and want the best for her. If I can help her out with something in some way, without too much effort or annoyance on my part, I'll always do it. But I know I'm not even close to the guy who can make her happy, and she knows it, too. So it's for the best she's found the guy who can."

Georgie lets out a long exhale, like she just made it to the ledge after a long walk across a high wire. "Do you have any tips for me, for when I talk to her at the party? Anything at all to help me close the deal?"

"Well, for one thing, I wouldn't mention you're fucking me."

Georgina rolls her eyes. "Yeah, I figured that one out all by myself. Engaged or not, no woman would ever want to give an in-depth interview to her ex's..."

Georgina trails off, apparently not sure of the appropriate word to finish that sentence. And I don't blame her. I have no idea how she should finish it, either.

"Here's a tip for you," I say. "Something that will work like a charm on her." I pull on Georgina's arm, guiding her to lie in my arms. "Tell Isabel you heard her franchise deal set a record in terms of salary for a female lead. Tell her she'll go down in history as breaking new ground for women in Hollywood. Call her a 'trailblazer' for women in Hollywood."

"Ooooh, that's good."

"Actually, that's a great hook. Tell her you're going to pitch the idea of a special 'Women in Hollywood' issue of *Dig a Little Deeper*, with Isabel as the cover interview."

"Oooh!"

"I'm positive both CeeCee and Isabel would *love* that idea. In fact, if you want to guarantee Isabel will give you a pound of flesh in an interview, rather than her usual guarded talking points, then dangle her possibly being the face of a prestigious issue like that... only if her interview is in-depth and revealing enough."

"Holy crap. You're a genius! My Fairy Godfather!" She grabs my face and lays an enthusiastic smack on my mouth. "Thank you so much for this!"

"I only planted the seed. You're going to have to go in, guns blazing, and close the deal."

"ABC, baby!" Georgina says enthusiastically. "That means 'always be closing.'"

"Yes, I know. *Glengarry Glenross* is one of my all-time favorite movies. Finally, a pop culture reference we both know."

Georgina looks at me blankly, and I know she's a broken clock that happens to be right at the exact right moment.

"Aw, come on, Ricci! You can't say ABC, if you've never seen *Glengarry Glenross!*"

She giggles. "I just thought it was a cute thing hustlers say."

I pull her to me, laughing, and kiss the top of her head. "What am I going to do with you?"

She pinches my nipple. "I'm sure you'll think of something."

"Seriously, though. How do I even tolerate you, let alone like you so damned much?"

My heart lurches into my mouth. Oh, shit. What did I just say? Panic. It's rising inside me. Too much. Too soon. She's gotten under my skin way too fast. And way too deep.

Sighing happily, Georgina lays her palm on my chest and shoots a wide, glorious smile at me, her hazel eyes sparkling. "I like you so damned much, too, Reed. So damned much, I feel like I'm going to burst when I'm with you."

And, just like that, my rising panic disappears... supplanted by butterflies in my stomach. No, bald eagles this time. Fucking condors.

Georgina's stomach rumbles loudly, making her giggle.

"Was that *you*?" I say, laughing.

She blushes. "I'm *hungry*."

"Well, damn, let's get you fed, before the alien living inside your stomach bursts out and eats my face."

She laughs, but, again, I know she's clueless.

"You have no idea what movie I just referenced, do you?" I say.

"You referenced a movie?"

Oh, God, I can't get enough of this girl. I touch her cheek. "What am I gonna do with you?"

"In the immediate future, feed me," she says "After that, do what ever you please."

I kiss her full lips gently, my heart soaring around the room. "Come, come, little kitty. Let's get you some food."

FORTY-THREE
GEORGINA

"I can't believe how good this is," I say, eating another mouthful of Amalia's amazing soup.

"It's my all-time favorite," Reed says. "The word 'soup' doesn't do it justice."

We're sitting across from each other at Reed's small kitchen table. I'm wearing a tank top and a pair of soft shorts. Reed is shirtless and in sweats, looking like a god. And for the past twenty minutes or so, I've been peppering him with follow-up questions about what Leonard told me at his office today. I've asked my questions out of genuine curiosity. But also, they've been my way of easing into asking Reed about an even greater topic of interest: the lawsuits I got earlier today at the courthouse.

Thus far, I've read two out of the three lawsuits the court clerk copied for me. I ran out of time to read the third, before it was time to head back to Reed's house. But what I've read so far in the first two lawsuits has raised some serious questions for me. Well, actually, not the first one involving a lease dispute. That one was a total snoozefest, as expected.

But the *second* lawsuit, the one filed eight years ago by a former employee of River Records claiming sexual harassment and wrongful termination? Yeah, I've got some burning questions about that one. All of which I plan to ask Reed about during this meal. Just as soon as I muster the courage.

In her lawsuit, Stephanie claimed Reed pressured her into having a sexual relationship for several months, and then fired her when she refused to continue. Which means, if her claims were true, then Reed was, and *is*, an asshole of epic proportions. A dirtbag who'd shamelessly abuse his power.

But Stephanie's version of Reed doesn't ring true to me. Yes, he's harsh at times. And arrogant. But the kind of boss who'd force an employee into a sexual relationship? Reed himself told me he never has sex with his employees. Also, when I toured River Records with Owen, back when Reed was still in New York, it was clear to me everyone on Reed's staff, including a bunch of women, respect their boss. Yes, they said he's exacting and tough and pulls no punches. Yes, one person laughingly said Reed can flash-freeze a room with one withering glare. But it was obvious to me they all admire their fearless leader, and would follow him to the ends of the earth.

I mean, I recognize I might not be the best person to accurately assess Reed on this topic, since the man started hitting on me the second he saw me. But he's not my boss. And, in fact, expressly told me he wouldn't have agreed to the special edition if it meant he would be.

Plus, I've never felt taken advantage of by Reed, even when we've gone toe to toe. For instance, backstage at the RCR show, when we were engaged in hard-nosed "negotiations," Reed stopped me several times, when I made a misstep, to tell me I'd said the wrong thing—basically, to give me a free pass—because he knew he's got far more experience at negotiations than I do.

Frankly, if it weren't for the fact that Reed settled Stephanie's case, and has told me his philosophy regarding settlements, I'd be thinking Stephanie's complaint was almost certainly a pack of lies, every bit as much as the copyright infringement lawsuit against Red Card Riot. But Reed *did* settle it. And Reed *did* tell me he only settles cases when they've got merit, or he thinks a jury will believe it.

The bottom line? I'm dying to ask Reed what the hell happened between him and Stephanie Moreland. Will Stephanie's lawsuit make it into my article? It's unlikely. But, either way, Reed is the man I've been sleeping with. The man I've been swooning over. Feeling addicted to.

The man who gives me butterflies like crazy. If it turns out he's an asshole who'd force an employee into a sexual relationship, then, regardless of my article, I want to know about it.

I eat the last spoonful of my soup and push my empty bowl to the side.

"Would you like another bowl?" Reed asks.

"No, I'm good."

"Another beer?"

"Yeah. Thanks."

Reed gets up and heads to the stove with his empty bowl.

"So, I did something kind of clever today," I say.

"Oh, yeah?"

"After you said I wouldn't believe it if I saw the list of lawsuits you've had to deal with over the past ten years, I popped over to the courthouse to see for myself."

It's a little white lie. In truth, I'd already had the printout when Reed made that specific comment this afternoon. But Reed already thinks I'm freaking Bobby Fischer, and I don't want to give him more reasons to think that. Let him think I'm smart and sneaky, sure, but not *that* smart and sneaky.

Reed returns to the table, puts down his refilled bowl, and hands me a beer bottle. "And? The list is as thick as a phone book, right?"

"Well, I've never actually seen a phone book, but I get your meaning. Yes, it was crazy-thick. I don't know how you sleep at night with so many people gunning for you, claiming you've done them dirty."

Reed takes a swig of his beer and shrugs. "Getting sued is one of the costs of doing business, especially in California. I don't take it personally."

"I was amazed at how many different kinds of lawsuits there were," I say, my pulse quickening. I'm circling the runway, getting ready to land. "There was everything from personal injury to breach of lease to copyright infringement to wrongful termination."

I watch him closely at those last words... but he doesn't flinch. Indeed, he smoothly takes a bite of food, as relaxed as ever.

"I've got a great team of lawyers," he says. He swigs his beer. "Also, I rest easy knowing almost all of it is total bullshit. The truth shall prevail, right? And if not, then I pay what needs to be paid, and move on."

My breathing hitches. *Does that mean Stephanie's lawsuit was the truth?* But I don't have the courage to land the plane yet. I'm still circling like a coward. "The printout noted you'd settled a lease dispute?"

He takes another bite of food. "Yeah. That was years ago. At my very first office space, I'd stupidly signed for way too long a lease period, thinking my business would expand much more slowly than it did."

At my urging, he tells me about the case. And, as expected, it's a big ol' nothing-burger. In summary, Reed's business blew up like crazy, way faster than he thought it would, and the space he'd been renting became way too small for his operations. So, he vacated that space, in order to rent a much bigger one—the one he's in now, actually—thereby breaching his lease.

"I never denied I'd broken the lease," Reed says. "I told the landlord I was willing to pay him what I owed him. But he wanted to gouge me. So I said, 'Here's what I rightfully owe you. Sue me for the rest, motherfucker.' And he did."

"And?" I say. "Did the guy get everything he'd wanted in the settlement?"

"No. Not even close."

"Was it all worth it in the end?" I ask, still trying to figure out how to broach the topic of Stephanie Moreland.

Reed's eyes light up. "Oh, God, yes. I had to act fast when the space I'm in now became available. It was the exact one I used to drive by in college and dream of occupying one day. Every day I get to walk into my lobby at River Records, every day I get to see my name above the door on *that* particular office space, every day I get to see all those framed gold and platinum and diamond records on those walls, I feel like I've made all my dreams come true."

Goosebumps erupt on my arms. Not only about what Reed just said, but how lit up he looked while saying it. "Hold that thought," I say, grabbing my phone. "I've got to make some notes. You just gave me goosebumps."

He laughs. "Knock yourself out, Intrepid Reporter."

I make a bunch of notes. Ask him to repeat a few things. And when I finally put down my phone and look up, I find Reed smiling broadly at me.

"What?" I ask.

He bites back his smile. "Nothing."

"Why were you smiling like that?"

"If I tell you, are you going to get angry?"

"It depends what you say."

"Are you going to flip me off?"

"No. I'll refrain, no matter what you say."

Again, he bites back a smile. "I just find you incredibly entertaining. And adorable. And, yes, amusing. And sexy. And smart. And, on occasion, all of that just makes it impossible for me not to smile."

I return his wide, beaming, beautiful smile. "Oh."

"Does any of that make you want to punch me in the face?"

"No. It makes me want to kiss you."

He laughs. "Progress."

"I'd say so."

I take a sip of beer. Shit. If I don't ask about this now, the moment will pass and I'll fall hopelessly under his spell again. It's now or never.

"So, one of the lawsuits on the printout caught my eye, in particular." I take a deep breath. "One you settled. The case was filed by a woman named Stephanie Moreland. She said you sexually harassed and wrongfully terminated her."

Boom.

Reed's demeanor changes. His jaw sets. His posture stiffens. And I know, without a doubt, I've stumbled upon something Reed doesn't want to talk about.

FORTY-FOUR
GEORGINA

"What happened with Stephanie Moreland?" I ask. "You settled it. So, that means there was some truth to her claims... or you thought a jury would believe her... right?"

Reed drags his palm down his face. He takes a long sip of his beer. Puts down his bottle. And exhales. "If I tell you about this, Georgina, you have to promise me this conversation will be off the record. I know what you said about me being able to nix anything I don't like in your article. But this particular thing..." He shakes his head. "It's the most humiliating thing that's ever happened to me, besides my father's arrest and conviction. And I don't want to have to read about it, or think about it, or see it reflected back to me through your eyes. I'll talk about it with you, to ease whatever doubts I'm assuming you're now having about me. But I'm only going to tell the woman I'm sleeping with this story. Not the reporter who's trying to get herself a permanent position at *Dig a Little Deeper*."

I feel short of breath. Sick to my stomach. What choice do I have?

I exhale. "Okay."

"Off the record?"

I nod. "Yes."

Reed takes another long swig of beer. Takes another deep breath.

"Stephanie was my first full-time hire at River Records. A marketing manager I hired right after RCR's debut rocketed up the charts. Early on, I could tell we had chemistry. But I never made a move on her because I was her boss. But then one night, Stephanie comes into my office and closes the door. This was right before RCR's second album was set to come out, and I was totally stressed out. Sophomore albums are notoriously dicey, and I was determined to catch lightning in a bottle again. So, I was working round the clock. Sleeping on a couch in my office. Doing way too much coke."

My eyebrows ride up.

"I don't do that anymore. Ever. But I was a big fan back then, especially in times of extreme stress. So, anyway, Stephanie comes in and says she knows I've been stressed out, and she wants to help me relax."

I cringe.

"Yeah, it's what you're thinking. I was sitting in my desk chair at the time, and she kneels in front of me and gets busy. I hadn't come on to her in the slightest before then, so it was totally out of the blue. And I was shocked. I knew I should say, 'No, Stephanie. Bad idea.' But I didn't. She was hot, and I was high as a kite. And I thought, 'Fuck it. She's the one coming on to me. What could go wrong?'" He rolls his eyes at himself. "Well, from that moment on, she owned my ass, although I didn't know it at the time." He shakes his head, rolling his eyes at himself. "For the next few months after that first BJ in my office, we'd fucked around at the office. I never saw her outside of work. Never took her on a date. Never took her to my place or went to hers. But we had some fun, now and again, after everyone else had gone home. But then things got out of control. Every time I turned around, even during normal working hours, she was unzipping my pants, or begging me to fuck her over the copy machine. It was like she wanted us to get caught. Like she wanted everyone to know she was fucking the boss. And then, *boom*. RCR's second album comes out and it's a global smash. I mean, holy shit, Georgie. I'd thought their first album was big, but that sophomore album took things to another level. And then came the debut of Danger Doctor Jones, which hit top ten. And then 2Real hit number one with 'Crash.' And I swear to God, I thought I must have made a deal with the devil, without remembering it. Which, it turns out, I did. Thanks to my coked-out pecker. A devil named Stephanie Moreland."

"Oh, Reed."

"She comes into my office and closes the door. She wants to give me a blowjob to celebrate 2Real's number one. But by then, I was sick to death of her. Sick of messing around. Sick of the distraction. Sick of myself. I wasn't even physically attracted to her anymore. Just disgusted. So I told her it was over. That we had to go back to being completely professional. And, to my shock, she said, 'You think you can get rid of me that easily? Guess what, asshole? I *own* your fucking ass now.' So, I said, 'I'm not getting rid of you, Stephanie. You're good at your job. I just mean I'm done *fucking* you. I've been an idiot to mess around with an employee, a coked-out idiot, and I've decided to clean up my act and never do it again.'" He shakes his head. "It turned out, she was recording that conversation, and a whole lot of others. Plus, every sex act. Every bit of dirty talk."

I grimace with him. "No wonder you settled the case."

"No, the recordings weren't the reason I settled, actually. I knew they were illegal. Both parties have to consent to recording in California, thank God. But what they made me realize was she'd totally set me up. From day one, I'd been her mark. She came into *my* office to give me that BJ, knowing she was ultimately going to come after me. And that freaked me out. I knew it was going to be her word against mine, if she accused me of something. And normally, I'd take on that challenge. But what would someone like *that* be willing to say about me?"

"Why didn't you turn her in for making those illegal recordings? That's a crime, right?"

"And let the police hear all that shit? Ha! No, thanks. Plus, I knew I was guilty as shit. I was her boss, and I'd fucked her. No getting around that."

"So what happened? Did she demand hush money?"

"Not at first. Instead, she decided her job duties had become 'optional.' For a couple months, she came and went as she pleased. Never made deadlines. Took days off, without calling in. I knew she was daring me to fire her, so she could sue me. Obviously, I didn't want a lawsuit. I just wanted to move past the sex thing and have her do her job, as required. But then she went MIA for a week, without a word, so I fired her, and she sued my ass a day later, making me sound like a monster. But guess what? Under California law, I *was* a monster, and I fully acknowledge that. When you're the boss, you can't fuck your employees. Period. There's no gray area. It's a strict liability state, meaning there's no defense. No saying, 'Hey, it was consensual.' No saying, 'Hey, she came onto *me*.' If you're the boss, and you've fucked an employee, then you've committed sexual harassment."

"Oh, Reed."

"It's actually a fair system, ninety-nine percent of the time. Sociopaths like Stephanie are rare. I've thought about this quite a bit."

"I'm sure you have."

"And I've realized something big. As the boss, I can never know, for sure, if an employee genuinely wants to sleep with me, or if she's only saying yes because she's afraid of losing her job if she says no. She could say yes. She could even come on to me. But I've realized there's no way to separate the fact that I hold all the power, when it comes to my employees. So, in the end, I've got no quarrel with the way the laws are written. The rules are clear and there for a reason. Just because I'm an idiot who let myself get played by a con artist, doesn't mean the laws aren't fair. Which is exactly what Stephanie was, by the way: a con artist. Leonard's investigator did some digging and found out she'd done the exact same thing twice before."

"No way."

"Yep. She'd slept with her boss, made secret recordings, and then threatened a sexual harassment lawsuit to get herself paid. I was the only one who didn't pay her off right away, so she'd never filed anything before. But, still, it was the same MO."

"Why the heck did you settle when you realized she's a con artist? Surely, the jury would have believed you, when they found out she'd done it before!"

"That's exactly what I said to Leonard. But he and his team convinced me those other instances wouldn't get into evidence, and I'd get reamed at trial. He said, even without the recordings being admissible against me, any jury would hate my guts for fucking around with an employee. Leonard said my cocaine use would come out. And that would make them believe Stephanie's version of events. He said I could get hit for ten million or more in punitive damages, given how my company had just skyrocketed. So, I caved." He rubs his forehead, looking distraught. "I paid her off in a confidential settlement that required her to destroy all the illegal recordings she'd made of me, got my ass to rehab, and tried not to think about Stephanie fucking Moreland, ever again."

My heart is physically aching at the expression on Reed's face. "You haven't done coke since then?"

"No. Never."

"How much did you wind up paying her?"

Reed pauses. "It was a confidential settlement, so I'm technically not allowed to talk about it, any more than she is. I'll tell you the number, but only if you swear you're just Georgie right now. Not the Intrepid Reporter. Not playing me, in any way. Look me in the eye, and promise this will stay between you and me, forever, and I'll tell you."

My heart is thumping. "I promise, Reed. I'll never tell a soul."

"You're not recording this conversation?"

Oh, my heart. This poor man. "I'm not. I'll never record anything you say without your knowledge and express permission. I promise."

He looks down at his hands on the kitchen table. "I paid that bitch a cool million."

"Wow. An expensive life lesson."

"Yeah. Honestly, the whole thing screwed with my head. Before Stephanie, I'd already had a hard time trusting people. Women, especially. I was always positive they were out to get something from me. But after Stephanie, my paranoia with women went to a whole new level. Ever since then, I'm just super careful. Always on guard."

Oh, my heart. I rise from my chair and go to him. I slide into his lap and touch his cheek. "I'm sorry she messed with your head."

"I've never told anyone about her," he whispers. "Well, other than my lawyers."

I press my forehead against his. "Not even Josh and Henn?"

"No. I was too embarrassed to tell them. I fucked up. Royally. In the end, it was my fault for being so stupid and reckless."

My heart feels like it's going to burst from my chest. I feel so close to him right now, so connected. So much so, I feel the need to reciprocate. To tell him something I've never told anyone, as well. "I've got my own Stephanie Moreland," I whisper, my heartbeat increasing. "I've never told anyone this story. But it's something that's made it really hard for me to trust. Something I can't stand thinking about. Something I want to forget." I swallow hard. "But I want to tell you about it. I want to tell you, because I feel really close to you right now."

He strokes my hair and looks deeply into my eyes. "You can tell me anything, Georgie."

I open my mouth... determined to tell him the thing I've never told anyone. Ever. But I close my mouth, too nervous to begin my story. "I think I'm gonna need some liquid courage to do this." I motion to my beer. "Something a bit stronger than that."

FORTY-FIVE
REED

We're sitting on barstools at the bar in my game room. Holding our second shots of Patrón.

"On the count of three," Georgina says. And when she counts us off, we both throw the tequila back.

"Beer chaser?" I ask.

"Hell yeah."

I grab bottles for both of us from a mini-fridge behind the bar, and she takes a long swig as I resume my stool.

"Okay. I'm ready to tell you my story now," she says, shaking out her hands. "I can't feel my face or toes."

I laugh. "You don't have to tell me this story, you know."

"I know, but I want to." She takes another long swig of her beer. Laces her fingers together on top of the bar. And exhales. "In high school, I wrote for the school newspaper the first three years. And I absolutely loved it. At the end of my third year, Mr. Gates, the teacher who supervised the paper, selected *me* to be editor-in-chief for the next year, over this total brainiac guy who'd also wanted the position. I was so freaking excited and proud to be selected, I could barely keep it together. I'd worked my ass off for three years, unlike the brainiac guy. He was way smarter than me, but he'd just phoned it in."

"Hustle beats talent, when talent doesn't hustle," I say. I grab her hand. "Although you've got both talent and hustle, so never mind."

She squeezes my hand. "Thank you." She pauses. "As it turned out, some of the kids at the newspaper—particularly, this group of mean girls—didn't think I deserved the editor position. So, they started a rumor that Mr. Gates had only selected me because he wanted to sleep with me."

"Oh, Georgie. Those girls were bitches."

She looks down at her beer, and it's immediately clear those mean girls aren't, collectively, her Stephanie Moreland, like I was just thinking. No, apparently, there's more to this story. I wait, my pulse thumping.

"I just tried to ignore the rumors and gossip and put my head down and work harder than anyone else, you know? I was so embarrassed they'd say that. I just wanted to work extra hard to prove them all wrong about me. To show them I *had* deserved the promotion." She looks up from her hands. "And then, one day, in the middle of my senior year, when I was working after school in the newspaper room, all by myself... Mr. Gates came in... and he..." She takes a shallow breath. "He cornered me, and he... pinned my arms behind my back, and he... he kissed me."

I'm flooded with rage. Disgust. A fierce urge to protect. I need to fix this. Protect Georgie. *Kill that motherfucker.*

Georgina wells up. "He said all this crazy stuff about me teasing him and flirting with him. He said I wore sexy clothes to turn him on. But I swear I didn't!"

I get up and hug her and she collapses into me. "Of course, you didn't. No matter what you wore, no matter what you did or said, ever, he had no right to touch you. Georgie, he was a fucking monster and you did absolutely nothing wrong."

"I was so shocked and scared... So ashamed."

"*Ashamed?* You had nothing to be ashamed about. He assaulted you."

"Yeah, but those girls were right about me the whole time. He picked me over the brainiac only because he wanted to sleep with me!"

"Oh, sweetheart."

"You want to hear the craziest part? That's what I was thinking when he did it. 'Those mean girls were right.'"

"Did you report him?"

"No. I knew nobody would ever believe me. Plus, I was embarrassed. The same as you with those illegal recordings."

"You had nothing to be embarrassed about. He *assaulted* you, Georgie. You should have reported him."

"You don't understand. Mr. Gates also coached football, and the team had won two championships in four years. Everybody loved Mr. Gates. If I thought those mean girls were on my ass before, I couldn't even imagine what would happen to me if I told anyone about what Mr. Gates did. Plus, there was no way I wanted those girls to find out they'd been right. It was the most humiliating, embarrassing, horrifying thing I could imagine."

I'm losing my fucking mind. A hair's breadth away from jumping in one of my cars and driving in a blind rage to the Valley to find this Mr. Gates and wrap my bare hands around his throat and squeeze the fucking life out of him.

"I quit the paper the very next day," she says flatly. "I knew I couldn't tell anyone what he'd done. And I didn't want to be in the same room with him, ever again. Thank God, I'd already gotten into UCLA, and my second-semester grades didn't matter. Because the entire rest of the school year, I couldn't concentrate. I was always on edge. If I saw Mr. Gates across campus, I ran the other direction and hid in a bathroom. At first, my father thought my grades plummeted because I was having boy problems. Then, he figured it was because I'd gotten into college and had senioritis. But the truth was, I was a wreck the entire rest of the school year because of Mr. Gates and this horrible secret I was keeping."

"You poor, poor baby." I wipe her tears. "I'm so sorry this happened to you." I stroke her cheek. "You've never told anyone any of this before?"

She shakes her head. "Not even Alessandra. You're the only person I've ever told."

I pull her to me and hold her tight. My heart is thundering. Aching. Breaking. Bleeding. My blood is boiling. I'm out of my head. "Does Gates still work at the school?"

"Yes. But please don't try to get me to report him. I just can't do it, Reed. No one would ever believe me. You need to trust me on this. He's a god at that school." She breaks free from our embrace and wipes her eyes. "It's okay. I've moved on. Honestly, getting this internship has worked wonders for me. Getting to work for CeeCee. A kickass woman. Knowing, for a *fact*, she offered me this internship based on my talent and nothing else... because she loved my writing, and my personality, not because she wanted to get into my pants. Having that kind of validation has meant everything to me and my confidence and helped me move on so much. But Mr. Gates is part of the reason why I've been so adamant about not wanting your artists to know about us while I'm working on the special issue. I just want everyone I'm interviewing to respect me. I don't want them thinking I got assigned to the special issue, specifically, because you requested me for personal reasons."

Oh, fuck.

I feel physically sick.

On the outside, I might be stroking Georgina's back calmly, kissing her cheek, holding her close... but, on the inside, I'm freaking the fuck out.

Prior to this moment, I didn't want Georgie to find out I'm the one who funded her grant and made it so that her internship is a paid one. But now, all I can think, on a running loop, is: *Georgie can never, ever find out. Never, never, never.*

"You knocked CeeCee out when she met you, baby," I say soothingly. "When CeeCee and I first talked about the special issue, she specifically said she loved your writing samples. And she also said you're the most charismatic and charming newbie she's met in a long time. Maybe, ever."

She squeezes me tight. So tight, in fact, I suddenly feel overcome with emotion.

"CeeCee really said all that about me, Reed? You swear?"

"She really did, baby. I swear. In those exact words."

Holy fuck. I've never been more relieved to be able to honestly quote anybody's exact words in my entire life.

"That's so amazingly wonderful to know. Ever since Mr. Gates, I've been so paranoid and filled with self-doubt. Not only that, I've had such a hard time trusting anyone. The same way you've felt after Stephanie Moreland. I think Mr. Gates is part of the reason why I went so batshit psycho on my boyfriend, Shawn, when I discovered he'd cheated on me.

Because I'd let down my guard with him and trusted him. And it's so, so hard for me to do that."

I pause. And disengage from our embrace. "Um. So... how 'batshit psycho' are we talking here?"

She smiles through her tears. "Pretty fucking psycho."

I wait, but she says nothing further. All she does is giggle.

"You're not planning to elaborate?" I say.

"Not really," she says. And then she laughs again, still wiping tears.

I kiss her cheek. "Come on, Ricci. If I've invited a psycho into my home, I think I should know about it."

She twists her mouth adorably. Takes my hand, and kisses the top of it. "Okay, Mr. Rivers. I'll tell you this story, too. Why not? But let's talk about this next thing in the pool. I'm suddenly feeling the urge to float."

FORTY-SIX
REED

Georgie, the most beautiful girl in the world, is naked and floating silently in my moonlit swimming pool, while I stand next to her, looking down on her. Feeling like I'm staring at an angel sent straight from heaven. A batshit psycho angel, apparently. She hasn't told me the story yet. We had some champagne while sitting on the pool ledge together. And then peeled off our clothes. Made out a bit. And now, she's floating and in some sort of meditation, while I stand next to her, lightly supporting her naked, horizontal frame, thinking two things on repeat. One, I'll never let anybody hurt you again. And, two, I've never seen anything so fucking beautiful in my life.

Finally, Georgie opens her eyes and stands. Without saying a word, she wraps her arms and legs around my neck and torso, like a monkey clinging to a tree, and nuzzles her nose into mine. "I feel better now."

"Good. That's all I want for you. I want you to feel good and nothing else."

"Thank you. I feel good when I'm with you."

My heart skips a beat. "I feel good when I'm with you."

"Good. Now, walk me around the pool, while I lay my cheek on your shoulder and tell you about the time I went batshit psycho on my cheating ex."

"I can't wait to hear the story."

I begin walking a loop around the shallow end of my pool, as Georgina tells me about the time she awakened one fateful morning and discovered a string of texts and photos on her then-boyfriend's phone that confirmed her long-simmering suspicions: he was cheating on her like she didn't exist.

"Actually," she says, "confirming Shawn was cheating on me was a huge relief. Twice before that morning, I'd told Shawn he was acting really weird and suspicious and secretive, but both times he said I was crazy and paranoid. So, I was kind of thrilled in a weird way to finally know I wasn't insane—that he was cheating on me. And not just cheating on me. The dude had *four* side chicks."

"Four? Oh my God. No wonder you went batshit psycho on him."

"Right? Who could blame me!"

"So, what'd you do to the guy?"

She laughs. "I'm scared to tell you. I don't want you to be scared of me and send me packing."

Oh, God. She's so fucking adorable. "No worries about that. Your invitation to stay here for the whole summer is irrevocable."

She lifts her cheek from my shoulder and beams a radiant smile at me.

"Come on baby," I coo. "A little psycho won't scare me off. To be honest, I get turned on by a little bit of crazy. It keeps things from getting boring for me."

"Yeah, well, this wasn't a little bit of crazy, sweetie. It was a shit-ton of batshit psycho."

I wince. "Okay, I admit you're starting to scare me a tiny bit."

She giggles uproariously. "One more glass of champagne and then I'll tell you *everything*," she says with gusto, clearly savoring the fact that I'm on the edge of my proverbial seat, waiting to hear this story from her.

But, of course, since her wish is my command, I carry her to the ledge, where I fill our empty flutes from a bottle of Cristal we brought down to the pool with us.

"Aah, that's good," she says after taking a long sip. "Best champagne I've ever had."

"I should hope so. This stuff ain't cheap. It's liquid gold. Now, come on. Tell me what you did to the guy. No more stalling. I know you're enjoying torturing me. But enough is enough."

She looks at me flirtatiously. "Okay, but in my defense, keep in mind that my dad was in treatment at this point. So I was on the brink of a nervous breakdown, as it was. And, like I said, I was more enraged at the betrayal of my trust, in my time of need, than about the cheating itself."

"Just tell me the story already. I'll consider all mitigating factors once I know the extent of your batshit psychosis."

She returns her empty flute to the ledge and leans her shoulder against the side of the pool. We're both standing now. Facing each other. Her hair is wet and slicked back. Her breasts just above the water line. And I can honestly say whatever's about to come out of her mouth won't scare me off in the slightest.

"Okay, so, I saw all those texts on Shawn's phone while he was taking a shower, and I—"

"Hold up. Sorry. How, exactly, did you see those texts and photos? Wasn't Shawn's phone passcode protected? If not, he's the world's stupidest serial cheater."

Georgina snickers. "Yeah, he had it passcode protected. And, trust me, he never punched in the code at an angle where I could peek over his shoulder. But where there's a will, there's a way."

"Oh, shit. His passcode was all zeroes, wasn't it? Or something like 1-2-3-4?"

She giggles. "Nope. It wasn't an obvious code. I'm just a brilliant, devious hacker."

I pause to let her elaborate, and when she doesn't I say, "Come on. Give it up. What'd you do?"

She giggles happily, sounding very much like a woman with an abundance of beer, tequila, and champagne in her bloodstream. "If I tell you, then I won't be able to hack into *your* phone, when *you* start acting weird and suspicious on me."

Oh, Georgie. I put my palms on her cheeks and her lips part in surprise.

"Sweetheart, I'm a lot of things, some of them not so admirable, but a cheater isn't one of them. I promise."

She swoons in my palms, so I lean down and kiss her bee-stung lips. And, for a moment, fireworks are going off so violently and deliciously inside me, I feel physically dizzy. When our lips break apart, I nuzzle her nose and whisper, "Also, I use facial recognition."

She bursts out laughing, and throws her arms around my neck again. And, just like that, she's clinging to me again... which I don't need to be told means she wants me to walk laps around the shallow end again.

"Okay, so here's how I hacked Shawn's phone," she says. "The night before, when he fell asleep, I cleaned his phone screen immaculately, until there wasn't a single smudge on it. And then, after he'd logged in several times the next morning, I peeked at the new smudges when he was in the shower." She shrugs. "Once I had the pool of numbers to work with, I was able to figure out his code on the third try."

"You're a genius."

She runs her fingers through my wet hair. "Are you scared of me now?"

"Not at all. Just impressed."

"So, anyway, I saw those texts and photos, and lost my shit. I went straight to his closet and grabbed all of his jerseys. Shawn played basketball for UCLA, so he had—"

"Hold the fuck up. 'Shawn' is Shawn *Gordon*? This whole time we've been talking about motherfucking Shawn *Gordon*?"

"Oh, God. Not you, too."

"Georgie, he's been UCLA's top scorer the past two years. He's a freak. A beast."

"Yeah, well, he's also a dickheaded cheater. If you're so in love with him, then *you* date him and see what kind of boyfriend he is to you."

I chuckle heartily. "Sorry. Josh, Henn, and I still follow UCLA sports religiously. Shawn Gordon is one of our favorites."

She glares at me.

"But not anymore. Now, I hate him."

She laughs.

"Continue. Please. You took all of his jerseys out of his closet, and..."

"I went outside to the barbeque set up at the back of Shawn's apartment complex... and I burned them all!"

"Oooh. What a psycho," I say sarcastically.

"Reed. I burned *all* his jerseys."

"Yes. I heard you the first time. But I hate to tell you, that's not batshit psycho. That's just run-of-the-mill anger."

"Yeah, well, I haven't told you the rest. Wait until you hear what *else* I did."

"Can't wait to find out."

She bites her lower lip, relishing whatever she's about to say. "There was a screwdriver sitting next to the barbeque, for some reason. And I picked it up, and marched straight to the parking structure, where Shawn's beloved Jeep was parked. He was so proud of that thing. It was his version of a Bugatti." She pauses for dramatic effect. "And I took that screwdriver and I punctured all four tires on his car! *One puncture for each side chick!*" She opens her mouth wide. As wide as it will go. As if to say, *Can you believe it?*

But I'm not the least bit impressed, and I'm sure my face shows it. "That's *it?*" I say.

"What do you mean, 'That's it'? Reed, I gave his beloved car *four* flat tires! Do you know how expensive tires are? And I made it so he'd have to replace the *entire* set, all at once!"

I can't help laughing uproariously at her beautiful innocence in this moment. Her stunning beauty. I kiss her cheek, still laughing. "Oh my God, Georgie girl. I thought you were going to say you keyed the fucker's car. Maybe scratched 'liar' onto his car doors."

She looks utterly shocked at the suggestion. "Well, first of all, his Jeep didn't really have doors. But, second of all, why would I do that? I could have gone to jail for a very long time if I did something as serious as that. I think that would be a felony!"

I laugh again. "And here I thought you were such a badass."

"I am." She pouts. "I gave him *four* flat tires and burned *three* jerseys. I was proud of myself for that."

I laugh. "Well, yeah. I'm glad you did *something* to the guy. He cheated on you with *four* women. I'm just saying that was your chance to go full-on 'Left Eye' Lopes on the guy, and be perfectly justified. I'm just saying you didn't really seize the opportunity as fully as you could have. That's all."

She looks up from her pouting. "Full-on 'Left Eye' Lopes? I'm sure it won't shock you to learn I have no idea what you're talking about."

I throw my head back. "No!"

She giggles. "Sorry."

I return to her. "Lisa 'Left Eye' Lopes. She was in TLC—the female R&B trio from the '90s."

She grimaces. "Nope. Sorry."

I drag my palm over my face. "Please, at least tell me you've heard of TLC?"

She shakes her head, so I sing the chorus of "Scrubs." And when that elicits nothing, I switch to the chorus of "Waterfalls," which, thankfully, she instantly recognizes.

"I *love* that song," she declares.

"Okay, well, the rap in the middle of that one was performed by Lisa 'Left Eye' Lopes."

"Ooooh. Quick question. What's the point of that song? When they say you shouldn't chase waterfalls, are they saying you shouldn't follow your dreams?"

"No, they're saying you shouldn't engage in self-destructive behaviors."

"Aaaaah. Okay."

"So, Lisa 'Left Eye' Lopes. You need to learn this."

"Yes, sir."

"Lisa 'Left Eye' Lopes had a boyfriend named Andre Rison. He was a pro football player. And one night, after they'd had a huge fight, Left Eye burned Andre's very large house in Atlanta completely to the ground."

Georgina gasps.

"She claimed she'd only intended to burn a pair of sneakers in a bathtub, but that the fire had spread and burned out of control."

"Holy crap."

"Guess how long she went to prison for felony arson?" I raise my eyebrow. "*Not a single day.*"

"What?"

"Andre knew he deserved it, apparently. He supported her in court."

"What the hell did Andre do to her?"

"She said he'd beaten her. He denied it."

Georgina's jaw sets. "Well, if he did, he got off easy, if you ask me."

In a flash, I'm thinking about that fucker Mr. Gates again. "I couldn't agree more," I say, my jaw tightening. I set Georgina down onto her feet, and put my fingertip underneath her chin. "Listen to me, Georgie girl. Listen close. Nobody is allowed to hurt you, ever again. You got that? If any man ever dares lay so much as a pinky on you, that you don't want on you, or if someone you trusted hurts you in any way, then I want you to go full-on 'Left Eye' Lopes on his fucking ass. Or, if you're too scared to do that. If you just want to get away, then you do that. But then, I want you to promise me, no matter how far in the future this scenario might come to pass, you'll come to me. Straight to me. No matter where I am in the world. And you'll tell me what happened, so I can go full-on *Reed Rivers* on the motherfucker's ass."

She's shaking against my fingertip. She nods, her hazel eyes flashing.

"Nobody—*nobody*—is allowed to hurt you, Georgina Ricci. Never, ever again. Do you understand me? *Never.*"

She nods again, just before lunging at me and crushing her gorgeous lips to mine.

FORTY-SEVEN
GEORGINA

My head is swimming. And not just from all the booze I've had tonight. The conversations I've had with Reed... our incredible make-out session in the pool, after I told him about Shawn... All of it has been electrifying. Intimate. Like a fairytale. And the night isn't even over yet.

We're out of the swimming pool now, sitting in the hot tub, gazing at the sparkling view of Los Angeles. And I swear I don't remember the last time I felt this alive—this safe and protected and adored—in my entire life.

I take a long swig from the bottle of Cristal and hand it to Reed.

"Tell me about Isabel."

"I already did. Tell her she's a trailblazer. She'll eat that shit up."

"No, no. I mean, tell me what happened between the two of you. Tell me about your relationship. Why did you break up?"

Reed takes a long sip from the champagne bottle. "Because our relationship ran its course, as these things always do. We realized we'd be better as friends. So, we called it quits. The End."

"'We' called it quits? Or *you* called it quits?"

"If you put Isabel into the article about me, I'm taking her out."

"I'm not asking you about her for the article. If I'm going to meet her and try to convince her to let me interview her in-depth, I should know about potential landmines. I should know what happened between the two of you."

"Bullshit. You want to know because you're jealous."

I bat his shoulder. "That's so absolutely... *not*... false!"

Reed laughs uproariously, and so do I.

But when his laughter dissipates, and it's clear he has no intention of answering my question, I slide into his lap and flash him my most charming, drunken smile.

"Aw, come on, Mr. Rivers. I told you about my ex, Shawn *Gordon*. Tell me about your ex, Isabel *Randolph*."

He shrugs. "There's not much to tell. We had fun for a while, but it eventually ran its course, so I ended it. And we've remained friends ever since." He takes another swig from the champagne bottle and hands it to me. "And, obviously, that turned out to be for the best, for both of us, seeing as how she's now marrying the man of her dreams, and I'm here with you."

My heart stops. *Holy crap*. "Where did you and Isabel first meet?"

"At that black-tie birthday party for CeeCee. The one I told you about already. The one I crashed, so I could meet CeeCee and convince her to write about RCR."

I giggle. "Just think. Ten years later, I crashed a music school event to meet CeeCee and convince her to read my writing samples. We're equally diabolical."

"Yes, we are." He kisses me. "Okay, it's my turn to ask a question. And I want your brutally honest answer this time, okay?"

My stomach clenches in anticipation. "Okay."

"This is important, Georgina. No fibbing." He puts his fingertip underneath my chin and looks at me sternly. "Georgina Ricci, did you *truly* have a poster of C-Bomb on your teenage wall—or did you tell me that to fuck with me?"

I burst out laughing, both in amusement and relief, and shake my head. "I was totally fucking with you."

"I knew it!" Reed says, joining me in laughter. "You're evil!"

"I really did love RCR as a teenager, though. That part wasn't a lie."

"You'll say or do *anything* to get what you want, won't you? You're shameless. Shameless and evil."

"You can't blame me for lying about that. I had to make sure you wouldn't let me walk out that door and go to C-Bomb. I didn't want to be Caleb Baumgarten's Penny Lane for a week." I nuzzle my nose against Reed's. "I wanted to be *yours*."

Reed runs his palm down my arm, before it disappears into the warm water of the hot tub and rests on my tailbone. "I was never going to let you go to Caleb, baby. Over my dead body." He kisses me passionately, sending my spirit swirling through the night sky. "What the hell are you doing to me, Georgina?" he mutters.

I'm drunk. On all the alcohol I've ingested tonight, and on Reed himself. "I don't know," I whisper back, my smile hurting my cheeks "All I can hope and pray is it's half of what you're doing to me."

FORTY-EIGHT
REED

I lay Georgina's sleeping, drunken frame onto the bed in her guestroom. Oh, how I wish I were laying her naked body down onto the four-poster in my room. But, of course, that's not an option. When she was perfectly sober last night, she asked for a room of her own, much to my extreme disappointment. And she didn't retract that request before passing out in my arms in a lounger by the pool.

I get her situated comfortably in bed underneath a sheet, and then move to the foot of the bed to grab a folded blanket... when my foot bumps into something hard on the floor by the bed. The room is too dark for me to make out what I've bumped into, but it's definitely not Georgina's suitcase, the outline of which I can see across the room by the door.

Curious, I head to the nightstand and flip on a small lamp. Momentarily, when the lamp illuminates, I worry the light will awaken Georgina. But a quick glance at Drunken Sleeping Beauty tells me, no, this girl is out for the night.

I return to the mysterious obstacle at the foot of Georgina's bed and discover it's a cardboard box emblazoned with *Courthouse Copy Service* on its side. The exact same kind of box Leonard always has in his office. And, instantly, even before I've peeked inside the box, I know what I'm going to find inside. Stephanie Moreland's lawsuit. But, still, just for kicks, I look anyway. And, yep. No surprise. There it is. Stephanie's complaint, sitting right on top a stack of documents.

A puff of air escapes from my nose. I should have known Georgina had it. There's no way Georgina would have seen reference on that printout to a *settled* sexual harassment lawsuit and not beelined to the clerk's office to get a copy of it. But why didn't she tell me she'd read it, when she asked me about the case? *Because she thought, if I didn't know she'd already read it, then I might lie to her about Stephanie. And she wanted to catch me in a lie.*

For a moment, I feel betrayed. Hurt. Angry. I feel the old familiar urges bubbling up. The ones I feel whenever a woman gets too close. When I feel my walls being threatened. The urge to run away, push away, shut down. That's what I'm feeling. As usual.

But then, I take in Georgina's beautiful, sleeping face and I remember the secret she shared with me tonight. The way she laid herself bare to me. And the panic inside me vanishes. The urge to run away, push her away, shut down subsides.

Okay, so she got the printout of lawsuits and noticed I'd settled a sexual harassment case. Considering what that asshole Mr. Gates did to her, it's no wonder she was especially determined to find out everything she could about Stephanie's claims. At least, to Georgie's credit, she came straight to me and asked me for *my* side of the story, rather than jumping to conclusions and instantly believing Stephanie's lies like they were gospel.

My heart rate is slowing again.

This is not a problem.

Georgina is simply doing her job.

And doing it well.

After what she's been through, I can't blame her for wanting to know what kind of man she's been sleeping with. Good for her for following the breadcrumbs. She might be young. And she might be smoking hot. But Georgina Ricci is nobody's fool.

I grab the blanket from the foot of the bed and gently cover her with it. I bend down and kiss her cheek gently, and turn off the light. Goodnight, Intrepid Reporter.

I stare at her for a long moment, not wanting to leave her side. But, finally, I drag my ass to my room. Which is where I brush my teeth, shower, and, finally, blessedly, crawl into my bed with an exhausted groan. But before flipping off my light, I grab my phone and send a text to Henn:

I need another favor, brother. Find out where Georgie went to high school. It's in the Valley somewhere. A guy named Gates is the football coach. They won two championships in four years. I need you to hack into his phone and computer and dig around. See if you find a vulnerability. I don't know exactly what I'm looking for. All I know is I want you to find something, anything, I can use to go Left Eye Lopes on the guy's ass. I want to burn this motherfucker's entire life to the ground, Henny. Just like Left Eye burned Andre's house. No mercy.

FORTY-NINE
GEORGINA

"Good afternoon," I chirp to CeeCee's personal assistant, Margot. She's seated at a desk, holding down the fort while CeeCee is still on vacation in Bali.

"Georgie!" Margot replies warmly. She hops up and gives me a hug. "How are you?"

It's a standard question, obviously. One I've been asked in polite conversation countless times in my life. One that *should* be answered with a simple, "I'm great! And you?" And yet, today, upon hearing that simple question, every fiber of my being wants to shout maniacally, "I think I'm falling for Reed Rivers!"

It's the same maniacal reply I wanted to shout at Amalia this morning, when she kindly asked if I'd slept well. And the same thing I wanted to scream at the top of my lungs at the barista in Starbucks, who asked if I wanted my coffee drink hot or cold. Truly, I don't know how many more times I can be asked how I'm doing or how I slept or how I want my coffee, and be expected to *not* shout in reply, "I think I'm falling for Reed Rivers!"

Because... I think I am.

Hard.

Obviously, I don't want to fall for Reed. Indeed, I'm trying very hard *not* to do that supremely stupid thing. But it's a hard thing to resist doing, after the amazing conversations we had last night, followed by the magic of this morning.

This morning, after Reed woke me up (and kindly gave me a couple ibuprofen for my slight hangover), he led me into his home gym for our morning workout... and then shocked the living hell out of me by giving me yet another piece of exercise equipment. This time, a top-of-the-line Pilates reformer! Which I happen to know costs around four grand. I protested, of course. Said I couldn't possibly accept it. But he insisted and wore me down. Obviously, I'll never collect it from him. As far as I'm concerned, that thing will stay in Reed's home gym forevermore. But just the thought that he bought it for me? *Swoon.*

But the amazingness didn't end here. After our workout, and after some delicious sex on my new machine, Reed and I headed to a recording studio in Hollywood. Which was where 2Real, aka Will Riley, was hard at work on his third album. Apparently, Will had asked Reed to swing by the studio today, saying he desperately wanted Reed's input on a particular track that was giving him fits. So, of course, Reed dropped whatever he'd been planning to do today, and headed straight there, with his eager shadow in tow.

And, oh, God, it was mind-blowing to watch those two work together. After brief introductions, I sat quietly in a corner for three hours that felt like three minutes, and watched in awe as they played a portion of the track in question. Stopped it. Went back. Talked. Tried something else. Talked again.

I came away from the experience with even deeper respect for Reed. Clearly, he's a meaningful partner to his artists. A genius at far more than business and marketing, or music scouting and strategizing. He's a genius at pulling the best out of his artists, as well.

Granted, I didn't understand most of what Reed said to Will during those three hours. For example, at one point, Reed said: "What if we were to saturate the vocals and make them extra dirty?" And I was like, *Huh?* Another time, Reed said, "We could turn up the flux on the Echo to around 300, playback level at zero. Let's try that and see if it makes our balls vibrate." It was another *huh?* But even without understanding the conversation, I could plainly surmise, thanks to Will's reactions to

Reed's comments, Reed was making a powerful contribution to Will's art.

But our amazing day together didn't end after the studio. From there, Reed spoiled me by taking me to lunch at the nicest restaurant I've ever been to—a hotspot frequented by the Hollywood elite. And when we ran into several movers and shakers, all of whom Reed knew and introduced me to, he said to each one of them, "This is Georgina Ricci, a brilliant new writer for *Rock 'n' Roll*. CeeCee hand-picked her to write an in-depth feature on me, so she's following me around to get the goods." Of course, I swooned at that introduction, each and every time.

After lunch, Reed had a meeting with his business partners on a bunch of nightclubs. He said I could come, but I decided to use the time to head over to *Rock 'n' Roll's* offices for a few hours.

"I'll drive you over there," he said. "It's not too far out of my way."

And that's when I said something awkward and embarrassing... that would have been mortifying to me if it hadn't led to Reed saying something so swoony, it made an egg pop out of my ovary.

The thing I said to Reed was this: "Thanks for the ride over there. I don't know how long I'll be there, though, so I'll plan to grab an Uber back home afterwards."

Back home.

I called Reed's house my home.

Of course, I was instantly mortified I'd let that word slip out. So, I quickly stammered, "I mean, back to *your* house. I'll take an Uber back to *your* house afterwards."

At first, Reed didn't even acknowledge my slip. He simply opened the passenger door to his Bugatti and gestured for me to get in. Which I did, and then promptly covered my face in embarrassment as he walked around the back to his own door.

But when he dropped me off in front of *Rock 'n' Roll's* offices, and called to me as I got out of the car, I forgot all about my embarrassment. Because that's when Reed called out, "I'll see you back home around five, baby! Don't keep me waiting this time!"

Yeah. I swooned pretty hard in that moment. It's when I knew *not* falling for Reed was going to be a tall order. Which brings me to this moment with Margot. To her question, "How are you doing?" and my raging impulse to shout, "I think I'm falling for Reed Rivers!"

Somehow, though, through sheer force of will, I manage to take a deep breath and reply, in a calm voice, "I'm great, Margot. How are you?"

"I'm swamped," Margot says dramatically. "It's always bananas when CeeCee is out of the country. But this week, especially, has been insanity. Are you here to see Zasu?" She's referring to the veteran reporter who's been assigned as my mentor this summer. "She just left."

"No, I texted with Zasu earlier today. I'm actually here to see if a box of documents I've been waiting on from the courthouse has arrived."

"I haven't seen anything addressed to you. I'd be happy to text you if something arrives." Margot makes a note on a pad. "Is it legal documents?"

"Yep."

"What is it, out of curiosity?"

"Just an old court case that might have some interesting information in it. To be honest, I'm probably just chasing a wild goose. Speaking of which, do you guys keep old issues of *Rock 'n' Roll* on the premises?"

"Of course. We have every issue ever published, filed in chronological order, in a storage room."

My heart leaps. "May I take a look?"

"You bet. Follow me."

I look around me, taking in the small storage room, its shelves filled to bursting with back issues of *Rock 'n' Roll*. I don't know which issue I'm looking for—from which month or year. Or, for that matter, if there will be anything of value in the article I've got in mind, if it exists at all. But not knowing what I'm doing has never stopped me before, and it won't stop me this time, either.

I head to Wikipedia on my phone and discover that CeeCee turned sixty a few months ago, in March. Which leads me to conclude the birthday party Reed crashed, where he met both CeeCee and Isabel, must have been CeeCee's fiftieth. I can't imagine CeeCee would have thrown herself a huge, black-tie affair for her forty-ninth or fifty-first.

So, that line of thinking gives me the *year* of the issue I'm looking for. Also, a two-month window, since my mentor, Zasu, told me the production cycle of most *Rock 'n' Roll* issues is thirty to sixty days. If an article about CeeCee's fiftieth birthday party, thrown in March, was printed in *Rock 'n' Roll* at all, I'm assuming it would have appeared in the April or May issue.

Obviously, it's a long shot to think such an article exists. And that, if it does, it includes a photo spread. But Reed did say he posed in his rented tux for "all the photographers" on the red carpet outside the party. So I think it's *possible* the magazine featured an article about the party, including photos... although I'm sure it's equally possible those photographers were only there to snap photos for CeeCee's social media or personal memories.

And why am I looking for this, at all? For several reasons, I think. The one I keep telling myself is my primary motivation is that any photos, if they exist, would allow me to trace Reed's professional path to glory, starting from the very beginning. Which, in turn, could lead to me painting a better portrait of Reed in my article. And, actually, I think that rationalization—that this wild goose chase is legitimate journalism— is plausible.

Unfortunately, though, I think the *higher* truth here is that I'm shamelessly stalking Reed. Dying to see a photo of the wildly successful man who's knocked me flat on my ass, from when he was nothing but a hungry, twenty-four-year-old hustler in a rented tux. Not too long ago, I crashed an event to meet CeeCee in an effort to change my life. And I can't deny I'm dying to see a photo of Reed on the night he did precisely the same thing a decade ago. In truth, I think I simply want to feel closer to Reed. To get to know him, inside and out.

But that's not everything, and I know it. There's one more reason I'm here, looking for a needle in a haystack like a St. Bernard looking for a skier buried beneath an avalanche. A reason I'm not proud of. But one I simply can't deny. *Isabel.*

I know the odds are slim I'll find a photo of the pair on the night they first laid eyes on each other. Neither of them had yet become famous or important that night. So, why would the magazine include a photo of either of them, let alone the two of them together? But I can't help thinking it's *possible* they were snapped in a group shot, or maybe in the background of someone else's shot, perhaps dancing together on the dance floor. If so, then I want to see the shot. I want to see what kind of electricity coursed between them in those first moments after they'd laid eyes on each other. I want to know how Reed's chemistry with Isabel compared to his chemistry with me. I want to know if Reed looked at me in the lecture hall the same way he looked at Isabel at CeeCee's birthday party.

Okay, yes, I know. Obviously, I have zero chill. I'm a psycho bitch who's jealous of one of the most beautiful, glamorous, famous actresses in the world. A woman who shagged the man I'm falling for, for years, and also, I suspect, snagged his heart at some point, too. I know she's engaged to the love of her life now. And that Reed has said he wouldn't want her anymore, regardless. But, still, I'm almost positive Reed loved Isabel at some point. And maybe still does. And I guess I'm grasping at straws here, irrationally trying to figure out if, maybe, Reed could one day, possibly, love me, too.

After some poking around, I figure out the filing system used in the storage room, and five minutes later, hit pay dirt.

The magazine in my hand has George Michael on its cover. On the left side of George's head, a small headline reads, "Meet your new obsession: Red Card Riot." In larger print above that, another headline reads, "CeeCee Rafael Knows How to Throw a F*cking Birthday Party!"

My heart in my mouth, I flip to the article about the birthday party, and squeal loudly when I see *five* full pages of photos.

"Jackpot," I whisper, my voice cutting through the air of the empty storage room.

Ravenously, my eyes search and scour. But, not surprisingly, I don't see any photos of Reed or Isabel. But then I see it. In a shot of Justin Timberlake. He's arriving at the party. He's just gotten out of a limo, and he's starting to traipse down the red carpet. And what I see in the background of the photo, behind Justin, snatches the air out of my lungs.

What the hell?

I pull out my phone and take a photo of the photo. And then I spread the background image on my phone wide with my fingers to zoom in. But it's no use. Thanks to the camera's focus on Justin, the background image is slightly blurred. Which means I'm only ninety percent sure of what I'm seeing. But, still, that's pretty damned sure.

Holy fuck.

If this photo shows what I think it does, then that could mean only one thing: Reed lied to me. Right to my face. About something I would have thought was totally innocuous.

And, for the life of me, I can't understand *why*.

FIFTY

REED

Georgina is late, once again. Caught up in traffic. This time, because she lost track of time while reading a bunch of articles at Rock 'n' Roll's offices.

To distract myself while awaiting her return, I've been sitting on my couch with my laptop, going over the marketing plan for Fugitive Summer's upcoming release. As I've been working, I've been sipping a glass of Bordeaux. Occasionally, glancing up at the sunset painting the floor-to-ceiling windows on the far side of the living room.

Surely, if someone were to see me right now, not knowing anything about Georgina, they'd think I'm the perfect portrait of a man in relaxation mode. But it couldn't be further from the truth. If Georgina doesn't get here soon, I'm pretty sure I'm going to die from anticipation. I'd probably feel that way, regardless. Just because I'm physically craving her after being away from her for several hours. But my impatience is amplified by the flat, square box hidden underneath my couch cushion at the moment. The box I hid there when I got home, so I can give it to her at just the right moment tonight.

Georgina won't keep my gift. Not this one. Not for long, anyway. She'll take it from me with a beaming smile and turn around and sell it, the first chance she gets. But that doesn't mean I don't want to give it to her. Or see that beaming smile of hers when she first opens the box and sees the sheer perfection of what's inside. Whether Georgina winds up keeping my gift for a day or a week, her gift to *me* will be the look on her face when she first opens the box.

Finally, just as I'm reaching the end of Fugitive Summer's release package, I hear my front door open. When I turn my head, it's just in time to see Georgina bursting into the expansive room. And, just like that, every cell in my body simultaneously jolts with a tsunami of reactions. Arousal, joy, relief. *She's home. She's safe. She's mine.*

"Sorry, sorry, sorry," Georgie says adorably, barreling over to me, her computer bag clanking against her hip as she moves. "I got caught up reading a bunch of stuff, and totally lost track of time."

Frazzled, she kisses me in greeting, and I calmly rise and hand her a goblet of wine.

"What were you reading?" I ask, settling next to her on the couch.

"Every past article I could get my hands on about every River Records artist," she says. "Including the article that started it all—the one CeeCee wrote about Red Card Riot's debut."

"Oh, wow. I haven't seen that one in forever. I'd love to read it, for old time's sake."

"I thought you might say that..." Waggling her eyebrows, she reaches into her computer bag and pulls out a sheet of paper. "So, I made a high-resolution color copy for you!"

"No way," I say, as she hands me the page. "This is amazing, Georgie! Thank you." I kiss her cheek. "That was awfully sweet of you."

"Well, you're awfully sweet to me, so... "

Oh, Jesus Christ. Those condors in my belly are back again, full-force. I read the entirety of the short article, stopping once to make a comment to Georgie, and, finally, place the page on the coffee table. "What a walk down memory lane. Wow."

"I was actually thinking you might like a framed copy for your home office," Georgie says. "You have all your major 'firsts' in there, so I thought..."

"That's a fantastic idea. Thank you. I'll give this to Amalia to get framed."

"Oh. No. I was thinking I'd get it framed for you, if that's okay." She smiles shyly. "I know a framed article isn't much of a gift, but you've given me so much. I'm dying to give you something special. Something that might be meaningful to you."

My heart skips a beat at the sweetness in Georgina's expression—even as my heart leaps and bounds at the perfect segue she just lobbed to me. I'd planned to give Georgina my gift after dinner. But after a segue like that, how could I possibly resist giving it to her now?

"Speaking of gifts, I have one for you."

"Oh, Reed. No."

"Just listen. My meeting this afternoon was in Beverly Hills." I take a deep breath. Holy shit, my heart is racing. "And when I was walking the couple blocks back to my car afterwards, I happened to pass a store window that was displaying something that instantly reminded me of you. So, I walked inside the store and bought it for you."

"Reed, no. No, no, no."

Ignoring her protests, I reach under the couch cushion and pull out the box I've been dying to give her. "This is for you. I hope you love it."

Her wide eyes dart from the blue box to my face and back again. "I can't accept that, whatever it is. Thank you so much for thinking of me, but it's way too much."

"Why don't you decide what's 'way too much' after you see it?"

"Reed, it's from Tiffany's."

"So what? It could be a bottle opener."

She's frozen. In shock.

"Come on, Georgie. Open the box. Are you going to deny me that pleasure?"

She looks deeply conflicted. But, still, she doesn't move.

"Aren't you the least bit curious what item in a store window reminded me of you so much, I felt called to buy it for you, on the spot?"

That does it. Her curiosity gets the best of her. With a trembling hand, Georgina takes the box from me and slowly opens it—and then sucks in a sharp inhale when she beholds the stunning treasure inside: a baroque-style ruby necklace set in Spanish gold, its multitude of deep-red gems cascading down in golden dripping, chandelier settings.

"Oh my God," she whispers. She puts her free hand on her heart. "Reed. This is... *exquisite*."

And so are you, I think. And it's the truth. The look on her face is everything I dreamed it would be and more. Even though I know she's going to sell it, this moment made buying the perfect piece of jewelry for her, rather than some placeholder that happened to be of the right monetary value, well worth it.

Georgina's eyes prick with tears. "It's the most beautiful thing I've ever seen," she whispers. She's shaking. Flushed. *Beautiful.*

"The crazy thing is," I say, my chest heaving every bit as much as hers, "I didn't even know rubies are your birthstone when I first saw it. The saleswoman inside the store told me about rubies after I asked her to show me the necklace. Did you know rubies are called 'the king's gem'?"

Georgina shakes her head, looking like a teary-eyed deer in headlights.

"It turns out, the king's gem is highly symbolic. They symbolize power and blood. Passion, desire, and fire. All of which is perfect for you, Georgina, because you're passion and power embodied. A human flame." *And you've infiltrated my blood.* I grab Georgina's limp hand. "Ever since I first laid eyes on you, I've wanted to tie you to my bed and show you what your body can do, if only you're willing to surrender completely. But then I got to know you, and I realized I had to wait to do that with you. I knew you'd enjoy it and have fun, to be sure, which is good enough for some... but with you, I didn't simply want to show you a good time. I wanted to show you something that would transform you." I squeeze her hand. "Tonight's finally the night, Georgina. You're ready to let go completely. You're ready to trust me. And I can't wait another night. Tonight, you're going to wear that necklace for me—a necklace dripping in the king's gems—and let me worship you as my queen."

I've rendered her speechless.

"Say yes, Georgie."

She swallows hard. She looks deeply conflicted. Which is exactly as expected. Indeed, I fully expected and counted on Georgina's conflicting emotions when I bought this necklace in the first place. "I can't," she says. "I mean, yes, tie me up. *Please*. I've wanted you to do that since you mentioned it the other night in front of your gate. But I can't accept this gift from you. It's too generous."

"I won't take no for an answer."

She frowns. "The truth is, I can't own thousands of dollars in rubies when my father is on the brink of losing his condo, any day now. If I took this necklace from you, I wouldn't be able to resist selling it behind your back at my first opportunity, so I could give the proceeds to my father."

I force myself not to smile. *Damn, I'm good.*

When Henn called this afternoon to give me the grand total of what Georgie's father owes on his condo, and also to tell me that a third notice had just gone out to him from the bank—meaning the guy is mere days away from being foreclosed upon, I knew I had to act fast. But I also knew paying off the guy's loan would be a bit tricky.

Georgie would never accept a straight-up check from me. That much I know. Nor could I anonymously pay off the loan. Georgie would instantly know who'd paid it... and then, quite possibly, quickly put two and two together, and think, "If Reed covertly paid off Dad's loan, maybe he also covertly paid for Dad's medication... *and my salary.*" Which, obviously, isn't something I want Georgina to be thinking, especially now that I know the story of Mr. Gates.

But, still, there was no question I had to pay off that damned mortgage somehow, as soon as possible, but in a way that didn't lead Georgina straight back to me. I needed a creative solution... a way Georgina would accept the money from me, in the first place, and also that wouldn't make her suspect my prior "donations" to her and her father.

And then it came to me. A perfect solution. *Don't rich men impulsively buy the women they're fucking sparkling baubles all the time? Isn't that a trope nobody ever questions?*

Now, granted, *I've* never bought a single piece of jewelry for any woman, other than my mother. Who, by the way, never wears the thing I bought her. But Georgina doesn't know that. Indeed, as far as she knows, I'm the kind of rich dude who sees a sparkly ruby necklace in a window at Tiffany's and buys it for his flavor of the month on the spot, just because he can. Georgina has no idea I'd never actually do that.

Although, come to think of it, maybe I *would* do that. Because, hell, I did. Today. Yes, my ultimate plan was to give Georgina a gift she could sell off, a gift that would yield the perfect payday for her and her father, without Georgina suspecting my endgame. But if paying off the mortgage had truly been my only motivation, then why did I buy *this* particular necklace—a piece of jewelry with almost triple the price tag of Georgina's father's debt? Why ask the saleswoman to see whatever pieces they had in the range of eighty grand, but then immediately ignore all the pieces she'd laid out for me the instant I happened to notice this particular ruby necklace, worth over two hundred grand, sitting in a display case on the opposite side of the store?

Obviously, when I bought the necklace, instead of one of the options in the range of eighty grand, I wasn't thinking about the loan any longer. I wasn't thinking about my brilliant plan. All that mattered to me in that delirious, impulsive moment was seeing Georgina open the box that held *that* particular necklace. All that mattered to me was seeing *that* particular necklace on Georgie's slender neck, if only for one night, and having the pleasure of fucking her in my bed while she wore it. I knew Georgie wouldn't keep the ruby necklace for long, exactly according to plan. But, in that moment, I knew seeing Georgina wearing the *perfect* necklace in my bed was worth far more to me than my two hundred twenty grand.

"I'm sorry," she whispers. "I feel terrible admitting I'd sell it. Please forgive me."

I'm quiet for a long moment. Partly, because I'm pretending to process Georgina's "shocking" confession. But also because I'm genuinely shocked. Not by the content of Georgina's confession, but by the fact that she's making it to me at all. Yes, I knew she'd sell the necklace. That was the point of me giving it to her in the first place. But I thought Georgina would take the necklace from me and then sell it behind my back.

I clear my throat. "I didn't realize things were so dire for your father."

Her shoulders droop. "He just got a third notice from the bank. I don't know what that means, exactly. But I know it can't be good."

"How much does your father owe, if you don't mind me asking? Because, whether you like it or not, this necklace is yours, to do with as you please, even if that means you're going to return it to the store for cash."

"Oh, gosh, no, Reed. I couldn't possibly—"

"Yes, you could. Unfortunately, the necklace probably won't cover your dad's full debt. It only cost me eighty grand. But it might help."

She's flabbergasted. "Reed. Oh my God! You're not going to believe this, but... *my father owes exactly eighty grand!*"

I palm my forehead. "No."

"*Yes!*"

"Holy shit." I shake my head in disbelief. "Well, that settles it, then. You have to return it and use it to pay off the mortgage. Now, I *really* won't take no for an answer. Me seeing this necklace in the window was fate!"

She chokes back a sob, and then another, but then loses her battle. She bursts into big, soggy, beautiful tears and throws her arms around my neck. "Thank you, thank you," she murmurs into my shoulder, her body wracking as she weeps.

"You're welcome." I pull back from our embrace, apparently struck by an idea. "Actually, you know what? I should return it for you. I have another meeting in Beverly Hills tomorrow. I'll return it and immediately wire the money straight to his bank. The loan will get paid off more quickly this way. And it sounds like time might be of the essence here."

It's a pack of lies, of course. I don't have a meeting in Beverly Hills tomorrow, any more than I had one there today. My meeting today was actually in Century City, and I left midway through to head to Tiffany's in Beverly Hills, the minute I got my brilliant idea. But I can't let Georgie walk into that store with a ruby necklace worth over two hundred grand, when she thinks it's only worth eighty, and find out the truth.

Georgina pulls back from me, her face contorted with anxiety. "I just realized my dad is going to ask me how the heck I got eighty grand. And what will I say? 'Oh, um, the CEO of River Records gave it to me as a gift, Dad!'" She scoffs. "He'll immediately know I'm sleeping with you, Reed. And that's not something I'm eager for him to know. I wouldn't want him to think, even for a second, that you've somehow taken advantage of his precious little girl. No offense, but you're not only rich and powerful. You're also, you know..." She grimaces. *"Thirty-four."*

"What happened to 'Age is just a number'?"

She pulls an adorable face. "Yeah, well, that may be *my* philosophy, but my father doesn't share it. At least, not when it comes to his baby girl. He thinks I'm far more naïve and inexperienced than I am. If he found out we're sleeping together, he'd think you've been taking advantage of me somehow."

"And he'd be right."

She smiles, assuming I'm joking. But, unfortunately, I'm not. How could I not be taking advantage of this naïve, sweet, inexperienced twenty-one-year-old? I know Georgina thinks she's seen it all, but she's wrong about that. Adorably, amusingly wrong. I keep telling myself the end justifies the means. I tell myself I've helped her and her father immeasurably. That my intentions, in the beginning, weren't *solely* lascivious—I also had other, parallel intentions, that were altruistic and good. All of which means I'm helping her, not taking advantage of her, even if I've also reaped some benefits along the way. It's what I tell myself. But with each passing day, as Georgina's hazel eyes increasingly fill with trust and affection toward me... I'm beginning to worry I might be barreling toward a catastrophe here. One I won't be able to fix.

"I wouldn't blame your father for thinking I'm too old for you," I admit. "To be honest, I'm thinking the same thing. I'm deeply conflicted about how young you are, Georgina. A month ago, I never would have believed I'd be dating a twenty-one-year-old. And yet, here I am."

Her face lights up. "You're *dating* me, Mr. Rivers?"

Shit. What did I just commit to? And how can I get myself uncommitted, if needed, without ruining this good thing?

"I thought you said you're merely 'seducing me,'" she sings out happily, and the look of unadulterated joy on her face instantly shoos away my threatening anxiety, the way a shaken broom shoos away a stray cat.

"Yes, I said that," I say. "But, at this point, I think we can both agree: *seduction complete.*"

She straddles me on the couch and throws her arms around my neck. "I'm glad you're dating me." She bats her eyelashes. "Even if it's got to be a secret for a little while." She gasps. "Oh! I just got a great idea! I could tell my father the money to pay off his mortgage came from that same cancer charity that paid for his medication!"

My heart stops. Shit. Fuck. No. Shit. *This is it.* Holding my breath, I scrutinize Georgina's face for any sign she's figured me out. Is this a test? Is she daring me to confess sins she already knows I committed? Is this the same as when she asked me about a sexual harassment lawsuit I'd settled, when she'd already had Stephanie's complaint sitting in a box in her room? But, no. I don't see anything on Georgina's lovely face except beautiful, blissful ignorance.

"That's a great idea," I say, regarding Georgina's idea to credit the cancer charity. "Do you have your father's account information, so I can wire the funds to the bank tomorrow?"

"I do."

"Great. The loan will be totally paid off by close of business tomorrow."

She can't contain her effusive joy. She hugs me and kisses every inch of my face, making me hard as a rock. I put my palms on Georgina's cheeks. "But before I return that necklace tomorrow, you're going to take off those clothes and slip on that ruby necklace. We're going to dine in the formal dining room. And then I'm going to take you upstairs and give you a night you'll never forget."

FIFTY-ONE
REED

Georgina rises from the couch and begins peeling off her clothes. So, I peel off mine. When we're both naked, I turn her around, brush her dark hair to the side, and lay soft, sensuous kisses along the nape of her neck before finally placing the necklace around her neck. The necklace in place, I push my cock into her ass and kiss her neck and shoulder. I reach around and touch her breasts. Pinch her nipples. Whisper to her that she's perfect. And, soon, she's so aroused, her knees are buckling.

Still kissing her neck and shoulders, I begin gently stroking her slit, until she's swollen and trembling. Aching for me. Dying for me. Until, finally, I touch her clit. Two seconds later, she cries out, digs her fingernails into my arm, and comes.

"You only get little ones for now," I whisper, pushing my cock into her ass. "To get you excited for the big ones to come later."

She shudders. "I'm so wet for you, Reed."

"And you're going to stay that way. Turn around."

She complies. And, when I see the fire in those hazel eyes, the fire in those rubies dripping off her neck toward her pink, erect nipples, my cock twitches with arousal. The head of my cock is already beaded with pre-cum. Its shaft is straining for her. My skin is hot. But tonight is all about the slow-burn. It's a night to savor, every bit as much as the special bottle of Bordeaux we're going to drink.

"You need to see yourself right now."

I take Georgina's hand in mine and lead her to a nearby mirror, and then stand behind her, the tip of my cock brushing her ass, as she takes in her glorious, glowing reflection.

As she stares at herself, she touches the necklace, in awe of it. "It's so beautiful. Thank you for seeing it and thinking of me."

"I had no choice. It was made for you. It belonged to you, even as it sat in the store window." I kiss her shoulder, making her shudder with arousal. "Amalia left an incredible meal for us in the oven. Eggplant parmigiana. Another favorite of mine. We'll eat at the big table, on opposite ends." I nuzzle my nose into her hair and inhale her glorious scent. "And then, I'm going to carry you upstairs, my queen, and give you a night that will change you forever."

Georgina, my queen, is wearing nothing but her ruby collar. I'm wearing nothing but a smile. We're sitting in high-backed upholstered chairs at opposite ends of my long dining table, the air between us crackling with sexual heat. And we're eating and chatting and sipping a bottle of Bordeaux, like all of this is the most natural thing in the world.

In fact, I think it's the apparent normalcy of this meal, while we're both naked and fully aroused, that's making it so scorching hot. It's the calm before the storm, the ultimate foreplay, and we both know it.

Finally, when both our plates are empty and Georgina's second glass of wine is gone, I push my empty plate and goblet aside and rise, showing her my erection.

"Come to me," I say, my eyes locked with hers. "Crawl across the table on all fours and come to me."

She doesn't hesitate. She pushes her plate and glass aside, the way I just did, places her linen napkin onto her plate, and rises. With her eyes trained on mine, she climbs onto the table on all fours, and proceeds to crawl slowly across it, like a cat.

Well, isn't that fitting, I think. Because, since the moment we met, Georgina and I have been engaged in a game of cat and mouse—a game in which both players have thought, at one time or another, they were the cat. But now, watching my glorious feline traversing the length of my table, I feel our roles cementing. Georgina is the cat in our relationship. There's no doubt about it. *And I'm the wolf.*

She comes to a halt in front of my straining cock, licking her lips. Her eyes ablaze, she whispers, "I've been fantasizing about—"

I put up my palm. "From here on out, you won't speak except when given a command or asked a question. When I give you a command, you'll reply 'Yes, sir.' When I ask you a question, you'll answer it fully, but say nothing more."

Her hazel eyes flicker with heat. "Yes, sir."

I run my thumb over her full lower lip. "You never have to do anything you don't want to do, Georgina. Not with me or anyone else. *Ever.* I have no desire to hurt or humiliate you. I only desire to give you the most outrageous pleasure of your life—an extreme form of it you didn't know was possible. If you don't want me to do something, tell me so. It's as simple as that. I don't want to force you to do anything. I don't want to cause you discomfort, let alone pain. If you feel pain, which you shouldn't, tell me so, and I'll immediately stop whatever I'm doing. If you're scared, say so—and, again, I'll stop whatever I'm doing so you can catch your breath and decide if you want to proceed. At which point, you'll tell me so, clearly and without equivocation. Do you understand?"

She nods, looking relieved—and incredibly turned on. "Yes, sir."

"Do you trust me to take good care of you?"

"I do." She softens. "I really do trust you, Reed. I'm nothing but excited."

I hold her trembling face in my hands. "You loved the swing, right?"

"I loved it."

"Then you're going to love this, too. Even more." I trace the contours of her striking cheekbones, before dropping my hand to my side. "Now, suck my cock, kitten. And make it the best fucking blowjob you've ever given."

Unbridled lust washes over her features. "Yes, sir." She dips down, sending her round ass into the air, and her breasts and necklace against the table, and gets to work. And, soon, I'm on the cusp of total Nirvana. Hurtling toward a release my body wants, but the rest of me knows won't serve my greater purpose.

"Stop," I choke out.

She obeys, her chest heaving.

"Come here."

I put my arms out and Georgina comes to me, wrapping herself around me the way she did in the swimming pool. When I've got her firmly in my grasp, I carry her out of the dining room, through my living room, and up my staircase, taking the steps two at a time. Finally, when I reach my bedroom, I lay her down on my bed, the head of my cock dripping, and open the top drawer of my nightstand.

FIFTY-TWO
REED

I've lost count of the number of orgasms I've pulled out of Georgina tonight. The number of times I've gleefully licked up the evidence of her complete and total surrender. I've marked her tonight. Literally, with my teeth and cum. Figuratively, with the tattoo I left on her deepest desires. Maybe even her very soul. *Property of Reed Rivers.*

She's mine now. Sex with anyone else will never measure up to what she's found with me. I've ruined her for anyone else. The same way I ruined Audrey. And Isabel after her. And then Natasha and Corinne and Veronica, and anyone else who's been fortunate enough—or, perhaps, *unfortunate* enough—to attract my undivided attention for any length of time. The only difference with Georgina is that, for the first time, ever, I'm pretty sure I've been ruined, too.

It's a thought that would terrify me, if I weren't so exhausted. If I weren't so drunk on Georgina and the perfection we shared tonight. As it is, though, in this moment, after this incredible night, in addition to exhausted, I'm feeling high. The kind of high an explorer feels after discovering, and conquering, a new land. I led Georgina to The Promised Land tonight, in a way she couldn't have fathomed. I showed her pure ecstasy, repeatedly, and watched with glee as her flames turned into a raging forest fire, and as that forest fire burned out of control. I watched everything she previously thought about her sexuality, and deepest desires, turn to ash. And, finally, I watched Georgina rise like a Phoenix from those ashes and unabashedly claim her new sexuality, without apology. There's no turning back now. Georgina Ricci will never be the same again. And, almost certainly, neither will I.

After one last, lingering kiss, I remove the soft cuffs from Georgina's ankles and wrists. I sit on the edge of the bed, pull her slack body to mine, and cradle her. And she wraps her legs around me and melts into me.

Still holding her, I lean toward my nightstand and grab a water bottle for her, which she gulps down greedily when I give it to her. I remove her ruby necklace with a soft kiss on her shoulder, and place it on my nightstand, next to her now-empty water bottle. And finally, holding her tightly, I carry her into my bathroom, to the shower, and wash my little kitten in warm water from head to toe.

Our shower done, I dry her off, stopping occasionally to suck her nipples or kiss her belly or thighs, and then wrap her in a thick white towel and carry her back into my room.

I place Georgina in an armchair. Change my bedsheets. Clean and put away my various cuffs and toys. I send a quick text to Owen, telling him to cancel my morning meetings. And then I bring the shades on my large windows down, turning my room into a dark cave. I carry Georgina's sleeping frame from the armchair to my bed, crawl next to her, pull her backside into me. And, finally, I exhale from the depths of my soul.

Holy shit.

I'm sure I'll start panicking tomorrow. Freaking out she's going to start demanding things from me I can't possibly give her. But I can't be bothered to feel any of the usual shit right now. I'm too exhausted. Too relaxed. Too... *happy*. And so, I simply clutch Georgina to me, just a little bit tighter, and revel in the overwhelming desire I'm feeling to *protect, protect, protect* what's mine... and, slowly, drift into the deepest sleep of my entire life.

A blood-curdling scream rips me out of a deep sleep, and my eyes fly open. In a heartbeat, my mind clicks into place. Georgina. She's lying next to me in bed. She's safe. Asleep. The scream came from her.

"No!" she shrieks. "No, no!"

I grasp her shoulder. "Georgie, wake up. You're having a nightmare."

Her eyes fly open, and when she sees my concerned face staring back at her, and realizes whatever was terrorizing her is gone, she crumples into my bare chest.

"You're safe," I whisper, holding her tight. "You're here in bed with me. Nothing can hurt you."

She shakes in my arms and whimpers, and with each tortured sound that comes from her, my heart feels like it's physically cracking.

"What was your nightmare about?" I ask.

"Mr. Gates," she says. "Telling you about him... I think it made everything I've been stuffing down bubble up and come to the surface." She pauses. "After he kissed me, he tried to do more, Reed. He tried to do a lot more, but I screamed and kicked him and ran away, as fast as I could."

I'm so full of the carnal urge to kill, I can't speak, so I lay my cheek against hers.

"I was terrified," she squeaks out. "I ran and ran, and never looked back."

I turn my head and kiss her cheek. "You're safe now, baby. You're safe, and I'm not going to let anything happen to you, ever again."

FIFTY-THREE
GEORGINA

It's finally here! The morning of Reed's party. I'm so freaking excited, and not just about the party. About life! About *Reed*. I can't believe how close I feel to him. How much I've opened up and let him in. I never would have believed it possible, but... I think I'm no longer falling for him. I think the fall is complete.

Which is so stupid, I want to slap myself silly. What sane, intelligent woman would ever let herself fall for Reed freaking Rivers—an intensely guarded, "non-committal" older man music mogul whose every third sentence is a bald-faced lie? The answer to that question is: no sane, intelligent woman would do that. Only an idiot. A felony stupid moron who's clearly let her foolish heart hijack her rational mind.

It's why my mind keeps shrieking at my heart to snap the fuck out of it! But my heart won't listen. And, really, I can't blame it, after everything that's happened in such a short amount of time between Reed and me. How could my heart possibly hold back, after the night of the necklace, and the way he comforted me after my nightmare? I didn't *want* to wake up the next morning and look at Reed's sleeping face on the pillow next to mine and think, *"My love."* But that's what happened, whether I wanted it or not... and has kept happening, at random moments over the past couple of days, ever since.

My ruby necklace is gone now. As promised, Reed brought it back to the store the next day and used the proceeds to pay off my father's condo in full. Which, *hello*, is even more reason for my heart to ignore my brain when it comes to my feelings for Reed. But I don't need the physical necklace around my neck to feel its phantom weight against my skin. Surely, I'll feel the power of those rubies, the power of that magical night with Reed, for the rest of my days.

I don't plan to tell Reed any of this, of course. My feelings for him have turned me stupid, but not dumb. I just wish I could stop *feeling* so damned smitten with him all the time. It's actually annoying me to constantly feel like I'm swooning, even when I'm trying to work. I spent most of the morning in my room, researching the first half of the guest list for tonight. But the whole time, I felt physically buzzed. After that, I left my room and, for the past hour, I've been following Reed around the house as he's made sure the various workers are preparing for the party to his exacting standards. I figured watching Reed manage the nuts and bolts of an event like this might be a cool metaphor for his hands-on management style, in general. And it has been. I've made several notes for my article. But, still, even as I've been working, I haven't once stopped feeling that crazy buzz—that simmering in my blood and skipping of my heart that constantly makes me swoon.

"No, no," Reed says to a worker, his voice dripping with annoyance. "The bass rig needs to be set up there, next to the drum kit. Have you never set up a live music performance in your life? Bass and drums. Peanut butter and jelly."

"Sorry, Mr. Rivers."

"Owen?" Reed shouts over his shoulder.

Owen arrives, looking irritated.

"Get someone over here who knows what the fuck they're doing, for fuck's sake."

"I'll handle it, Reed."

Owen pulls the red-faced worker aside, just as a large black man taps Reed's shoulder from behind. Which, of course, makes Mr. Cranky-Pants turn around to see who's dared touch him. But when he sees his assailant, Reed's demeanor instantly brightens.

The two men clap each other on their shoulders warmly and exchange quick pleasantries before Reed turns to me, a wide smile on his face.

"Georgina, this is Barry Atwater, the head of security for both my label and nightclubs. Barry, this is Georgina Ricci, a brilliant writer for *Rock 'n' Roll* who's doing a feature on me."

Ah, it never gets old, hearing Reed introduce me like that. I exchange brief small talk with Barry, and quickly surmise he's a teddy bear underneath all that muscle. And then, Barry and Reed drift into conversation about logistics for tonight.

As the men talk, I check the time on my phone. *Crap.* Alessandra should be here in about an hour to "pre-party" with me, and I still haven't finished going through the names on the guest list. Before the party starts, I want to be sure I know at least the basics about every name on the list, as well as being able to identify each person on sight, without needing an introduction. The last thing I want is to be introduced to some huge A-lister, without me realizing it. Or, even worse, with me asking something stupid like, "And what do you do for a living?"

"Hey, Reed," I say, pulling on his shirt sleeve. "I'm going to head up to my room for a bit to finish going through the guest list before Alessandra arrives. It was great to meet you, Barry. Reed has said wonderful things about you." I return to Reed. "Hey, can I talk to you privately about something for a sec?"

"Don't go anywhere," Reed says to Barry. "I want to finish our conversation."

Reed and I walk a few feet away, until we're in a semi-private spot.

"Is everything okay?" Reed asks, looking mildly concerned.

"Everything's great. I just wanted to let you know I haven't told Alessandra you listened to her demo. I want her to be able to enjoy the party, without feeling self-conscious or awkward around you. I'm going to tell her everything on Monday, before she heads back to Boston."

Reed rolls his eyes like I've said something ridiculous. "One of the conditions of you inviting Alessandra to the party was neither of you talking to me about her music tonight. Remember?" He glances over his shoulder and then, to my shock, reaches around me, and pinches my ass. "God, you turn me on."

I leap out of his clutches and immediately look over at Barry, worried he might have seen our clinch. But, nope, Barry is busy on his phone. I return to Reed and waggle my finger at him. "No more grabby hands, Reed. From this moment forward, until we're safely in your bedroom tonight, I'm nothing but a reporter from *Rock 'n' Roll* to you."

"I'll do my best to control myself." He flashes me a completely unapologetic smile. "The caterer should have a lunch buffet set up in the kitchen by now. I asked for a spread for whatever pre-partiers come by. Why don't you fuel up? I don't want you drinking on an empty stomach."

"There's going to be a pre-party?"

"Yeah, I told a small group to come by early. Not sure who's coming, for sure, beyond Josh and Henn." He looks at his watch. "Shit. I've got a conference call. Get yourself some food, baby."

I glance at Barry, my cheeks flushing, hoping he didn't overhear Reed's endearment. But it's clear he did. Because the minute my eyes meet Barry's, he looks down at his phone, and *pretends* not to have heard a thing.

"Barry knows about us, doesn't he?" I whisper.

"Barry is my personal bodyguard, whenever I need one," Reed says matter-of-factly, as if that explains everything. "Now, get yourself some food and do some work before Alessandra gets here. I'll catch up with you soon."

"Okay. See you later." I float happily into the kitchen to grab a bite, and to my surprise, discover Amalia standing at the island with the caterer. "Amalia!" I say, loping toward her, my arms extended. "I didn't think you came in on Saturdays!"

Amalia hugs me. "I always come in on party days to coordinate with the caterer."

After a bit of small talk, I load up a plate, and Amalia joins me at the small kitchen table to keep me company while I eat. She tells me a cute story about one of her grandsons, who just discovered the word "ridiculous." I tell her about Alessandra, and how excited I am she's coming over shortly, and will be staying overnight with me in the blue room.

After about fifteen minutes, in the midst of my conversation with Amalia, the kitchen door swings opens and two young women bound into the room. A woman with long, strawberry blonde hair, and another one with a dark bob with bangs and bright blue eyes.

"Amalia!" the brunette says.

"Hello, sweetie!" Amalia says warmly, leaping up from the table to administer hugs. Amalia introduces the women, and I learn the brunette is Reed's sister, Violet, and the blonde her best friend.

"And this is Georgina," Amalia says to the women. She opens her mouth, like she wants to elaborate, but closes it. And I don't blame her. In this context, it would be weird to introduce me in relation to *Rock 'n' Roll*. But who am I to Reed? And what am I doing here? It's obviously not for Amalia to put a name to it.

"I'm writing about Reed for *Rock 'n' Roll*," I say, trying to sound casual. "And also staying here with Reed." Ugh. That was awkward.

"Reed mentioned the article," Reed's sister says. "And also that you're staying here. He seemed excited about both."

My heart leaps. "I'm excited about both, as well."

"That's good." She flashes me a warm smile. "We're going out to the pool. Would you like to join us?"

"Oh, thank you for the invitation. But I've got to finish some work before my stepsister, Alessandra, arrives."

"Maybe when Alessandra gets here, then."

"Sounds good. I'll see you then."

Back in my room, I text Alessandra and ask her to pack bathing suits for both of us, so we can join Reed's sister and her friend at the pool later today. And, luckily, my timing is good—I've caught her before she's left her mother's place.

Swimsuits handled, I sit on my bed with my laptop, open the guest list, and pick up where I left off earlier. The next name on the list? *Laila Fitzgerald*. Well, there's no need to look her up. Laila is a superstar, thanks to a sophomore album that's spun off hit after hit this past year.

Aloha Carmichael. No need to look her up, either. After years of watching her Disney show *It's Aloha!* as a kid, and nowadays seeing Aloha's ubiquitous face on viral music videos and shampoo commercials, I'd know that pop star's gorgeous face and famous green eyes anywhere.

Keane Morgan. Okay, that's a name I don't know. But after a search, I quickly realize he's an actor from a show I binge-watched last year. In that show, he was in a small, but pivotal role. But, now, it seems he's moved on to a co-starring role on a hugely popular show I've never seen. Well, good for him. I'm glad to see he's doing so well.

Madelyn Morgan. I'm assuming from the name she's Keane's wife. I google her, and find out I'm right about that. But I also find out she's a kickass woman—a documentary filmmaker who was nominated for an Oscar last year. I'm a bit surprised, actually. In the show I saw, Keane came off like a total "bro." But, obviously, if he's married to a woman like Madelyn Morgan, there must be more to him than meets the eye.

Dax Morgan. Well, that's another easy one. 22 Goats has been one of my favorite bands for the past few years, ever since they broke onto the scene with a music video that went viral. With his gorgeous face and long, blond hair, Dax Morgan, their frontman, is instantly recognizable to me and half the world. But even so, I look him up, just to see if he's related to the actor, Keane Morgan. And, yup. Wikipedia tells me Dax and Keane are the two youngest brothers of five siblings in the Morgan clan.

Colin Beretta. Another easy one. He's the drummer of 22 Goats.

Matthew Fishberger. Hmm. I don't recognize the name, so I google it, and, instantly feel like an idiot. That's Fish! The bassist for 22 Goats who's come across as easygoing and likeable in every interview of the band I've read this past week.

Josh Faraday. Another easy one. Reed's "male model" best friend from college, whom I met at the bar.

Kat Faraday. I google her and find out Josh's wife is a gorgeous blonde bombshell who recently published her first romance novel—a romantic comedy entitled *Suck It.*

Well, this I've got to see. I find Kat's book online, and when I behold the smoking hot cover, and read the sassy synopsis, I buy that sucker on the spot.

"Kat Faraday," I murmur. "I think we're going to be two peas in a pod."

Ten minutes later, I'm flying through the names on the list, until I reach one that stops me in my tracks.

Isabel Randolph.

Gah. On the one hand, I'm dying to interview her. She's been one of my favorite actresses since before she became a massive movie star. On the other hand, though, I'm not sure I'll be able to pull off an interview of her, to the best of my abilities, when I have these feelings for Reed. Will I be distracted the entire interview, with feelings of jealousy and insecurity? Will I imagine Reed doing all the things he does to me... to *Isabel?* I don't want to wonder these things, but I can't help it. Did Reed tie Isabel up, the way he did to me? Did he fuck her in a sex swing? Did Reed give Isabel whatever might have been her equivalents of a Peloton, a Pilates reformer... and the most perfect, breathtaking ruby necklace the world has ever seen?

My heart pangs.

Why am I torturing myself? She's engaged now, for God's sake! And Reed explicitly told me he and Isabel have become more like siblings than ex-lovers. But, see, that's the thing. The idea of them being like siblings simply doesn't ring true to me. How could Isabel get fucked by Reed the way I've gotten fucked, and then, somehow, magically, desire nothing more from his hot body than a brotherly peck on the cheek? I don't care how badly Isabel might have gotten hurt by Reed at some point in their relationship—how big an asshole Reed might have been to her in the end. I can't imagine she'd turn down the chance to fuck Reed senseless again, regardless, if the opportunity presented itself...

If Reed cheated on Isabel, then, yes, maybe I could imagine her never wanting him to lay another pinky on her. That's how I feel about Shawn. Physically ill at the thought of him touching me. But that's not what happened between those two, or they sure as hell wouldn't be "like siblings" now. And, anyway, Reed says he's not a cheater, and I believe him. But if things between them really did simply peter out, if things really did just "run their course," as Reed said, then I can't imagine Isabel being completely over Reed. Unless, of course, she's now so madly in love with her new fiancé, she can't imagine wanting anyone else, ever again, even someone as swoon-worthy and smoking hot as Reed.

Which brings me to the next name on the list. *Howard Devlin.* The guy Reed told me is Isabel's fiancé. As I recall, Reed said Howard Devlin is a big shot billionaire movie producer and studio owner. Which made me retort, "Oh, then he's the Reed Rivers of the movie industry?"

I input Howard's name into Google, excited to see how this guy matches up to Reed, and when I see his photo, I gasp. Howard Devlin looks like Isabel's pervy grandpa! Gaping like a fish on a river bank, I read the guy's Wikipedia page and quickly learn he's *sixty-five* years old —thirty-four years older than Isabel!

Holy hell. I know I'm the one who always says "age is just a number." But, damn. I'm having a hard time believing a woman as young and vibrant and successful as Isabel said yes to spending the rest of her life boning *that* guy. Although, I suppose Isabel only said yes to spending the rest of *Howard's* life boning him. Which, when you're talking about your pervy grandpa, maybe isn't all that big a commitment.

Okay, I'm being a total bitch right now, and I need to stop. Looks aren't everything. And age really *is* a number. For all I know, Howard Devlin is a lovely, kind, generous man who's a tiger in bed. A guy who treats Isabel like his queen. Plus, who the hell do I think I am to judge any woman for being in a relationship with a wealthy, powerful, older man? Come on, Georgie. A girl who lives in a glass house—or, in my case, a house with a whole lot of floor-to-ceiling windows overlooking the Hollywood Hills—shouldn't throw stones.

I read a bit more on Howard Devlin and suddenly realize I've seen his face before. But where? I pause. Stare at the wall. And, then... Oh, yes! In that photo spread from CeeCee's fiftieth birthday party!

I pull out my color copy of the article and scan the photos... and sure enough, Howard is standing in a group shot with a slew of music and movie stars. Wow. How crazy is that? Isabel and Howard were *both* at that party ten years ago. Is that where they first met? Or is this a case of future spouses crossing within inches of each other, never realizing it? Isabel wasn't a successful actress back then. Not even close. Plus, Reed was at that party, too. So, it wouldn't surprise me if Isabel and Howard never said two words to each other that night.

On the other hand though, Isabel had to have had acting ambitions back then. Did she spot Howard, a famous movie producer, and try to charm him, or was she too young and inexperienced to recognize him at a party attended by far more recognizable faces?

And what about Howard? Did he spot Isabel that night, from afar, perhaps when she was talking to a young, gorgeous stud in an Armani tux, and think to himself, *One day, that woman will be my wife*?

Okay, my imagination is running wild now. But, regardless, I make a mental note to ask Isabel about that party. I doubt there's any sort of "written in the stars" or "love at first sight" angle there in regards to Isabel and Howard, but, still, I'd be remiss if I didn't at least poke around to find out.

Peter Hennessy. That's the next name on the list. And one I don't recognize. But when I google the guy, and see his photo, I palm my forehead. *He's Henn!* Reed's nerdy-looking best friend from college. When I met him at the bar, he instantly put me at ease with his authenticity and sweetness.

Hannah Hennessy. Henn's wife, I assume. I google and find out she is, indeed, Henn's wife—an adorable brunette with glasses who works in the publicity department of a movie studio... the same studio owned by Howard Devlin, as a matter of fact. Huh. What a small world! Or is it? Did Reed have something to do with Hannah getting that job? Did Reed pick up the phone and use his connections to help Hannah get an interview? Because that's exactly the kind of thing I could see Reed doing: pulling strings behind the scenes to help his best friend's woman get her dream job . . .

Ping.

A murky thought raps gently at the back of my brain. *Ping.* The thought is like a soft cotton ball lobbed at me from ten feet away...

It's only a blurry idea at the moment, tugging at the outer fringes of my consciousness. But before the cotton ball hardens into an actual pebble, my phone buzzes with an incoming text that makes me squeal and forget all about the fuzzy thought gently pinging in the back of my head. It's a message from Alessandra that reads:

I'm at Reed's front gate, baby! LET ME IN! It's time to pre-party like ROCKSTARS before we party with ACTUAL ROCKSTARS! (But first, a sandwich. Please. For the love of all things holy, I'm starving.)

FIFTY-FOUR
GEORGINA

"Oh my *God*," Alessandra says, gaping at the seven gleaming cars lined up before us in Reed's massive garage. We're at the last stop of the house tour I've been giving Alessandra for the last thirty minutes. And Alessandra is clearly as blown away by the spectacle of Reed's glittering car collection as she was the rest of the house.

I lead her down the row of vehicles, expertly rattling off whatever I know about each make and model—all the same factoids Reed told me during my house tour, plus some stuff I think I might have made up—and Alessandra "oohs" and "aahs" and makes snarky comments about Reed's over-the-top "bougie-ness" the whole time.

When we come to a standstill in front of Reed's yellow Ferrari, the second-to-last entry in the collection, I say, "Reed finally got this beauty back from the body shop yesterday. A few weeks ago, he was driving it too fast around a curve and, according to him, a tree 'leaped out into the middle of the road,' right in front of him."

"Oh my gosh. Was Reed hurt?"

"No, thankfully. But the right front of the car wasn't as lucky. Apparently, it was really smashed up... right through *there*."

I crouch down and peer closely at the area in question, and

Alessandra bends down and joins me in scrutinizing the body shop's handiwork.

"You can't even tell it was ever busted," Alessandra marvels.

"Yeah, it looks as good as new. Wow."

We straighten up and walk a few steps to our left.

"And last but not least... this is Reed's favorite, by far." I motion to Reed's beloved Bugatti. "It's a Bugatti *Chiron*. Which, believe me, is far superior to the Bugatti *Veyron*. The Bugatti folks *really* upped their 'pickup' game with the Chiron."

Alessandra scoffs and rolls her eyes along with me. "Like I always say, the Veyron is a straight-up piece of shit."

I burst out laughing. *"That's exactly what I said!"*

We laugh and laugh.

"Wow, Georgie," Alessandra says. She pauses to look around the expansive space. "Reed really did make you his Cinderella, didn't he? Just like he said that night at the bar."

I inhale sharply. *Holy crap.* Alessandra is right. *He did.* Indeed, that's exactly how I've been feeling this entire week with him. Like Cinderella at the ball.

Alessandra walks a few steps away to inspect Reed's sporting equipment on the far wall, but I stand frozen and flabbergasted by my epiphany. Have I been a fool to let myself get swept into a fairytale with a man like Reed Rivers—a man who's made it quite clear he's got no desire to be anyone's Prince Charming? There can't possibly be a happily ever after at the end of this fairytale I've been play-acting with Reed. I really need to remind myself of that fact, and prepare myself for the alternate ending. I need to pull back. Stuff these feelings down. Guard my heart so it won't get hurt. I glance at Reed's sparkling yellow Ferrari, and think, *If I give my heart to Reed and he smashes it, I can't imagine I'd come out the other side looking as good as new, the way this Ferrari did.*

"Earth to Georgie," Alessandra says.

I look at her blankly.

"I asked if you're ready to go to the pool now, Cinderella?"

"Oh." I take a deep breath. "Yeah, great. But, please, don't make Cinderella my nickname. It only makes me think I'm one midnight away from everything around me turning into a pumpkin."

After changing into our swimsuits, Alessandra and I arrive at the pool to find Reed's sister and her friend enjoying the sunny day, joined by Josh and his pregnant wife, Kat, who's rocking a white string bikini with her baby bump, and Henn, who's here with his adorable, bespectacled wife, Hannah.

Introductions are made, and easy conversation ensues. After some preliminaries, Kat asks me about the special issue and how I got my cool gig, so I tell the group the story of how I ambushed CeeCee at an on-campus event for music students.

"Sounds like she's your spirit animal, Kat," Josh says to his wife. "A woman who knows how to get shit done."

"He's complimenting you," Kat assures me. "Josh loves my devious side."

"Oh, absolutely," Josh says, laughing. "The way Kat cleverly gets what she wants is one of my all-time favorite things about her. Kat's family calls itself the Morgan Mafia. And she's definitely 'The Godmother' in that clan."

"Oh, you're a *Morgan*?" I say to Kat, putting two and two together. "Are you related to Keane and Dax?"

"They're my brothers. My two little brothers. I've also got two big brothers. I like to say I'm the meat in a Morgan brothers sandwich." She giggles at her own joke.

"Are your two older brothers coming to the party tonight, too?"

I don't recall seeing any other Morgans on the guest list. But, then again, I didn't make it through the entire list before Alessandra showed up.

"No. My oldest brother, Colby, isn't a big partier. And my second-oldest brother, Ryan, loves to party, but not with Reed."

My stomach clenches. "Oh."

Kat looks embarrassed. "Oh, no, it's nothing big. Reed flirted with Ryan's wife, a million years ago, and Ryan's never forgotten about it."

"*Oh,*" I say again, at a loss for words. Reed hit on a married woman? And not just any married woman, but his best friend's sister-in-law? I'm well aware Reed's always liked the ladies, but, come on, there's an entire planet of women who'd fall at his feet. There was no need for him to hit on Josh's sister-in-law.

"Oh, Georgie, no, no," Kat says, apparently reacting to the look on my face. "Tessa wasn't even Ryan's wife back when Reed flirted with her! She wasn't even Ryan's *girlfriend!*" Kat cackles with laughter. "My brother, Ryan, is a lunatic when it comes to his wife. A crazy-man with a grudge. Reed did nothing wrong. Tessa was single and fair game when he flirted with her. It was at our destination wedding in Maui, and everybody was hitting on everybody." She laughs uproariously, and I exhale with relief.

More conversation ensues, drink orders are taken by some dude, and more people arrive. First, the three guys of 22 Goats—Dax, Fish, and Colin—waltz in, nearly making both Alessandra and me pee in the pool. Shortly after that, the actor Keane Morgan and his cute documentarian wife, Maddy, arrive, along with their two best friends... who, get this, are none other than former Disney-star-turned-pop-star, Aloha Carmichael, the woman Alessandra and I both watched on *It's Aloha!* throughout our childhoods, plus, Aloha's bodyguard-husband, Zander.

More drink orders are taken. Music begins blaring out of hidden speakers. And, suddenly, we've got ourselves a legit pool party.

At first, I'm nervous and stiff around so much star power. And Alessandra is a mute. But soon, it's impossible not to loosen up in this easygoing group. We find out Keane's wife, Maddy, is the younger sister of Henn's wife, Hannah. We find out Kat is the one who introduced Henn to Hannah—that Kat used to work with Hannah in Seattle. "The minute I met Henny," Kat declares, "I knew he'd fall ass over tea kettle for Hannah!"

With the group looking on and laughing their asses off, Keane tells Alessandra and me a long, twisted, bizarre story about the day he first met Zander when they got stuck together in an elevator at a porn convention... before finally bursting out laughing at our expressions and telling us, no, actually the pair met in math class in eighth grade.

And on and on it goes, with music blaring and cocktails flowing all the while. And through it all, I find myself feeling more and more relaxed and like myself, despite all the glamour and star power around me. Even Alessandra begins to find her groove after a while. Mostly, thanks to Fish, the lanky, shaggy bass player of 22 Goats, with whom she's now chatting in a corner of the pool.

"So, do you mind if we talk about my interview of 22 Goats for a second?" I ask Dax.

I'm standing in the shallow end of the pool with him and his sweet wife, plus, Colin and his adorable girlfriend. Also, Josh and Kat, and Henn and Hannah. Behind us, Zander, Aloha, Keane, and Maddy are playing an enthusiastic game of chicken.

"Sure," Dax says. "Reed mentioned you're trying to come up with unique angles for all your interviews?"

"That's the idea," I say. "For instance, with Dean Masterson, I'm going to hang out with him at his house in Malibu. I'll watch him surf. He'll make me some stir-fry and show me some personal photos. I'm hoping to be able to write something really different about him than the world has seen before."

"That sounds cool," Dax says.

"You guys could show Georgina around Seattle," Kat suggests. "It could be an 'origin story' type thing. You could show her where you guys used to rehearse in Mom and Dad's garage. And where you used to skateboard. I have a thousand photos I could show you, Georgie."

Dax says he's in favor of the idea, and his drummer, Colin, agrees.

"Should we ask Fish if he's okay with it?" I ask, glancing across the pool at Fish and Alessandra.

"Nah," Dax says. "Fish is always cool with whatever."

And, just that fast, it's settled: In the near future, I'm going to spend the day in Seattle with 22 Goats!

"You should stay with Josh and me when you come," Kat says. "That way, we can hang out and relax while I show you all my photos and tell you all the stories the Goats would never want you to hear."

I laugh with her. "That sounds amazing, Kat. Thank you."

"Let's exchange numbers, so you can use me as your point of contact to schedule everything," Kat says. "It'd take you five times as long to get anything done if you had to go through official channels."

And off we go to the ledge of the pool to grab our phones and exchange information.

"So, hey," Kat says, after she's input my number. "I think I might have put my foot in my mouth earlier, when I said that thing about my brother, Ryan, not liking Reed. Josh overheard that and got pissed at me. He doesn't want you thinking badly of Reed, and neither do I. Reed is actually a good guy, Georgie. A sweetheart, once you get past all that swagger."

I open my mouth to reply, but quickly close it again. Kat knows about Reed and me? Or is she simply concerned she's said the wrong thing about her husband's best friend to the woman assigned to write an article about him?

Kat continues, "Honestly, Georgie, I can't even count all the times I've seen Reed being a fantastic friend or brother. Did you know he paid for all his sister's schooling? He also hosted Henn and Hannah's wedding here at his house. Also..." She looks behind her, apparently making sure nobody is within earshot. "This is off the record, okay? Not for your article."

"Sure."

"Don't tell my brother, Keane, but Reed really helped his career behind the scenes." She looks behind her again. "When Keane first moved to LA to try his hand at modeling and acting, his agent wouldn't send him out to audition for anything serious. Every role he auditioned for was a dumb jock or stripper or frat boy. Keane was grateful for the work, and excited at first, but after a while, he really wanted to throw his hat in the ring for more serious roles. So, he took acting classes, and really worked hard, but, still, his agent wouldn't take him seriously. So, Maddy told me about Keane's predicament. She said Keane was getting discouraged. So, I mentioned it to Josh, just, you know, to catch my husband up on my life. I didn't expect Josh to *do* anything with the information. But Josh, being Josh, he immediately took action and called Reed. Who then called the head of Keane's talent agency—because Reed knows *everybody* in this town—and Reed told the guy it would be a *personal* favor to *him* if Keane's particular agent would start taking a chance on him and send him out to a few serious auditions. And guess what happened? Keane got hired for the first serious role he tried out for! And that led to the next role, and the next. And now he's starring in a hit show!"

Of course, none of this surprises me. Indeed, everything Kat just said sounds *exactly* like something Reed would do. Like Reed told me that day in the gym, he won't compromise his professional judgment, but he'll do just about anything else for the people on his short list. And since Josh Faraday is one of the people on that list, all he had to do was give Reed a call to send him into action.

"And that's Reed for you," Kat says, her blue eyes twinkling. "And Josh, too. Both of those guys are so generous."

"Why don't they want Keane to know they helped him? Wouldn't Keane want to know, so he could thank both of them for helping him out? If someone helped me with *my* career behind the scenes, I'd want to know about it, so I could thank them profusely."

"Josh and Reed don't want to take anything away from Keane. Especially Reed. He never wants the spotlight for himself. He loves pulling strings behind the scenes."

Ping.

That soft cotton ball from earlier *poofs* softly against the back of my head again. A fuzzy idea is once again trying to sharpen and take root inside my brain. But before the amorphous thought crystallizes, Kat speaks again.

"And Keane is just another example on a long list of them. When Hannah first moved from Seattle to LA to be closer to her then-boyfriend, Henn, do you know what Reed did for her, simply because she was Henn's girlfriend?"

"He helped her get a job?" I throw out.

Kat looks surprised. "Actually... yes. I was going to say Reed gave Hannah a smoking good deal on an apartment in one of his buildings. But, yes, Reed *also* helped Hannah get her current job, too. I guess he knew someone who knew someone, and that got her in the door for an interview. Oh! He also got Zander an interview with Big Barry, when Zander first moved to LA, too. That's how Zander became Aloha's personal bodyguard." Kat grabs her club soda off the ledge and takes a long sip. "Seriously, if you've got Reed Rivers vouching for you, you can't lose."

"The Man with the Midas Touch," I say.

"Exactly. But, see, most people don't realize Reed's golden touch extends to far more things than music. Oh! Maddy is another example. Reed brokered the distribution deal for one of her documentaries—the one she did with Aloha—and he also introduced her to one of his producing partners for her next project. And, *boom*, Maddy's very next film, she wound up getting nominated for an Oscar!"

"Wow."

"The same kind of thing happened with Isabel Randolph. Josh told me Reed brought Isabel to one of Josh's parties, way before she was famous. Josh said Reed introduced her as a 'rising star' and 'one to watch'... and, well, you know how that turned out. I'm telling you, Reed is *never* wrong about spotting talent. He can spot it better than anyone."

I force a smile, but my stomach is tight.

"Oh, crap," Kat says. "I did it again, didn't I? Put my foot in my mouth. Georgina, Reed and Isabel are ancient news. You have nothing to worry about there. I don't know if this is public knowledge yet, so don't post about this, but she's getting married. In fact, Josh said she's bringing her fiancé to the party. And, regardless, Reed has no interest in her. Josh says Isabel is the one who's always carried a torch for Reed. Not the other way around. So, now that she's getting married, I guess that's that, right?"

Jesus Christ. Does *everyone* at this little pre-party know I'm having sex with Reed? Do the three guys of 22 Goats, who I'll be interviewing, know? Do they think I got this job, thanks to Reed pulling strings for me behind the scenes, the same way he did for Keane and Zander and Hannah?

Ping.

That cotton ball knocks me in the back of the head again... Only this time, it's a tiny pebble. But before another pebble hits, and the thought takes shape, a hurtling body cannonballs into the pool, immediately to my left, dousing Kat and me with a virtual tsunami that makes us squeal.

I didn't see the cannonballer, but I'm instantly assuming it had to be Keane Morgan, or maybe his best friend, Zander, since those two have been goofing around like kids in the pool for the past twenty minutes. But, to my shock, it's *Reed* who suddenly breaks the surface of the water next to me, like a great white shark breaching the ocean's surface to nab a frightened seal in its gaping mouth. Laughing at my shocked reaction, Reed swoops me into his arms and plants an enthusiastic kiss on my mouth, right in front of his entire group of friends.

For a split-second, I'm aggravated. I've been adamant with Reed that I don't want anyone knowing we're sleeping together. But then, I remember Kat almost certainly already knows about us, which means Josh and everyone else probably does, too.

And just that fast, I realize I'm feeling electrified, not upset, that Reed wants the people closest to him to know about us. In fact, I couldn't be happier about it. With a swooning sigh, I wrap my legs around Reed's waist and my arms around his neck and kiss the hell out of my gorgeous man, so everyone he cares about can plainly see I'm every bit as attracted to him, as he is to me.

FIFTY-FIVE
GEORGINA

Reed's party has been like a dream. A perfect fantasy. Everything Reed promised it would be, and so much more. The people-watching has been insanity. The impromptu performances and jam sessions have been mind-blowing. And, best of all, at least from a personal standpoint, I've felt like an actual guest tonight, as opposed to an awkward bystander or voyeur. And that's thanks to Reed's friends—the ones who so enthusiastically welcomed Alessandra and me at the pool earlier. They've made me feel like I truly belong here tonight. Not as a reporter for *Rock 'n' Roll,* but as Reed's girlfriend.

Kat, especially, has been the president of my fan club tonight—hell-bent on making me feel like the little sister she never had. At one point, when I said something that made Kat hoot with laughter, she threw her arms around me and said to Hannah, "See, Banana? I told you: Georgie's me, if I were seven years younger and a hot as fuck brunette!"

And I'm not the only one feeling comfortable here tonight. I can tell Alessandra feels relaxed and happy, too, thanks to her amazing connection with Fish. He's been a dream to her. Introducing her around. Pulling her into conversations and games of ping pong and HORSE. Thereby drawing her out of her shell in record time.

And I can't forget the smashing success of the "business" side of this amazing party, as well. Reed said I'd be able to bond with his artists at this party, in a way that would elevate the content of the special issue. And he was exactly right. I've played ping pong with Savage from Fugitive Summer. Corn hole with members of Danger Doctor Jones. For God's sake, Laila Fitzgerald and I now have our own secret handshake—an intricate maneuver we concocted while teaming up to beat Aloha and Zander in beer pong.

And through it all, Reed has been perfect. As requested, he's treated me with nothing but professionalism tonight. Well, to the naked eye, anyway. Covertly, we've flirted like crazy with each other across the crowded party all night long, the same way we secretly flirted with each other throughout the entire panel discussion a lifetime ago.

The panel discussion.

Wow.

It really does feel like a lifetime ago, even though it's only been a few weeks. Since then, I've graduated college. Met my idol. Snagged my dream job. I've moved into Reed's mansion, and befriended famous, glamorous people like it was a totally normal thing to do. I've breathed a sigh of relief to have my father's medicine and condo paid for, and worn a ruby necklace worth *eighty thousand dollars* around my neck. I've experienced a kind of pleasure I didn't know existed, and found a powerful new kind of confidence in the process...

And, of course, last but not least, I've fallen head over heels for an incredible, generous man with a huge heart. A man who makes me feel safe and adored in a way I needed so badly, but didn't even realize. Yes, I've fallen head over heels for Reed. I can't deny it any longer. I belong to him—mind, body, and soul.

Will everything turn into a pumpkin at the stroke of midnight? My brain is telling me the odds are high. But my heart doesn't give a crap. My heart is barreling ahead, with zero ability to swerve. At this point, I'm Reed's yellow Ferrari. And if Reed is the tree that's going to leap out into the middle of the road, then so be it.

The crowd at the party cheers wildly, jerking me from my thoughts. I'm standing at the foot of the stage with some of my new friends, while the current "super-group" of musicians onstage—a group that includes Fish, Aloha, 2Real, Dax, and more—finishes their performance.

The musicians pile offstage to back slaps and high-fives, and the minute Fish sees Alessandra standing next to me, alongside Hannah, Maddy, and Kat, he heads straight for her.

"I could use some fresh air," Fish says to Alessandra. "You want to go outside with me?"

"Absolutely," Alessandra says, looking as happy as I've ever seen her.

He puts his hand out. She grabs it like it's the most natural thing in the world. And off they go.

"Well, that was the cutest thing I've ever seen in my life," Hannah says.

Maddy, Kat, and I agree.

"They're like Bambi and that female doe, when they first meet as babies," Kat says.

"Faline," Hannah supplies.

"Yes!" Kat says, laughing. "They're like Bambi and Faline. Both of them are so sweet and awkward and bashful together."

"I can't believe how quickly Fish has already drawn Ally out of her shell tonight," I say. "She went to an all-girls' high school, where she had literally zero experience with boys. And now, in college, she says half the guys are gay, and the other half have friend-zoned her, so she's still a big-time newbie when it comes to boys."

"Hey, just like you," Hannah jokes to Kat, and Kat pats her big belly and laughs.

"Well, if Alessandra is a newbie, then Fish is a perfect starter kit for her," Maddy pipes in to say. "Just the other night, he and the Goats were over, and Fish said he's sick to death of the kinds of girls he meets on tour. 'Star-fuckers,' is what the Goats call them. Fish said he's done with girls who like him just because he's in 22 Goats."

My heart is fluttering with excitement for Alessandra. "Well, Fish is barking up the right tree with my stepsister. She's—"

"Excuse me," Reed says, appearing at Kat's side. "Sorry to interrupt. Georgina, I want to introduce you to a couple friends of mine." He steps aside and gestures to the two figures to his right. "This is Isabel Randolph and her fiancé, Howard Devlin."

FIFTY-SIX
GEORGINA

Inwardly, I feel like I'm going to hyperventilate at the sight of Isabel Randolph standing before me. But, outwardly, I manage to keep it together and smile like a normal person.

Reed gestures to me and says, "This is Georgina Ricci, a brilliant writer whom CeeCee has personally tasked with coming up with content for *Dig a Little Deeper,* in addition to the River Records special edition of *Rock 'n' Roll.*"

"Hello!" I say, a bit too enthusiastically, shaking the pair's offered hands, and they laugh and say hello.

"Hey, I work for you!" Hannah blurts next to me. She's speaking to Howard. "I work in your PR department, Mr. Devlin."

Howard chuckles at Hannah's enthusiasm. "What's your name?"

"Hannah Hennessy, sir."

He smiles graciously, but it's clear he's never heard of Hannah in his life. "Come get a drink with me, Hannah Hennessy. While Isabel chats with Georgina, you can tell me all about what it's like to work for me."

Panic flashes across Hannah's adorable face. She grabs Kat's hand and says, "Sounds great. My friend Kat has always wanted to meet you, too." And off the trio goes, as Isabel and I move to a quiet corner to talk.

Of course, I tell Isabel I'm a fan, right off the bat, and she thanks me and tells me a couple behind-the-scenes anecdotes about my two favorite movies of hers that thrill me and make me laugh—and, also, make me feel genuinely comfortable and relaxed in her presence. Or, heck, maybe it's the massive rock on Isabel's left ring finger that's relaxing me and calming my green-eyed monster. Either way, I quickly decide I genuinely like her. And that I'm elated at the prospect of interviewing her. Indeed, as she's been telling me those anecdotes, I've hardly imagined her sucking Reed's dick at all.

"So, Reed tells me CeeCee is contemplating a 'Women in Hollywood' issue of *Dig a Little Deeper*," Isabel says.

Ah, sneaky Reed. He set us both up, did he? He told Isabel that CeeCee is contemplating such an issue while telling *me* I should pitch the idea to CeeCee. But rather than being upset with Reed for his maneuverings, I'm only grateful to him. If this idea could ultimately impress CeeCee, and lure Isabel into giving an in-depth interview to me, all of which might lead to me getting onto the permanent writing staff of *Dig a Little Deeper*, then I don't care who might have concocted the idea first.

Obviously, I have no way of knowing if CeeCee would run with the idea of a "Women in Hollywood" issue. Or, if so, if she'd put Isabel on its cover. But CeeCee *did* say she'll consider "anything" I might submit to her for *Dig a Little Deeper*... So, fuck it. I decide to run with the idea with Isabel and ask for her forgiveness later, as needed.

"CeeCee was very clear she wanted me to submit interviews for *Dig a Little Deeper* that will blow her away," I say carefully. Yes, I'm letting Isabel assume that conversation was in the context of a special issue, but oh well. "And I genuinely think we could come up with something amazing together. Something that shows a new side to you." As an example, I tell her what I'm doing with Dean Masterson and 22 Goats for *Rock 'n' Roll*. "But for *Dig a Little Deeper*, we have to go deeper, obviously."

"Maybe I could give you a tour of my house?" she suggests.

But I've already seen her do that exact thing in one of the articles I read about her last night. "I think we should do something that's never been done before," I say. "With you getting married, maybe I could tag along on a day of wedding planning. We could talk about love, and marriage. Generally and specifically. We could talk about your childhood, and what you saw of marriage growing up . . .?"

Isabel is stone-faced, and I know I'm losing her.

"Or, maybe... is there something you've never done before, but always wanted to do? A hip hop dance class? Knitting? Archery? Or, maybe, is there something that scares the crap out of you, but you could conquer it for the article?" I gasp. "Yes! Isabel! You're about to play a superhero! That could be our angle. 'Isabel Randolph. A Superhero Onscreen. All Too Human in Real Life.'"

She's visibly elated with that last pitch. And suddenly, we're caught up in enthusiastic brainstorming that concludes with our decision to go skydiving together, even though she's terrified of heights and they're most definitely *not* my favorite thing.

"Oh, Isabel," I say. "I bet the conversation we're going to have after you've faced down a gigantic fear will be the best interview of your life."

"Wow, Georgina. Reed told me you're CeeCee's favorite, and I can see why."

"Thank you. That's so nice."

"How did you meet Reed, exactly?" she asks. And, instantly, I can tell she's wondering if there's something going on between Reed and me.

"Through CeeCee," I say smoothly. "CeeCee assigned me to write for the River Records issue, as well as for *Dig a Little Deeper*, so, I met Reed backstage at the Red Card Riot concert. Actually, my boyfriend was super jealous about me hanging out with RCR. He was worried I was going to run off with C-Bomb—their drummer."

Isabel visibly relaxes when she hears the words "my boyfriend" come out of my mouth. Which pisses me off, actually, even though that was my intended effect. She's engaged, for fuck's sake! And isn't Reed nothing but a brother to her now? Why should she be relieved to find out the reporter hanging around River Records for the summer has a jealous boyfriend?

"Well, C-Bomb *is* hot as hell," Isabel says. "I can see why your boyfriend was a bit worried there. I'd certainly do him."

How about you stick to your fiancé, hon? "Naw, my boyfriend is even hotter than C-Bomb. He doesn't have anything to worry about. Not regarding C-Bomb or anyone else."

Isabel looks pleased. Very, very pleased. Which, again, pisses me off.

"How did *you* meet Reed?" I ask. "You know, way back when, for the first time?"

She sips her drink. "Through a mutual friend."

And that's it.

She says nothing more.

The hairs on the back of my neck stand up. That's strange. If the mutual friend who introduced Reed and Isabel was CeeCee, as I'm thinking she means, then why not name CeeCee to me, seeing as how I just now said *I* met Reed through CeeCee? Wouldn't it be a natural thing, given the circumstances, for Isabel to say, "What a coincidence! I *also* met Reed through CeeCee, the same as you!"?

Hmm.

The investigative reporter inside me is suddenly awake and very alert.

"Who was the mutual friend?" I ask casually, trying not to sound like I feel—like a hungry shark smelling blood.

Isabel pauses. Ever so briefly. "Josh Faraday. Have you met him? He's around here somewhere. He's one of Reed's best friends."

Liar. "Yeah, I met him earlier. How did you know Josh?"

She sips her drink again. "From the party circuit. I met Reed at one of Josh's parties."

"And the rest, as they say, is history," I say brightly.

"Yep," she replies.

"Life can be crazy that way. You never know when someone you meet at a party will be in your life for years to come."

"So true."

Okay, seriously now. What the fuck is going on here? Kat didn't seem the least bit confused in the pool when she told me, quite clearly, that *Reed* had brought *Isabel* to one of Josh's parties, as *Reed's* guest, and then told Josh she was a "rising star" and "someone to watch."

My mind is whirling. Clacking. Processing. *Isabel just lied to me.* There's no doubt about that. And, based on what I saw in that photo of Justin Timberlake, I'm almost positive Reed's lied to me, too, about the very same topic. But, *why*? Why, why, why to all of it?

I take a long sip of my drink to hide my scowl, before saying, "I think CeeCee is a person like that for Reed. You know, someone he happened to meet at a party and then she unexpectedly became a deeply important person in his life. Well, correction. He didn't 'happen' to meet her. Reed actually told me he crashed CeeCee's fiftieth birthday party to get her to write about Red Card Riot's debut. But the fact still remains, after that one encounter, they've been genuine, great friends ever since."

"That's a great story," Isabel says.

And that's it again. She doesn't say another word. She doesn't say, "Hey! I was at CeeCee's fiftieth birthday party!" She doesn't say, "Hey! Wait! I just remembered *that's* the party where I met Reed, not a party thrown by Josh!" And she certainly doesn't say, "You want to hear something crazy? My future husband, Howard, was at that same party!"

Quickly, I decide to press the eject button and get myself out of this crazy-making conversation. Because, holy fuck, I'm not going to be able to keep a poker face for much longer.

"Well, I'll let you enjoy the party," I say, smiling. "I can't wait for our interview, Isabel."

We talk logistics briefly. She gives me the number of her publicist, and we say a warm and hearty goodbye, sealed with a you're-my-new-best-friend hug.

"Sincere congratulations on your engagement," I say, pulling out of our embrace. "I'm so happy for you."

"Thanks," she says. But her smile doesn't reach her eyes.

With a little wave to me, she takes a few steps into the crowded party, and stops. She scours the crowd, presumably looking for Howard. But when her eyes obviously land on him at one of the bars, where he's talking to several high-profile people from the entertainment business, she turns and strides purposefully away, in the exact opposite direction of her future husband.

FIFTY-SEVEN
REED

After leaving Georgina with Isabel and Howard, I do a quick lap around the party, looking for Henn. But when I spot Aloha, chatting with the other writer from *Rock 'n' Roll* assigned to the special issue, I decide to intervene.

It's been a bit of a juggling act to gently steer certain artists to Georgie, rather than Zasu, seeing as how I'm not technically supposed to be involved with interview assignments. But, still, I've managed to finesse things to my liking. Specifically, I want Georgina to interview my highest profile artists. People like Aloha. Because, of course, I want Georgina to get the lion's share of the glory and accolades when the special issue comes out.

That said, however, there are a couple high-profile *males* on my roster I don't want coming within ten yards of Georgina. Lady-killers with big swinging dicks. Savage from Fugitive Summer is definitely one of them. Also, Endo from Watch Party.

"Hey, ladies," I say to Aloha and Zasu. "Aloha, Georgina was looking for you. She wants to nail down what you're going to do for your interview with her."

"Oh. Zasu and I were actually—"

"Hey, Zasu. I think Georgina's idea for Aloha's interview sounds great. Would you mind letting her take that one?"

"Of course not. That's fine with me."

"Great. How about you interview Savage and Endo? They're both around here somewhere. Maybe you could touch base with them now."

"Oh. Okay. Sure thing."

"I saw Endo playing corn hole a few minutes ago," Aloha says.

"I'll wander over there now," Zasu says.

"Great idea." When she leaves, I turn to Aloha. "Nail something down with Georgina. I want her to get the best interviews."

She bats her eyelashes. "Aw, Reed. Is someone a smitten kitten?"

"Just do it, Aloha."

I head back to the main room to look for Henn, and spot Georgina talking to Isabel across the room in a corner. Of course, I stop and watch for a moment. It's something I've been doing all night—secretly watching Georgina as she charms my artists and friends. I've loved seeing how seamlessly Georgina fits into my world. How she lights up everyone who encounters her, the same way she lights up my house when she walks through the front door.

But, also, I've been watching Georgina from afar all night because I've been guarding her. Making sure nobody hits on her.

Georgina wants my artists to think my relationship with her is purely professional—so I've respected her wishes and kept my distance tonight. But the downside of me keeping my distance is that none of my artists knows the hot-as-fuck reporter from *Rock 'n' Roll* is taken. Indeed, they think she's fair game. Frankly, it's been a crazy-making situation for me, not being able to kiss her in front of everyone to make it abundantly clear she's all mine.

As I watch Georgina and Isabel talk, it seems to me things are going well. They're smiling and looking friendly. After a bit, the women hug, which tells me Georgina has landed an in-depth interview, and then Isabel heads off into the party.

I take two steps toward Georgina, intending to head over to her, when Savage from Fugitive Summer swoops in on his mark. Motherfucker. The pair high-fives enthusiastically, which tells me this isn't their first meeting of the night. Fuck. They chat enthusiastically, their body language familiar and highly friendly. But I keep my distance, out of respect for Georgina's wishes. I let her do her job. But when Savage puts his hand on Georgina's shoulder—*and then nonchalantly moves a lock of Georgina's hair off her shoulder*—all bets are off.

My heart thundering, I march through the crowd, and straight to the pair.

"I need to speak with you," I bark to Savage.

"Can it wait? Georgina and I—"

"It can't wait. Follow me."

I grab his sleeve and pull him with me, leaving Georgina standing in shocked stillness, her mouth in the shape of a perfect "O."

"Reed, come on, man. You're cock-blocking me."

Damn straight, I am.

I lead him around a corner and into an empty hallway and whirl around.

"Do *not* hit on the *Rock 'n' Roll* reporter."

He shakes me off him. "She's hot as hell."

"She's hands-off."

"Who says?"

I pause. *Fuck.* I promised Georgie. "She's here to do a job. Not to get hit on. I promised her boss nobody would hit on her."

He scoffs. "I think we should let her decide if she wants to get hit on or not."

"Go find the other writer. Her name is Zasu. She's been assigned to do your interview."

"Georgie and I have great chemistry. And we already have the whole thing figured out."

"You're doing an interview with Zasu. It's not a request."

He leans his shoulder against the wall of the hallway. "You want Georgina for yourself, don't you?"

"My motivations don't matter. The only thing you need to know is the owner of your label is telling you she's off-limits. Now, go find Zasu."

He pulls out a cigarette and slips it into his mouth. "Got a light?"

"No."

He pulls the cigarette out of his mouth, winks at me, and saunters out of the room, throwing over his shoulder. "You're too old for her, anyway, man. She's only twenty-one."

Fuck.

I run my palm through my hair and take a deep breath and leave the hallway.

Quickly, I spot Henn at one of the bars with Hannah, Josh, and Kat, so I beeline over there.

"Old Man Rivers!" Josh calls out when he sees me. He's been calling me that nickname since our college days, but, in this particular moment, I'm not amused.

"Don't call me that tonight. And order me a shot of tequila."

Not surprisingly, everyone but preggers Kat enthusiastically joins me in doing a shot. After which, I lean into Henn's shoulder. "Have you gotten access to his devices yet?"

Henn rolls his eyes. "Not since you asked me about it at the pool this afternoon."

"Why hasn't the bastard clicked on any of your phishing emails yet?"

"Sometimes, these things take time. But don't worry. There are other ways to skin this cat. I'll focus on it first thing Monday morning, once Hazel's party is behind me."

"Can you work on it tomorrow before Hazel's party? I'm going to explode if I don't get the ball rolling on this as soon as possible, Henny. I need you to do this for my mental health."

"Who is this guy?"

I pause, weighing how much I can divulge to my best friend without feeling like I'm betraying Georgina's confidence. Henn is one of two people in the world—the other being Josh—I trust completely. One of two people who get me completely. And, besides all that, if I expect Henn, a white hat hacker, to use his superpowers to completely destroy someone, I'm going to have to convince him he's using his superpowers for good.

"This is confidential."

"Of course."

"Not even Hannah, Henn."

"I understand."

I pause. "Gates was Georgie's teacher in high school. Her senior year, he pinned her arms behind her back and kissed her against her will. He tried to rape her, but she ran away screaming."

"Holy shit."

My heart is pounding. My blood simmering. "It fucked her up, Henn. I don't want to go into too much detail, but she's traumatized."

"Understandably. There's so much that's wrong about all that. I don't even know where to begin."

"I want to destroy him, Henny. Well, actually, what I really want to do is strangle the life out of him with my bare hands. But since I don't want to go to prison, I'll settle for ending life as he knows it."

Henn's jaw sets. "I'm on it. I'm pretty drunk right now, and I've got Hazel's party to deal with tomorrow. But I'll get access as soon as possible."

"Thanks, brother. I don't know how much longer I can keep myself from driving to the Valley and handling him myself."

"Don't do that." He pats my shoulder. "Have a drink. Actually, have several."

"I already have."

"Have some more."

He turns to the bartender and orders a gin and tonic for me, just as the Fantastic Four, as they call themselves—Aloha and her husband, Zander, and Keane Morgan and his wife, Maddy—reach the bar where my group is standing.

"No, I haven't talked to Georgina yet," Aloha says to me, before I've said a word. "We've been dancing."

"Well, chop, chop."

"Okay, okay." But when the DJ starts playing "Sweet but Psycho" by Ava Max, Aloha shrieks and pulls Maddy, Hannah, and Kat to the dance floor.

When the ladies are gone, Henn addresses Zander and Keane. "Hey, do either of you have any weed on you? Reed needs to take the edge off."

"Are there dicks in gay porn?" Keane says, holding up a joint.

"Do me a favor and take Reed onto the patio to smoke that thing. He needs something more than a gin and tonic to keep some homicidal thoughts he's having under wraps."

"Homicidal thoughts?" Keane says. "That's no bueno. Come on, Reed. Z and I will fix you right up."

FIFTY-EIGHT
REED

Once outside on the patio, Keane, Zander, and I move toward a dark, isolated corner by a low retaining wall, where we can smoke out and gaze at the amazing view without a hundred people approaching to kiss my ass, or bum a hit off the joint, or gush over Keane. But when our threesome comes to a stop, Fish's voice rises up from the ground only a few feet away.

"Well, hello there, fellas," he says. And when I look down, there he is, camped with Georgina's stepsister on the opposite side of a low retaining wall, their backs against the wall as they gaze out at the sparkling view.

Keane, Zander, and I look at each other, nonverbally acknowledging what we all instantly understand: we're totally cockblocking Fish right now.

"Sorry, brother," Zander says. "Carry on. We came out here to smoke a joint, but we can certainly find another spot."

"Oh, no need to do that," Fish says, hopping up with a laugh. He pulls his girl up with him. "Did everybody meet Alessandra at the pool?"

"Yeah," Keane says. "Hey, Ally Cat."

She waves shyly.

"Hello again, Alessandra," I say. I met her briefly this afternoon, but she was so intimidated, she barely held my gaze. And this time isn't much better. Which, frankly, annoys me. Whether she's intimidated or not, she needs to put on her big girl panties and try to impress me. She's a music student, for fuck's sake! And I'm the head of River fucking Records. If she can't pull her shit together enough to at least *try* to seize this once-in-a-lifetime opportunity, how is she ever going to make it in the music business? Has this girl *never* heard the phrase "seize the day"? How about "fake it till you make it"?

Exhaling with frustration, I take the joint from Keane and inhale extra deeply and then hold it out to Zander, who takes an extra-long hit, too. He offers it to Fish, who does his thing, before offering it to Alessandra, who, not surprisingly, politely declines.

"Give Reed her share," Keane says. "Murder can really fuck up a guy's life."

"Not if they don't catch ya," I say, taking the joint from Fish. Another inhale. Another hand-off. A long gulp of my gin and tonic. And I'm feeling pretty good. I smile at Alessandra. "If you're worried about breaking the law, don't be."

She looks at me blankly.

"Weed. It's legal in California."

"Oh," she says, catching my meaning. "Only if you're twenty-one, right? I'm nineteen."

We all chuckle, thinking she's kidding. But when her face blasts with color, we all have the good sense to respectfully pipe down.

"You want another bottle of water?" Fish asks, looking at his girl. "Something to eat?"

Alessandra looks relieved Fish has just offered her an eject button out of this stressful situation. "Yeah, I could use a water. I'll come with you."

"Why don't you stay here and chat with me for a minute, Alessandra," I say.

She freezes, looking like she's about to crap her pants.

"Just for a couple minutes," I say soothingly.

"Uh oh," Keane says. "What'd you do to get called to the principal's office, Ally Cat? You done fucked up, sis. *Godspeed*."

"She didn't fuck up anything," I say. "I just want to chat with her for a minute about music. Georgina mentioned you're studying music at Berklee."

"Yes," she manages to say.

"I know a lot of people who graduated from there," I say. "It's a great music school."

She nods.

I address the three men. "Will you boys excuse us for a few minutes?" I look at Alessandra. "That is, if you've got a couple minutes to spare?"

She looks like she's going to throw up, but she says, "Of course. Great."

"I'll come back in a bit," Fish says. He looks excited, like he's thinking this could be a once in a lifetime opportunity for this girl, if only she plays her cards right.

"Okay," she squeaks out.

"If you're not here when I get back for some reason, I'll find you."

"Great," she replies, but her red cheeks make it clear she's inwardly freaking out.

When Fish and the other guys are gone, I lead Alessandra to a nearby bench in a quiet corner. Once we're situated, I take a long swallow of my drink, finishing it off. I put the empty glass on the ground next to me, gaze for a long moment at the view, and then say calmly, "I've heard your demo, Alessandra. All three songs." I look at her. "And you've got some work you need to do, if your dream is to make a living as a professional artist."

She presses her lips together, her eyes wide, but says nothing.

"The good news? I like the quality and tone of your voice. I love your vocal control. Very impressive. I also think you've got a good sense of melody and how to build a song. But if you don't figure out who you are as an artist—as a *person*—then these next two years of time and tuition are going to be wasted, assuming you went to Berklee because you want to make music your career. As things stand now, I could get you work as a demo singer. Maybe even a backup singer. You could write songs for other artists. But if you want to be an artist in your own right, if you want to perform your songs and make a living doing that, then you've got a lot of work to do."

She opens her mouth. But closes it. Her nostrils flare.

"Some of those vocal tics you do? Knock that shit off. That's not *you*, and you know it. You're copying the artists you admire. Being a Laila knockoff. Strip that bullshit off your vocals and tell the truth, whatever it is—good, bad, or ugly. If you get real, you'll get confident, Alessandra. The two things go hand in hand. And then maybe you'll smoke the proverbial joint of life when it's offered to you. Or you'll turn it down, if that's truly what you want to do. But when you turn down the joint of life, don't do it because you're nineteen, and the legal age is twenty-one. For fuck's sake, turn it down because you don't want the fucking joint! Which is a perfectly valid thing, by the way, as long as it's the truth."

She's clearly holding back tears.

"I'm talking about the joint as a metaphor, Alessandra. I'm not the bad guy in an after-school special." I smile, but she's not even close to being able to return the gesture. "Look, I'm trying to do you a favor here. You get that, right? You're hiding behind your music, rather than revealing yourself through it. Fix that, and I think you could have a shot. But, as it is, until you get real, and get the confidence boost that will come from that, I can't imagine you'd be able to command a coffee house full of people as an artist, let alone an entire stadium."

She swallows hard, fighting to keep her emotions from seeping out her eyes. And I momentarily feel bad to see my words make her want to cry. But I've come too far to stop now. I'm helping this girl. Giving her the keys to the kingdom, actually. And I'm not going to stop now, without saying everything that needs to be said. The truth hurts. But it also sets you free. And this girl, most definitely needs to be set free.

"If I'm full of shit, then prove me wrong." I point toward the house. "Go in there, grab one of the acoustic guitars onstage, and sing the shit out of one of your songs the way I'm telling you to do it. Be *you,* not a Laila knockoff. Show me you can *reveal* yourself through your music, rather than hide behind it, and maybe today will turn out to be your lucky day."

"I couldn't possibly do that," she whispers.

"I get that it's an intimidating room. But so what? They're just people. They were in your shoes once. Grab this opportunity I'm giving you. Get up there and knock me out. This is the chance of a lifetime. Grab it."

She looks down at her hands and shakes her head.

"If you're too nervous to play solo, then pull Fish onstage with you. He plays acoustic guitar and sings. You two could sing anything together. 'Hey, Jude' or 'Stand by Me,' for all I care. All that matters to me is you have the balls to get up there and grab this shot I'm giving you. Show me you've got what it takes, Alessandra. Prove me wrong."

I get up from the bench, praying she'll follow suit—hoping she'll rise, literally and figuratively, and square her slender shoulders and march her shy little ass straight inside and onto that stage and knock it out of the park with a performance she didn't even know she had inside her.

But, no.

She's crumbling before my eyes.

Her chin trembling and her eyes pricking with tears, she stammers, "Thank you for taking the time to explain all this to me." Before lurching off the bench and sprinting away into the night.

"Alessandra," I call out after her. But only half-heartedly. Shouting at her isn't going to make her stop running away. And I'm certainly not going to physically chase her. If she's intimidated by me, then hunting her down is the last thing I should do. Plus, fuck it. I'm not here to hand out participation trophies. I tried to help her, but some people can't be helped. Yes, I was honest with her. But if she can't handle honesty, then she can't handle the music industry. And that's a fucking fact. My heart pounding, I sit back down on the bench, grab my empty glass, and take an ice cube into my mouth. Fuck.

"Where's Alessandra?" Fish says, appearing before me with two water bottles. He looks around. "Did she go inside?"

"Yeah, I think so," I reply. "I'm not sure."

"She didn't say where she was going?"

"No. But I can tell you where she hopes *I'm* going. To hell."

Fish's face falls. "What happened? What does that mean?"

"It means I said something that upset her, apparently. She ran off, on the verge of tears."

Anger flashes across Fish's usually congenial face. "What'd you say to her?"

"I told her the truth, without sugarcoating it. I told her I listened to her demo and, basically, that she's got to get past the bullshit if she wants any shot—"

"Goddammit, Reed!" Fish booms, shocking the hell out of me. "Why are you always such a prick, man? Before you came out here, Alessandra and I were having the most amazing conversation! She was telling me how she got into music after her dad died when she was a kid. She was telling me about her stage fright. Asking me for tricks to overcome it. And then you had to come out here and tell her she sucks and her music is bullshit? Goddammit, Reed! Fuck you, you fucking prick."

With an angry wave of his hand, he turns on his heel and sprints away, presumably to find Alessandra, his lanky body moving faster than I've ever seen it move it before.

"Well, that was unexpected," I mutter to myself.

Shaking my head, I gaze at the sparkling view for a long moment. Fuck. That sucked. I must say, though, I'm thoroughly impressed with the way Fish just told me off. Not because he's right, of course. I wasn't a prick to Alessandra. I was actually being *kind* to her. Cruel to be kind, as they say. But kind, nonetheless. I'd swear to that under oath.

But, still, it was cool to see Fish climb aboard his white horse. That dude hasn't raised his voice to me once in the entire time I've known him, let alone called me a prick. Well, not to my face, anyway. I think it's now obvious he's called me that, and worse, plenty of times behind my back. But that's fine. He's not the first person to think I'm a prick. He won't be the last. If, somehow, me being the bad guy lets him be the good guy with this girl, then I'm happy to oblige.

Although... Shit. I suddenly realize... *Georgina*.

When she hears Alessandra's version of this story, will she assume I treated Alessandra the way I treated that blonde at the bar? Because I didn't. Yes, I was honest with Alessandra, but I took special care to be gentle with her. I flashed her several reassuring smiles, which is something I never do. I was careful to use a calm and soothing tone of voice. Also, not my typical MO. But will Georgina understand any of that, or will she hear some disjointed, emotional version of the story from her stepsister and immediately assume I'm the devil incarnate?

My heart pounding, I rise from the bench, intending to head back into the party to find Georgina. But I've no sooner taken two steps than Isabel appears from around a corner.

"There you are!" she says.

"Not now, Isabel."

"Yes, *now*. It's important. A matter of life or death."

"I've got something important I've got to do," I say.

"It's an emergency," she says. "I need five minutes."

I exhale in frustration. "Five minutes. Not a second more."

The sound of people laughing nearby wafts toward us, emanating from the other side of a hedge.

"Not here," Isabel says. She grabs my hand. "Come on, love. Let's go somewhere we can talk in private."

FIFTY-NINE
GEORGINA

Where the heck is Reed? I've been looking for him for the past ten minutes, but I can't find him anywhere. And I can't find Alessandra, either. I'm guessing she's off in a quiet corner, chatting with Fish. Or maybe even *smooching* Fish. Which, of course, would tickle me pink. And would also provide a damned good reason not to be answering my texts. But Reed is a different story. This is his party, so, why has he disappeared?

I'm bursting at the seams to talk to Reed—to tell him the news that I landed the interview of Isabel. And, also, yes, to try to get to the bottom of the lies I think he and Isabel have both been telling me. Does it matter to me how they met? No! But it sure as heck matters to me they both seem to be lying about it.

Thus far, I've done two laps around the ground floor areas, including the patio and pool, in my pursuit of Reed. And now I'm doing a lap of the entire upstairs, too—even though I can't fathom Reed would have come up here while his party raged on below. But, again, I'm coming up empty. Crap.

I descend the staircase, feeling more and more frustrated with every step I take. At the bottom of the stairs, I run into Aloha Carmichael. She's with Barry, Reed's head of security. Getting a piggyback ride from him, actually. And when she sees me, she calls my name warmly.

"Reed told me to talk to you," she says.

"Have you seen him recently?"

"Not recently. I saw him at the bar a while ago."

"Which one?"

"The one by the French doors." She points. "That one."

I feel deflated. I passed that bar, not too long ago on one of my laps, and Reed was nowhere to be found. "Did Reed say where he was going, from there?"

Aloha purses her lips. "No, but while I was dancing after that, I saw him head out those French doors over there with Keane and Zander. Which can only mean one thing."

She puts her index finger and thumb to her lips, like she's smoking a joint. But I don't think she's right about that—because when I did a loop outside, not too long ago, I didn't see Reed out there. Not with Keane and Zander or anyone else.

"So, about my interview," Aloha says, laying her cheek on Barry's broad shoulder from behind. "Daxy told me he and the Goats are going to give you a tour of Seattle. And Laila told me she's going to make pottery with you. And Savage told me he's taking you ATVing... "

I force myself to look into Aloha's emerald green eyes, rather than looking around the party maniacally for Reed. "Yeah, the idea is for the interviews to be fun and different and really personal. I'm hoping getting a glimpse of you guys doing something that's meaningful to you, that's outside of music, will inspire a different kind of conversation than the typical interview."

"I love that idea." She pauses. "I go to children's hospitals quite a bit, to cheer up sick kids. Would you maybe want to tag along on a day like that?"

"Sounds great. Let's also make sure we talk about the success of your documentary. And I don't mean the financial success. The impact it has had on mental health awareness."

"Oh, absolutely."

"Someone told me Reed helped get distribution for that film?"

"He sure did. Some people have said Reed only threw his weight behind the documentary for business reasons—you know, because a hit film would lead to more music sales, which, in turn, would line his pockets. And a few years ago, I probably would have believed that narrative. But the last few years, I've started to think there might be an actual beating heart inside Reed's chest. I think he genuinely believed in the movie's message and cause."

"Of course, he did," Barry says.

"I know Reed comes off as all business sometimes," Aloha says. "But, behind the scenes, he's pretty generous with a bunch of charitable causes."

Ping.

That cotton ball from earlier today turns into a stone.

Behind the scenes, Reed is pretty generous with a bunch of charitable causes.

"Do you know if Reed donates to a charity that helps families affected by cancer?" I ask, my heart racing.

"I'm not sure," Aloha says. "But I wouldn't be surprised. I know for sure Reed donates to several cancer charities. Of course, he's extremely involved with The Superhero Project. And then there's also…"

But I've stopped listening. Because, all of a sudden, that cotton ball that turned into a stone has now turned into a motherfucking brick.

Crash.

In rapid-fire succession, my brain connects the dots between several comments made by Kat, Aloha, and Reed himself.

Reed likes pulling strings.

Reed likes playing star-maker behind the scenes.

Reed secretly pulled strings to help Keane get the auditions he wanted.

Reed pulled strings to get Zander a job interview with Big Barry.

Reed pulled strings to help Hannah get a job interview at a movie studio.

Everybody's got a price.

I clutch the banister on the staircase, feeling faint. Reed had something to do with that cancer charity paying for my salary! *If there's a cancer charity at all.* Did he pull strings to get me my internship… because he wanted to fuck me?

But how could that be? CeeCee hired me, because she believes in me. She told me so herself, and she wouldn't lie to me.

I'm so confused. Why would CeeCee hire me… but Reed secretly pay my salary? Why the secrecy? Am I crazy? Paranoid? Oh, fuck. *Did*

Reed find CeeCee's price? Did Reed offer CeeCee unparalleled access to his entire roster for the special issue, plus, an in-depth interview of himself, if only she'd hire the fuck buddy of his choice?

No. I can't believe CeeCee would have gone along with that! I simply won't believe it. But my mind is reeling. My insecurity is raising its ugly head. Did I get this internship solely because some asshole—in this instance, Reed—wanted to get into my pants?

"Excuse me," I say to Aloha, cutting her off mid-sentence. "I'm sorry. I just remembered I have to talk to Reed about something important."

"No problemo. Just get my number from Reed or Owen." She pinches Barry's ear. "Come on, Big Barry! This cowgirl wants to *dance!*"

Practically hyperventilating, I sprint toward a set of French doors leading outside. But when I get outside and race around like a chicken with my head cut off, I still don't see Reed anywhere. Not on the patio. Not by the pool. Not in the area just outside the garage where some of the members of Fugitive Summer and Watch Party are playing a rowdy game of corn hole. Frustrated, I turn around, intending to march back toward the house... but freeze on a dime.

The garage.

It's the only place I haven't looked for Reed.

But what the hell would he be doing in there, with the party raging on out here? Oh! Maybe he's showing someone his car collection! Yes, that must be it. Reed is giving some buddy or VIP a tour of his beloved cars.

My heart exploding, I turn around again and head down the path, telling myself the whole time I'm being paranoid—that there's no way Reed had anything to do with my salary or CeeCee's decision to hire me. CeeCee would never betray me like that. *And neither would Reed.* He's a liar, for sure. But only about highly personal things. Also, small things, sometimes, as well, for reasons that elude me. But he would never lie to me about something so important. But if he *did*, he certainly wouldn't continue lying to me, after I told him about Mr.—

The side door to the garage opens, and to my shock—and *heartbreak* —Reed and Isabel step through the doorframe, exiting the garage.

I'm standing, frozen, about ten feet away from them. And the minute Reed and Isabel see me, they freeze, too. And, instantly, from Reed's stiff body language and the guilty expression on his face, I know he's just been caught red-handed. Remorse washes over his guilty face. Followed immediately by barely contained *panic*.

I shift my gaze to Isabel, hoping whatever I see there will make everything okay. But, no, Isabel's face only makes matters worse. Her lipstick is smeared. Her hair disheveled. In short, she's a hot mess—a woman who just got fucked. She wipes her mouth—apparently trying to remove the evidence of Reed's mouth on hers—and a cavalcade of emotions flood me. Rage. Hurt. Rejection. *Heartbreak*. And then nothing but rage, rage, rage, rage, rage. But, somehow, I manage to disassociate from my white-hot emotions, long enough to get through this mortifying moment.

"Hello, Isabel," I say calmly, like a sniper looking through a scope. I shift my gaze to Reed, my eyes like lasers. *"Reed."*

"Hello again!" Isabel says, sounding nervous. Is she worried I'll run straight to her billionaire fiancé and tell him what I've just seen?

"Reed was just showing me his cars," Isabel blurts.

"Oh, yeah?" I say. "I've heard about them, but haven't seen them for myself. Are they pretty?"

"Very pretty."

I return to Reed, my nostrils flaring. "Would you be willing to show me your pretty cars, Mr. Rivers? I'd love to see them. Maybe I could feature them in my article about you."

Reed's Adam's apple bobs. "Sure."

"I should probably find Howard," Isabel says, walking briskly past me. "I'm sure he's looking for me."

When Isabel is gone, Reed steps toward me, his palms raised. He whispers, "Georgina, I know how this looks."

I point toward the garage. "Turn your lying, cheating ass around and get into that fucking garage. I'm not going to do this out here."

SIXTY
REED

My heart crashing, I close the garage door behind me and turn around to face Georgie's wrath. "I know how this looks, baby, but—"

"Don't you dare call me baby!" she seethes, her eyes like meteors. "When your dick is still wet from another woman's pussy!"

Oh, Jesus. "I didn't fuck her, Georgie."

"*Liar.* I saw her flushed face, Reed. Her smudged lipstick. Her tousled hair. That look in her eye like she just got fucked. You not only fucked her, you fucked the living shit out of her!"

"No. Calm down and listen to me."

"Why? So you can tell me I'm crazy and paranoid? So you can look me in the eye and lie through your teeth?"

"I'm not lying to you, Georgie. I didn't fuck Isabel."

She crosses her arms over her chest. "You expect me to believe you and Isabel came into your garage, while *your* party was raging in *your* house, for who knows how long... because you suddenly felt the need to show her—a woman you've known for ten years—your car collection?"

My stomach twists. Shit. Fuck. Shit. *Fuck.* I run my hand through my hair. *Fuck!*

Georgina's eyes are wild. "If I hadn't stumbled upon you two at exactly the right moment to catch you red-handed, would you have come clean about what you did? Or would you have taken me to your bed after the party, and fucked me right after fucking her? Would you have at least done me the courtesy of showering before you fucked me, to get her off your dick and lips?"

"You need to listen to me. Isabel asked me to talk in private, about something important, and the garage was the only place I knew nobody would barge in on us."

"Do you think I'm stupid?" she screams. "I saw her smudged lipstick, Reed!"

Oh, God. I feel the ground giving way underneath my feet. Panic streaks through me. Regret. Remorse. But there's no way around it. If she saw Isabel's smudged lipstick, then I have to come clean. I have no choice. "Yes, I kissed her," I admit, my stomach twisting and churning. "But, I swear, I didn't fuck her."

"Liar!" she shrieks.

She pushes on my chest and whizzes past me, racing past the hoods of my cars, and I follow her, my panic spiraling.

"She asked me to give her a goodbye kiss, for old time's sake, and I did it," I blurt, keeping step with her. "How could I say no to that? But it meant nothing to me."

She whirls around in front of my Porsche, her eyes aflame. "I don't believe you only kissed her as far as I can throw you. But let's pretend you're telling the truth, for a minute. *How could you say no?*" she asks, echoing me. "How could you *not* say no, Reed?" Tears fill her eyes. "You said it made you crazy to think of me kissing anyone else. You promised exclusivity was a two-way street, and I believed you. You said you're not a cheater! You said that to me, and I trusted you!"

Anguish grips me. Why did I do this? Why did I fuck up the best thing that's ever happened to me? I want to rewind the clock. Take it all back. *I have to fix this.* "I'm so sorry, Georgie. I admit I fucked up. But you have to believe me, I only kissed her, and it meant absolutely nothing to me. In fact, I told her—"

"Even if you 'only' kissed her, which I don't believe, does that really make it okay in your book? If I secretly disappeared with someone... Let's say Savage. He's hot as hell. Let's say I disappeared with Savage into your garage, in the middle of the party tonight, without telling you, and I made out with him in here until my lips were swollen and my lipstick smeared and my face bright red and my hair tousled—*but it meant nothing to me!*—that would be perfectly fine with you? That wouldn't break your heart, after everything that's happened between us this week?"

"Georgie," I choke out, the enormity of what I've done slamming me. "Please, put yourself in my shoes. The example of Savage isn't the same thing. I've known Isabel ten years. She's getting married and wanted one last kiss. It was a goodbye kiss, Georgie. It's unreasonable for you to expect me *not* to give her that, after ten years of knowing her, when I've only known you a matter of weeks."

She looks crushed. Furious. *Heartbroken.* "Obviously, this past week meant a whole lot more to me than it meant to you." She throws her hands over her face. "God, I was so stupid to let my guard down with you. I was so stupid to think this week could have meant anything to you."

I feel like my heart is physically cracking in two. "Georgie, don't say that. Please don't doubt how much this past week with you has meant to me. It's been the best week of my life. Every minute with you, Georgie—"

"Save it!" She marches away, whizzing past my cars, all the way to the back wall filled with sports equipment, which is where she whirls around to face me. "How'd you meet her, Reed?"

"Who?"

"Isabel!"

"I told you how I met her. At CeeCee's birthday party."

"Josh didn't introduce you to Isabel?"

I pull a face of confusion. "No. Why are you asking—"

"Josh didn't introduce you to Isabel at one of his parties?"

"No. *I* introduced *Josh* to Isabel at one of Josh's parties. Why are you asking me this?"

"Because Isabel told me she met you through a mutual friend. And when I asked the name of the friend, she said *Josh Faraday.* She said she went to one of Josh's parties, and *he* introduced her to *you* that night."

My stomach is twisted into knots. My breathing is shallow. Fuck. "Isabel is mistaken," I say. "Which is understandable, since it was ten years ago."

Georgina throws up her hands. "Why are you both lying to me

about this? It's something so meaningless and insignificant! I don't get it!"

"We're not both lying. I'm telling the truth, and Isabel is simply mistaken. Why are we even talking about this?"

"Because it's just further proof that every word out of your mouth is a fucking lie. You didn't take Isabel into your garage, in the middle of your party, to kiss her goodbye. You fucked her goodbye. And you didn't meet Isabel at CeeCee's birthday party, either. I saw the photo spread in *Rock 'n' Roll* from CeeCee's party, and in one of the shots, behind Justin Timberlake, you and Isabel were arriving *together* to the party. Reed, you were getting out of the limo *with* Isabel. Ergo, you did not 'meet' her at that party, as you've told me. You cannot meet someone you've arrived with. Ergo, you *lied* to me about that. And you're lying to me about this."

I feel like I'm going to throw up. "Isabel and I were on a blind date that night," I blurt, desperation seizing me. "We hadn't met before that night, but I'd seen her photo. She didn't want me to pick her up at her house. So, she asked me to pick her up in the limo a mile away from the party. I think I picked her up in front of a McDonald's. And that's why that photo showed us arriving together. But, in my mind, when I told you I'd 'met' Isabel at CeeCee's party, I was telling the truth. I mean, technically, we met a few blocks away, yes, but I wasn't intentionally *lying* to you. It was just too complicated to explain the logistics. Yes, she was my date that night. Yes, we arrived together. But I swear to God, I also met her that night. I was telling you the truth about that night, Georgie. And I'm telling you the truth about tonight. I'm sorry I kissed her. I shouldn't have done that. But, trust me, if you'd seen the way it went down, you'd understand it didn't take anything away from the amazing week we've had—and the amazing summer—"

"I told you about Mr. Gates!" she screams, a sob lurching out of her. "I told you about Shawn, and you said you're not a cheater! You said nobody is allowed to hurt me, ever again, and then you came in here and threw me away like I never mattered!"

My heart feels like it's physically shattering. I take a step toward her, determined to convince her. To fix this mess I've created. "I'm sorry. I think maybe, in part, I was sabotaging myself. I think a piece of me maybe got scared of how much I'm feeling for you, Georgie. Because, I swear, I've never felt the way I do with you before."

She stares at me with disdain for a very long moment, before saying, calmly, "I have one question. And I want you to answer it with complete honesty."

My heart leaps. Is she throwing me a lifeline? If I answer this question right, will she forgive and forget that stupid kiss ever happened?

"Whatever you want to know, I'll tell you."

Her nostrils flare. "Did you have anything to do with me getting my internship, including but not limited to donating the money that ultimately went to me as my salary?"

Oh, fuck. "Yes. But let me explain..."

But she's done listening to me. As quick as lightning, she grabs a golf club out of my bag and marches straight for my Bugatti, the club raised high above her head.

"Not the Bugatti!" I shout at the top of my voice. "Georgie, please! *Not the Bugatti!*"

To my surprise, Georgina stops mid-swing, barely missing the hood of my Bugatti, and marches to the next car in line. My yellow Ferrari. The first expensive car I bought when I started making some real money. Up Georgina's golf club goes... and then down it comes, smashing into the Ferrari's newly repaired right front fender.

"You told me to go Left Eye Lopes on the next guy who hurts me?" she shrieks. "Well, guess what, asshole? You're that guy!"

As I stand to the side, watching in shocked silence, Georgina raises her club and smashes my Ferrari's windshield. "This one's for you, Reed!" Panting, she heads to the car's passenger door. "And this one is for Shawn!" She brings the club down again. Next up, the passenger window. "Another one for Reed!" She walks around to the back of the car and whacks both taillights and the bumper with her club. But this time, the name she yells breaks my fucking heart. "Mr. Gates! Mr. Gates! Mr. Gates!" From there, she marches to the driver's door and whacks it with all her might, yet again in Mr. Gates' name. The same thing with the driver's side window and left front bumper. "Mr. Gates! Mr. Gates!"

And through it all, I say nothing. Do nothing. I stand back and watch, and take my punishment. It kills me to hear her scream my name along with Mr. Gates'. And worse, it shatters me to know I deserve it. Indeed, I deserve every single dent in that car. Every drop of her rage.

She trusted me completely. I asked her to surrender to me, without holding back. And she did. In body, heart, and soul. And I knew it. And then, I turned around and betrayed her. What's wrong with me? Women have been asking me that my whole life. And now I'm wondering the same thing. *What's wrong with me?*

As I watch Georgie turning my three-hundred-thousand-dollar car into a pile of scrap metal and shattered glass, I feel pain and remorse and regret like nothing I've felt before. But I also feel two unexpected emotions, too.

One, I feel pride. I'm damned proud of Georgie for going Left Eye Lopes on me, and on all the men who've hurt her. As she should. Smash that Ferrari, baby. Smash it and never let anyone hurt you again.

And, two, as strange as it sounds, even as I watch Georgina decimate my Ferrari, I feel a twinge of hope. Because, even in the midst of her justifiable rage and confusion, *Georgina didn't bring her club down on my beloved Bugatti.*

Yes, Georgina is heartbroken and angry and deeply confused. She doesn't know what happened between Isabel and me in this garage tonight. She doesn't understand how or why the money for her salary came from me. All of which isn't good for me. Obviously. But, thanks to my Bugatti, and the fact that there's not a scratch on it, I have reason to believe it's not hopeless for me. Indeed, thanks to my pristine Bugatti, I have reason to believe Georgina is holding out hope I'll eventually be able to win her back.

SIXTY-ONE
REED

I'm panting as I follow Georgina out of the garage and toward the house.

"Hey, Georgie!" Savage calls to her as she passes.

He's at the ping pong table with Davey from Watch Party. And I swear to God, I'm this close to wringing his fucking neck.

"Hey there, handsome!" Georgina calls back to Savage. "I can't wait for you to take me ATVing!"

Savage looks at me, and I shake my head, letting him know whatever they've planned is never going to happen.

"Let's do dinner and drinks afterwards!" Georgie calls to Savage as she continues marching toward the house.

"Stop it, Georgie," I whisper-shout to her. "You're not going anywhere with Savage. Zasu is doing his interview."

"I'm done taking orders from you, asshole. *Ciao, stronzo.* I'm not only going to interview Savage, I'm going to fuck him, too, and then lie to you and say I only 'kissed him goodbye.' But it won't matter, right? As long as it meant nothing to me?"

She barrels into the house and, immediately, gets greeted by Kat and Hannah, who happen to be standing just inside the French doors. And the minute Kat sees Georgie's tear-stained cheeks and puffy eyes, she morphs into a grizzly bear protecting her cub.

"You've been crying," Kat says, her face etched with concern. "What happened?"

"I haven't been crying. I'm just drunk."

"You don't look drunk. You look *devastated*." Kat's blazing blue eyes dart to mine. "Why has she been crying?" Her eyes narrow to murderous slits. "*What did you do?*"

Georgina looks frantically around. "Have you seen Alessandra?"

"Not for a while." Kat shoots me another death stare. "What happened, Reed?"

"We've had a disagreement."

"A *disagreement*." Georgina scoffs. She returns to Kat. "Have you seen Fish?"

As if on cue, Fish walks up, looking distraught. He shoots me a death stare that rivals Kat's, before addressing Georgie. "Alessandra needs you. Reed told her she sucks, and that her music is bullshit, so she ran upstairs to your room to cry."

Oh, for the love of fuck. "That's not how it went down *at all*," I blurt.

But nobody is listening to me, least of all Georgina. Indeed, suddenly, it feels like everyone around me is gathering up their pitchforks, and I'm the guy with a rather conspicuous hump on my back.

"I tried to comfort her," Fish says, "but she said she preferred being alone, until you could come."

"I was trying to *help* Alessandra," I say lamely. "I was *encouraging* her."

Fish flashes me a look that plainly says, *Prick*. Kat shoots me one that says, *I've seen your version of encouragement many times, Reed. And it ain't pretty.* And Georgie doesn't even look at me. Indeed, her skin flushed and jaw tight, Georgina marches away from me, without so much as a glance at me, through the packed party, straight to the staircase, and up the entire flight of stairs, like a woman possessed.

Of course, I clamber after her, desperate to clear my name on this one thing, at least. "I told Alessandra she's talented!" I shout from behind Georgie, matching her every bounding step. "I told her she has great vocal control. All I said was she's trying to be someone she's not and—"

"I told you not to say anything to Alessandra about her demo!"

Oh, shit. That's right. She did.

"Are you capable of keeping *one* promise to me?" she shouts. "Why do you even bother pretending to make promises, if you're literally *never* going to keep any of them?"

"I forgot you said that. I think I was stoned? I'm sorry. I was just trying to help her, and I guess I just... forgot what you said about that. I don't know." I run my hand through my hair. "Georgina, if you'd just let me tell you *exactly* what I said to her, you'd know I was actually doing her a favor."

But she doesn't stop. She keeps bounding down the hallway toward her room.

"All I said was she needed to tell the truth in her art. That she shouldn't try to mimic—"

She stops in front of her closed door and whirls around on a dime, making me nearly run into her. "You told Alessandra to 'tell the truth' in her art? Oh, that's rich, seeing as how you don't even know the meaning of the fucking word." She turns and swings open the door to her room, and gasps at what she finds inside: her stepsister lying on the bed in tears. "Ally!" she shouts as she runs into the room, leaving me in the doorway, like a vampire who hasn't been invited inside.

Georgina takes her beloved stepsister into her arms, while I stand watching helplessly from the doorway. After a moment, though, when she notices me, she gets up, marches to me, and slams the door in my face. And that's when I know: all hope is lost. If Georgie were standing over my Bugatti now, holding a golf club raised above her head, she'd smash it to Kingdom Come, even more so than she did to my Ferrari. And no command or plea from me would stop her.

I place my palms flush against the closed door, my heart feeling like it's physically bleeding onto the wood. *Let me in, Georgie. Please, please, let me in.*

After what feels like forever, the door swings open, making me lurch back into the hallway, and Georgie and Alessandra barge out of the room.

Georgie's wheeling her suitcase behind her, her regal head held even higher than when she wore that ruby necklace. Alessandra's wearing a backpack on her back, and holding the cardboard box Georgie doesn't know I know about. The one containing the documents from Stephanie Moreland's lawsuit, plus, God knows what else.

"Where are you going?" I choke out.

"None of your business," Georgie tosses over her shoulder.

I follow the girls down the hallway. "Alessandra, you misunderstood me. I'm sorry if my words seemed harsh, but—"

"Don't speak to her," Georgie hisses. "And don't speak to me, either. Ever again."

Down the stairs they go, with me following behind like a stray dog.

A new "super-group" is performing onstage now, which means, thankfully, everyone at the party is crowded in the main area, blissfully dancing and cheering with their backs to us. It's the perfect time for the girls to make a getaway, completely unnoticed. Which is exactly what they do. Indeed, they walk straight out my front door, past security, and into the cool night, without anyone noticing a damned thing.

I follow the girls, of course, talking the entire time. Explaining. Apologizing. Defending. Rationalizing. Fixing, convincing, *begging*. Yes, fuck it. I'm *begging* Georgina to stay. To listen. To forgive. It's something I swore I'd never do with Georgina again. But now isn't the time to be proud. Now is the time to make her understand. To fix this mess I've gotten myself into. To make her forgive me.

But Georgina isn't having any of it. And Alessandra follows her lead, looking straight ahead like she can't hear my pathetic pleas.

The girls march down my circular drive toward my iron gate, where four security guards greet us.

"Hello, Mr. Rivers," one of the guards says. "Ladies."

"Hello," Georgina says brightly, her tone oozing with sex appeal. "My, you look handsome tonight, sir."

"Thank you."

"We're here to wait for our Uber," Georgina explains.

"That's fine."

"Are you wearing cologne? You smell amazing."

"It's just soap."

"Well, whatever it is, it smells good enough to *eat*."

"Georgie, that's enough," I say calmly. "Come inside, so I can explain—"

"No, thank you, Mr. Rivers. I think you've explained more than enough."

Fuck. Begrudgingly, I shut up. If I don't, it's quite possible she'll offer to suck a security guard's dick, just to watch me commit murder and go to prison for it.

Headlights.

They're shining on the guards' faces. And then on the girls'. And then on mine. They're shining in my eyes. Illuminating the blackness of my fucking soul.

The car stops. The girls pile into its backseat and slam their doors, without looking back or saying a word to me. And off they go, just like that, into the night. Leaving me standing at my gate in the cool night with stinging eyes and a lump in my throat.

I stand frozen as Georgina's car drives away, watching its retreating taillights and holding my breath. *Turn around, Georgina. Flip me off through the back window, so I know you still care. Flip me off, baby. Please. Hate me, if you must. Just care enough to flip me off.*

It's my last hope—that Georgina will grace me with the tiniest flicker from her glorious flame.

But, no.

The car is gone now.

And Georgina never turned around.

She never met my eyes, so they could tell her how sorry I am. She never met my eyes, so they could beg her to come back to me. She never met my eyes so I could tell her I'm fucked up in ways I don't understand. Ways I can't help. Ways I can't fix. She never turned around so my eyes could tell her I've never felt the way I do with her. She never turned around so my eyes could explain I don't know how to do this. I don't know how to *feel* this. I simply don't know.

"Is everything okay, Mr. Rivers?" one of the guards asks.

I look down at the ground for a long beat.

If any other girl had left me standing here, I'd look directly at the guard, smile, and say, "Yes, everything is great. Everything is perfect. I'm on top of the world, motherfucker. The Man with the Midas Touch."

But I can't say any of it now. Not when the girl who's left me is Georgina. Not when the girl I betrayed, the girl I hurt, is the same girl I'd move heaven and earth to protect. I can't say it now, when it's

Georgina who thinks I'm a liar. Even though, I swear, a solid three quarters of what I said to her was the God's truth.

I look up and meet the guard's eyes. "No. Everything's not okay." I drag my palm across my jaw and take a deep breath. "In fact, Jeremy. To be honest with you, everything just turned to total fucking shit."

SIXTY-TWO
GEORGINA

The moment the Uber is out of sight from Reed's house, I crumple into the backseat. *Everybody's got a price.* Reed warned me that was his life philosophy. Why didn't I listen to him when he told me exactly what kind of monster he is? Why did I trust him with the most vulnerable, sacred parts of myself? *Why, why, why?*

Everybody's got a price.

What was CeeCee's price, I wonder? Did she ever truly believe in me, as she and Reed both claimed, or was she all too happy to help her good friend, Reed, get the tits and ass he desired, if it meant she could get a River Records special issue, including a Reed Rivers interview, for herself? I thought CeeCee was my friend, my hero, my inspiration—and it turns out she was my pimp.

"I can't believe you lied to me," Alessandra says, looking out her window.

I swivel my head to look at her, at a loss.

"About my demo. Why didn't you tell me Reed had already listened to it? Why did you lie to me? You thought I couldn't take it? You think I'm so weak and pathetic I can't handle the truth? I was totally blindsided, Georgie. I couldn't speak."

I wipe my eyes. "I'm sorry. I didn't tell you because I didn't want you to feel awkward at the party around Reed."

"That's not why."

"What do you mean?"

"You were a coward. You didn't want to have to break the news to me."

"Well, of course. But, mostly, I didn't want you to lose faith in yourself. Reed's opinion isn't the gospel."

Alessandra shakes her head and looks out the window. "I missed out on a great chance to have an honest discussion with him. To ask him questions. Maybe even try to impress him. But I was too blindsided to say or do anything. I just sat there, like an idiot. And now, thanks to you, he thinks I'm mentally deficient, in addition to being a 'Laila knock-off.'"

"He called you that? Asshole! He swore he wouldn't say anything to you tonight."

"So, the answer to this problem is for Reed to have lied to me, too? Guess again, Georgina. Frankly, I'm glad Reed told me the truth. I only wish you had, too, so I could have been ready for him. He told me to get up on that stage and knock his socks off. If I'd known he'd listened already, maybe I would have... I don't know. Maybe I would have *done* something."

I wipe my eyes. "I'm so sorry."

She scowls at me. "I said from the start he'd never want to sign me. Remember? I never once thought I'm good enough."

"You are. He's stupid."

"He's *right*."

"No, Ally."

She looks out the window for a long moment. "Just, please, don't lie to me again. Not about anything. I know you think you need to protect me, but you don't. I don't want your protection. I want your respect."

I choke back a sob. "I'm sorry."

She looks at me and melts when she sees the emotion ripping through me. "Aw, sweetie. What happened to you tonight? What did Reed do?"

I shake my head, too mortified to say it out loud, even to Alessandra: *he broke my heart.* "I don't want to talk about it." I rub my eyes. "Tell me about Fish. Did you kiss him?"

She sighs wistfully. "No. I was positive he was *finally* about to kiss me, when stupid Reed showed up with Keane and Zander to smoke a joint, and the moment was lost."

"Oh my God. Reed was freaking Godzilla tonight. Smashing everything in his path."

"Even if we'd kissed, nothing could have come of it, anyway, with me going back to Boston on Monday." She exhales. "But, dang it, I just wanted to kiss him so much, even if I never saw him again. I just wanted to cap off the perfect night, with the perfect boy, with the perfect kiss..."

"Fucking Reed! In addition to everything else, he fucked up a lifelong memory for you? God, I *hate* him."

"Okay, Georgie. Come on. You have to tell me what the hell he did to you." She grabs my hand. "Because the way he was following us out of the house, babbling and begging, he seemed so desperate and pathetic. So *sincere*."

A dam breaks inside me. "He fucked Isabel Randolph!"

Alessandra gasps. "When?"

"Tonight. During the party. In his garage!"

"No."

"*Yes*. He said he only kissed her, but I don't believe him. But even if he *did* only kiss her, it doesn't matter. Either way, he's a liar and a cheater and I can't trust him." I wipe my eyes. "I gave him my whole heart, Ally. I trusted him like I've never trusted anyone. But none of that mattered to him. He took my heart and stuffed it into his pocket like a pack of gum." I shake my head at my stupidity. "I bet it drove him *crazy* when he found out Isabel was engaged. I bet he dragged her into that garage, the first chance he got, to remind her what she'll be missing out on when she marries her pervy grandpa."

"Did you actually walk in on them in the garage?"

"No, I saw them as they were coming out. Her lipstick was smudged. Her hair all messed up. She was a hot mess, and he looked like a dog who'd just shit the bed."

"What did they say when you saw them?"

"Well, Isabel ran off to find her fiancé. I'm sure she was freaking out I might tell him what I saw. And then I dragged Reed into the garage and read him the Riot Act. Which is when he swore he only kissed her and it 'meant nothing.'" I pause. "And then I went 'Left Eye' Lopes on his ass."

Alessandra's jaw drops. "You burned down his garage?"

"You know 'Left Eye' Lopes?"

"TLC. Georgie, what did you do?"

I smile. "I totaled his Ferrari with a golf club."

She gasps. "The yellow one that just got back from the shop?"

"That's the one. I'm thinking maybe Reed should take it back to the shop. Although I don't think they'll be able to fix it this time."

"You seriously *totaled* it? Or you just gave it a couple dents?"

"I smashed the crap out of it. I literally broke a sweat, I was swinging that damned club so hard and so many times."

She laughs. "Holy shit. And what did Reed do while you were murdering his Ferrari?"

"Nothing at all. He just stood there watching me, not saying a word."

"Not a word? Not even 'no!'?"

I shake my head. "Nope. He didn't tell me to stop. He stood there with his arms crossed, silently watching me."

"Now that's a guy with money to burn."

"No, that's a guilty man. He didn't say anything because he knew he deserved every swing of that club. Because he knew he was lucky I wasn't swinging the club at his head. Or his Bugatti." I look out the car window at the passing cars on the freeway. "His non-reaction reaction was an admission of his guilt, Alessandra. I mean, what man, I don't care how rich he is, lets a woman total his Ferrari over a freaking *kiss*?"

"Good point." She winces. "On the flipside, though. If he *did* only kiss Isabel—not that I'm okay with that at all—but, if he did only kiss her, then, holy fuck, Georgina, you totaled a Ferrari over a freaking kiss. If that's not going 'Left Eye' Lopes on a guy, then I don't know what is."

She giggles, but I stare at a car passing us in the adjacent lane.

There's more to this story, of course. Namely, that Reed is the one who paid my salary. And, quite possibly, pulled strings behind the scenes to get me this job, in the first place. What strings, exactly? I'm not entirely sure. What I do know is that Reed wanted to fuck me, and he arranged things to make that possible, unbeknownst to me. Was it unbeknownst to CeeCee, as well? Again, I'm not entirely sure. The only thing I'm sure about is Reed wanted me, so he paid whatever price, and pulled whatever strings, to get me. And once he got me, he got bored of the game, as he warned me he always does, and moved on.

But I have no desire to tell Alessandra the truth about any of that. It's far too mortifying to say out loud. Even more so than the idea of Reed having sex with Isabel in that garage.

Is the fact that Reed cheated on me painful? Yes. Embarrassing, too. But it's a betrayal I can wrap my head around, thanks to Shawn. But admitting I was some sort of purchase to Reed, every bit as much as his Ferrari or Bugatti? Admitting I might not have earned my dream job, like I thought, but, instead, got hired because Reed wanted to sleep with me... and, also, that, *maybe*, CeeCee was perfectly willing to go along with that plan? Well, shit, all of that is downright soul-crushing.

Alessandra sighs and grabs my hand. "I'm so sorry, Georgie. I know you really liked him."

No, I loved him, I think. But what I say is, "I really did. And I stupidly thought he was feeling the same way." Another sob lurches out of me. And then another. Until, suddenly, I'm a weeping mess and the Uber driver is handing me a box of tissues.

"Aw, sweetie, come here," Alessandra says. She opens her arms and I dive into them, and then proceed to sob from the depths of my soul the rest of the drive to my father's condo—the tiny two-bedroom in the Valley that, thanks to Reed, is now bought and paid for... every bit as much as me.

Beloved LIAR

USA Today and International Bestselling Author
Lauren Rowe

PLAYLIST

Playlist for Beloved Liar

"You and Me"—James TW
"Oh, Darling"—The Beatles
"I Don't Want to Get Over You"—The Magnetic Fields
"Bad Liar"—Imagine Dragons
"Love the Way You Lie"—Eminem
"Ready to Let Go"—Cage the Elephant
"Golden"—Harry Styles
"Adore You"—Harry Styles

SIXTY-THREE
REED

It's a temperate Sunday afternoon in the Hollywood Hills. The perfect day for Hazel Hennessy's first birthday party on her parents' small backyard patio. The birthday girl is sitting in a highchair, wearing a bib that reads, "I'm the Birthday Girl, Bitches!" Her party guests, other than me, are crowded around her, singing "Happy Birthday," while her proud mommy stands over her with a white cupcake topped with Elmo and her smiling daddy records the occasion on his phone.

And where is Uncle Reed in this happy moment? Nowhere good. He's slumped in a chair in a corner of the patio, slugging his third Bloody Mary, while drowning in a dark and stormy sea of soul-searing regret.

Because... *Georgina*.

It's been sixteen hours since she took off in that Uber with her stepsister, without looking back, leaving me to wallow in a brand of pain I didn't even know existed. What I'm feeling in this torturous moment is the kind of pain artists sing about in their most tormented breakup songs. The kind of pain I've heard other people talk or sing about and immediately thought to myself, "Get over it, you fucking pussy. Move on to the next and you'll be fine."

And now, here I am, wallowing in misery, drowning in Bloody Marys, and certain I'll never "get over it" or "move on to the next and be fine" ever again.

My phone vibrates in my hand, and I look down, praying I'll see Georgina's name. But, no. It's Owen, telling me something I don't care about. Goddammit! Why won't Georgina respond to any of my texts or voicemails? I mean, yes, I know *why*. Because, last night, in a space of mere minutes, Georgina got hit by a shit storm trifecta that made her question everything. In rapid-fire succession, Georgina figured out I'd funded the grant, she found her stepsister sobbing in an upstairs guest room, thanks to a speech I'd given to her about her demo, and, worst of all, Georgina discovered me coming out of the garage with Isabel, right after I'd kissed her. In that horrible moment that's now running on a permanent loop in my brain, Georgina saw Isabel's smudged lipstick and the guilty expression on my face and decided, *wrongly*, that I'd fucked the living hell out of Isabel in that garage, rather than merely giving her an ill-advised goodbye kiss. And, just like that, Georgina's trust in me was shattered, along with her precious heart. And now, I'm rightfully paying the price for my stupidity.

Out of nowhere, an idea pops into my head. A lifeline. An ingenious idea that will prove to Georgina I did nothing more than kiss Isabel. Granted, this idea wouldn't fully exonerate me in Georgina's eyes, since touching Isabel at all was wrong. A betrayal I wish, more than anything, I could take back. But, still, at least this idea would put an end to Georgina thinking I screwed the crap out of Isabel in that garage. At least, Georgina wouldn't be thinking I cared so little about her, and our magical week together, that I took the first possible opportunity to screw my ex. And, maybe, knowing I'm not *that* big a monster would soften the blow a bit for Georgina and then, hopefully, pave the way for her to eventually forgive me.

My mind begins turning this idea over. Looking at it from every angle. Weighing the pros and cons. And, soon, much to my dismay, I conclude it's a non-starter. Surely, it would create more problems than it solved. Shit.

I take another long swig of my Bloody Mary, and sigh from the depths of my tormented soul. I just wish Georgina would call me, if only to chew me out or interrogate me about the grant. CeeCee is still in Bali, so I'm presently Georgina's only source of enlightenment about the grant. Doesn't she want to hear what I have to say about how that happened? Does she hate me so much she *literally* never wants to hear my voice again? Because, if so, then I've got some bad news for her. She's still assigned to the special issue—including writing an in-depth article about *me*—and I fully intend to hold her to her professional obligations.

The crowd reaches the last note of their song, and I let my eyes drift to Josh's former assistant, T-Rod. Theresa "Tessa" Rodriguez. Nowadays, Morgan. The Woman I've Wanted to Fuck for Ten Years. She's standing next to her asshole husband, Ryan, holding a dark-haired baby on her hip, as Ryan holds their toddler's hand. And, man, she's smoking hot. Hotter than ever. Motherhood definitely suits her. But there's no doubt about it: I don't want T-Rod. Not even in a fantasy. Sitting here now, I know, without a doubt, the only woman I want, the only one my heart and body are *capable* of wanting, is Georgina.

It's a mind-blowing thing to realize, considering how long T-Rod has been my gold standard of hotness. My go-to masturbation fantasy. But it's the undeniable truth. Georgina owns me now. Georgina is my new gold standard. My queen. Before today, I knew Georgina had burrowed herself underneath my skin and slithered her way into my bloodstream. But now, as I sit here trying in vain to "move on" and "get over it" and "be fine," I realize something shocking: *Georgina has embedded herself into the very tissues of my heart.*

T-Rod laughs, along with everyone around her, so, I shift my gaze to the birthday girl to see what's up and discover Hazel has just smashed a large glob of white frosting into her face. She was aiming for her mouth, and missed, apparently. And the crowd loves it. I don't blame them. It's a cute moment. Objectively humorous. But I don't give a shit. Because... *Georgina.* If only she'd call me to let me explain!

I glance at T-Rod again, and marvel at how much she reminds me of Georgina. In ten years, I bet that's exactly how Georgina will look. T-Rod is a crystal ball showing me Georgina as a mommy. Georgina as a wife.

Out of nowhere, while I'm still staring at T-Rod, her asshole husband gives her a kiss and then glares at me. I quickly look away. Was that a not-so-subtle message to me? Did Ryan notice me staring at his wife and decide he needed to stake his claim? *Fucker.* Calm down, man. I don't even want your fucking wife anymore. I was just imagining she was someone else. Someone who used to trust me.

Aw, fuck. Out of nowhere, I'm having a horrible thought. If I don't win Georgina back, *pronto,* if I don't fix this mess I've created, Georgina is going to "get over it" and "move on to the next" and "be fine." Maybe one day soon. And then, one day, ten years from now, she's going to be standing at a kiddie birthday party alongside her asshole husband, holding his baby on her hip, getting kissed by him when he notices some pathetic loser staring at her. And I won't be Georgina's asshole husband in this scenario. *I'll be the pathetic loser staring at her, wishing she were mine.*

Testosterone whooshes into my bloodstream. White-hot jealousy. Aching regret. And all of it followed by a tidal wave of panic. If I don't fix this right away, Georgina is going to move on to the next. She's going to fuck someone else. Fall in love with someone else. Get married to, and have babies with, someone else.

In a flash, most likely to avoid my head physically exploding, my brain transforms T-Rod across the patio into Georgina. And Ryan into *me.* That's *my* baby on Georgina's hip now. Nobody else's. Georgina fucked *me* to make that baby happen. Nobody else. In fact, in this fantasy, Georgina never fucked anyone else, after me. Ever again. And she certainly never pledged her undying love to some other motherfucker. Hell no. She pledged her undying love to *me.*

Calm washes over me. Obviously, I've got no desire to get married or have a baby, not even with Georgina. But I sure as hell don't want her doing either of those things with someone else.

I finish off my Bloody Mary and check my phone again. But, still, nothing from Georgina. Just more shit I don't care about from Owen.

I shouldn't do it, I know, but I can't help myself. I tap out yet another ill-advised text to Georgina. And then, just because I'm in my texts, I answer Owen, too, including telling him he's fired, just for kicks. But it's no use. Nothing, not even "firing" Owen, is numbing this searing pain. The only thing that could possibly help me now would be seeing Georgina's name lighting up my phone.

"I've brought reinforcements," a voice says, and when I look up from my screen, Henn is standing before me, holding two drinks. In reaction to whatever misery he's seeing on my face, his features contort with concern. "Aw, Reed. If you feel half as miserable as you look, then I'm sincerely worried about you."

SIXTY-FOUR
REED

Henn gives me a choice between his two proffered drinks. When I pick the gin and tonic, he sits across from me with the vodka soda. "You're not planning to join the party today at all?"

"It's for the best. I can't imagine anyone wants me walking around, scaring all the little kiddies. Have you made any progress on hacking the football coach yet?"

Henn looks annoyed. "When would I have worked on that for you, since the last time you asked me about it—which was last night, at your party, when I was shitfaced?"

"I think I'm going crazy, Henn. I can't stand the fact that he's out in the world, living his best life, and not suffering at all for what he did to Georgie. She was *seventeen*. He was her *teacher*. *She trusted him*." Georgina's words as she screamed at me last night slam into me, yet again: *I trusted you, Reed!* And, once again, my heart twists painfully. I whisper, "I swear, if I could take a hit out on this guy, and know I wouldn't get caught, I'd do it."

Henn rolls his eyes. "Okay, I'm ninety-nine percent sure you're not stupid enough to start searching the dark web for a hired killer. But just in case: don't do it. You *will* get caught. And from what I've heard about prison, you wouldn't like it. No Egyptian cotton bedsheets and the veggies, if you get them at all, come from a can." He sighs sympathetically. "I'll get into his devices, okay? And when I do, the odds are high I'll find something we can use to sink him."

"But, see, I don't want 'high' odds. I want a *guarantee*."

"If that's code for 'I want you to plant evidence,' then fuck off. You know I'd never do that. Will you please just trust me? I'm amazing at what I do. Let me do my thing and stop acting like Tony Soprano."

I lean back in my chair. "I have to do *something* with this manic energy. If I don't focus it on taking down Gates, then I'll have no choice but to focus on what a fucking idiot I am. And I don't want to think about that. I can't believe this is a self-inflicted wound."

Henn looks sympathetic. "What, exactly, did you do? I'm so confused. One minute, you were making breakfast for Georgina and telling me she's breakfast-worthy. And the next thing I know, Hannah is telling me Georgina stormed out of the party, looking distraught over something *you* did."

Midway through Henn's comment, Josh walks up, holding his one-year-old, Jack. "You're talking about Georgina?" He looks at me. "What happened?" He settles himself into a chair. "I don't get it. One minute, you were cannonballing into the pool and kissing her in front of everyone, and the next thing, Kat was telling me you'd done something to make her cry her eyes out."

I groan. "I don't want to talk about it, guys. Suffice it to say I fucked up, royally. And I regret it from the depths of my soul."

Kat appears, out of nowhere. "Exactly *how* did you fuck up? Spill it, Reed. Whatever you did to my beautiful Georgina, I could strangle you for it. I liked this one. I wanted to keep her!"

"I was just explaining to the guys I'm not interested in talking about this."

"Too bad. Tell me everything."

"News flash, Kitty Kat. That's not *my* ring on your finger." I point to the baby on Josh's lap, and then to Kat's baby bump. "And those aren't my kids. Which means I don't have to tell you jack shit."

Kat doesn't flinch. She's a girl who's grown up with four brothers, after all. Plus, she's long since learned to take me in stride when I'm in one of my bad moods. "It's in your best interest to tell me everything. Have you forgotten Georgina will be staying at my house when she comes to Seattle to interview Dax and the Goats? Well, when your name comes up, which it surely will—because that's what women do: we shit-talk the idiots we love—don't you want me to know your side of the story, so I can gently try to steer Georgina toward saintly forgiveness?"

Feigning shock, Josh says, "Wait. Women shit-talk the idiots they love?"

"Oh, honey." Kat pats her husband's thigh. "It's our favorite sport."

Damn. I think Kat has a point. She's uniquely positioned to influence Georgina's opinion of me. Plus, Kat's fiery temperament and personality are a lot like Georgina's. Kat's the only person I know who's as gifted at twisting people around her finger as Georgina, not to mention ripping them a new asshole with a smile. Come to think of it, yeah, I should probably use Kat as a sounding board—as a proxy for Georgina—to help me figure out my best strategy for winning Georgina back.

"All right. I'll tell you everything. But this stays between us, guys." I look at Henn. "Although, of course, you can tell Hannah." With that, I proceed to tell Kat and my two best friends the whole story. Everything from the panel discussion to the grant, and how it came about, to my conversation with Alessandra, to my regrettable kiss with Isabel in the garage. "The irony," I say, in wrap-up, "is that kissing Isabel made me realize I only want Georgina."

Kat snorts. "Good luck convincing Georgina of *that*."

"Why? It's true."

"Maybe, but that's the thing cheaters *always* say after they get caught. 'Yes, baby, I cheated on you. But it only made me realize how much I only love *you*.'"

My shoulders slump in defeat.

Kat asks, "Before the party, did you and Georgina exchange 'I love yous'?"

"No. Is that good or bad for me?"

"It's a double-edged sword. On one hand, if you'd already exchanged the magic words with Georgina when you cheated on her, she'd think those words meant nothing to you."

"Can we not say I 'cheated' on Georgina? I feel like that's a bit dramatic for what I actually did. It was nothing but a stupid goodbye kiss."

"It was *cheating*, Reed."

I slump in my chair.

"As I was saying," Kat says, "it's a *good* thing you hadn't already said the 'L' word to Georgina when you cheated on her. That saves you from Georgina thinking the words are meaningless to you. But, on the flipside, if you were to say 'I love you' now, *after* cheating on her, then Georgina will think you're only saying that as a ploy to win her back."

I exhale with exasperation. "This isn't helping me. What's your point? That I can *never* tell Georgina I love her now? That I'm fucked forever?"

Kat's face lights up. "So, you *do*, in fact, love her?"

I pause. I've never said "I love you" to a woman before. I've said, "You drive me crazy" and "I can't get enough" and "I care about you." But, in this moment, there's no doubt the word "love"—and nothing less —is the one that accurately describes my once-in-a-lifetime feelings for Georgina. "Yeah. I love Georgina like I've never loved anyone before."

Kat clutches her heart. "Aw, sweetie." She looks at me sympathetically for a beat, before her features contort sharply with anger. She swats at my shoulder. "What the hell is wrong with you, Reed? Why did you go into that garage with Isabel, in the first place?"

What the hell is wrong with me? Women have been asking me that same question my entire adult life. And I'm no closer to being able to answer it now. "How is this helping me?" I whisper-shout. "You told me to tell you *everything* so you can convince Georgina to *forgive* me. Flogging me for my stupidity isn't useful." I wave at the air. "You know what? Forget it. I'll figure it out myself." I stand. "Someone who isn't drunk, drive me to Georgie right now. She's got to be at her father's condo in the Valley. I'll go there now and tell her I love her and win her back."

Kat stands and points at my chair like she's commanding a misbehaving dog. "Sit your ass down, you clueless, impulsive, drunken fool! Do you want Georgina to swoon or scowl when you tell her the magic words for the first time?"

"I want her to swoon," I admit softly.

"*Then sit down.*"

I flop down, feeling dejected.

"You can't say 'I love you' to Georgina until you're completely out of the doghouse, or she won't believe you. She doesn't trust you, Reed. You need to regain her trust before you're allowed to say those magical words."

"But when will she trust me again?" I boom—but then, I look around the party, realizing I said that far too loudly. I lean forward and whisper-shout, "How can I get myself out of the doghouse with Georgie when she won't even call me back? *Help* me, Kat, for the love of fuck!"

Kat looks at Josh. "Have you ever seen him this pathetic before?"

"Not even close."

She puts her hand on mine. "Okay, Reed. I'm going to help you. But you need to look me in the eye and *swear* you only *kissed* Isabel in that garage, and nothing more."

I look into Kat's blazing blue eyes. "I swear on my life. On my mother's. *On my nephew's.*"

And that's it. Kat clearly believes me now, without question. Because she knows, for all my faults, I'd never swear falsely on my beloved nephew.

"Okay," she says decisively. "Let's figure out how to get Georgie back."

"Oh, thank God. Thank you, Kat. Bless you."

Kat taps the little indentation in her chin. "Okay, first off, I think it's important to realize the kiss is your biggest hurdle. I'm sure you were a bit rude with Alessandra, knowing you. But I have to believe Georgie will talk to her stepsister and find out what you *actually* said, versus what she *thinks* you said, and all will eventually be forgiven."

"Good. Yes. That's my thinking, too. Same thing with the grant."

"I agree. I'm sure Georgina felt blindsided about the grant last night—and understandably so—and now she's thinking worst-case scenario about you and CeeCee. But, eventually, she'll talk to CeeCee and find out what *really* happened and forgive you on that score, too. Heck, she might even *thank* you."

My spirit is rising and filling my chest. "CeeCee is still in Bali. But I'll text her now..." I pull out my phone. "And tell her to call Georgina the minute she lands and tell her—"

"No, no, you stupid man!" Kat booms, snatching my phone out of my hand. "You have to let Georgina contact CeeCee, *organically*. And when she does, you need CeeCee to be able to say, honestly, she hasn't spoken to you about any of this. Otherwise, Georgina will think you tampered with the witness. Look, I know you're a control freak who's used to pulling strings every which way. But, this time, you need to release that impulse and have faith the truth will come out, on its own, and set you free."

"But what about the kiss? How do I convince Georgina I'm telling the truth about that? And, then, how do I make her forgive me for it?"

Kat twists her mouth. "Yeah, that's a toughie. Even if you could convince Georgie it was only a kiss, she's going to think you're full of shit if you say it made you realize you only want her."

"But nothing's impossible, right? Come on, Kat. You think like Georgina. You're a hotheaded psycho, just like her. A demon spawn."

"Thank you."

"So, use that brilliant, evil, demonic mind of yours to channel Georgie. Tell me what would work on *you*, in this same situation."

"If *Josh* were the dumbass who'd kissed his ex in a garage?"

"Yes."

She looks at Josh. "If Josh had kissed his ex in a garage, during Josh's party, when our relationship was still brand new, and we were still building trust, and I'd been staying at Josh's house for a week, falling head over heels in love with him, and I'd *just* told him things I'd never told anyone else...? Hmm." She taps her chin again, deep in thought. "That's a tall order, Reed. Not gonna lie."

I groan in pain and crumple over. "It sounds so bad when you say it out loud like that."

Kat shrugs. "I think, if the situation were exactly as I've described, then there's only one solution. Only one thing Josh could possibly do to even have a *shot* at winning me back." She pauses for dramatic effect. "*Grovel*. Reed, trust me on this: you need to grovel, grovel, grovel your arrogant ass off, like you've never groveled before. It's the only way."

I throw up my hands, exasperated. "I've already done that! *Repeatedly*. And it hasn't worked."

"What do you mean you've already done that? That's impossible."

"I groveled my ass off last night! The whole time I was following Georgina from the garage, into my house, upstairs to her room, downstairs to the front door, across my driveway, to my front gate! I groveled like a pathetic fucking idiot."

Kat scoffs. "All of that wasn't *groveling*! It was explaining. Apologizing. Maybe begging and pleading. But real groveling takes time. It takes grand gestures. It takes humbling yourself until the woman knows you're in it to win it, for real. She needs to see you're willing to get down on your hands and knees, over a lengthy period of time, and beg and plead for forgiveness in a way that makes it indisputable you're willing to sacrifice your ego completely, all in the name of winning her back!"

I look at Josh, and he shrugs, making it clear he's deferring to his wife on this one. But I can't sign onto this madness. Yes, I'm willing to do "anything" to get Georgina back. *But only within reason.* I'll apologize profusely. I'll even beg Georgina for forgiveness. *But* I can't give myself a personality transplant! I'm Reed Rivers. A survivor. A fighter. A *hustler*. I'm a man who transformed his name from a badge of shame into a badge of honor—from a cross to bear into a designer label. I'm not a guy who's going to *grovel* in the way Kat's describing. And even if I were, why would I do that, when I'm certain it wouldn't work! Georgina fell in love with me this past week, every bit as much as I fell in love with her. I'm sure of it. Which means, to win her back, I can't turn myself into a guy she doesn't even recognize—some simpering version of myself with no swagger and no game and no pride. The only thing weeks and weeks of groveling would do is make Georgina lose respect for me. Which, in the end, wouldn't help my cause at all.

Once again, that same idea from before, the one that would vindicate me, pops into my head as my best option. But, quickly, my rational brain discards the idea as a non-starter, for all the same reasons as before. No. That's not the answer. But neither is *groveling*. What I need is to get back to basics. And what's the most basic thing I know in life? *Everyone's got a price.* All I've got to do to win Georgina back is figure out her goddamned price in *this* particular situation... which, I admit, is a tall order, like Kat said. But, still, I'll do it. I'll figure out her price, whatever it is. And once I do, I'll give it to her. *I'll bribe her with it.* And that's how Reed Rivers, The Man with the Midas Touch, is gonna play—and *win*—this particular game of chess.

SIXTY-FIVE

GEORGINA

Monday, 7:16 pm

"**G**eorgie," Dad whispers, rubbing my arm. The edge of my bed lowers with the weight of his body. "There's a delivery guy at the front door. He says he's got a stationary bike for you. Does he have the right address?"

"Oh. Um." I rub my eyes and glance out the window. It's dusk. Nearly dark. When did that happen? When I crawled into bed it was just past noon. "Yeah, uh, the bike is mine. It was a gift."

Dad's eyebrows shoot up—a sure sign he knows that bike wasn't cheap.

"It's from my boss," I add quickly. "CeeCee Rafael gives every new intern a stationary bike. She says it helps with productivity." I hate lying to my father, but I don't have a choice. There's no way I'm going to tell him the bike was a gift from the CEO of River Records.

Dad turns on the lamp beside my bed. "That's quite an employment perk, especially for a summer intern."

"CeeCee is generous."

Dad looks at me for a long beat, his eyes letting me know he thinks

I'm full of crap. But, whatever he's thinking, he doesn't say it. Instead, he stands and says, "I'll accept the delivery, then. I thought for sure there had to be some sort of a mix-up."

"Nope. It's mine."

When Dad leaves the room, I grab my phone to check the time. But my phone is still turned off. I turned it off two days ago while sitting in the back of that Uber—right after I'd started receiving frantic voicemails and texts from Reed—and I haven't turned it on since.

When my phone springs to life, a backlog of text- and voicemail-notifications comes up—a bunch of them, not surprisingly, from Reed. My stomach churning, I slide into my texts, and, consciously ignoring Reed's messages, head to one from Alessandra.

Landed safely in Boston. I hope you're feeling better. I love you.

I tap out a reply.

I just woke up. I got back into bed after driving you to the airport this morning. Don't worry. I've decided to stop wallowing now. I love you, too. I'll call you tomorrow.

Next up, I've got a text from Zasu, my co-writer on the special issue.

I've secured a 2:00 meeting with CeeCee on Wednesday, so we can go over all the interviews we've got lined up. It was hard to get onto CeeCee's calendar that day, since it'll be her first day back from vacay, so the meeting will be short. Make sure you're super prepared with your pitches!

I write back to Zasu to say I'll see her on Wednesday, and I'll be ready to slay.

Next up? A text from CeeCee's assistant, Margot.

There are three boxes here for you from the courthouse. I put them into Conference Room D.

I reply to Margot, thanking her for the information and telling her I'll come to the office tomorrow, Tuesday, to go through the boxes.

Next up, there's a text from Kat Faraday, giving me some options on dates for my trip to Seattle. One, as early as the end of this week. I reply to Kat, telling her I adored meeting her on Saturday and can't wait to see her again. I write:

Let's tentatively plan on Friday for my interview in

Seattle. I'll confirm after I meet with my boss on Wednesday.

And that's everything in my inbox... *except* for that slew of texts and voicemails from Reed. With a heavy sigh, I steel myself for whatever bullshit I'm about to read and then swipe into his first text. It's time-stamped mere minutes after I'd hopped into that Uber with Alessandra.

But before I've read more than two words, Dad pokes his head into my bedroom. "I had the guy leave the bike in the living room. I was thinking I might want to try it out, if that's okay with you."

"Of course. Enjoy it."

Dad enters the room and stands over me, his bullshit detector visibly flashing "RED ALERT." He crosses his arms over his chest. "That's a *really* nice bike, Georgina Marie."

Uh oh. It's never a good sign when Dad uses my middle name. "Mmm hmm. My boss is *really* generous."

Dad sits on the edge of my bed. "Are you sure that's not an apology of some sort, maybe from whoever made you crawl into bed and cry for the past two days?"

Oh, jeez. Each and every time I cried these past two days, I put a pillow over my face. Damn the paper-thin walls of this condo.

Dad strokes my hair. "I could tell you were trying to muffle your crying, but I couldn't help hearing. You want to talk about it?"

I exhale. "I'm sorry, Dad. I lied to you about the bike. It was actually from a guy I really liked." *No, a guy I loved,* I think. But, of course, I'd never say that out loud. I continue, "I thought this boy liked me the same way I liked him. But it turned out, he didn't. He rejected me at a party on Saturday night. That's why I came home and cried my eyes out."

"Aw, honey." Dad grabs my hand. "You can't let a boy rejecting you send you to bed crying for two days. It's the same thing you did when that stupid basketball player broke your heart. You came home for a weekend and cried your eyes out the whole time. And before that, the same thing happened during your senior year of high school, only worse. You crawled into bed for a *week* that time, after whatever stupid boy broke your heart."

My stomach clenches at my father's unwitting reference to Mr.

Gates, and the way I imploded after he attacked me. For a solid week after Mr. Gates shoved his tongue down my throat and his fingers into my body, I felt literally dysfunctional. I couldn't sleep or eat or concentrate. I couldn't stop tears from streaming down my cheeks or my stomach from twisting into knots. So, I went to bed and told my father I had the flu. But when he said, "This isn't the flu. Did something happen with a boy?" I took the bait and nodded. And said nothing else.

Dad continues, "That time in high school, you'd just gotten the news you were accepted into UCLA! You should have been on Cloud Nine. But, instead, you were in bed, crying your eyes out for a week over some stupid boy."

Bile rises in my throat. My stomach physically twists. "I don't want to talk about that, Dad. Please."

Dad's face softens. "I'm not trying to upset you. I'm saying you can't let boys get you down the way you always do."

"I don't *always* do that. That's a massive exaggeration."

"My point is only that there are plenty of fish in the sea. And if this latest dumb boy isn't smart enough to want you, then you're lucky to be rid of him. *Ciao, stronzo*, right? Time to move on."

Despite my clenching stomach, I can't help smiling at my father's invocation of my mother's favorite expression. Literally translated, *Ciao, stronzo* means, *Bye, asshole*. But Mom always said it in a broader sense, not just in relation to people. It was her way of saying "good riddance" or "I'm done with you" to any person, place, or thing, even something as small as a malfunctioning can opener that might have broken her nail.

I look down at my mother's wedding ring on my hand and hear her feisty voice, telling me to move on from Reed. *Ciao, stronzo*, she says. *He cheated on you, love. He thought he could buy you with that grant.*

But it's no use. My head might be conjuring my mother's voice to help me move on. But my heart still only wants Reed, despite everything. I could have sworn he was falling in love with me the way I was falling for him this past week. My brain knew it was a long shot, given his renowned womanizing and public declarations of eternal bachelorhood. But, still, my heart *felt* so sure he was experiencing my exact feelings.

Dad brushes his fingertips against my cheek. "What about your job?"

"What about it?"

"Nobody expected to see your pretty face in the office today? It's Monday."

"No. Don't worry, Daddy. I'm not screwing up at work. I worked on Saturday night, into the early morning hours of Sunday, so Zasu told me to take Sunday and Monday off. I just now texted the office to let them know I'm coming in tomorrow to look through some documents."

Dad looks relieved.

"Plus, nobody expects to see me at *Rock 'n' Roll's* offices, just to show my face—not unless I've got a specific meeting. They know I'll be working mostly out of the office this summer. Out in the field, or at home, or at a desk set up for me at River Records."

"Speaking of home, where is that these days? You never texted me the name of your hotel. You know I like knowing where you are."

"Oh, yeah. I wound up staying with my co-worker, Zasu, this past week."

"Oh. How fun. Send me that address, would you?"

"Sure. Of course."

Crap. I think I might be a sociopath. Over the years, I've lied to my father, here and there. Simply because he's always been crazy-strict with me and girls just wanna have fun. But I've never lied to my father about *important* stuff. And I've certainly never told this many lies to him in rapid-fire succession.

I squeeze my father's hand. "Don't worry about me, okay? My job is going great. I'm going to be doing a whole bunch of cool interviews of famous artists in the next few weeks. One of them, as early as this Friday in Seattle, if my boss gives me the green light on Wednesday."

Dad's face lights up. "Any artists I might know?"

"Remember that show I used to watch: *It's Aloha!* on Disney?"

"Oh, sure. You loved that one."

"Aloha Carmichael is a pop star now, signed to River Records, and I'll be interviewing her."

Dad flips out.

"Have you heard of Laila Fitzgerald?"

Dad shakes his head.

"Oh. Well, then I guess you won't be excited to learn I'm interviewing her, too. How about the rock group 22 Goats?"

Dad shakes his head again. "They're called '22 *Goats*'? As in, the farm animal?"

"Yep. They're super popular, Dad. If my boss says yes, I'll be flying to Seattle on Thursday to interview them on Friday."

"Are there twenty-two people in the band?"

I chuckle. "No, only three. You know how random band names can be."

"That's true. What the hell is a 'Led Zeppelin'?"

We talk about nonsensical band names for a bit, and, with each passing minute, my mood lifts and brightens.

"Don't worry, Daddy. I know this job is the chance of a lifetime. I promise I'm not going to blow it. Not for anyone. Least of all, some stupid boy who doesn't love me back."

Dad juts his lower lip, making a classic "sad face." "Aw, I didn't realize you *loved* this boy."

Crap. How did I let that slip? "I thought I did."

"Aw, honey. I'm sorry."

I shrug and say nothing. Because... what is there to say? I was a fool to give my heart to Reed Rivers, any way you slice it.

Dad says, "Well, then, this *stronzo* is obviously more than dumb. He's crazy."

"It's for the best," I say, trying to convince myself, even more than him. "I should be focusing on my career, not trying to make some dumb, crazy boy fall in love with me."

"Amen. Focus all your energy on your internship and getting hired for that magazine you've always wanted to work for."

"That's exactly what I'm going to do." I bolt upright. "In fact, I'm going to get back to work right now." I point to the cardboard box in the corner—the one filled with the three settled lawsuits I got from the courthouse the other day. For some time now, I've been meaning to read the third lawsuit Reed settled—the one filed by Troy Eklund for breach of contract, fraud, and assault—but I haven't had a spare moment to dig into it. "Could you hand me that box? There's something I've been dying to read, and there's no time like the present."

"Nope. You're going to eat something now and read whatever is in that box later."

"No, I'll eat later. I want to capitalize on this burst of energy."

"What have you eaten today, Georgina Marie?"

My middle name, again? "Coffee this morning, when I took Alessandra to the airport. And a banana."

"And that's it?"

I nod, grimacing.

"That's what I thought. Your appetite is always the first thing to go when you're upset. Well, you're in luck, *Amorina*. I've been slow-cooking meatballs all day."

I fist-pump the air, and Dad chuckles. He doesn't always know how to talk through my feelings with me, though he tries. He doesn't always know how best to console me when I'm down. But the man sure as hell knows how to feed me.

"I'll put together meatball sandwiches for us," Dad says. "While you take a shower and get into some fresh jammies."

"It's a date." I hug him. "Thank you, Daddy. You're the sweetest."

Dad kisses my cheek. "I know you wish Mommy were here to talk to you about boy stuff. And I don't blame you. But I'm here. Any time. If you want to talk."

"Thank you."

"Now, shower while I make us dinner."

"I'll shower after dinner. I've got some texts and voicemails to go through, real quick."

"All right." Dad rises from the bed and points at the cardboard box in the corner. "As long as you don't start reading whatever's in there. I know how laser-focused you get when you work. Two hours pass without you even realizing it."

"I'll deal with my texts and voicemails and come right out."

"Good girl."

Dad kisses my forehead and heads out. And the minute the door closes behind him, I grab my phone, steel myself for whatever bullshit explanations and apologies Reed has left me over the past two days, and swipe into his first voicemail.

SIXTY-SIX
GEORGINA

I must admit, the desperation in Reed's voicemails makes me smile. He's miserable? Desperate? Tormented? Full of remorse and regret? Good.

After listening to his voicemails, all of which say basically the same things he said to me at the party, I swipe into Reed's first text, which tells me only that he's left me a voicemail that "requires my attention." Pfft.

I move on to Reed's next text, sent an hour later, after he hadn't heard from me regarding his voicemails. This time, his text is about Alessandra. But he doesn't apologize. On the contrary, he says he's got "nothing to apologize for" in regard to my stepsister. "If she follows my advice," he writes, "she could be great. If not, she'll be stuck singing demos her whole career, if she's lucky."

"That's your idea of an *apology*, you prick?" I say out loud. But, truthfully, I know he's right. I'm still annoyed he said anything at all to Alessandra about her demo, given his promise not to do that very thing. But when I drove Alessandra to the airport this morning, she told me everything Reed said to her. And, by the time she was done talking, I knew in my bones, at least in regard to Alessandra, Reed didn't do anything unforgiveable. He was clearly only trying to help her, just like he said.

But so what? Even if I were to forgive Reed for making Alessandra cry, he's still got two other strikes against him. The grant and *Isabel*. In Reed's voicemails, he said he "refuses" to explain himself about either topic, via text or voicemail, but, instead, "demands" that I call him to hear him out. But I'm not in the mood to meet his "demand." Nor am I inclined to let him try to sweet-talk me. He already tried to do that as I was leaving the party, and I wasn't impressed.

I move on to Reed's next text, which he sent around noon yesterday (Sunday):

I get that you're upset, and you have every right to be. But I'd appreciate the courtesy of a reply to my voicemails and texts, even if it's just to tell me to fuck off. I'm worried about you and want confirmation that you're safe and sound. Call me.

Obviously, he received no reply to that command. And so, he sent another text, this one about an hour later.

Per our initial agreement, I've booked a hotel room for you for the summer, at the W in Hollywood. I've also decided it would benefit the special issue if you had access to a car, so I've rented a little convertible for you. It's already sitting in the hotel's parking garage. Keys at the front desk. No need to thank me. I've done all of this for business reasons. All I ask is that you call me, the CEO of River Records, to let me know you're safe and sound.

When Reed received no reply from me about the hotel and car, he sent yet another text, four hours later. This one, on Sunday afternoon.

Guess where I am, Georgie Girl? At Hazel Hennessy's 1st birthday party! Drinking like a fish, sitting in a corner, wishing you were here. You were supposed to come with me to this shindig, remember? In fact, you were excited to come. And now, here I am, a lone wolf. Looks like The Man with the Midas Touch has lost his golden touch, huh? Sure would be awesome if you'd answer one of my fucking texts or voicemails.

Reed's next text came an hour later, at 5:26 pm on Sunday.

I swear I've never wished I could rewind the clock and get a 'do-over' more than I wish that right now. I'm sorry, Georgie. Please, call me. XO

Fifteen minutes later, he sent this:

Georgie, I'd walk a million miles, barefoot, over the shards of my Ferrari's shattered windshield, if it would make you forgive me. Please, call me. Scream at me. Tell me you hate me. Just call and let me hear your voice. I'm losing my mind. I'm sure you're happy about that. I'm sure you're smiling at my misery, and I don't blame you. But if you ever cared about me at all, please, just call me and let me explain. I'm physically sick with the need to talk to you. XO

When he *still* didn't receive a reply from me, Reed sent this little gem at 2:13 a.m. today (Monday):

Congratulations. You've now ignored me for a full twenty-four hours. Are you alive? Are you safe? Should I file a missing person report? I think the punishment far outweighs the crime, at this point. I mean, I get that you're pissed at me. But guess what? I'm pissed at you for smashing my Ferrari as punishment for a fucking kiss! So, let's call it even. A kiss for a Ferrari. Call me, even if it's to tell me to fuck off and die. CALL ME.

I can't help smirking. God, he's terrible at this. Doesn't he realize he should be groveling right now? Not lashing out. Not being cocky. Not telling me he's angry with me. Jesus, he's infuriating. But so am I. Because the pathetic truth is that I kind of like Reed's bad attitude. In fact, knowing he's grouchy and angry and cantankerous and lashing out... all of it kind of makes my heart go pitter pat. How screwed up is that?

When Reed didn't hear from me, yet again, he sent me another text. Surprise, surprise. This one, about thirty minutes later.

I lied. I'm not mad about my Ferrari. Never was. I just texted that to piss you off, so you'd call me. Please, Georgie. Have mercy on me. I've never done this before. I've never felt this before. There was no way I was going to be able to do this, and to feel this, without stumbling. I fucked up. I know that. Give me another chance. Please.

But I didn't call. Not because I have willpower of steel. Not because

I'm heartless or the Bobby Fischer of breakups. But because... I had my phone off. Because I was in bed, wallowing in self-pity.

Well, guess what? My non-strategy strategy finally wore Reed down and forced him to do the one thing he *swore* in his voicemails he wouldn't: explain the grant to me over text. In four messages, all of them sent in rapid-fire succession, he unloaded on me, as follows:

I didn't want to explain any of this to you in a text, but you've left me no choice. CeeCee was going to hire you, regardless. When I called the day after the panel, she'd already fallen in love with you and your writing samples. The only problem? She never pays summer interns and didn't want to open a can of worms by doing it for you. On the other hand, she'd heard about your father's situation, and didn't feel right about offering you a standard unpaid internship. I suggested a solution that would benefit all three of us: I'd donate to CeeCee's favorite cancer charity to get you paid, in exchange for RnR doing a special issue about my label. CeeCee countered that the deal had to include an in-depth interview of me. I said okay. She suggested you as the interviewer. I said yes, because, unbeknownst to CeeCee, that would give me a chance to try to seduce you. And that was that. A win-win-win. So sue me.

You once told me you had parallel motivations the first time we met. Well, so did I. Yes, I wanted another shot at seducing you, but I ALSO wanted to help CeeCee, and you, and your dad. I regret the way the grant turned into such a big secret. That wasn't my intention. I didn't say anything about it because I didn't want to steal your thunder or make you think, even for a second, you hadn't earned your job. Also, I didn't want you feeling any kind of pressure to sleep with me. Yes, I wanted it to happen. Hell yes. But only if you genuinely wanted it, too. Not

because you felt a financial obligation to me. That's the truth. On my nephew. Now, stop acting like a petulant child and reply to this text so I know you're safe.

PS I sent the Peloton to your dad's place. If you don't have room for it there, let me know. Also, let me know if you want your Pilates machine. It's much bigger than the bike, so I figured it'd be better to ask before sending.

I'm assuming you're coming to today's team meeting, seeing as how you're still obligated to write an article about me. Please allow me to take you to lunch before the meeting. We'll talk and forgive. I'll forgive you for ignoring me for two days. And you'll forgive me for being a stupid idiot. I'll make a reservation at Nobu. You'll love it. Please reply to confirm. I can't wait to see you. XO

I look up from my phone. Damn that man. He's persuasive. I still need to talk to CeeCee, to hear her unbiased account regarding the grant. But I can't deny Reed's texts have made me cautiously optimistic about that. I'm sure Reed spun some of the facts to make himself sound as innocent as possible. But, even so, I'm feeling pretty sure CeeCee wasn't my pimp, but instead leaped at the chance to create a win-win-win with her trusted friend, for my benefit, and theirs. But so what? None of that would absolve Reed of whatever happened in that garage with Isabel. Sighing loudly, I scroll to Reed's next text, which landed in my inbox about an hour and a half ago—at 6:13 pm this evening:

Miss Ricci, I'm sending this text in my professional capacity. I'm deeply disappointed you didn't come to this afternoon's weekly team meeting. Even if you despise me for personal reasons, you've still got a job to do, and I expect you to fucking do it. You're a writer for the world's

top music magazine and you need to start behaving like it. Whatever has transpired between us, personally, it's time for you to put your feelings aside and behave like a fucking professional. I'll expect you to attend next Monday's team meeting. I'll also expect you to respond to all business-related texts from me, going forward, including confirmation that you're safe and sound, within the next fifteen minutes.

I look up from my phone, gritting my teeth. Reed wants me to act like a "fucking professional," does he? Well, all righty, then. How about this? I'll write an article about him that kicks so much ass, CeeCee will have no choice but to publish it in *Dig a Little Deeper*!

Determination flooding me, I hop out of bed and plop myself onto the floor next to the cardboard box and begin sifting through its contents like a madwoman. Quickly, I find the documents pertaining to Troy Eklund's lawsuit. It was filed six years ago, against Reed and River Records, and alleges four causes of action: breach of contract, breach of the implied covenant of good faith and fair dealing, fraud, and assault.

But before I've gotten past the second paragraph of Troy's complaint, Dad pops his head into the room. And the minute he sees me on the floor, surrounded by legal documents, I know I must look to him like a chocolate-smeared kid surrounded by a mountain of candy wrappers on Halloween.

"*Georgina Marie*. You promised not to look at whatever's in that box!"

I grimace. "Sorry. I wasn't lying to you. I just... *forgot*."

Dad points toward the hallway. "Get your butt into the kitchen and eat the meatball sandwich I've made for you. *Dinner is served*."

"Sorry, Daddy. I need five minutes. There's a text for work I need to send."

"No."

"It's for work. I swear. I need to send it."

Dad exhales. "You swear on Mommy it's for work?"

Damn it. I hate it when he does that. He knows it's the one thing I'll never, ever fib on. But, luckily, the text I want to send is to Margot. Not about a work-related matter, actually. But, hey, since she works for *Rock 'n' Roll,* I still think a text to her should qualify as something "for work." I say, "Yes. I swear. I just need five minutes."

Satisfied, Dad leaves my doorway, and I pick up my phone, intending to send my text to Margot. But before I've started typing, my phone pings with yet another incoming text from Reed:

The hotel informs me you haven't checked into your room or retrieved your car keys. I'm assuming that means you're staying at your father's condo. Please confirm. If I don't hear from you by 8:00 tonight, then I'll have no choice but to call your father to confirm your whereabouts. If you're not at his place, and he hasn't heard from you, then my next call will be to the police. Your choice, Miss Ricci.

"Bastard!" I whisper-shout. The clever man has found my Achilles' heel. He knows I'd never want the CEO of River Records calling my father about me. How would I explain that to my dad, after the loan on his condo got magically paid off? After a fancy stationary bike showed up at his house? And, especially, now that my father knows I've been in bed, crying for two days because a stupid boy didn't love me back? Damn that relentless man! Gnashing my teeth, I bang out an angry reply to Reed's missive:

Hello, Mr. Rivers. Yes, I'm at my father's condo. I'm planning to stay at the hotel starting tomorrow night. Thank you for the room and rental car. Thank you for having the Peloton delivered. Keep the Pilates machine, please. I missed today's team meeting because I've determined I've got enough information from you, directly, for my article and will now begin gathering information from other sources. Going forward, please keep future communications on a professional basis. Thank you for everything you've done for me and my father. We both appreciate it very much. However, as I hope you have

discerned by now, my affection and trust do not have a price tag.

I press send on my message, and not ten seconds later, my phone rings with an incoming call from Reed—which I decline—and then breathlessly tap out a text to CeeCee's personal assistant, Margot:

I know CeeCee will be slammed on Wednesday, since it's her first day back, but I'm hoping to grab a few minutes of her time, one-on-one, before her scheduled meeting with Zasu and me at 2:00. I'm sorry to ask for this favor, but it's an urgent personal matter. Thank you.

After pressing send, I toss my phone onto my bed and march into my father's kitchen, my stomach growling and my head held high. Reed wants me to act like a "fucking professional"? Fine. Great. Then that's exactly what I'll do, *stronzo*.

SIXTY-SEVEN
GEORGINA

Tuesday, 1:04 pm

I lean back in my chair, blown away. Heartsick. Devastated. How am I going to remain angry with Reed after reading all of *this*?

I'm sitting in a conference room at *Rock 'n' Roll*, having just read the documents comprising the twenty-year-old legal malpractice suit filed by Eleanor Rivers against her divorce attorney—which, in turn, set forth the basic facts of the underlying divorce and custody battle between Eleanor and Terrence Rivers. And I'm feeling like I've just been run over by a Mack truck. I can't imagine what Reed had to do—the fortress he had to build around his heart—to overcome the chaos and abandonments of his childhood.

It's taken me half a day to read everything in the three boxes sent from the courthouse, all of which can be summarized as follows:

Two years before Reed came along, Terrence and Eleanor Rivers had a son named Oliver. When little Oliver Rivers was born, Terrence and Eleanor hired a weekday, live-in housekeeper/nanny named Amalia Vaccaro. Two years later, when Reed joined the family, a weekend nanny named Celeste was added to the payroll. Why did Terrence and Eleanor feel they needed so much assistance with their two young children, when Eleanor didn't work outside the home? Well, according to Eleanor, it was because Terrence wanted his young wife to be able to "dote on their children" while also having plenty of time to "paint and nap, and read poetry," and, basically, not have to worry about pesky things like cleaning toilets or making the family dinner, or anything else that might cause Eleanor a moment of worry or stress.

According to Terrence, however, he insisted on round-the-clock help for his "unstable and emotional" wife because he knew, from the start, she would make an "unfit mother, if she were left to handle the pressures of motherhood without a lot of help."

Not so, Eleanor retorted in a deposition, pointing out that she'd grown up babysitting her younger sisters and her neighbors' children. "I've always adored babies," Eleanor insisted. "And I absolutely adored mine." According to Eleanor, it was Terrence, *not* herself, who was the unfit parent. "Terrence never showed any genuine interest in being a true father to our boys," Eleanor claimed. "He loves having a family for Christmas cards. But that's about it." Moreover, Eleanor claimed, the reason Terrence "insisted" on hiring their weekend nanny, Celeste, wasn't because *Eleanor* needed her. But because Celeste was "young and beautiful, and Terrence wanted to get her into bed."

But no matter what Eleanor argued in the divorce, it fell on deaf ears. At least, that was my impression when reading the documents—and all because of one tragic fact, which Terrence and his army of lawyers relentlessly hammered on: it was Eleanor who was home alone with her two young sons on the fateful Saturday when little Oliver Rivers drowned in his family's backyard swimming pool.

On that day, the weekend nanny, Celeste, had called in sick, and Terrence was off playing golf. At least, according to Terrence. According to Eleanor, Terrence was off screwing Celeste, the "sick" weekend nanny, that fateful day. In the legal malpractice case, one of Eleanor's biggest beefs with her own divorce lawyer was that she hadn't tracked down Terrence's actual whereabouts that day, either through hotel receipts or witnesses. Eleanor claimed Terrence was a liar and a cheater in the divorce—which, of course, isn't a hard thing to believe, in retrospect, considering Terrence's criminal conviction three years later. She argued proof of Terrence's infidelity on that particular Saturday, and his lies about it in the divorce, would have debunked his entire case, all of which centered on Terrence being a devoted and exemplary husband and father—a pillar of the community. To Eleanor's thinking, proving Terrence was an unfaithful husband and a liar under oath would have given her a fighting chance to retain the right to care for her son, Reed.

Personally, I'm not sure if Eleanor was right about any of that. I have to think, even if the judge had ruled Terrence *was* a liar and a cheater in relation to his wife, it wouldn't have made him decide Terrence was an unfit parent. Otherwise, half the divorced people in the world would lose custody of their kids. But, either way, I felt bad for Eleanor while reading the malpractice case. It was undisputed she'd been alone with her two boys the day Oliver died, which was a tragedy, in itself—and one she was desperately trying to grapple with and explain. But, unfortunately, for Eleanor, that horrible tragedy was all the judge in the divorce case needed to know about, seven years later, to grant Terrence full legal and physical custody of Reed. What did Eleanor get? Once-weekly supervised visitations with her son, for two hours at a time.

Honestly, I have no idea if Oliver's death was Eleanor's "fault," as Terrence claimed. Maybe it was. But I can't help thinking children die tragically in swimming pools every day—sometimes, even in the presence of lifeguards. Sometimes, at a party, when a bunch of parents are standing nearby. Are all parents whose children slip silently underwater, never to rise again, *de facto* unfit parents to their surviving children, based on a few seconds of tragic inattention? And if so, are they *still* unfit parents, a full seven years after the tragedy?

I don't pretend to have answers. I'm just saying, from what I just read, I feel like the judge in the divorce case believed Terrence's version of events, hook, line, and sinker, without giving Eleanor's version of events, and her desperate pleas for him to listen to her, a moment's sincere consideration. And, in light of what we've since learned about Terrence, one of the world's most notorious liars, I feel in my bones Eleanor was probably given a raw deal.

In Eleanor's version of events, she had the stomach flu the day Oliver died and could barely keep her eyes open. Eleanor testified she "begged" and "pleaded" with her husband to stay home and help her with their children, since the weekend nanny, Celeste, had called in sick. "But Terrence told me to 'suck it up, Buttercup,'" Eleanor testified in a deposition, an excerpt of which was attached to a motion in the malpractice case. "So that's what I did. I put the boys down for their regular morning nap, the same as always, set an alarm so I'd wake up before them, the same as always, and then, I crawled into bed and crashed."

Tragically, when Eleanor woke up and went to check on her boys, she found Reed still fast asleep in his crib... and Oliver nowhere to be found. She testified she looked high and low for her missing son, becoming increasingly panicked, and finally found him in an unthinkable spot. The poor woman described her desperate dive into the swimming pool. She testified about how she pulled Oliver from the water and tried frantically to resuscitate him... But it was too late. She testified, "I had no idea Oliver knew how to open the lock we'd put up high on the sliding door. He'd pulled up a chair to reach it. He'd never done that before!"

A week after Oliver's death, Eleanor tried to commit suicide. She was hospitalized thereafter for a week, and, then, sent to a long-term "mental care" facility in Los Angeles for the better part of a year. While she was away, Terrence was Father of the Year, according to him. Although, according to Eleanor, it was Amalia, not Terrence, who cared for Reed during this period. But since nobody called Amalia as a witness in the divorce case—yet another grievance for Eleanor in the later malpractice lawsuit—the divorce judge, once again, sided with Terrence, even going so far as to praise him for being Reed's "rock" during this time.

Poor Eleanor. She testified in the divorce, "I fully admit I wasn't capable of caring for Reed during the first year after Olly's death. But I knew Amalia was there for him, and that I needed to focus on getting better so I could get out and be a good mother to him. So that's what I did. I got the help I needed. And then I came home and took care of my son for the next six years. I'm not a perfect mother, but who is? Judge, I want to be with my son. I want to be his mother. Please, please, let me do that."

It wasn't enough to convince the judge. Not when Terrence, a man regarded as a "pillar of the community" testified that Eleanor was "useless and non-functional" when she returned home from her year away, and then remained that way for the entirety of the six years preceding the divorce.

In the end, Eleanor got bitch-slapped at every turn by Terrence and his team of lawyers. And then by the divorce judge. And then she got bitch-slapped again in the legal malpractice case. The same way, it seems to me, if I'm reading between the lines correctly, she'd gotten bitch-slapped by Terrence during their marriage.

After the judge in the divorce case granted Terrence full legal and physical custody of Reed, Eleanor swallowed a bottle of pills. It was the same thing she'd done after Oliver died seven years prior. And, again, it ultimately led to her institutionalization in a shitty facility in Los Angeles. Against all odds, she bounced back after about a year and came out with her boxing gloves on. She filed a legal malpractice action against her divorce attorney, the one I've just read, as some sort of last-gasp attempt to prove she'd been railroaded in the divorce, and that she did, in fact, have the wherewithal to care for Reed.

But when the judge in the *malpractice* lawsuit ruled against Eleanor, the same way the divorce judge had, it was game over for Eleanor's mental health. She snapped for the last time. Once again, she tried to end it all. And wound up in that same, shitty Los Angeles institution. This time, for good, until her hard-working, loyal, and generous son moved her to a posh facility in Scarsdale.

Was Eleanor capable of caring for Reed at the time of the divorce, as she insisted vehemently at trial? I have no idea. All I know is it strikes me as awfully unfair that Terrence had Amalia's full-time help with Reed, and yet the judge expressly commented in his ruling against Eleanor, "A woman shouldn't need a paid nanny to help her care for her own children."

Also, I can't help feeling irate that the judge believed *everything* Terrence said, without question, given that, a mere two and a half years later, the FBI raided Terrence Rivers' sprawling mansion at dawn and arrested him in his underwear for staggering, truly evil financial crimes, thereby rendering his thirteen-year-old son, Reed, whom he'd fought so hard to claim for himself in the divorce, an effective orphan. Was Terrence Rivers any less of an "unfit parent" for mercilessly stealing from countless innocent families who'd trusted him, as Eleanor was for taking a nap, along with her two sons, when she had the stomach flu? I mean, assuming Eleanor's version of the story was true. Which, granted, I don't know.

I scrub my face with my palms, overwhelmed and aching for Eleanor. And Amalia. And Oliver. And, of course, for my beautiful liar, Reed. I've always found his hard outer shell immensely attractive, because it's what makes the rare glimpses of softness and vulnerability all the more breathtaking. But now, I'm realizing Reed's patented poker face, the steely mask he wears so well and often, must have been forged early on in his life as a coping mechanism. A way to survive the chaos. The abandonments. The lack of control he must have felt, at all times.

Even though I lost my mother at a young age, I nonetheless had the good fortune to observe her passionate, happy marriage with my father before she died. But what has Reed observed of marriage that would make him believe it's possible for one to be happy? If I'd experienced everything Reed has, I'd probably have ten layers of cement around my heart, too. Frankly, after reading all this, I'm in awe of how kind and generous Reed is... exactly as Amalia said to me, that time we were cooking together in the kitchen.

I love him so much.

The thought pops into my head and streaks through my heart.

I love Reed. Even though I fervently wish I didn't.

But so what if I do? I simply have to get over it. Because loving Reed isn't enough. For our relationship to work, I need to love *and* trust him. And I don't see how I could ever get there. Not really. If I were to give Reed another chance, I know, deep down, I'd slowly become jealous, paranoid, and possessive. I'd grow to despise the woman I'd become with him. And he'd despise her, too. Which means it really is time for me to move on.

Ciao, stronzo.

It's what my brain keeps telling me to do. The thing I know is for the best. *Move on, Georgie. There are other fish in the sea. You're too young to have met the great love of your life, anyway, no matter what your foolish heart is telling you. Yes, Mom met her Prince Charming at nineteen. But Mom and Dad's fairytale was the exception, not the rule.*

I tell myself all of these things, as I stare at the conference room wall in a daze. I tell myself these things and stuff down the urge to call Reed and tell him I miss him. I love him. I forgive him. But no. I can't wave a magic wand and make everything the way it was before. Even as my heart wants to hug the tragic, neglected, abandoned little boy who grew up to be a wildly successful, sexy, breathtaking man, my brain knows it's time for me to move on.

SIXTY-EIGHT
REED

Tuesday 10:12 pm

I'm grunting. Sweating. Shaking as I finish a savage set of clapping pull-ups in my home gym. Henn texted yesterday to say he'd have something on Gates by Friday. So, at least, there's that. But regarding Georgina herself, I still haven't heard from her, other than that one soul-crushing text she sent twenty-four hours ago, after I threatened to call her father.

To entice her to call me, I did something yesterday morning that's surely going to piss her off when she finds out about it. Hopefully, enough to make her call me and chew me out. Obviously, I'd rather Georgina call me to whisper sweet nothings into my ear. But at this point, I'll do whatever I have to do to hear her voice, even if she's screaming at me.

I finish my pull-ups and look down at my phone on the floor, checking to see if I somehow missed a call from Georgina. But, nope. Grunting with annoyance, I grab my phone and head to a workout bench in a corner. But as I'm getting into position with some heavy dumbbells, it finally happens. *My phone rings with an incoming call from Georgina!*

Gasping like a fish on a hook, I scoop up my phone and briefly fumble with it, like some kind of electrocuted circus clown, and, finally, gather enough control of my fingers to connect the call.

"Georgina," I blurt, far more enthusiastically than intended. "You're alive!"

"What the hell do you think you're doing?" she shouts.

I close my eyes and take a deep breath. The sound of her voice, even when she's shouting angrily at me, is a balm for my tortured soul "Whatever do you mean?" I ask, even though I know exactly what she means.

"I don't have a price, Reed!" she shrieks. "Get it through your head. *You cannot buy me.*"

I feel physically dizzy. I'm a junkie getting his first hit of the good stuff after three torturous days of withdrawal. I sink into the workout bench, feeling blissed out. "What crime have I committed to elicit this shrieking reaction from you, Miss Ricci?"

"You know exactly why I'm screaming at you. My father just called. His email address is the one on record for all my student loans. Apparently, two minutes ago, he checked his inbox for the first time today and discovered he'd received a 'paid in full' notification at noon regarding *all* my student loans!"

I smirk. *God, I'm good.*

"You can't pay off my student loans!"

"It appears I can. Quite easily, in fact."

"I won't let you."

"I already did it."

"Then, *undo* it. Tell the banks to return your money and restore the original loans."

I chuckle. "It doesn't work that way. That money belongs to the banks now. It's theirs."

Georgina mutters something expletive-laden under her breath that makes me smile even wider. "All right," she says, her voice brimming with resolve. "As of this moment, I owe that same exact amount of money to *you*. I don't care how long it takes me, I'm going to pay you back every cent, with interest."

Oh, how I've missed this back and forth with my beautiful fireball. I've only been without her for a matter of days, but it feels like years. "You know I won't accept a dime from you."

"I'm not giving you a choice. I'm going to Venmo payment to you every month, on the first."

"Which I'll decline with the push of a button."

"God, you're impossible! Do you have any idea the trouble you've caused me?"

"Trouble?"

"With my father! He saw that email and freaked out. He was like, 'How did you get your hands on a hundred thousand bucks, Georgina Marie?'"

"Did you tell him about me?"

"Of course, not! I told him that same cancer charity from before came to the rescue again. But he didn't believe me this time. He barely believed me last time, regarding the pay-off on his condo. He was like, 'Tell the truth, Georgie. Where is all this money coming from? Did that same jerk who sent you the expensive stationary bike also pay off your student loans?'"

Admittedly, knowing that Georgina's father thinks I'm a jerk isn't optimal. But, hey, at least, Georgina told him about me. And, even better, she's talking to me again. Which means I can now see a path forward to convincing her to take me back. "Ah, so your father knows of my existence?"

"Only because I couldn't avoid telling him where I got the Peloton."

"So, what did you finally tell him about the loans?"

"That I'm secretly working for a drug cartel."

"What?"

"That was a joke. I wish I could have told my father that. Telling him I'm working for a drug cartel would have been preferable to telling him I fell head over heels for the asshole CEO of River Records, and that, unfortunately, that asshole sneaked off and had sex with a movie star, and now thinks he can buy my trust and affection by paying off my student loans."

Okay, I realize a whole lot of what Georgina said wasn't good for me. Particularly, the part where she's *still* convinced I had *sex* with Isabel. Also, it's not ideal she called me an asshole. But I can't focus on negativity when Georgina started her diatribe with the amazing words: *I fell head over heels for the CEO of River Records.* During our magical week together, Georgina and I never said we were "falling" for each other. We said we felt "addicted." And that we were "crazy about" each other. We said we liked each other "so damned much." But we never once said "I'm *falling* for you"—which, of course, is a close cousin of "I'm falling *in love* with you"—which, in turn, is only one tick shy of "I love you."

"So, how'd you explain the loan getting paid off, if you didn't say you were a drug mule?"

"Well, since my father wasn't buying the cancer charity anymore, I told him the head of River Records is an eccentric billionaire who loves doing random acts of kindness. Which is actually kind of true. So, I told him you'd paid off my student loans, along with the student loans of Zasu, the other reporter working on the special issue."

I scoff. "And he bought that?"

"No. He's not a moron. Don't insult my father's intelligence."

I laugh. "You're the one who told him the lie. Not me."

"I'm his *daughter*. I've been insulting my father's intelligence since I was sixteen and putting pillows under my covers to make it look like I was in bed, fast asleep, when I'd actually sneaked out a window to go to a party."

I chuckle heartily. "You were Ferris Bueller. Oh, God. Please tell me you know that reference."

"Of course."

"There's no such thing as 'of course' when it comes to you and pop culture references. Did you put pillows under your covers a lot, little Miss 'Sneaky' Ricci?"

"Probably, like, ten times. And it always worked like a charm. Until it didn't. Hoo boy, the day I finally got caught wasn't a good one."

I laugh, and so does Georgie, which then makes every cell in my body electrify with excitement. Hope. *Love.* "I'm not a billionaire, by the way."

"Huh?"

"You told your dad an 'eccentric billionaire' paid off your loans. I'm not a billionaire. Give me twenty years and I will be, though."

"You're a *millionaire*, though, right?"

"About five hundred times over."

"Why are you correcting me on this? Isn't it 'on-brand' for the world to think you're a billionaire?"

My stomach tightens. "I'm not 'on-brand' with you, Georgina, and you know it. I'm just me."

She's silent on the other end of the line, tacitly admitting she knows I'm speaking the truth.

"Georgie, I know you don't trust me as far as you can throw me—which I'm sure would be out a third-story window, if you could swing it—but, please, come home. Sleep in the blue room, while we work this out. My house feels so empty without you. My heart feels like it's rubbing against a cheese grater. Come *home*."

"I can't do that. I'm way too hurt. As sad as it is for me, I think we should agree to be friends and business colleagues, and nothing more."

I scoff. I can't be Georgina's friend and business colleague. Not in a million years. I want every inch of this woman. But, hey, at least she's not telling me to fuck off and die. And she did say it would be "sad" for her to be nothing but my friend.

She says, "Thank you for paying off my student loans. I appreciate it. But don't you get it? It doesn't change anything between us because I was never with you for your money. We could have been staying in a mud hut for a week, or a rundown motel, and I still would have fallen for you. We could have been eating Taco Bell for every meal, taking hikes with peanut butter and jelly sandwiches, or working out at some local gym filled with nothing but soccer moms. *And I still would have fallen for you*. It still would have been the best week of my life. A fairytale." Her voice cracks. "Because I would have been with *you*."

Oh, God, what have I done? My heart feels like it's physically breaking. "Georgie, I feel the same way. I know you don't believe it was just a kiss with Isabel, but it was. I know you won't forgive me for that kiss, even if you did believe me. But can you at least forgive me about the grant? You got my texts explaining that, right?"

"Have you talked to CeeCee about that?"

"No."

"Good. Don't say a word to CeeCee about the grant, please. I want to hear what she has to say, in her own words, without any undue influence on your part."

Damn. Kat is good. "Of course. I assumed as much. What about the thing with Alessandra? Can you forgive me for talking to her about her demo?"

"Yes. I was actually about to text you about that, right before my dad called me about the student loans. She's back in Boston now, and she called me earlier today with some fantastic news. She got hired for a weekly gig at a popular coffee place near campus. And she said it was all thanks to you."

"To *me*?"

"She said she almost didn't go through with her audition, she was so nervous. But then, she heard *your* voice in her ear—telling her the same stuff you said at the party—and she realized you were right about all of it. So, she marched onto that stage, the way she wished she'd done at the party, and wound up giving the performance of her life."

My heart is soaring. For Alessandra, of course. For Georgie, who's so obviously elated for her stepsister's victory. But, mostly, selfishly, for myself. The way Georgina is talking to me right now, the joy she's expressing to me, without holding back—it's like she's my Georgie again. We might as well be sitting at my kitchen table, talking while eating a delicious meal Amalia left for us. This, right now, we're *us* again. And Georgie's trying to convince me we're going to be nothing more than *friends* and *business colleagues*? I take a deep breath to gather myself. "Tell Alessandra I'm ecstatic for her."

"I will. The Man with the Midas Touch strikes again. Whatever you said to her, it really helped her out. Thank you so much for breaking your promise not to talk to her about her demo. If you hadn't done that, she never would have gotten this gig."

Oh, my heart. It's physically straining to fuse with hers across the phone line. I swallow hard. "Please, Georgina, come home to me. I'm wrecked without you. I swear, I've learned my lesson."

She exhales audibly. "What would be the point? If we got back together, I'd always feel paranoid and mistrustful. I'd never be able to let go completely with you, like I used to do. I'd always be holding back. And what fun would that be, for either of us, when the thing that was so amazing about us was the way neither of us was ever holding back?"

I'm hurtling toward despair. Feeling like my heart is being wrung out like a sponge. Only, it's my crimson blood, my very happiness, that's oozing from its twisted wreckage. "I don't want Isabel. I only want *you*. And that's exactly what I told Isabel in the garage."

"Oh, yeah? Did you tell her that *before* or *after* you had sex with her?"

I close my eyes. I can't believe I had heaven in the palm of my hand and threw it away. "*I didn't have sex with her*. Hate me. Wish me dead. As long as you believe me when I say I only kissed Isabel goodbye, and it meant nothing." I know Kat told me not to say this next thing, but I don't care. It has to be said. "Georgina, I swear, kissing Isabel only made me realize, without a doubt, I only want *you*."

Georgina snorts with disdain. And now I know, for certain, Kat was exactly right. Georgina thinks I'm only saying what every cheater says when he gets caught. And can I blame her, really? If the situation were reversed, and Georgina had gone into that garage with her ex and "kissed him goodbye," how would I be feeling right now? Decimated. Betrayed. Rejected, beyond repair. That's how. And nothing, no words from Georgina, not even swinging a golf club against one of Georgina's prized sports cars, if sports cars were her thing, would have lessened the pain of that dagger to my heart.

As if reading my mind, Georgina sighs and says, "I wish so badly smashing your car could have made us even. Or maybe given me amnesia, or rewound time. But, unfortunately, it turns out it doesn't work that way."

"I know. I'm so sorry."

"I wish swinging that golf club could have solved every problem I have." She pauses. "I wish it could have made my nightmares about Mr. Gates go away." She sniffles. "I wish it could have brought my mother back to me."

My heart pangs. "Oh, sweetheart. I'd let you smash every one of my cars, including my Bugatti, and then I'd buy another fifty Bugattis for you to smash, if it would bring back your mother to you."

She sniffles again.

"I mean that, sincerely."

"I know you do. Thank you." Another sniffle. "You're really not mad at me *at all* for totaling your Ferrari?"

"No. I'm grateful you spared my Bugatti."

I can hear her smile over the phone line. "The punishment has to fit the crime. I'm psycho but not crazy. You didn't *murder* anyone, for crying out loud."

I clutch my heart, feeling physical pain. I love this woman. I do. I know it as well as I know my own name. I love her, and I betrayed her, and, now, I'm rightly suffering for it. Seriously now, what the fuck is wrong with me?

"I have to go," Georgina says softly. "Thanks again for paying off my loans. But I'm warning you: don't spend another dime on my father or me, or I'm going to come over and smash your Bugatti."

"As long as you come over," I whisper.

"Bye, Reed."

"Wait. Georgie, come on. Can't you feel what's happening between us? We're still *us*. I know I've got to prove myself to you, but I will. The most important thing is that our chemistry, our electricity, it's the same as it ever was. Come home and let's talk until sunrise and figure this out."

"I can't come over."

I look at the clock on my phone. 10:56. "Yeah, okay, that's probably a good call. I don't want you driving late at night. I'll come to your hotel." Without waiting for her reply, I march out of my gym and race toward my bedroom, planning to take a lightning-quick shower and then drive like a bat out of hell to her hotel.

"Don't go to my hotel, Reed. I'm not there."

I freeze in the middle of my bathroom, already half naked. "Where are you?"

She sighs. But doesn't answer me.

The hairs on the back of my neck stand on end. "*Where are you?*"

"I wasn't planning to tell you this, but, since you're asking, I'm sitting in my rental car, outside a bar, about to head inside."

My heart stops. "It's almost eleven."

"Yeah, that's the time of night when bars have people inside them."

I can barely breathe. I feel sick. "Are you meeting someone? A friend from school? One of my artists?"

"No, none of the above. I'm flying solo tonight."

An odd cocktail of relief and panic swirls inside me. I'm thrilled Georgina doesn't have a date... that she's not, for instance, meeting Savage or Endo for a drink. But if she's truly going to walk into a bar alone at eleven at night, then she won't be alone for long. Is she going to a bar, alone, on a Tuesday night, because she's looking for a casual hookup? Does she intend to have revenge sex tonight, with some random stranger, in retaliation for the sex she *thinks* I had with Isabel?

"To be clear, if I *were* meeting up with someone at the bar tonight, it wouldn't be any of your business," she says. "When you hooked up with Isabel, you released me from my obligation not to hook up with 'anyone on Planet Earth.'"

Jealousy explodes inside my veins like a Molotov cocktail tossed onto a puddle of gasoline. "Tell me where you are," I say, trying, and failing, to keep my voice calm.

She scoffs. "Why would I do that?"

"What's the name of the fucking bar?" I shout.

"*Calm down*," she says, and I can hear the smirk on her sultry lips. "All I'm going to do is have a drink—only *one*, because I'm driving—and listen to some live music to unwind. I *might* chat with a nice-looking stranger, if the opportunity falls into my lap. But when the musician is done, the plan is for me to head back to my hotel and go to bed, all by myself."

I exhale the equivalent of the Pacific Ocean. "Thank you for telling me that. I almost had a heart attack, imagining you—"

"*Although*... you know what they say about plans, right? Make one, only if you want to make God laugh."

"Georgina."

"I suppose it's *possible* I could meet a handsome stranger at the bar tonight who charms my pants off... *literally*. In which case, I *might* find myself at his place later tonight, screwing the hell out of him... *while thinking of you and Isabel*."

My head explodes. I feel like I'm stroking out. I'm literally blinded by my panic. "That's enough! You're going to head back to your hotel right now to wait for me. Do you hear me? I'm leaving my place now. Meet me at your hotel!"

She giggles with glee. "Goodbye, Reed. I'm hanging up now, and then I'm going to turn off my phone until morning. So, don't blow up my phone all night with texts and voicemails, ya freakin' psycho. *Ciao, stronzo*! Sleep tight!"

I'm stumbling. Tripping as I race to my walk-in closet to throw on clothes over my sweaty body. Forget showering. My house is burning down around me, and I need to grab only my most valuable possession. *I need to grab Georgie!*

"Tell me the name of that bar, Georgina Marie! That's a *command* from the head of the label that's making his artists available to you!" I hop on one foot as I try to throw on jeans with one hand while holding my phone to my ear with the other. "Georgie? Georgina Marie Ricci!"

But it's no use. The line has gone dead.

Georgina Marie Ricci, the most diabolical woman alive, a woman who takes scorched-earth tactics to a whole new level, is gone.

SIXTY-NINE
GEORGINA

Tuesday 10:57 pm

After I hang up with Reed, I get out of my parked rental car and begin walking the three blocks to my destination: a small bar in West Hollywood called Slingers that features live music every night. Hopefully, Troy Eklund is performing tonight, as Slingers' online schedule promises, because I've got a crap-ton of questions for him.

I haven't decided if I'm going to come right out and tell Troy I'm a writer for *Rock 'n' Roll*, researching an article about Reed Rivers—and, oh, by the way, I've got a bunch of questions about a lawsuit you filed against Reed six years ago!—or if, instead, I'll pretend to be some random chick in a bar with a boner for musicians. My gut tells me I'll get a whole lot more information out of Troy if I play Star-Struck Groupie. But I figure I'll play it by ear and decide on the fly.

Everything I know about Troy, I've learned from two admittedly unreliable sources—the internet and the pages of his six-year-old lawsuit—all of which can be summarized, as follows:

Ten years ago, when Troy was eighteen, he started a band called

The Distillery in Sacramento. Troy was his band's front man and guitarist, and, even at eighteen, had so much swagger, you'd have thought the kid had arrived in our world via the future, already knowing his rock stardom was in the bag.

For three years in Sacramento, The Distillery played local bars and gigs, until finally catching the eye of one Reed Rivers—a shrewd and brilliant young businessman with an up-and-coming indie label that had recently scored back-to-back smash debut albums from two young bands: Red Card Riot and Danger Doctor Jones, as well as a number one smash debut single from 2Real.

With the ink barely dry on The Distillery's deal with River Records, Troy and his bandmates moved to LA—into Reed's house, as a matter of fact—where they began writing, and then recording, their debut album with Reed's guidance.

Troy's complaint didn't list the address of Reed's house, but, given that Reed purchased his present hilltop castle five years ago, and the events alleged in Troy's lawsuit happened *seven* years ago, Troy and his band must have stayed in Reed's much smaller first house. A place Reed once told me would have fit inside his present garage. Which means Reed and those Distillery boys almost certainly got up close and personal during those several months together.

According to Troy's complaint, Reed and the band had many "detailed" conversations during the band's stay with Reed, about music, in general, and the band's bright future, specifically. According to Troy, Reed always said the "sky was the limit" for the band—and for Troy, in particular. Troy claimed Reed made multiple promises to him during this time period. Promises Reed didn't wind up keeping.

According to my research, Reed wasn't shy about expressing his admiration for The Distillery during those early months. Reed was variously quoted as saying The Distillery was "lightning in a bottle" and "like nobody else." Regarding Troy, in particular, Reed called him a "future star."

For their part, Troy and his bandmates returned Reed's enthusiasm, calling their deal with River Records a "dream come true" and Reed, specifically, "a genius."

After several months of hard work, The Distillery's album was completed, and Reed teed up everything for the upcoming release, including having the guys shoot a music video for their debut single. By all accounts, the stars were aligned for The Distillery to take the world by storm in the same way Red Card Riot and Danger Doctor Jones had already done.

But, then, out of nowhere, mere weeks before the band's debut album was scheduled to drop, something happened that made Reed abruptly scrap the album, unceremoniously dump the band from his label, and physically beat the shit out of Troy. What was it that made Reed turn so viciously on a band he'd so vocally supported and admired? *Well, a woman, of course.* What else? Specifically, an "unnamed woman" with whom Reed had previously "been involved"... and with whom Troy had apparently had sex within two weeks of the scheduled debut album release.

In other words, according to Troy, Reed dumped Troy and his band, and physically assaulted Troy, thereby forfeiting all the time and money Reed had invested, merely to exact revenge upon Troy for screwing the wrong woman. Now, really. Does all that sound like something Reed would do?

Hell yes, it does! *Duh.* I saw the way Reed looked at C-Bomb that night at the RCR concert. Like he wanted to kill C-Bomb for merely flirting with me. I also saw the way Reed handled that PA who'd walked in on us. He was absolutely ruthless with that poor girl. Like a mob boss. Plus, backstage at the RCR concert, Reed himself told me he'd "trained" his artists not to hit on anyone he'd been involved with. Well, now I know what he was talking about. He was referring to the incident with Troy.

But even without all that direct evidence to make me believe Reed did precisely what Troy accused him of doing, I'd still believe it, if only because Reed settled Troy's lawsuit. Reed himself told me he doesn't settle a case, unless it has merit, or Reed believes a *jury* will think it does. In regard to Stephanie Moreland's lawsuit, Reed settled because Leonard advised him a jury would hate him. Also, because California law is clear about the consequences of a boss screwing an employee. But, in this instance, my gut tells me Reed settled Troy's lawsuit because it was flat-out *true.*

What happened to The Distillery after they got unceremoniously dumped by River Records? They broke up. Apparently, Troy's bandmates were too pissed at him for fucking the "unnamed woman," whoever she was—*cough, cough,* Isabel Randolph—to want to continue making music with him. They couldn't release their existing debut album, since River Records owned it, according to the ironclad terms of their record deal. And everyone in the band was far too pissed at Troy at that point to sit down and try to write new music. For crying out loud, the band was even prohibited from *performing* any of the songs on that debut album, without the label's written consent—which, of course, it refused to give. And not only that, according to the complaint, Reed went so far as to "blackball" Troy in the music industry, thereby ensuring Troy's present *and* future music career was DOA.

So, that was that. The Distillery was dead, and Troy thereafter became a lone wolf pariah who eked out a meager music career by performing in small bars. I don't know what Troy received in settlement there were no details on that in the court file. But whatever payment he got, it obviously wasn't enough to keep Troy off the schedule of dive bars like Slingers a full six years later.

Speaking of which, I reach the front door of Slingers and show my ID to the bouncer, who stamps my wrist and allows me to enter the darkened bar. And there he is. Troy Eklund. Playing an acoustic guitar and belting out a song on a small stage in the corner.

I stand, stock still inside the door for a moment, blown away. No wonder Reed signed this guy. He's mesmerizing. Talented and hot as hell. I already knew what he looked like, thanks to YouTube. But, still, in person Troy Eklund is a smoke show. No wonder the "unnamed woman" screwed him. I'd screw him, too. In fact, who knows? Maybe, if Troy plays his cards right, I'll screw him tonight.

I take a seat at the bar and order a beer, and then swivel around to watch Troy's performance. It doesn't take long for him to notice me staring at him like a hungry dog.

When his gaze mingles with mine, I flash him my most brazen "I'm looking for a sexy good time" smolder. And in response, Troy winks at me, not missing a beat in his song.

Well, damn, that was easy.

Looks like I'll be playing Star-Struck Groupie tonight.

SEVENTY
GEORGINA

Wednesday 12:37 am

"**G**ood night, everyone!" Troy says into his microphone. His blue eyes flicker to me, the same way they've been doing for the past hour and a half. "I'm Troy Eklund, and I'm here every Tuesday and Friday night! See you next time."

There's a smattering of half-hearted applause, the most energetic of it, coming from me. Troy notices my enthusiastic clapping and raises his beer bottle to me from the stage. So, of course, groupie that I am, I raise my beer to him in reply with a bold wink. And that's all it takes. After sliding his guitar into its case, Troy heads straight to me at the bar.

"Is this stool taken?" he asks.

"I was hoping you'd ask me that. Sit, please. I was supposed to meet a blind date tonight, and he never showed up. So I've been saving that stool for you."

Troy settles onto the seat next to me. "That guy made the biggest mistake of his life, and he'll never know it." He raises his near-empty beer bottle toward the front door of the bar. "Thanks, dipshit! Whoever you are."

I giggle and bat my eyelashes shamelessly. "I think we're both feeling grateful to that dipshit for standing me up. Here's to silver linings."

We clink.

"What's your name, beautiful?"

"Georgina. You're Troy?"

He nods. "I've never seen you here before."

"Mr. Blind Date picked the place."

Troy raises his beer bottle toward the front door again. "Thanks again, dipshit! I owe you one!"

"*Ha, ha, ha,*" I laugh flirtatiously

"You want another one?" he asks, motioning to my beer.

"No, thanks. I'm driving. But let *me* buy *you* another one to thank you for all that incredible music. Seriously, Troy, you're amazing." It's the truth, actually. The guy is indisputably talented.

"Sure. I'll take another one."

I flag down the bartender and order his preferred beer and a club soda for me. And then settle onto my stool as Troy proceeds to talk my ear off. About himself. And how amazing he is. He tells me about his musical inspirations, not that I asked, and why he wrote such and such song he performed earlier, not that I remember it. He talks about how he first realized he's a natural on guitar. Oh, and did I notice he has perfect pitch? He tells me story after story about himself, and his talent, and his musical inspirations and philosophies, almost all of it unsolicited. And never once does he ask me a goddamned thing about myself. Which is why it takes all of ten minutes for me to realize, with certainty, he's an arrogant asshole. And not the good kind. Not like Reed. No, the kind I genuinely want to punch in the face.

When I manage to sneak in any words into Troy's monologue, it's obvious he's only waiting for me to finish talking so he can say whatever he's got cued up on the tip of his tongue. When, against all odds, I'm able to sneak in a little joke or snarky comment, which I've done about four times, Troy's chuckle isn't sincere. It's made of tin. Nothing more than a ploy to get himself into my pants.

All of which makes me think about Reed, even more than usual. I miss him so much, even though I'm bound and determined to hate him for what he did. But, see, when I talk to Reed, he actually listens. Mostly, anyway. Yes, occasionally, he sits there, smiling like a Cheshire cat while I'm talking, and it's obvious he's thinking I'm silly or amusing or fuckable. But, at least, even at those times, he's *listening*, even if his eyes are blazing with amusement or heat. But this guy? His brain is an echo chamber, filled with nothing but self-congratulations.

Also, Reed *always* laughs at my jokes, no matter how stupid they might be. And Reed's laughter is *always* sincere. True, Reed is always thinking about getting into my pants, every bit as much as this guy is. But it always feels with Reed like he's as attracted to my brain and personality as my body. That might not have been the case in the very beginning. When Reed first saw me in the lecture hall, I know he wanted to bone me, based on nothing but animal attraction. But I'd say the same thing about myself. It certainly wasn't Reed's heart I wanted to bone in that lecture hall. But by the end of our amazing week together, there was no doubt Reed wanted to "bone" my soul, along with my body, every bit as much as I wanted to bone his. Or, at least, that's how it felt to me.

Also, who does this Troy dude think he is? Reed has built an empire from scratch. He started with nothing and put *everything* on the line, because he believed in himself and his vision so much. And then, through sheer force of will and talent and drive, Reed came out the other side a king. *That's* why *Reed* is an arrogant prick! Because he's a legit god among men. But what's Troy's excuse? What has he built from scratch? Sure, Troy's got a soulful voice and he plays guitar well. And he's definitely got that "I know you want to fuck me" smolder down pat. But big whoop. Guys like him are a dime a dozen in this town.

For all Troy's bragging, you'd think he'd cured cancer with his songs. But Reed has *literally* been trying to cure cancer by donating huge amounts of money to cancer charities. And yet, Reed *never* brags the way this guy keeps doing. I only learned about most of Reed's biggest accomplishments and awards and milestones from snooping through his memorabilia and reading up on him online.

Frankly, the more I sit here listening to Troy, the happier I am that Reed eviscerated him. Reed plucked Troy, and his band, out of obscurity and helped them write and record a top-quality album. Reed moved them to LA and opened his personal *home* to this little twat for *months*. And this was a small house, too, so it's not like Troy and his bandmates had their own wing of the house. I'm sure they practically lived on top of each other. Not to mention, Reed invested a ton of time and money in Troy's band. Probably, his whole heart, too, assuming those interactions I witnessed between Reed and 2Real in the studio were indicative of Reed's usual contributions to his artists.

And Troy thanked Reed for all that by *betraying* him? By fucking an "unnamed woman" Reed had been involved with? I can't imagine, after living with Reed for months, Troy didn't *know* the "unnamed woman" had been involved with Reed. There's no way Troy didn't know he was stabbing Reed in the back. But, obviously, he didn't care.

I suddenly realize Troy is staring at me, like he's expecting me to say something.

"Wow, you're so amazing," I say, figuring that's a pretty safe thing to reply, no matter what he just finished saying. "Please don't take this the wrong way. But you're so amazing, I can't believe you don't have a deal with a record label. If you ask me, you should be headlining a world tour."

"I had a record deal once, actually. A big one."

Here we go. "That's so cool! What happened?"

"Oh, you know. The music business is crazy."

I wait, but that's all he says. "Actually, no, I don't know anything about the music industry."

Troy shrugs. "The label holds all the power. No matter how talented you might be, the label can decide to shelve your debut album. And that's that. You're done."

"Really? I didn't know that. That's terrible."

"Yep. They have full control."

"So, they shelved your album?"

He nods.

"But why would they do that for someone as talented as you? Don't they want to make money, every bit as much as you do?"

"Not if the owner of the label decides he doesn't like you for personal reasons and wants to fuck with you out of spite. When that happens, when the owner of the label is a fucking dick, then you're done, no matter how good the album is. Because the contract says the label owns and controls the album, and has the absolute right *not* to release it, ever, if that's what they decide to do."

"Holy hell. That sucks. What label was it?"

"River Records."

I look at him blankly.

"It's a good one. You've heard of their bands, I promise you."

"Let's see." I pull out my phone and google it. "Oh, wow! Red Card Riot, 2Real, Laila Fitzgerald, Danger Doctor Jones, 22 Goats! Holy crap, Troy!"

"Yep. They didn't have all those bands when I signed. The guy who owns the label was planning to build his entire label on my band, Red Card Riot, 2Real, and Danger Doctor Jones."

I point to a photo of Reed on my phone, my heart aching at how excruciatingly handsome he is in the shot. "Is this the guy who screwed you over?"

"Yup. That's him. Reed Rivers. Fucking dick."

Despite everything, hearing Reed's name sends butterflies racing into my belly. "Yeah, that guy looks like he'd be a fucking dick."

Troy chuckles. "He's more than a dick, actually. He's a fucking psychopath."

My eyebrows shoot up. "A *psychopath*? In what way?"

Troy pauses. "I'm actually not allowed to talk about this in any detail. I sued that guy's ass after he shelved my album, and we reached a confidential settlement. If I say too much, and it gets back to him, I'll owe him a shit-ton of money."

"Whoa. You *sued* him? You're such a baller."

Troy looks enamored with himself. "Yep. I brought that bastard to his knees."

"Oh my gosh. I'm *dying* to hear this story. Something tells me it's super-hot." I bite my lower lip suggestively. "Hey, aren't lawsuits public record?"

"Yeah...?"

"So, you're allowed to tell me stuff that's already in the public record. You can't get in trouble for doing that, if it's right there for anyone to find it."

Troy considers that logic for a beat. "Good point."

He empties his beer bottle, and I order him another one. We talk some more. I flirt and laugh and nudge him a bit. And, soon, hallelujah, the floodgates open for me. *Blah, blah, blah,* Troy says, telling me everything I already know from reading his lawsuit, except for a few noticeable edits. First off, he refers to the "unnamed woman" as "the record guy's ex-girlfriend." Which, again, makes me think it has to be Isabel. And, second off, seeing as how he's trying to pick me up, Troy gallantly says he "hooked up with" Reed's ex, rather than explicitly saying they had sex. "And the next thing I knew," Troy says, "the bitch went straight to Reed and told him we'd hooked up, and that's when all hell broke loose. The guy went fucking psycho on me!"

My mind is racing. Reed's ex went straight to Reed after fucking Troy, huh? Now, why would she do that? Could it be she'd only screwed Troy to make Reed jealous? "How did the record label guy go psycho? What'd he do?"

"He dropped my band from his label, shelved our album and music video, and totally blackballed me in the industry, so I couldn't get signed anywhere else, or hired for any tours or festivals."

I gasp like I'm shocked. "What a dick!"

"Yep."

So, is Troy going to mention Reed beating his ass, too? He made a huge thing about that in his lawsuit, after all. Or does he not want me imagining that smoking hot record label guy kicking his emo ass? "Is that everything the label guy did to you? Anything else?"

"I think he did more than enough. Don't you?"

"Oh, yeah. I just mean, *how* did he blackball you? What did he say?"

Troy takes a drink of his beer. "Oh, you know. He just talked a bunch of shit about me to all his powerful friends in the music industry."

I scoff. "None of it true?"

"Nope."

"What a jerk."

Hmm. Troy just lied to me. I believe most of what he's told me about Reed, actually... but something about this thing—the blackballing—doesn't ring true to me. I can't imagine Reed picking up the phone and spreading flat-out lies about Troy. Reed cares too much about his reputation and name to do something like that. But then again, Reed is a scorched-earth kind of guy. And he *did* settle with Troy, so who knows how far Reed might have taken his vendetta.

Troy babbles for a bit longer, about how great his band was and how big they would have been if Reed hadn't been such a wack job asshole psychopath who thought he "owned" his ex-girlfriend's body for eternity. And while Troy talks, I google Reed on my phone, pretending to get up to speed.

When a photo of Reed and Isabel lands on my screen, I gasp. "Wait. This guy dated *Isabel Randolph*? She's my *favorite!*" I look up, wide-eyed and whisper, "Was *Isabel* the one you hooked up with?"

Troy smirks devilishly, telegraphing the answer to my question is a resounding *yes*. But then he leans forward and whispers, "The woman isn't identified in the public record, though. So you guessed that. I didn't tell you anything."

"Gotcha," I say, returning his wink.

I was already almost positive the "unnamed woman" had to be Isabel, of course. The timing was exactly right. Plus, several articles about Reed and Isabel mention they dated off and on for a while before finally entering into their well-documented two-year relationship. So, it makes sense Isabel could have slept with Troy during an "off" period with Reed, which then brought the pair together again. This time, for two years. But, still, even if I was expecting to hear Isabel's name in relation to all of this, it's nonetheless a blow to actually hear it, and realize Reed went *that* ballistic when another man slept with her.

For a moment, I feel like I'm going to burst into tears at the sense of loss I'm feeling. The rejection. The betrayal. Why did Reed pick a stolen moment in a garage with Isabel over a future with me? I would have given him *everything*. All of me.

I take a deep breath, force my emotion down, and plaster a fake smile on my face. "Here's what I don't get, Troy. Why'd that record label guy settle your lawsuit? Seeing as how he went so scorched earth on you for hooking up with his ex-girlfriend, it seems like he's the kind of guy who'd go equally scorched earth on you in the court case, as well."

Troy takes a swig of his beer and empties it. So, I quickly buy him another one, to keep him nice and loose. "Actually, he told me he'd 'never' settle with me—'not in a million years.' He said he'd 'see me in hell' before he'd pay me a dime." Troy smirks. "Little did he know, though, I had an ace in my pocket, which I used to bring him to his knees."

I lean forward, egging him on. "Oooh, this is gonna be good."

Troy pauses. "Shoot. Sorry. As much as I want to tell you, this part isn't in the public record."

"So, help me *guess* it. What sort of thing was this 'ace in your pocket'? Information?"

He nods. "Confidential information he didn't want anyone to know."

My eyebrows ride up. "About *him*?"

Troy smiles deviously. "No. About his ex."

"The one...?" I point to my phone, referencing the photo of Isabel Randolph I showed him earlier, and Troy nods.

"It was something, to this day, she'd never want the world to know about her. So, I thought, 'Hey, if he cares so much about me hooking up with his ex, then he'll probably pay to keep the world from finding out her secret.' And guess what? I was right."

My heart is thumping. I'm on the bitter cusp of blowing this thing wide open—whatever "this thing" is. "Holy crap, Troy. You're a genius." *And a disgusting blackmailer.* "She told you this secret?"

Troy shakes his head. "Not intentionally. She and I were watching TV together one night, just her and me, when a news story came on TV that made her gasp in shock. It was a news story about a particular woman. So, I was like, *Do you know her*? And his ex said, no, she didn't know the woman in the news story. But it was obvious she was lying." He snorts. "So much for her being a talented actress, huh? So I told her, 'Hey, I know you're lying. And I know why you must be lying. But don't worry, your secret is safe with me.' And I swear I was planning to keep my promise to her. But then, when she went straight to her ex to tell him we'd hooked up, and he went fucking crazy on me, I was like, 'Well, fuck my promise.' So, I told the label guy I'd sell her secret to the highest bidding tabloid, if he didn't settle my lawsuit. And that was that. He settled with me the very next day."

Holy shit. Doesn't this idiot realize what he just described to me was textbook extortion? Reed didn't settle Troy's *lawsuit*, he succumbed to a brazen blackmail scheme... and only to protect Isabel!

Oh, God. I'm reeling. I don't want to swoon over Reed being Isabel's white knight. I don't want to hear that Reed would slay any dragon for that woman—because it only twists the knife already lodged in my heart. But I can't help swooning, just a little bit, despite myself, to realize, yet again, Reed really is a ride or die kind of guy for the people he loves. Like he told me once, if you're on his short list, he'll do *anything* for you.

Too bad I never made it onto his short list. I clear my throat. "Good for you, Troy. That label guy screwed you over, so you screwed him over, even harder. That's *so* hot."

Troy licks his lips. "*You're* so hot." With that, he leans forward, obviously intending to kiss me. Abruptly, I jerk back and take a long drink of my club soda, pretending not to realize I just stiff-armed him.

"So, come on. Give me a little hint about that secret."

I jut out my breasts, and Troy's gaze drifts directly to them, right on cue.

But, dammit, he shakes his head. "For all I know, you could sell the secret to the tabloids, or tell someone else who'd do that. One way or another, the information could get out, and then the psycho would know I'd talked, and he'd sue me for breaching the confidential settlement."

Damn. I bet if I slept with Troy, I could get him to sing to me like a canary about this secret. But that's never going to happen. Not in a million years. Even if I found Troy attractive, which I *don't*, it's clear to me now my heart still belongs to Reed, whether I like it or not. And that means my body belongs to him, too—simply because that's the way I'm wired. When I love, I do it with everything I am. My heart, mind, body, and soul.

Troy touches my arm, making me stiffen, and leans into me. "You have really pretty eyes, Georgia."

I feel no need to correct him on my name. In fact, I'm glad he got it wrong. "Thank you, Troy. So do you."

Troy leans forward, *again*, obviously intending to kiss me, so, I jerk back, *again*, and sip my water. But it's obvious my little jerk-back-cluelessly maneuver isn't going to work a third time. Next time, Troy is going to get up and find someone else to hit on. Someone who'll give him the green light. Which means I need to pry this secret out of this bastard's blackmailing mouth right now, before it's too late.

I put my elbow onto the bar and bat my eyelashes. "I don't normally tell people this, Troy, but I'm super close with someone who writes for *Rock 'n' Roll*. You know, the music magazine?" Troy perks up like a Labrador whose owner is holding up a tennis ball. "I bet if I told this writer about you—and how talented and sexy you are, and how this Reed guy screwed you over—she'd be interested in interviewing you for a featured article."

"Oh my God. That would be *huge*."

"The only thing is," I say coyly. "She's not easy to impress. Honestly, she's always saying she's got a line around the block of musicians wanting her to write about them. So, I think I'd need to tell her you're willing to divulge something more than what's in the public record for the article—or at least, to drop a sizeable hint that will allow *her* to figure it out on her own—*wink, wink*—if you want to have any chance of her coming down here to meet you."

Troy looks pained. "I really can't say anything too specific about that secret."

"Oh, yeah, I totally get it. But you figured it out, based on a news story on TV, right?"

He nods.

"Well... What was the news story? That's got to be in the public record. Maybe this *Rock 'n' Roll* reporter could follow the same breadcrumbs you followed, without a word from you, and figure it out for herself. Maybe this writer for *Rock 'n' Roll* was researching an article about Reed Rivers, so she went to the courthouse to look at the lawsuits filed against him, and she noticed *your* lawsuit, and she read it, and then *happened* to see whatever news story *you* saw... And then, *she* put two and two together, *without a word from you*."

Troy is lit up. *He gets it.* "Yeah, I think that could work!"

"Of course, it'll work." I lean forward conspiratorially and put my fingertips on his forearm. "Who was the woman in the news story? I'll tell this writer her name, and she'll research it, and take it from there."

Troy pauses, his wheels turning. But, finally, it's obvious his ambition has won out over his fear of Reed. "Francesca Laramie."

My heart is racing. "Francesca Laramie?"

He nods. "Tell your friend to look her up. It won't be hard for her to put two and two together, from there."

With that, he licks his lips and goes in for a kiss.

But I'm outta here. "Let's not," I say, popping up from my barstool. "It kills me to do this, Troy, since you're so hot and talented, and I want nothing more than to go home with you right now and screw the living hell out of you. But if this label guy is as big a psycho as you say, then you have to be extra careful. There shouldn't be any connection between you and me and this writer for *Rock 'n' Roll*." I jut my chin at the bartender. "For all we know, he's reporting back to the record label guy. We shouldn't be seen leaving together." I gather up my purse. "I'm going to tell this writer about you *right now*. Bye!"

"Wait! Georgia! Take my number, at least, so your writer friend can call me!"

"No, no, that's way too risky. If this writer is interested in the story, she'll come to Slingers on a night when you're performing. That way, if Reed ever comes down here, after the article comes out—or God forbid, sues you for breaching the confidential settlement agreement—you'll be able to swear truthfully, under oath, that's how you first met her. She showed up at the bar."

Troy looks vaguely convinced by that. "Yeah... Okay."

I tap my temple and wink. "Bye now, hon. So awesome talking to you!"

And off I go, sprinting out the door, as fast as my devious little legs will carry me, and then laugh to myself like a madwoman as I sprint to my nearby car in the cool Los Angeles night.

SEVENTY-ONE
REED

Wednesday 2:35 am

I roll onto my opposite side and look at the clock on my nightstand. This is pointless. I'm not going to be able to fall asleep while my brain is still wracked with images of Georgina having sex with someone else. Oh, God. I roll over again, feeling like I'm going to puke from stress.

After my horrifying phone call with Georgina ended, I drove straight to her hotel, thinking maybe she was lying to me about not being there, simply to keep me from coming. But she wasn't there. So, I chatted up the concierge in the lobby, trying to figure out what nearby clubs or bars had live music. Specifically, what places might have featured a solo musician tonight, since Georgina said, "And when *the* musician is done performing..." But, unfortunately, the concierge didn't have any useful suggestions.

After that, I drove around aimlessly, like a madman, scoping out random hotspots, in search of Georgina's parked car. And when I didn't see Georgina's car anywhere—not surprisingly, considering I was looking for a needle in a haystack in a city of four million people—I simply kept going. Driving. Searching. Freaking out.

When my search of Hollywood came up empty, I drove to Westwood—the neighborhood immediately adjacent to UCLA—figuring Georgina might have gone back to her old stomping grounds. I even went into Bernie's Place, looking for her. But, nope. She wasn't there, either. At every turn, I came up empty-handed. No Georgina.

And that's when I had a batshit crazy, paranoid thought: what if, when Georgina casually referenced "the musician," she meant to do it? What if that wasn't a slip or an incidental bit of information I'd cleverly picked up on? What if that telltale phrase had been the entire point of Georgina's little speech to me? What if Georgina was actually calling me, *specifically* to tell me, in code, she was heading into a bar to watch a performance... by *Troy Eklund*?

The very thought of Georgina being in the same room with Troy nearly sent me into cardiac arrest. My rational brain knew I was being paranoid, and that the chances were slim. But then again, Georgina did know all about Stephanie Moreland. So, why wouldn't she know about Troy, too?

I googled Troy's name and quickly found out he was scheduled to play at some dive bar called Slingers in West Hollywood tonight. So, off I went, all the way back to that side of town. Even though I knew I'd *literally* commit murder, thereby ruining my life, if I walked into that bar and found Troy with his hands or lips on Georgina.

Thankfully, though, when I got to Slingers, I didn't see Troy, or Georgie, anywhere. And when I chatted up the bartender, I found out Troy had played his set earlier, as scheduled, thereafter flirted with several women, per usual, and then left about fifteen minutes before my arrival with a blonde who'd practically swallowed his face in the few minutes before they'd cut out. Also, per usual. It was all excellent news, obviously. Also, proof I'm losing my damned mind.

Finally, when I'd exhausted all my ideas, I drove to Georgina's hotel. Which was where I saw her convertible in the parking lot. I was glad to see she'd returned to the hotel... but sick to my stomach to think she might not be alone in her room. Oh, God, how I toyed with the idea of going to Georgina's room and knocking on her damned door. But, somehow, I refrained. I forced myself to leave and drive home, even though my heart felt like it was bleeding.

And now, here I am. Tossing and turning as I await a return text from Georgina—confirmation she's alone in that fucking hotel room.

Exhaling in resignation, I grab my phone and tap out another text to her, asking her if she's home yet, even though I know she is... Also, even though I've already sent her three similar texts, none of which she's answered.

Are you back at your hotel yet? PLEASE REPLY.

This time, Georgina texts back immediately.

I told you not to text me, Mr. Rivers.

A huge smile spreads across my face. If she's answering me, then she's alone. Has she been alone all night... or did whatever guy from the bar just now leave?

Me: Just want to make sure you're safe and sound.

Georgina: Do I need to sic my lawyers on you? That's four texts tonight. You've long since crossed into stalker territory, dude.

Me: I thought you said you were turning off your phone until morning.

Georgina: I lied. That's this thing where a person says one thing but does another. Oh, wait, I don't need to explain that to you. You know all about lying, don't you?

Again, I smile. Even when Georgina is bitch-slapping me, she turns me on.

Me: Are you back at your hotel?
Georgina: None of your business.
Me: Just want to be sure you're safe.
Georgina: My safety isn't your concern.
Me: Yes, it is. You're my friend, remember? Also, you're working on the special issue. While you're doing that, your safety is my top priority. If you don't tell me where you are, then I'll call your father to ask him if he

happens to know how to use the "Find My iPhone" feature. I'm assuming you're on your father's phone plan?

Georgina: Goddammit! You can't keep doing that! Yes, I'm at my hotel, you wack job! I've been here for well over an hour, doing research on my laptop.

Me: Did you get hit on at the bar?

Georgina: What do you think?

My heart rate spikes.

Me: But did you come back to your room alone?

Georgina: None of your business. But because I'm a saint, and we're friends, I will admit the guy who hit on me at the bar was a turd. He was good looking, but within two minutes of talking to him, I hated his guts. And not in a good way. Not the way I hate your guts. Like, for real.

I sigh with the force of a thousand hurricanes. And smile at the backhanded compliment.

Me: Thank you for telling me that. I had a semi-psychotic breakdown tonight, imagining you going home with someone else. The thought damn near gave me a stroke. I actually drove around for hours tonight, aimlessly looking for your parked car outside random bars.

Georgina: You did not.

Me: I did. Bernie says hi, btw.

Georgina: You went to Bernie's Place? Well, that's not crazy or anything.

Me: You drive me crazy.

Georgina: Good.

Me: Georgie, let me come to your hotel now. I need to see you.

Georgina: It's almost 3:00.

Me: I don't care.

Georgina: Well, I do. I've got important meetings at work tomorrow, including one with CeeCee and Zasu. I need to get some sleep, so I can kick ass tomorrow.

I feel oddly encouraged about this entire exchange. She isn't shutting down the concept of seeing me, really. She seems to be saying now isn't a good time.

Me: Okay, let me take you out to dinner tomorrow night.

Georgina: Zasu and I are doing a working dinner tomorrow night, probably until late into the night.

Me: Lunch tomorrow, then.

Georgina: Like I said, I'm going to be in meetings at RnR tomorrow.

Me: Still, you need to eat.

Georgina: I'll grab a sandwich at my desk.

Me: When can I see you?

Three little dots wiggle underneath my text, signaling Georgina is typing. But, suddenly, the dots disappear. And no text from her arrives for a long moment. I stare at the screen for what seems like forever, willing something to appear, until, finally:

Georgina: I'm sure our paths will cross organically, thanks to the special issue. Let's let fate take the wheel.

Me: Fuck fate. I'm taking the wheel.

Georgina: I've got to get some sleep. Goodnight, Reed.

. . .

I stare at my phone. Excitement, disappointment, determination, relief coursing through me. Finally, I tap out my reply.

Me: Goodnight, sweetheart. Sweet dreams. XO

Again, those three little wiggling dots appear underneath my text, and I hold my breath, praying for a little "XO" from Georgina in reply to mine. But another text from Georgina never comes. And so, finally, I put my phone on the nightstand, roll over and force myself to sleep.

SEVENTY-TWO
GEORGINA

Wednesday 11:34 am

"Welcome back, CeeCee!" After hugging her enthusiastically, I take the chair across from her at her large glass desk. "Thank you so much for agreeing to see me privately, before our meeting with Zasu."

"Margot said it was an 'urgent' personal matter. Are you okay?"

"Yes, I'm fine. How was Bali?"

"It was wonderful. But let's talk about this personal matter." She looks anxious. "Do you have a problem with Zasu?"

"Oh, gosh, no. Zasu is a goddess. I worship her. No, it's... I don't really know how to say this, so I'm just going to spit it out." I take a deep breath. "It's about Reed Rivers."

"Oh?"

"We had a bit of a fling, CeeCee. A highly mutual, consensual, amazing, fun fling for a week at his house. And then he was an asshole. And now it's over."

CeeCee furrows her brow. "I'm sorry to hear that."

"No, it's fine. It couldn't have ended any other way. But my fling with Reed isn't what prompted me to ask for this meeting, specifically. That's merely context so you understand what I'm about to ask you."

Anticipatory dread overtakes CeeCee's elegant face. "Okay..."

I take a deep breath and proceed to unload the entire, embarrassing, enthralling, heartbreaking story. All of it. Including my discovery that Reed donated the money for my grant. "Honestly, knowing Reed funded the grant is making me question if I got this job on the merits of my writing. Forgive me if this is an insulting question, but did you and Reed broker a deal where you both got the special issue, Reed got access to some tits and ass he wanted, and you got that coveted interview of Reed you've been wanting for two years?"

CeeCee looks ashen. "Oh my gosh, Georgina. *No!* I'm heartbroken you've even had to wonder these things! I promise you, the way the grant happened wasn't like that at all—though I totally understand how it looks that way to you. Darling, I would have hired you, regardless. You're a star. I knew it the minute I met you. And then I read your writing samples, and I knew I had to have you, no matter what."

My shoulders soften. My spirit expands. "Oh, I'm so relieved to hear you say that."

CeeCee explains everything to me, all of which is right in line with what Reed told me in his texts.

"Yeah, that's pretty much what Reed told me in some texts," I admit. "I just wanted to hear it from you before I let myself believe it."

"Do you mind letting me read what Reed texted you about all this?"

"Sure. It's everything you just said."

I pull out my phone and she reads all of Reed's lengthy messages about the grant.

When she's done reading, CeeCee hands my phone back to me. "I agree with almost everything Reed wrote. But, in the interest of transparency, I should tell you there are a couple places where my narrative differs from his." She threads her manicured fingers together onto her glass desk. "First of all, Reed doesn't know this, but I was kind of messing with him during our initial discussion about you. I was going to hire you, no matter what, Georgina. *With* pay, by the way, one way or another. I'd already decided that when Reed called and started asking me about you. I acted like I was on the fence when Reed brought you up, simply because he seemed so damned interested in talking about whether I was going to hire you, and then he was so adamant I should pay you. It was so out of character for him, I wanted to test the waters and see what the hell was motivating him. But the truth is, I wasn't going to let you slip through my fingers, whether Reed had called me or not."

"Thank you so much. That means the world to me."

"It's the truth. But then Reed offered to pay your salary! Ha! And I knew my hunch was right. He'd seen you at the panel discussion and had been flirting with you the whole time, just like I'd thought."

I gasp. "You saw us flirting?"

"Darling, Reed wasn't subtle. And neither were you." She chuckles. "But, still, I never would have assigned you to work on the special issue—effectively serving you up on a silver platter to that horny heathen of a man—were it not for a few things. First off, when I told you about the special issue, you let it slip you'd already looked up Reed on Wikipedia. Well, that's when I knew I'd seen things correctly at the panel. You'd been flirting with Reed, every bit as much as he'd been flirting with you. Why else would you already have looked him up at that point? And then, you expressly *asked* if you could sleep with an interview subject. Ha!" She snorts. "I loved that you did that, by the way. But, again, I knew at that point I wasn't sending Little Red Riding Hood straight to the Big Bad Wolf."

I blush.

"But there was something else that sealed the deal for me. Something that made me feel especially confident about assigning you to River Records." She leans forward and places her forearms onto her desk. "Your father's expensive medicine, darling. Paying for that was Reed's idea, not mine. And that told me you'd caught the attention of more than Reed's libido. I knew, somehow, you'd caught the attention of his generous heart."

My heartbeat is thrumming in my ears. I can barely breathe.

"Plus, your father wasn't the only person Reed helped that day. That generous man donated a quarter million dollars to my favorite cancer charity, even though only a fraction of that sum was needed to cover your salary and your father's medication."

I clutch my heart, feeling overwhelmed with love for Reed.

"And *then,* as if all that weren't enough, Reed agreed to let you peel a layer of his onion. And that was the last straw for me. I knew, for certain, even if Reed didn't realize it himself: you'd caught his attention in a way that far exceeded lust. Frankly, I don't know how you did that from across a crowded lecture hall. That's some special kind of magic, darling. You cast a spell on that man in a way I'd never seen anyone else do, in ten years of knowing him. Now, did I *also* get what I wanted out of the deal? Yes, I did. The special issue was a coup for me. And getting him to agree to a more in-depth interview than he'd given before was also a huge coup. But I did *not* serve you up to Reed as a sexual object. And I did *not* hire an intern I didn't already desperately want to hire. And I did *not* pimp you out or otherwise sell you like a piece of meat."

I bite my lower lip. "I have a confession to make. I didn't cast my spell at the panel discussion. Reed and I ran into each other later that night at the bar where I worked. We talked and flirted quite a bit and really hit it off."

CeeCee palms her forehead. "Now everything makes sense! I was wondering how you'd managed to knock him onto his ass from across a crowded room."

"Well, yeah. I'm good, darling. But I'm not *that* good."

We both laugh uproariously.

"I left the bar with him that night, intending to sleep with him. He drove me to his house, but we never made it inside. We got into a heated argument at his front gate, and I took off in an Uber."

CeeCee hoots with gleeful laughter. "No wonder he was willing to move heaven and earth to get another bite at your glorious apple." She smirks. "And if I'm not mistaken, the apple was rather desperate to get herself bitten, too?"

I blush and nod. "After I cooled down, I was pissed at myself for leaving that night."

Again, CeeCee laughs deliriously. "Oh, my sweet Georgina. You're endlessly entertaining." She sighs. "I'm sorry if all of these shenanigans made you doubt yourself, and the fact that you got hired on your merits. I'm also sorry you doubted Reed. He's actually a wonderful man."

"Except for the fact that he messed around with Isabel when he'd promised to be exclusive with me."

CeeCee frowns sharply. "I'm honestly shocked by that. I never would have expected that of Reed. He's a bit of a fibber sometimes. A good salesman who's spectacularly adept at getting what he wants. But

I've never once thought of him as an actual liar or cheater. On the contrary, when it comes to important things—the people he cares deeply about—I've always known Reed's word to be golden."

I press my lips together at the painful thought flickering across my mind: *Yeah, well, ipso facto, I guess that proves Reed never really cared deeply about me.*

CeeCee juts her lower lip in sympathy with whatever she's seeing on my face. "Aw, sweetheart, I don't know what happened between Reed and Isabel in that garage. The only two people who will ever know for sure are Reed and Isabel, unfortunately. But whatever he's been telling you about that, I think it's highly likely he's telling you the truth, the same way he told you the truth about the grant. I'd bet anything on it."

I shrug. "Reed says he kissed her goodbye, and that it only made him realize he only wants me. But I've been cheated on before, CeeCee. And that's *exactly* what my ex said. Plus, I know myself. I'm not going to be able to forgive and forget. I'm not the kind of person who trusts easily in the first place. So, no matter what 'epiphanies' Reed might have gained from kissing Isabel—or doing whatever else he might have done with her—I'm not going to be able to trust him completely, again. And that will doom us. So why hop aboard that train again, when I know it will ultimately lead to Misery Town, USA?"

She nods. "I get it."

"If I knew for *certain* Reed only kissed Isabel, and that it truly made him realize he only wanted me... I think I could forgive and forget and move on. Everyone makes mistakes. We were still so new, and he was saying goodbye to someone he'd been linked to for a long time. I think I could process that. But like you said, the only two people who will ever know for sure what happened in that garage are Reed and Isabel. And I don't want to jump back into a relationship where there's not one hundred percent trust."

She looks pained. "Will this affect your ability to complete Reed's interview?"

"No. I've already got everything I need for my article. I just need to write it now. And it's not like I hate Reed. Honestly, I still like him, despite everything. I'm not sure how that's possible, but I do."

"I know how. He's fatally charming."

"Yes, he is. We've agreed to be 'friends.'"

CeeCee and I exchange a look, both of us acknowledging that's a crock.

"So, did I address all your concerns?" CeeCee asks.

"Yes. Thank you. I'm excited to get to work on all my artist interviews."

She looks at her watch. "Speaking of which, shall I buzz Margot to have Zasu come in? It's still a bit early, but I'm sure Zasu is here somewhere, and I can't wait to hear what you two have come up with."

"Actually, can I run a quick idea past you? Something for *Dig a Little Deeper*?"

She withdraws her hand from the intercom. "Of course."

"What do you think about an in-depth interview of Isabel Randolph?"

CeeCee looks at me like I just threw up on her desk. "As in, the woman who walked into Reed's garage and blew your fairytale fling with him to Kingdom Come?"

"Okay, hear me out on this. Isabel doesn't know I had a fling with Reed, and I won't tell her, or anyone else. I met her at Reed's party, before everything between Reed and me blew up, and she said yes to an interview. She promised to go deeper than her usual interview, CeeCee. To give me something she's never given to anyone. So, why should I pass up this golden opportunity, just because a guy I had a fling with did who knows what with her in a garage? I'm a professional. I can separate my personal and professional feelings."

CeeCee narrows her eyes. "Could it be you're dying to get her alone so you can ask her what happened between her and Reed in that garage?"

My face blasts with heat. If I'm being honest, I have, indeed, *fantasized* about myself doing that very thing. But it doesn't take a brain surgeon to quickly realize that little fantasy would backfire spectacularly on me. First off, Isabel would never tell me the truth, anyway. She's engaged to Howard, after all. So, of course, she'd cling with white knuckles to the story she told me outside the garage—that Reed was showing her his car collection.

Also, asking Isabel about what happened would require me to reveal my fling with Reed. Maybe even that I've developed serious feelings for him. Which, in turn, would cause Isabel to feel duped about the interview and storm out, probably. And then what? Who knows what kind of fit Isabel might pitch for having been ambushed like that? Would she blast *Dig a Little Deeper* and CeeCee for my unprofessional behavior? I think it's likely. And so, in the end, I've realized I can't risk torpedoing my fledgling career, or splashing mud on CeeCee or her magazine, to pull a stunt like that.

"CeeCee, I swear on my mother I wouldn't ask Isabel about what happened between her and Reed. It would almost certainly be a pointless exercise, anyway, and might even backfire on me."

CeeCee shakes her head. "It's still not a good idea for you to interview Isabel, even putting Reed aside. Isabel's not even a good interview subject, Georgina. I know she's a huge star. And with that big franchise deal she signed, I'm probably a fool not to jump at the chance to put her on a cover. But she's notoriously wooden and guarded in interviews. A real dud."

"Yeah, I've heard that. But I think she might open up to me about her engagement to Howard. Maybe I could ask her about that?"

CeeCee makes a face like she just bit into a lemon. "I have no desire to put that man's name inside the pages of my beloved magazine."

I knit my eyebrows together. "You mean Howard?"

"Correct."

"I thought you and Howard were friends. Did you have a falling out in the past ten years?"

CeeCee looks surprised. "Howard Devlin and I aren't friends, and never have been. Who told you we're friends?"

"Oh. Nobody. I assumed it because he was one of the guests at your fiftieth birthday party. I read the article in the George Michael issue."

CeeCee rolls her eyes. "A guest of mine brought Howard to my party as their plus-one. And, trust me, I was livid about it. I can't stand that creep. All my friends know that." She points her finger at me. "Stay away from him, Georgie, if your paths ever cross. From what I've heard, he's all hands with pretty young things like you. Stay. Away."

"Oh, don't worry about me. As a bartender, I've handled more than my fair share of dirty old men."

CeeCee's face turns dark and serious. "No, honey. You don't understand. I've heard some very disturbing rumors about Howard, regarding the young actresses who've worked with him over the years. Nothing I can personally confirm. The rumors have all been second and third hand. But, still, I believe what I've heard. In fact, I've been wanting to do an exposé on that bastard for years. But nobody I've talked to will confirm the rumors. And who could blame them? What young actress would want to torpedo her budding career by pointing her finger at one of the most powerful producers in Hollywood—especially regarding something that would pit her word against his, or maybe even confirm she succumbed to his advances, and slept her way to the top? Howard can make and break careers, at his whim. Look at Isabel! She's been his favorite forever and look at her now. She's landed the biggest four-picture deal any lead actress has ever had. Imagine that."

"All the more reason for me to do that interview of Isabel. I could subtly try to get information out of her about those Howard rumors."

CeeCee scoffs. "Isabel is the last person who'd rat out Howard. Obviously, she's firmly hitched her plow to his wagon. Truth be told, that's one of the reasons I've always said no to Isabel's publicist. Because I'm so annoyed with her for being in Howard's pocket. Especially now that she's wearing his ring, I have zero respect for her. She did what she had to do to get ahead, obviously, but that doesn't mean I respect her."

I think back to my conversation with Isabel at the party. To how charming she seemed. How genuinely sweet. Of course, minutes later, my impression of her was shattered by her smeared lipstick and tousled hair, coupled with Reed's guilty-as-sin expression. But, still, there was genuine sweetness about her when we spoke at the party. And a deep sadness about her, too, especially when her eyes fell on Howard across the party... and she turned and walked in the exact opposite direction.

"Maybe she's more sympathetic when it comes to Howard than you think. Maybe he's been a creep to her, too. Maybe she's marrying him because, it's like, if you can't beat 'em, join 'em."

CeeCee's features soften. "You're kind, Georgina. That's a very kind take on the situation, especially given the fact that Isabel played a part in breaking your heart."

I shake my head. "Isabel isn't the one who broke my heart. Reed did that. For all Isabel knew, Reed was single when they went into that garage together. Yeah, Isabel cheated on her beloved fiancé, but that's her business."

CeeCee studies me for a long beat, her wheels visibly turning. "You really think you could interview Isabel, without breaking down and asking her about Reed?"

"I know I could. I swear to you, I wouldn't ask her about that."

CeeCee narrows her eyes. "All right. Go for it, Georgina."

"Woohoo!"

"Fair warning, though. I might scrap the interview, if it's not interesting enough. But feel free to give it the ol' college try. With those superhero movies all over the news, it's actually a coup for us to get this interview."

"Do I have permission to poke around, gently, about Howard, if I see an organic opening?"

"Yes. But do it subtly, Georgina. I know you're brilliant at that. Don't let her know what you're doing."

"Yes, ma'am. Her publicist already texted me some dates. Isabel's not available until much later in the summer, unfortunately. So, in the meantime, how about I snoop around and see if I can make any progress with some of those young actresses you've heard rumors about?"

"No," CeeCee says firmly, wagging her finger at me. She shoots me a little *Tsk.* "I appreciate your enthusiasm. It's exactly what attracted me to you in the first place. But the Howard exposé is too hot for a newbie to handle on her own. Get yourself some experience and we'll revisit the idea another time. Maybe you'll get something from Isabel that might prove helpful and we'll circle back."

I sigh with resignation, and CeeCee chuckles at my dejected reaction.

"Darling, you've got plenty to do, without running around trying to talk to actresses about their experiences with Howard Devlin. You've got artists to interview for the special issue. Plus, a mind-blowing article to write about Reed for *Dig a Little Deeper*. And who knows? Maybe you'll wind up bringing me something fantastic about Isabel Randolph, too."

SEVENTY-THREE
REED

Wednesday 3:17 pm

I'm sitting at my desk at River Records, listening to some demos forwarded to me by my team. But my heart isn't in it. Because... *Georgina.* Right this very minute, she could be meeting with CeeCee. *And talking about me.*

I've got no doubt CeeCee's recollection of our initial conversation about the special issue and the grant will match everything I told Georgina in my texts. The truth is the truth. But, still, I'd be lying if I said I wasn't a little stressed about their conversation. Is Georgie telling CeeCee that she caught me coming out of my garage with Isabel? And if so, is Georgina erroneously saying I *fucked* Isabel? God, I want to crawl into a hole to think CeeCee is hearing either version of the story. But I'd be especially ashamed for CeeCee to think I fucked Isabel after having the best week of my life with Georgie.

An email notification from Leonard with the notation "URGENT" on the subject line flashes across my screen, so I quickly click out of the marketing plan I've been reviewing and into Leonard's email. It's about the copyright infringement lawsuit against Red Card Riot. We filed a motion for summary judgment on Monday, and it seems the plaintiff's attorney has now offered to dismiss the case, even before the motion gets ruled on by the judge. His only request? We have to agree not to pursue reimbursement of our attorneys' fees from his clients, which is something we'd be entitled to do under the applicable copyright infringement statute, if we were to win the motion.

I type out a quick reply, telling Leonard to take the deal, just to put the thing behind us. "But tell that motherfucker he'd better dismiss his lawsuit within twenty-four hours, or I'm riding that summary judgment motion all the way up his ass until it's coming out his mouth."

I've no sooner pressed "send" on my email to Leonard, when my phone rings with an incoming call—and the minute I see Georgina's name on my screen, my heart leaps and bounds, even as my palms begin to sweat with anxiety.

"Hey, baby," I say, trying to make my voice sound casual, even though I'm freaking out. "Did you talk to CeeCee yet?"

"Yes. At length. And, please, don't call me baby."

"What'd she say?"

"She said she loved every idea Zasu and I pitched for the special issue."

"What'd she say about the grant?"

Georgina pauses. "Yeah... about that. That part of our meeting was... disappointing, Reed. To say the least."

My stomach clenches. *Fuck.* "How so?"

There's another long pause, during which I feel like my stomach is turning inside out.

"Ha! I'm just screwing with you, dude. CeeCee said 'ditto' to everything you said in your texts."

I groan loudly with relief. "Oh my God, you evil woman. Are you trying to make me stroke out? So, CeeCee backed up everything I told you?"

"All of it. Although she did make a few clarifying comments."

My stomach somersaults. "*What* clarifying comments?"

"It doesn't matter. All that matters is that I not only forgive you for paying my salary and for all my father's expensive medication, I thank you profusely for doing both. Thank you, Mr. Rivers. Sincerely. You're an incredibly generous man, and I'm grateful."

My eyes widen in shock. I look around like a cartoon character for a moment, even though nobody is here with me in my office to see the gesture.

"Hello?" she says.

"Yeah... I was waiting for you to say you're kidding again."

"I'm not kidding. Thank you."

"Wow. That's way more than I was expecting. Thank you."

"No, no, no. Thank *you*." She laughs again. "Look, I know you donated to that cancer charity because you wanted to get laid. But guess what? I wanted to get laid, too. I understand how a person can have *concurrent* motivations, as we've discussed. The bottom line is CeeCee would have hired me, no matter what. And that's the most important thing."

I feel dizzy with relief. "Let's celebrate my complete vindication. Let me take you to dinner tomorrow night."

"I can't. Sorry. I'm flying to Seattle tomorrow, so I can interview 22 Goats on Friday."

Sorry, she said. Was that a figure of speech, or is she really sorry to miss the chance to have dinner with me? "When will you be back from Seattle? We'll do it then." I've managed to keep my tone casual, I think. But, inside, my body is a riot of excitement and hopeful anticipation.

"I'll be back from Seattle on Saturday," she replies, her tone as breezy and casual as mine.

"Great. I'll take you to dinner on Saturday night, and then to New York on Sunday morning."

"Excuse me?"

My heart is racing. But there's no turning back now. I'm taking my shot. "I promised to take you to an RCR concert this summer, remember? Well, RCR is playing at Madison Square Garden on Sunday night. Your birthday is at the end of this coming week, right?"

"Yes."

"Well, then, we'll call the trip a birthday present. I'll get tickets to some Broadway shows, too. How about *Hamilton*? You should see that one, if you haven't." I hold my breath, awaiting Georgie's reply. For the first time since I dropped an atomic bomb onto my own happiness, I feel hopeful. I feel *optimistic*.

But then I hear Georgina's voice, and I know I'm sunk.

"Reed," she whispers on an exhale. "We shouldn't do this."

"Why not? You said yourself, we're friends now. Well, let me take my *friend* to New York City as a birthday present."

"If I go on this trip with you, and let you try to 'seduce' me again, then what? It won't end well. We're doomed. So, what's the point?"

We're not doomed, I think. *We're destiny*. "Please, Georgie. I won't hurt you again. I promise." She's silent. And I'm desperate. "All right, then. This trip isn't a birthday present. It's a work obligation. I've got full discretion as to when and where I make my artists available for interviews. And I'm only making RCR available to you backstage before their concert at Madison Square Garden. Take it or leave it."

She scoffs. "Seriously?"

"Seriously."

"Wow, great plan, Mr. Rivers. Bully me into falling in love with you again."

My heart stops. It's the first time Georgina's used the "L" word. And it only makes me want to come at her that much harder. "Take it or leave it, Miss Ricci," I say sternly. "You can still interview Dean, individually, in Malibu, like we discussed. But this is the only way I'll serve up RCR to you, as a full band."

I can practically hear her eye roll over the phone line. "Fine, ya big dickhead. I'll take it. But I won't have dinner with you on Saturday night. And I won't fly to New York with you. I'll meet you backstage at the concert on Sunday, with my press pass around my neck."

"God, you're even more stubborn than me. I want to take you to my favorite restaurant in Manhattan."

"And I want to punch you in the face. Sometimes, we can't have everything we want in life."

I chuckle, despite my misery. "Georgina, this is stupid. Every time we talk, the chemistry between us is through the roof, and you know it."

"So what? Chemistry is a shortsighted thing to chase. If I can't trust you with my heart, there's no point in moving forward. Honestly, I wish I could trust you with my heart again, because, apparently, it still belongs to you, whether I like it or not. Along with my body. But I have to get over you, Reed. For my own good. You're nobody's Prince Charming. And yet, that's how I started thinking about you when I was following you around like a smitten puppy for a week. Is that really what you want? For some pie-eyed smitten puppy to start imagining you're her Prince Charming?"

Yes. The word pops into my mind, unbidden. *Yes, yes, yes.* That's exactly what I want, as long as the pie-eyed smitten puppy is *you.*

Georgina continues, "Now, stop trying to bully my affection out of me. Stop trying to buy it. And stop trying to wear me down with all this sweet-talk and razzle dazzle. The answer is *no.*"

"Georgina, you've got to know turning a 'no' into 'yes' is my favorite thing to do, when I want something badly enough. *And what I want is you.*"

"No, you don't. You want the *old* version of me. The one who let go for you, completely, the night of the necklace. Well, guess what? I won't be able to let go like that again, because I'll be imagining you screwing Isabel in that garage."

I feel too defeated to speak. Too full of despair and remorse. For the hundredth time since this disaster happened, I think about doing that thing... the thing that would almost certainly exonerate me... but also risk unleashing the kraken on me, and on Isabel, too, in a way I'd live to regret. Yet again, I decide I simply can't risk it.

"I'll see you in New York, Mr. Rivers," she says, breaking the thick silence. "Backstage at the RCR concert on Sunday night."

"I'll book your travel."

"No. It's official business, remember? *Rock 'n' Roll* will cover it."

Emotion threatens. My eyes sting. But I clear my throat and bite back the wave of emotion gripping me. "All right. I'll see you in New York, Miss Ricci. Travel safe."

SEVENTY-FOUR
GEORGINA

Wednesday 4:14 pm

After quite a bit of driving around, I find a parking spot in downtown LA and then start trekking the few blocks to my destination—a little hole-in-the-wall restaurant called "Dee-Lish." The eatery opened by Francesca Laramie after her release from prison three years ago. What were the crimes that sent Francesca to The Big House? Procurement of prostitution, conspiracy, tax evasion, and money laundering, all stemming from the high-end escort service she ran in Los Angeles for almost twenty years. All of which leads me to the inescapable conclusion, based on what Troy Eklund told me, that Isabel's secret—the one Troy used to blackmail Reed into settling his lawsuit—was that, at one time or another, America's Sweetheart worked for Francesca Laramie as a paid escort.

But so what? Assuming it's true, is it something I'd write about? No. Just because I've discovered a secret about someone, that doesn't give me the right to reveal it to the world. Even if that someone happens to be a world-famous actress. Even if that someone happens to be the woman who fooled around with my man.

No matter how much Reed hurt me, I'm not going to ruin Isabel's life for a kiss. Or whatever happened in that garage. And I'm sure as hell not the kind of woman who'd shame another woman for doing whatever she wanted with her own body. Isn't that what CeeCee taught me, when I asked her if it was okay for me to sleep with an interview subject? Not to shame another woman for doing whatever the hell she wants with her own body? Well, then, I'm paying it forward. You're welcome, Isabel.

I admit I was devastated when Reed kissed Isabel. Or did whatever he did with her. But what I said to CeeCee was the truth: my issue is with *Reed*. Reed is the one who slipped that ruby necklace around my neck and called me his "queen." Reed is the one who told me nobody is allowed to hurt me, ever again, and then turned around and did just that.

Also, and this isn't a small thing, I have to think Reed hired Isabel as his paid escort the night of CeeCee's birthday party. Why else would they *both* lie about how they met? Why else would Reed say he and Isabel went on a blind date that night, and Isabel say she met Reed through Josh Faraday? Really, it makes perfect sense. Reed had a rented tux that night. A rented limo. So, why not a rented woman, too? He had a plan to convince the power players at that party, especially CeeCee, he belonged there. Apparently, he figured a hot blonde on his arm was the ultimate status symbol. And guess what? He was probably right.

Frankly, this realization about Reed doesn't shock me at all. Reed once told me he figured out how to be an "influencer" before the term was coined. He explained he figured out how to use his curated image as a "cool kid" to conquer the world. Well, bravo, Reed Rivers. If hiring Isabel was part of that strategy, then good for you. Look at you now. I know Reed has hurt me. But he's also done amazingly wonderful things for my father and me. Life-changing things. And for that, he'll always have my loyalty and love. Which means Isabel's secret—and Reed's, too, if I'm right about him hiring Isabel—are safe with me.

So, why am I walking to Francesca's restaurant, then? Curiosity, I guess. Because she's a breadcrumb to follow, which is my favorite thing to do. And also because... who knows? Maybe talking to Francesca will lead me to something of interest to write about for *Dig a Little Deeper*. And if not, then, oh well. I'll have wasted a couple hours getting to meet a famous madam. No big deal.

I reach Francesca's small restaurant and peek in the window. And there she is. The woman I recognize from my online research. She's standing behind a counter, talking to a stout man in a white apron. As I was hoping, the place isn't bustling at this time of day. In fact, Francesca looks downright relaxed behind the counter.

As I grip the door handle, my stomach ripples with nerves. But I've come this far. I'm not turning back now. "Hi there, Ms. Laramie," I say, coming to a stop before her. "My name is Georgina Ricci. I was wondering if—"

"If you're a reporter, don't bother. I don't talk to reporters."

"Oh, no, I..." *Crap.* What now? "Can we go to a quiet spot? I just need five minutes of your time."

"For what purpose?"

It's a great question—one I don't know how to answer.

"The film rights to my story have already been sold," Francesca says, her arms crossed over her chest. "And I'm not interested in doing any more interviews about my life story."

"I'm not here to interview you like that. I'm just here to... get information for... someone. A friend of mine. One of the girls who used to work for you. She was targeted by a blackmailer. She's too famous to have come here herself. Could we speak privately, please? This is sensitive."

Francesca looks me up and down. And just when I think she's going to tell me to piss off, she turns to the stout guy in the white apron. "Mind the counter for me." She looks at me. "You've got five minutes."

I follow her through the restaurant's tiny kitchen to an even tinier office that's barely big enough for a small desk and chair. She closes the door, refolds her arms over her chest, and glares at me with hard, suspicious eyes. "Which girl?"

"Isabel Randolph."

Francesca nods. It's a subtle movement of her head, but unmistakable. Which is how I know my assumption about Isabel is spot-on: she did, in fact, work for Francesca at some point.

"Someone figured out she used to work for you, and now he's blackmailing her."

I've fudged the truth a bit. Made it sound like Troy is *presently* blackmailing Isabel, which I don't believe is the case. But I had to think of *something* to justify my presence here.

"Sorry to hear that. But it's not my problem."

In a flash, my mind sorts through the various interviewing tactics I learned in school—ways to get an interview subject to open up—and quickly settles on *confrontation*. "Candidly, Francesca, I thought maybe *you* could be the one blackmailing Isabel. Her four-picture deal has been all over the news. She's a big target now." Francesca opens her mouth, clearly ready to curse me out, but I add quickly, "Although Isabel told me, quite vehemently, you'd never do that to her. I just wanted to come here and meet you and get a read on you myself."

Francesca scoffs. "It's well documented I went to prison for eighteen months longer than I needed to, simply because I wouldn't give up a single name. Not of my girls, or my clients. And I never will." She narrows her eyes. "What are you? A paralegal? Some sort of private investigator?"

I shake my head. "I'm just trying to help Isabel. All her dreams are coming true, and now someone is threatening her."

Francesca shakes her head and exhales. "You know what really pisses me off? That anyone even has any leverage to blackmail her at all. There shouldn't be any shame attached to what she did. Same with what *I* did. There was a demand for a particular service, and I filled it. Simple as that. My girls were adults who came to *me*. I never solicited or trafficked anyone. They were all models and actresses who wanted to earn extra cash in between jobs. And I always told them, they had absolute discretion regarding what they would, or wouldn't do. That's what I told the clients, too. 'Treat my girls right, because if you don't, they won't do anything with you, no matter how much money you offer.' And yet, just because money changed hands, these girls, some of whom went on to become highly successful and famous, like Isabel, have to deal with assholes threatening to 'expose' them for their pasts? Where is the justice in that?"

"It's not fair at all."

"Are the men who used my services looking over their shoulders, worried someone might expose them? No, they're not. Because nobody cares about them. And yet, here I am, a *felon*, just because I ran a business in LA that's perfectly legal in New Zealand. It infuriates me that *I'm* the felon here, when I can think of a client who should have been thrown in jail a long time ago for hurting several of my girls. But does the

DA want to pursue *him*? Nope. That asshole terrorized my girls, without consequence, and yet I'm the one who had to go to prison and watch him collecting his Academy Awards on TV."

Holy crap. Was that a reference to Howard Devlin? I have a hunch it was. So, I decide to act like I'm in the know, to suss out more information. "Howard," I say matter-of-factly. Like there's no doubt in the world that's who we're talking about. "Yeah, I know all about him. I've actually been warned to stay away from him, for my safety."

Francesca's eyebrows shoot up. "By *Isabel*?"

And there it is. Confirmation my hunch was right. Because she didn't say, "Howard who?" Or, "I don't know what you're talking about." Nope. She immediately linked the name Howard to the name Isabel. Which tells me everything I need to know. "No, Isabel's never mentioned Howard's grabby hands. An older woman warned me. Someone I trust implicitly, who's very well connected in Hollywood. She told me he's rumored to have assaulted several young actresses—and that she fully believes the rumors to be true."

"She's right to believe them. You're an actress, then? A model?"

"No, I work for the older woman who warned me about Howard. My boss knows lots of celebrities."

"A word of advice? Listen to your boss and steer clear of Howard. Certainly, never accept a drink from him, if you know what I mean."

I inhale sharply, and she nods ominously.

"I didn't know what he was up to for a long time, or I never would have let him near my girls. None of them told me anything, at first. Apparently, he was masterful at dangling all sorts of carrots to get my girls—all of whom were aspiring actresses—to do all sorts of things they didn't want to do, off the books." She rolls her eyes. "And when they finally started tiring of his dangling carrots, and started refusing him services, he'd say he understood, and then invite them to his hotel room to 'have a drink' and 'discuss a part' he supposedly had in mind for them. And the next thing they knew, they were waking up in his bed, naked, groggy, with a terrible headache... and scorching pain in every hole."

My stomach physically revolts. "Oh my God. He needs to be stopped, Francesca. Maybe he's still doing it."

"Who would come forward to accuse him? They all know it'd be their word against his—and career suicide. Add to that, plenty of women are worried he'd out them for having worked for me. Or, possibly, saying yes to him to further their careers."

Crap. I know CeeCee told me not to pursue an article about Howard, but I can't imagine she'll stand by that position, once she hears all of this.

"Francesca, if any of the women who used to work for you came forward to—"

"They won't."

"But, if they *did*, would you—"

"They *won't*. Trust me on that."

"Just hear me out. Please. In a fantasy, a fairytale, an alternate reality where they *did* speak up about Howard, would you be willing to back them up and reveal what you know?"

"It's a pointless question. Nobody's going to say a word."

"Could you play along? *If* I could get some of the women who worked for you to speak up, maybe band together, would you come forward to support them with whatever you know?"

A puff of air escapes Francesca's nose. "I'm a felon, remember? My word is shit, according to the world."

I can barely stand still. *This is it.* The big story I've been waiting for! I feel it in my bones.

"I have a confession to make. My boss, the older woman I mentioned, is CeeCee Rafael—the owner of *Rock 'n' Roll* and another magazine called *Dig a Little Deeper*. I'm a summer intern at *Rock 'n' Roll*, assigned to write about music artists, but CeeCee's given me the green light to find interesting stories for *Dig a Little Deeper*, too. And I think this story about Howard is the one I've been searching for."

Francesca looks annoyed. But, thankfully, slightly amused by my exuberance, as well. "I don't talk to reporters. I told you that, right from the start."

"Yes, I know. Sorry. I didn't mean to mislead you. I really do know Isabel. And someone really *did* blackmail her about her connection to you. Which is what brought me here. Also, my boss really did tell me to stay away from Howard Devlin. But the full truth is that I'm trying to get hired onto the writing staff of CeeCee's magazine that's devoted to investigative journalism. I swear I have no desire to write about you, in particular. You're entitled to your privacy. And your story's already been written about quite a bit. I also promise I won't write about any of the girls you employed or the men who hired them. Except for *one* client. Howard Devlin. Who needs to be exposed and taken down by someone." I puff out my chest. "And that someone is *me*."

Francesca looks outright amused now. She can't hide it.

"Francesca, please. I'm a person who follows my gut. And it's telling me this is my purpose. My *calling*. My destiny."

Francesca presses her lips together. "Show me some proof you work for CeeCee Rafael."

I scramble into my purse and breathlessly pull out my ID and press pass. Also, as further proof I am who I say I am, I also hand her my student ID and a "membership card" from my favorite frozen yogurt place on campus. It's got eight stamps on it at the moment. One shy of getting my next yogurt free. Which proves, I think, I really did attend UCLA, just like my student ID would suggest.

Francesca looks over everything and hands it back to me, seemingly satisfied. "So, one minute you're worried about some asshole blackmailing Isabel, and the next you want to take down her fiancé?"

"I'm not entirely sure how Isabel fits into all this. All I know is she's engaged to a monster, and I'm going to take him down. I have no desire to hurt Isabel, but if she happens to get humiliated because she's engaged to a sexual predator, then sorry not sorry. Was Isabel one of the women who told you about Howard?"

"Like I said, I don't talk about my former girls or clients. Everything I've said in this room has been off the record, and totally confidential, and I'll sue your fucking ass, and your boss's, if you print a word of it."

My stomach twists. "I won't print a word of this conversation. I just want to do the right thing. This is highly personal for me. In high school, someone I trusted tried to rape me and I didn't say anything because he was far more powerful than me and I thought nobody would believe me. Looking back, I realize he was counting on me feeling too powerless to report him. And that's what Howard counts on, too. Well, fuck him. *Ciao, stronzo.* That's Italian for—"

"Yes, I know. Bye, asshole." For a long moment, Francesca stares at me, her face unreadable. Finally, she says, "As I've said, Georgina, I make it a firm rule to *never* name any of my clients."

My heart falls. Dang it. For a second there, I thought I had her. "I understand. Thank you for your time."

She puts her palm up. "But if you really think it will help your 'destiny' to be able to tell my former girls I'll corroborate their stories, then, yes, I'll do it. I'll make an exception to my firm rule, just this once. Only for Howard."

SEVENTY-FIVE
REED

Thursday 8:48 pm

After our waiter leaves our table, CeeCee leans back and says, "All right, my darling." She pushes aside her empty plate with purpose. "Now that I've got you nice and loose on a fabulous bottle of red, and your belly nice and full on a fantastic meal, it's time to talk about my magical unicorn of an intern. Georgina is obviously head over heels in love with you, Reed. And yet, you were stupid enough to do God knows what with Isabel in your garage?"

Damn. I've been waiting for CeeCee to bring up Georgina, ever since we sat down in this restaurant. Up until now, we've talked about Bali and the special issue. And, stupid me, when CeeCee hadn't yet chastised me for being a dipshit by the time our entrees were served, I started thinking maybe Georgina hadn't told her about The Garage Debacle, after all.

"What did Georgina say I did in that garage, exactly?" I ask calmly, even though my pulse is pounding.

"She doesn't know for sure. So, tell me. What did you do?"

My stomach tightens. "I kissed Isabel. It was a goodbye kiss."

"A little peck?"

I flash her a look that says, *What do you think?* And she smirks and flares her nostrils, nonverbally calling me a cad.

"She's marrying Howard, and I gave her a whopper of a kiss goodbye, to prove my point that she shouldn't marry Howard. Not to be with *me*, mind you. But I gave Isabel a kiss to remind her what it feels like to actually *feel* something. But, damn. The moment my lips touched Isabel's, I knew I was in love with Georgina."

CeeCee swoons. "Well, that's actually kind of romantic, in a twisted sort of way."

"It is, right? That's what I thought!"

"Oh, simmer down. I'm not the one you need to convince. And I'm sixty, for goodness sake. I've been around the block enough times to make your head spin, little boy. To me, one drunken goodbye kiss with an ex would merit an eye roll. But to sweet little Georgina, something like that is the Apocalypse. And understandably so. You broke her trust, Reed. Shattered her little newbie heart. Shame on you."

"Please, don't pile on, CeeCee. I'm well aware I've blown it. By the way, you'll be happy to know that little newbie totaled my Ferrari with a golf club that night in retribution for my transgression."

CeeCee's face lights up. "Seriously?"

"Yep."

CeeCee laughs uproariously. "Ha! My kind of woman."

"Mine, too."

"Yes, you made that abundantly clear, from the minute you first saw her—*at the lecture hall*. Yeah, that's right, Mr. Sneaky Pants. I saw the sparks flying between you two at the panel discussion. And then you called me, feigning curiosity about why I left the hall that day without saying goodbye to you. You actually had the audacity to say you'd only seen Georgina from the back? Ha! And *then* you offered to pay for Georgina's father's medical expenses, not just her salary?" She waves at the air. "Forget about it. I knew you were a goner."

"You knew I was full of shit from the moment I called you?"

"Do you think I'm stupid?"

"You played me like a violin."

"I did. If it makes you feel any better, though, you're a Stradivarius, darling."

"Is that why you sent Georgina straight to C-Bomb, as her 'top priority interview'?"

CeeCee bursts out laughing. "Guilty as charged. Did it work? Did you fall all over yourself, promising Georgina the best interview you've ever given, to lure her away from interviewing—and getting seduced by—C-Bomb?"

"You wicked woman."

"Thank you. That's high praise, coming from you."

"The highest."

We clink wine goblets.

"Don't pat yourself on the back too hard," I say. "I didn't give Georgina anything I wasn't already planning to give her." *Other than my heart.*

CeeCee juts her lower lip. "Aw, Reed. You're miserable."

"I am."

"Well, nothing's fatal except death. Win the girl back."

"That's the plan. When I finally see Georgina again, this Sunday at the RCR concert in New York"—I smile broadly—"I'm going to tell her, for the very first time, I love her." I'm rather impressed with myself. But CeeCee, not so much. "Well, shit. If you've got a better idea, let's hear it."

"I do, actually. Georgina told me she'd be able to forgive and forget, if only she knew for sure you gave Isabel a goodbye *kiss*, and nothing more."

My heart lurches. "Georgina said that?"

"She did. So, I know this sounds crazy, but—"

"CeeCee, did she actually *say* it, or *imply* it?"

"She said it. In those exact words. So, my idea is this: why not ask Isabel to call Georgina and tell her exactly what happened, in confidence? She's marrying Howard now, so she knows she can't have you for herself. Maybe she still cares enough about you to want you to be as happy as she is."

I drag my hand through my hair, buzzing with adrenaline. "No. I know exactly what I have to do now. I've been going back and forth for days on this idea. But I kept nixing it, because I know it'll open Pandora's Box. But now that I know Georgie said that..."

I tell CeeCee my idea—the one I first considered, and rejected, at

Hazel's birthday party. And CeeCee expresses extreme support for the idea. In fact, she tells me I'm a fool for not having done it sooner.

"The thing is," I say, "even though I'll be vindicating myself, I'll also be throwing Isabel under the bus—telling Georgina a secret she could use to hurt Isabel."

CeeCee waves dismissively. "So what if Isabel kissed you while wearing Howard's ring. She made her bed. Now she has to lie in it. The same way you've had to lie in your bed with Georgina."

I press my lips together. Isabel cheating on Howard isn't the "secret" I was talking about. I was talking about the same secret of Isabel's I've been guarding for ten years. Can I really divulge that information to Georgina, and trust her to keep it confidential, forevermore, in order to save myself? If I'm wrong about Georgina choosing her loyalty to me, over her shot at writing something salacious for *Dig a Little Deeper,* then it's *Isabel's* life and career that will be decimated, not mine. I *think* I can trust Georgina with this bombshell... but I also know how ambitious Georgina is... and also that she probably hates Isabel's guts for that kiss and would almost certainly revel in taking Isabel down.

But since I can't tell CeeCee about any of that, I decide to reply in a way that lets her continue thinking my concern is Georgina possibly outing Isabel to Howard. "I just need to feel certain Georgina won't use confidential information to try to take Isabel down with a hit piece."

"Have you forgotten I'm Georgina's publisher? I'm not going to publish gossip about Isabel's love life. I'll leave that to the tabloids. If you give Georgina this information and she immediately runs to Howard or includes it in an article on Isabel she submits to me, then I hate to say it, but maybe she isn't the woman you think she is. Or the writer *I* think she is. Which is all the more reason for you to do this. Either you trust her completely, including with this sensitive information, or you don't. It's as simple as that, Reed. You want Georgina to trust *you?* Well, you've got to trust her, too. Trust is a two-way street, sweetheart."

My chest tightens. "You're right. If I want Georgina to trust me, then I have to trust her first."

"Of course I'm right. I'm always right." CeeCee raises her wine glass. "To trust. True love is based on it, my dear. Which, I do believe, has been Georgina's point, all along."

After sending CeeCee off in her car, I get settled into my Porsche. Before starting my car, I check my phone, just in case I've missed something important during my dinner with CeeCee. I have. A text from Henn:

Call me ASAP. I've got news on the asshole.

My heart rate spiking, I start my car and immediately place the call.

"Hey," Henn says.

"You found kiddie porn, didn't you?"

"Worse."

Henn tells me the situation, and I'm blown away.

"That's why it took me so long to get back to you," he says. "Once I saw what we were dealing with, I knew I had to follow the clues and hack everyone involved. So, it took a little time."

"You've got everything now?"

"Yep. I've got it all."

"Send it to me. I'm driving home now. I'll look at everything when I get home."

Henn pauses. "You realize this is bigger than your personal vendetta now, right? We have a higher duty than just ruining this asshole's life on the down-low to avenge Georgina. You get that, right?"

"Send me the stuff and we'll talk next steps."

"We're going to have to tell Georgina what I found. This isn't as simple as tipping off the FBI about some kiddie porn. She deserves to know."

I exhale. "Yeah. I know. I'll be seeing Georgina in person in New York in a couple days. I'll talk to her about it then."

"Good. Keep me posted."

"Will do. Thanks, Henny. Seriously. You never let me down."

I end the call with Henn and place another one. This time, to my head of security, Barry Atwater. Unfortunately, though, I get Barry's voicemail.

"Hey, Big Barry. It's Reed. I need your help with something personal and confidential. It's urgent and highly important. Call me as soon as you can."

SEVENTY-SIX
GEORGINA

Friday 9:24 pm

"And this was when Dax and I dressed up as the Wonder Twins for Halloween," Kat says, showing me a photo. "I was sixteen. Dax, twelve."

I'm in Seattle. Sitting on Kat's couch in her stunning home. Earlier today, Dax and the Goats gave me a tour of "their" Seattle, while I interviewed them. Tonight, Kat is regaling me with story after story.

"You two look so much alike," I say, grinning at the photo. "You're both spitting images of your mom." I know this because I met Kat and Dax's mom, Louise Morgan, last night, when I went to "Casa Morgan" for a family dinner.

"Oh, I know. Everyone says that. Gracie, too." That's Kat's spitfire of a daughter. "My mom always says the four of us are Russian nesting dolls. Oh! This is a good one. Dax at age two." She shows me a photo of Dax as a toddler on a couch, looking like he's playing air guitar, while little Kat in the photo, a tow-headed blonde, cheers on her little brother enthusiastically. "According to family lore, Dax saw some hot shot guitar player on TV, and he jumped up and started mimicking him. It's how Daxy got his lifelong nickname: Rock Star."

I giggle. "The Morgans sure love their nicknames."

"Oh, Georgie girl, you have no idea." She pulls out another photo. "This is the Goats rehearsing in my parents' garage. A very common occurrence back in the day. They used to come home from high school every day and head straight to the garage to practice for hours."

"How old are they here?"

"Fifteen or sixteen."

"And Dax already had long hair."

"He always loved having long hair, from day one. My mom said at his very first haircut, he started bawling when he saw his long locks floating to the ground. My mother swears he said, 'But now how will you know which one is me?'"

I laugh and laugh. The same way I did yesterday, when I toured Seattle tourist spots with Kat and her kids, and Kat's best friend, Sarah, and her kids. The same way I did last night, during dinner with Kat's family. Also, during today's fun-filled interview with the band, which Kat tagged along on. Seriously, any time I'm in Kat's presence, I can't stop smiling.

"Do you think Dax would mind me using that 'first haircut' anecdote in my article?"

"Go for it. Dax already told me I could tell you anything."

"Thank you so much. When you offered to put me up in Seattle, I had no idea you'd go all out like this. You've made me feel like family."

"That's because you *are* family, Georgie." She returns to her photos, like she didn't just take my breath away. "Oh, this is a good one. It's from my destination wedding in Maui. This is the night Reed watched 22 Goats play a show for our wedding guests." She smiles. "He signed them to River Records that very night."

Reed. Oh, God, he's gorgeous in the shot. Tanned and relaxed. *I love him.* That's all I can think as I stare at his chiseled face. *I. Love. Him.* Immediately followed by *Why did you screw everything up, you stupid man?*

When I look up from the photo, Kat is staring at me. Scrutinizing my face. Probably looking for signs of heartbreak, since yesterday, while touring Seattle with her and Sarah, I spilled my guts, in nauseating detail, about what happened between Reed and me.

"I'm sorry I showed you a photo of Reed," Kat says. "I didn't think."

"It's fine. Reed and I are friends."

Kat flashes me a look that tells me she doesn't buy that.

Blushing, I return to the photos splayed out before us. "May I use any and all of these for my article?"

"Use whatever you want. The Goats said to give you 'full access.'"

"Thank them for me. I feel like I won the lottery. Not just in terms of my article, but also because I've found you. You're so amazing, Kat."

She touches my shoulder. "The feeling is mutual. You're my spirit animal." She winks. "So, do you have everything you need?"

"For my article about 22 Goats, yes. More than I ever dreamed possible." I pause. "Although... there's another article I'm gathering information for... something for *Dig a Little Deeper*. Would you mind giving me Hannah Hennessy's number? This is highly confidential, but I'd like to ask her about her boss."

Kat grabs her phone. "I just sent you Hannah's contact info and texted her that you want to talk to her."

"Thank you."

She looks up from her phone. "So, by 'Hannah's boss,' do you mean that gray-haired guy who's marrying Isabel?"

I nod. "Howard Devlin."

"You're going to interview him?"

"No. I'm investigating some rumors I've heard about him. I want to ask Hannah if she's heard the rumors, too."

Kat arches an eyebrow. "What kind of rumors?"

"I shouldn't say."

"The ones about him being a pervert groper?"

I gasp. "Oh my gosh! You know about that?"

"Hannah told me. When Howard invited her to get a drink with him at the party, she dragged me along. Later, she told me she did that because it's well known at her company women should always use the buddy system around him."

"Holy hell."

"She said she's almost certainly safe around him, since she's only in PR. Not an actress. Plus, he's apparently a fan of big boobs, and, if you didn't notice, Hannah's Flatty Mcgee. But, still, she didn't want to be alone with him. She's actually looking for a new job. She's heard too much bad stuff about him to want to keep working there."

"Why the hell has nobody reported him? He's the worst kept secret in Hollywood!"

Kat shrugs. "He's a powerful old guy. Those guys always get away with murder." Her phone buzzes and she looks down. "Hannah says she's just putting Hazel down for the night, but we can call her in ten minutes."

My stomach clenches. "Oh, wow. I didn't expect to hear from her quite this fast."

Kat looks perplexed. "Is something wrong?"

I grimace. "The truth is my boss told me not to pursue the Howard story yet. I'm kind of 'going rogue' by talking to Hannah about him."

"She told you not to pursue the story, because she's trying to cover up for whatever he's been doing?"

"Oh, gosh no. My boss wants to take him down, with all her heart. She just thinks I'm too green, and the story too explosive, for me to try to tackle it just yet. But she said that *before* I'd landed my ace in the hole—this woman named Francesca Laramie." I google Francesca and show Kat some articles. Of course, I don't mention Isabel's connection to Francesca, or tell Kat how I found Francesca in the first place. But I tell Kat the gist of my conversation with Francesca about Howard, and the amazing news that Francesca has agreed to lend support to my efforts, if I can get anyone to come forward.

"Impressive," Kat says. "Maybe what Francesca knows about Howard will dovetail with what Hannah knows."

"That's my hope. I'm thinking maybe putting their two lists of names together will crack the whole thing wide open."

"Ooh, I'm getting pumped," Kat says. "Can I be on the call with Hannah?"

"I'd love it. I'm sure Hannah will feel more comfortable talking to me, if you're on the call."

Kat claps her hands and hoots. "Wonder Twin powers, activate!" Laughing, she rises from the couch, her adorable baby bump leading the way. "I'm gonna check on my kiddos real quick, before we call Hannah. Gracie sleeps like a ton of bricks, but Jack always wakes up around this time of night, wanting me, so I want to check on him before we make that call. Why don't you pour yourself another glass of wine while I'm checking on my babies, and then we'll call Hannah to see if she's got any information that might be useful for us to take this motherfucker down."

I could cry. *Us.* That's the word Kat just used. Such a tiny word. But so powerful.

"Oh, hey, you know what?" Kat says, stopping in the entryway of her living room. "Why don't I call Sarah to come over, too?" She's talking about her best friend and sister-in-law, Sarah Faraday, who happens to be a lawyer. The one we toured Seattle with yesterday. "Sarah is crazy-smart—a whiz at research and strategizing. She only lives ten minutes away, and I'm sure her babies are down for the night."

"Wow, Kat. I can't tell you how much your support means to me. I've been really stressed out about tackling this story as an army of one, especially since I'm kind of going rogue here, like I said."

Kat laughs. "The fact that you're willing to go rogue to pursue this story is the best indicator that you *should*." She smiles warmly. "And you're not an army of one anymore, sweetie. You're now an army of *four* —you, me, Hannah, and Sarah." She pats her belly. "Actually, make that four and a *half.* Don't tell my family this, because Josh and I are going to surprise them, but this little peanut is a girl. Arabella."

"Aw, I love it. Congratulations."

She pats her belly. "And you know what I'm going to tell my two daughters one day? And Jack, too. My son needs to know this, too. I'm going to tell them that, once, a long time ago, their mommy helped their Auntie Georgie bring down a truly evil man."

SEVENTY-SEVEN
GEORGINA

Saturday 2:46 pm

When my flight from Seattle touches down in LA, I turn on my phone, the same as everyone seated around me on the plane. And when I see an email from Reed, with a subject line that reads, "Personal and HIGHLY confidential," my heart stops. My breathing shallow, I read the body of the email:

My dearest Georgina, Attached, you will find a confidential video that's for your eyes only. Audio quality is poor, so watch with sound turned all the way up. It's critically important you watch this video when you're alone, in a quiet place, where you won't be interrupted. Please, I beg you not to share this video with anyone, or even describe its contents. At least, not before you've spoken to me and given me a chance to explain what you've seen. Thank you in advance for granting this request. Please call me after you've watched. RR

. . .

I look around me on the crowded airplane, where passengers have just started grabbing their bags, and realize, much to my dismay, I'll have to wait until I reach my parked car to watch this mysterious video. After shuffling off the plane, I make my way through the maze of LAX and onto a parking-lot shuttle. I get off at the appropriate overnight lot, slip inside my rental car, turn the sound on my phone all the way up, and, finally, breathing hard, press play on the video.

Grainy, black and white video of Reed's garage comes up. It's surveillance video, time-stamped in the bottom right-hand corner with a date from exactly one week ago. In other words, the date of Reed's party. I hold my breath with anticipation, and, a few seconds later, Reed and Isabel enter the garage through the same side door they exited through when I stumbled upon them.

As Reed closes the door, Isabel marches into the expansive garage, looking agitated. She comes to a stand, facing the camera, and Reed stops in front of her.

"What's this supposed 'emergency'?" he says, sounding deeply annoyed. "Make it quick. I've got something important to do."

"That reporter you introduced me to. She mentioned CeeCee's birthday party."

"So?"

"Did you tell her I was with you that night?"

"She asked me how I met CeeCee, so I told her the story of how I crashed the party. And, yeah, I mentioned you were my date. So what?"

"Goddammit, Reed!"

"You're being paranoid, Isabel. It's perfectly fine you were my date. Nobody would ever guess how that came to be."

"She's really smart. I can tell."

"Yes, she is. And she wants to write a flattering interview about you. That's all. She's not looking to write a hit piece. You're being paranoid."

Isabel wrings her hands. "Can you blame me? Every day of my life, I'm waiting for the next Troy to come along to blackmail me."

Reed's back is to the camera, but his shoulders soften. "Isabel, I understand why Troy messed with your head. But he was a one-off. If someone was going to threaten to expose your secret again, they would have done it by now. It's been ten years since you worked for Francesca. If I thought there was an army of Troys out there, lying in wait to take you down, I wouldn't have paid him so much to stay quiet. I'm rolling in money, sweetheart, but even I can't afford to pay off the entire world."

Isabel rubs her face. "Yeah, you're right. I'm being paranoid. I am, right?"

"You are."

"Just don't tell this reporter anything else about me."

"I won't. Now, can we please go back to the party? I just made a little girl cry and I need to fix it."

Isabel steps forward and slides her arms around Reed's neck. "What's the rush? Now that we're here, how about we have a little fun, for old time's sake?"

I hold my breath and squint my eyes, convinced I'm about to see something deeply traumatizing to me. But I needn't worry. Reed immediately disentangles himself from Isabel and says, "That's not gonna happen." He grabs her hand, the one with Howard's massive rock on it, and holds it up. "This means nothing to you?"

She yanks her hand away. "You know I don't want him. I want *you*."

Reed throws up his hands. "Goddammit. Not this again. Things are different now than when you fucked Troy to make me jealous. It's not going to work this time."

She puts her hands on her hips. "You're not going crazy to think of me marrying someone else?"

He scoffs. "No. Would I prefer you marry someone you actually love? Yes. Because I care about you and want you to find happiness. But do I wish you were marrying *me*? Fuck no. Isabel, like I keep telling you. *I'm over you*. I've moved on. So, if you're marrying Howard to manipulate me into action the same way you did when you fucked Troy, only bigger and better this time, then don't bother. Don't marry anyone to try to get a rise out of me. The only thing that strategy will get you is a husband you don't love."

"Why are you always so mean to me?"

"I'm not mean to you. I'm *honest*. I don't want you anymore. We'll *never* get back together. *Never*."

"I don't believe that."

"Believe it. If you must know, I'm with someone else now. I'm in a serious, committed relationship."

Even in the grainy footage, I can tell Isabel is crushed.

"I'll always care about you," Reed says. "I'll always protect you, as best I can. And your secrets are always safe with me. But the truth is you're more like a sister to me now, than anything else."

Isabel slaps Reed across his face, but he doesn't even flinch. "Who is she?" she shrieks, her tears matching mine as I watch the scene unfolding. "Is she here at the party?"

"No, she's not here," Reed lies. "But if she were, I'd expect you to be nice to her. We haven't been together in *years*, Isabel, and you're engaged to another man. Why do you think you still have any claim on me?"

"Because I'm still in love with you!"

He's exasperated. Irritated. "Why the hell are you marrying Howard?" he booms. "I don't get it! You don't need his money, and you certainly don't need his connections anymore. You're a huge star now. The biggest star on the planet. *You don't need him.* You can get cast in anything from blockbusters to indies, without his help or blessing. I get why you flirted with him when you were starting out, but don't you think saying yes to marrying a man you don't love is taking the casting couch a bit far?"

She shakes her head. "You don't understand."

"I think I do. He's made marriage part of the deal for the superhero movies, hasn't he?"

She drops her head, looking defeated. But says nothing.

"Screw the superhero movies! If he drops you from them, so what? There are ten other producers who'd hire you in a heartbeat."

She shakes her head. Rubs her face. "You cheated on this girlfriend of yours with me in the Hamptons?"

"No. I hadn't met her yet back then."

Isabel is flabbergasted. "How new is this relationship? Were you lying to me last month when you said you were having dinner with your friends? Were you actually seeing *her*?"

"No. I didn't lie to you that night. I was having dinner with my friends. But then we went to a bar, after dinner, and that's where I met her. She was the bartender."

Isabel gasps. "You want a *bartender* over *me*?"

"Fuck you," I whisper to my screen. At the same moment Reed says something I don't catch because I was talking. I rewind the video to hear whatever I missed, and what Reed says makes me smile from ear to ear: "Fuck you, Isabel." Which he follows with, "I'm not going to talk about my girlfriend with you anymore. All you need to know is she makes me feel things I've never felt before." He pauses for dramatic effect. *"Ever."*

The meaning is clear. *Not even with you.* And, obviously, by the devastated look on Isabel's face, his message has been received, loud and clear. She bows her head and bursts into tears. And, sweet man that he is, Reed wraps his strong arms around her and squeezes her tight. And, suddenly, I find myself quaking with dread about whatever I'm going to witness next.

They remain still for a long time, holding each other. They're whispering to each other, but I can't make out their words. Finally, Reed pulls back from their tender embrace. He takes Isabel's gorgeous, iconic face in his hands and looks deeply into her eyes for a very long moment, causing her body to visibly wrack with sobs.

"If I could have flipped a switch and made myself fall madly in love with you, Isabel Schneider, I would have done it years ago. You're gorgeous and talented. You've got the world on a string. I know what you went through as a kid. I know how bad it was, and I want nothing more than to see you safe and happy and successful, for the rest of your life. You deserve a happily ever after. But I'm truly not your Prince Charming, and I never will be."

Isabel closes her eyes and tilts her face up. "Kiss me goodbye. One last kiss. Just so I can remember what it feels like to kiss you. What it feels like to actually *feel* something with a man. Please, Reed. At least, give me that."

Reed looks into her tear-streaked face for a long moment, and then leans in and presses his lips to hers. And, somehow, the vision doesn't repel me. It doesn't enrage me. No, in this moment I'm actually in awe of Reed's kind heart. I know this isn't a betrayal of me, as much as one final act of generosity toward a woman he's loved for a very long time. Just like he told me, this truly is a goodbye kiss. Yes, he's technically breaking his promise to me in this moment. That fact hasn't escaped me. But seeing the way the kiss unfolded, I know he didn't kiss her because he doesn't want me. He kissed her because he *does*. Because he's closing the book on their tumultuous relationship, forever.

Um...

Okay, Reed, this kiss is far lengthier, and more passionate than required to close that fucking book. Come on, now. *Enough.*

Finally, Reed pulls away, having given Isabel the kiss of her life. She swoons and wobbles, looking dazed, and I can plainly see Isabel is now wearing the same expression she wore when I stumbled upon her and Reed coming out of the garage. She looks like a woman who just got fucked.

Reed puts his fingertip underneath Isabel's chin. "Don't marry anyone who doesn't kiss you like *that.*"

I roll my eyes. Okay, Reed. That was wholly unnecessary, sweetheart. It's time to move along now.

"How can you deny our magic?" Isabel chokes out. "You felt it, every bit as much as I did, during that kiss. Admit it."

"No. The only thing I felt while kissing you was complete clarity that I'm head over heels in love with my girlfriend. I felt guilty while kissing you, to be honest. Because the only one I want to be kissing—the only one I *should* be kissing—is her."

Isabel clutches her heart. And so do I.

Even in grainy black and white, it's clear Reed just dealt her a death blow.

And I couldn't be happier about it.

Reed is unmoved by the expression of pure devastation on Isabel's face. She might as well be the blonde at the bar who tried to give him her demo. He looks at his watch, and sighs. "I need to get back to my party now. Come on. I'm sure your beloved fiancé is wondering where you are." With that, he opens the door to the garage, his urgency to get the hell out of there wafting off him. With a heavy sigh, Isabel drags herself out the door, and Reed follows, at which point the surveillance video ends.

I look up from my screen, practically hyperventilating. Reed told me the truth about everything. *Reed loves me. And he figured it out while kissing Isabel.*

And that's a damned good thing. Because, despite everything, I love him, too. With all my heart.

Breathing heavily, I tap out a text to my man, my love, asking him if he's home. And when he replies instantly, telling me he's not home, but can be there in fifteen minutes, my heart gallops with joy.

Me: Go home now. I'm coming home.
Reed: You got my email?
Me: Yes. Just landed at LAX and watched the video in my car. I'm coming straight to you now. See you soon! XO
Reed: I can't wait to see you, my love. XOXOXO

SEVENTY-EIGHT
REED

Saturday 4:23 pm

I peek down my street again, awaiting the appearance of Georgina's convertible turning the corner. But, still, nothing. For the past ten minutes, I've been standing in front of my iron gate, staring down my street like a Labrador awaiting his owner's return from work while trying not to freak out. I *think* the "XO" Georgina tacked onto the end of her "see you soon!" text message, combined with the exclamation point she used, and the fact that she said she's coming "home," meant she's coming here to forgive me completely and pick up where we left off. But, when it comes to Georgina, and her temper, I never know for sure what she's going to do or how she's going to react. For all I know, after watching that surveillance video—and the whopper of a kiss I laid on Isabel—she's coming here to take a golf club to another one of my cars.

Either way, I'm surely going to have to field a thousand questions from Georgina about the confusing, and highly intriguing, things Isabel and I talked about in that video. Things like "Troy" and "blackmail" and "Francesca" and "secret." All the things that initially kept me from sending that damned surveillance video to Georgina in the first place, even though I knew it would prove I'd been telling Georgina the truth about that kiss, and what it made me realize. Although, yeah, if I'm being honest, I was also highly skittish about Georgina witnessing the actual kiss. It's one thing for me to tell Georgina I "only kissed" Isabel, and to let Georgina *imagine* it, and another thing for her to *see* it, and get confirmation that, to put it mildly, that smooch wasn't a brotherly peck.

I lean against my gatepost, staring down my street. But, still, there's no sign of Georgina. I look at my watch. She must have hit traffic. *Welcome to LA.*

I've never told a woman I love her before. But, today, for the first time in my life, I've told Georgina. Albeit, indirectly, through that video. Plus, I called her "my love" in my text. Which I'm now thinking might have been a bit premature. I *think* Georgina's "XO" meant she feels the same way I do. I *think* Georgina is coming here to say she's mine. But after this torturous week, and a lifetime of shit hitting fans in ways I never expected, I should know by now, better than anyone, not to count my chickens.

Hallelujah! I see Georgina's car turning onto my street! As she draws near, I wave and smile broadly, the sight of her glorious face sending my heart galloping and my skin buzzing. And, in return, Georgina shoots me a wide, beaming smile that tells me everything I need to know.

She's home.
She forgives me.
She loves me.
She's all mine.

I know we're going to need to talk in detail about everything, including the mysterious things Isabel and I talked about on that video. But, after seeing the smile on Georgina's face, I know we'll talk about all of it later. First things first, I'm going to take that woman into my arms and kiss the hell out of her and tell her I love her, to her face, while looking into her gorgeous hazel eyes. And then, I'm going to take her upstairs and show her, with every inch of me, how much she means to me.

Shaking with excitement, I tap out the gate code and wave Georgina's little car through, and then sprint after her tailgate as she traverses my circular driveway and comes to a stop in front of my house.

When Georgina's car door opens, I'm already there, my arms extended. I swoop her into my embrace, and every atom of my body electrifies at the touch of her.

"Welcome home," I murmur into her lips, just before crushing my mouth to hers. As our tongues tangle, a tsunami of love slams into me. Followed immediately by a hurricane of pent-up arousal. My heart thundering in my chest, I disengage from Georgina's hungry lips and take her magnificent, tear-streaked face in my palms. "I love you, Georgina. I love you madly. Completely. And only *you*."

Her smile is beaming. Radiant. Breathtaking. "I love you, too. Only you."

"I'm so sorry I hurt you. I'll never do it again."

She smiles. "We'll call it a fair trade: a kiss for a Ferrari."

I chuckle. "Deal."

"That's a one-time deal, by the way."

"It'll never happen again."

She arches her eyebrow. "Can we talk about that kiss, though? Holy hell, Reed."

I grimace. "Yeah. Sorry about that."

She smiles. "It's all right. What you said right afterward made it all worth it." She winks. "But just barely."

Sighing with relief, I kiss her again. And, soon, our kiss becomes voracious. I scoop her up like a bride, making her squeal, and stride into my house like a stallion running for the barn. When I get to my staircase, I take the steps two at a time and then barrel down the hallway toward my bedroom, whispering the entire time to Georgina about how much I've missed her, how much I want her, need her, *love* her, can't wait to touch her, lick her, fuck her.

In my bedroom, I lay Georgina down onto my bed and begin energetically ripping off her clothes, and then mine. In short order, we're a naked blur of greedy fingers and lips and tongues. Warm, bare skin against warm, bare skin. In record speed, I make her come with my fingers, which, not surprisingly, makes her beg me to fuck her.

But not yet.

I open the second drawer of my nightstand and retrieve something I've been keeping there for this exact moment. I return to Georgina, holding up her ruby necklace. And the moment she sees it, she gasps in shock.

"You went back to Tiffany's to get it for me?"

I chuckle. "No, baby. I never returned it."

Her jaw drops comically, making me laugh.

"Sit up. I want you to wear it while I fuck you. My Ruby Queen."

"You've already done too much. I can't accept that."

"Sweetheart, look at my boner. I don't have patience for this conversation. Please, let's fast-forward to the part where you let me have what I want."

She sits up, sighing. "Oh, Reed."

After clasping the necklace around her neck, I kiss her neck and shoulder. And then, finally, do the thing I've been fantasizing about for half my life. I pull Georgina on top of me and guide her to ride me, and as she does, as her body gyrates, and her hips snap back and forth, and her tits bounce with her movement, I tell her, over and over again, that I love her. And it's the best sex of my life, even without the ropes and toys and harnesses.

We're fire together, Georgina and me. We're a pyre. I sit up as her body moves on top of mine and devour her pebbled nipples with fervor. I grab her ass and bite her neck. Inhale her scent and lick the hollow at the base of her neck. I'm delirious with desire for her. Overwhelmed to feel white-hot lust intertwining with all-encompassing *love* inside me, for the first time in my life. Oh, God, the sensation of loving to fuck someone, while actually *loving* them, as a person. I mean, totally and completely and unconditionally *loving* everything about them, and knowing they love me back... oh, fuck. I can't get enough of this sublime pleasure.

I run my fingertips over the dripping gems around Georgina's neck. And then caress her tits and pinch her hard nipples, and suck on her breasts and neck and gorgeous bottom lip, again and again. I grip her hair and run my teeth along her jawline, wanting to physically consume her. To ingest her into my body and keep her there, beholden to me, and only me. I want to fuse with her, in every way possible. I want to capture this beautiful butterfly in my net and never, ever let her go. My nerve endings on fire, my body lit up, I gaze up at the mirror above us and tell her, in graphic detail, what she looks like as she fucks me. I tell her about the way her ass is moving as she rides me. I tell her she's my queen.

Finally, Georgie screams my name and comes, hard, and when I feel her muscles clenching and rippling with her orgasm, it's sheer bliss for me. A direct line to a God I've never believed in, until now. I give myself permission to let go. And not just physically. To let go of fear. I'm hers now. Committed to giving her all of me now, no matter what.

When our bodies slacken, Georgina and I flop onto the bed, onto our backs, and stare at our smiles—and our heaving, panting, naked bodies—in the overhead mirror.

Wracked with euphoria, I grab Georgina's hand. "Please tell me you're home now."

She smiles seductively. "Are you inviting me to stay here, for however long?"

"No, I'm *begging* you. No limitations or expiration date. As in, I want you to go down to the DMV, right after we get back from New York, and change the address on your driver's license."

She opens her mouth and eyes as wide as they'll go.

"Yep," I say, chuckling at her shocked expression. "This is DMV-serious, baby."

Georgina bites her lip. "You're serious? Because I'm not willing to go back down to the DMV again any time soon. It's hell down there."

I sit up and look down at her. "Seriously, Georgie. I'm in it for the long haul with you. I'm sure. Please, tell me you're sure, too. It's you and me, from now on."

She nods. "I'm sure."

I lean down and kiss her. But then pull away excitedly and grab my phone off the nightstand with a loud hoot.

"What?"

"I'm telling Owen to get your bike back here ASAP. I want the Ginger Rogers of Spin to start kicking my ass again, as soon as possible."

Georgina sighs like a Disney princess. "I'm so happy."

"I'm also telling Owen to add you to my flight tomorrow."

"Don't do that. I mean, I'd love to travel with you. But I've already got a flight booked. No sense wasting money."

I roll my eyes. "You're coming with me. We're flying first class."

"Oooh, I've never flown first class!" She giggles. "Okay, I'm coming with you."

We both laugh.

As I get settled onto my back again, she turns onto her side and drags a fingertip down the center groove of my abs. "So... I hate to say this and ruin the afterglow... but I think, before we get too swept away on endorphins, we should talk."

My stomach clenches with dread. Shit. Here we go. Isabel's secrets weren't mine to reveal. But what choice did I have but to send that video? If I'm going to love Georgina, all the way, then I've got to trust her to choose me, and our love, over the chance to use the information on that video to try to land her dream job. Or, worse, to try to destroy Isabel out of sheer spite. I know Georgie didn't fully understand anything she heard on that video, but she heard enough to realize Isabel has a secret. And that some guy named Troy blackmailed her because of it. "Yeah, you're right," I say. "We definitely need to talk."

Georgina looks stressed. "I don't want there to be any secrets between us, Reed. Not anymore. No more lies—even if it's only through omission. It's time to come clean about everything."

"Yeah, I agree," I say, my words overlapping with Georgina's, as she says, "I need to talk to you about *Troy*."

Wow. She's jumping right in. Shit. I take a deep breath. "Yeah, I figured you'd ask me about him. In fact, I'm sure you've got a whole bunch of questions about the confusing stuff you heard on that video. But before I explain who 'Troy' is, I need to emphasize that—"

"Oh, no," Georgina says. She lays a palm on my chest, pausing me. "When I said it's time to come clean about Troy, I meant *me*. *I* need to come clean about Troy."

I blink several times, utterly confused. *Did I hear that right?*

Georgina leans onto her elbow and props her head with her fist. "What you and Isabel talked about wasn't confusing to me at all. I already know all about Troy Eklund."

"Uh." I blink again, my synapses exploding. "What, exactly, do you know?"

"Everything. The fact that he slept with Isabel. And figured out Isabel's secret—which I also know about, by the way. I know he blackmailed Isabel. Well, technically, he blackmailed *you*, and you gallantly paid him off in exchange for him signing a confidential settlement of his lawsuit." She shrugs. "I know everything, Reed."

My brain feels like it's melting. "How...?" But I'm too shocked to complete the sentence.

Georgina continues, "Normally, I wouldn't have said anything. I'd have pretended to be clueless, so you wouldn't fully realize the true nature of the demon you've fallen in love with. But if we're truly going to make this relationship work, if I'm really going to brave the DMV for you—then I feel like I should come clean to you about how clever and diabolical and relentless and... *brilliant*... I truly am." She winks. "I know you've *suspected* all along I'm Bobby Fischer. But I feel like, before I put your address onto my driver's license, which is, to me, as serious as a relationship can be, I should come clean and tell you that... no matter how much you've been thinking I'm Bobby Fischer? Oh, honey. You have no freakin' idea."

SEVENTY-NINE
GEORGINA

I tell Reed everything I know about Troy Eklund. How I read his lawsuit and then tracked him down at Slingers and cleverly pumped him for information without him realizing it. I tell him about Troy's unmistakable hints and body language, and finally, those two little words—Francesca Laramie—that sent me straight to Google, which then led me to deducing Isabel's secret, as well as causing me to assume that Reed must have hired Isabel to be his "blind date" on the night of CeeCee's fiftieth birthday party.

And, last but not least, I tell Reed about my visit to Francesca's restaurant downtown, although I don't drop the bomb on Reed, just yet, about my firmly held belief that Howard Devlin is a sexual predator who's been getting a free pass for decades because he happens to be a wildly successful billionaire movie producer. I'm going to tell Reed about Howard during this conversation, of course. But later. I feel like Reed and I have plenty to talk about, before we get to that.

I take Reed's hand. "I want you to know Isabel's secret is safe with me. And so is yours. Assuming I'm right about you hiring Isabel through Francesca."

"Yes, you're right about that."

"I figured. Rented tux, rented limo, rented girl..."

He nods. "CeeCee's party was actually the last time Isabel ever worked for Francesca. We spent the night together after the party. We hit it off. And I got to feeling a bit protective. Not to mention, possessive."

"You? Shocker."

He smiles. "I offered to pay Isabel's rent for the next year, so she could quit her gig with Francesca and afford to live on nothing but modeling and waiting tables, while she went to auditions and tried to get her big break."

My heart melts. Why doesn't it surprise me to learn Reed forked over a year's worth of rent for Isabel? Or, that Isabel took the deal and quit working for Francesca for him. I can only imagine how hard Isabel must have fallen for the dashing, young client she met the night of CeeCee's party. The smoking hot, scrappy dude who looked better in a rented tux than every millionaire or billionaire at that party with ten tuxes in their closets. In fact, I'd bet anything it was love at first sight for Isabel, when Reed got out of that rented limo to pick her up in front of McDonald's. And, judging from that surveillance video, she never fell *out* of love with him, for the next ten years. I can relate. Lying here naked with Reed, I'm certain I'll never fall out of love with him, either. God help me.

"Isabel and I weren't even an exclusive couple when I told her I wanted to pay her rent, so she could quit Francesca. Our serious relationship came a couple years later. But, right from the start, no matter what, or *who*, she was doing, I didn't want her doing it for money. I always knew she was going to be a star. I wanted to free her up from taking shitty jobs just to pay the rent. I wanted her to make smart decisions for her career."

Oh, Reed. Some things never change. He was a star-maker, right from the start. A man who took intense pleasure from helping others achieve their dreams and shoot for the stars. And he doesn't think he was Isabel's Prince Charming? Clearly, he was, right from night one.

Reed says, "It's funny, at one point, I had a feeling you knew about Troy. But I convinced myself I was being paranoid. Remember that night I drove all over town, looking for your car outside of bars and clubs? I drove to Slingers that night, looking for you, because I found Troy's name on their performance schedule."

I gasp. "We must have just missed each other!"

"When I got there, the bartender said Troy had left with a blonde fifteen minutes before."

"Holy hell. Thank God you didn't run into him. Now that I know what I do, I never would have dropped that hint about what I was doing that night. I'd never want you and Troy to be in the same room. It wouldn't have ended well. And rightly so. He's such a douchebag."

Reed glowers. "If I'd walked into that bar and found that fucker hitting on you, it's fifty-fifty I wouldn't have been able to stop myself from wrapping my hands around his throat and squeezing the life out of him, right then and there." His dark eyes flicker, and I know he's dead serious.

"Is it wrong I get turned on when you look like you're genuinely capable of committing murder?"

"Everyone is capable of murder, under the right circumstances." His eyes flash. "And *you're* my right circumstance."

I bite my lip.

"As it is, I might have to settle this time for suing Troy's punk-ass for breaching his confidentiality agreement. Tell me again everything he said to you that night. This time, word for word."

I tell him everything Troy told me, and, when I'm done, we both conclude Reed probably wouldn't have a legal leg to stand on, thanks to the fact that it was mostly Troy's facial expressions and body language, combined with my clever deductions, that led me to discover the most salacious and sensitive nuggets of information. Plus, would Reed *really* want to reopen that particular wound, in a forum as public as a lawsuit, now that Reed's fame is a hundred times what it was when Troy sued him six years ago? The answer to that question, we both decide, is a resounding no.

"You were enraged Troy slept with Isabel, huh?"

"I was pissed he slept with Isabel. Yeah. Not gonna lie. But, more than that, I was enraged he betrayed me. When Troy slept with Isabel, I'd already broken up with her months before. So, she wasn't cheating on me. I didn't care if she fucked other people. I was doing the same. But *Troy* fucking her? That was a dagger to my heart." He shakes his head. "I'd loved that asshole like a little brother. I'd taken him into my *home* and under my wing. I'd poured obscene amounts of money into his band and guided him every step of the way. I'd *believed* in him and backed him with my name and reputation. And then, Troy had to pick *Isabel*, of all the women in LA, to fuck? And more than that, he had to do it a mere *two weeks* before his debut album was set to drop? I couldn't believe it. She'd come over lots of times while Troy and his band were staying at my house. He knew all about our relationship. I'd even told him about her one night over tequila. Pfft. Talk about a backstabber."

"Her plan worked, though. You got back together with her after that. Exclusively. For two years."

"Yep. It worked like a charm."

"So, as pissed as you were at Troy, I can't imagine you would have gone *that* scorched-earth on him, if it weren't for your love for Isabel."

He looks at me like I've just said two plus two equals five. "That's what you think? That I dropped Troy's band, and tanked his release, and lost all that money, and all that time and effort because he fucked Isabel? Because you think I *loved* Isabel, that much?"

"Well... *yeah*."

He scoffs. "I beat the shit out of Troy because he betrayed me with Isabel. And because I was jealous as fuck. But the reason I destroyed Troy's career had nothing to do with Isabel. I'm a businessman, Georgie. I ruined that motherfucker because I'd discovered, thanks to Isabel, he'd put my reputation—my entire *label*—everything I'd worked so hard to create—at risk. More than anything, that's the reason I'll always be grateful to Isabel and have her back. Because she had mine regarding Troy, *big-time*."

I furrow my brow. "But she slept with him."

"To make me jealous. Yeah. But it's what she did afterwards that's the true measure of her heart. Her loyalty. Apparently, when Isabel and Troy were spending some 'alone time' together in the sack, he played her his band's upcoming debut album. According to what Isabel told me, Troy started bragging about how he'd come up with each song on the album, what his 'inspirations' were, blah, blah. And during that conversation, that little shit started bragging to her about how he'd basically ripped off some no-name band's lyrics and melodies on three tracks!"

I gasp.

"Thank God, Isabel had my back, despite everything. She came straight to me to tell me what he'd said to her. And I immediately went and listened to the songs that had 'inspired' Troy, and, holy fuck, he'd literally *stolen* them, practically note for note and word for word."

"Oh my God."

"I mean, all music is derivative in some way. All new songs have been influenced by whatever came before. But there was no question this was outright thievery. Textbook copyright infringement. And on *three* fucking songs." Reed scoffs. "That I knew of. God only knows how many more songs he'd ripped off. So, anyway, right then and there, I knew I couldn't release the album. No way. If someone had figured out the link to those stolen songs after release, River Records never would've weathered the shit storm. We were too new. Still building our reputation. It would have been fatal."

I'm blown away. "This whole time I thought you destroyed Troy because of how much you loved Isabel."

Reed scoffs. "No. I would have released that album, despite Troy sleeping with Isabel, if it hadn't been for those stolen songs. Although, admittedly, I still would have beaten the shit out of him for fucking Isabel."

I can't help chuckling. "What happened with that? Did you head out, expressly planning to beat him up? Or was it a spur of the moment thing?"

Reed smiles wickedly. "I went out, specifically to beat his ass. Isabel came to me and told me about Troy's thievery. And, of course, she made sure I understood she'd acquired the information from Troy while naked in his bed. So, I freaked out, for all the reasons I've described, not just about them having sex. All of it. So, I knew C-Bomb was having a party that night. So I headed over there, and beelined to Troy, and beat the hell out of that punk-ass little bitch, just for the sheer pleasure of it."

I bite my lip. "I guess I'm not the only one who knows how to go 'Left Eye Lopes' on someone, eh?"

He winks.

"Troy didn't tell me about the beating he took at your hands. I guess he didn't want to come off as weak to the woman he was trying to pick up. He also didn't tell me about the copyright infringement stuff. He only said you'd 'blackballed' him to your 'powerful friends' in the industry by telling them a pack of unspecified lies."

Reed scoffs. "Oh, I blackballed him, all right. But only with the truth. I warned anyone who'd listen, even my rivals at competing labels, to steer clear of Troy because he was a liar and a thief." He shrugs. "If that's 'blackballing' someone, then so be it. He deserved it."

"And now he plays every Tuesday and Friday night at Slingers."

"Yeah, when I saw that place, and the bartender confirmed that's his regular gig, I admit I was damned happy about it. I hope that little shit never plays a venue bigger than Slingers, as long as he lives."

"Backstage, at the RCR concert, when you told me you've 'trained' the guys on your roster not to sleep with anyone you've slept with, you were talking about Troy, I presume?"

"Of course. The guys on my roster have all heard the legend of how Reed dumped a guy's band, and beat his ass, solely for sleeping with his ex. Why should I tell anyone the whole story? The legendary version adds to my mythos as a hard-ass prick. It helps keep everyone in line, in all sorts of ways. Plus, it's a disgrace I never realized Troy's songs were stolen in the first place. Believe me, I'm much more careful and knowledgeable about that sort of thing now. But, yeah. For a whole bunch of reasons, I let everyone think I'm just that ruthless."

I laugh. "I love you so much."

"Glad to hear it. Because I love you."

"So..." I say. "There's something else I want to talk about. Two things I need to come clean about, actually." I take a deep breath. "Stephanie Moreland. I already had a copy of her complaint when I asked you about her in your kitchen."

"I know," he says. "After you got drunk and passed out that night, when I put you to bed, I noticed her complaint sitting in a box at the foot of your bed."

"Oh, snap." I wince. "Were you mad?"

"For a split-second. But quickly, I felt nothing but proud of you. I knew you'd been hired to 'peel my onion.' And that's exactly what you were doing."

Butterflies whoosh into my stomach. God, I love this man. "I hope you know I'd never write about Stephanie in my article about you, any more than I'd write about Troy or Isabel. I only got copies of those three lawsuits—that lease dispute, Stephanie, and Troy—because I was following breadcrumbs. It's what I do. I can't help it. But I've never once considered writing any sort of exposé on you."

"I know that. You were smart to follow every breadcrumb, for both professional and personal reasons. The first night I met you, I told you I admire hustlers. And I meant it."

I beam a huge smile at him. "If you'd snooped a little more into that box, you would have found Troy's complaint at the bottom."

Reed shrugs. "I saw Stephanie's lawsuit on top and didn't have the stomach to root around further. So, what's the second thing you feel the need to 'come clean' about?"

"Yeah. Uh." My cheeks blast with heat. "Howard Devlin. I'm investigating him. Hoping to write an article about him for *Dig a Little Deeper*."

Reed looks confused. "What's the nature of your 'investigation'? You think Howard has committed financial crimes of some sort?"

I shake my head. "No. I'm gunning for Howard Devlin because I'm ninety-nine percent sure he's a serial sexual predator, and that it's the worst kept secret in Hollywood."

Reed looks deeply shocked, and I know, in my bones, he has no idea about Howard's reputation among the women who've interacted with him.

I tell him everything I know thus far, told to me by CeeCee, Hannah, and Francesca, fully admitting all my information is based on hearsay. All of it adding up to the same conclusion: Howard Devlin almost certainly regularly harasses and/or assaults women. Sometimes, as part of a "casting couch" scenario. Other times, when he's not getting what he wants through coercion and manipulation and dangling carrots, he resorts to flat-out roofie-ing his victims.

"CeeCee gave me the green light to pursue my investigation, full steam ahead, this morning. I called her before boarding my flight and told her about my conversations with Francesca and Hannah. So, I'm a full-fledged investigative reporter now, chasing a story. But I want you to know, I'm not doing it to get back at Isabel, or to hurt or humiliate her in any way. She's irrelevant to my reasons for pursuing this article. But I admit she'll probably feel humiliated, and most likely want to break her engagement, if I'm successful. But I'm not going to hold back on writing this, simply because Isabel happens to be Howard's fiancée and your beloved ex-girlfriend."

"As well you shouldn't. And, to be clear, I didn't love her, Georgie. I never fell in love with her. Now that I love you, I know that for sure."

I touch his cheek. "Do you think Isabel knows about any of those rumors?"

Reed screws up his face. "I can't imagine she does. We've had several conversations about Howard over the years. I used to be annoyed about how obsessed he was with her, and told her so, and she never once said a word about any of this kind of stuff."

"Well, if that's the case, then she's going to get blindsided. People are going to wonder how much she knew, and if she looked the other way, simply because Howard was helping her career. That narrative won't be a good look for 'America's Sweetheart.'"

Reed scrubs the stubble on his chin. "Shit. Maybe I should warn Isabel about him. Or at least, that a potential shit storm is coming her way. I don't know when she's planning to marry him, but she can't go through with it."

"No, Reed. Please. I'm trusting you by telling you about this article. CeeCee told me not to tell anyone. And she specifically told me *not* to let Isabel find out about it, because she's worried Isabel might run to Howard and warn him. And then who knows what Howard might do? What hush money payments he might make to the witnesses I'm going to try to interview?"

Reed looks physically nauseated. And my stomach twists in response.

"If you're thinking of asking me *not* to write this article, then don't. Just like you won't compromise your business judgment for anyone, not even someone you love, I won't compromise my journalistic integrity. This is going to be a huge story. I can feel it. So, please, don't ask me to choose between my love and loyalty to you, and your loyalty to Isabel, versus my convictions and ambition and moral code."

Reed's face softens. He smiles and takes my hand. "So feisty. I love it." He sighs. "Sweetheart, I wasn't thinking, even for a second, of asking you not to write this article. If Howard has done any of this stuff, then I want him taken down, every bit as much as you do."

I exhale with relief. "Really?"

"Of course."

"I thought, maybe, since he's Isabel's fiancé, and you obviously still care about her, you wouldn't want her hit by any sort of scandal."

"I'd rather she's embarrassed by a scandal than married to a monster." He touches my cheek. "And let me be clear about something else, my love. I still care about Isabel. I'm still her friend, whether she believes that or not. But at every turn, at every fork in the road, I'll always, *always* choose *you*, and *us*, and our love, over Isabel or anyone else. *Every fucking time*. That's what I was trying to tell you by sending you that surveillance video. I had the idea to send it to you days ago. But I only did it when I was finally ready to trust you, completely, with the information. Besides trying to vindicate myself, I was telling you I pick you—I pick *us*—over protecting Isabel's secret."

I hug him. "I love you."

"I love you. I choose you, Georgie. Above anything and everyone else."

I kiss his cheek. "I choose you too."

"Write this article about Devlin, baby. Take him down. I'll be with you, cheering you on, every step of the way."

I take a deep breath to quell the surge of adrenaline I'm feeling. "I'm so excited. I really think this article is going to be huge. Plus, I think writing it will give me some much-needed closure about Gates, you know? I need that so much."

Anguish flickers across Reed's chiseled face. He lets out a long, controlled breath. "There's something I need to tell you, love. Something about Gates."

My stomach drops into my toes. "About *Gates*?"

He touches my chin. "Come on. We'll talk about it over dinner. Amalia left food in the fridge for the weekend. Let's eat and have a really nice bottle of wine and I'll tell you everything."

EIGHTY
REED

"Have you ever heard the term 'white-hat hacker'?" I ask. Georgina and I are dressed in soft clothes now, sitting at my kitchen table with one of Amalia's meals and a bottle of red. And I'm nervous. Yes, *I* know Henn is completely trustworthy. Even more so than a priest or lawyer. But *Georgie* doesn't know that. What if she finds out I told Henn about Gates, out of pure necessity, and decides, once and for all, she can't trust me to keep a promise? If me telling Henn about Gates is the straw that breaks Georgina's back, and she leaves me again—for good, this time—*after* I've said those three little words to her—words I've never said to another woman—then I'm positive I won't survive it.

Georgina says, "White-hat hackers are the ones who help companies find vulnerabilities in their online systems, so the bad guys can't hack them."

My heart is thundering. "That's right. Well, Henn is one of the best white-hat hackers in the world. Sometimes, he does favors for good friends, including me. In fact, if he believes in the cause enough, he'll even don a grey—or maybe even *black*—hat, on occasion."

Georgie lights up. "Oooh! You think maybe Henn would hack into Howard's computer for me?"

Damn. I probably shouldn't have led with that. "Uh... No. I mean, maybe. But Howard wasn't the reason I mentioned Henn." I take a deep breath. "Georgie, I had Henn gather some information for me about Gates. So I could find something to destroy him with."

Georgina's nostrils flare. But she says nothing.

"When you told me what Gates did, I wanted to kill him. Literally. I still do. But since murder is apparently hard to get away with, according to Leonard, and I very much enjoy my freedom—I decided to destroy Gates in a more indirect way. I figured he'd have a stash of child porn, or maybe Henn would find proof he'd embezzled from the school or something. I didn't know what Henn would find. All I knew, in my bones, was a guy like Gates couldn't be living a squeaky-clean life."

Georgina blinks slowly... and exhales.

"I'm sorry I breached your confidence by telling Henn your secret."

"What, exactly, did you tell him?"

"The gist of what you'd told me. Gates was your teacher in high school, someone you trusted, and he tried to rape you, but you got away. I also told him you've been deeply traumatized by the incident."

"He's the only person you've told about this?"

"Yes. And I told him not to tell anyone, not even Hannah. And I know he hasn't. Please, don't be angry. Please, Georgina, don't leave me."

Her features soften with pity. "Oh, Reed." She gets up and slides into my lap. "I'm not going to leave you. This is DMV-serious, remember?" She touches my cheek. "I like that you felt so protective of me, you roped Henn into helping you." She smiles. "It turns me on that you did that, if I'm being honest."

I'm so relieved, I can only exhale loudly.

Georgina chuckles. "You poor thing. You really thought I'd *leave* you for telling Henn?"

"Georgina, when it comes to you, I never know what you're going to do. And I know we're only just beginning to rebuild trust. I don't want there to be any reason for you to doubt me, ever."

She presses her forehead against mine. "Don't cheat on me. Don't lie to me. Don't you dare smack me. But anything else, we'll work it out. I'm not going anywhere, ever."

Again, I breathe a sigh of relief. "Don't cheat on me. Don't lie to me.

Feel free to smack me, any time. Especially in bed. But, please, for the love of all things holy, do not put a scratch on my Bugatti."

"Deal." She kisses my cheek and returns to her chair. "So, did Henn find something useful?"

"He did. And what he found led him to hacking the principal of your high school and another guy—a renowned criminal defense attorney named Steven Price. AKA the father of the Price Brothers: Brody, Brendan, and Benjamin."

"I remember Brody. He was a year behind me. The star quarterback. I don't remember his brothers, though."

"You wouldn't. Brendan was two years behind Brody, and Benjamin a year behind him, so you were long gone by the time the two younger Price brothers got *their* starting quarterback gigs."

"What does the father of the Price brothers have to do with Gates?"

"Steven Price confidentially paid hush money to two female students who'd been assaulted by Gates."

Georgina gasps.

"There might be more victims besides those two other girls and you. Maybe more girls, like you, who told nobody. But, thanks to Henn, we know, for sure, there were at least three total girls, including you. One before you. One after you. The before you was a sixteen-year-old named Katrina Ibarra. Gates raped her a year and a half before he tried to rape you."

"Oh my God."

"It was smack in the middle of football season, when scouts from all the top colleges were actively trying to recruit Brody Price. Hence, the motivation for Steven Price to keep that information from coming out and disrupting his son's football program."

"This is... crazy."

"The second girl, the one after you, was a fifteen-year-old named Penny Kaling. It's not clear exactly the nature of Gates' sexual assault of her. All we know, for sure, from some text messages, is that Gates forced himself on Penny in some way, and she was scared and ashamed and extremely upset about it the next day."

Georgina looks ashen. "You realize what this means, right? If I'd reported Gates, I could have saved Penny from whatever happened to her."

"Not necessarily. Katrina reported him and it got her nowhere. She told a teacher, who told the principal, who then called Katrina and Gates into his office for separate interviews. After those interviews, the principal, in his infinite wisdom, determined Katrina's claim 'wasn't credible.' And that was that. He swept it under the rug and didn't send it up the flagpole to anyone else."

"How is that possible?"

I shrug. "Gates denied all wrongdoing, and the principal believed him. Gates said Katrina was an unstable girl with a crush who'd thrown herself at Gates and gotten rejected—and, now, she was getting back at him. Lucky for Gates, Katrina wasn't a star pupil. She'd been suspended the prior year for plagiarism. Plus, she was known for being a 'drama queen' after a couple breakups. So, the principal decided it was a 'he said, she said' situation, where the accuser wasn't credible, and the accused was a 'well-respected and admired pillar of our community.' Oh, and by the way, the football team was having an undefeated season at this point."

Georgina hangs her head. "I should have known he'd do it to someone else."

"Look at me, Georgina. You were seventeen and in survival mode. If you'd said something, I doubt it would have made a difference. There were no witnesses to your assault, any more than there were to Katrina's. If you'd accused Gates of trying to rape you, maybe those mean girls from the newspaper class would have come forward to say you'd always had a 'thing' for Mr. Gates. Maybe you would have been labeled a 'drama queen,' the same as Katrina. Has there ever been a time in high school when you lost your temper, or maybe got highly emotional, or displayed some sort of behavior Gates or the principal could have pointed to in order to paint you as an 'overly emotional' and 'unstable' drama queen, too?"

"Well, of course. I was a teenage girl who wound up breaking down every year on the anniversary of her mother's death."

"Well, there you go."

Georgina sighs. "So, how did Steven Price get involved?"

"Gates contacted him and told him some 'crazy' girl was making accusations against him. At the time, Brody was being courted by the best colleges in the country. So, Steven Price told Gates not to worry about it. He'd take care of it. And he did. He paid Katrina off. Well, Katrina and her mother, since Katrina was a minor."

"I can't believe her mother took that money."

"Don't judge her too harshly. Katrina's father wasn't in the picture. Her mother, an immigrant, worked three jobs. So, a hundred grand was life-changing money to that family. All Katrina had to do was transfer schools and shut the fuck up about Gates forevermore. I can't really blame them for taking the deal, especially after the principal had basically called her a liar. I'm sure Katrina figured a hundred grand in her and her mother's pockets would help her a whole lot more than going to the police and being called a liar again."

Georgina looks down at her wine glass on the table, shaking her head. "What about the other girl? Did she get paid off, too?"

"She did. Penny was fifteen when Gates did whatever he did to her. A sophomore on the newspaper staff. Unlike Katrina, she didn't report him to anyone. But we have text messages between Penny and Gates, where she tells him she feels 'sick' about what she 'let' him do to her and that she'd been crying nonstop about it all day. She says she'd never done anything like that before and she feels like throwing up every time she thinks about it. Next thing you know, Steven Price was wiring Penny and her mother two hundred grand as part of a confidential settlement."

"No father in the picture?"

"No father. Not sure if that was a coincidence or a sign of Gates' MO. Maybe he figured girls with one parent at home, like you, had less of a support system. Or maybe he thought one parent would be easier to convince, later on, that nothing happened. Either way, by the time Gates assaulted Penny, he was Steven Price's man. Brody had gone on to play football at Purdue. His first pick. And the next Price brother, Brendon, was having a golden season and getting courted by top colleges."

"And the principal?"

"It's not clear what he knew about Penny. We found nothing to indicate he knew anything. But who knows?"

Georgina picks up her wine glass and takes a long gulp. When she replaces her glass, she puts her elbows onto the table and sinks her face into her hands. "This is... horrible."

I get up and pull her to me. Take her into my arms. Hold her tight and kiss her cheek. "Don't beat yourself up about not telling anyone. You did the best you could under the circumstances."

"But I'm not seventeen anymore."

"No, you're not."

"But what good would it do to speak up now? It's been almost five years since he tried to rape me—and it'd still be my word against his because those other two girls signed confidentiality agreements. I'd be on my own, the same as always. He said, she said. Only, now, five years later."

"The truth is the truth, whether anyone believes you or not. Maybe, if you speak up, you'll save the next girl. And if you don't, at least you tried."

She makes a tortured sound. "I need some time to think. Can you send me everything Henn sent you?"

"Of course. How about you read it *after* we get back from New York, though? Like you said, it's been almost five years. Surely, it can wait another five days. In the meantime, let's have fun and celebrate your birthday and forget about this shit."

She looks grateful for the suggestion. "Yes. I'd like that."

"In fact, let's kick off that game plan, starting now." Without hesitation, I scoop my beloved butterfly into my arms like a bride, making her swoon audibly. "Come on, beautiful. One giant dose of pleasure-induced amnesia, coming right up."

EIGHTY-ONE
GEORGINA

I'm deliciously tipsy as I stare at Reed's gyrating, muscular ass in the mirrored ceiling. My wrists are bound. So are my ankles. I'm spread eagle as Reed fucks me. Staring at that mouthwatering ass. The way his hard muscles clench and unclench magnificently with each beastly thrust is sublime. And the best part? As Reed claims me, he keeps whispering to me in a husky growl. He tells me he loves me. That he worships me. He says I own him. And in reply, I'm groaning out words like "I love you" and "so good" and "that ass!" And, of course, the words Mr. Hottie told me to say the first time he laid eyes on me at the panel discussion: "Yes... yes... *yes*."

When I reach climax this time, I feel like I'm having a seizure. Which, in fact, I think I am. And, of course, my release sends Reed over the edge, too.

With a soft kiss to my lips, Reed unties me and pulls me to him, and I cleave my naked body to his, leaving not even the slightest space between us, literally or figuratively.

We talk about tomorrow's trip to New York. About how excited Reed is to show me the City for my first time.

"And then you know what we're going to do?" he says excitedly. "On your birthday itself, we'll swing by Boston to see Alessandra."

I shriek with joy and pepper his face with kisses and then, just because I know it's his favorite thing, leap up and do a particularly jiggly happy dance that makes Reed hoot and guffaw and applaud. And, finally, I dive back into bed and assault my man with enthusiastic kisses.

"If it turns out Alessandra isn't comfortable around me," Reed says, "then no worries. I'll give you two money to have a nice lunch or dinner without me."

"Oh, honey, Alessandra will be thrilled to see you. You're the reason she got that gig at the coffee house. I know she's dying to thank you."

Reed looks genuinely thrilled. "Well, in that case, why don't you ask Alessandra if she can get onto the schedule to perform at the coffee house the night we'll be in Boston. We'll do lunch that day, and watch Alessandra that night."

My heart lurches. Oh, man, this could be a *huge* opportunity for Alessandra! If she hits it out of the park, who knows what Reed might do? I take a deep breath and try not to sound like I'm totally freaking out. "Yeah, good idea. I'll tell her. But only if you promise me one thing."

"Anything."

"Don't give me any more gifts, okay? You've already given me too much, and I've given you nothing. This trip to New York and Boston—that's my only birthday present, okay? Nothing else."

"Okay, first off. You haven't given me *nothing*. Every time you give me a happy dance, especially a naked one, it's the best gift *ever*."

I giggle.

"And, second off, nobody—not even you—is going to tell me what I can and can't give the woman I love. So fuck off with that shit."

I feign shock and flip him off. And he feigns outrage and lurches at me like a bear and then proceeds to eat my extended middle finger, and then my arm, making comical "nom, nom, nom!" noises, as he does.

Finally, when Reed is done devouring my arms and neck and breasts and ears, he pulls back from our silliness and looks down at me with twinkling brown eyes. "This is going to be so much fun," he says. And I know he's not talking about our trip to New York.

EIGHTY-TWO
REED

"Georgina!" Owen says warmly, embracing her. "It's great to see you!"

"It's great to see you! You look dapper."

Georgina and Owen are having this conversation in front of me in a backstage hallway at Madison Square Garden. Owen has been in New York the past few days, working as the point of contact for a documentary film crew shooting tonight's RCR concert for a Netflix special. And, of course, the Intrepid Reporter is here to do a quick interview of RCR.

"And you're perfection!" Owen coos to Georgina. "The lady in red. That ruby necklace is a show-stopper."

Georgina touches the gems around her neck and looks at me. "It was a gift from my generous boyfriend."

Owen already knows that, of course. He's the point of contact for both my accountant and bookkeeper, so he's well aware of any large purchase I might make. But Owen, smart man that he is, plays along. "That was quite a gift. Sounds like someone is smitten. And I can see why."

"Sorry to interrupt this lovefest,'" I say dryly. "Is everything all set for filming? Did Andrew get my notes on those shots I want him to get?"

Owen nods. "Andrew's got a skeleton crew in the guys' dressing room now, capturing that behind-the-scenes idea you had." He looks at

Georgina. "The band is expecting you. I told them to allot forty-five minutes. Is that enough time?"

"Double what I need, probably. The special issue will be focusing a lot more on Dean, individually, than the full band, so we only need a quickie with all four."

We head off toward the dressing room, at which point Owen leans into me and whispers, "Wow, boss, this is quite a 'purely professional relationship' you're having."

Inside the dressing room, we find all four guys of Red Card Riot, as expected, plus their usual entourage, plus, a skeleton crew for the documentary. And, last but not least, there are several PAs flitting around the room... including, to my delight, the little waif who walked in on Georgina and me backstage at the Rose Bowl, when I was camped between Georgina's naked thighs.

"You remember Georgina." I say to RCR. And all four of them—Dean, Clay, Emmitt, and C-Bomb—immediately come over to greet her. But nobody more enthusiastically than C-Bomb—Caleb Baumgarten—who strides over, hugs Georgina with fervor, like she's his long-lost lover.

As small talk ensues, I steal a glance at the little PA from the Rose Bowl to find her looking at me like she's a mutt at the pound who just took a crap in her food bowl. I smile at her reassuringly, but it's no use. She's terrified of me. Not at all happy to see me, to put it mildly.

When I return my attention to the band and Georgina, they've already moved to a nearby sitting area, so I follow them and take a chair behind Georgina, where I've got a direct line to C-Bomb. *Keep your friends close and your enemies closer.*

C-Bomb asks Georgina—but not me—if she'd like a drink. Georgina declines, explaining, "I drank too much champagne on the flight here. It's my first time in New York, plus my birthday week, so I went a little crazy with the bubbly."

C-Bomb looks like a shark smelling blood. "Your first time in New York *and* your birthday week? This calls for celebration. Come to our party after the show tonight, and we'll make you our guest of honor."

Motherfucker.

"Oh, that's sweet of you!" Georgie says. "But I've already got plans tonight."

C-Bomb is undeterred. "How about tomorrow, then? We're not

leaving New York until Wednesday. I'll show you all the tourist spots by day. And take you for the best pizza you've ever had by night."

I'm a hair's breadth away from launching out of my chair, grabbing C-Bomb by his mohawk, and dragging his tattooed ass out of the dressing room. But, quickly, it's clear there's no need for me to intervene. My baby's got this.

"Thanks for the offer," Georgina says sweetly. "But I'm here with my boyfriend. He knows New York really well. I'm sure he'll be taking me to a great pizza place."

Oh, how I love this brilliant, gorgeous woman. And, ooooh, how I love seeing Caleb look like he just got punched in the balls.

"Cool," Caleb says. And that's it. He sinks into his chair, looking defeated.

"What are you and your *boyfriend* planning to do while you're in town?" Clay, the bassist, asks, and it's clear his question is only designed to razz his drummer.

"Oh, the usual tourist things," Georgina says. She rattles off everything we've talked about doing during our stay, and then adds, "Plus, we're going to visit family." I'm assuming her comment refers to our planned detour to Boston, until she says, "My boyfriend's mother lives in Scarsdale and he always visits her when he comes to the East Coast."

My heart stops.

No.

How did I not see that one coming?

Georgie has made it clear she wants us to "come clean" with each other—to trust each other "completely," as she keeps saying. And, of course, I'm fully on board with that plan. But only in regard to stuff that *directly* affects Georgina. Not *everything* about me. And certainly not about my mother. I've spent my entire life lying to people about my mother! Literally, my *entire* life. And I can't suddenly stop doing it, just because I've fallen head over heels in love.

When I was in grade school, I remember telling classmates my mother was a firefighter who worked crazy hours down at the station, which was why my nanny, Amalia, and not my mother, was the one who showed up for school functions. Also, why I had to be so quiet during the day—so my mother could sleep at odd hours. Looking back, it was an interesting choice of profession for her, but my undeveloped brain thought it was a stroke of brilliance at the time.

By middle school, I'd grown savvy enough to realize my mother's slight frame made the firefighting story wholly unbelievable. So, *voila,* she became the US Ambassador to France.

After that, during my first year of high school, once I'd started living at that horrid group home, I remember telling the other kids both my parents had died in a plane crash. Which, in my mind, was a whole lot better than admitting I was in foster care because my mother was in a mental facility and my father in prison for bilking innocent people out of their life savings, and all my relatives had decided I was too big a pain in the ass—my anger issues way too difficult to manage—to deal with me. Not to mention, they'd all figured out there was no pot of gold at the end of the rainbow for anyone who took me in.

Granted, lying about my father's death in high school came back to bite me in the ass a few times, whenever I happened to be talking to a kid who followed current events, and therefore knew all about my notorious father. But, mostly, my lie that I was an orphan worked out just fine, especially in relation to my dead mother. Which was good. The fewer questions about her, the better.

After my father killed himself during my first year of college, I abruptly stopped telling people Mom was dead. Instead, she became the mother of my current lies. The one living her best life. The one who does yoga and paints and plays Scrabble like a boss. And that's the mother she's going to remain, even with Georgina. Especially with Georgina. Because, now that I'm truly happy and in love for the first time in my life, the only thing I want to do, more than ever, is look *forward,* not back. Why would I want my relationship with Georgina to get dragged down by the shit that's always dragged me down my entire fucking life?

I take a deep, calming breath. It's fine. I'll simply tell Georgina my mother isn't available for a visit this time. I'll say she's got a friend staying with her. Or that she's out of town, visiting a friend in Paris. Or Toronto. And on our next visit to New York, I'll make excuses that time, too. And then, again and again. And if Georgina starts asking me why she *still* hasn't met my mother, down the line, I'll deal with it then. Who knows? Maybe I'll feel ready at some point to tell Georgina the truth.

Maybe one day I'll tell her about all the tragedies that have left my mother irrevocably broken. The tragedies sitting like an elephant on my chest every day of my life. But today isn't that day.

Everyone around me chuckles, drawing me out of my thoughts—and I realize Georgina is in the midst of a raucous interview of RCR. I watch her for a moment, marveling at her confidence and charisma. At how obviously she's charmed each and every one of them. Not just C-Bomb.

After a moment, my eyes drift to that PA, the one who walked in on Georgina and me. She's sitting in a far corner, watching the interview. And when her eyes happen to land on mine, she flashes me a pitiful look that practically screams, *I swear I didn't tell anyone what I saw!* before quickly looking away, her face flushed.

I resist the urge to smile at her misery—because, man, it's highly amusing to me—and, instead, shift my eyes to Dean. My golden goose. The face and voice and brilliant mind that launched my empire. He's a fucking genius, that man. And a great guy, too. Can't say the same thing about his best friend. Speaking of which... my eyes snap back to C-Bomb to find him glaring at me.

Fuck you, I shoot him nonverbally, with a little lift of my chin.

He returns the glare and the gesture. And then does something that makes my blood simmer. He looks at Georgina lasciviously, and then back at me, and flashes me a look that plainly says, *Looks like we both missed out on that one, eh?* He winks, like he's taking great pleasure in knowing I won't get to tap that ass, any more than he will.

And that's it. My blood flash-boils. I look away, forcing myself not to shoot him a smug look that will telegraph I've already tapped that ass, motherfucker... and it was the best ass I've ever had.

Goddammit. Clearly, my scare tactics with that little PA worked *too* well, because there's no doubt in my mind she didn't tell C-Bomb, or anyone else, what she saw going down in that dressing room. Or, rather, *who* she saw going down. When C-Bomb heard I'd nixed Georgina's plans to attend his party and tag along on tour, he must have figured I did that because I wanted Georgina for myself... but *not* because I'd *already* successfully gotten her. And that pisses me off to no end. Sitting here now, I *want* Caleb to know I've fucked Georgina. I want him to know I'm fucking her every night of my life. In fact, I want every fuckboy on my label to know it. Even the nice guys, too. I want the whole *world* to know Georgina is mine. In fact, I want to take out a full-page ad in *Rock 'n' Roll* to broadcast the truth: *I love Georgina Ricci... and, miraculously, she loves me, too, motherfuckers!*

There's more laughter that draws my attention. I look at Georgina. She's having a great old time with the band. And, suddenly, I feel like a man possessed. Obsessed with the idea of C-Bomb, and the other band members, knowing *I'm* the "boyfriend" Georgina just mentioned.

"Awesome, guys," Georgina says. She rises from her seat. "That's all I need."

The guys thank Georgina. Dean wishes her a great time in New York and a happy birthday. The other guys follow suit, with Clay specifically telling her to have fun with her "boyfriend." Georgina wishes the band a great show. And in the middle of all that, Owen arrives with a small group of VIPs who've come to meet the band.

I shake hands with the VIPs and introduce them to the guys, and then to Georgina—but only as a reporter for *Rock 'n' Roll*. Not as my girlfriend. Because that's what Georgina has specifically said she wants, whenever we're interacting with my artists. But this time, unlike all times before, not getting to call Georgina my *girlfriend* is driving me batshit crazy. I want—no, I *need*—the world to know she's mine.

As the VIPs take their selfies with the band, I pull Georgina aside. "I need to talk to you about something."

She looks concerned. "Are you okay?"

I glance at C-Bomb, and force myself, through sheer force of will, not to kiss Georgie, right here and now, so he can see me do it. "No, actually, I'm not. Come on, Miss Ricci. Follow me."

EIGHTY-THREE
GEORGINA

Reed leads me down a hallway into an empty dressing room, where he closes the door and guides me to a couch. "I can't do it anymore," he blurts. "I can't hide that you're mine and I'm yours. I want everyone, especially my artists, to know it."

I exhale with relief. "Oh, God. I thought it was something serious."

He pulls on me roughly, animalistically, sending arousal whooshing between my legs, and guides me to straddle him on the couch. "I want to shout from the highest rooftops, 'She's mine!' I know you don't want my artists to know, but I—"

"Go for it," I say, and Reed's face ignites. "I don't want to hide our relationship, either. If someone thinks I'm too young for you, or they don't take me seriously as a writer because they think you pulled strings —screw 'em. *Ciao, stronzo.*"

Reed crushes his mouth to mine, and we kiss passionately. Until, soon, predictably, we're both on fire. Making out energetically. Groping. Grinding. Devouring. You know. Being us.

Reed pulls my shirt up and deftly unlatches my bra. With a growl of arousal, he buries his face in my breasts and sucks on my nipple, making me moan—

"Oh, no!" a female voice blurts in the doorway, making me leap off Reed onto the couch and scramble to cover myself.

"Don't leave, little PA," Reed says calmly. "I want to speak to you about this."

And that's when I see her. The *same* PA from the Rose Bowl. Standing in the doorway, her ashen face turned away.

"I didn't see anything, Mr. Rivers!" she shouts. "Not a thing!"

"You can go," I say. "I'm sorry you had to see this again."

"No, you may *not* go," Reed corrects firmly. "Come here. Miss Ricci's got her shirt on now. I want to speak to you."

"*Reed*," I chastise. "Let her go."

"Not a chance. Come here, little PA. Right now."

With a loud sigh, the poor PA drags herself across the room like a shackled prisoner and stands before us, her brow furrowed with anxiety. "I didn't see anything except two people having a conversation."

Oh, man, Reed is smiling like a possum with a sweet potato. Obviously, he's *loving* this. "What's your name, again?" he asks, his dark eyes glinting with the purest form of glee.

"Amy O'Brien. Mr. Rivers, I don't know how this happened again. There must have been a mix-up. Owen told me to come in here, right away, to talk to you. He said you texted him that you needed to see me *urgently*. In *this* dressing room."

Full understanding of Reed's wickedness slams me upside the head. I swat Reed's broad shoulder. "Reed Rivers! You're evil!"

He bites back a smile and calmly addresses Amy. "Remember that time at the Rose Bowl, when you *thought* you saw Miss Ricci and me doing something in a dressing room, but you were mistaken, because we were only talking?"

"Yes, sir. I didn't say a word to C-Bomb or anyone else about—"

"Yes, I know. I believe you. I want to remind you that you're still bound by your NDA with respect to that incident."

"Yes, sir. Same as now."

"No, not the same as now," he says, shocking me. "I mean, you *are* bound by your NDA, of course. But I'm giving you special permission to talk about what you just saw. In fact, I *want* you to talk about what you saw, just now, to anyone and everyone on this tour. *Especially C-Bomb.*"

I inhale sharply, floored by Reed's diabolical machinations. But I must admit, I'm holding back a smile. He's evil, yes. But he's damned sexy, too.

Reed says, "In fact, if you blab to C-Bomb about what you just witnessed, before he takes the stage tonight, I'll personally make sure you get a thousand-dollar bonus added to your next paycheck."

Amy's eyebrows shoot up. Obviously, that's a lot of money to her. "What, exactly, do you want me to say to C-Bomb, sir?"

"The truth. What you saw when you poked your head into the room. For real. Now, to be clear, last time is still off limits, Amy. But *this* time, fire away. In fact, let me give you a little something else to gossip about." He turns and smiles devilishly at me. "Georgina Ricci, I love you, baby."

I can't help smiling broadly. "I love you, too, Reed Rivers."

"And I don't mean that platonically," he adds. "I very much enjoy having sex with you, every single day."

I giggle. "I'm glad. Because I very much enjoy having sex with you."

Reed kisses me briefly, but sensuously—definitely *not* platonically—before returning to Amy with a smirk. "Did you catch all that, Amy O'Brien?"

She makes a face that plainly conveys her mistrust. Like she's wondering, *Is this a trap?* "Uhh," she says. "I think so?"

"We can do it for you again, if you're not clear."

"No, I am. And, congratulations. You two are an incredibly attractive couple. But... I just want to make sure I understand, out of an abundance of caution. You want me to be *honest* about what I've seen and heard tonight... with *Caleb*?"

"Correct," Reed says. "Tell everyone and anyone, as you like. But if you want to earn that bonus, you'll tell Caleb *tonight*."

She looks at me. "Are you okay with me doing this, Miss Ricci?"

"I'm thrilled about it, Amy. But thanks for asking."

"Okay, then. Sure. I'll head straight to C-Bomb now."

"Actually, hold on." Reed grabs his wallet, counts out ten bills, and hands them to Amy. "I trust you to earn it. There's no need for us to deal with payroll on this."

Amy takes the cash with a shy smile and disappears out the door, presumably to babble to C-Bomb about the shocking thing she's just witnessed.

"You're a sadist," I say. "That poor girl was nearly crapping her pants *again*. And you clearly enjoyed it."

"She's a PA on tour with a rock band. If she can't handle walking in on a make-out session a few times, she needs a new profession." He smirks. "Now, where were we, sexy girl?"

"Not so fast. When you texted Owen and arranged for that poor girl to walk in on us again, you didn't know I was going to say yes about you telling the world about us."

He shrugs, not understanding my meaning.

"*What if I'd said no?*"

"Then I would have put the fear of God into Amy O'Brien about her NDA, *again*. But, either way, I would have had the pleasure of getting walked-in on again. One of my all-time biggest turn-ons."

My jaw drops to the floor.

"Oh, please. You love getting walked-in on as much as I do."

"I do *not*."

"Liar. You love it."

"No, I don't."

"Yep. And you can't convince me otherwise."

I twist my mouth. "Okay, I admit it's a turn-on for me to see how much it turns *you* on. But that's as far as I'll go." Laughing, I slide onto his lap again, and we begin making out enthusiastically... until I remember the door to the dressing room is unlocked. "Hold on. Who knows who else you've arranged to 'accidentally' walk in on us." With a little bite to Reed's earlobe, I get up and lock the door—a move that elicits a booming and fervent "Boooo!" from Reed. And when I return to my hot boyfriend, his face, and the bulge behind his pants, tell me he's as aroused as I am.

Standing over him, I reach inside my skirt, pull off my cotton undies, and fling them onto the floor with gusto. And then, licking my lips, I slowly kneel before him, unzip his fly, pull out his hard shaft, lick him from his balls to his mushroom tip, and get to work. I lick and suck and deep-throat him with everything I've got, enjoying every groan and shudder and yank of my hair, until Reed is growling and quaking so fervently, I know he's on the bitter edge.

My heart pounding along with my clit, I get up, straddle him, and slide myself down onto his hardness. And the moment I'm positioned, Reed grabs my hips and roughly leads my movement, until we're both losing our minds. Release comes for Reed first—which isn't a surprise, considering the epic blowjob I just gave him. But after he comes, he kisses and touches me to a rolling, rocking orgasm that curls my toes and makes me wish he already had another erection I could suck.

I collapse onto him, feeling utterly euphoric. Swept away. Closer to him than ever. We're not going to hide our love anymore. From *anyone*. It's a dream come true.

I kiss his cheek. "So, I'm assuming you're planning to visit your mother during this trip, like always, right?"

Reed stiffens against me. "Uh. No, actually. Not this time. My mother is out of town. She's visiting a friend."

I bite my lip, trying not to smile in reaction to his lie. Oh, Reed. My beautiful, beloved liar. . . I was hoping he'd tell me the truth without coaxing. But I suppose old habits die hard. "Oh, yeah? How nice for her. Where does this friend of your mother's live?"

Reed pauses. His chest heaves. "In... I don't know, actually. I didn't ask. She's out of town. Somewhere."

I press my forehead against Reed's and exhale. "My love. I know all about your mother."

His breathing hitches. "What do you mean?"

"I know your mother isn't visiting a friend. I know she lives in a mental facility in Scarsdale. And I know and understand why you don't like to talk about that."

Reed has turned into a trapped animal, looking for a way out. With a soft whisper of reassurance, I caress his chiseled face. Kiss his cheek. Skim his lips with mine. "You don't have to spill your guts to me about her. Or about anything else that's been hard for you in your life. You're a private person, and I get that. I respect it. But you can't flat-out lie to me anymore, okay? Those days are over. We don't lie to each other about *anything*. You don't want to talk about something? You say so. *But you will not lie.* And neither will I. Which is why I'm confessing to you: I know all about your mother. And your childhood. I know about Oliver. And the divorce. I know *why* your mother lives in that mental facility, and why she's lived in one, almost continuously, since you were nine."

Somewhere in the arena, Red Card Riot launches into their first song. But I don't react. Because I don't care if we miss this entire concert *again*. All I care about is making my beloved Reed understand that I love him unconditionally. For real. The good, the bad, and the ugly.

I put my palms on his cheeks. "I'm not trying to force you to talk about this stuff with me. I just want you to know I love you. The *real* you. And, also, that I *admire* and *respect* you for overcoming so much to become the glorious man you are."

Reed looks flabbergasted. "How the hell do you know all this?"

I tell him about the legal malpractice lawsuit—which, to my surprise, he knows nothing about. He asks me some questions about it, which I answer. He asks me how long I've known about his mother being in a facility, and I tell him I've known since almost day one, thanks to a conversation with Amalia, during which I coaxed her into revealing certain things without her realizing I didn't already know them. "But I didn't read the malpractice lawsuit until a few days ago," I say. "That's where I got a far more thorough understanding of your childhood and everything your poor mother's been through."

Red Card Riot begins playing their debut hit, "Shaynee," in a distant part of the arena. My favorite RCR song. But, again, we don't react.

"I'd like to read those documents from the legal malpractice case," Reed says.

"Of course. You were so young during the divorce. I think reading them now will help you understand your mother, so much better. The deck has always been stacked against her, one way or another. I feel so bad for her." Reed looks like he's fighting his emotions, so I take his hand and bring his knuckles to my lips. "I think *not* talking about, or thinking about, things that are painful for you, has been your coping mechanism for a long time. I can relate. But, speaking for myself, I don't want to do that anymore. Not with *you*. I want to tell you everything. I want to show you every part of me. And I'd love for you to do the same with me. Reed, when we say, 'I love you' to each other, I want us to know the word 'you' means '*all* of you.' Not only the good parts we show everyone else."

Reed's Adam's apple bobs.

I feel overwhelmed with love for him. "Do we have a deal? No more secrets?"

Reed opens his mouth like he's going to say *yes*. But then he closes it and scowls. "No more secrets *at all*... about *anything*?"

I can't help chuckling at his facial expression. It's as if I've asked him to bring me a slice of the moon to put onto a cracker. "Correct. *Zero* secrets. No gray area."

Reed looks dubious. "I don't know, baby. Don't you think that's unrealistic? A guy's got to have *some* secrets. At least, small ones."

"Why? If they're little ones, all the more reason not to have them. Let's be open books."

Reed scrubs his face and exhales.

"What is it?" I say. "Spit it out, already."

He sinks into the couch in surrender. "Your necklace."

"Those aren't real rubies?"

He rolls his eyes. "Don't insult me. Of course, they're real. It's just that..." He exhales. "The necklace is worth quite a bit more than I told you. I wanted to pay off your father's mortgage, and I figured if the price tag for the necklace happened to be the same amount as what he owed, you'd think it was fate and let me 'return it,' so you could use the proceeds to pay off the loan."

I'm slack-jawed. "Our *entire* conversation about the necklace was—"

"A set-up. Yes. I knew what you'd say and do, so I arranged a situation that would lead to you saying and doing all of it, so you'd let me pay off the loan, without you being stubborn and contrary."

"And you think *I'm* the Bobby Fischer in this relationship?"

"Takes one to know one, baby. Don't bother asking me the actual value of the necklace. I think the monetary value of gifts should be exempt from our new 'open book' policy, don't you? But if we're truly going to tell each other the truth about 'everything,' other than the value of gifts, then I guess I should come clean about the necklace being part of my clever strategy to save your dad's condo from foreclosure."

I kiss him enthusiastically. "*Thank you.* You're the sweetest, most generous, most adorable man in the world."

"Only for you. Honestly, I was initially planning to buy something worth exactly eighty grand, so I could return it, and use the proceeds, just like I said. But then, I saw the ruby necklace on display on the other side of the store, and, the minute I saw it, I knew it had to be yours, no matter the price."

I gasp. "You didn't walk past Tiffany's and see the necklace in the store window?"

He snorts. "No. My meeting was in Century City. Not Beverly Hills."

I laugh uproariously, and so does he.

"I'm so relieved," I admit. "When you said you didn't think complete honesty was realistic, I thought you were going to drop a bombshell on me."

"Nah. I've got no more bombshells to drop, sweetheart. I'm done with those."

"So am I." I kiss him again, feeling like my soul is soaring around the small dressing room. "So, it's a deal. No more lies, from either of us. Ever again. Unless it's about the price tag of a gift or, you know, like about a surprise party or something like that. *But that's it.*"

Reed pauses underneath me, and I know he's thinking, *Shit.*

"What now?" I say. I pull out of our embrace and look at him sternly. "Whatever it is, spit it out, dude. Let's get it all out in the open."

Reed flaps his lips together. "It pertains to a gift, so I feel like it could very well be exempt."

"Except you know that's not true, or else you wouldn't look guilty as sin right now."

He grunts.

"Tell me." I pinch his face between my finger and thumb, making his lips part. "The truth shall set you free. *Speak.*"

Reed exhales and I release his face.

"The 'rental car' I got you for the summer?"

I gasp. "No. *Reed.*"

He winks. "Happy birthday, baby. It's all yours."

EIGHTY-FOUR
REED

"Feel free to go to a diner or something," I say to my usual New York driver, Tony, as he parks the sedan in front of my mother's facility. "I'll text you when we're about fifteen minutes out."

"You got it, Mr. Rivers."

I look at Georgina sitting next to me in the back seat. Never in a million years did I think I'd bring a girlfriend to meet my mother. How did Georgina convince me to do this?

"This is going to be great," she says, reading my mind. "You've briefed me for three days, love. I know what to expect."

She's right. Over the past three days, as Georgina and I have painted Manhattan red, visiting all the usual tourist spots, watching Broadway shows, and eating at fabulous restaurants, she's slowly, but surely, peeled every layer of my onion, all the way down to the nub. Down to my deepest core. To my darkest secrets and sources of shame and embarrassment and pain and insecurity. And to my surprise, with each new layer uncovered, I've found myself feeling *more* comfortable and in love with Georgina. Not less. And, slowly, I've felt that lifelong elephant, who lives on my chest, getting up and wandering off into parts unknown.

"Did you tell your mother I was coming today?" Georgina asks.

"No. I didn't want to answer any questions in advance. So, don't take it personally when she stares at you, mouth agape, like you're an alien from Mars." I look at the front door of the facility, without moving.

"It's going to be great," she says, patting me reassuringly.

I exhale and open the car door. "Well, here goes nothing."

Inside the lobby, the orderly behind the front desk, Oscar, looks shocked as we approach. And I'm not surprised. In all my years of coming here, I've never once shown up with a plus-one.

I introduce Georgina, calling her my girlfriend, which feels amazing, and then set about leafing through the logbook, as usual, to confirm my mother's paid "best friend" has been doing her job. When I'm satisfied she has, I slide the logbook to Georgina for her signature, and ask Oscar where I might find my mother.

Oscar glances at the wall clock. "With such nice weather, I'd try the garden first."

And off we go.

Once inside the garden, Georgina and I immediately spot my mother from afar, sitting before an easel in a far corner, looking engrossed and attentive.

"She's so beautiful," Georgina whispers. "She looks every bit as lovely as in that framed photo on your desk."

I shrug. "Mom always looks the most beautiful when she paints. It's like a time machine for her. It's when she's not painting that she's lost."

We begin crossing the lawn, and when we're close enough for Mom to notice our approaching movement, she does a classic double-take—followed by her face lighting up in a way I've never seen before. Squealing, Mom puts down her paint brush and rushes toward us. But, to my surprise, she doesn't hug me. She hugs *Georgina*, like she's known her forever.

"You're finally here!" she says. "I'm so glad you came!"

Oh, Jesus. Well, this is new. My mother has a lot of issues, including some cognitive dysfunction, but she's never before mistaken a stranger for someone she knows. Does she think Georgina is one of her long-deceased sisters, come back from the dead?

"Mom, no. This is my *girlfriend*, Georgina Ricci. You've never met her. She came with me from LA."

"Hi, Mrs. Rivers," Georgina says, putting out her hand. "I'm so happy I'm 'finally' here, too."

"*Eleanor.*"

"Eleanor."

"You're beautiful, Georgina."

"Thank you. So are you, Eleanor."

Mom hugs me. "Hello, dear. Yes, I know I've never met Georgina before. You think I don't know that?" She pulls back from our embrace and flashes me a chastising look. "I said I'm glad she's *finally* here because you've *finally* found a woman you like enough to bring her to meet me." Chuckling at my stunned expression, she addresses Georgina. "Please, tell me you like my son, as much as he likes you, or I'll never forgive him for bringing you here, only to tease me."

"I do like your son. I also love him very much. With all my heart."

Mom claps. "*Finally*! And you?"

"I like Georgina, and love her, too. With all my heart. To the moon and back again."

Mom squeals and grabs Georgina's hand. "Come. Sit and talk to me while I continue painting the ocean." She tosses over her shoulder, "Grab a couple chairs, Reed."

"Yes, Mother."

I carry two chairs over and get Georgina settled next to my mother, and myself settled next to Georgina, and then take a good, long look at this week's opus. Not surprisingly, it's more of the same. A Happy Family Portrait, featuring Mom's lost loved ones. This time, set at the seashore.

As usual, a younger version of Mom sits on a red blanket with her two young sons—Oliver and me—and both of us are happily licking ice cream cones. One of Mom's sisters wades in the ocean up to her knees. Another sister turns cartwheels in the sand. A third sister throws a colorful beach ball with her ill-fated mother.

Mom's father is in this happy scene, too, as usual. Although, per protocol, he's set apart from his other family members, just in case the pesky rumor about him setting the house fire that claimed his wife and three daughters was true.

Mom picks up her brush and begins filling in the gray-blue of the ocean. And as she paints, she peppers Georgina with questions. How did Georgina and I meet? How long have we dated? When did she know she was in love with me?

At first, I pipe in, here and there, to supplement Georgina's replies. But, quickly, it's clear I'm a third wheel. *Persona non grata.* So, I sit back and listen, feeling relieved and amused and, surprisingly, relaxed. After a bit, Mom starts asking Georgina personal questions that have nothing to do with me. Does Georgina have siblings? What do her parents do for a living? Which, of course, ultimately leads to Georgina revealing her mother's death.

"Oh, dear. I'm so sorry," Mom says. "My mother died, too." She points to her mother's happy avatar on her canvas. "When I was sixteen."

I brace myself. This is a topic I've avoided talking about with Mom my whole life. Like the plague. Same with Oliver's death. Because, obviously, I don't want to upset Mom or trigger a meltdown.

But Georgina jumps right in. "Oh, no," she says. "How did your mother die?"

I brace myself again. But to my surprise, Mom answers Georgina, in detail, without crying, and then proceeds to regale Georgina with stories about everyone in her painting. When Georgina asks follow-up questions, Mom not only answers them, she tells Georgina lovely, lighthearted stories about her family members, most of which I've never heard. And, suddenly, I realize something huge: Mom has been *dying* to talk about these people!

My eyes drift to Mom's painting again. To her family members, enjoying the sun and surf. To her younger self, sitting on that red blanket with Oliver and me. And I feel deep compassion for my mother washing over me, not disdain or shame or embarrassment. Not only that, I feel pissed at myself for never doing exactly what Georgina is doing right now. *Asking questions.*

"Tell me some happy stories about Oliver," Georgina says. And to my surprise, Mom leaps right in, treating us to three adorable stories about him, which then leads to her telling one about *me* I've never heard before—a story in which I played a concert with pots and pans on our kitchen floor for an enraptured audience of teddy bears.

A bell rings in the distance, signaling lunch is ready in the dining hall, and Mom stands like a Pavlovian dog, saying she's so hungry she could eat a hippo. But for some reason, for the first time, ever, seeing

Mom's avatar sitting happily on a blanket with her two young sons has given me an idea.

"Why don't we have a picnic? Right over there, on the grass?"

Mom loses her mind at the idea.

"You two continue chatting and enjoying the sunshine. I'll head inside and get everything we need."

Mom claps with glee, while Georgina flashes me a smolder that somehow simultaneously lights my very soul and sends rockets of desire into my dick. And I know, without a doubt, I just hit a grand slam homerun in the bottom of the ninth.

Feeling light as a feather, I practically skip into the dining hall, where Gerta, the woman in charge of the kitchen, hooks me up with the good stuff, all of it packed expertly into a beautiful basket.

But when I return to my mother and Georgina outside, holding the basket in one hand and a red blanket in the other, Mom bursts into tears at the sight of me.

My stomach drops. Shit. "It's okay, Mom. We don't have to do this if—"

She launches herself at me. "This is the best day of my life!" She pulls back from our hug, smiling broadly. And I'm relieved to realize her tears are happy ones. She asks if I got a sandwich for Lee, her boyfriend.

"Of course. And don't worry, I remembered you telling me once that he hates mustard with a fiery passion, so I specifically made sure Gerta didn't put a drop on his sandwich."

Mom touches her heart, looking like the name "Eleanor Rivers" was just announced after the phrase "And the Oscar goes to..." And, again, Georgina flashes me a look that makes me feel like I could jump, from standing, straight to the moon.

Biting back a wide smile, I say, "Come on, Mom. I know we can't have a picnic without *Lee*. That dude's the life of the party."

Mom looks like she's about to cry again, so I tell her to go find Lee while Georgina and I set up our feast.

Wiping her eyes, Mom heads off, leaving me alone with Georgina... who's now staring at me like I'm Superman who's just saved the world from a hurtling meteor.

"It's just a picnic," I say, my cheeks burning.

"It's not just a picnic."

I'm blushing too much to reply, so I hold up the blanket. "Help me spread this out, will you?"

"My pleasure."

We spread the blanket and lay out the food, and by the time Mom appears with Lee, the blanket looks ready for a photo shoot with *Better Homes & Gardens*. Brief introductions are made between Lee and Georgina, and a conversation about yoga ensues. At first, Georgina tries to include Lee in the discussion, but when she realizes that's a fool's errand, she leaves the silent man alone to quietly eat his mustard-free sandwich and stare at my mother like she walks on water.

And what am I doing in this Happy Family Portrait? A whole lot of nothing, really. Smiling. Looking around at the trees and flowers and birds and bees. Enjoying a damned good sandwich while listening to my mother and Georgina chatter away. *And it's amazing.* I tilt my face up toward the sun and enjoy the sensation. The peace infusing me. The certainty I feel that I've found The One. I can't believe Georgina is here. And that she knows *everything* about me, and loves me, anyway. No, actually, as she's told me repeatedly, she loves me even *more* because of what she's learned about me.

All of a sudden, I feel like I've been hit by a lightning bolt of pure joy and peace and certainty, and I realize this, right here, is the happiest moment of my life. Which is a crazy thought, considering it's such a big, fat *nothing* of a moment. A simple picnic in a garden with my mom and the woman I love. Plus the man my mother loves. But it's enough. It's not the way the storybooks show families. Or love. But this is what I have. And it's mine.

Moisture threatens my eyes, but, as usual, I push it away. I look at Georgina. She's laughing with my mother—who, in this moment, looks ten years younger than she did when I visited her by myself last month. How did Georgina do this? Nobody in my "real life" has *ever* entered this secret vault, this place where I visit my mother and wish in vain she could be different.

But, contrary to my fears, the sky isn't falling to have Georgina here. I feel nothing but good. Happy. *Free.* My eyes drift to a little brown bird hopping across a nearby tree branch. And then to a rosebush that's bursting with colorful blooms. I look at my mother's smiling face as she chats with Georgina. And I know, as surely as I know my name, I truly do love Georgina Marie Ricci with all of me.

EIGHTY-FIVE
REED

"Are you flying out of LaGuardia or JFK this time, Mr. Rivers?" Tony, my driver, says, as Georgina and I settle into his backseat.

"Teterboro, actually. We're flying private today."

"Yes, sir." Tony pulls away from the curb. "Did you have a good visit with your mother today?"

I look at Georgina and smile. "We had a wonderful visit. My mother wouldn't let Georgina leave until she promised to come back with me next time. Or without me. Either way."

Tony's eyes crinkle in the rearview mirror with his smile. "You're heading back to LA now?"

"No, we're stopping in Boston first. LA, after that."

"Oh, I love Boston. Make sure you walk the Freedom Trail, if you've never done that. Do you need a restaurant suggestion? My cousin lives in Boston."

"No, I've got it covered. It's Georgina's birthday tomorrow, so I'm taking her and her stepsister out to an extra special lunch."

"Ooh. Nice." Tony's dark eyes shift to Georgina in the rearview mirror. "Happy birthday, Miss Ricci."

"Thank you. I'm excited I get to see my stepsister." She tugs on my sleeve and mouths, *Thank you.*

"Your stepsister lives in Boston?"

"She's a student at Berklee. The music college?"

"Oh, yeah. That's a good one. She must be talented."

"Oh, she is." Georgina flashes me a salty look that makes me chuckle, before adding, "My stepsister is a singer-songwriter, and she just got hired to play at a popular coffee house near campus. She beat out lots of other talented people for the job."

"Good for her."

"Tomorrow evening, Reed and I are going to watch her perform there."

"Sounds like a great birthday to me."

"Doesn't it? It's been a great birthday *week*. The best, ever. Tomorrow will be the icing on the cake."

"So, you met Reed's mother today and he's meeting your stepsister tomorrow? This sounds serious, Mr. Rivers."

"That, it is, Tony. That, it is."

"Reed has already met my stepsister," Georgina says. "But he's never seen her perform, so that will be particularly exciting."

"What about your parents, Miss Ricci? Has Reed met them? If so, I'm assuming your father grilled Reed about his intentions, and then threatened to break his legs if he breaks your heart."

Georgina chuckles. "Reed hasn't met my dad yet, no. But that's *exactly* what he'd do. How'd you know that?"

Tony shrugs. "You're *Ricci*. I'm *Borelli*. I've got three daughters of my own, so I know how Italian fathers think. My daughters are still young, but if they brought home a suave guy like Mr. Rivers, I'd let the guy have it. No offense, Mr. Rivers."

"None taken. I've been called far worse things in my life than 'suave.'"

Georgina says, "I've brought home exactly *one* boyfriend in my life. And my father went so freaking Italian on that guy, I've never had the stomach to bring anyone home again."

Tony chuckles. "Sounds like your father is a good egg."

"The best. He was right to dislike that guy I brought home, by the way. He turned out to be a first-class jerk."

"Daddy always knows best."

Tony's eyes in his rearview mirror shift to me, and I flash him a look that says, "Wrap it up."

"Well, I'll leave you two alone now," Tony says. "Would you like some air? Music?"

"Music," I reply. "Something mellow, not too loud."

"You got it, Mr. Rivers."

Soft, soothing music begins playing and Georgina sinks back into the leather seat. "Whew. I was more nervous about meeting your mom than I let on. I'm so glad it went well."

"Let's do it, Georgie."

She glances at Tony and mouths, "*Here?*"

I chuckle, realizing she thinks I want to have sex. "No, sweetheart. Take me to meet your father."

Georgina makes the exact face I'd expect her to make if I'd just now asked her to shave my balls.

"Why is that such a ridiculous request?" I say, laughing at her expression. "We said we're not going to hide our relationship anymore. And you said yourself you don't care what anyone thinks."

"My father isn't 'anyone.' I care very much what he thinks."

"Aw, come on. I brought you to meet my mother, and I was scared to death to do that. And look how fantastically that turned out."

"That's different."

"Why?"

"Because your mother would never think I'm your boss. Because *I* haven't paid off *your* student loans, and your mother's condo, or paid for your mother's expensive medicine."

"Well, I'm not your boss. So, that's not an issue."

"My father won't understand that."

"And I can't fathom your father will have a problem with me taking care of you, and someone you love dearly, to the best of my abilities. Plus, you really shouldn't care what he thinks, Georgina. In the end, all that matters is what *we* think. What *we* feel."

"Yes. That's true, in relation to everyone in the world, except my father."

"Are you planning to see him for your birthday when we get back?"

"On Saturday. I'm going to his house for dinner and cake."

"Then I'm coming with you."

She winces.

"Stop being a coward. We're doing this. We're both open books now, remember? We've got nothing to hide."

"*From each other.*"

I laugh. "Come on, Ricci. Put your big girl panties on. Stop being a wimp."

"He's going to grill you, exactly like Tony said. He won't be happy with anything except you saying I'm the great love of your life."

"Great. Then, we've got nothing to worry about."

Georgina makes that face I love. The one where she opens her mouth all the way, like she can't believe what she's heard.

"Is that a yes?" I say.

She flashes me a million-dollar smile. "Okay, let's do it. But don't you dare tell him I've moved in with you. He still thinks I'm living at the hotel. Let's not give the poor man a stroke."

Tony's eyes crinkle in the rearview mirror at that.

"Don't worry." I touch Georgina's thigh. "I thought today would be a disaster, and it was the best day of my life."

Georgina bites her lip. "It was?"

"Yup. Thank you for pushing me to do it. You were right. It was beautiful. *Freeing.*"

She takes my hand. "What'd I tell you? *The truth shall set you free.*"

We rhapsodize about today's visit for a bit. But after a while, Georgina says she's tired, and I open my arm to her and let her crumple against me for a nap. After a few minutes, when I'm sure she's out like a light, I pull out my phone and tap out a text to Josh and Henn.

Me: Georgie and I just finished visiting my mother. It went fantastically well. Tomorrow, we're visiting her stepsister in Boston. Saturday, I'm going to dinner at her father's condo in LA.

Henn: HOLY SHIT!

Josh: Whoa. Mutual meeting of the parents? This is a first for you, right?

Me: Yep.

Josh: Damn, dude. This is as serious as you've ever been with someone, isn't it?

Me: I just told her she's the great love of my life. And saying it felt good, not scary.

Henn: I have no words.

Me: Josh, send me your brother's phone number, por favor. I want to ask him a question.

Josh: You can't ask me?

Henn: Or me? I'm the smart one, remember?

Me: You're not the right guys to answer this particular question.

Josh: Well, now I'm intrigued.

Henn: Ditto.

Me: Don't read too much into this, but I want to ask Jonas what made him decide to propose to Sarah, as opposed to continuing to shack up with her.

Henn: HOLY FUCK! You're thinking of proposing to Georgina?

Josh: Henn, no. Don't be stupid. He's obviously thinking of proposing to Sarah.

Henn: I knew it! When we talked and you said she's breakfast-worthy, I said you sounded like I did after meeting Hannah. I'm a genius.

Me: Calm down, Peter. I'm simply gathering information, out of curiosity.

Josh: Last time I checked, Henn and I are every bit as married as my brother. We can tell you why we proposed.

Me: But Jonas' situation is the closest to mine. Henn's always known he'd get married and have kids one day. And you, Josh, only proposed after knocking Kat up. Yes, it turned out great for you, but you didn't put a ring on it out of the blue, like Jonas did. I want to talk to a dude who wasn't always planning to get married, same as me, and also didn't knock his girlfriend up.

Josh: I didn't ask Kat to marry me because she was preggers. I was perfectly fine with having a baby momma.

I only proposed when I realized I wanted Kat to be my wife.

Henn: And I didn't ask Hannah to marry me because I had some thumping need to marry just anyone. I only asked Hannah because I knew, for sure, she was The One.

Me: I'm not questioning your undying love for your wives, fellas. I just want to know what makes a guy who's never been interested in marriage, like me, suddenly do an about-face and pop the question.

Henn: I'm answering it, whether you like it or not. I knew it was time to pop the question when "girlfriend" wasn't nearly enough.

Josh: Perfect way to explain it. That's how I felt, too. Girlfriend/baby momma wasn't enough. Even fiancée kind of bummed me out after the novelty wore off. I couldn't wait to call her my wife. Mrs. Faraday.

Henn: Same. Mrs. Hennessy. Couldn't wait.

I look down at Georgina, at the top of her dark head. She's the best thing that's ever happened to me. The great love of my life, like I implied a moment ago. But, at least for now, I've got no problem calling her my girlfriend. In fact, when I introduced Georgina as my girlfriend to Tony, and then Oscar, the orderly, and then to my mother, I felt nothing but buzzed and excited each time. But before I've answered my friend's latest texts, my phone buzzes with one from Henn.

Henn: I wanted to propose to Hannah after knowing her for a week. I only waited out of fear of rejection. But, really, the minute I saw her, I thought, Hello, Wife.

Again, I look down at Georgina against my shoulder. I didn't think, "Hello, Wife," when I saw her in that lecture hall. I thought, *Oooh, I want to fuck that one.*

Me: See? That's exactly why you're not helpful to me, Peter. What sane man sees a woman and thinks, "Hello,

wife"? Back me up, Faraday. What did you think when you first saw Kat?
Josh: I thought, "OH, GOD, I WANT TO FUCK HER!"

I chuckle. Josh and I have always shared a brain.

Me: So, Josh, how'd you get from that to "I want to call her Mrs. Faraday?"
Josh: It's too much to explain in a text. Can you talk?

I gently lift Georgina's chin to make sure she's fast asleep, and when it's clear her head is dead weight in my hand, I tap out a text, telling my friends I'll call them both, on a three-way call. The call connects. My friends express shock and excitement that I've opened this line of discussion. And, again, I tell them to pipe the fuck down.

"There's no need for you to call Jonas," Josh says, referencing his fraternal twin. "I know exactly what he'd tell you, because he's already said it to me. It was back when Jonas had just proposed to Sarah, after a month or two of dating, and he was hell-bent on having the wedding right away. So, I was like, 'Dude, what's your rush? And why do you need the piece of paper at all? Do you think it makes your love official?' And Jonas looked at me, all intense—you know how he is when he flashes those serial killer eyes—and he goes, 'Josh, I'm not marrying Sarah because I think I need a piece of paper to make our love *official*. I'm marrying her because I want to be there for her, for better or worse, for richer or poorer, in sickness and in health—and I want to let her know that's my eternal promise to her, in the most irrevocable and sacred way known to mankind.' Or something crazy like that."

I chuckle. "And *that* made you want to propose to Kat?"

"No. At first, I was like, 'Well, okay, dude, you do you. That's not how I feel about Kat, so I guess that's further proof I'm *not* the marrying kind.' And then, I saw Kat standing there at Jonas and Sarah's wedding, looking so damned beautiful, and I just... I don't know. Out of nowhere, it hit me like a ton of bricks. I suddenly felt exactly the way Jonas had described it to me. Plus, the thought of Kat marrying someone else made me fucking homicidal."

"I feel like that didn't improve at all on my succinct, but powerful, answer from before," Henn says. "Deep thoughts, by Peter Hennessy: 'You know it's time to pop the question when the word "girlfriend" simply isn't enough.'"

"Yeah, I admit that's pretty damned good," Josh says. "So, do you still want Jonas' number?"

"No, I think I've got what I need."

"What does that mean?" Henn says. "Is the word 'girlfriend' not nearly enough?"

I look down at Georgina sleeping next to me. "No, it's enough. At least, for now. Like I said, I was just curious. Gathering information. Don't read too much into it, boys."

My eyes meet Tony's in the rearview mirror. He looks away quickly, but not before broadcasting his sincerely held belief that I'm full of shit.

"Of course, we won't read into it," Henn says sarcastically. "Why would we think there's any correlation between you introducing Georgina to your mother, and her introducing you to her father, and you wondering how you'll know if it's time to put a ring on it?"

"I gotta go, guys," I say, my cheeks flashing with heat. "I'll talk to you later."

"Let us know the *minute* 'girlfriend' isn't enough!" Henn says.

But I don't reply. In fact, I disconnect the call, without saying goodbye. And when I see Tony's eyes in the rearview mirror again, I quickly look out the window at a car in the adjacent lane of the expressway.

What the hell am I doing? Georgina is way too young to want the fairytale. I'm sure she wouldn't even want an engagement ring, if I offered her one. Not at her age. I kiss the top of Georgina's head and pull her into me. For fuck's sake, I admitted this woman is the "great love of my life" today. If that's not *enough*, then I don't know what is.

EIGHTY-SIX
GEORGINA

When Reed and I enter the packed coffee house, Alessandra is getting herself situated on a tiny stage. When she sees us, she waves enthusiastically, and Reed and I return the gesture, before joining the back of the line for the counter. Normally, upon seeing my stepsister, I'd rush to her and hug her. But since the three of us spent hours together today, enjoying my magnificent birthday lunch and walking The Freedom Trail, an enthusiastic wave from afar seems natural and appropriate.

After several minutes of waiting, Reed and I finally reach the counter, and when our cashier lays eyes on Reed, her face ignites. "You're Reed Rivers!"

"Last time I checked. Hello"—he looks at her nametag—"Reena. How are you? We'll have a mocha and a cappuccino, please."

But the girl is too frazzled to take Reed's order. "I'm such a huge fan of all your artists. Your label is amazing. *You're* amazing."

"You attend Berklee?"

She nods profusely. "I'm a singer-songwriter. Oh my God. Can I send you my demo? Or will you check out my Instagram?"

She scrambles for her phone, but Reed puts up his palm, making me brace myself for whatever harsh and/or rude thing he's about to say to her. Surely, it will be something along the lines of what he said to the blonde at Bernie's Place.

"Sorry, Reena," Reed says. "If I check out your Instagram, I'm going to be bombarded with similar requests all night. And that would make me cranky for two reasons. One, I'm here to scout tonight's performer, Alessandra, and I want to give her my undivided attention."

The cashier and I exchange a look of excitement for Alessandra.

"And, two..." Reed continues. He puts his arm around me. "I'm on a date, with my girlfriend, Georgina, here—the great love of my life—and I'd like to relax with her tonight without being interrupted."

Predictably, the cashier looks disappointed she won't be able to capitalize on this potentially life-changing chance meeting. But she manages to say, "I understand. Enjoy your night, Mr. Rivers."

"Thanks."

I'm thinking that's that. Which, I must admit, is a bummer, simply because this girl is so darling and charismatic.

But when Reed's gaze meets mine, whatever he sees on my face makes him exhale and return to the cashier. He leans over the counter. "Okay, kid, it's your lucky day. Georgina here likes you and wants me to give you a shot, so..." He pulls out his phone. "Tell me your Instagram handle, and I'll send it along to my music scout to take a look. If she likes you, and tells me to take a look at you, then I promise I will."

"Oh, wow. Thank you, Reed! That's amazing."

The girl tells Reed her Instagram handle and he taps out a text onto his phone. And two seconds later, my phone vibrates in my hand with a text from Reed.

Look at this girl's IG for me, Music Scout. Thanks.

"Okay, I just sent a text to my music scout," Reed says to the girl, shoving his phone into his pocket.

"Thank you!"

"As a return favor, would you make an announcement that I don't want to be bothered tonight?"

"Sure thing."

"Aw, Reed," I say. "I'm sure your music scout wouldn't mind checking out a bunch of Instagram profiles for you. In fact, I'm sure she'd be happy to do it."

"Whatever floats her boat."

I address the cashier. "Why don't you make an announcement you'll be collecting Instagram handles and YouTube links for Reed's music scout, to ensure Reed himself won't be bombarded tonight." I turn to Reed. "And in exchange for Reena being a doll and gathering all those links for your scout, maybe you could do something you hardly ever do and check out her Instagram account, *personally*, without using your scout as a middlewoman?"

"I can do that."

"Oh my gosh! Thank you!"

"Maybe you'll even give Reena some brief feedback and guidance about her music, one way or the other?" I look at Reena. "Would that be helpful to you?"

"That would be a dream come true. Good or bad. Please. Just give me brutal honesty."

"That happens to be my specialty, Reena. I'll look it over in the next few days and be in touch."

"Thank you so much! Oh my gosh."

"Reed, as long as you're feeling benevolent tonight, why don't you grab the mic and talk to everyone for a couple minutes about the music industry, before Alessandra starts her performance? When Reena introduces you, that's when she can make the announcement about her collecting handles and links for your music scout."

Reed says no. "It's Alessandra's night to shine," he insists. Blah, blah. But I know he's only being cranky, so I insist he'd be doing a huge kindness for every person in the coffee house. And Reena backs me up.

"Fine. Just a few words, though. This is Alessandra's night."

As I pop over to Alessandra to tell her the plan, Reena heads to the small stage. She introduces Reed and tells everyone they should give any demos and Instagram handles to her, to be forwarded to Reed's music scout. "So, without further ado," Reena says. "I give you... Reed Rivers!"

Enthusiastic applause erupts, during which Reed traipses onstage. He takes a stool and grabs the mic, and begins talking to the crowd about what he believes they all need to focus on as aspiring musicians, if they hope to make an actual career in music. And, just like at the panel discussion, every person in the room is riveted to him. Mesmerized. In awe. After about ten minutes of speaking, Reed opens it up for questions, and, instantly, he's deluged with a roomful of raised hands.

As Reed answers questions, Alessandra leans into me at our small table. "He's so nice to do this."

"I know. He's such a sweetheart."

"He's so much nicer than I thought. I can't believe I thought he was such a jerk."

"I know the feeling."

"I can't wait to show him just how much I've grown since my demo, thanks to everything he said to me at the party."

My stomach twists. "Whatever happens, don't take his word as gospel, okay? A lot goes into Reed's decision-making that has nothing to do with talent."

Alessandra winks. "You don't have to protect me, Momma Bear. I'm scared to death to perform in front of him, but I'm also excited. Whatever happens, I'll be okay."

"Okay, guys," Reed says onstage. "Let's let Alessandra do her thing now. Be sure to tip her, okay? I'll get things started." He pulls out his wallet and stuffs a wad of bills into Alessandra's tip jar, and everyone laughs and applauds and marvels at his smoothness. And I can't help giggling to myself to see my Reed, the man I know and love, morph into Panel Discussion Reed before my eyes. It's not an act, actually, when Reed turns into this dazzling version of himself. The suave, charming, debonair guy who says all the right things, and elicits chuckles and applause at all the right times. That guy is sincerely him. But what I've come to learn is it's only one facet of him. A facet I love... although, I must admit, I've come to love the parts of him that aren't quite as perfect even more.

"Now, if you'll excuse me," Reed says, "I'm going to take a seat with my beautiful girlfriend and enjoy the show."

Alessandra gapes when Reed calls me his "beautiful girlfriend," and I blush.

"He's been calling me his girlfriend every chance he gets during this trip," I whisper.

"Swoon!" Alessandra whispers back.

A moment later, Reed appears at our table, which prompts Alessandra to head to the stage. With rosy cheeks and a heaving chest, she pulls her acoustic guitar into her lap.

"Hi, I'm Alessandra. Happy birthday, Georgie." She takes a deep breath. "This is called 'Blindsided.'" With that, she takes another deep breath, clears her throat, glances at Reed—which only makes her look like she's going to barf, so she quickly looks at me, instead—and then, begins to play.

It's a new song. One I've never heard before. And, holy crap, it's the best damn song Alessandra's ever written. *By far.* Not only that, she's singing it in a way I've never heard her sing before. With less vocal acrobatics and more soul. In fact, as I listen to her, goosebumps form on my skin. Tears well in my eyes. She's magic up there. And anyone who doesn't see that, including Reed, is just plain dumb.

Speaking of which, I steal a look at Reed. And what I find isn't his usual poker face. He's not Business Reed right now. He's not Discussion Panel Reed. He's *my* Reed. My lover. My man. The generous, kind, sweetheart I've come to know and adore. And, much to my thrill, that man, *my* Reed, is smiling from ear to ear.

EIGHTY-SEVEN
REED

So far, so good. Although I can't help feeling like I'm waiting for the other shoe to drop. Or, perhaps, a hammer. Onto my head.

I'm at Georgina's father's condo, sitting at a small table with Mr. Ricci and Georgina, eating homemade spaghetti Bolognese for Georgina's birthday dinner. It's one of the man's specialties, apparently. Also, one of Georgie's favorites. Which is why I've been shoveling my meal down enthusiastically, even though I rarely eat red meat or simple carbs. But, hey, whatever it takes to get onto this man's good side. Because, frankly, he hasn't welcomed me with open arms thus far. Not that I blame him.

When Georgina and I first arrived this evening, and Georgina introduced me as her "boyfriend," her dad took one look at me and made a face I'd caption as, *You've got to be fucking kidding me.* Which, right away, told me this was going to be an uphill battle. Although, in the man's defense, I wasn't particularly thrilled to hear Georgina call me that word, either. The minute Georgina uttered it in her father's presence, I couldn't help feeling exactly the way Henn and Josh described it to me the other day, only in reverse. *It's not nearly enough.*

I was shocked to think that way. By all rights, I should be thrilled to be introduced as Georgina's boyfriend, seeing as how, mere days ago at the RCR concert, that's the word I coveted. But the thrill is gone now.

I've realized "boyfriend" is actually a stupid, juvenile, overly vague word. For crying out loud, it's the same fucking word Georgie used when introducing that bastard, Shawn, to her father.

Also, thanks to the bombshell Georgina dropped on her father fifteen minutes ago—namely, that I'm the guy behind all their recent financial windfalls—he seems suspicious as hell of me. Although, he did thank me profusely for my generosity. But, still, it was abundantly clear he was feeling deeply worried and conflicted. He's already said "I don't know how I'll ever be able to repay you" at least ten times. To which I've replied, every time, "The payments were gifts. No strings attached."

The last time he made the comment, I told him I donated a whole bunch of money to that cancer charity, not just to him and Georgina, in an effort to make him feel less singled out. But, immediately, I could tell the comment had backfired on me. Rather than reassuring him, it only served to make me sound like I was bragging about my wealth. And so, realizing I was only digging a hole for myself, I shut up and let Georgina change the topic. Which she did. To Alessandra. Specifically, to Alessandra's performance at that coffee house in Boston the other day. And that's what she's still talking about, a solid ten minutes later.

"You should have seen Ally's face when Reed told her he wanted to sign her to his label!" Georgina gushes. "She was so excited, I thought she was going to pass out!"

Georgina's father looks at me, his face impassive. "Add that to the list of generous things you've done for my family."

"Oh, it wasn't charity, Mr. Ricci," I say. I pause, hoping he'll correct me regarding his name this time. But yet again, he doesn't. Which annoys me to no end. I mean, I get it. This is his home, and Georgina's his beloved daughter, so, he's clearly exerting his alpha status in this pack. But, come on, this man is only seventeen years older than me, and he's been letting me call him "Mr. Ricci" all fucking night? I continue, "I was genuinely blown away by Alessandra. Specifically, by a song she performed called 'Blindsided.' To be clear, I've only offered to produce and release that one song, as a single. I told Alessandra, if the single goes well, we'll talk about what comes next, if anything."

"Daddy, trust me, this is such a *huge* deal. Every student at Berklee—every aspiring artist in the *world*!—would sell their soul to have a single released by River Records!"

"Very kind of you, Reed."

Did the dude not hear a word I just said? Forcing myself not to scowl, I say, "It wasn't charity. Alessandra earned her spot. I listened to a demo of hers a while back, and the improvement and growth between then and now was staggering. With the right mentoring and guidance, I think Alessandra will do great things. If I didn't wholeheartedly believe that, I wouldn't have signed her. Not even for one song."

"It's true," Georgina says. "Reed's name and reputation are too valuable to him, not to mention his investment of time and money, to throw it away on anyone he doesn't believe in wholeheartedly. He says that all the time."

"It's the truth."

"A while back, Reed told me he makes it a rule never to take on young artists who need to be coaxed out of their shell. 'Ponies who need to be led out of the barn,' is what he called them. And look at him now, talking about mentoring Alessandra, and breaking his rule, because she's just that good."

Georgina's father shoots me a look like he can see right through me, and I can't help flashing him a look that concedes, *Okay, okay, maybe Georgina is being a bit naïve here.* In truth, Alessandra's performance at the coffee house was amazing. Honestly, I was blown away by her growth, and thrilled with how brilliantly she'd implemented every one of my suggestions. But does Georgina *truly* think I would have given Alessandra this shot, and committed to investing my valuable time and money and mentorship, if it weren't for my all-encompassing love for her? *Really?*

Mr. Ricci smiles at me, ever so subtly, letting me know he saw the white flag I offered, the concession I made, and he appreciated it. Maybe even respected it. He peels his gaze off me and smiles warmly at his clueless daughter, who's still babbling about Alessandra's amazing performance.

Finally, when Georgina stops rambling, Mr. Ricci says, "That's wonderful, honey. I'm so proud of Alessandra. But, as great as she performed, I'm sure part of Reed's motivation to sign her was knowing how much it would mean to you."

"No, Daddy. *Stop.* Reed doesn't compromise his business judgment.

Ever. Not for anyone. Not even me." She looks at me with little hearts in her eyes. "Not even for someone he *loves.*"

Mr. Ricci's eyebrows ride up. "Oh, you two are in love, are you?"

"We are," Georgina says.

"We are," I confirm. I feel myself blush, but I press on. "In fact, as I've told Georgina, she's the great love of my life."

Mr. Ricci looks shocked.

"And I feel the same way about Reed," Georgina says, her chest heaving. "I met his mom in New York, and she welcomed me into the Rivers family with open arms. And now, Reed is meeting you, and I want you to welcome him into the Ricci family, the same way."

Mr. Ricci gathers himself. He puts his elbows on the table. "How old are you, Reed?"

And there it is. The elephant in the room. He thinks I'm a dirty old man.

"I'm thirty-four."

"Have you been married before?"

"No, sir."

"Any children?"

"No. I've been in some committed relationships. I'd say I've cared deeply. But now that I'm in love with Georgina, I know I've never actually been in love. Never like this."

Georgina swoons, but her father looks unconvinced.

There's silence in the room for a long beat before Mr. Ricci exhales and says, "Georgie, will you excuse Reed and me? I'd like to chat with him, man to man."

Georgina looks at me, and when I nod, she rises, flashes a warning look at her father, and then an apologetic one at me, and heads out of the room.

"Don't eavesdrop, Georgina Marie," her father calls after her. "I'm well aware the walls are thin."

"I won't eavesdrop," Georgie tosses over her shoulder. But even I can tell she's lying through her teeth.

"Swear on Mommy."

Georgie stops in the doorway and whirls around, looking annoyed. "You can't constantly pull that out for things that aren't critically important."

"This is critically important," he says. And it's clear to me he's dead serious about that.

Georgina seems surprised by that retort. She softens. "Okay, I swear on Mommy. But be nice to him, Dad. *Please*. I didn't bring him here to meet you because I need your permission to love him. That ship has sailed. I brought him here because I want him to be part of our family. Because I love him."

"I understand, *Amorina*. Please, give us a minute—*without* you pressing your ear to the kitchen door."

Georgina rolls her eyes. "I'll be in my room."

"With headphones on and music blaring."

"Fine!"

When Georgina is gone, Marco Ricci leans back in his chair. "These grand gestures of yours, Reed... Aside from the fact that I don't know how I'll ever be able to thank you or repay you—"

"Like I said before—"

"Yes, I know what you said. And I don't want to appear ungrateful to you. I can't deny you've saved my life. *Literally*. I'll never be able to thank you enough for that. But that's totally separate from my job, as Georgina's father, to protect her to the best of my abilities. I'm sure you can appreciate that."

"Of course."

"So, let's talk about what these grand gestures are communicating to my impressionable daughter. She's obviously enthralled with you. Totally under your spell."

"It's not a spell. This isn't smoke and mirrors. We've gotten to know each other, in a deep and meaningful way, without any bullshit, and we're now as close, and in love, as two people can be."

He sighs. "Georgina doesn't give her heart away easily, but when she does, she falls hard. Which means she gets utterly destroyed on the back end, when she gets rejected. She'd kill me if she knew I was saying this to you, but Georgina isn't always the firecracker you think she is. On occasion, she gets knocked on her ass like you wouldn't believe. Her senior year in high school, some stupid boy rejected her, and whatever happened, she crawled into bed and cried for a full *week*. And then, at UCLA, when..."

He continues talking, but I'm too devastated to continue listening.

This man thinks his fierce daughter was nothing but a silly high school girl with a flair for dramatics for a week, when, in actuality, she was trying to deal, all by herself, with a sexual assault?

"My point is this," Mr. Ricci says. "How bad will Georgie get knocked on her ass *this* time, with you—a glamorous man who took her to New York, and signed her stepsister to his label, and paid off all her and her father's expenses? It's one thing for a twenty-year-old to say his girlfriend is the 'great love of his life.' But when *you* say it, under the circumstances, you're creating a much higher expectation. Painting yourself as her knight in shining armor on a white horse. Don't you see, you're implicitly promising my daughter 'forever.'"

Forever.

It's the first time that word has been in play in relation to my love for Georgina. A mighty big word that should, by all rights, terrify me. And yet, it doesn't. It only feels right.

"If Georgina thinks I'm promising her forever, then she's right. I am."

He arches an eyebrow, clearly surprised by that reply. "Answer me this, Reed. What did you do, mere days ago, that made Georgina crawl into bed and cry for two days?"

Shit. My stomach drops into my toes. "I made a couple mistakes. But we worked through them and came out the other side, stronger for it. Whatever crying Georgie did here, with you, you should know, when dealing with me, she was nothing but strong and forceful about the level of respect and honesty she required from me, going forward. Despite what you obviously think, Georgina is an equal in this relationship. In fact, I think it would be fair to say she has the upper hand in some ways. Although, please, don't tell her that, or God knows what she'll do to me."

He doesn't return my smile.

"Look, you don't have to worry about my intentions. All I want to do is to love and protect Georgina, for as long as she'll have me. You asked Georgina to swear on her mother. Well, for me, my most sacred promise is on my nephew. I swear on him, Mr. Ricci, that I love Georgina and my intentions are honorable."

Mr. Ricci remains quiet for a moment, until, finally, he smiles and says, "Marco. Call me Marco."

My heart leaps. "Thank you. But if it's okay with you, I'd prefer to call you 'Dad.'"

Marco can't help himself. He chuckles. So, I chuckle, too. And, just like that, we're both laughing, and all tension between us is gone.

"Do you have any questions of me, Marco? Ask me anything. I'm an open book."

Marco shakes his head. "Nothing else. Just don't hurt my daughter."

"I won't."

He rises from the table. "Why don't you get our little force of nature from her bedroom, while I put some candles on her birthday cake and open a bottle of champagne? It sounds like we've got a lot to celebrate."

EIGHTY-EIGHT
REED

I knock on the door to Georgina's bedroom, and say her name, but when she doesn't reply, I poke my head inside the room. She's lying on her bed, earbuds in, her eyes trained on an e-reader.
"Georgina?"
Nothing.
I cross the small room, detecting the faintest sound of 22 Goats blasting from Georgina's ears. When I reach the edge of the bed, I stand over her for a beat, waiting for her to look up, but she's too engrossed in whatever she's reading to notice me. Out of curiosity, I peek at the book title in the upper corner of the page she's reading and discover it's a biography of a New York City mobster. The sight makes me smile broadly. How is it possible for someone so gorgeous to also be so damned smart, adorable, and curious?
I could stand here all night, watching Georgina's various facial expressions as she reads. But since her father is waiting on us, I gently tap the top of her head to announce myself.
At my touch, Georgina jolts, tosses down her e-reader, and pulls out her earbuds.
"What'd he say?" she gasps out, her cheeks flushed with anticipation.

"Remember what Tony said a good Italian father would say to a 'suave' dude like me? That's basically what he said."

Georgina winces. "Was it super weird and cringey for you?"

"Not at all. It was awesome, actually. The conversation ended well. And it helped me further clarify my thoughts and feelings about you. About *us*."

Her eyebrows ride up. "What does that mean?"

I sit on the edge of the bed. "Your father told me all these grand gestures I've been doing for you, and him, would imply I'm promising 'forever' to you. And I said, good. That's precisely my intention."

Georgina makes that wide-mouthed, astonished face I love so much. "You actually used the word 'forever' when talking to my *father*—about *me*?"

I nod. "And I meant it." I take her hands. "If I haven't made this clear to you, Georgina, let me do it now. I'm not going anywhere. You're my last stop on the train."

Her chest heaves. "You're mine, too."

"Glad to hear it. But, listen, love. There's something else your dad said... something we should talk about."

I'd noticed Georgina reading everything Henn sent to me about Gates during our flight home from New York, and it was clear to me the information was deeply distressing to her. But she said she didn't want to talk about it yet, so I didn't press. Instead, I simply put my arm around my baby and invited her to sleep on my shoulder for the rest of the flight.

But now, after hearing that thing Marco said to me a moment ago—that thing about Georgina supposedly melting down for a solid week in high school, due solely to some dumb boy—my gut tells me it's time for her to speak up about Gates. At least, with her father.

"While your father was warning me not to break your heart," I say, "he told me a cautionary tale about some unknown boy in high school who broke your heart so badly you crawled into bed and cried for a week."

Georgina scowls. "Ugh. My dad made a similar comment the other day. You realize he's talking about the week after Gates attacked me, right?"

"Yeah, that's my point. I understand why you didn't tell your father about Gates at the time. And I'm not trying to push you to do something you're not ready to do. But do you really want your father thinking his daughter spent a week in bed because some stupid high school boy dumped her? No wonder he thinks you're more fragile and naïve than you are. He has no way of knowing what a badass you are, Georgina. A grown man attacked you, at seventeen—a man in a position of power—and you fought him off. Don't you want your father to know *that's* the badass daughter he raised, all on his own?"

"But if I tell my father what Gates did, he'll want me to go to the police. And what good would that do? Like I said before, it's my word against his only now, a full five *years* later."

I hold her anxious gaze. "Here's what I think, love. Go out there and tell your dad what happened, simply because he loves you and doesn't fully understand you as an adult. From there, I admit, I don't have the expertise to guide you. But you know who does? Leonard. Let's set up a meeting. We'll show him everything Henn found and ask his recommendation on next steps. Should you file a police report? A civil complaint? I have no idea. But I trust Leonard. I know he'll be able to help us figure out what to do next."

Tears moisten Georgina's eyes. "Thank you. Yes, I'd love to talk to Leonard. I trust him, too." Her face contorts, like she's holding back the weight of the world. But only barely.

"Aw, baby. Come here." I hug her to me, and, when I hear sniffling, my heart physically palpitates with love for her.

"Thank you," she ekes out.

"You don't have to thank me. Don't you get it? *I love you.* Your pain is mine. Your happiness mine." I pull back and meet her teary eyes. "The only thing I want is for my beautiful, colorful butterfly to be set free, and to get to see her flying loop-de-loops against a brilliant blue sky, the way she was meant to do."

"*Loop-de-loops?*" She chuckles through tears. "Whatever happened to you wanting to capture your beautiful butterfly and pin her to paper and enclose her in an airtight frame?"

I brush the tear streaking down her cheek with my thumb. "Well, I guess that right there is the difference between lust... and *love*."

EIGHTY-NINE
REED

Music is blaring. Bright lights flashing. And I'm a little bit drunk. Not because I'm having fun at this stupid birthday party at my Las Vegas nightclub. But because I'm *not*. Because after the past six weeks of bliss with Georgina, I can't stand being away from her. Because I'd rather be shitfaced than have to stand here, completely sober, wishing I were home with my baby. Because, as this five-day business trip has taught me, I'm now hopelessly incapable of being away from Georgina for even one night—let alone, *five*.

The Old Reed traipsed around the world for weeks at a time, without a care in the world. Not missing anyone. Fucking whoever. Never truly letting anyone get to know the man behind The Man with the Midas Touch. But now, it's abundantly clear: The Old Reed is dead. And The New Reed is totally, madly, irrevocably in love with the siren, the bombshell, the fireball known as Georgina Ricci.

It's been a productive trip, from a business standpoint. In San Francisco, Seattle, Phoenix, and Boise, I've scouted bands, checked out potential real estate investments, and attended meetings. All stuff I really needed to do, after six weeks of ignoring far too much work to hunker down in my house with Georgina. I've survived it all, but just barely, knowing it was all stuff I legitimately had to do for work. But, tonight, I'm losing my mind, since this party isn't work related and I'd much rather be home with Georgina. I'm hosting a birthday party for an old fraternity brother named Alonso in my nightclub tonight, and, I swear, if it weren't for an important meeting tomorrow with some business partners here in Vegas, I'd already have hopped a plane back to Georgina.

I tried to get her to come with me on this trip, but she said she had too much work to do. Her final artist interviews to polish. Her Gates article to finalize. Also, the one about me to edit. Plus, on top of all that, Georgina said she's *still* trying her mighty best to get *someone* to talk to her, on the record, about Howard Devlin. It's looking pretty unlikely she's going to be able to pull that particular rabbit out of her hat, despite how hard she's tried over the past six weeks. But, still, she's not ready to give up. Which doesn't surprise me. Georgina Ricci is nothing if not persistent.

Someone jostles my shoulder on their way to the dance floor, and I'm jolted back to my present surroundings. I'm standing near the dance floor with three of my old fraternity brothers—Henn, Luke, and the birthday boy, Alonso—plus, Ethan, an old friend from UCLA who wasn't in my fraternity, but is friendly with that whole group, thanks to regular poker parties at my house the past several years.

I tune into the conversation happening around me and discover Ethan, a successful producer of indie flicks, is telling the group a "behind the scenes" story from one of the films he's produced. Luke and Alonso are listening intently and laughing. But not Henn. He's glued to his phone, looking anxious.

As I watch Henn furiously tapping out a text, my drunken eyes fixate on the gleam of his metal wedding ring. And, much to my shock, I find myself *envying* him for that ring. For being a marked man. For getting to broadcast to the world, he's got a wife somewhere in the world. A woman who pledged her eternal love to him in a legally binding ceremony.

I look down at my bare ring finger and think it must be cool to have a ring like Henn's. I mean, assuming the woman wearing my ring, in return, was Georgina.

"Reed?"

I look up. It's Alonso talking to me. The birthday boy. He's pointing at my empty glass, asking me if I want a refill.

"Yeah. Sure."

"Henn?" Alonso asks.

Henn barely looks up from his phone. "No. Thanks."

Alonso takes my empty and heads to the bar, at which point I lean into Henn.

"Everything all right, buddy?"

Henn sighs and looks up from his phone. "Hazel's running a high fever. Hannah's at Urgent Care with her now. I'm totally freaking out." He rubs his forehead and, again, my drunken eyes notice the gleam of his wedding band. "Hazel's never had a high fever. Only low-grade ones when she's teething."

"Reed!" a female voice says, drawing my attention away from Henn.

It's Corinne. An ex-girlfriend of mine. An actress I dated exclusively for about three months a couple years ago, until boredom set in—at least, for me.

I hug Corinne hello. She kisses my cheek and links her arm in mine as I quickly introduce her to my friends. After introductions have been made, she pulls me aside and tells me she's elated she ran into me tonight because she's been thinking about me *a lot* lately—a *ton*, actually. In fact, she had a dream about me, just the other night! A really sexy one! Ha, ha! Which made her wonder if maybe we should—

I cut her off. Tell her I've got a girlfriend. And that's when it hits me, like a Mack truck. *Girlfriend isn't enough.* Even as I say the paltry word, I can plainly see Corinne's lack of respect for it. And why not? It's what *Corinne* was to me, once, not that long ago. And she wasn't anything special to me, though I liked her well enough. She was nothing but a brief distraction. Not even in the same universe as Georgina.

Suddenly, I can't stand the hideous word. *Girlfriend.* How can I use that word to describe Georgina, when I've already used it on someone like Corinne? And so many others before her? Georgina is the sun. And every woman who came before her, an LED lightbulb. And yet, here I am, slapping Georgina with the same label used for Corinne and everyone else? Shame on me.

In a flash, I'm desperate to get away from Corinne. So, I tell her there's someone she has to meet. I tell her it's "serendipity" she ran into me tonight, so she could meet this particular friend of mine. Without waiting for her reply, I lead her to Ethan at the bar. I tell Ethan

Corinne is an actress. "A talented one." Which is true. I tell Corinne Ethan is a "hot-shot producer" of some of the "best independent films I've ever seen. Some of which have made me a shit-ton of money." Also, true. And then I bid them adieu. And why not? Besides the obvious business connection, Ethan is rich and powerful and young and good-looking. And Corinne is talented and magnetic and gorgeous. I hope they fall madly in love and make a minivan full of babies together. *Peace out.*

I turn to go, but before I do, Ethan catches my eye and flashes me a look that plainly asks if she's fair game.

I nod and flash him a resounding, *Godspeed,* in reply. And then I'm gone, heading back to Henn to find out the latest on Hazel.

But Alonso finds me before I've reached Henn and hands me my refilled drink.

"Thanks."

"No need to thank me," Alonso says. "You're the one who bought it." He motions to Ethan and Corinne at the bar. "What the hell, man? I'm the birthday boy. If you didn't want her, why not introduce her to *me* as a birthday present?"

"Because she's an actress, and you sell life insurance."

"All the more reason to help a brother out."

"She's out of your league, Alonso. Actresses don't date insurance salesmen, any more than squirrels date bumblebees."

As I gulp my drink, Alonso babbles a bunch of shit I don't care about. So, when my drink is done, I ditch Alonso and stride over to Henn. Not surprisingly, he's still tapping furiously on his phone, looking worried and frazzled.

"Any update?"

"Yeah. Thankfully, the doctor isn't too worried. She told Hannah exactly what to do. So, she's heading home with Hazel now."

"Keep me posted."

Henn runs a hand over his face, looking distraught. "I've got to go, man. I'll say a quick goodbye to Alonso. Do me a favor and say my good-byes to everyone else."

"You bet."

We head over to Alonso. Henn says, "Hey, man, I'm sorry, but my baby has a fever and I need to go home."

"The last flight to LA has already left," Alonso says. "Why don't you go back first thing in the morning?"

Without hesitation, as Henn and Alonso continue talking, I grab my phone and start making arrangements.

"I'm gonna rent a car and drive," Henn says. "This time of night should be smooth sailing. I'll make it home in four and a half hours. Perfect timing for my wife to crash and for me to take over for her with Hazel."

Henn turns to me, clearly intending to hug me goodbye. But I put up an index finger, asking him to hold on for a second. Quickly, I finalize what I'm doing on my phone, and then look up.

"No rental car required," I say. "I just booked you a car and driver, so you can sleep on the way home. It'll be at the front of the club in exactly fifteen minutes."

"Oh my God, Reed. It didn't even occur to me to do that! I'll pay you back."

"Don't be stupid. Go get your suitcase from upstairs and meet me out front. I'll wait outside for the car, in case it gets here before you're out front."

"You're the best. Thanks, brother."

With that, Henn heads toward the front exit of the club, looking like a man on a mission.

Alonso shakes his head as he watches Henn's departing frame. "What the fuck has happened to all of us? Faraday couldn't come to Vegas because his wife is in her third trimester and he won't leave her, even for one night. Henn is running off to hold his sick baby, even though his wife is already there. Cory stayed home because his wife's *sister* is about to have twins. Jake is standing over there, showing everyone a video of his baby's first fucking steps. And you just now turned down a smoking hot actress with the most perfect tits I've ever seen because you have a *girlfriend* waiting for you at home? Seriously now, am I the only one whose balls are still attached to his body?"

"Fuck you," I mutter. "You were always trash in college, and now you've grown up to be a *Peter Pan* asshole motherfucker. I never liked you, Alonso. Not even in college. Not even when I was high on blow. So, why am I here? Why am I *hosting* this birthday party for you?"

Alonso laughs heartily, apparently thinking I'm joking. But I'm not.

Why am I wasting my precious time on this planet doing *anything* I don't want to do? More to the point, why am I doing *anything* that takes me away from *Georgina*?

"I'm going outside to wait for Henn's limo," I toss out, and then stride toward the front door without waiting for Alonso's reply.

Outside in the warm Las Vegas night, I bum a cigarette off the security guy out front, even though I don't smoke. Just as I'm stubbing the cigarette out, Henn's limo comes. Two minutes after that, Henn appears with his suitcase, looking frayed. I give my sweet best friend a bear hug and tell him to keep me posted. And then, I send Henn off into the night, on his white horse.

Deciding I'd rather have FaceTime sex with Georgina in my room than return to the excruciating birthday party, I begin crossing the street toward my hotel. But just as I'm heading into the lobby, my phone buzzes with a text from CeeCee that stops me dead in my tracks.

CeeCee: I saw on Instagram you're in Vegas. Francois and I are here, too, for his friend's birthday dinner tomorrow night. Let me know if you have time for a drink.

Me: I have time right now, as a matter of fact.

CeeCee: Perfect timing! We just got back to our room. Bellagio. Penthouse 8. See you soon, darling!

NINETY
REED

Not surprisingly, given that CeeCee's husband is a multi-billionaire, CeeCee's penthouse at the Bellagio is the biggest, most luxurious hotel suite I've ever beheld. Which is saying a lot, considering how much I like to treat myself to the finer things in life.

At first, CeeCee, Francois, and I chat as a threesome while gazing at the neon view of The Strip below. But, after a while, Francois heads downstairs to meet some friends in the casino, leaving CeeCee and me to booze it up as a dynamic duo.

"Okay, darling," CeeCee says when her husband is gone. "Tell me what's going on with you. You're not yourself tonight."

"Yeah, I've got some blood in my boozestream."

She laughs. "No, I've seen you drunk, plenty of times. There's something bothering you. What's wrong?"

I sigh. "I can't stand being away from Georgina. She's my disease and there's no cure. I'm lovesick."

CeeCee pats my arm. "What a glorious reason to be miserable."

"How the hell do you and Francois live on different continents? Are you not in love with him? I won't tell, if you're not. Just tell me the truth."

She bats my shoulder. "Don't insult me. Of course, I'm in love with my darling Francois! I hate being away from him, every bit as much as you hate being away from Georgina. But I've got no choice, at least for now. I'm not ready to retire yet. Not even close. So, we make it work."

I shove my empty glass at her. "Another one, bartendress. Help me numb the pain of my acute lovesickness."

Chuckling, CeeCee gets up to refill my glass. "I don't blame you for falling head over feet for Georgie. So have I. I knew she was going to knock my socks off this summer, the minute I met her. But she's blown away even my highest expectations with everything she's submitted to me. Especially that piece she wrote on Gates! Have you read it, Reed? It's incredible."

My chest swells with pride. "Yeah, I read every draft along the way. It's amazing, isn't it? I'm so proud of her."

She hands me a drink and resumes her seat. "I made it a double."

"Bless you, Saint CeeCee."

"Did Georgina tell you? If she's able to incorporate my final edits and turn in her final draft by tomorrow, we'll be able to sneak it into the next issue of *Dig a Little Deeper*, just under the wire."

"She told me. She's beyond elated about it. Georgie's been dreaming of getting published in *Dig a Little Deeper* for a long time."

"Well, cheers to dreams coming true."

We clink and drink.

"Does this mean you're going to hire Georgina full-time at *Dig a Little Deeper*?"

"Of course, I am. But don't you dare steal my thunder and tell her. When her internship is officially over in two weeks, I'm going to throw her a little surprise party at the office to tell her. I already told Margot to order a cake."

I feel euphoric, like this victory for Georgie is my own. "She'll love a party. She doesn't have a mom, CeeCee. Little things like a party with a cake... the way you've taken her under your wing. That stuff means the world to her. More than you could possibly realize."

"Aw, Reed. You look so smitten right now. Like you're bursting with pride."

"I am. This Gates article... It's been so inspiring to watch her journey. When Georgina told her dad about Gates six weeks ago, she was so nervous and timid. And look at her now. She's unstoppable. That article doesn't pull any punches. It's incredible."

"That, it is." She raises her glass. "Everyone drink to Georginaaaa!"

"Heeeey!"

Again, we clink and drink.

"Can I ask you a kind of weird question?" I ask. "Why did you marry Francois?"

CeeCee looks highly offended. "Because I love him more than life itself. And he asked."

"Yes, I know all *that*. Don't get your designer panties in a twist."

She giggles.

"What I mean is, you've both been married twice before. His main residence is in France. Yours is in LA. And you're both at an age where you're not going to have any babies."

"Francois and I aren't going to have babies? Oh, crap. Don't tell Francois! He only married me for my fertile womb!"

We laugh and laugh.

"But, seriously," I say. "I don't get it. Okay, you both fell head over heels. Woohoo. Congratulations. But why not be 'jet-setting lovers'? Wouldn't that be far more romantic than trying to make a trans-continental marriage work?"

CeeCee looks at me like I'm trying to glue false eyelashes onto a pig. "You think being 'jet-setting lovers' is *more* romantic than exchanging vows of *forever* with the person you're head over heels in love with? And doing it in front of family and friends, in a ceremony that dates back hundreds of years and is *legally binding? And,* in my case, getting to exchange those vows of forever, and thereafter partying with said family and friends, in a seven-hundred-year-old castle in the South of France? Pfuff. I mean, to each their own. But I, *personally,* think there's nothing more romantic than any of *that*. Especially considering Francois's wealth. He owns half the world, and yet, he told me his life wouldn't be complete if he didn't spend the rest of it with *me*."

"But, see, that's my point. Spend the rest of your lives together. Great. Wonderful. *Why get married?* You and Francois both know, for a fact, marriage isn't necessarily forever, no matter what you say in your vows. CeeCee, Francois is your *third* husband."

"He is? Oh, shit! Please, don't tell him that! He thought I was a virgin when he married me." She flashes me a snarky look. "Yes, I'm fully aware marriage might not last *forever*, but the thrill is that it *could.*

Did you not hear a word I just said? Marriage isn't about *logic*. It's a leap of faith, you fool."

I bring my drink to my lips as my drunken brain feverishly tries to ignore the crazy shit my lovesick heart is saying to me.

CeeCee arches an eyebrow. "You're planning to propose to Georgina?"

My heart shouts, *Yes!* But I ignore it, as best I can. Because, obviously, that would be a ridiculous thing to do. Georgina is too young for that. And I don't even believe in the institution of marriage, as a matter of principle. "No," I manage to say in a calm voice. "I don't believe in marriage. But even if I did, Georgina is *twelve years* younger than me. She's got a lot of life to live before she'd be ready to commit to 'forever' with me."

"I'm fifteen years younger than Francois, and I was ready to commit to him forever."

"Yes, but you're twenty-*five*, darling. Not twenty-*two*. That's a big difference."

We both laugh at my silly, drunken joke.

"I was twenty-two the first time I got married," CeeCee says wistfully. "And it was so much fun."

"CeeCee, you got *divorced*!"

"Yes, but it was fun while it lasted. And the wedding was a damned good party."

I can't help laughing.

"Have you asked Georgina what she thinks about all this 'forever' business? She's been through a lot at such a young age, you know. Losing her mother. Taking care of her father through his cancer battle. And let's not forget what she went through with Gates. I think maturity has more to do with what's happened to a person in their years of life, rather than how many years of life a person has had."

I swirl my drink. "I'm not going to ask Georgina's permission to *ask* her to marry me. That'd take all the fun out of it."

CeeCee chuckles. "Oh, so you *are* a romantic, underneath it all."

I shrug. "Maybe I am. I decided tonight I hate the word 'girlfriend.' It isn't even close to enough to describe what Georgina means to me. In fact, the word feels like an insult, at this point. A hideous slur."

CeeCee laughs. "Well, I think that's a tad bit dramatic. But okay."

I look out at the neon-lit view, gathering my thoughts. There's something on my mind... something I didn't realize I thought about, until this very moment. But now, suddenly, it's crystal clear. "I think my parents' marriage, and bitter divorce, has messed me up in the romance department. My father was thirty-two when he knocked up my nineteen-year-old mother and married her. I was too young during my parents' marriage to understand the dynamics of their age gap, but looking back, as an adult, I can plainly see my father steamrolled my mother at every turn. He lorded over her, controlled her, squeezed the life out of her. In fact, I'd even venture to say he gaslighted her. Finally, my mother discovered his mistresses—one of whom was nineteen, by the way. Oh, and then *he* divorced *her* when she found him out, as if *she'd* done something wrong because *he* had mistresses. I was only nine when they divorced, so I didn't fully grasp everything, but Georgina recently showed me some legal documents that shed some light on my parents' divorce and custody battle, and I got to see how nasty it was. How scorched earth my father was. And I guess, if I'm being honest, I'm terrified of history repeating itself with me and Georgina. Either with me as the controlling older husband who squeezes the life out of his young wife. Or with me as my mother, who falls apart, completely, when the fairytale doesn't work out."

"Oh, Reed. Who says the fairytale wouldn't work out?" She grabs my hand, her face awash in sympathy and love. "Not every love story ends the way your parents' did. You're not your father, and you're not your mother. You're *you*. A beautiful, brilliant man with a huge heart and a whole lot of love to give. You've kept the best of your love bottled up for thirty-four years, like the finest wine. It's time for you to finally pour that delicious wine into someone's goblet, without holding back. Whether that will translate to marriage for you, I have no idea. Just, please, don't let your parents, and your childhood, keep you from doing whatever is truly in your heart. Whatever that might be."

My eyes feel as though they're on the cusp of tearing up. So, I take a deep breath, and then another, to ward off my threatening emotion.

"Forever is a beautiful thing to promise to someone you love," CeeCee says. "If you're feeling the urge to propose to Georgina, then get yourself a prenup and roll the dice."

Yes! my heart screams at me. But, again, my brain tells me, *No, it's a non-starter. She's too young. And marriage only ends in pain.*

I wipe my eyes. "I've actually got a better idea than making Georgina sign a fucking prenup."

"Marriage *without* a prenup?" CeeCee gasps. "Reed, being romantic is one thing. Being *stupid* is another."

"Cool your jets, woman. I'm not proposing to her. Why give her a ring to symbolize forever when she could take it *off*?" I drain my glass and put it on a side table. "Come on, Ceece. I'm a man on a mission. I'm going to get something for Georgina that symbolizes forever that she can't take off. Something far better than a stupid ring."

NINETY-ONE
GEORGINA

I'm sitting on the couch in the living room of Reed's house—or, rather, "our" house, as Reed keeps calling it—reading the final version of my article about Gates and his two enablers—the principal of my high school and Steven Price—before submitting it to CeeCee. And I love it. When I met with Leonard the day after telling my father about Gates, Leonard recommended I write this article as my best course of action—and reading it now, six weeks later, I never dreamed I'd write something this powerful.

"What's your goal here?" Leonard asked me six weeks ago.

I replied, without hesitation. "I want to expose Gates and the men who covered up for him, so there will never be another Katrina, Penny, or Georgina at my high school."

"Well, then," he said, "if that's your goal, then I don't think walking into a police station and reporting you were the victim of an attempted rape almost five years ago would be nearly as effective as writing an in-depth, airtight account of what happened. Most people in your shoes don't have a national platform like you do. Use it. I predict all appropriate dominoes will fall after that."

So, that's exactly what I decided to do: write my story, without holding back.

After our meeting with Leonard, Reed and I went straight to

CeeCee's office, where I told her about Gates, in detail. After that, after hugging me and saying some truly beautiful things to me, CeeCee immediately gave me the green light to write the article... *provided* I could get Katrina and/or Penny to contribute, *on* the record.

"Consider it done," I assured CeeCee, brimming with confidence... and then quickly discovered my confidence was a bit premature. In actuality, when I tracked down Katrina and Penny, neither girl wanted to talk to me about Gates. Thankfully, though, after I told each girl about the other, and also about my own harrowing experience at the hands of Gates, both girls ultimately poured their hearts out to me... but only *off* the record. They said they *wanted* to take him down. They truly did. But they were scared to death they might have to pay Steven Price's money back.

And that's when Reed, my knight in shining armor, stepped in to save the day. He told both girls he'd cover any and all legal expenses arising from them speaking up and breaching their "hush money" agreements with Steven Price, and promised they'd never have to come up with that money. And that did it. Both girls agreed to take a leap of faith with me and let me include their courageous, heartbreaking, stomach-churning, no-holds-barred stories in my article.

And now, after six weeks of blood, sweat, and tears, not to mention daily pep talks to myself to be brave, I've finally finished writing my article. It's a five-pager entitled, "Football at All Costs: How a Winning High School Coach Got Away with Sexual Assault with a Little Help from His Friends." And I couldn't be prouder of it. I read the article one last time, attach it to an email, and send it to CeeCee. And the moment I press send, a torrent of pride and relief surges inside me. Also, a touch of fear. But the good kind of fear. The kind that tells me I'm alive. It's a one-of-a-kind moment for me. So, of course, I want to share it with Reed.

My heart bursting, I pick up my phone and tap out a text:

I just submitted my Gates article. I'm terrified, but mostly excited. I can't wait to celebrate with you. Let me know the minute you've landed. XO

As I await Reed's reply, I send the article to my father and Alessandra, and then wind up chatting with Alessandra on FaceTime. Alessandra gushes about the article. She tells me she loves me and is proud of me. And then, at my request, she sends me the latest mix of

"Blindsided," which, she says excitedly, Reed is planning to release in about three weeks. Finally, though, after about twenty minutes of chatting with Alessandra, my phone pings with a reply from Reed and I tell Alessandra I've got to go.

Reed: Landed. Coming straight home to celebrate. SO proud of you!

Me: Woohoo! Can't wait to see you. I've been dying without you here.

Reed: I've been miserable without you, sweetheart. Can't wait to touch you. I'm not going to make it two steps past the front door before I rip your clothes off.

Me: Promise? XO

Reed: Hell yes. XO

My body is vibrating with excitement. I knew I'd miss Reed during his business trip. But I didn't think I'd miss him *this* much—like missing a limb. I thought I was "adulting" when I said I should stay home to finish my mountain of work. In retrospect, though, I wish I would have done the irresponsible thing and joined him on his trip. Because these past five days have been pure torture.

To pass time until Reed gets home, I open my laptop and edit an article I've been writing, off and on, for the past several weeks—a secret article I haven't told anyone about, not even CeeCee or Reed. I'm hoping to ultimately get this piece into *Dig a Little Deeper*. But if not, I'll still be awfully proud of it, and happy I took the time to investigate and write it.

As I'm engrossed in the words on my screen, I hear the best sound in the world: the front door opening behind me. Squealing, I close my laptop with gusto, sprint across the living room, and hurl myself like a missile into Reed's waiting arms. In a flash, we're kissing and ripping off our clothes, right inside the front door, exactly as Reed promised.

Reed unties his tie and unbuttons his shirt with frenzied fingers. He peels off his shirt, breathing hard… and that's when I see it: a new tattoo to join Reed's collection. This one, on his left pec. *ReRiGeRi*. Instantly, I know what the seemingly random letters mean. They're a tribute to us. To our love. The beginning letters of both our names, inked onto his flesh—over his heart—forever.

"I love it!" I exclaim, bending down to kiss the tattoo. From there, I work my way down Reed's abs, to his treasure trail, and then to his hard penis. But before I take him into my mouth, Reed pulls me up and backs me into the door. His eyes ablaze, he binds my wrists with his necktie and raises them above my head. He opens the front door slightly, throws the long end of his tie over it, and shuts it again, pinning me in place with my back against the closed door and my hands trussed over my head.

With eyes like hot coals and flaring nostrils, Reed sinks to his knees and greedily kisses my belly. And then my thighs. He lays fervent kisses around my clit, never actually touching it, until I'm moaning and begging for more. Finally, he begins lapping at my bull's-eye with confident strokes, until, soon, I'm shuddering and bucking and whimpering with pleasure. I'm wet for him now. Swollen and throbbing and aching. He slides his fingers inside me, and, still devouring me with his mouth, begins stroking my G-spot, over and over again, without reprieve. Without letting up or changing speed. He's a laser beam. An oncoming train. Until, finally, my orgasmic screams echo throughout the expansive living room.

Reed's initial job complete, he rises, grabs me by my naked ass, and fucks me against the door like he's trying to kill me with his cock, growling into my ear with each thrust about his love for me, how good I feel, how hot I am, how much he missed me.

When Reed comes, it's with a primal roar that sends me hurtling into a release of my own, thanks to a little help from Reed's talented fingers. Finally, we're finished and breathing hard. Glowing with sexual satisfaction. Reed frees my wrists from the door and unbinds them, and the minute I'm free, I throw myself into his hard chest and clutch him to me, overwhelmed by the intensity of my feelings. It scares me to know I not only love and want Reed. I physically *need* him. I wish I didn't. It's terrifying to realize someone's got the power to decimate me. To shatter my heart into a billion pieces with one word. *Goodbye*. But it can't be helped. I'm undeniably at his mercy. All-in. Laid bare.

"Never leave me," I whisper, still clutching him.

Reed chuckles. "Don't you worry, little kitty. From now on, you're coming with me on every work trip. I was miserable without you."

"No. I meant... *never leave me*." I pull back and look him in the eye, my own eyes pricking with moisture. "Never leave *us*. I *need* you, Reed. Like air. It scares me to think how badly I'd drown if I ever lost you."

Reed's features soften. He puts his fingertip underneath my chin. "Georgina Marie, why do you think I got the tattoo? If stamping our combined names onto my flesh for eternity doesn't tell you I'm not going anywhere, then I don't know what would."

Without meaning to do it, I make a face that says, *Well, actually...*

Because, damn, without intention, my mind was just now hijacked by this distinct thought: *Well, actually... I can think of one thing that would say "forever" even more than a tattoo.*

Ugh. Who am I right now? I should be nothing but thrilled and grateful about Reed's tattoo, not thinking, *It's not enough.* The man inked our combined names onto his chest as a surprise gift, as a permanent testament to our love, and I've got the nerve to think, basically, *Thanks, but I'd rather you put a ring on it?* Shame on me. Plus, that's so *not* me. I've never had any thumping desire to get married. I'm not the kind of girl who sits around dreaming of her future wedding. But I can't deny I've had the thought. And, even worse, based on Reed's expression, he knows it.

The air in the room feels thick and still for a moment, like an elephant wearing a sign that reads "Put a ring on it!" just galloped between us.

For a split-second, we're both frozen. Red-faced and stilted.

"I want to get the same tattoo!" I blurt, pointing at his chest. Desperately trying to fill the awkward silence with something that will convince Reed he's misread me. "We're Fred and Ginger. We need to be a matched set. A promise of 'forever' will only work if both of us make it."

Reed exhales with relief. It's subtle. But it's there. "Are you sure? You don't have to do that."

"I'm sure. I want to. In fact, let's go right now."

A wide smile splits Reed's handsome face. "Sounds good. I need a shower, and then we'll go." Chuckling, Reed bends down and begins gathering his scattered clothes, so I follow suit, my heart stampeding. "I'll call my usual tattoo guy now and tell him we're on our way. After the tattoo parlor, how about I take you to a nice dinner to celebrate you submitting the Gates article to CeeCee?"

Our clothes gathered, we head toward the staircase.

"Actually, if it's okay with you, I'd rather do a quiet dinner at home. That's all I've wanted for five days. To be home, alone, with you."

Reed takes my hand and squeezes it as we climb the stairs. "Have I ever mentioned you're perfect?"

I swoon. "I'm so relieved you're home. This house felt so big and lonely without you."

We've reached the top of the staircase. Reed stops walking. He looks down at me, his dark eyes a window into his beautiful soul. He lays a gentle fingertip against my lip. "Now you know how I felt living in this big and lonely house for five years before you walked through the door and finally made it a home."

NINETY-TWO
REED

We're back from the tattoo parlor now. Sitting in our comfy clothes at my kitchen table, eating Amalia's delicious meal and drinking Cristal from crystal flutes. And, as Georgina eats and talks and repeatedly brings her fork and champagne flute to her lips, I can't help staring at those tiny letters inked along the inside of her left ring finger... *ReRiGeRi*... and, to my surprise, thinking, over and over again, *It's not nearly enough.*

What's wrong with me? Matching tattoos should be more than enough! Especially considering Georgina got hers on *that* finger. The one reserved for a wedding ring. The one that tells the world she's taken, for life. But, nope. I don't feel the surge of pure elation I thought I would. I don't feel sated. *I still want more.*

Georgina puts down her champagne. "I finished writing my article about you while you were gone."

Shit. My gaze jerks from Georgina's tattooed finger to her eyes, as my spirit thuds into my toes. To be honest, I've been dreading Georgie's article about me for weeks. I've asked to read her early drafts, seeing as how she let me do that with her Gates article, but she's always said no. "I want to surprise you," she's told me. And now, holy shit, the "surprise" is finally upon me.

"I'd like to send it to CeeCee tomorrow," Georgina says, unaware of the intense anxiety brewing inside of me. "I'd love it if you'd read the article tonight and let me know what you think about it."

"Sure thing."

"I had such a hard time writing this one. You know, getting it right. I kept going back and forth on what information to include. What to exclude. It was important to me that the piece has journalistic integrity and a strong voice. I didn't want it to be nothing but a sappy love letter to my boyfriend."

She smiles. But I can't muster one in return. Now that I love Georgina more than life itself, now that her dreams are mine, how could I possibly nix a single word of this damned article—even if she's included information about me I don't want to share with the world? If I'm forced to choose between supporting Georgina's career and ambition, versus guarding my own need for privacy and control, how could I possibly choose anything but what Georgina wants?

She stands, her excitement palpable. "So, can I grab my computer now?"

I take a deep breath. "Of course."

Hooting with glee, Georgina bounds out of the kitchen like a gazelle. And a moment later, she returns and places her opened laptop before me on the table. "Promise you'll read it with an open mind, okay? Fair warning, parts of it are almost certainly going to freak you out, at first. But if you give it a fair chance, and read it with an open mind, I'm sure—"

"Enough," I say, more harshly than intended. "We'll let the article speak for itself."

As Georgina resumes her chair, wringing her hands, I exhale a long, slow breath, place my elbows onto the table, on either side of the laptop, and let my eyes settle on the title of the article that's surely going to hurtle me into a massive existential crisis. It reads, "Reed Rivers: The Man with the Midas Touch Unexpectedly Has a Heart of Gold."

I look up, frowning sharply. "What the hell is this?"

"The article I wrote about you."

"I thought you said you want your article to have journalistic integrity, and not be a sappy love letter to your boyfriend."

She winks. "How about we let the article speak for itself? Read to the end before providing commentary, please. Thank you."

Exhaling with annoyance, I return to the screen, and, after reading only a few paragraphs, easily surmise this article is a fucking travesty. A fluff piece. Shameless propaganda. Georgina describes how "brilliant" and "hands-on" I am, in every aspect of running my "empire." She says I'm "gifted," not only at holistic marketing, scouting, and negotiations, but also, at assisting my artists with "honing, maximizing, and developing their unique talents."

She writes, "But Reed's greatest talent lies in something that's hard to encapsulate in words. Something that's awfully hard to perceive about him, unless you've spent days observing him in his natural habitat. As crazy as it might sound to a casual observer, Reed Rivers is genuinely inspirational. Through more than his words—though his *example*, his persistence, his drive—he inspires the people around him to reach for their best selves and conquer the world."

Georgina goes on to admit I'm not perfect. I can be "shockingly harsh" and "grouchy." "At the office, annoyance and impatience are Reed's default modes. But all of that's okay with his team," Georgina writes, "because Reed's artists, and everyone who works for him, understand and respect his mission." Which, she goes on to explain, is fundamentally built on an "uncompromising commitment to greatness." Georgina further writes, "Everyone who works with Reed is well aware he only commands from others what he commands of himself. Excellence. And that makes them respect the hell out of him, both personally and professionally."

I look up from the computer, scowling. "CeeCee will never publish this tripe in *Dig a Little Deeper,* and you know it."

"Which is why I'm submitting this for *Rock 'n' Roll*. For the special issue."

I pull a face like that's the most moronic thing I've ever heard. "CeeCee explicitly assigned you to covertly try to unpeel my onion and bring her something on-brand for *Dig a Little Deeper*. Come on, Georgina. You're still vying for a spot at *Dig a Little Deeper*. Don't dim your light for anyone. Not even me. You know very well an article about me in *Rock 'n' Roll* isn't an A-plus result for you."

Georgina shrugs. "A's are overrated. C's get degrees, dude."

I stare at her blankly, incredulous. I've told this shark of a woman every fucking thing about me, every embarrassing, sensitive, excruciating, torturous thing... and *this* piece of shit is what she decided to write about me? I'm flabbergasted. Shocked. *Annoyed.* "You're sincerely proud of this... *article?* And, yes, I'm using that term loosely."

She laughs. "Yes, I'm very proud of it. Keep reading, please. No further commentary until you're finished. Thank you."

My pulse thumping in my ears, I return to Georgina's screen and continue reading at the point where I left off. It's the turning point of the article, it turns out. The place where Georgina gets to her true thesis: "But Reed isn't merely a wildly successful and brilliant mogul-innovator-influencer-genius, he's also, surprisingly, a truly good, generous, and kind human being, as well." According to Georgina, I'm a "devoted son" who plays Scrabble and does yoga with his "beloved mother." A loyal big brother who put his little sister through school and adores his nephew. "Reed is loyal as the day is long," Georgina writes. "A man who's had the same best friends since college and who grew up to hire his childhood nanny as his housekeeper, as soon as he could scrape together the funds to do so."

To drive her thesis home, Georgina quotes several of my employees, including Owen, all of whom babble about whatever exceedingly nice thing I've done for them, or their family members, over the years, without fanfare or taking credit for it. Owen, in particular, goes on and on about my over-the-top generosity. "He's a dream boss," Owen is quoted as saying. "There's never a dull moment with that guy. I learn something new every day by watching him."

"This is hideous tripe," I spit out. "I feel like I'm reading my own fucking obituary."

Georgina giggles with glee. "Read to the end, *stronzo*. What part of that instruction do you not understand?"

Begrudgingly, I return to Georgina's screen, only to discover I'm not only a "philanthropist" who "generously" supports such and such causes, I'm also a guy who "regularly" helps good friends and family, and *their* friends and family, with whatever they ask of me, while never seeking acknowledgment or praise for any of my covert good deeds.

"Not true," I mutter under my breath. But I know better than to look up from the screen again. I continue reading: "Why does Reed help so many people, without seeking credit or adulation? As far as this writer can tell, he does it simply because he can. Because helping people gives his life purpose. Because he's a genuinely good man who likes watching other people soar. Of all the wonderful things I've discovered about Reed this summer, I think that's the thing I like best about him. The thing that made me fall in love with him the most.

"Yes, you read that right. This writer has fallen hopelessly and totally in love with Reed Rivers. I didn't mean to do it. In fact, I tried very hard *not* to give him my heart. But it couldn't be helped. He's irresistible. Thankfully for me, though, luck was on my side. When I gave Reed my heart, he gave me his in return. And let me unpeel it, down to the nub. And that's why I'm able to tell you, with certainty, The Man with the Midas Touch truly does have a heart of gold."

And that's it. The article ends that way, without any mention of my father—not even the golf story I explicitly gave her permission to use. She doesn't bother to mention the fact that I play all that Scrabble and do all that yoga with my "beloved mother" in a mental facility. Similarly, there's no mention of my parents' divorce or Troy Eklund or Stephanie Moreland. For crying out loud, Georgina's article is so *opposite* a hit piece, so unabashedly—and *explicitly*—a sappy love letter to her boyfriend—I mean, for fuck's sake, she *literally* declares her love for me! —it's an embarrassment. Not only to *me*, but also to Georgina.

And then it hits me. *She's playing a prank on me.* Ha! I look up, chuckling. "Good one. You *almost* got me. Now, show me the real article."

Georgina smiles. "This is the real article."

"No more joking around, sweetheart. I'll cherish this forever. It's sweet. But, please, show me the one you're actually planning to submit to CeeCee."

"This is it. I swear on my mother."

I pause, utterly floored. Not to mention, disgusted. "Are you insane? You can't submit this!"

She laughs. "Why not?"

"Because it's everything you said you *didn't* want to write. Propaganda. A love letter to your boyfriend. Not to mention, it's full of brazen fabrications and untruths."

"Name one thing that's not true."

"All of it! It's not any one thing. It's the total effect of it, put together. You've made me sound like a saint."

"The article is well-researched and every word is accurate."

I scoff. "I funded your grant because I wanted to fuck you. Did you forget about that?"

Georgina folds her arms over her chest and leans back from the kitchen table. "Then why'd you pay for my father's medication, on top of my salary? Why'd you donate so much money to the cancer charity, if your only goal was getting me into bed? Surely, you could have paid my measly little salary and nothing else, if you sincerely didn't have *any* altruistic motivations."

Well, shit. She's got me there. I've already told her, repeatedly, I had parallel motivations on that front. So, fuck, I guess I need another tack. "Yes, okay, but you make it sound like I'm *never* selfishly motivated, in anything I do, and you know that's a bald-faced lie. There's *always* something in it for me."

"Is that so? Why'd you help Keane with his career? His agent wouldn't send him on any serious auditions, so you pulled strings, without a moment's hesitation. What'd you get out of *that*?"

"Where'd you hear about that?"

"Kat."

I roll my eyes. Fucking Kat. It's no wonder her family calls her The Blabbermouth. "Did Kat bother to mention *Josh* asked me to do it?"

"You also helped Hannah get a job."

"Because *Henn* asked me to do it. Whoop-de-do, I sometimes do favors for my two best friends. It hardly makes me a saint. Do you know how many favors they've done for *me* over the years? Josh paid for *every* fun thing we ever did in college. He flew a group of us to Thailand for spring break! Did you know that, after graduation, he's the one who gave me a loan to help me get River Records off the ground? I owe *everything* to Josh for that loan. Just as much as I owe CeeCee for putting *Rock 'n' Roll's* reputation behind a nobody-band called Red Card Riot. And don't get me started on Henn. You already know that guy helps me left and right, in a million ways. And not just regarding occasional hacking. He's my conscience. He keeps me sane and on the right track. So, okay, yes, I do nice things for my friends, sometimes. It doesn't mean I have a 'heart of gold.' It only means I'm not a sociopath. But that's hardly something to praise me for in a gushing piece of tripe."

She giggles. "It means you're fiercely loyal. Which is how I've described you in the article. Yet another thing I've said that's totally true."

I scoff. "I'm almost always motivated by selfishness, Georgina. One way or another. I just mask it well."

She flashes me a look of total incredulity. "What about Zander? Were you being selfish when you helped him land a job as Aloha's bodyguard?"

"Actually, yes! Ha! Aloha needed a bodyguard on her upcoming tour, and I knew Zander would be a perfect fit for her in terms of personality. And I *also,* selfishly, didn't want Barry going on tour with Aloha himself—which was exactly what Aloha, little miss diva, was demanding. I *selfishly* wanted Barry to stay in LA and work on *my* shit. So, I pulled strings and arranged a win-win-win-win."

"That doesn't sound selfish. It sounds brilliant. Which, again, is exactly how I've described you in my article."

"Georgie, I get what I want by giving other people what they want, too."

"Exactly." She laughs. "Wow, Reed, you're such a dick."

I run my hand through my hair. "Why didn't you at least tell the golf story?"

"Do you *want* me to tell the golf story?"

"No. Not particularly. But I don't want you to compromise your journalistic integrity by excluding it."

Georgina shrugs. "I decided that story wasn't on-brand for *Rock 'n' Roll.* Which is the publication I decided to write this for."

I lean back in my chair, bewildered. "This is insane. You make me sound so *nice.* And we both know I'm not. I mean, I am. But not *this* nice. I'm short-tempered. Harsh. Vaguely annoyed at all times."

"I've said all that."

"But not enough. Oh! I'm arrogant, too. But you didn't bother to say that."

"Okay, I'll add it. Fair point. Anything else?"

"Just paint an accurate picture of me, for crying out loud. Come on. *Drag me.*"

"Why would I do that? I had a thesis, which is that you have a heart of gold. Anything not supportive of that thesis isn't relevant."

"Not *relevant?*"

"This isn't a biography, Reed. It's a short little piece for *Rock 'n' Roll* about how unexpectedly wonderful you are—which is something the world doesn't already know about you. And *that,* my darling, was my *actual* assignment from CeeCee. To uncover a side of you nobody has seen before."

I shake my head. "I won't approve the article unless you make it a more accurate depiction of me. You need to dick me up a bit."

"No. If I do that, I'll look like an idiot for falling in love with you."

I grunt. "Yeah, about that ending..."

Georgie's face falls in earnest. "You don't like it? You want me to take it out?"

Oh, my heart. Fuck. "Come here, sweetheart." I pat my thigh, and Georgina leaves her chair and slides into it. "It's my favorite part. Thank you. But you can't leave that part in for the version you send to CeeCee."

"Why not? It's the truth."

"CeeCee will never print that."

"Well, I guess there's only one way to find out." She nuzzles her nose into mine. "Please, let me submit this article, as is. If CeeCee doesn't like something, she'll tell me to change it. But this is the article I want to submit. This is my truth." Before I can reply, she begins laying soft kisses up my jawline to my ear, licking and nipping and kissing as she goes, until I'm rock-hard and feeling incapable of saying no to her. "Say yes," she purrs. "Let me submit this, as is."

"It's propaganda of the worst kind," I whisper, but I'm smiling. Paradoxically, turning to steel underneath her while melting into a puddle of pliable goo.

Georgina's lips find mine and skim softly, making me shudder. "I've peeled your onion, down to your very core, my love. And what I found there, is what I wrote about." She places both palms on my cheeks. "Say yes."

I still can't believe *this* is what The Intrepid Reporter came up with, after everything she's discovered about me. Especially given that she thinks her dream job at *Dig a Little Deeper* is still on the line. Yeah, *I* know CeeCee is planning to offer Georgina a full-time slot, but *Georgina* doesn't know that. And, yet, Georgina is nonetheless willing to submit this puff piece for *Rock 'n' Roll*, rather than something that would surely lock down her dream job. "I just don't want you compromising your professional judgment for me."

She smirks. "Says the man who's about to release a single for my stepsister."

My cheeks flush. "But I'm not compromising anything to do that. Alessandra has all the makings of a quirky little indie star. She just needs some guidance and coaching."

"And you're willing to take the time to give Alessandra that 'guidance and coaching,' *personally*, because... *why?*"

I bite back a smile. She's got me there.

Georgina presses her forehead into mine. "I've written this article about you, for *Rock 'n' Roll,* because I love you with all my heart *and* I believe in this article. Which is the same thing as you producing and releasing Alessandra's song because you love me *and* believe in her. That's love, Reed. It's a two-way street."

Oh, my heart. If anyone is a saint here, it's Georgina. I press my lips to hers. And as I do, a dam breaks inside me. *Girlfriend* isn't enough. Matching tattoos aren't enough. I want it all, and I can't deny it a second longer. I want Georgina to take my name and wear my ring. I want us to pledge forever to each other in the most sacred way known to humankind. *I want her to be my wife.*

I've tried my damnedest to avoid reaching this conclusion. I've shucked and jived and thrown shiny objects into my own path to divert myself from reaching it. But the truth is, with each new ploy designed to convince myself I'm perfectly satisfied with shacking up, with each new label I use—whether it's girlfriend, lover, or partner—and each tiny letter we get permanently inscribed onto our bodies, all of it keeps bringing me to the same place. The same inescapable conclusion. *It's not nearly enough.* I want Georgina to be my one and only wife. Forever. And I won't settle for anything less.

"So, can I submit this article, as is? *Please?*"

I look into her hazel eyes, feeling overwhelmed with love and excitement about the decision I just made. "Just be prepared for CeeCee to say it's not what she wanted."

"I'll take that chance."

"Okay, you win, you relentless force of nature. Submit it. But only if you do a happy dance for me."

Squealing, Georgina gets up and gives me what I've demanded, making me laugh and clap. Breathlessly, she slides back into her chair, as I refill our champagne glasses and say a toast to the "godawful" article.

"So... there's actually one more thing I've been wanting to talk to you about," she says, putting down her champagne glass. "I figured I'd wait until you got home to tell you about it in person."

My stomach tightens. *What now?* "Okay..."

Georgina exhales loudly. "It's Isabel."

NINETY-THREE
REED

Georgina strokes the stem of her glass. "Remember I told you Isabel's PR person had contacted me a few weeks ago and said she didn't want to do the skydiving thing, after all? That she decided she wanted to do a conventional lunch interview?"

"Yeah. I thought you said you were going to cancel the whole thing. You said you didn't feel right interviewing Isabel, now that we're together."

"Yeah, and I meant that when I said it." She grimaces. "Turns out, though, I never got around to actually cancelling. I started having this fantasy I could show up to the lunch, and tell Isabel we're together, and let her decide if she wanted to proceed with the interview." She makes an adorable face I'd caption, *Sorry, not sorry.* "And now I've dragged my feet so long on cancelling, I'm in a bit of a pickle." She winces. "I'm scheduled to meet Isabel for lunch tomorrow."

"Georgina Marie."

"I know, I know. I'm a bad girl. It's just that texting her PR woman to cancel feels so anti-climactic and unsatisfying compared to getting to tell Isabel, to her face, I'm your girlfriend, and then watching her expression as she puts two and two together and realizes *I'm* the woman you were talking about in that surveillance video. Although, I promise, I'd *never* mention the video itself or what I saw or heard in it."

Ah. I get it. Georgina can't help wanting that delicious moment of revenge for herself, every bit as much as I wanted the pleasure of making that PA scurry back to C-Bomb to let him know I'm the "boyfriend" Georgina mentioned during her interview of RCR. And you know what? I don't blame her. Frankly, after the shit I pulled in that garage, I think it's only fair Georgina should get to enjoy a triumphant moment like that.

"If I'm being immature and vindictive, tell me so," Georgina says. "But the truth is, I want Isabel to realize, if she's only marrying Howard to try to win you back, she's going to have to go through *me* to do that."

Oh, my gorgeous fireball. She's a blazing pyre before me. Physically glowing with passion. "You know what?" I say. "Go for it."

"Really?"

"Why not? Once your article about me comes out in *Rock 'n' Roll*, Isabel will find out about us, anyway. You might as well experience the pleasure of telling her yourself, in person. But, if you don't mind, I'd like to come along, so she understands we're a team—that I'm as committed to you, as you are to me."

"Oh my gosh! I'd love that."

"Just be prepared for Isabel to get pissed off and feel like we've ambushed her."

Georgina's eyes ignite. "Yes, please."

I laugh.

Georgina's face flashes with mischief. "Actually, now that an actual interview of Isabel isn't going to happen, I can't see the downside of me asking her about Howard. I still haven't been able to get a single actress who's worked with Howard to talk to me on the record, although several of them have told Hannah and me horror stories, *off* the record. CeeCee said she won't publish anything based solely on anonymous sources. So, I might as well go for broke and ask Isabel if she's heard any of the rumors and see what she says."

"Why not? Although I can't imagine she's heard a thing. Isabel is screwed up in a lot of ways, but I don't believe she'd marry Howard if she knew any of that stuff, no matter what superhero franchise he'd offered her."

"She's truly never said *anything* to you about Howard being a creep?"

I shake my head. "Not in the way you mean. Sure, she's always laughed about how obsessed he was with her, right from the minute he met her at her first big audition. She called him a 'stalker,' but she laughed about it."

Georgina furrows her brow. "Isabel met Howard at an audition?"

"Yeah. It was her big break. He happened to be at the audition, by chance. Usually, that's below his paygrade. But he happened to be there, and when he saw her, he immediately demanded the director give her the part."

Georgina squints. "Did that audition happen before or after CeeCee's fiftieth birthday party?"

"About a year after. Why?"

"Oh, nothing. I'd convinced myself Isabel met Howard at CeeCee's birthday party. I had this whole storyline in my head about that. But I guess not."

"No. She met him at an audition. Howard wasn't even at CeeCee's party."

"Yes, he was. I saw him in a group photo from the party. Hang on." Georgina leaves and comes back with a color copy of the article, which she places before me on the kitchen table. "See?" She points to Howard's face. "That's definitely him. Plus, CeeCee confirmed he crashed her party and she was livid about it."

"Well, I'll be damned. I had no idea. I didn't even know who he was that night, so I never would have noticed him. But I can't imagine Isabel didn't know who Howard was at the time. She was always savvy when it came to…"

I trail off, as my brain starts connecting dots. Suddenly, I remember that twenty-minute gap during the party when Isabel disappeared on me, and later told me she'd been in line for the toilet. Was she talking to Howard then? Did she contact him after the party, and stay in touch with him during that entire next year, working him, hustling her ass off, until he finally agreed to give her that first big break? And did she do all of this, while I was paying her fucking rent because I didn't want her working for Francesca anymore?

Georgina sits in my lap and looks at the smiling group photo that includes Howard. "Maybe Isabel was in the same boat as you. Too young and naïve to realize she was in the presence of a hugely successful movie producer." She runs her fingers through my hair. "Or maybe she was just too damned smitten with her gorgeous date for the evening to notice—"

"No, she noticed," I say, my jaw tight. "Trust me, she knew exactly who he was that night. Isabel is, and always has been, the most ambitious person I know. She's always wanted to be a star, come hell or high water." Again, my brain catalogs the countless times I felt like Isabel was lying to me, early on. The times I felt like what she was telling me didn't add up. But since I was regularly lying to her, too—about my father, mother, childhood, lack of funds—I always let it go.

"Are you okay?" Georgina says.

"I'm fine." I stroke her arm and exhale. "I think it's a great idea for you to keep your lunch date with Isabel tomorrow, and for me to tag along. We'll tell her about us, and, after that, I definitely think you should ask her any goddamned thing you want about her beloved fiancé."

NINETY-FOUR
REED

I wake up and look at Georgina's sleeping face next to me. *Hello, wife.* The thought pops into my head, without me consciously putting it there. Which means the thumping urge I felt last night to make Georgina my wife hasn't abated in the slightest. In fact, it feels even stronger inside my veins this morning. Which means... hot damn. I need a ring.

I grab my phone off the nightstand and send a quick email to Owen, asking him to set up a private showing with a high-end jeweler this week. After a few gifs expressing excitement and shock, he asks me my budget, to which I reply, "Something between a Bugatti Chiron and a Lamborghini Veneno." Owen replies to that bit of news with two gifs from Disney's *Aladdin*. One of the Genie, granting a wish. Another of Aladdin tossing up a pile of gold coins. And I send him a gif of Leonardo DiCaprio from *Titanic*, where he's shouting that he's king of the world.

Next up, I send CeeCee a text, telling her I've decided to pour every proverbial drop of me into Georgina's wine goblet, and asking her to join me ring shopping this week. As I'm reading her enthusiastic reply, a photo of Hazel Hennessy, looking happy in a bathtub, flashes across my screen, along with a message from Henn:

Hazel's fever broke this morning. Thanks for the limo

ride. When I got home, I was well rested and ready to take over for Hannah. You're the best.

I tell Henn I'm relieved to hear the news, and then rope Josh into the chat, at which point I tell my two best friends the shocking news that I've decided to propose to Georgina. The three of us exchange texts and gifs for a while, trying to come up with the perfect location and plan for my proposal, until Georgina stirs next to me in bed and I quickly tell my friends I've got to go.

"Hey, good lookin'," Georgina says, her voice husky.

I put down my phone. "Hey, beautiful. How'd you sleep?"

"Like a baby." She rubs my thigh underneath the covers. "Who were you texting with?"

"Henn. He left early from our fraternity brother's birthday party in Vegas the other night because Hazel had a high fever. He was just updating me. Her fever's broken and she's doing great."

"Aw, that's great. I'm so impressed he left Vegas early to be with his sick baby."

"Yeah, all flights had left already for the night, so he booked a limo and hightailed it home." Okay, yes, Georgina and I have decided to be open books. But there's no reason for me to mention I'm the one who booked the damned limo for Henn. For all I know, she'd slip that little nugget into her atrocious "Reed Rivers Can Turn Water Into Wine" fluff piece.

Georgina snuggles up to me and the touch of her warm flesh against mine makes my heart rate increase.

"Henn is such a good daddy."

"Same with Josh. Both of them love being fathers."

She runs her fingertip down the ridges and grooves of my abs for a long moment. "So, what are your thoughts about becoming a father one day? Is that a firm 'never'? Or is it more like, 'Never say never'?"

Wow. I didn't see that coming. I open and close my mouth a few times, sincerely unsure how to answer the question.

She adds quickly, "Everything I've read says you're not interested in having a kid. But, you know, rule number one of journalism is to go straight to the source, whenever you can."

My heart is clanging against my sternum now. "I think I'll answer your question with a question of my own. Would *you* like to have a baby one day? If your answer is yes, then my answer is, 'Yes, I'd be willing to have a baby with you one day. Not in the near future, please. But, yes. One day.' And if your answer is that you don't want a baby, then my answer would be, 'I'm perfectly fine with not having a baby.'"

I'm thinking this is a monumental answer. Shocking. Earth quaking. But Georgina looks wholly unimpressed.

"I'm asking what *you* want, in your heart of hearts. Not what you think *I* want."

"I just told you what I truly want. What I said is my honest answer."

Georgina flushes, the enormity of what I've said hitting her, full force.

I sit up and look down at her. "So, what do you truly want? Do you want to have a baby one day, in your heart of hearts? Don't tell me what you think I want to hear. Tell me the truth."

She bites her full lower lip, and the sparkle in her hazel eyes makes it abundantly clear what she's about to say. "Well, not any time soon... but, yes. I can't imagine not being a mommy one day. Like, maybe when I'm thirty?"

And just like that, I see my future in Georgina's hazel eyes. I see my future family. And, to my extreme shock, the vision doesn't terrify me. It only makes my heart skip a beat to imagine Georgina with a baby on her hip, the way T-Rod had one at Hazel's birthday party.

"Then I guess we're gonna have a baby one day, baby."

She touches my arm. "I'd never want to bring a child into the world with you, though, if that's not truly what you want."

I take her hand. "Am I chomping at the bit to have a kid, in this moment? No. I'm not. But, sweetheart, if you get to the point where you truly want one, and you honestly feel ready, then, *boom*. Decision made. We're having a baby. I mean, come on, I'm sure as shit not letting you have one with someone else."

She pulls me down and snuggles into me with glee. "I love you so much."

"Good. Because I love you. Just, promise me, we're not boarding the baby train any time soon. I want you all to myself for a while. I want to show you the world. Fuck you in forty countries."

She sighs happily. "Sounds great to me. I want you all to myself for a long while, too. Plus, I want to get established in my career."

"Can't wait to see you do it." I kiss the top of her head. "Now, come on. We don't have tons of time for our workout before we have to meet Isabel for lunch. Annihilate me, Ginger."

Georgina flashes me a wide smile that makes my heart burst wide open. "You got it, Freddie Boy." She hops up and heads to her closet, swishing her naked ass as she goes. And the minute she disappears, I grab my phone, eager to see what I've missed in my conversation with Josh and Henn.

Not surprisingly, my two best friends have roped their wives into our conversation, and all four of them have been littering our group chat with gifs—images of people popping champagne and jumping for joy and getting down on bended knee. Finally, I reach the end of the long text chain, and tap out a reply.

Me: Thanks for the enthusiasm, guys. I can't wait to blow her away. CeeCee already said she'll help me pick out a ring.

Kat: I'M SO EXCITED!!!

Me: Really? I couldn't tell.

Hannah: When, when, WHEN are you going to ask her?

Me: I don't know yet. Once I have the ring, I'll take her somewhere with white sand beaches.

Henn: Josh, you owe me $1000.

Josh: No, the bet was RR getting married, not engaged. I don't have to pay until RR actually says, "I do."

Me: Josh, pay Henny on the bet now.

I look up. Georgina's just now re-entered the bedroom in her workout gear, looking like a wet dream. And there it is again. *Hello, wife.* I return to my phone and quickly finish tapping out my text: **Because, I assure you, the deed is as good as done.**

NINETY-FIVE
REED

I'm in an upscale restaurant with Georgina. We're sitting in a private dining room, awaiting Isabel. When she finally walks into the room, twenty minutes late, and sees me with Georgina at our table, her features contort with surprise.

"Reed?" Isabel says. "What are you doing here?"

"I came to sit in on the interview," I say, rising and giving her a polite hug. "Also, to tell you some news, so you won't hear it first on social media."

Isabel looks anxious. "Okay." She politely hugs Georgina. "Hello again. Nice to see you."

"You, too."

We take our seats at the linen-covered table, just as a server appears to take our drink orders.

"Water for me," Isabel says.

"Why don't we have martinis all around?" I suggest. "I think you might thank me later, when you hear what I have to tell you."

Isabel's face drops. She looks at Georgina. And then again at me. But since she's an actress by trade, she forces a stiff smile and says, "It's five o'clock somewhere. Martinis it is."

When the waiter leaves, Georgina motions to me, giving me the floor. So, I put my elbows on the table and jump right in.

"I thought you should know Georgina and I are in a committed relationship. She's the one I told you about at my party. The one I'm head over heels in love with. Actually, my love for her has only grown exponentially since that night."

Isabel swallows hard, but otherwise remains stoic.

"Georgina lives with me," I continue. "We're as committed and serious as two people in love can possibly be."

Well, that does it. Isabel can't keep her poker face intact any longer. Her chin trembles. Her eyes flash with acute rejection. And I'm not surprised. How many times did Isabel declare her love for me over the years, and I told her I'm not cut out to say those words in return? "It's nothing personal," I'd always say. "I've never been in love. I'm not cut out for it." How many times did Isabel say she wanted to move in with me, and I'd say, "I value my space and privacy too much to share my bed and home with anyone. It's nothing personal." How many times did Isabel say I "broke her heart" because I wasn't capable of loving her the way she so clearly needed to be loved? And now, here I am, breaking her heart one last time—forcing her to hear that I've given everything she's ever wanted from me to another woman. And not just any woman, but someone who's Isabel's physical opposite in every way. Plus, Georgina is ten years Isabel's junior—a fact that's probably hitting Isabel where it counts, considering how much she's been using Photoshop lately to smooth away all signs of her actual humanity.

But it can't be helped. As much as I don't have any impulse to brutalize Isabel, she needs to understand, without a doubt, my heart is now irrevocably taken. Not to mention, I feel like I owe this moment to Georgina as my final act of penance.

"Why are you telling me this in front of *her*?" Isabel spits out. "Did she demand you do this, and let her watch, as some sort of test of your—"

"Here we go," the waiter says, arriving with our martinis, and we lean back from the table to let him put them down.

"Bring me another one," Isabel says, picking up her glass.

"Make that three," I say.

"Of course," the waiter says. "Would we like to order some appetizers?"

"No, we won't be ordering food," Isabel snaps. "Bring the next round of drinks and then leave us alone."

"Yes, Miss Randolph."

As he scurries away, Isabel trains her ice-blue eyes on mine. "Doing this in front of her is cruel."

"Nobody is trying to hurt you," Georgina pipes in. "We thought it would be more respectful to tell you this, in person, before we started posting 'happy couple' photos on Instagram. And, by the way, I don't see how Reed telling you he's in love and happy could possibly be considered 'cruel' to you, when *you're* the one who's engaged to be married, and you and Reed haven't even been together in *years*."

I bite back a smile. *That's my girl.*

"It's not like you and I are besties," Georgina continues. "So, I don't feel like either one of us owes you an apology for falling head over heels in love with each other and then giving you the *courtesy* of an in-person heads-up about it."

I take Georgina's hand underneath the table, letting her know I've got her back. "I understand you're feeling blindsided," I say. "But Georgina is right. You've got no reason to be upset with me or throw shade at Georgina. You've moved on with Howard. I've moved on with Georgina. Congratulations to us both." I raise my martini. "Cheers."

Georgina clinks with me, but Isabel doesn't.

"You told me your girlfriend wasn't at the party," Isabel says, her nostrils flaring.

"I didn't want you heading straight to Georgina to confront her. I also wanted Georgina to have a shot at getting a good interview out of you."

Isabel scoffs. "*Why?* Why did you care about that?"

"Because I thought it would be a win-win."

Isabel looks at Georgina. "I hope you know you can forget about that interview now, sweetie."

"Yes, I've gathered that, sweetie. Although I do have a couple questions for you. Not for an article about *you*. For something I'm writing about your fiancé."

"Ha! Howard's not going to let you interview him! Not after I tell him—"

"No, no," Georgina says calmly. "My article about Howard isn't going to be an *interview*. It's going to be an exposé."

Isabel pauses, clearly taken aback. "About *what?*"

"I'm glad you asked. But first, a little background, so you understand how this idea was born. I was researching an article about Reed, actually. So I went to the courthouse and got copies of some lawsuits he'd settled. One of which, was this one." She reaches into her computer bag, pulls out Troy Eklund's lawsuit, and slides it across the table in front of Isabel. And the moment Isabel sees the name at the top, she gasps and looks at me, hurtling into full panic mode.

"I want to be clear, I found this lawsuit, all by myself. Without Reed or anyone else saying a word about it. And when I read it, I found it so interesting and mysterious, I decided to track down this Troy Eklund dude and hear his side of it. I went to a bar in West Hollywood, where he was playing on a Tuesday night. Troy and I chatted after his set. Man, he's a chatty motherfucker. Also, a douchebag. But, anyway, based on *that* conversation, I then headed downtown to a restaurant owned by a woman I think you know. Francesca Laramie."

Isabel looks ashen. She looks at me and whispers, "*You told her?*"

"Reed didn't say a word to me about any of this," Georgie says. "He didn't even know I was sniffing around about any of this. I figured everything out for myself."

"Oh my God," Isabel says, burying her face in her hands.

"There's no need for you to worry," Georgina says reassuringly. "I swear on my mother, and that's my most sacred promise, that I'll never tell anyone your secret. No matter what. The only reason I'm telling you about all this is because—"

"Here we go," the waiter says, bringing us the second round of drinks. "Are we sure we don't want to order—"

"We're sure!" Isabel shrieks. "Now go, and don't come back unless you've been expressly summoned!"

"Yes, miss." He scurries away.

"This isn't a shakedown," Georgina says. "I wasn't going to mention this next thing, but I suddenly feel like it would be for the best if I do. I already know that you and Reed kissed in his garage at the party, Isabel. And I want you to know this isn't about that. I want to assure you I'm not going to find out about that kiss later, and snap, and then go back on my word not to divulge your secret. My promise is ironclad. I come in peace. I'm not here to hurt you and I'll never tell *anyone* what I figured out. I love Reed. And whether he realizes it or not, he loves you. And that means, no matter what, I'm not going to hurt or humiliate you. Not directly, anyway. Which brings me to Howard and the reason I'm telling you all this." She takes a deep breath. "When I was talking to Francesca at her restaurant, Howard's name came up. Francesca said she never talks about her girls, or her former clients. But she did say there was one client who used to assault her girls. And when I mentioned Howard's name, she confirmed that's who she meant."

Isabel's lips part in surprise.

"You know why I knew Francesca had to be talking about Howard? Because my boss, CeeCee Rafael, had already warned me about him. She told me not to be alone with him. And then, a young woman who works at Howard's company told me every young woman who works for Howard knows not to be alone with him. In fact, all the young women who work at Howard's studio know to use the buddy system when interacting with him."

Isabel looks like she's having a hard time taking air into her lungs.

"Thanks to this insider at Howard's company, I've now interviewed five actresses who told me detailed stories about Howard sexually assaulting them. Everything from unwanted groping and kissing to coerced sex to being roofied and raped."

Isabel groans like she's about to throw up.

"The only problem? They're all too scared to come forward." Georgina leans forward. "He's a predator, Isabel, and my gut tells me you know it."

"No."

"Don't you want to stop him? Because he's not going to stop, unless someone brave, someone the world will believe, leads the charge. Isabel, that someone is *you*."

Isabel looks frantic. "You think I know about all this? I don't!"

"Yeah, well, you know something. At the very least, you know what he's done to you, personally. But I'm here to tell you, you're not alone. He's done stuff to others. And he won't stop, just because he's marrying you. He'll never stop."

"What do you want from me?"

"I want you to tell the truth, on the record. Either to the police, or in an interview, or in a press conference. I don't know. I want you to stop him. Because once you speak out, everyone else will, too. And that's the only way we're going to take this man down. If we band together."

Isabel is trembling. And there's no doubt in my mind Georgina is right: Howard's done *something* to Isabel. The thought physically pains me.

"For what it's worth, I have a glimmer of understanding about how hard this is for you," Georgie says. She reaches into her computer bag and pulls out a copy of her Gates article. "This is going to be published in a couple days in *Dig a Little Deeper*. It's an article I wrote about the forty-two-year-old man who tried to rape me when I was seventeen. He wasn't a billionaire movie producer, and I wasn't a young actress with big dreams, who felt like she had no other choice. But he was very powerful in my little world. After he assaulted me—and to be clear, he came as close to forcibly raping me as a person can get, before I wiggled free from his clutches and ran away—after that happened, I was too terrified to say a word to anyone. So I kept it bottled up inside me for almost five years. But, recently, I found out he's hurt other girls, too. And that made me realize he's going to do it again and again, unless someone stops him. So, I decided that someone is going to be *me*."

Isabel picks up her martini with a shaky hand and drains it. But she doesn't speak.

Georgina taps the article on the table. "Pretty soon the whole world is going to read this article and know what he did to me, and to those two other girls. And I can't begin to tell you how fucking proud I am, how *freeing* it is, to know I'm not hiding this secret anymore. And not only that, I'm doing everything in my power, however small, to protect other girls from suffering at the hands of that fucking prick." Georgina reaches across the table and takes Isabel's hand. And to my surprise, Isabel doesn't flinch or jerk away. "You're about to play a superhero on screen. But on your deathbed, won't you be far prouder of yourself for playing a superhero in real life?"

Isabel slides her hand away. But not forcefully. Her demeanor is dejected. Scared. "I'm sorry. I can't help you."

"You can do this," Georgina says. "If I can do it, then you can, too. And, by the way, I don't want you to do this to help *me*. I want you to do it to help yourself. To help the other women he's hurt and the ones he hasn't yet but will."

Isabel's features harden. "You don't understand. You're not *me*. I've got too much to lose."

All of a sudden, I get it. "Howard has been blackmailing you, hasn't he? You met him at CeeCee's party, not at an audition a year later. Howard found out you were a working girl at that party, and he's been blackmailing you about your past, ever since."

Isabel's breathing halts, and, just that fast, I know I'm right. Isabel did, indeed, meet Howard the same night she met me. The night we went back to my hovel of an apartment and fucked like rabbits and talked until sunrise about our dreams and ambitions. The night I told her I didn't want her working for that fucking escort service any longer. The night I told her I'd pay her rent, even though I could barely afford to pay mine, so she could stop selling her body and concentrate on her auditions and making her dreams come true. The night I told her I'd always protect her and have her back, no matter what. And she let me say all that. And do all that for her. She let me think I was her knight in shining armor... and all the while, she was fucking Howard on the side. Or, if not fucking him, then flirting with him. Stringing him along. Wrapping him around her finger until he finally gave in and gave her the big break she'd been trying to coax out of him for a fucking year.

"Did you fuck Howard at CeeCee's party?" I choke out.

"No," Isabel says. "Reed, no."

"But you met him that night."

She exhales and nods. "I flirted with him and gave him my number."

"Why did you lie to me?"

"You'd made it clear to Francesca your date that night wasn't allowed to network for herself. You told Francesca that was rule number one—your date had to be there to support you, and only you, and not her own agenda. I knew you'd be furious with me for hunting Howard down and slipping him my number. I thought you might even demand your money back from Francesca."

I take a deep breath. "You told him you worked for Francesca that night?"

"Yes. And he liked it. It turned him on."

I look down at the table. I can't believe Isabel let me pay her rent that entire year, when she knew how hard I was working to keep my own dreams afloat. I can't believe she did that to me, when Howard was probably slipping her gifts and God knows how much money, at the same time.

"I really did quit Francesca's when I told you," Isabel says. She begins to cry, but I don't believe a single tear. "Howard was my only client after that. But he hired me directly. After a while, though, I told him I'd fallen in love with you and wouldn't be doing anything with him, anymore. And that's when he drugged me. The first time. When I woke up, I told him I'd go to the police, and he said, go ahead. He said he'd tell them, and everyone else, I'd worked for Francesca. He said he'd make sure I never got hired for anything but porn. And that's when he finally gave me that first big role. And then another one. And another. Until my career really started taking off... But then I felt trapped. Like I couldn't get away, even if I wanted to... Which I did, Reed. I swear, I did. But I was in a gilded cage." Isabel wipes her eyes. "He said he'll finally let me go if I marry him. He said he'd never let a 'scandalous' secret like mine come out about his *wife*. Not even his ex-wife."

"And when will that be?" I ask flatly. "What does the marriage contract say, Isabel?"

She looks down. "Five years."

I shake my head. I can't believe how stupid I've been. For so long, I thought I was defective, thanks to my childhood. I thought I was literally incapable of falling in love. I knew I'd felt a glimmer of something special with Isabel that first night. Something I'd never felt before. Not quite that thing everyone writes about in love songs. But, still, it was definitely *something* more than I'd ever felt before. But then, as our relationship progressed, I felt myself constantly butting up against an impenetrable wall. And I thought that was because of *me*. Because *I* was too fucked up to let someone get too close to me. Because *I* was too guarded to ever let someone in, all the way. But now, suddenly, I realize it was never going to work for Isabel and me, not because *I'm* too fucked up to love. I mean, yes, I'm fucked up. But not to the degree I've always thought! No, Isabel and I were doomed because our entire relationship was built on lies, from day *one*. Because Isabel was playing me, and using me, and a piece of my heart always sensed it, and held back out of self-preservation.

"I'm sorry, Reed," Isabel chokes out. "I've always loved you. Only you."

"You don't know what love is," I say. I look at Georgina, my eyes plainly telling her: *But you sure do.* I return to Isabel, my jaw muscles pulsing. "If you're hoping I'll save you from Howard, the same way I've always saved you, then stop hoping right now. I'm not here to save you this time. *Georgina* is. *She's* your white knight. She's the one throwing you a lifeline. So, grab it with both hands." With that, I grab Georgina's hand under the table and squeeze. "Nobody can blackmail you about something you're not hiding. Set yourself free. I don't know if you'll find true happiness by doing that. But what have you got to lose? You're obviously miserable now."

As Isabel sits quietly, her chest heaving, Georgina reaches into her computer bag, and pulls out a pad. She scribbles on it, tears off a sheet, and slides it across the table to Isabel. "I don't blame you for not wanting to talk to me about any of this. So, call my boss, CeeCee Rafael. This is her number. CeeCee's been wanting to expose Howard for years. I've also confidentially listed the names of the women I've spoken to about Howard, several of whom were on Francesca's roster, early in their careers. Talk to them. Hear for yourself what Howard did to them. See for yourself if you feel okay with staying silent after you speak to them."

To my relief, Isabel takes the paper. But, again, she says nothing.

I say, "If Howard's got you brainwashed into thinking you're nothing without him, he's dead wrong about that. You're a brilliant actress, Isabel. And everyone knows it. I know for a fact my buddy Ethan Sanderson—you remember him, right? I know for a fact he's got at least four films in the pipeline he'd *kill* to hire you for. Wouldn't you rather do movies you can sink your teeth into, anyway? That's what you always used to dream about when we were young and poor—not doing *superhero* movies. Chase your *real* dreams, Isabel. Fuck Howard."

After stowing the scribbled paper in her purse, Isabel stands, throws back the entirety of her second martini, and says. "I've got to go."

"Take Georgie's article," I say.

Isabel pauses and eyes the pages on the table. But she doesn't move.

"As a favor to me," I say. "If you ever truly loved me, as you claim, then take that article and read it tonight. It's the only thing I've ever asked of you."

Nodding, Isabel picks up the pages and folds them into her purse.

She holds my gaze for a long moment, her blue eyes full of longing and regret, and, finally, leaves the room without saying another word.

The moment the door of the private dining room closes, Georgie melts into her chair. "Holy crap, that was intense."

"You were amazing."

"I was?"

"A superhero."

She smiles from ear to ear. "So were you. We're a dynamic duo."

"Let me take you somewhere, Georgie. Some place where we can relax and fuck and eat and think of nothing but each other."

"Sounds amazing. When?"

"As soon as possible. Your internship is officially over at the end of the week, right? So, let's pick up and go then."

"Where?"

"St. Barts... Santorini... the Amalfi Coast? You pick. Anywhere, as long as it's got sun and beaches and is easy to get to from the East Coast. We'll stop in New York, on our way, pay a quick visit to my mother, and then head to paradise."

Her face is glowing with excitement. "I've still got one more article to finish up. A secret something I've been working on as an 'audition' piece for *Dig a Little Deeper*. I should be done with it on Friday."

"We'll head out on Saturday, then. That's actually perfect timing. Several of my bands are performing in New York at a big charity concert this coming week. Why don't we add a few days in New York to our itinerary before we fly to paradise?" My wheels are suddenly turning. "Actually, you know what? I'll fly Alessandra to NYC to catch the charity show with us. And the next day, we'll shoot a simple little music video for her upcoming single."

Georgina shrieks. "What? Oh my God!"

"Don't get too excited. The video won't be anything fancy or complicated. Just a simple little 'performance' video we can throw onto YouTube, to show people how cute Alessandra is. I'll ask Maddy Morgan if she's available to fly in and direct the thing for me. I've always wanted to give her a shot. This is a perfect opportunity."

"Oh my gosh! This is so exciting!"

"And after all that, we'll swing by Scarsdale for an afternoon, and then jet off from there to paradise to relax." *And get engaged.*

"Amazing."

"Now come here, my little kitten." I coax Georgina out of her chair and bring her to my lap, where I kiss her passionately. And, soon, it's clear our kiss is barreling toward something a whole lot more than that.

"We can't do it *here*," Georgina whispers playfully, but she's purring as I reach underneath her skirt and massage her clit. "Reed, the waiter might walk in on us."

"Oh *no*," I say with mock horror, my fingers making her swollen and wet. "That would be *terrible*." I skim her lips with mine, as my fingers continue making her eyelids flutter. "Relax," I coax. "Isabel put the fear of God into the waiter. He won't come back, unless called."

"But what if he does?" she groans out, her pleasure apparent.

"Oh *no*," I say softly, my voice low and oozing with arousal. "Whatever would we do?"

Georgina groans and gyrates into my fingers. "You'd love for us to get caught, wouldn't you?"

I suck on her lower lip. "So much."

With that, I guide her belly against the table, pull off her panties, unzip my pants, and enter her from behind. And then, I proceed to fuck her, hard. She's the woman I'm going to ask to be my wife. The woman who's most likely going to have my baby one day—Jesus fucking Christ! The woman I love. I fuck her without mercy, while continuing to massage that hard, swollen bundle of nerves. Until the sounds of her pleasure become so loud, I have to shove a linen napkin into her mouth to muffle them. Finally, Georgina comes. As her body milks mine, I release and growl loudly and then collapse into her back, seeing stars.

Sadly, our waiter never walks in to discover us fucking like animals against the white-linen-covered table. Nor does he enter the room as we're putting ourselves back together. The consolation prize, though? As we pass the guy on our way out of the private room, the look on his face tells me he heard every telltale sound Georgina made in that room, and he's well aware of what I did to get her to make them.

NINETY-SIX
GEORGINA

"I did it! I finished writing my last article of the summer!" I walk across Reed's home office and stand over his desk, holding up the printed pages—the secret article I've been working on for the past six weeks. "I never told you about this one. I wanted it to be a surprise. I think you're going to love it."

Reed looks up from whatever he's doing on his laptop. "Uh... what? Hold on." He clacks on his keyboard for a moment. And then looks up again. "Sorry? What?"

I hold up the printed pages of my mystery article. "I just finished writing a super-secret surprise article and I'm wondering if you'll read it now."

"Oh. Wow. Congratulations. Of course, I'll read it."

My chest heaving with anticipation, I slide the pages across Reed's desk, and he calmly picks them up. But when he looks down at the page, and sees the title at the top, his mouth hangs open.

"How did you...? Oh my God, Georgie."

"I know. Crazy, right? Read it. Please. I'm dying."

Still looking flabbergasted, Reed leans back in his leather chair and begins to read, and, in short order, it's clear he's thoroughly engrossed. Mesmerized, I'd even say. After a while, he looks up from the last page. "I can't believe you did all this. I'm in shock."

He asks me some questions about the article. How I gathered the information set forth in it. And I answer him.

"Holy shit," he says. "Would you do me a favor and give this to my mother before submitting it to CeeCee?"

"Of course. That's always been my plan. First, you. Then, your mom. And then, CeeCee, but only *if* Eleanor gives me the green light. I'm planning to give it to your mom, in person, during our upcoming visit, if that's okay with you."

"Perfect." Reed's mind is visibly racing. "My mother is going to have a thousand questions for you. Every bit as much as I did."

"And I'll happily answer them. Do you think she'll like it?"

"I think she'll be as blown away as I am."

My heart is thundering. I'm so relieved Reed likes this article and thinks his mother will, too. My biggest fear was Reed would say this topic was none of my business. I say, "Okay, but, if, for some reason, Eleanor doesn't love it, or wants her privacy, I won't submit it to CeeCee." My phone rings and I look down to find CeeCee's name on the screen. "Speaking of CeeCee, her ears must be ringing." I connect the call. "Hi there. Reed and I were just talking—"

"Sorry to cut you off. I've got big news. Are you at Reed's?"

"Yes."

"Stay put. I'm coming now."

I give CeeCee the passcode for the front gate and disconnect the call. And then drag Reed into the living room, where I pace circles around the cavernous space as we await CeeCee's arrival. Finally, CeeCee knocks on the front door. And the minute I fling it open, she barges into the room and blurts, "I sent advance copies of your Gates article to a few friends in the media, and we've caught two huge whales on our line! Both *NPR* and *Good Morning America* want to interview you about the Gates article, Georgina!"

"No!"

"*Yes*! You'll do a radio interview with *NPR* on Monday morning in Philadelphia. Which is perfect timing because the article will be published online that same morning. From Philly, you'll head straight to New York and do a nationally televised live interview on *Good Morning America* the following morning!"

I'm practically hyperventilating. "You'll come with me to all of that, right?"

CeeCee laughs. "I wouldn't miss it for the world."

I look at Reed, feeling like a deer in headlights. "And you, too?"

Reed chuckles. "Of course I'm coming. And don't worry. We'll rearrange our trip itinerary to make everything work."

CeeCee claps. "We have so much to do! I'll set up a prep session with my PR woman, Jane. She and I will go over talking points with you for both interviews, and also get you camera-ready." She looks me up and down. "Which, obviously, won't be hard to do." She slides into an armchair, a wide smile splitting her elegant face. "Now, listen, Georgie girl. I was going to tell you this tomorrow at the office—Margot and I were going to throw you a little party with a cake when I told you. But I've obviously got to tell you now: you're officially a full-time writer for *Dig a Little Deeper!*"

I leap up from the couch, shrieking with joy. I hug CeeCee exuberantly, and then Reed, and then perform the most enthusiastic happy dance of my life, making Reed and CeeCee guffaw.

"Holy shit, guys," Reed says, looking down at his phone. "When it rains, it pours. I just got a text from Isabel. She's read the Gates article and wants me to tell Georgina she found it 'deeply moving and inspiring.'" He reads, "'After some soul-searching, I reached out to the women Georgina listed for me. I've now met with several of them and decided I can't stay quiet any longer. Let the chips fall where they may. I'm ready to tell the truth. And so are they.'"

"Oh my freaking God," I breathe.

Reed continues reading, "'We're going to consult a lawyer, and then give statements to the police. After that, we've all agreed we're going to do one, exclusive interview, as a group. Please ask CeeCee Rafael if she wants the exclusive. I don't want to text her, or anyone else. This is highly confidential, and I only trust you. Delete this message right after you get it. I'm sending it from a burner phone.'"

"Tell her yes!" CeeCee shrieks. "Tell her I'm sitting here now, and that I say yes!"

Reed begins tapping away on his phone, while CeeCee looks at me, astonished.

"You're a miracle worker!" CeeCee says. "The *Woman* with the Midas Touch!"

"Okay," Reed says. "I told Isabel you're one hundred percent in, CeeCee." He looks at me. "Isabel wanted me to tell you she's proud of you for coming forward about Gates. She says she wouldn't have made this decision if it weren't for that article."

I feel electrified. On the verge of tears. "Tell her I'm proud of her, too. Tell her we're not enemies. We're *sisters*." Tears well in my eyes. "Tell her she's more of a superhero now, than if she played one in *forty* movies."

Reed pats his thigh. "Come here, little kitty."

I go to him, on the bitter cusp of bawling, and he wraps his strong arms around me. "The Intrepid Reporter strikes again," he coos. "I'm so proud of you."

I nuzzle my face into Reed's neck and inhale his musky scent, somehow, still managing to keep it together. But when I look down at my mother's wedding band on my hand, a tsunami of emotion slams into me. Pride. Relief. Longing for my mother to be here to see this. But, mostly, I feel a deep-seated certainty that I'm fulfilling my purpose in life.

Reed touches my mother's ring on my splayed hand. "She'd be so proud of you," he whispers. "She's watching over you right now and cheering you on."

"I can feel her," I squeak out. And that's it. I can't keep my emotions at bay any longer. I squeeze my beautiful Reed with all my might, nuzzle into his chest, and give myself permission to sob.

NINETY-SEVEN
GEORGINA

When my article about Gates and his enablers went live three days ago, early Monday morning, my phone lit up like crazy, and my father told me the reaction in our hometown community was like an atomic bomb had gone off. But I was already in Philadelphia by then for my radio interview with *NPR* that same day, so I ignored my phone and social media, choosing instead to focus on not sounding like a clown on live national radio.

Luckily, my *NPR* interview went fabulously well. Better than expected. But, right after that, Reed took me, CeeCee, and CeeCee's PR woman, Jane, to lunch to celebrate, followed by whisking us off to Manhattan. So, again, I didn't have a chance to focus too much on whatever the world was saying about Gates and my article and me.

But once Reed and I got settled into our penthouse suite overlooking Central Park, and CeeCee and Jane came over, we finally looked, as a group, at the world's reaction to the story. And that's when we realized the story of Gates, the high school football coach who was secretly a sexual predator, was rapidly becoming high-profile national news.

One major news outlet called the story "a sexual assault scandal" and summarized it this way: "Three female former students at a California high school allege the school's football coach sexually assaulted them, and also that the school's principal, and a wealthy parent, actively covered for him." I thought that summed it up nicely.

Luckily, according to the vast majority of online commentary, it seemed most people believed Katrina, Penny, and me, and wanted swift justice for Gates and anyone who'd covered for him. On social media, people were sharing the story like crazy, as part of several lines of discussion. One of them about the intersection between sexual assault and sports-hero worship. Another one focused on women often being scared to speak truth to power, for fear of being called a liar or slut. I felt heartened to read all of those discussions. Frankly, I felt immensely proud.

But it wasn't all rainbows and unicorns. In one line of general discussion, people lamented the ability, in the age of social media, for any "disgruntled" or "unhinged" woman to say "anything she wants" about any "innocent man," thereby unjustifiably ruining his life, without due process. Fair enough. I think, generally speaking, we can all agree that's a true statement, in concept. But, when people went so far as to *specifically* call Katrina, Penny, and me "fame-seekers," "opportunists," and "liars," that pissed me off.

A former player of Gates', a guy who went on to play in the NFL, posted his support for Gates on Instagram with the hashtags #innocentuntilprovenguilty and #myhero. Again, fair enough. I totally understood his point, in concept. Gates *is* innocent until proven guilty, in terms of the legal system. But to me, he's not a hero. He's the man who shoved his tongue down my throat and his fingers up my vagina, forcibly. The man who literally ripped my shirt as I tore myself away from his terrifying grasp. He's the man who made me hide, trembling, in bathrooms whenever I saw him across campus. The man who, to this day, occasionally visits me in nightmares that always cause me to break out in a cold sweat.

But that whirlwind is what happened on *Monday*. Day *one*. On day two, I opened a can of whoop-ass on not only Gates, and his two enablers, but also on the online trolls and detractors who said Katrina, Penny, and I are liars. That morning, I did my interview on *Good Morning America,* with one of my all-time idols, by the way, so, that was a personal thrill. And, thankfully, the TV interview went even better than the radio interview. So much so, by the time Reed, CeeCee, Jane, and I walked out of the studio and into the sunshine on 44th Street, the "high school football coach scandal" had indisputably become a viral story.

Within an hour of my TV interview, both my name and Gates' were trending on Twitter. Gates' name, mostly, because people wanted his head. My name, mostly, because people were supporting me for all the right reasons. But, also, because a popular dude on Twitter had posted a screen shot of me, taken during my TV interview, that captured me looking like a goddamned fire-breathing dragon. Apparently, the Twitter guy decided that particular angry shot of me was incredibly hot. His actual hashtag was #hotwhenangry. And, apparently, a massive amount of his followers wholeheartedly agreed with him.

After that first Twitter guy did his thing, a *second* Twitter guy, someone with the handle @AngelinaFan, picked up on the thread and expanded upon it. Even though @AngelinaFan agreed I was, indeed, "hot when angry," he also felt it vitally important to note I looked uncannily like a young Angelina Jolie—which then, bizarrely, inspired him to start tweeting out all sorts of photoshopped images of me soundly kicking Gates' ass, using screen grabs from the movie *Tomb Raiders* as his starting point.

Along with my actual name in his hashtags, and the other guy's hashtag #hotwhenangry, as well as #TombRaiderRebootPlease, @AngelinaFan *also* transformed me into some sort of Georgina action hero with his additional, numerous hashtags. Stuff like #DoNotFuckWithGeorgina and #GeorginaSaysNotTodayGates and #BadassHotChickGeorgina. So stupid. Did he not understand the point of my article was to push back against exactly that kind of objectification?

But, whatever. In truth, I liked all those images of me kicking Gates' ass, as well as that first screen shot of me looking like a fire-breathing dragon. Because, truth be told, those two Twitter dudes, every bit as much as the radio and TV interviews, are what pushed my article into The Viral Stratosphere.

By the time Tuesday afternoon rolled around, all hell broke loose, in the best possible way. Leonard called to tell us that a young woman had come forward to accuse Gates of kissing and groping her when she was sixteen. The following morning, another young woman said Gates had forced her to give him a blowjob when she was fifteen, and also that she'd been paid off by none other than Steven Price to keep her mouth shut about it.

Well, that was when shit got real—when the story no longer lived in the world of Twitter or TV or radio—but, instead, started having real-world implications. Leonard called to tell me Gates and the principal had been put on leave by the school district, pending an internal investigation. Two hours after that, he called again to say authorities in Los Angeles had just announced—in a freaking press conference, attended by national media!—that they'd opened a criminal investigation into Gates *and* the principal. And *then,* shortly after that, Leonard called to report that Steven Price, the father of Brody, Brendan, and Benjamin, had lawyered up.

"I'm not sure what the charges against Price will be," Leonard told Reed and me. "My guess is money laundering and/or tax evasion. Maybe obstruction of justice."

"Oh, tax evasion, for sure," Reed said. "No way Price didn't cook his books to hide all those hush-money payments."

"So, listen, Georgie," Leonard said. "Some of Gates' victims are talking about filing civil lawsuits. Do you have any interest in that?"

I looked at Reed in that moment. Into his chocolate brown eyes. And, instantly, I knew my answer was a resounding *no.* Just that fast, I felt certain it was time for me to move forward. To build my career and a happy future with Reed, and not give another drop of my energy or time or soul to Mr. Gates. "No interest," I replied to Leonard. "I'll cooperate with any criminal investigations. But I'm done. *Ciao, stronzo.*"

Oh, the smile Reed flashed me then. If CeeCee and her PR woman hadn't been in our hotel suite at the time, I would have ripped Reed's clothes off and sunk to my knees to pleasure him, right then and there. Which is exactly what I did, only a few hours later, the minute CeeCee and Jane left.

And now, here I am, sitting in the back of a limo with Reed on Wednesday morning, scouring the curbside at JFK for Alessandra's beautiful face. I'm ready to put the past behind me now. For good. And to have a fantastic time, during the rest of this trip, to celebrate. Playing tourist today and going to the concert tonight. Visiting Eleanor in Scarsdale on Friday. And then heading off to Sardinia on Friday night to start a weeklong vacation in paradise with my man.

"There!" I say, pointing excitedly when I spot Alessandra on the curb with her suitcase.

The driver maneuvers and finds a spot, and I pop out of the car and race to my stepsister. When I reach her, we hug and kiss and jump for joy. And a few minutes later, we're heading off in the limo, excited to enjoy a carefree day of sightseeing in Manhattan, along with Reed's sister, Violet, and nephew, who we're going to pick up now, while Reed heads off, separately, to the venue for tonight's charity concert. It's going to be a huge show, featuring, among others, some of Reed's biggest stars. 22 Goats, Laila Fitzgerald, Danger Doctor Jones, Aloha Carmichael, Watch Party, and Fugitive Summer. I can't think of a better way to celebrate the first day of the rest of my life.

Laughter rises up from the other side of the long dinner table. Apparently, Davey from Watch Party has just told a joke to all the other River Records artists seated near him, as Davey often does—although this restaurant is too noisy, and our table too long, for the group at this end of the table to hear whatever joke Davey's told. But that's okay. I'm thoroughly enjoying my conversation with Alessandra and Fish. Who, by the way, have been joined at the hip since the moment Fish spotted Alessandra backstage at the concert earlier tonight.

This place is a chic eatery in Midtown. We're here to enjoy a post-concert dinner party, hosted by Reed. As I've been chatting with Alessandra and Fish to my left, Reed has been engrossed in an intense conversation with Maddy and Keane Morgan, to my right, about tomorrow's video shoot.

Without warning, however, Reed abruptly turns away from his conversation to address Alessandra. "Hey, Ally. Change of plans for your video tomorrow. I didn't know Maddy was bringing Keane to the shoot to help her. But now that I know he'll be there, I think we'd be missing a golden opportunity not to give him a starring role in the video. Keane says he's up for anything, so Maddy and I just now put our heads together and came up with an entire storyline for him."

Alessandra expresses excitement and enthusiastically thanks Keane.

"Happy to do it," Keane replies. "It sounds like a blast."

Alessandra looks at me, as if to say, *Can you believe this is my life?* And I don't blame her. Keane Morgan's show on Netflix is doing extremely well, from what I've gathered. With each passing day, he's becoming a bigger star. Having him star in her debut music video is huge.

"Now, don't feel any stress about tomorrow," Reed says soothingly to Alessandra, his little lamb. Over the past few weeks, as they've worked on Alessandra's song together, and fine-tuned it, exactly according to Reed's specifications, Alessandra has grown to trust him completely, and Reed has often told me he thinks Alessandra is "absolutely adorable." He continues, "From your end of things, Ally, you'll still mostly be doing what we talked about, okay? You'll still mostly be performing onstage at the coffee house."

"*Mostly?*" Alessandra says meekly.

"Yes. Maddy and I have come up with two storylines. A love triangle involving Keane. Also, a cute little love story involving you and Fish." Reed looks at Fish, who looks astonished to hear his name called. "If you're game, that is, Fish Taco."

Fish chuckles. "Sure. Count me in."

Thankfully, there's been no lasting tension between Fish and Reed, deriving from when Fish ripped into Reed at his party. Backstage at the charity concert earlier tonight, Fish pulled Reed aside and apologized for calling him a prick that night. To which Reed replied, in true Reed fashion, "I don't even know what you're talking about, Fish."

"What will Fish and I have to do for this 'cute little love story'?" Alessandra asks, looking on the verge of panic.

"Don't worry, honey," Maddy says reassuringly. "You'll be the performer onstage at the coffee house, as we discussed, and Fish will play the shaggy barista across the room. All you two will have to do is make googly eyes at each other, from afar, like you're totally smitten with each other."

Fish smiles shyly at Alessandra. "Well, speaking for myself, that shouldn't be hard to do."

Alessandra blushes the color of a vine-ripened tomato, and my heart skips a beat for her. "I think I could manage that," she says, through her lashes.

Reed looks at me. "Georgie, you're going to star in this thing, too."

"*Me?*"

"Yes. You and Laila are going to be in a campy love triangle with Keane. Laila already said yes. But we need *two* smoking hot women to pull this off, and it's too late to hire someone else on such short notice."

"But I'm not an actress."

"Oh, yes, you are," Reed says. "You're a better actress than half the professionals in Hollywood."

"Georgina, I saw you on *Good Morning America*," Maddy says. "The camera *loves* you."

I make a face that plainly telegraphs I'm freaking out.

"Sweetheart. Pull it together. This is happening. You're always saying you want to give me a present. Well, this is your present to me. From the first moment I saw you in that lecture hall, I fantasized about putting you into a music video. Well, this is my chance. Don't you dare deny me this pleasure."

I laugh. "Okay, okay. Count me in."

Reed smiles at Alessandra. "Wait till you hear this next thing." He motions to the array of artists seated at the far end of our long table, none of whom are paying a lick of attention to our conversation. "See all those rock stars down there? They've all agreed to stop by the coffee house tomorrow to shoot quick cameos for the video."

"*Whaaaat?*" Alessandra blurts, making Reed and Maddy laugh with glee.

"You've hit the jackpot, Alessandra Tennison," Reed says gleefully. "Having all these superstars in your debut video—plus, having Laila, Keane, and Fish in starring roles alongside you—is going to give you so much street cred, it's ridiculous. Without a doubt, all this star power is going to make this video go viral. Which, in turn, my dear, is going to rocket your song to the top of the charts."

Alessandra and I flip out, and then begin peppering Reed and Maddy with a thousand questions, asking them to describe their two storylines in detail. In response, Reed calls Laila over, so she can hear what he's about to tell the group. Plus, he calls Owen to come over, too.

"Hey, O," Reed says. "Do me a favor and arrange to buy a really cheap used car for use in Alessandra's music video tomorrow. We'll need it by midmorning or so. Laila and Georgina are going to beat it to smithereens with baseball bats."

Owen says he's on it, boss, no questions asked, and heads off to look online for some possible candidates. And then, finally, Reed leans back in his chair and, with an exuberant assist from Maddy, tells our group about the concept for Alessandra's music video:

The setting is a packed coffeehouse in Brooklyn. Alessandra is the performer on a small stage, her audience filled with famous faces. Fish is the shaggy barista behind the counter—Alessandra's "secret admirer" who covertly writes her love letters on distinctive pink stationery. Although, sadly, Fish never musters the courage to give Alessandra any of his pink love letters, but, instead, throws them, one after another, into a nearby trashcan.

Meanwhile, Keane is a hot douche-canoe customer who's been shamelessly two-timing *both* waitresses at the coffee house, Laila and me... by giving us both the distinctive pink love letters he finds in the trash. Throughout the video, we see Laila and me, pink letters in hand, separately following Keane into his beat-up love mobile, presumably for some hanky-panky.

Midway through the video, the love triangle explodes, and Laila and I confront Keane together, both of us standing shoulder-to-shoulder as we angrily hold up those distinctive pink love letters and let him have it. After soundly chewing him out—and looking hot as we do it—because, you know, angry women are hot—Laila and I drop our notes to the floor, and march outside the coffeehouse with purpose, as Keane trails behind us, pleading his case.

As the love triangle exits, Alessandra's gaze drifts to the pink love notes on the floor... and then to Fish across the room... who, at that very moment, is tossing yet another "secret admirer" love note into the bin. On that same pink, distinctive paper.

Alessandra connects the dots, and realizes *Fish* is the true author of those love notes on the floor. She also realizes, thanks to the many smitten looks Fish has sent her throughout the video, those notes on the floor must have been written to *her*.

Fish sees Alessandra's gaze migrating from the notes to him. He sees her putting two and two together. With a deep breath, he grabs his latest pink love letter from the trash, smooths it out, and marches toward Alessandra on the stage... who, as he's been doing that, has turned to grab something out of her guitar case. And that's when the audience sees a splayed stack of blue papers in Alessandra's case. A whole bunch of love songs she's secretly written about Fish. We see a shot of the handwritten lyrics, with titles like, "I'm Secretly in Love with a Barista" and "He Makes Coffee and Owns My Heart"—and we know Alessandra has always been every bit as in love with Fish, as he's been with her.

With their love notes in hand, Alessandra and Fish meet in the middle of the coffee house. They exchange their colorful declarations of love, smile like smitten kittens at each other, and then march, hand in hand, out of the coffee house... where they walk past Georgina and Laila furiously beating the crap out of Keane's love mobile with baseball bats, much to his chagrin.

"The End," Maddy says. And her enraptured audience instantly explodes with excitement.

"Can I ask a question?" Alessandra says. "I'm not trying to look a gift horse in the mouth here. I can't believe how lucky I am. But why are all these famous artists willing to make cameos in some nobody's video?"

"Every last one of them owes me a favor," Reed says. "But also, and this is the truth, Alessandra, none of them would do this if they didn't genuinely like you and believe in your song."

Alessandra couldn't be more effusive and adorable in this moment. She thanks Reed profusely and says she's going to hop up and thank each artist around the table, individually.

"No, no," Reed says, laughing. "Thank them tomorrow if they actually show up. Also, there's no need to thank me. I wouldn't be doing any of this if I didn't think I'd make my money back, and then some."

I smile at Reed. *Liar*. I love him for it, don't get me wrong. But I've come to realize Reed isn't trying to make Alessandra a star for money. He's doing it for himself. As a game. Just to see if he can. And, of course, he's doing it for me. The same way I wrote a sappy love letter about him for *Rock n' Roll*, rather than a hard-hitting, revealing piece for *Dig a Little Deeper*.

A waiter comes to refill water glasses and Reed gestures to him. "Open a case of your finest champagne. We're celebrating an amazing charity concert and the imminent birth of a superstar." He indicates sweet little Alessandra with his whiskey glass. "Mark my words, this girl here is about to make every person at this table look like a fucking amateur."

The waiter chuckles. "Yes, sir." He looks at Alessandra. "Congratulations."

As the waiter leaves, I lean into Reed's ear. "When we get back to our hotel room, I'm going to give you a blowjob that will make you pass out."

Reed grins. "Gosh, I wonder what prompted that reaction, Miss Ricci." He winks. His face aglow. "And you thought you didn't have a price."

NINETY-EIGHT
REED

"Wasn't Alessandra *amazing*?" Georgina gushes.

We're cuddled up together in the backseat of Tony's black sedan, heading to my mother's facility in Scarsdale. Throughout the drive, we've been talking enthusiastically about yesterday's music video shoot for Alessandra's single. Reliving it. Laughing about it. Marveling at how well it went.

"She was adorable," I say. And it's the truth. To my surprise, Maddy was able to coax a delightful performance out of shy little Alessandra. Actually, I think it's fair to say Maddy captured lightning in a bottle from everyone. "Props to Maddy for what she accomplished yesterday," I say. "She impressed the hell out of me."

"Me, too." Georgina lays her head on my shoulder. "You swear I didn't embarrass myself?"

I kiss the top of Georgina's head. "Sweetheart, I promise you were magnificent in the video. A bombshell. A siren." And, again, I'm telling the truth. Not surprisingly, Georgina was a star yesterday, just like I knew she'd be. When I watched her being interviewed the other day on *Good Morning America*, her star power was undeniable. Even CeeCee saw it. During the interview, she leaned into me and said, "I'm not going to be able to hang onto my unicorn for long. She's going to get a whole lot of TV offers after this... and, at some point, she's going to take one."

CeeCee didn't sound the least bit upset when she said that, by the way. Only proud. Because CeeCee knows, as do I, that dreams are inherently meant to grow and expand. Right out of college, Georgina thinks writing for *Dig a Little Deeper* is the highest peak imaginable for her career. But one day, probably soon, I'd guess, Georgina will realize she's standing at the base of a much, *much* higher peak. She'll realize she was born to take that *GMA* interviewer's job one day, or its equivalent. And when Georgina realizes that, and leaves *Dig a Little Deeper* to chase an even bigger dream, CeeCee will be as excited for Georgina as I'll be.

Tony brings the sedan to a stop in front of my mother's facility. "Will this be a long visit today, Mr. Rivers?"

I touch the ring box in my pocket, reassuring myself, yet again, it's still there. I'm not going to give it to Georgina until we're in Sardinia, standing on a beach at sunset with a photographer there to capture the once-in-a-lifetime moment. But when I took the ring box out of the hotel safe this morning, I didn't feel good about packing something so valuable in my suitcase. And so, here it is. Burning a hole in my pocket. Making me feel physically ill with excitement about what's to come every time it bumps against my thigh.

"It'll be a long visit today, Tony," I say. "Feel free to head to a diner or something. I'll text you when we're close to leaving." I look at Georgie. "You've got a print-out of your article?"

She pats her purse. "God, I hope Eleanor likes it."

I reassure her my mother will love it, even though, in truth, nerves are suddenly gripping me. I'm *almost* positive I'm right about that—that my mother will, indeed, love the article Georgina has written for her. But you never know with Eleanor Rivers. There's always the chance the article will send her spiraling into some sort of unexpected meltdown.

I lay my palm on the ring box again, subconsciously reassuring myself it's there. And then, with a kiss to Georgina's cheek, get out of the car, take Georgina's hand, and lead her up the familiar steps toward the facility.

NINETY-NINE
GEORGINA

There she is. Eleanor. Curled into Child's Pose, alongside her boyfriend, Lee, at the front of her yoga class. When the instructor sees Reed and me in the doorway, she says something to Eleanor that makes her sit up and look, and the moment Eleanor sees us, her face ignites with childlike joy. She leaps up, shrieking happily, and bounds over to us like a gray-haired gazelle. Only this time, unlike last time, Eleanor flings herself into Reed's strong arms, first—but only to chastise him for it being so long between visits.

"It's my fault," I say. "I had a bunch of deadlines for my summer internship, and I had to hunker down. I promise, I'll never let so much time pass between visits again."

"No, no, it's my fault," Reed says. "I should have come weeks ago, by myself. The truth is, I haven't traveled these past six weeks at all, other than one short business trip out West, because I've enjoyed staying home with Georgina so much." He looks at me and flashes a smile that sends my heart fluttering. "Georgina's living with me now, Mom. Permanently. And, suddenly, the only thing I want to do is stay home and hang out with her."

Eleanor looks pleased. "Well, if you're going to ignore me for way too long, I suppose that's a delightful reason." She waggles her finger at her son. "But never stay away this long again, Reed Charlemagne."

"I won't."

Eleanor looks at me, all smiles. "Did you wind up getting offered your 'dream job' at *Dig a Little Deeper*?"

"Oh my gosh. I can't believe you remembered me telling you about that. Yes, actually, I did. When Reed and I get back from Sardinia, I'll start full-time as a permanent staff writer."

Eleanor claps happily. "I knew it! After your last visit, I told all my friends you were going to nab your dream job. I even bought a subscription to *Dig a Little Deeper*, so I could see why you wanted to work there. I've now read every back issue, and, I must say, I'm impressed."

"Oh, wow. Thank you for doing that, Eleanor."

She leans forward. "I read your article in the last issue about that horrible football coach. I'm so sorry he hurt you and those other girls. But good for all of you for telling the world what he did."

I'm astonished. I've always thought of Eleanor as living in a sort of bubble here in Scarsdale, cut off from the outside world. It never occurred to me she would have read my Gates article. "Thank you so much for reading it. That means the world to me."

"Pish. I not only read the article, I also listened to your radio interview on Monday and watched your TV interview on Tuesday. And so did Lee, and all of my friends and nurses. I'm the president of your fan club." Eleanor pats my hand. "Oh, my, we're going to have such a glorious visit today. They're serving chicken pot pies for lunch. Reed's favorite. And after we eat, I'll introduce you around to the other members of your fan club. And then, we'll play *Scrabble* and cards."

Reed says, "Don't forget, Mom, Georgina and I have a flight to catch today. We're going to make this an extra-long visit, I promise, but it sounds like you've got three days' worth of activities on the itinerary for us."

Eleanor waves at the air, dismissing Reed's comment. "Let me tell Lee we're going to the dining hall, so he doesn't worry. He always worries about me when he can't find me, though I don't know where he thinks I'd go." Giggling, she prances off gaily to the front of the yoga class.

"What the hell have you done to my mother?" Reed whispers out the side of his mouth, his eyes trained on his mother.

"What do you mean? She's positively joyful."

"That's what I mean. That's twice in a row now. I figured her preternatural joy last time was a one-off. Never to be repeated. But here she is again, prancing and giggling like a kid at Christmas... *two* times in a row? That's some powerful magic you've got in your bag of tricks, Ricci. Please, always use your superpowers for good, or we're all screwed."

Eleanor returns and happily grabs my arm. "Come on, my beloved darling. We have so much to talk about!"

"I guess I'll come, too," Reed says dryly, trailing behind. But when I glance over my shoulder at him, Reed is smiling from ear to ear.

We reach the dining room and get situated with our food, and then proceed to talk for quite some time about the Gates article and the various ripple effects it's had over the past few days, including the latest bombshell—that Gates was arrested in Los Angeles this morning, after yet *another* accuser came forward. This one, with a surveillance video of some sort to back her up.

"And not only that," I say. "From what Leonard's been hearing, the arrest of Steven Price is imminent, as well."

"Oh, good," Eleanor says. "I hope all those men get everything they deserve in this life, and then go to hell after that. Especially that horrible football coach."

"I have full faith justice will be served," I say. And it's the truth. I tell Eleanor what Leonard told me this morning, thanks to information he obtained from a buddy at the DA's office. Specifically, that the line of women accusing Gates is so long and credible at this point, and the text messages and settlement agreements so damning, Gates is already apparently asking the DA for a deal in exchange for his guilty plea.

"A deal?" Eleanor asks.

"A lighter sentence than the worst-case scenario he could get, if he's convicted on all counts at trial," I explain. "But don't worry. Either way, Leonard said the DA will make sure, no matter what, Gates goes away for a very long time. The whole world sees him for what he is now. Nobody is going to let this man walk away from his crimes."

"When he goes to prison, I bet all the TV shows will want you to come on. Don't you think, Reed?"

"Absolutely."

She returns to me. "I think you should be on TV, all the time, Georgie. Not just about Gates. But as your actual *job*. You're a wonderful writer, and *Dig a Little Deeper* is a fantastic magazine, but you've got a face for TV. When we were watching you on *Good Morning America,* one of my friends said, 'Georgie should be on TV, every morning!' And I told her I agree and would tell you so when you *finally* came to visit me." She shoots Reed a withering look, nonverbally chastising him for staying away so long, and then returns to me, smiling. "Oh! What if you hosted that show where they 'catch a predator'? You'd be so good at that!"

I can't help smiling. She's so cute. "Definitely something to think about."

"Has *Good Morning America* asked you to come work for them yet? If not, I bet they will soon!"

I laugh. "Weirdly enough, not yet. And I've been waiting by the phone all day!" I wink.

"Did you like being on TV? It sure looked like it."

"I did. I loved it. I was super nervous, right before going on. But then, the minute I got out there, and that little red light above the camera turned on, I felt nothing but excitement."

"I could tell. You didn't seem nervous at all." She pats my arm. "It's settled, then. You're going to be a huge star on TV."

I giggle. "Don't rush me, please. I'm elated about my new job. Writing for *Dig a Little Deeper* has been my dream for a long time."

My phone, and Reed's, both ping simultaneously with incoming texts. I don't look down, since I'm engaged in a conversation with Eleanor and don't want to be rude. But Reed looks down. And when he does, he instantly blurts, "Ho! Maddy says she's uploaded a rough cut of Alessandra's video to the Dropbox!"

With excitement, I quickly explain to Eleanor the context—the backstory of the music video Reed is excitedly cuing up. And a moment later, the three of us are huddled around Reed's phone, watching Maddy's masterpiece.

It's *phenomenal.* Better than anything I could have imagined. When it's over, I look at Reed, and it's clear he's every bit as blown away as I am. In fact, I'll be damned, he's morphing into Business Reed before my eyes.

"This video is going to launch Alessandra to the moon," he declares, his dark eyes blazing. "'Blindsided' will hit Top Thirty in its first week.

Top Ten by its third. I'm calling it now." Reed's wheels are visibly turning. His excitement is palpable. "Real talk, Georgie. Do you think your stepsister will be able to handle overnight stardom? I'm talking about the kind of whirlwind success that's going to make her drop out of school. Will she crumple under the weight of that kind of success, or rise to the occasion?"

My heart is pounding. I'm euphoric. "She'll rise to the occasion, the same way she did at the video shoot. She's ready for this, Reed. I promise. It's what Alessandra's always wanted."

Reed nods, apparently reaching some sort of decision. "All right, then. I'll get the machine fired up for a full album. The minute we get back from our trip, I'll pull my team together and get everything scheduled. We'll want to capitalize on the success of the first single. Keep momentum going."

Squealing, I pepper Reed's handsome face with kisses, and thank him profusely.

"There's no need to thank me," he says, laughing. "This time I'm telling the truth. Alessandra is going to make me a mint."

Swooning, I check the time on my phone. "We'll need to call her in a couple hours. She's still on her flight back to Boston."

"This is so exciting," Eleanor says. She leaps up and grabs my hand. "Come with me, Georgie! I'm going to introduce you to all my friends and tell them you've agreed with me you belong on TV one day—and, also, that your cute little stepsister is about to become a star!"

In a pleasant, sunlit game room, filled with people playing Scrabble and dominoes and cards, Reed and I are making the rounds, making pleasant small talk with Eleanor's friends and nurses, when a newscaster on a TV in the corner reports something startling: "Breaking news. Howard Devlin, the billionaire studio head and movie producer, has just been arrested by LAPD for rape and various other sex crimes." My jaw hanging open, I snap my head toward the TV in the corner, just in time to see Howard Devlin, in handcuffs, being shoved like a common criminal into a cop car that's parked in front of his sprawling mansion.

I turn to Reed to find him looking as shocked as I feel. We quickly excuse ourselves from the game room and barrel into the hallway. First off, Reed immediately calls Isabel, but gets her voicemail. He calls Leonard, who says he's heard the news, but knows nothing more than what's being reported. Finally, Reed calls CeeCee and hits the jackpot. Confidentially, of course, CeeCee tells us Isabel and her posse went to the police station last night, through a back door and in the cover of darkness, and stayed for hours, giving their detailed statements.

"And this morning," CeeCee says exuberantly, "Isabel's lawyer called to schedule two interviews with me! An exclusive, one-on-one with Isabel, which we'll do on network television. I've already made arrangements. And a second, more comprehensive interview, which will be published in a special edition of *Dig a Little Deeper*, along with individual, exclusive interviews of all the other women, too."

"Holy crap, CeeCee. This is going to be the story of the year. A game-changer."

"I know. Now, listen, Georgina. I want you to do some brainstorming while you're in Italy. When you come back, you're going to need to write an opinion piece for the special edition. Something that draws parallels between Gates and Devlin, from your unique perspective."

"I'd love to. *Yes.*"

"I'll handle both Isabel's interviews, personally, but I'm going to want you to handle some of the other women's interviews for me. We're going to have a short turnaround time on this special edition to make it timely."

"You got it. Thank you for trusting me."

"Trusting you? This is all because of *you*."

"No, it's because *you* had a gut feeling about him. Because *you* warned me about him. And because, most of all, you've shown me what a kickass woman looks like."

Our excited lovefest continues for a short while longer. But, finally, we end the call and I hand Reed's phone back to him.

Reed looks at his watch. "We should think about catching our flight soon. If you're still planning to show my mom that article you wrote for her, I think you should do it now, sweetheart."

"Okay. Yeah, let's do it."

We head back into the game room, where Eleanor is chatting with her favorite nurse, Tina. After Reed tells her why that Howard Devlin news story sent us sprinting into the hallway, we lead Eleanor to a table in a quiet corner of the game room. And that's where I reach into my purse and tell her I've brought her a special surprise.

"Since I last saw you," I say, my heart thrumming in my chest, "I've been researching and writing an article inspired by something you told me." I hand her the folded pages of my article. "I wrote an article especially for you, Eleanor."

"For *me*?"

I nod. "If, for any reason, you don't want the world to read what's in your hand, then I promise, I won't submit it to my boss. The only reason I wrote it is to give you a tiny drop of some much-deserved peace."

ONE HUNDRED
GEORGINA

L ooking deeply perplexed, Eleanor puts reading glasses on, squints at the first page in her hand, and reads aloud the words printed at the top: "'A War of Fire: How a Battle Between Rival Mobsters Shattered Innocent Lives.'"

She looks at me blankly.

"It's about your family," I say nervously. "About the fire. After you told me about it during our last visit, I decided to poke around to see if I could solve the mystery of how it got started. I wanted to see if I could clear your father's name. And I did it, Eleanor. I figured out, without a doubt, your father *didn't* set that house fire. I'm positive."

Eleanor looks beyond flabbergasted. She looks at her son, and then at me, before throwing her hands over her face and bursting into wracking sobs.

"Aw, Mom." Without missing a beat, Reed gets up and takes his weeping mother into his arms. "Wait until you hear what Georgina figured out. You're gonna be so happy, Mom."

But Eleanor is inconsolable. Crying so hard, so violently, a nurse comes over to make sure she's okay. And, of course, I'm mortified to have provoked this horrifying reaction. All I wanted to do, the only thing, was to give this poor, tormented soul, who's suffered so much in her lifetime, the tiniest measure of peace. But, obviously, my unexpected news has had the exact opposite effect than intended.

Thank goodness for Reed. This ain't his first time at this particular rodeo, obviously, and he's smooth as silk with his mother. He holds her tenderly. Strokes her back and whispers to her in a calm, controlled voice. He's so simultaneously confident and nurturing, in fact, I can't help thinking as I watch him, "Damn, this man is going to make one hell of a father one day."

Eventually, Eleanor quiets down and becomes a rag doll in her son's muscular arms.

"How about Georgina tells you the gist of what she wrote, so you don't have to read the article itself?" Reed suggests. "She can tell you how she solved the mystery, like she's telling you a detective story."

Eleanor nods, rubbing her slack cheek against Reed's broad shoulder. "I'd like that."

My stomach somersaults. "Maybe you should tell your mother about the article. I'd hate to say something wrong."

Eleanor shakes her head. "No, I want you to tell me. You're the one who solved the mystery. I want to hear it from you."

I look at Reed and he nods encouragingly.

"Okay. Of course. Whatever you want."

But where to begin?

In my article, I start by setting the stage for the reader. I describe the ill-fated Charpentier family, and the tragic house fire that claimed four of six of them in one horrible night. I describe how Charles' insurance company refused to honor his property claim because of "suspected arson and insurance fraud." And how he fought to clear his name, and secure the funds owed to him, for the better part of the next year, because he wanted desperately to build a new house, and a new life, for his sole surviving teenager, Eleanor.

I explain in my article that, in the end, a defeated and beleaguered Charles Charpentier marshalled every last dime in his bank account and used it to send his bereft daughter to an art school in Paris. And that, when he knew she was safe and sound on another continent, painting family portraits while overlooking the Seine, he put a gun in his mouth and ended his life on the one-year anniversary of the fire.

But, obviously, Eleanor doesn't need to hear about any of those tragedies, seeing as how she lived them, plus many more, once she met Terrence Rivers—a strapping, smooth-talking thirty-year-old American—who happened to be vacationing in Paris.

I turn my article facedown on the table, deciding to ditch the format of the article, and, instead, walk Eleanor through my investigation, step by step.

I say, "After you told me about your family and your father during our prior visit, I couldn't help wondering what investigations might have been conducted at the time, either by the police or the insurance company. I called my favorite professor from UCLA, a woman named Gilda Schiff, and she was excited to help me. Right away, we discovered police records regarding the fire were nonexistent. So, we focused on trying to track down the insurance company's investigation. At my professor's recommendation, I hired a local investigator in New York to help identify the insurance company, and, pretty quickly, she was able to find an archive of old property records that provided the answer."

"Mom," Reed says. "What Georgina isn't telling you is that she hired that private investigator with her own money. I didn't even know she was doing any of this research."

"I didn't want to tell Reed, or anyone, in case I came up empty handed," I say. But the full truth is that I didn't want to say anything to Reed, or anyone else, in case I stumbled upon evidence that suggested, or possibly even confirmed, that Charles Charpentier had set that fire. I continue, "To be clear, though, I only paid for the investigator in the beginning. When my little pot of money ran out, she continued working on the case *pro bono* for me, simply because she'd become as obsessed with the case by then as me."

"I didn't realize that," Reed says. "Give me your investigator's address later. I'll send her a big, fat check to thank her."

I smile at Reed. "Thank you. She'll be grateful for that. She worked really, really hard on this case." I address Eleanor. "I should mention it was only because of Reed's generosity with me that I could afford to pay that investigator, at all. Thanks to him, I didn't have any expenses this summer."

I pause, thinking Eleanor might say something, but when she only stares at me, wide-eyed and visibly overwhelmed, I realize this isn't going to be a back-and-forth conversation. Plainly, Eleanor is too shell-shocked to do anything but sit and listen to an unending monologue. And so, that's what I give her. The full story, in one long, continuous ramble, summarized as follows:

The private investigator I hired, Carla, quickly figured out the Charpentier home had been insured by a long-defunct company called Shamrock Insurance, which went out of business within a year of the fire, when its owner, Henry Flannery, a renowned New York City mobster, was arrested for money laundering, racketeering, and other criminal enterprises.

After finding out the shocking news about Shamrock being owned by a mobster, I called Leonard with some general questions about money laundering and racketeering, and he told me criminals always run their "dirty money" through legitimate businesses, in order to "clean" it. Or, in other words, to make the money look, on the books, like it didn't come from a criminal enterprise. Leonard explained, "It sounds like Shamrock Insurance was one of the legitimate businesses Henry Flannery used to clean his dirty money."

At that point, I devoured every article I could find on Henry Flannery, and noticed that many of them mentioned his bitter feud with another New York mobster named Giuseppe Benvenuto, who'd famously owned a bustling restaurant in Lower Manhattan called "Sofia's"... until it burned to the ground in a raging fire a mere *six days* before the Charpentier fire.

Bam! For some reason, that fact hit me like a ton of bricks. Just that fast, the investigative reporter inside me knew I'd hit on something big. A restaurant in Manhattan, owned by one mobster, burned down in a *fire*, and less than a week later, a home insured by that mobster's rival *also* burned down in a *fire*? Rationally, I knew it was a stretch to link the two fires. But my gut told me there was almost certainly a connection.

Not knowing what else to do, I read a biography about Henry Flannery, written, with the help of a professional co-writer, by a high-ranking member of Henry's crime organization—a "lieutenant" who'd flipped on Henry during Henry's trial, and then disappeared into the witness protection program. And what I discovered while reading that lieutenant's biography broke the entire cold case wide open.

According to this "lieutenant" dude, Henry ordered Giuseppe's restaurant torched to the ground for some unknown offense. And so, in retaliation, Giuseppe decided to "take down" Shamrock by forcing it to pay out on a whole bunch of property claims, all at once. Specifically, claims that would be filed by Shamrock's handful of few "legitimate clients," whom the lieutenant described in his book as "suckers from rich suburbs, who'd bought cheap insurance from Shamrock, not realizing they were doing business with the mob."

Well, that was it for me. After reading that description, I knew in my gut poor Charles Charpentier had been one of those "suckers." I knew, in my gut, he hadn't set the fire that claimed his family. Giuseppe Benvenuto had. But, obviously, a gut feeling wasn't going to be enough. I knew I needed to find unquestionable *facts*.

When I tried to track down the professional co-writer of the Henry Flannery biography, I learned he'd died a decade ago. But, lucky for me, his adult daughter—a professor at Cornell—was more than happy to chat with me on the phone and relay to me all the detailed stories her beloved, and very talkative, father had told her about the legendary mobster, Henry Flannery.

According to the co-writer's daughter, ninety-five percent of Shamrock's clients were dummy profiles with bank accounts controlled by Henry or one of his family members. Only five percent of Shamrock's client roster was comprised of real people—poor saps Henry counted on, without their knowledge, to prove his company's legitimacy, if needed. Over the years, on the rare occasion when one of Shamrock's few real clients filed an actual property claim, the company always denied it on whatever grounds. And then, as necessary, bribed someone at the Insurance Commission to rule in Shamrock's favor on the claim, if the client persisted.

As Giuseppe correctly surmised, however, this strategy didn't work when *every* legitimate client filed a claim, all at once. As the co-writer's daughter explained to me, "There's only so much greasing the skids a mobster can do before people *not* on the take, whether at the Insurance Commission or NYPD, started noticing suspicious irregularities. That's what wound up happening, and ultimately took Henry down. Someone *not* on the take at the Insurance Commission noticed a whole bunch of denied claims, all at once, and picked up the phone to call a detective friend at NYPD. And the rest is history. Law enforcement saw a way to finally get their man."

By the time I hung up the phone with the co-writer's daughter, I knew I was *this* close to hitting the motherlode. But, still, I needed additional facts. I needed *proof*. So, I asked my investigator, Carla, to research any house fires that might have occurred during the same week as the Charpentier fire, in any "rich suburbs" near New York City. And when Carla got back to me on that task, I knew I'd finally hit the motherlode. I'd proved Charles Charpentier was innocent.

As it turned out, there were no less than *eight* other house fires within forty-eight hours of the Charpentier fire, in eight different nearby suburbs outside of New York City. Some in New York state. Others in New Jersey and Connecticut. But all within an hour of New York City.

"And do you know what company insured all *nine* homes that burned down, including your family's?" I ask, looking into Eleanor's dark brown eyes. "*Shamrock Insurance*."

I wait, expecting a "wow!" reaction from Eleanor. But she's still too shell-shocked to speak.

Reed says, "Do you understand, Mom? Your family's home was burned down as part of Giuseppe Benvenuto's revenge against Henry Flannery. Your family, and eight others, were unwittingly caught in the middle of a war between rival mobsters."

"Yes, I understand," Eleanor says softly. "Thank you for figuring this out, Georgina."

I nod. "I'm so glad I was able to get a definitive answer."

"Was anybody else hurt in the other fires?"

"Yes. One family lost two members. Another lost one."

Eleanor's face contorts. She looks down. And we're all silent for a long moment, paying our respect to the poor souls lost.

Finally, Eleanor lifts her head. "I need to change this week's painting. I need to move my father in the scene. He should be standing next to my mother—in this painting, and every future one." She looks at Reed. "Can you and Georgina come back to see the revised painting in a few days?"

"No, Mom," Reed says gently. "From here, Georgina and I are flying to Italy, remember? If you don't want us to see this week's painting, as is, that's fine. We'll see whatever masterpiece you've painted the next time we visit."

"No, no, you have to see *this* painting. I made it especially because I knew Georgina was coming." She stands and offers her hand to me, which I take, and then begins leading me out of the game room. "Promise me, when you look at this painting, you'll imagine my father standing next to my mother, with a big smile on his handsome face."

ONE HUNDRED ONE
REED

At the shocking sight of my mother's latest painting, I inhale a sharp breath. *She's painted something different this time.* I mean, not entirely. In some essential ways, this scene is the same as all those that came before: an idyllic setting—this one, a seashore—featuring Mom and me, and Mom's many loved ones lost, who are all busy frolicking and making merry.

Other than those general similarities, however, this particular painting is strikingly different than its countless predecessors. For one thing, my mother has painted herself at her present age. With gray hair. For the first time, ever, not as a young mother enjoying a picnic with her two young sons.

Also, Oliver isn't tethered to Mom's hip, as usual. This time, for the first time, Mom has allowed the poor kid to run off and play. Specifically, Oliver is throwing a beachball with Mom's youngest sister, down by the water's edge.

Shockingly, I'm not sitting on Mom's blanket, either. And I'm not a little kid. For the first time, she's painted me as a grown man. I'm standing on the sand, wearing a tuxedo, and doing something that makes my head explode: exchanging wedding vows with a beautiful brunette who's clad in a simple white gown and bridal veil.

It's a good news, bad news situation, obviously. On one hand, I'm elated and relieved to *finally* see something new in an Eleanor Rivers Original. It's huge progress. A welcome respite from the usual madness. On the other hand, though, I feel like I'm going to stroke out with my rising panic. Of all the days for my mother to have a massive breakthrough, she had to do it by painting me in a wedding scene with Georgina on the very day I'm whisking Georgina off to Sardinia to propose marriage to her? *Way to steal my thunder, Mom*! Now, when I propose to Georgina on that beach at sunset, she's going to think this painting forced my hand! Or, at least, that it gave me the idea. Hell, Georgina might even think I only asked her to marry me to win my mother's long-withheld approval and love.

Mom is presently babbling about where she wants to relocate her father in the scene, but I'm not listening. My mind is racing far too much to focus on her words. *This is a catastrophe.* I look at Georgina and it's clear the elephant in the room is sitting on Georgina's chest, every bit as much as it's sitting on mine.

"And what do you think about yourselves in the painting?" Mom says, looking mischievous.

Georgina looks at me, wide-eyed and rendered mute, so I say, "We look great, Mom. And so do you. I love your gray hair. Have you shown this one to Dr. Pham?"

"Yes. She liked it. She said I should keep painting myself, and you, too, as we are in the present. And she also liked that I included Georgina."

"So do I," I say.

"Thank you for including me," Georgina manages to say brightly. But her gaiety sounds forced to me. "I'm honored."

"You're family now." She looks at me. "Although I'd be very interested to know when—"

"Well, we've gotta head out now," I blurt. "Georgina and I have to get to the airport so we don't miss our flight."

"But I thought you said you're flying private today. You always say the best perk of flying private is that you can never miss your flight, because everyone is paid to sit around and wait for you."

My heart is crashing in my chest. "Yeah, but we've still got time constraints. You should take a nap, Mom. It's been an emotional day for you."

Mom exhales. "Well, that's true. A nap sounds nice, actually."

"Good. I'll help you get into bed."

I grip her frail shoulders gently and pointedly turn her away from her canvas and guide her straight to bed. My breathing labored, I adjust Mom's covers over her and kiss her forehead. I say one last goodbye. So does Georgina. And then, I grab my woman's hand in a death grip and pull her out the door, with more gusto than intended. But rather than turning left in the hallway, toward the front entrance, I turn right and practically drag poor Georgina toward the back door.

The last thing I want is for Georgina to doubt this proposal is *my* idea. My desire. Or for her to think it's some pathetic attempt to win my mother's approval. On the contrary, I need Georgina to know, without a doubt, I already had her ring in my pocket when I saw my mother's shocking painting, and that I didn't scramble upon landing in Italy to get something overnighted to me.

"Hey, Smart Guy," Georgina says. "The front door is that way."

"I need to talk to you about my mother's painting before we get into the car. I want to talk to you about it in a private spot."

"Oh, Reed. There's no reason to freak out. I've read your Wikipedia page, babe. I'm not expecting—"

"Stop talking, Georgina. Please."

"I'm just saying I'm fully aware—"

"*Stop. Talking.* If you love me at all, don't say another word until I've explicitly told you it's your turn to talk."

Georgina flashes me her patented "Well, you don't need to be a dick about it" look. But, thankfully, she clamps her lips together and stops talking as I guide her into a secluded corner of the garden.

When we come to a stop, anxiety rockets through me. Fear of rejection. When I called Georgina's father, Marco, to ask for his blessing two days ago, he gave it to me. Thankfully. But he also gave me a piece of unsolicited advice: "If I were you," he said, "I'd bring up the general topic of marriage with Georgina *before* popping the question. From what she told me at her college graduation party, she's not going to marry anyone before age thirty."

"Yeah, well, that was before she fell in love with *me*," I replied confidently. And from that moment on, I completely disregarded the man's stupid advice and went about my business, buying Georgina's four-million-dollar ring and planning the perfect proposal in Sardinia. I mean, please. Why would I ask Georgina's permission to ask her to marry me, when my favorite thing in the world is blindsiding her with surprises that provoke jiggling happy dances?

But now that I'm here, and the actual moment is upon me, I'm suddenly feeling a whole lot less confident. Was Marco right? Should I have broached this topic with Georgina, the same way she broached the topic of having a baby with me? Is that what normal people do? I don't *think* Georgina will turn me down. But, then again, I never thought, not in a million years, the FBI would raid my house that fateful morning and drag my father away in handcuffs.

"Are you okay?" she says, disregarding my request to remain silent. And when I look into her concerned hazel eyes, what I see there chases away my anxiety. She loves me. Totally and completely. The same way I love her. For crying out loud, she promised me forever, with letters inked permanently onto her ring finger. Which, I have to believe, whether she realized it or not, was her way of subconsciously asking me to put a ring on it.

"Yeah, I'm fine." I take her hands. "I was planning to say this to you in Sardinia in three days. But, now that I've decided to say it here, instead, I realize this is actually the perfect place. Because it's where I finally understood what it means to let down my guard all the way, and let someone in, without holding back." I take a deep breath and exhale a long, controlled breath. "Georgie, you're the great love of my life. My queen. I'll never want anyone but you."

She bites her full lower lip and whispers, "I love you, too."

"I called your father a couple days ago and asked for his blessing to ask you to marry me."

Her eyes widen like saucers as her mouth hangs open.

"And he gave it to me. Which means, I can now do *this*." With another deep breath, I pull the closed ring box out of my pocket and kneel before her. I look up at her, smiling. "Georgina Ricci, I'll marry you tomorrow, if that's what you want. I'll marry you in a year, or ten. Just, please, say yes to me today. Be my fiancée. And whenever you're ready, be my wife. Say yes." I open the ring box, revealing the fifteen-carat, Princess-cut, pink diamond I picked out for her, with CeeCee's help. And Georgina screams like I just poked her with a very large needle in her ass.

Laughing at her reaction, I choke out, "Georgina Marie Ricci, will you *please* marry me?"

Tearfully, she shrieks out her reply. The very thing I told her to say the first time I laid eyes on her at the panel discussion. "Yes, yes, yes!"

A shockwave of euphoria floods me. Quaking, smiling, swallowing down tears, I slip the rock onto Georgina's shaking finger, lurch up, and take my fiancée into my arms. As I kiss her, joy of a kind and magnitude I didn't know exists washes over me. I feel like I'm on top of the world. Or, perhaps, in the Garden of Eden. Because, surely, this moment, this place, and not any white sand beach in Sardinia, is paradise.

Finally, Georgina breaks free of our embrace to gift me with the best happy dance of her happy-dancing career. When she's done, I scoop her up and swing her around, making her squeal and giggle. I put her down and grab her hand and we both stare in awe at the ring on her hand.

"It's so *big*," she whispers. "I swear I would have been happy with something so much smaller."

I scoff. "Did you not understand the question? I asked you to *marry* me. Not go to *prom*. Go big or go home, baby. You know that."

"Honestly, I'm going to be scared to wear it, unless you're with me. I can't go to the gym wearing a ring like this. Or to the grocery store. This is for, like, the Academy Awards!"

I laugh. She's right, actually. It's pretty over the top. "Okay, when we get back from our trip, we'll go shopping and get you another ring—an 'everyday ring' you can wear to the gym or wherever, and you can wear this one whenever you're dressed up."

"What? No! I didn't mean you should buy me a *second* ring! I meant we should return this one and get something less expensive."

"You don't like it?"

"No, I love it! I just can't believe you—"

"Then that's the end of the conversation. What I spend on gifts for you is none of your fucking business, per an exception expressly delineated in our 'open book agreement.'"

She flushes and looks down at her hand again. This time, with unadulterated excitement. "Thank you so much."

"You're very welcome."

"Why did you have it in your pocket, if you weren't planning to propose to me today?"

"Because there was no way I was going to leave a ring worth more than a Bugatti in my luggage."

The color drains from Georgina's face. "No."

"Yes. Not that it's any of your business, of course." Laughing at her expression, I stroke her cheek. "Georgie, you're going to be the one and only *Mrs. Rivers,* forever. I'm not going to give my future wife a ring worth anything less than the most expensive sports car sitting in my garage." I scoff at the very thought. "Now, come on, fiancée." I put my hand in hers. "Sardinia awaits."

We practically float through the back door, into the facility, the air between us crackling with our mutual elation.

"Your dad put the fear of God into me when I called him, by the way. He gave me his blessing, no problem, but he suggested I should chat with you about marriage, before proposing, because, last he'd heard, you didn't want to get married to anyone before age thirty."

Georgina scoffs. "Well, yeah. I said that before I met *you.*"

"That's what I told him!"

Laughing, Georgina says, "It's easy for a girl to draw imaginary lines in the sand before she knows Reed Rivers exists in the world."

We reach my mother's door in the hallway and poke our heads inside her room, thinking we'll share our happy news before heading out. But Mom is fast asleep, so we decide to let her stay that way.

"We'll call her after we land," I say, as we make our way down the hallway toward the lobby.

"Let's call my dad and Alessandra in the car, though," Georgina says excitedly. "I'm bursting to tell them. I want to tell the whole world!"

"Me, too. We'll call CeeCee in the car, too. She helped me pick out the ring."

"She did? Aw, that means so much to me." Georgina looks at her hand and giggles. "No wonder it's so big. You and CeeCee shopping together must have been like fire and gasoline. I can only imagine how much she goaded you on to 'go big.'"

"Sweetheart, I didn't need anyone to goad me on to do that. Trust me. If anything, CeeCee kept me from buying something that would make your knuckles physically drag on the ground when you put it on."

Georgina laughs uproariously. "What about Amalia? Did she know you were going to ask me?"

"No. Only CeeCee, Josh, Henn, Kat, Hannah, my sister, and Dax."

"Let's call all of them from the car! I can't wait to tell everyone!"

We've reached the lobby now. But instead of heading out the front door, and straight to Tony's waiting sedan, we pause at the front desk.

"Hey, Oscar," I say. "When my mother finishes tweaking her latest masterpiece, will you do me a favor and ship it to me in California?" I scribble my address onto a piece of paper and hand it to him, along with a bunch of bills. "That's for shipping and your trouble."

"Thanks. Sure. No problem. If you don't mind me asking, why don't you want her latest painting tossed onto the heap, with all the others? Is there something special about this one?"

"Yeah, there's something special about this one." I look into Georgina's sparkling eyes. "This one is going to be a memento, forever, of the happiest day of my life."

ONE HUNDRED TWO

GEORGINA

One year later

"And now, it's time for you both to exchange your vows," Henn says. "At least, that's what the template says we should do now."

Everyone seated in rows on our patio chuckles. And I don't blame them. For his first time officiating a wedding, Henn is absolutely killing it.

There was never any serious question that Henn would officiate our wedding, while Josh served as Reed's best man, any more than there was a question that Alessandra would be my maid of honor and Kat my bridesmaid. Or that Reed and I would get married here, on our patio, surrounded only by the people we love the most. Reed and I both knew long distance travel would be difficult for my father, thanks to some lasting side effects from chemo. And also that Reed's mother would never want to fly internationally, even if Reed were to arrange a luxurious private flight for her. Plus, Eleanor hates hotels, so we knew she'd be most comfortable staying here, at our house, along with her favorite nurse, Tina. And so, in the end, Reed and I agreed to get hitched *here*, exactly like this, rather than in some far-flung exotic locale. And we couldn't be happier about it.

"Georgie?" Henn prompts. "Why don't you say your vows first. Show Reed how it's done."

Nerves rocket through me. Not because I have any doubt about pledging myself to Reed forever. But because I'm quite certain what I've come up with for vows won't come close to expressing the depth of my love for Reed—the gorgeous, generous, enthralling man who's become my world. My breathing stilted, I pull a piece of paper out of my cleavage. "Sorry," I mumble, indicating the paper. "I didn't want to mess this up."

"You can't mess it up," Reed says soothingly, squeezing my hand. "No matter what you say, it will be perfect."

I glance down at the paper. And then return to Reed's chocolate eyes. I clear my throat. "Reed, loving you feels like the most natural thing in the world—like breathing and blinking and smiling." I smile. "I never have to think about loving you, because I was born to do it. *Designed* to do it. But 'love' isn't a big enough word for how I feel about you. There's really no word for it, actually. No way for language to encapsulate the depth and endlessness of my devotion to you, any more than the word 'infinite' truly encapsulates the vastness of outer space. Please know that I love you as deeply as a human being can love. I adore you, with every drop of me. I admire and respect you. And I *like* you. My vow to you today is to love you fiercely and faithfully, forever. Until we're old and gray. Which, in your case, will be in about three years."

Reed hoots with laughter, along with Henn and Josh. Plus, I can hear Alessandra and Kat guffawing behind my back, as well, along with everyone in our audience.

"Try the veal, I'm here all week," I say, making Reed chuckle again. I crumple my paper and toss it behind me, and then grab both of Reed's hands. "It boils down to this. My beloved Reed, I promise to be yours, in sickness and health. For richer or poorer—"

"Don't jinx me, baby."

Again, everyone laughs, including me.

"Reed Rivers, I can't wait to spend the rest of my life with you, as your wife. I love you so much. I promise to give you, and only you, all of me. Forever."

"Perfect." He leans in and kisses me gently. "I love you so much."

"I love you, too. So, so much."

"That was so beautiful, Georgie," Henn says. He smiles at his best friend. "Okay, buddy. You're up. Make it good."

"I'll do my best." A huge smile overtakes Reed's face. "To start, I feel the need to correct a few things I've said in the past—things that were true when I said them, but aren't anymore. I once told you I'm a believer in 'going big or going home.' But now that I love you the way I do, I've realized that's not an either-or proposition. Going home *is* going big, as long as I'm coming home to you."

I clamp my lips together to keep my chin from trembling.

"Another thing," Reed says. "I once called you the 'Ginger Rogers of Spin.' But I've since realized that's too limiting. You're the Ginger Rogers of *Life*. A badass at everything you do. Far more so than me. From the outside, people might look at us and assume I'm the teacher here—that I'm some sort of Svengali. But the truth is you've taught me far more than I've taught you. You've taught me how to love, Georgie. You've taught me how to be happy."

Well, that does it. Tears spring in my eyes.

"You're my partner," he says, his chest heaving. But then, his mouth quirks up with a little half-smile. "My *sparring* partner, at times, yes. My partner in crime, for sure. But, always, my equal *partner*."

My breathing hitches as I try not to sob.

He cups my cheek in his palm. "I thought I knew it all when I met you, Georgina Ricci. I thought I had the whole world figured out. But you came along and showed me what I was missing. You completed me and brought me pure joy. And for that, I'm so grateful. My vow to you, my beloved Georgina, is that I'll always love and protect you and take care of you. You've got me, baby. All of me. And I promise, every day of my life, forever, to make sure I'm the Fred Astaire you rightly deserve."

Best. Wedding. Reception. *Ever.*

With a loud whoop, I throw my bridal bouquet up and behind my back. And when I spin around to see where my flowers landed, I'm thrilled to discover it's Zasu, the woman who mentored me during my internship at *Rock 'n' Roll,* who's caught them. It's a perfect result, since Zasu is always telling me horror stories from her "hellacious" dating life. Hopefully, those flowers will bring her a prince, the next time she swipes right on Tinder, rather than yet another frog. Although, given that Tinder is Zasu's primary vehicle for meeting men, I wouldn't count on it.

As Zasu raises her flowers into the air, a loud cheer rises up inside the house—a telltale sign that yet another "super-group" has walked onstage to perform another "typical wedding song" for the party. It's the only wedding gift Reed and I requested: for Reed's attending artists to get up onstage, at some point during the reception, in any combinations, and thrill our guests with their interpretations of classic party songs. Tunes like *Dancing Queen* and *Love Shack* and *Uptown Funk.* And that's exactly what these musical geniuses have been doing all night long. And it's been the best thing, ever.

The iconic piano intro to "I Will Survive" sounds from inside the house, followed by the smooth vocals of the one and only Dean Masterson of Red Card Riot singing the instantly recognizable first line.

"I have to dance to this one!" I shriek. I mean, come on. *Dean Masterson* is singing "I Will Survive"... at *my* wedding? My fourteen-year-old self would need smelling salts.

As if on cue, my new husband appears at my side, looking dapper in his perfectly tailored Armani tux, and leads me on his arm into the house.

As we walk toward the French doors on the opposite side of the large patio, I notice C-Bomb and Dax Morgan sitting on a bench together in a far corner, their body language relaxed and friendly. "Reed, look." I gesture to the unlikely duo, and Reed and I share a huge smile.

Before tonight, we already knew the guys of 22 Goats and Red Card Riot had received our wedding invitations and decided to put their differences aside to party under one roof for the first time in years. But *knowing* Dax and C-Bomb had finally decided to bury the hatchet, in our honor, and *actually* seeing them together, looking like old friends, laughing and smiling... well, those are two different things.

"That happened because of *you,*" Reed says.

I scoff. "No. They're here because celebrating with *you* was more important to them than hanging onto whatever originally pissed them off."

Reed chuckles. "Silly Mrs. Rivers. What I meant is they're all so shocked I landed a catch like you, they were dying to see for themselves if you actually went through with saying 'I do.'"

I roll my eyes and he laughs.

Inside the house, we find Dean singing his heart out onstage, as expected, backed by some of the most recognizable musicians in the world, all of them looking like they're having the time of their lives up there, making that campy song their own. When we reach the dance floor, we're welcomed enthusiastically by Josh and Kat—who looks svelte and gorgeous in her tight-fitting blue gown—and, also, by Henn and Hannah—who's sporting an adorable baby bump these days.

Not surprisingly, Henn begins performing one of his patented "break dance moves," making everyone around him laugh and egg him on. And, soon, our little dance party in the middle of the floor is *the* place to be. In rapid succession, we're joined by the Fantastic Four: Keane, Maddy, Zander, and Aloha, who, in turn, are accompanied by Kat's adorable parents, Thomas and Louise Morgan. Soon, the next wave shows up: Reed's sister, Dax, Colin and his date, and Alessandra and Fish, all of whom begin dancing like there's no tomorrow.

Still dancing, Alessandra comes over to me and grabs my hands, and we do a joyful little jig that makes me feel like I've got a jetpack on my back. As Reed predicted, Alessandra's single, "Blindsided," eventually rose as high as number eight on the charts and launched her in a big way. So much so, Alessandra's eventual album, which released four months ago, has already churned out three top twenty hits, including an adorable duet she co-wrote and recorded with Fish called "Smitten," which recently hit number one on the Alternative Chart.

When I disengage from Alessandra, I prance over to Owen, who's dancing with Zasu, and then my father, and Leonard and his wife, before returning to my husband to finish out the song. As I dance, my eyes drift around the room, grazing over all the familiar, happy faces. CeeCee and her husband, Francois. Professor Schiff and her date. Bernie, my old boss from the bar, with his sweet wife. Reed's mom is dancing with Amalia and her nurse, Tina, and the orderly, Oscar, who made the trip, at our invitation and on Reed's dime.

And, suddenly, it hits me like a ton of bricks what a truly magical thing a wedding is in a person's life. The one and only time—at least, when they're alive to see it—when a person is surrounded by literally *everyone* who loves them, from every segment and phase of their life, all under one roof—and *everyone* is full of pure joy.

Feeling overcome with love and gratitude, I hurl myself at Reed, pull his face to mine by his sexy scruff, and kiss him fervently. "Happy wedding day, my gorgeous hunk of a husband!"

Reed laughs. "Oh, shit. I'm a *husband*?" He looks down at the metal band on his finger. "Wait. Is that what all that ring exchanging and 'I doing' meant? Someone should have told me!"

I giggle with glee and kiss his ring. "Sorry, Mr. Rivers. The deed is done, and you can't take it back. I'm all yours, according to a legally binding contract. And you're all mine. Don't you know the first rule of negotiations? Careful what you ask for—you just might get it."

Reed nuzzles my nose, a huge smile on his face. "I wouldn't have it any other way. Happy wedding day, Cinderella."

I swoon. "I knew you were my Prince Charming, the minute I met you."

He laughs. "And this is the part of the fairytale where we get to ride off into the sunset and live happily ever after."

I look into Reed's sparkling, chocolate eyes. "There's no need for us to ride off anywhere, my love. We're already here."

EPILOGUE
REED

Eight years later

My heart pounding, I park my small suitcase inside our front door and tear through our moonlit living room. I take the stairs, two at a time, and barrel down the hallway toward Leo's nursery. As I approach the doorway, I hear the glorious sound of Georgina singing "Beautiful Boy" by John Lennon—the song I played for my beautiful wife the day she gave me Leonardo Ricci Rivers seven months ago.

As it turns out, I probably could have made Georgina a pop star, if she'd let me. I would have needed to rely heavily on Autotune, but I swear I could have done it, just for the sheer fun of it. As it is, though, Leo and I have been Georgina's sole audience of two, the lucky ones who get to enjoy Georgina's sweet, soulful voice behind closed doors. I swear, that woman singing to our son, especially this song, is in a three-way tie for my all-time favorite sound. The other two being every noise Leo makes, whether he's laughing, crying, babbling, or eating, and every sound Georgina makes when we have sex. Especially the ones she makes when she comes.

My chest heaving from anxiety and exertion, I enter the nursery, and discover Georgina sitting calmly in a glider, holding our sleeping son in her arms. When she senses my movement in the doorframe, she looks up and her features contort with apology.

"Oh, love. You didn't need to drop everything. I shouldn't have freaked you out like that."

I bend down and kiss her in greeting. "You think I'd stay in Vegas when Leo was running a fever and you were worried sick about it? You insult me." I press my lips against Leo's forehead, and to my relief, his skin feels only vaguely warmer than usual, not "on fire," as Georgina described it to me, earlier today, in a panic. "When was the last time you checked his temperature?"

"About thirty minutes ago. The doctor said to check it every hour."

"Check it now."

I pull up a chair, as Georgina presses a thermometer to Leo's temple. When it beeps, she holds up the reading, with a relieved smile on her face. "It's down again. This time, by point-three." She flashes an apologetic face. "I think it's distinctly possible I overreacted here. I'm sorry. I should have left you alone to have fun."

"Would you stop insulting me, please? I'm glad you called. I'd be upset if you hadn't."

"But your artists were up for so many awards. You should be at your after-party right now. Did anyone win?"

I scoff. "Nobody cares if I'm at the after-party. Truthfully, I was grateful to have an excuse to leave. And yes, we had lots of wins. Read about it on Google." I touch Leo's soft brown hair and gaze adoringly at his features. He's got his mommy's lips and nose. His daddy's dark eyes and face shape. And, man, does this kid have a stubborn, fiery spirit, probably inherited from both of us. "When did Amalia leave?"

"She never left. She's downstairs now, asleep in her old bedroom. You should have seen Amalia with Leo today. She was a baby whisperer. And my dad was so sweet to meet me at the doctor's office before I could get ahold of Amalia. I was so grateful to him." She kisses Leo's little hand. "You've got a lot of people who love you, little dude."

"He sure does. Including his daddy." I reach out. "Hand him over. I've been going through withdrawals. I need my fix." I unbutton and open my tuxedo shirt, and when Georgina hands him over, I press his tiny chest flush against mine—right over the ink on my left pec—which nowadays, as of seven months ago, reads, *ReRiGeRiLeRi*. The same as Georgina's tattoo on the inside of her left ring finger.

It wasn't easy to bring Leonardo Ricci Rivers into the world. It took three grueling rounds of IVF and a whole lot of prayers. Which was why, when I finally saw my son for the first time in that delivery room, I wept like a baby, shedding actual tears—and a whole lot of them—for the first time since age fourteen. And with each tear streaking down my face, I felt myself transforming—turning into the man I was always meant to be.

After Leo's birth, I assumed it'd be another twenty-eight years until my next round of tears. But I couldn't have been more wrong about that. Only four months later, I cried again. Just as hard. This time, when my mother's favorite nurse, Tina, called to tell me my mother had passed. She'd been taken in her sleep, unexpectedly, by a massive stroke.

Of course, I was devastated by the news. But I took solace in a few things. I was relieved to know Mom hadn't suffered. And that Georgina had cleared her father's name all those years ago. I loved knowing Mom had gotten to hold her grandson several times. It also made me smile to think she'd taken so much pleasure in watching Georgina on TV every week, for two years before Georgina took her current extended maternity leave. Mom absolutely loved bragging to nurses and friends that Georgina's skyrocketing TV career was all thanks to her. "Years ago, I was the one who told Georgie she's got a face for TV!" Mom always used to say. And Georgina, saint that she is, would always reply something along the lines of "Yep! I never would have thought to get into TV if it hadn't been for Eleanor's suggestion!"

Georgina and I have been sitting quietly for several minutes in Leo's nursery, both of us staring in awe at the little miracle in my arms, when Georgina's soft voice finally cuts the moonlit silence. "I talked to Amalia about that job offer today."

"Yeah?" I say, even though I know exactly what Georgina is going to say. She's going to tell me she's decided to take the job. Which is a no-brainer, by the way. High-profile TV jobs based in LA, like the one recently offered to Georgina, don't come along very often. Turning it down would be unthinkable, if you ask me. But I've kept my mouth shut this past month, letting her process the offer on her own, and providing input only when asked.

"My conversation with Amalia gave me some much-needed clarity," she says.

"Oh yeah? Good." I wait, and when she says nothing, I add, "Care to elaborate?"

Georgina takes a deep breath. "I've decided to take the job. They said I could work part-time the first year, and start when Leo turns one, so that's what I've decided to do."

"That's wonderful, Georgie. Congratulations."

"You think this is a good decision?"

"I think it's a spectacular decision."

She sighs with relief. "Amalia said she'll come out of retirement to take care of Leo when I go back to work."

"Oh my God. That's amazing."

"I know."

"Did she say she'd *think* about doing that, or she's fully on board?"

"She's fully on board. She said she'd never forgive us if we hired another nanny. So, of course, I told her we'd love it. But I made it clear she won't be Leo's *nanny*. I said, 'You'll be his grandma who just so happens to get a paycheck.' And she loved that."

"Good. I'm glad you said that. I'm sure she was touched."

Georgina smiles. "I told her we're going to teach Leo to call her 'Gramalia,' and she laughed with glee."

"That's perfect. I love it." I bite my lip. "Thank you."

"For what?"

"For preserving 'Grandma' for my mom. It means a lot to me."

Her features soften. "Oh, love. Of course. Your mom will always be Grandma. Mine will always be Nonna. CeeCee will always be CeeCee." She smiles. "And, now, Amalia will always be *Gramalia*. Every one of Leo's grandmas will have her own name."

We share a smile.

Georgina bites her lip and touches my thigh. "Do you think it would be okay if we put him down in his crib for a bit?" Her eyes flash with heat. And I know she's missed me as much as I've missed her.

"I think it's a great idea."

Georgie scoops Leo up and gently lays him down. She checks his diaper. Determines he's good. She turns on a white-noise machine. Double-checks the baby monitor. Adjusts the nightlight and thermostat. And, while she does all that, I take Leo's temperature again, just for good measure.

When we leave the nursery, we do it hand in hand. And as we walk the length of the hallway, the air between us becomes charged with three days' worth of pent-up desire.

We reach our moonlit bedroom, where I guide Georgina onto our bed, peel off her pajamas, and my clothes, and proceed to worship every inch of my wife. I kiss and lick and caress and taste, reveling in her curves and newfound softness, my body vibrating with each sultry sound that escapes her throat.

When she comes, I crawl over her writhing torso and plunge myself deep inside her, and then push myself deep, deep, deep, over and over again, as deep as a man can go. As I make love to my wife, I whisper words of adoration. If I were a bottle of wine, I'd be pouring every drop of me into Georgina's goblet. I'm giving her all of me. No holding back.

When we're done, and our bodies are quiet and still, I creep into Leo's room to find him sleeping soundly—butts up coconut—in his crib. I take his temperature again and sigh with relief at the reading. I change his diaper, through which he sleeps like a rock. And, finally, I return to my room, to the bed I share with my wife, and crawl in. "His fever went down again," I whisper, wrapping my arms around Georgina and pulling her body into mine.

"Thank you for coming home."

"There's no place I'd rather be."

The moonlight is wrapping the room in a serene, blue haze. Georgina's skin is warm against mine. My son is safe and sound and fast asleep, and the baby monitor is turned to high. And so, I close my eyes and give myself permission to drift off to sleep.

As my mind begins to float, a feeling of gratitude and serenity—*pure love*—washes over me. Many moons ago, this fireball in my arms saw something inside me I didn't see in myself. She saw something I didn't even know was there. And now, thanks to her, the one and only Georgina Ricci Rivers, I've become the husband and father—the *man*—I was always meant to be.

. . .

THE END

BONUS MATERIAL! Check out the River Records website here: http://www.laurenrowebooks.com/river-records

Do you want to read about Fish and Ally? Their romance *Smitten* is available now.

If you want to know more about the beef between **Reed** and **C-Bomb**, and between **C-Bomb** and **Dax Morgan**, then read the standalone ROCKSTAR, about Dax and his lady love.
Be sure to check out 22 Goats' original music and music videos from the book under the "MUSIC FROM ROCKSTAR" tab of Lauren's website.

If you want to read about Josh and Kat, you'll find their explosive and sexy trilogy beginning with INFATUATION.
Note: Henn and Hannah's love story also begins in INFATUATION, and continues as a side story in several books of The Morgan Brothers series. However, Henn and Hannah do not have their own separate books.

Be sure to sign up for Lauren's newsletter (http://eepurl.com/ba_ODX) to find out about upcoming releases!

Find Lauren on social media!
FACEBOOK - https://www.facebook.com/laurenrowebooks/
INSTAGRAM - https://www.instagram.com/laurenrowebooks/
TWITTER - http://www.twitter.com/laurenrowebooks

FACEBOOK GROUP - Lauren Rowe Books
BOOKBUB - https://www.bookbub.com/authors/lauren-rowe

A brief list of books by Lauren Rowe is located at the front of this book. Further details follow.

BOOKS BY LAUREN ROWE

Meet Me At Captain's Series of Standalone Romantic comedies

Who's Your Daddy?

When thirty-year-old patent attorney, Maximillian Vaughn, meets a sassy, charismatic older woman in a bar, he invites her back to his place for one night of no-strings fun. It's all Max can offer, given his busy career; but, luckily, it's all Marnie wants, too. But when Max's chemistry with Marnie is so combustible, it threatens to burn down his bedroom, he does the unthinkable the next morning: he asks Marnie out on a dinner date.

Mere minutes after saying yes, however, Marnie bolts like her hair is on fire with no explanation. What happened? Max doesn't know, but he's determined to find out and convince Marnie to pick up where they left off.

Textual Relations

When Grayson McKnight unknowingly gets a fake number from a woman in a bar, he winds up embroiled in a sexy text exchange with the actual owner of the number—a confident, sensual older woman who knows exactly who she is . . . and what she wants.

No strings attached.

But as sparks fly and real feelings develop, will Grayson get his way and tempt her to give him more than their original bargain?

My Neighbor's Secret

When Charlotte gets into her new dilapidated condo to start fixing it up for resale, she finds out the infuriating stranger who's thoroughly messed up her life is her new next-door neighbor.

Also, that he's got a big secret.

She confronts him and proposes they work together to get themselves out of their respective jams, even though they both admittedly can't stand each other. Yes, he's let it slip he thinks she's pretty. And, okay, she begrudgingly thinks he's kind of cute. But whatever. They hate each other and this is nothing but a business partnership. What could go wrong?

The Secret Note: A Spicy Standalone Novella with HEA

He's a hot Aussie. I'm a girl who isn't shy about getting what she wants. The problem? Ben is my little brother's best friend. An exchange student who's heading back Down Under any day now. But I can't help myself. He's too hot to resist.

The Morgan Brothers

Read these standalones in any order. Chronological reading order is below, but they are all complete stories. Note: you do not need to read any other books or series before jumping straight into reading about the Morgan boys.

Hero

The story of heroic firefighter, Colby Morgan. When catastrophe strikes Colby Morgan, will physical therapist Lydia save him . . . or will he save her?

Captain

The insta-love-to-enemies-to-lovers story of tattooed sex god, Ryan Morgan, and the woman he'd move heaven and earth to claim.

Ball Peen Hammer

A steamy, hilarious, friends-to-lovers romantic comedy about cocky-as-hell male stripper, Keane Morgan, and the sassy, smart young woman who brings him to his knees during a road trip.

Mister Bodyguard

The Morgans' beloved honorary brother, Zander Shaw, meets his match in the feisty pop star he's assigned to protect on tour.

ROCKSTAR

When the youngest Morgan brother, Dax Morgan, meets a mysterious woman who rocks his world, he must decide if pursuing her is worth risking it all. Be sure to check out four of Dax's original songs from ROCKSTAR, written and produced by Lauren, along with full music videos for the songs, on her website (www.laurenrowebooks.com) under the tab MUSIC FROM ROCKSTAR.

Dive into Lauren's universe of interconnected trilogies and duets, all books available individually and as a bundle, in any order.

A full suggested reading order can be found here!

The Josh & Kat Trilogy

It's a war of wills between stubborn and sexy Josh Faraday and Kat Morgan. A fight to the bed. Arrogant, wealthy playboy Josh is used to getting what he wants. And what he wants is Kat Morgan. The books are to be read in order:

Infatuation

Revelation

Consummation

The Club Trilogy

When wealthy playboy Jonas Faraday receives an anonymous note from Sarah Cruz, a law student working part-time processing online applications for an exclusive club, he becomes obsessed with hunting her down and giving her the satisfaction she claims has always eluded her. Thus begins a sweeping tale of obsession, passion, desperation, and ultimately, everlasting love and individual redemption. Find out why scores of readers all over the world, in multiple languages, call The Club Trilogy "my favorite trilogy ever" and "the greatest love story I've ever read." As Jonas Faraday says to Sarah Cruz: "There's never been a love like ours and there never will be again... Our love is so pure and true, we're the amazement of the gods."

The Club: Obsession

The Club: Reclamation

The Club: Redemption

The fourth book for Jonas and Sarah is a full-length epilogue with incredible heart-stopping twists and turns and feels. Read The Club: Culmination (A Full-Length Epilogue Novel) after finishing The Club Trilogy or, if you prefer, after reading The Josh and Kat Trilogy.

The Reed Rivers Trilogy

Reed Rivers has met his match in the most unlikely of women — aspiring journalist and spitfire, Georgina Ricci. She's much younger than the women Reed normally pursues, but he can't resist her fiery personality and drop-dead gorgeous looks. But in this game of cat and mouse, who's chasing whom? With each passing day of this wild ride, Reed's not so sure. The books of this trilogy are to be read in order:

Bad Liar

Beautiful Liar

Beloved Liar

The Hate Love Duet

An addicting, enemies-to-lovers romance with humor, heat, angst, and banter. Music artists Savage of Fugitive Summer and Laila Fitzgerald are stuck together on tour. And convinced they can't stand each other. What they don't know is that they're absolutely made for each other, whether they realize it or not. The books of this duet are to be read in order:

Falling Out of Hate with You

Falling Into Love with You

Interconnected Standalones within the same universe as above

Hacker in Love

When world-class hacker Peter "Henn" Hennessey meets Hannah Milliken, he moves heaven and earth, including doing some questionable things, to win his dream girl over. But when catastrophe strikes, will Henn lose Hannah forever, or is there still a chance for him to chase their happily ever after? *Hacker in Love* is a steamy, funny, heart-pounding, **standalone** contemporary romance with a whole lot of feels, laughs, spice, and swoons.

Smitten

When aspiring singer-songwriter, Alessandra, meets Fish, the funny, adorable bass player of 22 Goats, sparks fly between the awkward pair. Fish tells Alessandra he's a "Goat called Fish who's hung like a bull. But not really. I'm actually really average." And Alessandra tells Fish, "There's nothing like a girl's first love." Alessandra thinks she's talking about a song when she makes her comment to Fish—the first song she'd ever heard by 22 Goats, in fact. As she'll later find out, though, her "first love" was actually Fish. The Goat called Fish who, after that night, vowed to do anything to win her heart. SMITTEN is a true standalone romance.

Swoon

When Colin Beretta, the drummer of 22 Goats, is a groomsman at the wedding of his childhood best friend, Logan, he discovers Logan's kid sister, Amy, is all grown up. Colin tries to resist his attraction to Amy, but after a drunken kiss at the wedding reception, that's easier said than done. Swoon is a true standalone romance.

Misadventures Standalones (**unrelated standalones not within the above universe**):

- ***Misadventures on the Night Shift*** —A hotel night shift clerk encounters her teenage fantasy: rock star Lucas Ford. And combustion ensues.

- ***Misadventures of a College Girl***—A spunky, virginal theater major meets a cocky football player at her first college party . . . and absolutely nothing goes according to plan for either of them.

- ***Misadventures on the Rebound***—A spunky woman on the rebound meets a hot, mysterious stranger in a bar on her way to her five-year high school reunion in Las Vegas and what follows is a misadventure neither of them ever imagined.

Lauren's Dark Comedy/Psych Thriller Standalone

Countdown to Killing Kurtis

A young woman with big dreams and skeletons in her closet decides her pornoking husband must die in exactly a year. This is not a traditional romance, but it will most definitely keep you turning the pages and saying "WTF?" If you're looking for something a bit outside the box, with twists and turns, suspense, and dark humor, this is the book for you: a standalone psychological thriller/dark comedy with romantic elements.

AUTHOR BIOGRAPHY

Lauren Rowe is the USA Today and international #1 best-selling author of newly released Reed Rivers Trilogy, as well as The Club Trilogy, The Josh & Kat Trilogy, The Morgan Brothers Series, Countdown to Killing Kurtis, and select standalone Misadventures.

Lauren's books are full of feels, humor, heat, and heart. Besides writing novels, Lauren is the singer in a party/wedding band in her hometown of San Diego, an audio book narrator, and award-winning songwriter. She is thrilled to connect with readers all over the world.

To find out about Lauren's upcoming releases and giveaways, sign up for Lauren's emails here!

Lauren loves to hear from readers! Send Lauren an email from her website, say hi on Twitter, Instagram, or Facebook.

Find out more and check out lots of free bonus material at www.LaurenRoweBooks.com